NORTH CAROLINA

McDougal Littell

World Cultures and Geography

South America and Europe

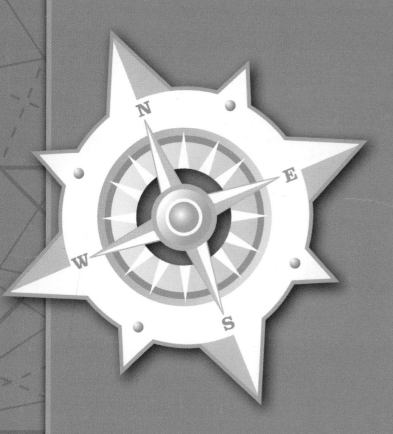

Sarah Bednarz

Marci Smith Deal

Inés Miyares

Donna Ogle

Charles White

CONTENTS IN BRIEF

North Carolina Standard Course of Study
6th Grade: South America and Europe

Senior Consultants

Sarah Witham Bednarz is associate professor of geography at Texas A&M University, where she has taught since 1988. She earned a Ph.D. in Educational Curriculum and Instruction specializing in geography in 1992 from Texas A&M University and has written extensively about geography literacy and education. Dr. Bednarz was an author of *Geography for Life: National Geography Standards, 1994.* In 2005 she received the prestigious George J. Miller Award from the National Council for Geographic Education.

Marci Smith Deal is the K–12 Social Studies Curriculum Coordinator for Hurst-Euless-Bedford Independent School District in Texas. She received the 2000 Distinguished Geographer Award for the State of Texas, and was one of the honorees of the 2001 National Council for Geographic Education Distinguished Teacher Award. She has served as president for the Texas Council for Social Studies Supervisors and as vice-president for the Texas Council for Social Studies. She currently serves as a teacher consultant for National Geographic Society.

Inés M. Miyares is professor of geography at Hunter College-City University of New York. Born in Havana, Cuba, and fluent in Spanish, Dr. Miyares has focused much of her scholarship on Latin America, immigration and refugee policy, and urban ethnic geography. She holds a Ph.D. in geography from Arizona State University. In 1999 Dr. Miyares was the recipient of the Hunter College Performance Excellence Award for excellence in teaching, research, scholarly writing, and service. She has just published a co-edited book on contemporary ethnic geographies in the United States.

ISBN-13: 978-0-618-88875-7   ISBN-10: 0-618-88875-6

02 03 04 05 06 07 08 09—CKI—12 11 10 09 08 07

Internet Web Site: http://www.mcdougallittell.com

Senior Consultants

Donna Ogle is professor of Reading and Language at National-Louis University in Chicago, Illinois, and is a specialist in reading in the content areas, with an interest in social studies. She is past president of the International Reading Association and a former social studies teacher. Dr. Ogle is currently directing two content literacy projects in Chicago schools and is Senior Consultant to the Striving Readers Research Project. She continues to explore applications of the K-W-L strategy she developed and is adding a Partner Reading component—PRC2 (Partner Reading and Content 2).

Charles S. White is associate professor in the School of Education at Boston University, where he teaches methods of instruction in social studies. Dr. White has written and spoken extensively on the importance of civic education, both in the United States and overseas. He has worked in Russia since 1997 on curriculum reform and teacher preparation in education for democracy. Dr. White has received numerous awards for his scholarship, including the 1995 Federal Design Achievement Award from the National Endowment for the Arts, for the Teaching with Historic Places project. In 1997, Dr. White taught his Models of Teaching doctoral course at the Universidad San Francisco de Quito, Ecuador.

Middle School Teacher Consultant

Judith K. Bock earned a B.A. in Elementary Education and an M.A. in Geography and Environmental Sciences from Northeastern Illinois University. She taught as a middle school educator in gifted education for 33 years and is currently an adjunct geography professor in college geography departments in metropolitan Chicago. Ms. Bock serves on several local, state, and national geography education committees, writes geography lesson plans and curriculum, and facilitates geography workshops and institutes. She received the Distinguished Teaching Award from NCGE and was awarded the Outstanding Geographer in Illinois–2004 from the Illinois Geographical Society.

Regional Reviewers

Edwin Bryant
Professor of Hinduism
Rutgers University
New Brunswick, New Jersey

Gary S. Elbow
Associate Dean of the Honors College
and Professor of Geography
Texas Tech University
Lubbock, Texas

Ibipo Johnston-Anumonwo
Professor of Geography
State University of New York College
 at Cortland
Cortland, New York

James A. Millward
Associate Professor of History
Georgetown University
Washington, D.C.

Mark Peterson
Associate Professor of Korean
Brigham Young University
Provo, Utah

Teacher Reviewers

Erik Branch
James C. Wright
Middle School
Madison, Wisconsin

Ann Christianson
John Muir Middle School
Wausau, Wisconsin

Jim Easton
Roscoe Middle School
Roscoe, Illinois

Ed Felton
Coopersville
Middle School
Coopersville, Michigan

Greta Frensley
Knox Doss Middle School
Gallatin, Tennessee

Todd Harrison
Hardin County
Middle School
Savannah, Tennessee

Esther Howse
Byron Center West Middle School
Byron Center, Michigan

Amber McVey
Antioch Middle School
Gladstone, Missouri

Ken Metz
Glacier Creek
Middle School
Cross Plains, Wisconsin

Suzanne Moen
DeForest Middle School
DeForest, Wisconsin

Tim Mortenson
Patrick Marsh Middle School
Sun Prairie, Wisconsin

Matt Parker
Eastgate Middle School
Kansas City, Missouri

Terry Rhodes
McNair Middle School
Fayetteville, Arkansas

Matthew J. Scheidler
Wayzata East Middle School
Plymouth, Minnesota

Don Stringfellow
Mobile City Public
School System
Mobile, Alabama

NORTH CAROLINA

OVERVIEW
North Carolina Student Edition

- Guide to Understanding North Carolina's Competency Goals and Objectives for South America and Europe
- Guide to Test-Taking Strategies and Practice

Lessons with Embedded North Carolina Objectives

 Look for the North Carolina symbol throughout the book. It highlights targeted performance indicators to help you succeed on your test.

Cape Hatteras Lighthouse, Hatteras Island, North Carolina © Craig Brewer/Getty Images

NORTH CAROLINA CONTENTS

Introduction to World Geography

Chapter 1
Understanding the Earth and Its Peoples

Chapter 2
Earth's Interlocking Systems

Chapter 3
Human Geography

Chapter 4
People and Culture

Online Activities
@ ClassZone.com

Animated GEOGRAPHY
Amazon Rain Forest

Explore life in a rain forest—the Yanomamo people, plants, animals, and the scientists who study them.

Interactive Review

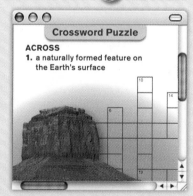

Solve a crossword of key terms and names related to Earth's physical geography.

Online Test Practice

Review test-taking strategies and practice your test at the end of every chapter.

UNIT 2
NORTH CAROLINA

Latin America

Online Activities
@ ClassZone.com

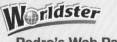

Pedro's Web Page

Visit Pedro's Web page to experience the sights and sounds of his world.

Interactive Review

Use interactive flip cards to review key terms and concepts related to Mexico.

Online Test Practice

Review test-taking strategies and practice your test at the end of every chapter.

UNIT 3 NORTH CAROLINA

Europe

Online Activities
@ ClassZone.com

Animated GEOGRAPHY
Victorian London

Enter the world of Victorian London and visit homes, shops, parks, and an underground railway.

Interactive Review

Play the GeoGame to test your knowledge of the geography of Western Europe.

Online Test Practice

Review test-taking strategies and practice your test at the end of every chapter..

UNIT 4
NORTH CAROLINA

Russia and the Eurasian Republics

Online Activities
@ ClassZone.com

Worldster
Zuhura's Web Page

Visit Zuhura's Web page to experience the sights and sounds of her world.

Interactive Review

Play the Name Game to test your knowledge of the Eurasian Republics.

Online Test Practice

Review test-taking strategies and practice your test at the end of every chapter.

FEATURES

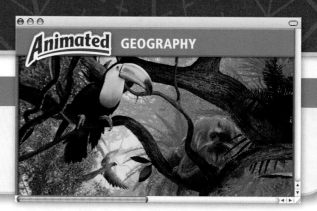

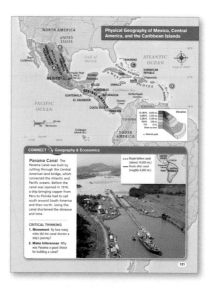

CONNECT Geography & Economics
Panama Canal The Panama Canal was built by cutting through the Central American land bridge, which connected the Atlantic and Pacific oceans. Before the canal was opened in 1914, a ship bringing copper from Peru to Florida had to sail south around South America and then north. Using the canal shortened the distance and time.

CRITICAL THINKING
1. **Movement** By how many miles did the canal shorten a ship's journey?
2. **Make Inferences** Why was Panama a good choice for building a canal?

Make a *Cuíca*

1. 2. 3. 4.

ANALYZING Primary Sources

HISTORY MAKERS

Fun Facts!

COMPARING

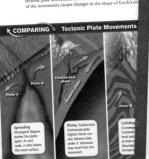

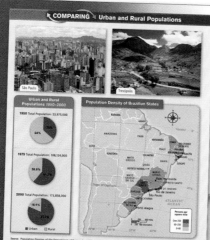

MAPS, GRAPHS, CHARTS and INFOGRAPHICS

MAPS

GRAPHS

TABLES AND CHARTS

INFOGRAPHICS

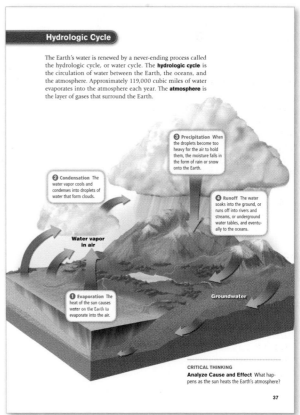

Hydrologic Cycle

The Earth's water is renewed by a never-ending process called the hydrologic cycle, or water cycle. The **hydrologic cycle** is the circulation of water between the Earth, the oceans, and the atmosphere. Approximately 119,000 cubic miles of water evaporates into the atmosphere each year. The **atmosphere** is the layer of gases that surround the Earth.

3 Precipitation When the droplets become too heavy for the air to hold them, the moisture falls in the form of rain or snow onto the Earth.

2 Condensation The water vapor cools and condenses into droplets of water that form clouds.

4 Runoff The water soaks into the ground, or runs off into rivers and streams, or underground water tables, and eventually to the oceans.

Water vapor in air

1 Evaporation The heat of the sun causes water on the Earth to evaporate into the air.

Groundwater

CRITICAL THINKING
Analyze Cause and Effect What happens as the sun heats the Earth's atmosphere?

37

READING FOR UNDERSTANDING

Four Steps to Being a Strategic Reader

These pages explain how *World Cultures and Geography* chapters are organized. By using the four key strategies below, you'll become a more successful reader of geography.

1 Set a Purpose for Reading

2 Build Your Social Studies Vocabulary

3 Use Active Reading Strategies

4 Check Your Understanding

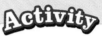

Can you find it?

Find the following items on this and the next three pages.

- **one** chapter Essential Question
- **two** places where important words are defined
- **three** online games
- **four** key strategies for reading

---

1 Set a Purpose for Reading

Key features at the beginning of each chapter and section help you set a purpose for reading.

A **Essential Question** This key question sets the main purpose for reading.

B **Connect Geography & History** This feature helps you to consider the relationship between geography and history.

C **Animated Geography** identifies the region or country you'll be studying.

D **Before, You Learned** and **Now You Will Learn** This information helps you to connect what you've studied before to what you'll study next.

E **Key Question** Each topic covered in the chapter is followed by a Key Question that sets your purpose for reading about that topic.

2 Build Your Social Studies Vocabulary

The Reading for Understanding pages provide three important ways to build your vocabulary.

A **Terms & Names** cover the most important events, people, places, and social studies concepts in the section.

B **Background Vocabulary** lists words you need to know in order to understand the basic concepts and ideas discussed in the section.

C **Visual Vocabulary** features provide visual support for some definitions.

D **Terms & Names** and **Background Vocabulary** are highlighted and defined in the main text so that you'll understand them as you read.

① GEOGRAPHY
The Earth and Its Forces

② GEOGRAPHY
Bodies of Water and Landforms

③ GEOGRAPHY
Climate and Vegetation

④ GEOGRAPHY
Environmental

CHAPTER 2

Earth's Interlocking Systems

A 🏴 **ESSENTIAL QUESTION**

How do Earth's physical systems make life on Earth possible?

B CONNECT ▶ Geography & History

Use the map and the time line to answer the following questions.

1. On which plate does most of the United States sit[...]
2. Which event on the time line is supported by the [...] evidence on this map?

C *Animated* **GEOGRAPHY**
Earth's Tectonic Plates

🖱 *Click here* to explore Earth and its systems @ ClassZone.com

Eurasian Plate

Arabian Plate

African Plate

Philippine Plate

Indo-Australian Plate

Ring [...]

External Forces Shaping the Earth

E ▶ **KEY QUESTION** What external forces shape the Earth?

External forces also reshape the Earth's surface. The two main external forces are weathering and erosion. **Weathering** is the gradual physical and chemical breakdown of rocks near or on the Earth's surface. **Erosion** is the wearing away and movement of weathered materials from one place to another by the action of water, wind, or ice. As you can see, weathering and erosion work together to shape the Earth.

Weathering Weathering occurs slowly, over many years or even centuries. The two types of weathering are mechanical weathering and chemical weathering. Mechanical weathering is a process in which rocks are broken down into smaller pieces by physical means. It takes place when ice, extremes of hot and cold, or even tree roots cause rocks to split apart. It also occurs when hard objects, such as other rocks or sand, scrape or rub against a rock, and pieces of the rock break off.

Chemical weathering is caused by chemical reactions between the minerals in the rock and elements in the air or water. This process changes the make-up of the rock itself. For example, most rocks contain iron. When iron comes in contact with water, it rusts, which helps to break down the rock. Water and elements in the air can cause other minerals in rocks to dissolve.

The Grand Canyon The Grand Canyon is located on the Colorado River in Arizona. It is an example of both weathering and erosion caused by wind and water.

UNITED STATES
○ Grand Canyon
ARIZONA
MEXICO

SECTION 2

Reading for Understanding

▶ **Key Ideas**

D BEFORE, YOU LEARNED
Internal and external forces shape the surface of the Earth.

NOW YOU WILL LEARN
Interaction between landform[...] of water makes life on Earth[...]

▶ **Vocabulary**

A TERMS & NAMES

drainage basin the area drained by a major river

ground water water found beneath the Earth's surface

hydrologic cycle the circulation of water between the Earth, the oceans, and the atmosphere

landform a feature on the Earth's surface formed by physical force

plateau a broad, flat area of land higher than the surrounding land

relief the difference in the elevation of a landform from its lowest point to its highest point

B
continental shelf the subme[...] at the edge of a continent

BACKGROUND VOCABU[...]

atmosphere the layer of gas[...] surround the Earth

C Visual Vocabulary landform

▶ **Reading Strategy**

Re-create the web diagram shown at right. As you read and respond to the **KEY QUESTIONS**, use the diagram to organize important details about the Earth's landforms and bodies of water.

📖 See Skillbuilder Handbook, page R4

FIND MAIN IDEAS

WATER BODIES

🖱 **GRAPHIC ORGANIZERS**
Go to **Interactive Review** @ Class[...]

③ Use Active Reading Strategies

Active reading strategies help you note the most important information in each section.

Ⓐ Reading Strategy Each Reading for Understanding page contains a Reading Strategy diagram to help you track and organize the information you read.

Ⓑ Skillbuilder Handbook Every Reading Strategy is supported by a corresponding lesson in the Skillbuilder Handbook section at the back of this book.

Ⓒ Active Reading Strategies in the Skillbuilder Handbook will help you to read and study *World Cultures and Geography*.

---

drainage basin the area drained by a major river

ground water water found beneath the Earth's surface

hydrologic cycle the circulation of water between the Earth, the oceans, and the atmosphere

landform a feature on the Earth's surface formed by physical force

plateau a broad, flat area of land higher than the surrounding land

relief the difference in the elevation of a landform from its lowest point to its highest point

continental shelf the submerged at the edge of a continent

BACKGROUND VOCABULARY

atmosphere the layer of gases that surround the Earth

Visual Vocabulary landform

▶ **Reading Strategy Ⓐ**

Re-create the web diagram shown at right. As you read and respond to the **KEY QUESTIONS**, use the diagram to organize important details about the Earth's landforms and bodies of water.

See Skillbuilder Handbook, page R4

FIND MAIN IDEAS

WATER BODIES   LANDF

GRAPHIC ORGANIZERS
Go to Interactive Review @ ClassZone.com

34 Chapter 2

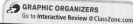

Skillbuilder Handbook

Ⓒ Contents

Reading and Critical Thinking Skills

NC20

Ⓑ 1.2 Finding Main Ideas

Defining the Skill

A **main idea** is a statement that summarizes the subject of a speech, an article, a section of a book, or a paragraph. Main ideas can be stated or unstated. The main idea of a paragraph is often stated in the first or last sentence. If it is the first sentence, it is followed by sentences that support that main idea. If it is the last sentence, the details build up to the main idea. To find an unstated idea, use the details of the paragraph as clues.

Applying the Skill

The following paragraph provides reasons why Japan and Australia make such good trading partners. Use the strategies listed below to help you identify the main idea.

How to Find the Main Idea

Strategy ❶ Identify what you think may be the stated main idea. Check the first and last sentences of the paragraph to see if either could be the stated main idea.

Strategy ❷ Identify details that support the main idea. Some details explain that idea. Others give examples of what is stated in the main idea.

TRADING PARTNERS

Australia is an island. Japan is also an island, though much smaller than Australia. Australia is not as densely populated as Japan. ❷ In Japan, an average of 881 people live in each square mile. Australia averages 7 people per square mile. ❷ Australia has wide-open lands available for agriculture, ranching, and mining. ❷ Japan buys wool from Australian ranches, wheat from Australian farms, and iron ore from Australian mines. To provide jobs for its many workers, ❷ Japan developed industries. Those industries ❷ sell electronics and cars to Australia. ❶ Australia and Japan are trading partners because each has something the other needs.

Make a Chart

Making a chart can help you identify the main idea and details in a passage or paragraph. The chart below identifies the main idea and details in the paragraph you just read.

Main Idea: Australia and Japan are good trading partners because each supplies something the other needs.
Detail: Japan's population density is 881 people per square mile; Australia's is 7 per square mile.
Detail: Australia has land, natural resources, and agricultural products.
Detail: Japan buys wool, wheat, and iron from Australia.
Detail: Japan has many industries.
Detail: Australia buys electronics and cars from Japanese industries.

4 Check Your Understanding

One of the most important things you'll do as you study *World Cultures and Geography* is to check your understanding of events, people, places, and issues as you read.

A Interactive Review includes a Name Game and provides online activities to test your knowledge of the geography you just studied.

B Section Assessment reviews the section Terms & Names, revisits your Reading Strategy notes, and provides key questions about the section.

Interactive Review

A CHAPTER SUMMARY

Key Idea 1
The Earth is composed of many layers, and its surface continually changes because of the drifting of the continents.

Key Idea 2
Interaction between landforms and bodies of water makes life on Earth possible.

Key Idea 3
The Earth's rotation and revolution influence weather, climate, and living conditions on Earth.

Key Idea 4
Human interference with physical systems causes problems with the environment.

For Review and Study Notes, go to Interactive Review @ ClassZone.com

NAME GAME

Use the Terms & Names list to complete each se on paper or online.

1. I am the hot metal center of the Earth. _____ core _____
2. I am a naturally formed feature on the Earth's surface. _____
3. I fall in the form of rain, snow, sleet, or hail. _____
4. I am an increase in the Earth's temperature. _____
5. I move weathered materials from one place to another. _____
6. I am the trapping of the sun's heat by gases in the atmosphere. _____
7. I am a large rigid piece of the Earth's crust that is in motion. _____
8. I am typical weather conditions over a period of time. _____
9. I circulate water between the Earth, oceans, and atmosphere. _____
10. I am plants that grow in a region. _____

Activities

Flip Cards
Use the online flip cards to quiz yourself on terms and names introduced in this chapter.

magma — melted or liquid rock

Crossword
Complete an online crossw your knowledge of Earth's

ACROSS
1. a naturally formed fe Earth's surface

Erosion New landforms and new soil are formed by erosion. It occurs when materials loosened by weathering are moved by water, wind, or ice to new locations. Currents in streams and rivers pick up loose materials and deposit them downstream or carry them out to sea. These tiny pieces of rock, deposited by water, wind, or ice are called **sediment**. Sediment can be sand, stone, or finely ground particles called silt.

Wave action along coastlines carries rocks and sand from one place to another. Waves also pound boulders into smaller rocks. Wind erosion lifts particles from the Earth's surface and blows them great distances. The wind's actions can reshape rock s Arizona's Grand Canyon is a result of both wind and water

Another type of erosion is caused by glaciers. **Glaciers** slow-moving masses of ice. They grind rocks and boulders un the ice and leave behind the rock when the ice melts. Pa central United States have been shaped by glacial erosion.

▲ **SYNTHESIZE** Explain how external forces shape the Eart surface.

ONLINE QUIZ For test practice, go to Interactive Review @ClassZone.com

B Section 1 Assessment

TERMS & NAMES
1. **Explain the importance of**
- continent
- tectonic plate
- weathering
- erosion

USE YOUR READING NOTES
2. **Categorize** Use your completed chart to answer the following question:

Are external or internal forces responsible for volcanoes? Explain your answer.

INTERNAL FORCES	EXTERNAL FORCES
1.	1.
2.	2.
3.	3.
4.	4.

KEY IDEAS
3. What are the five layers that make up the Earth's interior and exterior?
4. How were the continents formed?
5. What are the two major external forces reshaping the Earth?

CRITICAL THINKING
6. **Draw Conclusions** How does the movement of wind, water, or ice reshape the Earth's surface?
7. **Analyze Causes and Effects** What is the relationship between plate movement, volcanoes, and earthquakes?
8. **CONNECT to Today** In which parts of the United States are external forces shaping the landscape?
9. **ART Create a Puzzle** Make a copy of a map of the world. Cut out the continents. Use the continents as puzzle pieces to form the continent of Pangaea. When you have finished putting the pieces together, draw an outline around the entire supercontinent.

Exploring Geography Online

World Cultures and Geography provides a variety of tools to help you explore geography online. See geography come to life in the Animation Center. Find help for your research projects in the Research and Writing Center. Review for tests with the Interactive Review, or create your own activities in the Activity Center. Go to ClassZone.com to make ***World Cultures and Geography*** interactive!

ClassZone.com

is your gateway to exploring geography. Explore the different **ClassZone Centers** to help you study and have fun with geography.

A **Interactive Review**
provides you with flip cards, a crossword puzzle, section quizzes, drag-and-drop map activities, and more.

B **Activity Center**
lets you explore world cultures through a **Worldster** community and participate in **WebQuests** and geography games.

C **Activity Maker**
lets you create your own activities so that you can focus on what *you* need to review.

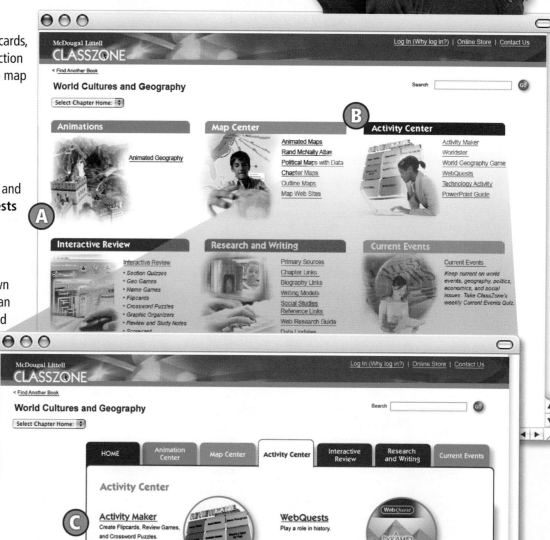

Animation Center

A rich collection of interactive features and maps on a wide variety of geographical topics at **ClassZone.com**

Ⓐ Roll-overs
Explore the illustration by clicking on areas you'd like to know more about. This Amazon Rain Forest animation includes features about biodiversity, life in the rain forest, and more.

Ⓑ Video and Photo Gallery
Explore the rain forest and the scientists who study it.

Review Game

- Create your own review game to study geography *your* way in the Activity Maker at **ClassZone.com**

- Select your own topics from any chapter to help you focus on specific regions, people, or events to review.

- Help your friends to explore geography online. Challenge them to play a review game that you create and modify!

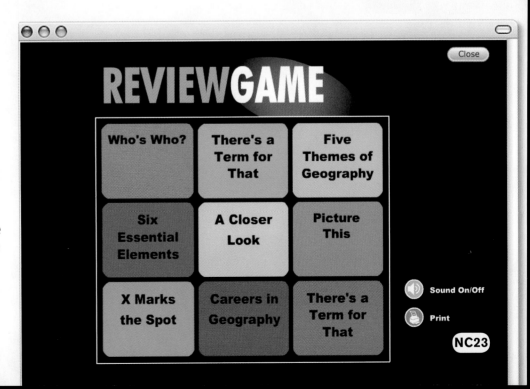

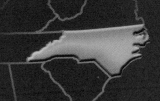
STEPS TO SUCCESS

Guide to Understanding
North Carolina's Competency Goals and Objectives for South America and Europe   NC27

- North Carolina's Competency Goals and Objectives are organized into thirteen goals. Each goal is divided into objectives.

Guide to
Test-Taking Strategies and Practice   S1

- These test-taking strategies and practice are designed to help you tackle many of the items you will find on a standardized test.

 For a complete list of North Carolina's Competency Goals and Objectives for South America and Europe, see page R91.

Cape Hatteras Lighthouse, Hatteras Island, North Carolina © Craig Brewer/Getty Images

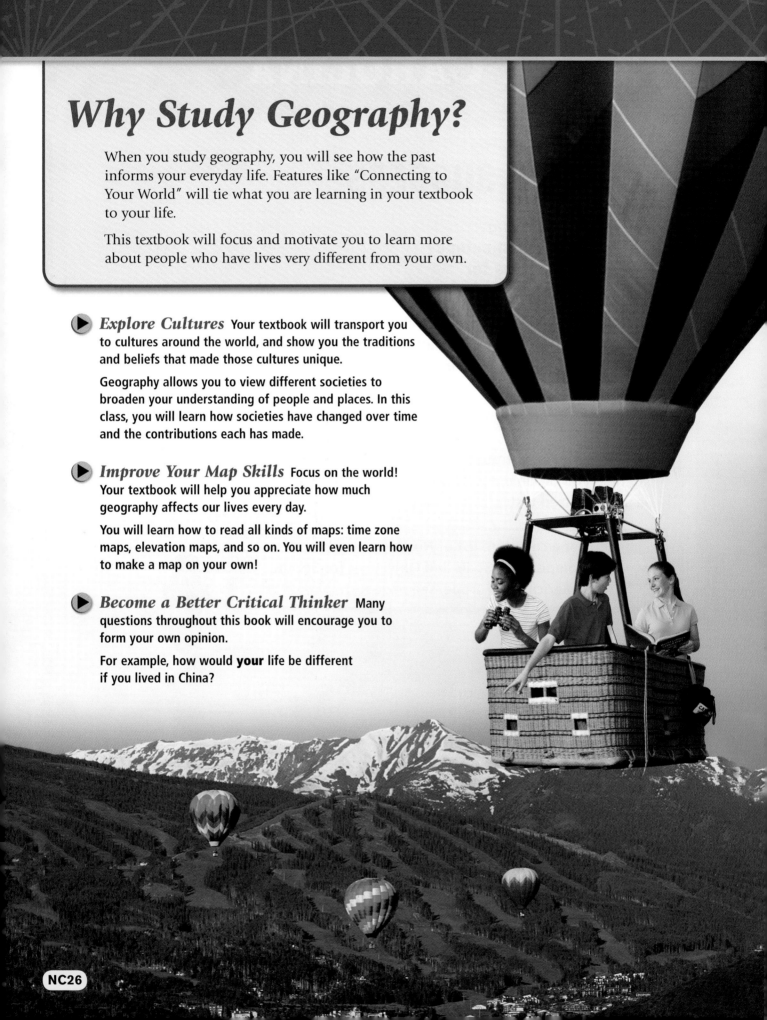

Why Study Geography?

When you study geography, you will see how the past informs your everyday life. Features like "Connecting to Your World" will tie what you are learning in your textbook to your life.

This textbook will focus and motivate you to learn more about people who have lives very different from your own.

▶ *Explore Cultures* Your textbook will transport you to cultures around the world, and show you the traditions and beliefs that made those cultures unique.

Geography allows you to view different societies to broaden your understanding of people and places. In this class, you will learn how societies have changed over time and the contributions each has made.

▶ *Improve Your Map Skills* Focus on the world! Your textbook will help you appreciate how much geography affects our lives every day.

You will learn how to read all kinds of maps: time zone maps, elevation maps, and so on. You will even learn how to make a map on your own!

▶ *Become a Better Critical Thinker* Many questions throughout this book will encourage you to form your own opinion.

For example, how would **your** life be different if you lived in China?

What Will I Learn?

Guide to Understanding

North Carolina's Competency Goals and Objectives for South America and Europe

▶ North Carolina's Standard Course of Study for 6th grade Social Studies is divided into thirteen competency goals.

▶ Each competency goal is divided into objectives.

Competency Goals and Objectives

COMPETENCY GOAL 1:

The learner will use the five themes of geography and geographic tools to answer geographic questions and analyze geographic concepts.

Objective

1.01 Create maps, charts, graphs, databases, and models as tools to illustrate information about different people, places and regions in South America and Europe.

Competency Goals are the broad categories of information you need to learn.

Objectives narrow the focus of what you need to learn.

Overview
North Carolina's Competency Goals and Objectives

The charts that follow provide a brief overview of the competency goals and objectives. The objectives are the skills and knowledge you need to succeed on the North Carolina End-of-Grade Test of Reading Comprehension.

 For a complete list of North Carolina's Competency Goals and Objectives for South America and Europe, see page R91.

COMPETENCY GOAL 1:	The learner will use the five themes of geography and geographic tools to answer geographic questions and analyze geographic concepts.
Objectives	**What It Means to You**
1.01 Create maps, charts, graphs, databases, and models as tools to illustrate information about different people, places and regions in South America and Europe.	You will use tools such as maps and globes to learn more about South America and Europe. You will also create maps and charts that will allow you to apply what you have learned to your everyday life.
1.03 Use tools such as maps, globes, graphs, charts, databases, models, and artifacts to compare data on different countries of South America and Europe and to identify patterns as well as similarities and differences among them.	

COMPETENCY GOAL 2:	The learner will assess the relationship between physical environment and cultural characteristics of selected societies and regions of South America and Europe.
Objectives	**What It Means to You**
2.01 Identify key physical characteristics such as landforms, water forms, and climate, and evaluate their influence on the development of cultures in selected South American and European regions.	You will learn how physical characteristics like mountains, rivers, and weather have influenced cultures in South America and Europe. You will investigate how similar characteristics impact where and how people live near you.
2.02 Describe factors that influence changes in distribution patterns of population, resources, and climate in selected regions of South America and Europe and evaluate their impact on the environment.	

COMPETENCY GOAL 3:	The learner will analyze the impact of interactions between humans and their physical environments in South America and Europe.
Objectives	**What It Means to You**
3.02 Describe the environmental impact of regional activities such as deforestation, urbanization, and industrialization and evaluate their significance to the global community.	You will examine the effects that people have on the environment. Discovering how tools and technology help people adapt to the environment will help you understand what you can do to preserve the environment.
3.03 Examine the development and use of tools and technologies and assess their influence on the human ability to use, modify, or adapt to their environment.	

COMPETENCY GOAL 4: The learner will identify significant patterns in the movement of people, goods and ideas over time and place in South America and Europe.

Objectives		What It Means to *You*
4.01	Describe the patterns of and motives for the migrations of people, and evaluate their impact on the political, economic, and social development of selected societies and regions.	You will examine the movement of people in South America and Europe. You will learn how trade affects the development of cultures and regions in the world around you.
4.02	Identify the main commodities of trade over time in selected areas of South America and Europe, and evaluate their significance for the economic, political and social development of cultures and regions.	

COMPETENCY GOAL 5: The learner will evaluate the ways people of South America and Europe make decisions about the allocation and use of economic resources.

Objectives		What It Means to *You*
5.02	Examine the different economic systems (traditional, command, and market), developed in selected societies in South America and Europe, and analyze their effectiveness in meeting basic needs.	You will compare and contrast different economic systems. You will also learn about the importance of global trade patterns and what they mean in your life.
5.04	Describe the relationship between specialization and interdependence, and analyze its influence on the development of regional and global trade patterns.	

COMPETENCY GOAL 6: The learner will recognize the relationship between economic activity and the quality of life in South America and Europe.

Objectives		What It Means to *You*
6.02	Examine the influence of education and technology on productivity and economic development in selected nations and regions of South America and Europe.	You will learn how education and technology have impacted economic development in South America and Europe. You will learn how over-specialization has impacted the standard of living.
6.03	Describe the effects of over-specialization and assess their impact on the standard of living.	

COMPETENCY GOAL 7: The learner will assess connections between historical events and contemporary issues.

Objectives		What It Means to *You*
7.01	Identify historical events such as invasions, conquests, and migrations and evaluate their relationship to current issues.	You will evaluate how events in the past influence the present. You will also investigate key events in South America and Europe and how they have a lasting impact on the world you live in.
7.02	Examine the causes of key historical events in selected areas of South America and Europe and analyze the short- and long-range effects on political, economic, and social institutions.	

COMPETENCY GOAL 8: The learner will assess the influence and contributions of individuals and cultural groups in South America and Europe.

Objectives		What It Means to *You*
8.02	Describe the role of key groups and evaluate their impact on historical and contemporary societies of South America and Europe.	You will discover the roles key groups in South America and Europe have played in their society. You will also learn how discoveries and inventions have changed past societies as well as your own life.
8.03	Identify major discoveries, innovations, and inventions, and assess their influence on societies past and present.	

NORTH CAROLINA COMPETENCY GOALS AND OBJECTIVES

COMPETENCY GOAL 9:
The learner will analyze the different forms of government developed in South America and Europe.

Objectives		What It Means to *You*
9.01	Trace the historical development of governments including traditional, colonial, and national in selected societies and assess the effects on the respective contemporary political systems.	You will learn about the different types of governments and how these governments impact the world today. You will analyze which types of governments you think are the best.
9.02	Describe how different types of governments such as democracies, dictatorships, monarchies, and oligarchies in selected areas of South America and Europe carry out legislative, executive, and judicial functions, and evaluate the effectiveness of each.	

COMPETENCY GOAL 10:
The learner will compare the rights and civic responsibilities of individuals in political structures in South America and Europe.

Objectives		What It Means to *You*
10.02	Identify various sources of citizens' rights and responsibilities, such as constitutions, traditions, and religious law, and analyze how they are incorporated into different government structures.	You will compare the rights of people in South America, Europe, and the United States. You will also think about the rights you have and how they shape your life.
10.03	Describe rights and responsibilities of citizens in selected contemporary societies in South America and Europe, comparing them to each other and to the United States.	

COMPETENCY GOAL 11:
The learner will recognize the common characteristics of different cultures in South America and Europe.

Objectives		What It Means to *You*
11.01	Identify the concepts associated with culture such as language, religion, family, and ethnic identity, and analyze how they both link and separate societies.	You will learn how differences in culture link and separate people in different societies. You will also learn the basic wants and needs that people have.
11.02	Examine the basic needs and wants of all human beings and assess the influence of factors such as environment, values and beliefs in creating different cultural responses.	

COMPETENCY GOAL 12:
The learner will assess the influence of major religions, ethical beliefs, and values on cultures in South America and Europe.

Objectives		What It Means to *You*
12.02	Describe the relationship between cultural values of selected societies of South America and Europe and their art, architecture, music and literature, and assess their significance in contemporary culture.	You will learn how cultural values, art, architecture, music, and literature in South America and Europe impact the world today. You will also learn how your culture learns and borrows from other cultures.
12.03	Identify examples of cultural borrowing, such as language, traditions, and technology, and evaluate their importance in the development of selected societies in South America and Europe.	

COMPETENCY GOAL 13:
The learner will describe the historic, economic, and cultural connections among North Carolina, the United States, South America, and Europe.

Objectives		What It Means to *You*
13.02	Describe the diverse cultural connections that have influenced the development of language, art, music, and belief systems in North Carolina and the United States and assess their role in creating a changing cultural mosaic.	Exploring North Carolina's diverse and rich culture will help you understand how your local culture affects the culture of the United States.

NORTH CAROLINA

Guide to
Test-Taking Strategies and Practice

The charts below provide a guide to the End-of-Grade Test categories and test-taking strategies that will help you prepare for the **End-of-Grade Test of Reading Comprehension**, and be successful in your social studies class.

- **Learn** about each category and strategy by reviewing the numbered steps on the page listed in the column.
- **Practice** the category or strategy on the following page.

North Carolina End-of-Grade Test of Reading Comprehension

EOG Test Category	Learn	Practice	Apply
Cognition	p. S2	p. S3	Essential Questions, Reading Strategies
Interpretation	p. S4	p. S5	Key Questions, Evaluate features, Key Ideas Questions, Document-Based Questions
Critical Stance	p. S6	p. S7	Critical Thinking Questions
Connections	p. S8	p. S9	Connect to Today features, Connect Geography & Culture features, GeoActivities

Test-Taking Strategies and Practice

Strategy	Learn	Practice	Apply
Multiple Choice	p. S10	p. S11	end of each chapter
Primary and Secondary Sources	p. S12	p. S13	p. 256, Chapter 9
Political Cartoons	p. S14	p. S15	www.ClassZone.com
Charts	p. S16	p. S17	p. 55, Chapter 7
Line and Bar Graphs	p. S18	p. S19	p. 251, Chapter 9
Pie Graphs	p. S20	p. S21	p. 214, Chapter 8
Political Maps	p. S22	p. S23	p. 23, Chapter 1
Thematic Maps	p. S24	p. S25	p. 135, Chapter 5
Time Lines	p. S26	p. S27	beginning of every chapter
Constructed Response	p. S28	p. S29	p. 175, Chapter 6
Extended Response	p. S30	p. S31	every Connect to Geography & History box, every Essential Question
Document-Based Questions	pp. S32–S33	pp. S34–S35	p. 323, Chapter 11

Cognition

Cognition refers to the strategies a reader uses to understand a text. These strategies include using context clues to figure out a word's meaning, identifying the main idea and supporting details, and summarizing.

1 Always read the title of a passage. It often provides clues to the main idea.

2 Skim the passage. This will give you an idea of what the passage is about.

3 Read the answer choices carefully. Then reread the passage to find the information you need.

4 The main purpose is similar to the main idea. The main purpose is the author's reason for writing the article.

1 Food Safety Facts

Below are some facts and tips to teach you the basics of food safety.

2 **1 Keep hot foods hot!** If a food is cooked and put out to serve, make sure that you keep the food hot if it is not going to be eaten right away. Perishable food should never be kept at temperatures between 40°F and 140°F for more than two hours. Bacteria can grow well at these temperatures and may grow to levels that could cause illness.

2 Keep cold foods cold! Cold salads, lunchmeats, dairy products and other foods which require refrigeration should always be kept cold (below 40°F).

3 Always wash your hands well with soap and warm water, both before and after handling food! Our hands naturally carry bacteria on them. If we transfer that bacteria to food, the food is a good place for those bacteria to grow! It is important not to let the bacteria from raw foods stay on your hands when you may transfer them to your mouth or other foods.

4 Don't cross contaminate! Cook meat and poultry thoroughly to kill the harmful bacteria that may be on them. That is why it is very important to make sure that you don't allow the juices associated with raw meat and poultry to contaminate other areas of your kitchen.

5 Thaw foods safely! Frozen raw meat and poultry should never be thawed by leaving them on the counter at room temperature. The proper way to thaw such products is to either thaw them in the refrigerator or thaw them in a microwave oven.

1. What is the *main* purpose of this selection? **4**

3 **A.** to tell readers how to thaw foods

   B. to warn readers about eating hot foods

   C. to tell readers how to prevent food borne illnesses

   D. to scare readers about cooking

   Thinking Skill: *Analyzing*

2. Which of the following supports the main purpose?

   A. Bacteria grows at temperatures between 40°F and 140°F.

   B. Food borne illnesses are preventable if food is handled safely.

   C. Cold lunchmeats should always be kept on the counter.

   D. Frozen raw meat should only be thawed in the refriegerator.

   Thinking Skill: *Analyzing*

answers: 1 (C), 2 (B)

From the North Carolina Department of Agriculture & Consumer Services Web site http://www.agr.state.nc.us/cyber/kidswrld/foodsafe/facts/Sffacts.htm. Reprinted by permission.

Directions: Read the article about the Wright brothers. Then answer the following questions.

In Mechanics

by Richard Sussman

Most people do not realize that the Wright brothers—Orville, born 1871, and Wilbur, born 1867—performed various scientific experiments before inventing their aircraft. For as long as anyone in their hometown of Dayton, Ohio, could remember, the Wright boys had worked on mechanical projects.

Luckily, the brothers had parents who had encouraged their love of science. Their mother, Susan, had studied mathematics in college and taught them to draw plans and to think through experiments. Their father, Milton, a church official who traveled a great deal, brought home presents that stimulated their interests.

Orville and Wilbur long remembered their favorite gift, a toy similar to today's helicopter that was made from cork, bamboo, and tissue paper. They called it "the bat." It was powered by two rubber bands attached to two propellers. Through their teenage years, a variety of projects kept the boys' interest. Orville tried his hand at making and selling kites, building a lathe with Wilbur, and constructing and using printing presses.

Then, after working together on building a large press, the brothers decided to publish a weekly newspaper in the spring of 1889. Before long, though, Orville discovered yet another interest: bicycles.

Bicycles enjoyed great popularity in America in the mid-1890s. Orville and Wilbur opened a series of four bicycle shops in Dayton. In 1896, the Wrights started building their own brands of bicycles—the Van Cleve and the St. Clair—with parts they manufactured themselves.

Still greater challenges drew the Wrights' attention away from bicycles after a few years. The brothers began experimenting with kites and gliders in 1899, hoping that they could invent the world's first practical airplane. As a matter of fact, the first airplane included many bicycle parts.

1. What is the main idea of this article?

A. The Wright brothers liked bicycles.

B. The Wright brothers were always interested in mechanical projects.

C. The Wright brothers owned a newspaper.

D. The Wright brothers had parents who encouraged them.

Thinking Skill: *Analyzing*

2. Which of the following interests did not help the Wright brothers invent the first practical airplane?

A. kites

B. gliders

C. bicycles

D. newspaper publishing

Thinking Skill: *Analyzing*

Interpretation

Interpreting a piece of literature means more than repeating information or understanding the context. You may be asked to discuss a selection's tone or explain why the selection is important.

1 Always read the introductory paragraph of an interview or an article. It often provides information about the person being interviewed or what is being written about.

2 When reading an interview, read the questions carefully. The questions often set the tone of the interview.

3 Read the questions and all of the answer choices carefully. Then reread the passage to find the information that you need.

4 You are being asked to interpret the tone of the interview. Skim the interview again. Ask yourself, what kind of questions does the interviewer ask?

5 Think about the answers Cal Ripken, Jr. gave to the interviewer. Do they give you clues about his personality or beliefs?

answers: 1 (B), 2 (A)

Batty About Baseball

1 Former professional baseball player Cal Ripken, Jr. talks about his career and his work with kids with *Time Magazine for Kids* (TFK).

2 **TFK: What advice do you have for kids who want to play pro baseball?**

Ripken: There are no shortcuts. You have to work hard, and you have to be honest with yourself. And you have to work on your weaknesses. And I wish there was a form that says if you follow A, B, C, and D, you'll make it to the big leagues but that's not true. Any goal, anything you do including trying to be a professional baseball player, you have to consider talent.

TFK: Do you think kids' sports are too competitive?

Ripken: Well, competition is part of sports, but I think if you emphasize winning too much, you lose the development of the kids. You have to let the kids play, let them experience their own mistakes. You have to let them make choices within the game.

TFK: What can kids and adults do to lower the competition?

Ripken: To me it's less about competitiveness and more about pressure. So if you push too much on the competitive side, if you push too much on the winning side, you create pressure. Pressure for kids takes the fun out of the game, so I think the best thing you can do as a coach or a parent [is] to remember it is for the kids, and take a step back and allow the kids to play.

3 **1.** Which word describes the tone of this interview? **4**

A. angry
B. honest
C. nervous
D. depressed

Thinking Skill: *Generating*

2. What can a reader tell about Cal Ripken, Jr. from reading the interview? **5**

A. He believes in hard work.
B. He doesn't think children should play baseball.
C. He wants everyone to fill out a form to play baseball.
D. He only cares about winning.

Thinking Skill: *Analyzing*

Directions: Laura Ingalls Wilder wrote books about her life growing up in South Dakota. Many children read her books and wrote her letters telling her what the books meant to them. Read the letter. Then answer the following questions.

March 15, 1952

Dearest Laura,

My name is Jeannie. I am 12 years old and in 7th grade.

How old is your daughter Rose? Is she still living? How old is she? Do you have any other children?

Are Ida and Elmer still living? What are their children's names? Where do they live?

Did you teach school after you were married?

How long did you and Almanzo live in South Dakota before you moved to Missouri?

I was very sorry to hear about Almanzo and Pa and Ma and Grace, Carrie and Mary passing away.

How old did Pa and Ma and Grace, Carrie and Mary live to be?

I have read all eight of the books you have written and enjoyed them very much. I read most of the time. Sometimes even when I am supposed to be studying Calif. Hist, and Geography. Mother [says] that I read [too] much and am a "Book worm."

I have one sister that is almost 2 years younger than I. Her name is Peggy. We have a gray and white cat named Smokey. He is real big and awful pretty.

I don't suppose I'll ever find out the answers to all these questions I have asked you, but I can always hope that you will have time to write a few lines to me.

Sincerely yours,

Jeannie
Lindsay, Calif.

P.S. Please write if you have time.

1. How can you tell that Jeannie thinks of Laura Ingalls Wilder as a friend?

A. She tells her about her cat.

B. She asks her about her children.

C. She asks her to write back.

D. She addresses the letter to "Dearest Laura."

Thinking Skill: Generating

2. What can you tell about Jeannie by reading the letter?

A. She is very curious.

B. She is lonely.

C. She doesn't like to study.

D. She only likes to read Laura Ingalls Wilder's books.

Thinking Skill: Applying

Critical Stance

You may be asked to take a critical stance on a piece of literature. You can do this by comparing and contrasting, distinguishing between fact and opinion, and trying to understand the way the author has constructed the piece.

❶ Read the introduction carefully to see if there are any clues about the selection you are going to read.

❷ Read the passage. Make notes and ask yourself questions as you read.

❸ Read the questions and all of the answer choices carefully. Then reread the passage to find the information that you need.

❹ Part of reading critically is to understand how the author constructs, or puts together, the piece. This question is asking why the author included the narrator's memory of Jamie in this selection.

❺ Another way to read critically is to compare and contrast. Comparing tells how things are alike; contrasting tells how things are different.

A Taste of Blackberries
by Doris Buchanan Smith

❶ *A Taste of Blackberries* **is a story about a boy dealing with the loss of his best friend.**

❷ Did the world know that Jamie was dead? The sky didn't act like it. It was a blue sky and white cloud day. Horses and lambs and floppy-eared dogs chased across the sky. Was Jamie playing with them?

What kinds of things could you do when you were dead? Or was dead just plain dead and that's all?

I looked across at Jamie's window. He would never flash me a signal again. We had learned Morse code, Jamie and I, and talked to each other at night. Before that we had taken cans and a string and stretched it across from his window to mine.

That had been a funny day. It had been so easy to string up one can and drop the string down from Jamie's window. It wasn't so easy getting the string up to my window.

We dragged the string across the street and Jamie tried to throw the can up to me.

Finally, I climbed my mother's rose trellis by the kitchen window careful to keep my foot at the cross pieces of the trellis where it was strongest. I picked my way up through the thorns until I was on the sun deck with the can and string.

"Yeah, smarty," Jamie laughed. "Now how are you going to get it to your room?"

"And you know what I just thought of?" Jamie asked when he came back over. "Why didn't we just drop an extra piece of string from your front window and tie onto this one and pull it up?" It was so simple we collapsed again and clapped our arms over our heads. We felt so stupid.

❸ 1. What is the purpose of the story about Jamie and the narrator trying to set up the cans in the window? **❹**

A. It shows how creative Jamie was.

B. It tells why the narrator learned Morse code.

C. It shows how the narrator and Jamie were best friends.

D. It explains why Jamie died.

Thinking Skill: *Analyzing*

2. How does the sky contrast with how the narrator feels? **❺**

A. The sky seems happy and the narrator is sad.

B. The sky is gloomy and the narrator is happy.

C. The clouds seem playful and the narrator is not allowed to play.

D. The sky is blue, which is the narrator's favorite color.

Thinking Skill: *Analyzing*

answers: 1 (C), 2 (A)

Directions: The following is an excerpt of a play about Anne Frank in which Anne discusses her situation with Peter, the boy who is in hiding with her. Read the selection. Then answer the questions below.

The Diary of Anne Frank

Anne: Where did you go to school?

Peter: Jewish Secondary.

Anne: But that's where Margo and I go! I never saw you around.

Peter: I used to see you . . . sometimes. . .

Anne: You did?

Peter: . . . in the school yard. You were always in the middle of a bunch of kids.

Anne: Why didn't you ever come over?

Peter: I'm sort of a lone wolf. *(He starts to rip off his Star of David.)*

Anne: What are you doing?

Peter: Taking it off?

Anne: But you can't do that. They'll arrest you if you go out without your star. *(He tosses his knife on the table.)*

Peter: Who's going out?

Anne: Why, of course. You're right! Of course, we don't need them any more. *(She picks up his knife and starts to take off her star.)* I wonder what our friends will think when we don't show up today.

Peter: I didn't have any dates with anyone.

Anne: Oh, I did, I had a date with Jopie this afternoon to go play ping-pong at her house. Do you know Jopie de Waal?

Peter: No.

Anne: Jopie's my best friend. I wonder what she'll think when she telephones and there's no answer? . . . I wonder what she'll think . . . we left everything as if we'd suddenly been called away . . . breakfast dishes in the sink . . . beds not made. . . . *(As she pulls off her star the cloth underneath shows clearly the color and form of the star.)* Look! It's still there! *(PETER goes over to the stove with his star.)* What're you going to do with yours?

Peter: Burn it.

Anne: *(She starts to throw hers in, and cannot.)* It's funny. I can't throw mine away. I don't know why.

Peter: You can't throw . . . ? Something they branded you with . . . ? That they made you wear so they could spit on you?

Anne: I know. I know. But after all, it is the Star of David, isn't it?

1. How are Anne and Peter different?

   A. Anne is serious and Peter is funny.

   B. Anne is quiet and Peter is friendly.

   C. Anne wants to wear the star and Peter does not.

   D. Anne has a lot of friends and Peter does not.

   Thinking Skill: *Organizing*

2. What is the significance of Peter telling Anne that he is a "lone wolf"?

   A. He is telling her to leave.

   B. He is telling her that he wants to be friends.

   C. He is telling her that he is lonely.

   D. He is telling her that he is afraid.

   Thinking Skill: *Generating*

Connections

Sometimes, you are asked to make connections between what you read and the outside world. You can make connections by comparing something that happens in the story and something that has happened in real life. Another way to make connections is to relate information you know from other sources to the piece of literature you are reading.

1 Read the poem. Ask yourself questions as you read.

2 Read the questions and all of the answer choices carefully. Then reread the poem to find the answers.

3 Part of making connections is to compare what happens in the selection to what could happen in real life. Think about each choice. Which one is *most* like the one described in the poem?

4 This question is asking what message the poet is trying to tell you. Read each choice. Which one best describe what is happening in the poem?

Soup

by Carl Sandburg

1 I saw the famous man eating soup.

I say he was lifting a fat broth

Into his mouth with a spoon.

His name was in the newspapers that day

Spelled out in tall black headlines

And thousands of people were talking about him.

    When I saw him,

He sat bending his head over a plate

Putting soup in his mouth with a spoon.

2 **1.** Which experience is *most* like the one described **3** in the poem?

    A. seeing a movie star signing autographs

    B. seeing the President at the grocery store

    C. seeing your neighbor mowing the lawn

    D. seeing your friend at the mall

    Thinking Skill: *Integrating*

2. What does the experience in the poem tell us? **4**

    A. Famous people like soup.

    B. Famous people are different from everyone else.

    C. Famous people have the same needs as everyone else.

    D. Famous people want to be left alone.

    Thinking Skill: *Integrating*

answers: 1 (B), 2 (C)

EOG PRACTICE

Directions: Read the poem. Then answer the following questions.

Moon of Falling Leaves

by Joseph Bruchac and Jonathan London

Long ago, the trees were told
they must stay awake
seven days and nights,
but only the cedar,
the pine and the spruce
stayed awake until that seventh night.
The reward they were given
while all the other trees
must shed their leaves.

So, each autumn, the leaves
of the sleeping trees fall.
They cover the floor
of our woodlands with colors
as bright as the flowers
that come with the spring.
The leaves return the strength
of one more year's growth to the earth.

This journey
the leaves are taking
is part of that great circle
which holds us all close to the earth.

---

1. Which experience is *most* like the one described in the poem?

    A. a rabbit having a litter of bunnies

    B. the rotation of the earth

    C. cutting down a tree

    D. a rose bush blooming every spring

    Thinking Skill: *Integrating*

2. What is the "great circle"?

    A. the trunk of a tree

    B. the change of seasons

    C. the revolution of the earth around the sun

    D. the earth

    Thinking Skill: *Integrating*

Test-Taking Strategies and Practice

Use the strategies in this section to improve your test-taking skills. First, read the tips on the left page. Then use them to help you with the practice items on the right page.

Multiple Choice

A multiple-choice question is a question or incomplete sentence and a set of choices. One of the choices correctly answers the question or completes the sentence.

1 Read the question or incomplete sentence carefully. Try to answer the question before looking at the choices.

2 Read each choice with the question. Don't decide on your final answer until you have checked all the choices.

3 Rule out any choices that you know are wrong.

4 Look for key words in the question. They may help you figure out the correct answer.

5 Sometimes the last choice is *all of the above*. Make sure that the other choices are all correct before you pick this answer.

6 Be careful with questions that include the word *not*.

1 **1.** Which of the following countries shares a border with the United States?

2 choices
- **A.** Brazil
- **B.** Canada
- **C.** Cuba
- **D.** Venezuela

3 Since Cuba is an island, you know that it cannot share a border with the United States.

2. Which language is spoken by (most) of the people who live in Latin America and the Caribbean?

- **A.** English
- **B.** French
- **C.** Portuguese
- **D.** Spanish

4 The word *most* is key here. All of the languages listed are spoken in Latin America and the Caribbean, but most people there speak Spanish.

3. The Andes mountains run through

- **A.** Colombia.
- **B.** Ecuador.
- **C.** Peru.
- **D.** all of the above

5 Before selecting *all of the above*, make sure that all of the choices are, indeed, correct.

4. Which of the following is (not) an island in the Caribbean?

- **A.** Barbados
- **B.** Cuba
- **C.** Hawaii
- **D.** Jamaica

6 First rule out all the choices that name islands in the Caribbean. The choice that remains is the correct answer.

answers: 1 (B); 2 (D); 3 (D); 4 (C)

Directions: Read each question carefully. Choose the best answer from the four choices.

1. Which of the following was *not* a result of the bubonic plague?

   A. Cities worked together during the plague.

   B. Europe lost one-third of its population.

   C. The Church lost its prestige among the people.

   D. The economies of many countries were ruined.

2. Martin Luther started a reform movement when he

   A. published the New Testament in German.

   B. criticized some of the Church's practices.

   C. wrote his 95 Theses and made them public.

   D. all of the above

3. The Ottoman Empire reached its greatest size and glory under the rule of

   A. Mehmet II.

   B. Selim the Grim.

   C. Suleiman the Lawgiver.

   D. Timur the Lame.

4. During the 1700s, England controlled which of the following?

   A. the sugar trade

   B. the Atlantic slave trade

   C. the cotton trade

   D. the coconut trade

Primary and Secondary Sources

Sometimes you will need to study a document to answer a question. Documents can be either primary sources or secondary sources. Primary sources are written or created by people who either saw an event or were actually part of the event. A primary source can be a photograph, letter, diary, speech, or autobiography.

A secondary source is an account of events by a person who did not actually experience them. Newspaper articles and history books are some examples of secondary sources.

1 Look at the source line to learn about the document and its author. If the author is well known and has been quoted often, the information is likely true.

2 Skim the article to get an idea of what it is about.

3 Note special punctuation. For example, ellipses (. . .) indicate that words have been left out.

4 Ask yourself questions about the document as you read.

5 Review the questions to see what information you will need to find. Then reread the document.

answers: 1 (B); 2 (C)

A Native American View of Nature

Plants are of different families. . . It is the same with animals. . . It is the same with human beings; there is some place which is better adapted to each. The seeds of the plants are blown about by the wind until they reach the place where they will grow best. . .and there they take root and grow. . . In the early days the animals probably roamed over a very wide country until they found a proper place. An animal depends on the natural conditions around it. If the buffalo were here today, I think they would be different from the buffalo of the old days because all the natural conditions have changed. They would not find the same food, nor the same surroundings. We see change in our ponies. . . Now. . . they have less endurance and must have constant care [unlike the past]. It is the same with the Indians; they have less freedom and they fall an easy prey to disease.

—Okute, at Teton Sioux (1911)

The Sioux were a Native American people who lived on the Great Plains of North America.

1. Okute thinks that horses and Indians now are different from those of early days because

A. the buffalo are gone.

B. natural conditions have changed.

C. they cannot roam to find the best place to change.

D. there is no water.

2. Which sentence *best* expresses the idea of this passage?

A. "Animals and humans must always roam."

B. "Each plant, animal, and human is different."

C. "Each plant, animal and human thrives in a particular place."

D. "Plants and animals were created for humans to eat."

Directions: Read this passage. Use the passage and your knowledge of world cultures and geography to answer questions 1 and 2.

Before World War I

In 1892, France and Russia had become military allies. Later, Germany signed an agreement to protect Austria. If any nation attacked Austria, Germany would fight on its side. France and Russia had to support each other as well. For instance, if France got into a war with Germany, Russia had to fight Germany, too. This meant that in any war, Germany would have to fight on two fronts: France on the west and Russia on the east.

If a war broke out, what part would Great Britain play? No one knew. It might remain neutral, like Belgium. It might, if given a reason, fight against Germany.

1. If Russia and Germany went to war, which country had to help Russia?

   A. Great Britain

   B. Belgium

   C. Austria

   D. France

2. What was a result of the military alliance formed between France and Russia?

   A. Belgium would have to fight a war on the side of Germany.

   B. Great Britain would remain neutral.

   C. Germany would have to fight a war on two fronts.

   D. France and Russia would support Germany in a war.

Political Cartoons

Cartoonists who draw political cartoons use both words and art to express opinions about political issues.

1 Try to figure out what the cartoon is about. Titles and captions may give clues.

2 Use labels to help identify the people, places, and events represented in the cartoon.

3 Note when and where the cartoon was published.

4 Look for symbols—that is, people, places, or objects that stand for something else.

5 The cartoonist often exaggerates the physical features of people and objects. This technique will give you clues as to how the cartoonist feels about the subject.

6 Try to figure out the cartoonist's message and summarize it in a sentence.

1 NEXT!

4 The cartoonist uses the swastika, a symbol used during World War II.

5 The swastika looks like a huge, frightening machine. It can easily crush Poland.

2 The label "Poland" tells which country is the subject of the cartoon's title.

Daniel Fitzpatrick / *St. Louis Post-Dispatch*, August 24, 1939.

3 The date is a clue that the cartoon refers to the beginning of World War II.

1. What does the swastika in the cartoon stand for?

    A. the Soviet Union

    B. Nazi Germany

    C. the Polish army

    D. Great Britain

6 **2.** Which sentence best summarizes the cartoonist's message?

    A. Germany will attack Poland next.

    B. Poland should stop Germany.

    C. Germany will lose this battle.

    D. Poland will fight a civil war.

answers: 1 (B); 2 (A)

PRACTICE

Directions: Study this cartoon. Use the cartoon and your knowledge of world cultures and geography to answer questions 1 and 2.

The Granger Collection, New York

Benjamin Franklin (1754)

1. What do the sections of the snake in the cartoon represent?

    A. army units

    B. states

    C. Native American groups

    D. colonies

2. Which phrase *best* states the message of the cartoon?

    A. "East is East, and West is West, and never the twain shall meet."

    B. "Taxation without representation is tyranny."

    C. "United we stand, divided we fall."

    D. "Out of many, one."

TEST-TAKING STRATEGIES AND PRACTICE

Charts

Charts present facts in a visual form. History textbooks use several different types of charts. The chart that is most often found on standardized tests is the table. A table organizes information in columns and rows.

❶ Read the title of the chart to find out what information is represented.

❷ Read the headings at the top of each column. Then read the headings at the left of each row.

❸ Notice how the information in the chart is organized.

❹ Notice that information from different years is used for different countries.

❺ Of all the countries listed, six took in the most immigrants. Think about what these countries have in common.

❻ Read the questions and then study the chart again.

❶ This chart is about the number of people who immigrated to different countries.

❹ Notice that information from different years is used for different countries.

Immigration to Selected Countries

Country	Years	Number of Immigrants
Argentina	1856–1932	6,405,000
Australia	1861–1932	2,913,000
Brazil	1821–1932	4,431,000
British West Indies	1836–1932	1,587,000
Canada	1821–1932	5,206,000
Cuba	1901–1932	857,000
Mexico	1911–1931	226,000
New Zealand	1851–1932	594,000
South Africa	1881–1932	852,000
United States	1821–1932	34,244,000
Uruguay	1836–1932	713,000

Source: Alfred W. Crosby, Jr. *The Columbian Exchange: Biological and Cultural Consequences of 1492*

❸ This chart lists countries in alphabetical order. Other charts organize information by years or by numbers.

❺ Of all the countries listed, six took in the most immigrants. Think about what these countries have in common.

1. The country that received the most immigrants was

A. Canada.
B. the British West Indies.
C. the United States.
D. Brazil.

2. Different countries received immigrants in different years. According to the chart, which countries received immigrants the earliest?

A. Argentina, New Zealand, and Canada
B. Canada, Brazil, and United States
C. Mexico, United States, and British West Indies
D. Brazil, South Africa, and Cuba

answers: 1 (C); 2 (B)

PRACTICE

Directions: Read the chart carefully. Use the chart and your knowledge of world cultures and geography to answer questions 1 and 2.

Mexico and the Nations of Central America				
Country	Capital	Area (sq. miles)	Population	Per Capita Gross Domestic Product (in U.S. dollars)
Belize	Belmopan	8,800	270,000	3,600
Costa Rica	San José	19,700	4,327,000	4,300
El Salvador	San Salvador	8,100	6,881,000	2,300
Guatemala	Guatemala City	42,000	6,881,000	2,200
Honduras	Tegucigalpa	43,300	12,599,000	1,000
Mexico	Mexico City	756,000	7,205,000	6,400
Nicaragua	Managua	50,200	107,029,000	820
Panama	Panama City	29,200	5,487,000	4,300

Source: World Statistics Pocketbook 2006
UN Department of Economic and Social Affairs

1. The largest country in terms of both area and population is

A. Guatemala.

B. Honduras.

C. Mexico.

D. Nicaragua.

2. Which correctly states the countries' rank from high to low in terms of per capita gross domestic product?

A. Honduras, Nicaragua, Belize, Guatemala

B. Mexico, Panama, El Salvador, Honduras

C. Panama, Costa Rica, Mexico, Belize

D. Mexico, Nicaragua, Panama, Guatemala

TEST-TAKING STRATEGIES AND PRACTICE

Line and Bar Graphs

Graphs are often used to show numbers. Line graphs often show changes over time. Bar graphs make it easy to compare numbers.

1 Read the title of the graph to find out what information is represented.

2 Study the labels on the graph.

3 Look at the source line that tells where the graph is from. Decide whether you can depend on the source to provide reliable information.

4 See if you can make any generalizations about the information in the graph. Note whether the numbers change over time.

5 Read the questions carefully and then study the graph again.

1 Exports of English Manufactured Goods, 1699–1774

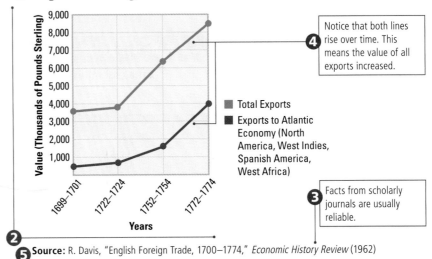

4 Notice that both lines rise over time. This means the value of all exports increased.

3 Facts from scholarly journals are usually reliable.

5 Source: R. Davis, "English Foreign Trade, 1700–1774," *Economic History Review* (1962)

1. Which of the following is a true statement?

A. Exports to the Atlantic economy declined over time.

B. Total exports stayed the same over time.

C. Total exports rose sharply after 1724.

D. Exports to the Atlantic economy fell sharply after 1754.

1 Nations with High Foreign Debt, 2003

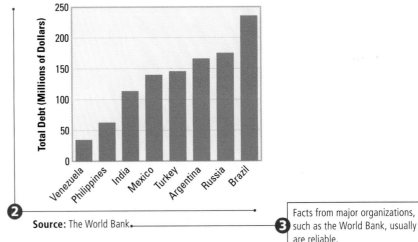

3 Facts from major organizations, such as the World Bank, usually are reliable.

Source: The World Bank

5 2. The nation with the second largest foreign debt is

A. Brazil.

B. Argentina.

C. Russia.

D. Mexico.

answers: 1 (C); 2 (C)

Directions: Study the graphs carefully. Use the graphs and your knowledge of world cultures and geography to answer questions 1 and 2.

Canada: Imports and Exports, 2000–2005

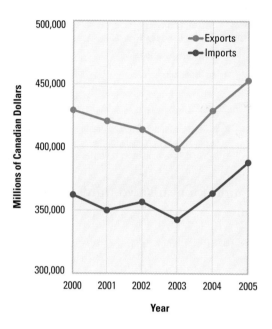

Source: Statistics Canada

Unemployment Rates for Selected Countries, 2005

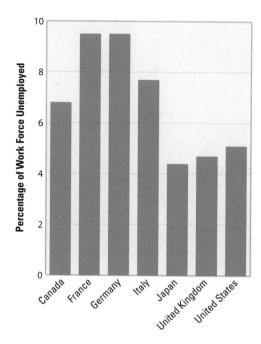

Source: Organization for Economic Cooperation and Development

1. In which year was the value of imports and exports the smallest?

A. 2001

B. 2002

C. 2003

D. 2005

2. Which country had the lowest unemployment rate in 2005?

A. Japan

B. Germany

C. United States

D. United Kingdom

TEST-TAKING STRATEGIES AND PRACTICE

Pie Graphs

A pie, or circle, graph shows the relationship among parts of a whole. These parts look like slices of a pie. Each slice is shown as a percentage of the whole pie.

1 Read the title of the graph to find out what information is represented.

2 The graph may provide a legend, or key, that tells you what different slices represent.

3 The size of the slice is related to the percentage. The larger the percentage, the larger the slice.

4 Look at the source line that tells where the graph is from. Ask yourself if you can depend on this source to provide reliable information.

5 Read the questions carefully, and study the graph again.

1 World Population by Region, 2006

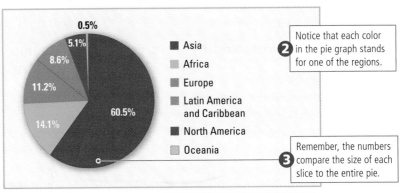

2 Notice that each color in the pie graph stands for one of the regions.

3 Remember, the numbers compare the size of each slice to the entire pie.

Source: Population Reference Bureau

4 The Population Reference Bureau studies population data for the United States and other countries.

1. Which region accounts for nearly two-thirds of the world's population?

A. Africa

B. North America

C. Europe

D. Asia

5

2. A greater share of the world's population lives in Latin America and the Caribbean than lives in

A. Africa

B. Europe

C. North America

D. Asia

For this question, find the "pie slices" for each of the regions listed in the alternatives. Compare each one to the "pie slice" for Latin America and the Caribbean.

answers: 1 (D); 2 (C)

PRACTICE

Directions: Study the pie graph. Use the graph and your knowledge of world cultures and geography to answer questions 1 and 2.

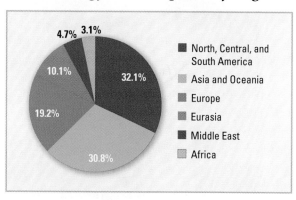

World Energy Consumption by Region

- 4.7%
- 3.1%
- 10.1%
- 32.1%
- 19.2%
- 30.8%

■ North, Central, and South America
▨ Asia and Oceania
▨ Europe
▨ Eurasia
■ Middle East
▨ Africa

Source: Energy Information Administration/Annual Energy Review 2005

1. Which region uses the least energy?

A. Europe

B. Asia and Oceania

C. Africa

D. Middle East

2. North, Central, and South America are grouped together because

A. they are in the same part of the world.

B. all three have about the same number of people.

C. all three are roughly the same size.

D. they use the same power sources.

Political Maps

Political maps show the divisions within countries. A country may be divided into states, provinces, or other kinds of segments. The maps also show where major cities are. They may also show mountains, oceans, seas, lakes, and rivers.

1 Read the title of the map. This will give you the subject and purpose of the map.

2 Read the labels on the map. They also give information about the map's subject and purpose.

3 Study the key or legend to help you understand the symbols on the map.

4 Use the scale to estimate distances between places shown on the map. Maps usually show the distance in both miles and kilometers.

5 Use the compass rose to figure out directions on the map.

6 Read the questions. Carefully study the map to find the answers.

1 Present-Day United States

3 The legend gives symbols for the nation's capital and the states' capitals.

2 The labels identify the states of the United States.

1. What state extends farthest east?

A. Oregon

B. Maine

C. Georgia

D. Alaska

2. About how many miles is it from the Great Lakes to the Pacific Ocean along the United States–Canada border?

A. 1,000

B. 1,500

C. 2,000

D. 2,500

answers: 1 (B); 2 (B)

Directions: Study the map carefully. Use the map and your knowledge of world cultures and geography to answer questions 1 and 2.

Present-Day Europe

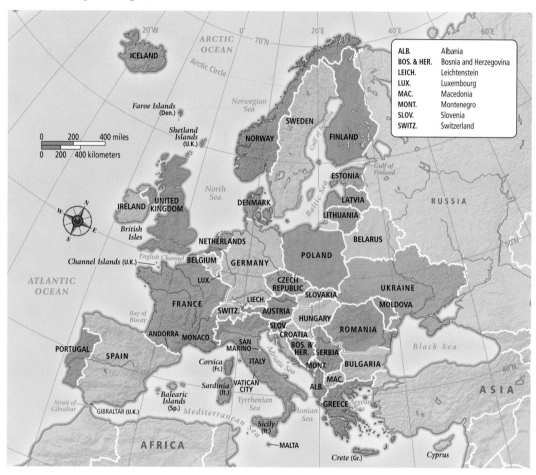

ALB.	Albania
BOS. & HER.	Bosnia and Herzegovina
LEICH.	Leichtenstein
LUX.	Luxembourg
MAC.	Macedonia
MONT.	Montenegro
SLOV.	Slovenia
SWITZ.	Switzerland

1. What body of water borders Poland on the north?

   A. North Sea

   B. Norwegian Sea

   C. Baltic Sea

   D. Adriatic Sea

2. The northernmost country in Europe is

   A. Ireland.

   B. Denmark.

   C. Iceland.

   D. Norway.

Thematic Maps

Thematic maps focus on special topics. For example, a thematic map might show a country's natural resources or major battles in a war.

1 Read the title of the map. This will give you the subject and purpose of the map.

2 Read the labels on the map. They give information about the map's subject and purpose. (The labels identify the three European empires.)

3 Study the key or legend to help you understand the symbols and/or colors on the map. (The legend shows the colors that indicate the three European empires.)

4 Try to make generalizations about information shown on the maps.

5 Read the questions. Carefully study the map to find the answers.

1 European Empires in North America, 1700

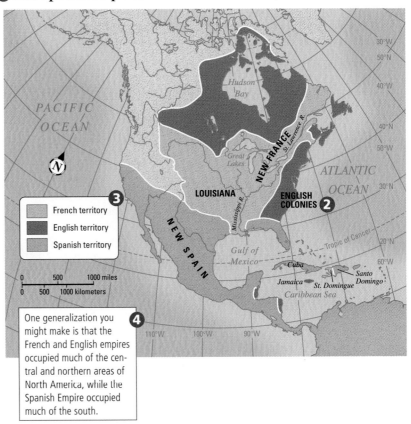

Legend:
- French territory
- English territory
- Spanish territory

0 — 500 — 1000 miles
0 — 500 — 1000 kilometers

4 One generalization you might make is that the French and English empires occupied much of the central and northern areas of North America, while the Spanish Empire occupied much of the south.

1. The land around the Great Lakes was controlled by

   A. England.

   B. France.

   C. Spain.

   D. all of the above

2. Which of the following statements about the English colonial empire in North America is *not* true?

   A. English lands shared borders with both French and Spanish lands.

   B. English lands did not stretch as far west as those held by Spain.

   C. England held no land on the Pacific Coast of North America.

   D. England held no lands east of 60° W longitude.

answers: 1 (B); 2 (D)

Directions: Study the map carefully. Use the map and your knowledge of world cultures and geography to answer questions 1 and 2.

The Roman Empire, A.D. 400

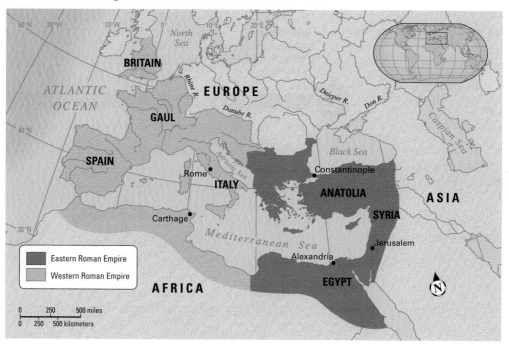

1. Which area was part of the Eastern Roman Empire?

   A. Spain

   B. Gaul

   C. Anatolia

   D. all of the above

2. The northernmost region in the Western Roman Empire was

   A. Syria.

   B. Gaul.

   C. Spain.

   D. Britain.

TEST-TAKING STRATEGIES AND PRACTICE

Time Lines

A time line is a chart that lists events in the order in which they occurred. Time lines can be vertical or horizontal.

1 Read the title to learn what period of time the time line covers.

2 Note the dates when the time line begins and ends.

3 Read the events in the order they occurred.

4 Think about what else was going on in the world on these dates. Try to make connections.

5 Read the questions. Then carefully study the time line to find the answers.

❶ The Struggle for Mexican Independence

1810 Father Miguel Hidalgo issues the "Cry of Dolores," launching the Mexican independence movement.

1813 Morelos calls a congress of representatives from all of Mexico's provinces. The congress writes a constitution for a Mexican republic.

1820 Spain sends large force, under the command of Agustín de Iturbide, to round up guerilla bands. Iturbide throws his support to the rebellion.

1810 — **1821**

1811 Spanish forces capture Hidalgo and execute him. Father José María Morelos takes over leadership of the revolt.

1815 Spanish forces capture and execute Morelos.

1815–1820 Vicente Guerrero, with a small band of followers, continues the rebellion against Spain.

1821 Iturbide and rebel leaders declare Mexico's independence.

2 Horizontal time lines show the earliest date on the far left.

3 Notice that the time period between 1810 and 1821 was one of conflict.

4 Note that Mexico, like other Latin American countries, was deeply influenced by the revolutions in the United States and France.

1. In which year did Father José María Morelos become the leader of the Mexican Independence movement?

A. 1810
B. 1811
C. 1813
D. 1815

2. Which of the following switched sides during the struggle for Mexican independence?

A. Vicente Guerrero
B. Father Miguel Hidalgo
C. Agustín de Iturbide
D. José María Morelos

answers: 1 (B), 2 (C)

Directions: Study the time line. Use the information shown and your knowledge of world cultures and geography to answer questions 1 and 2.

The Breakup of the Soviet Union

1985 Mikhail Gorbachev becomes leader of Soviet Union.

1989 In Soviet elections, many Communist candidates are defeated.

1991 Boris Yeltsin is elected president of Russia.

1991 Communist and army hardliners seize power; Yeltsin leads resistance that defeats them.

1991 Soviet Union ceases to exist. Over the next several months, 14 other republics become independent.

1985 ——————————————— 1991

1986 Gorbachev starts economic and political reforms.

1988 New Soviet constitutional amendments allow for open elections.

1990 Lithuania declares independence.

1. What happened after Lithuania declared independence?

   A. Gorbachev started economic and political reforms.

   B. Many other republics became independent.

   C. New constitutional amendments allowed for open elections.

   D. Gorbachev defeated Yeltsin in a new election.

2. In which year did Communist and army hardliners try to seize power?

   A. 1985

   B. 1988

   C. 1990

   D. 1991

TEST-TAKING STRATEGIES AND PRACTICE

Constructed Response

Constructed-response questions focus on a document, such as a photograph, cartoon, chart, graph, or time line. Instead of picking one answer from a set of choices, you write a short response. Sometimes, you can find the answer in the document. Other times, you will use what you already know about a subject to answer the question.

1 Read the title of the document to get an idea of what it is about.

2 Study the document (including any caption, if it is an image).

3 Read the questions carefully. Study the document again to find the answers.

4 Write your answers. You don't need to use complete sentences unless the directions say so.

1 The Temple of Inscriptions, Palenque, Mexico

2 Constructed-response questions use a wide range of documents. These include short passages, cartoons, charts, graphs, maps, time lines, posters, and other visual materials. This document is a photograph showing ruins in Palenque, Mexico.

The Temple of Inscriptions stands over the tomb of Pakal, a great Maya king. The Maya used the temple for religious purposes. Such flat-topped, pyramid-like buildings are typical of Maya architecture.

3 1. Palenque, with its massive pyramid structures, was one of the city-states of what civilizations?

4 *Maya*

2. For what purpose was this building used?

religious purposes

3. This civilization went into decline around A.D. 900. Which great civilization arose in its place?

Aztec civilization

Directions: Read the following passage from *Zlata's Diary*, a diary kept by Zlata, a 12-year-old girl. Use the passage and your knowledge of world cultures and geography to answer questions 1 and 2. You do not need to use complete sentences.

Saturday, May 2, 1992

Dear Mimmy,

Today was truly, absolutely the worst day ever in Sarajevo. The shooting started around noon. Mommy and I moved into the hall. Daddy was in his office, under our apartment, at the time. We told him on the intercom to run quickly to the downstairs lobby where we'd meet him . . . The gunfire was getting worse, and we couldn't get over the wall to the Bobars', so we ran down to our own cellar.

The cellar is ugly, dark, smelly. Mommy, who's terrified of mice, had two fears to cope with. The three of us were in the same corner as the other day. We listened to the pounding shells, the shooting, the thundering noise overhead. We even heard planes. At one moment I realized that this awful cellar was the only place that could save our lives. Suddenly, it started to look almost warm and nice. It was the only way we could defend ourselves against all this terrible shooting. We heard glass shattering in our street. Horrible. I put my fingers in my ears to block out the terrible sounds. I was worried about Cicko. We had left him behind in the lobby. Would he catch cold there? Would something hit him? I was terribly hungry and thirsty. We had left our half-cooked lunch in the kitchen.

—Zlata Filipovic, *Zlata's Diary: A Child's Life in Sarajevo* (1994)

1. What does Zlata say is happening in the city of Sarajevo?

2. How does the war affect Zlata and her family?

TEST-TAKING STRATEGIES AND PRACTICE

Extended Response

Extended-response questions, like constructed-response questions, focus on a document of some kind. However, they are more complicated and require more time to complete.

Some extended-response questions ask you to present the information in the document in a different form. You might be asked to present the information in a chart in graph form, for example. Other questions ask you to complete a document such as a chart or graph. Still others require you to apply your knowledge to information in the document to write an essay.

❶ Read the title of the document to get an idea of what it is about.

❷ Carefully read directions and questions.

❸ Study the document.

❹ Sometimes the question and/or example may give you part of the answer. (The answer given tells how inventions were used and what effects they had on society. Your answers should have the same kind of information.)

❺ The question may require you to write an essay. Write down some ideas to use in an outline. Then use your outline to write the essay. (A good essay will contain the ideas shown in the rubric to the right.)

> Read the column heads carefully. They offer important clues about the subject of the chart. For instance, the column head "Impact" is a clue about why these inventions were so important.

❶ Inventions of the Industrial Revolution ❸

Invention	Impact
Flying shuttle, spinning jenny, water frame, spinning mule, power loom	Spun thread and wove cloth faster; more factories were built and more people were hired ❹
Cotton gin	Cleaned seeds from cotton faster; companies produced more cotton
Macadam road, steamboat, locomotive	Made travel over land and water faster; could carry larger, heavier loads; railroads needed more coal and iron
Mechanical reaper	Made harvesting easier; increased wheat production

❷ 1. Read the list of inventions in the left-hand column. In the right-hand column, briefly state what the inventions meant to industry. The first item has been filled in for you.

2. The chart shows how some inventions helped create the Industrial Revolution. Write a short essay describing how the Industrial Revolution changed people's lives.

❺ **Essay Rubric:** The best essays will point out that progress in agriculture meant that fewer people were needed to work the farms. As a result, many farm workers went to the city looking for work in factories. As cities grew, poor sanitation and poor housing made them unhealthy and dangerous places to live. Life for factory workers was hard. They worked long hours under bad conditions. At first, the Industrial Revolution produced three classes of people: an upper class of landowners and aristocrats; a middle class of merchants and factory owners; and a large lower class of poor people, including factory workers. Eventually, conditions improved even for the lower class. This was partly because factory goods could be sold at a lower cost. In time, even the poorer people could afford to buy many goods and services.

PRACTICE

Directions: Use the drawing and passage below and your knowledge of world cultures and geography to answer question 1.

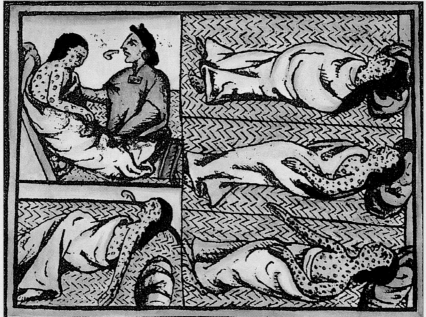

Smallpox Spreads Among the Aztecs

European diseases were like a second "army" of conquerors. Native people had no way to treat diseases like smallpox, typhoid fever, or measles. This "army" was more deadly than swords or guns.

—Based on P. M. Ashburn, *The Ranks of Death* (1947)

The Granger Collection, New York.

1. What role did disease play in the Spanish conquest of the Aztec and Inca?

Document-Based Questions

To answer a document-based question, you have to study more than one document. First you answer questions about each document. Then you use those answers and information from the documents, as well as your own knowledge of world cultures and geography, to write an essay.

1 Read the "Context" section. It will give you an idea of the topic that will be covered in the question.

2 Read the "Task" section carefully. It gives you the topic for your essay.

3 Study each document. Think about the connection the documents have to the topic in the "Task" section.

4 Read and answer the questions about each document. Think about how your answers connect to the "Task" section.

1 Introduction

Historical Context: South America is made up of 12 very different countries. However, these countries have many features in common. The ways of living in these countries are quite similar. The challenges they face are similar, too.

2 Task: Identify and discuss the common features that make the countries of South America a culture region.

Part 1: Short Answer

Study each document carefully. Answer the questions that follow.

3 Document 1: The Countries of South America

Country	Main Language	Major Religion	Colonized by	Date Became Independent
Argentina	Spanish	Catholic	Spain	1816
Bolivia	Spanish	Catholic	Spain	1825
Brazil	Portuguese	Catholic	Portugal	1822
Chile	Spanish	Catholic	Spain	1818
Colombia	Spanish	Catholic	Spain	1819
Ecuador	Spanish	Catholic	Spain	1830
Guyana	English	Catholic	Great Britain	1966
Paraguay	Spanish, Guarani	Catholic	Spain	1811
Peru	Spanish	Catholic	Spain	1821
Suriname	Dutch	Christian	Netherlands	1975
Uruguay	Spanish	Catholic	Spain	1828
Venezuela	Spanish	Catholic	Spain	1830

4 **1.** What are the dominant language and religion in South America?

Spanish; Catholicism

3 **Document 2: The Government in South America**

Oligarchy (government by the few) and military rule have characterized the governments of many of the countries of South America since they won their independence. . .

Although many South American nations gained freedom in the 1800s, hundreds of years of colonialism had its effects. Strong militaries, underdeveloped economies, and social class divisions still exist in the region today.

—Daniel D. Arreola, et al., *World Geography*

4 **2.** What kinds of governments have ruled in South America for much of the time since independence?

Oligarchies and military governments

3 **Document 3: Crowded São Paulo**

Over the last 60 years, South Americans have moved to the cities. Today, nearly 80 percent of the people live in cities. More than 18 million people live in the Brazilian city of São Paulo.

4 **3.** What is one of the major challenges facing the countries of South America today?

rapid urbanization and overcrowding of cities

5 **Part 2: Essay**

Using information from the documents, your answers to the questions in Part 1, and your knowledge of world cultures and geography, write an essay identifying and discussing the features that make South America a culture region. **6**

5 Read the essay question carefully. Then write a brief outline for your essay.

6 Write your essay. The first paragraph should introduce your topic. The middle paragraphs should explain it. The closing paragraph should restate the topic and your conclusion. Support your ideas with quotations or details from the documents. Add other supporting facts or details from your knowledge of world cultures and geography.

7 A good essay will contain the ideas in the rubric below.

7

Essay Rubric: The best essays will begin by noting that a culture region is a large geographic area marked by a common culture. Essays will go on to discuss the common historical and cultural background of the countries of South America (Document 1). Essays also will note that most South American countries share similar experiences in political and economic development (Document 2). Finally, essays will point out that the major challenges that South American countries face today are alike (Document 3).

Introduction

Historical Context: For many centuries, kings and queens ruled the countries of Europe. Their power was supported by nobles and armies. Then European society began to change. In the late 1700s, those changes produced a violent revolution in France.

Task: Discuss how social conflict and new ideas contributed to the French Revolution and why the Revolution turned radical.

Part 1: Short Answer

Study each document carefully. Answer the questions that follow.

Document 1: Social Classes in Pre-Revolutionary France

LE GRAND ABUS

1. This cartoon shows a peasant woman carrying women of nobility and the Church. What does the cartoon say about the lives of the poor before the revolution?

_____

_____

_____

Le Grand Abus. Engraving of a cartoon held in the collection of M. de baron de Vinck d'Orp of Brussels/Mary Evans Picture Library, London.

Document 2: A Declaration of Rights

1. Men are born and remain free and equal in rights . . .

2. The aim of all political association is the preservation of the natural and [unlimited] rights of man. These rights are liberty, property, security, and resistance to oppression . . .

—*Declaration of the Rights of Man and of the Citizen* (1789)

2. According to this document, which rights belong to all people?

_____

Document 3: The French Revolution—Major Events

July 1789 Crowd storms the Bastille.

Aug. 1789 National Assembly abolishes feudalism, approves *Declaration of the Rights of Man and of the Citizen.*

June 1791 Royal family is arrested in escape attempt.

Sep. 1791 France is made a constitutional monarchy.

Jan. 1793 King is executed.

July 1793 Robespierre and allies gain control of government, begin to arrest rivals.

1793–1794 Reign of Terror: about 300,000 are arrested and 17,000 are executed.

1789 ———————————————— 1794

July 1790 Church is put under control of government. National Assembly seizes lands of Catholic Church.

Aug. 1792 Paris mob captures King Louis XVI.

Sep. 1792 Crowds kill priests, nobles in September Massacres; monarchy is abolished.

July 1794 Robespierre is executed, Reign of Terror ends.

3. Over time, the revolution became more violent. How does the information in the time line show this?

_____

Part 2: Essay

Write an essay discussing how social conflict and new ideas led to the French Revolution and why it became so violent. Use information from the documents, your short answers, and your knowledge of world cultures and geography to write your essay.

Map Basics

Maps are an important tool for studying the use of space on Earth. This handbook covers the basic map skills and information that geographers rely on as they investigate the world—and the skills you will need as you study geography.

Mapmaking depends on surveying, or measuring and recording the features of Earth's surface. Until recently, this could be undertaken only on land or sea. Today, aerial photography and satellite imaging are the most popular ways to gather data.

Satellite Imagery A satellite image is a photograph taken from a satellite. This image shows Latin America. The color of the land indicates whether it is desert, forest, farmland, or mountains.

Reading a Map Most maps have these parts, which help you to read and understand the information presented.

A Title The title indicates the subject of the map and tells you what information it contains.

B Symbols Symbols may stand for capital cities, economic activities, or natural resources. Check the map legend for more details.

C Labels Labels are words or phrases that name features on the map.

D Colors Colors show a variety of information on a map. The map legend tells what the colors mean.

E Lines of Longitude These are imaginary lines that show distances east or west of the prime meridian.

F Lines of Latitude These are imaginary lines that show distances north or south of the equator.

G Compass Rose The compass rose shows you north (N), south (S), east (E), and west (W) on the map. Sometimes only north is shown.

H Locator Globe The box shows where the area on the map is located in the world.

I Scale A scale compares a unit of length on the map and a unit of distance on Earth.

J Legend A legend, or key, lists and explains the symbols and colors used on the map.

A Economic Activity of Latin America

Land use
- Commercial agriculture
- Livestock raising
- Subsistence agriculture
- Forestland
- Limited agriculture

Major resources
- Bauxite
- Fish
- Copper
- Gold
- Iron ore
- Natural gas
- Oil
- Silver
- Timber
- Tin
- Other minerals
- Manufacturing center

PACIFIC OCEAN

ATLANTIC OCEAN

Gulf of Mexico

Caribbean Sea

Monterrey
MEXICO
Mexico City

BAHAMAS
CUBA
DOMINICAN REPUBLIC
BELIZE
JAMAICA
HONDURAS
HAITI
GUATEMALA
EL SALVADOR
NICARAGUA
COSTA RICA
PANAMA

Caracas
VENEZUELA
COLOMBIA
GUYANA
SURINAME
FRENCH GUIANA (FRANCE)

Equator

ECUADOR
PERU
BRAZIL
BOLIVIA

Belo Horizonte
Rio de Janeiro
São Paulo
PARAGUAY
CHILE
ARGENTINA
Santiago
Buenos Aires
URUGUAY

Tropic of Cancer
20°N
0°
Tropic of Capricorn
20°S
40°S

120°W   100°W   80°W   60°W   40°W   20°W

0   500   1,000 miles
0   500   1,000 kilometers

N W E S

A1

The Geographic Grid

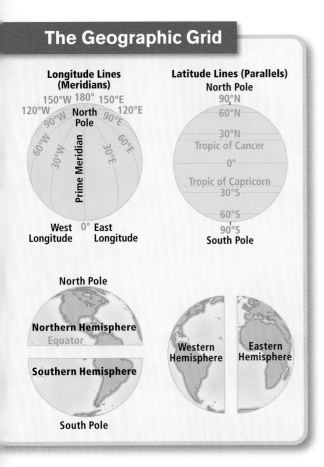

Longitude Lines (Meridians)

150°W 180° 150°E
120°W   120°E
90°W North   90°E
      Pole
60°W   60°E
30°W   30°E
Prime Meridian

West   0°   East
Longitude   Longitude

Latitude Lines (Parallels)

North Pole
90°N
60°N
30°N
Tropic of Cancer
0°
Tropic of Capricorn
30°S
60°S
90°S
South Pole

North Pole
Northern Hemisphere
Equator
Southern Hemisphere
South Pole

Western Hemisphere   Eastern Hemisphere

Longitude and Latitude Lines These lines appear together on a map and pinpoint the absolute locations of cities and other geographic features. You express these locations as coordinates of intersecting lines. These are measured in degrees.

Longitude Lines These imaginary lines run north and south; they are also known as meridians. They show distances in degrees east or west of the prime meridian. The prime meridian is a longitude line that runs from the North Pole to the South Pole through Greenwich, England. It marks 0° longitude.

Latitude Lines These imaginary lines run east to west around the globe; they are also known as parallels. They show distances in degrees north or south of the equator. The equator is a latitude line that circles Earth halfway between the North and South poles. It marks 0° latitude. The tropics of Cancer and Capricorn are parallels that form the boundaries of the tropics, a region that does not have a change of seasons.

Hemisphere The word *hemisphere* is a term for half the globe. The globe can be divided into northern and southern hemispheres (separated by the equator) or into eastern and western hemispheres. The United States is located in the northern and western hemispheres.

Scale What scale to use depends on how much detail is to be shown. If the area is small and many details are needed, a large scale is used. If the area is large and fewer details are needed, a small scale is used.

Large Scale: London

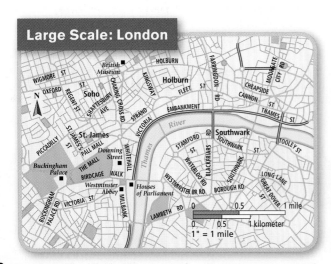

Small Scale: Europe

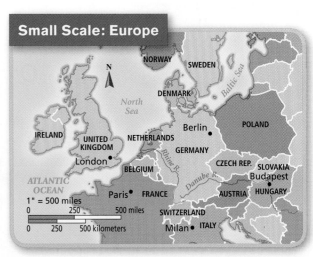

Projections A projection is a way of showing the curved surface of Earth on a flat map. Flat maps cannot show sizes, shapes, and directions with total accuracy. As a result, all projections distort some aspect of Earth's surface. Below are four projections.

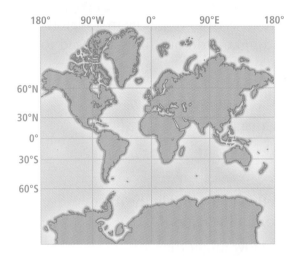

Mercator Projection The Mercator projection shows most of the continents as they look on a globe. However, the projection stretches out the lands near the North and South poles. The Mercator projection is used for navigation.

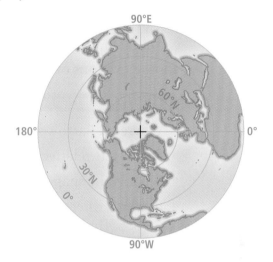

Azimuthal Projection An azimuthal projection shows Earth so that a straight line from the central point to any other point on the map corresponds to the shortest distance between the two points. Sizes and shapes of the continents are distorted.

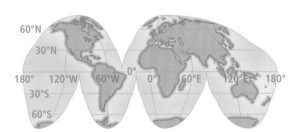

Homolosine Projection This projection shows landmasses' shapes and sizes accurately, but distances are not correct.

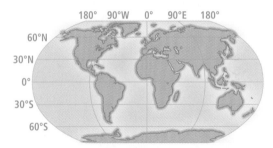

Robinson Projection For textbook maps, the Robinson projection is commonly used. It shows the entire Earth, with continents and oceans having nearly their true sizes and shapes. However, the landmasses near the poles appear flattened.

Map Practice

Use pages A1–A3 to help you answer these questions.

MAIN IDEA

1. What information is provided by the legend on page A1?

2. What do latitude and longitude lines show?

CRITICAL THINKING

3. Why do you think latitude and longitude are important to sailors?

4. How do the depictions of Antarctica in the Mercator and Robinson projections compare?

Different Types of Maps

Physical Maps Physical maps help you see the landforms and bodies of water in specific areas. By studying a physical map, you can learn the relative locations and characteristics of places in a region.

On a physical map, color, shading, or contour lines are used to show elevations or altitudes, also called relief.

THINK LIKE A GEOGRAPHER

- Where on Earth's surface is this area located?
- What is its relative location?
- What is the shape of the region?
- In which directions do the rivers flow? How might the directions of flow affect transportation in the region?
- Are there mountains or deserts? How might they affect the people living in the area?

Northern South America: Physical

Political Maps Political maps show features that humans have created on Earth's surface. Cities, states, provinces, territories, and countries are included on a political map.

THINK LIKE A GEOGRAPHER

- Where on Earth's surface is this area located?

- What is its relative location? How might a country's location affect its economy and its relationships with other countries?

- What is the shape and size of the country? How might its shape and size affect the people living in the country?

- Who are the region's, country's, state's, or city's neighbors?

- How populated does the area seem to be? How might that affect activities there?

Northern South America: Political

Thematic Maps Geographers also rely on thematic maps, which focus on specific topics. For example, in this textbook you will see thematic maps that show climates, types of vegetation, natural resources, population densities, and economic activities. Some thematic maps show historical trends; others focus on movements of people or ideas. Thematic maps may be presented in a variety of ways.

The Division of Poland *1795*

SWEDEN
Baltic Sea
Gdansk
PRUSSIA
Warsaw
RUSSIA
N
W   E
S
.Kiev
AUSTRIA
HUNGARY
OTTOMAN EMPIRE
OTTOMAN EMPIRE

0   100   200 miles
0   100 200 kilometers

To Russia   To Austria
To Prussia   Poland before
                 partition, 1772

Qualitative Map On a qualitative map, colors, symbols, dots, or lines are used to help you see patterns related to a specific idea. The map shown here shows how Poland was divided among other countries in 1795.

THINK LIKE A GEOGRAPHER

• What does the map title suggest about the theme of the map?

• What does the legend tell you about the information being presented?

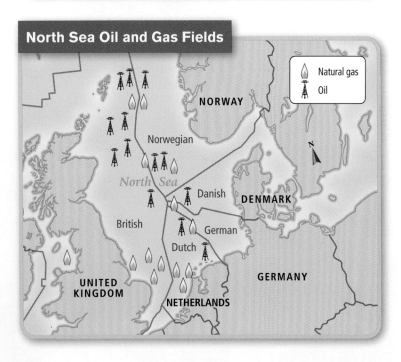

North Sea Oil and Gas Fields

NORWAY
Norwegian
North Sea
Danish   DENMARK
British
German
Dutch
UNITED KINGDOM
NETHERLANDS
GERMANY
N

Natural gas
Oil

Point-Symbol Map On a point-symbol map, a symbol is used to show the location of a particular feature. This map shows the locations of oil and gas fields in the North Sea.

THINK LIKE A GEOGRAPHER

• How do the map title and legend help you know the theme of the map?

• How might the presence of oil and gas fields affect the countries located near them?

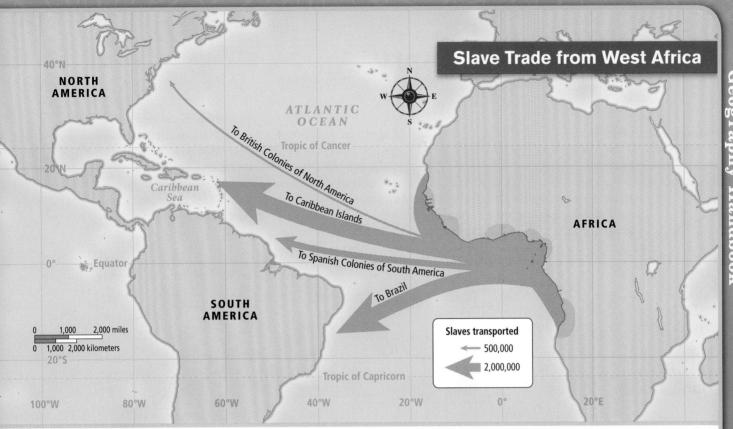

Slave Trade from West Africa

NORTH AMERICA

ATLANTIC OCEAN

Tropic of Cancer

To British Colonies of North America

20°N

Caribbean Sea

To Caribbean Islands

AFRICA

0° Equator

To Spanish Colonies of South America

To Brazil

SOUTH AMERICA

0 1,000 2,000 miles
0 1,000 2,000 kilometers

20°S

Tropic of Capricorn

Slaves transported
500,000
2,000,000

100°W   80°W   60°W   40°W   20°W   0°   20°E

Flow-Line Map Flow-line maps illustrate movements of people, goods, or ideas. The movements are usually shown by a series of arrows. The map may show locations, directions, and scopes of movement. The width of an arrow may show how extensive a flow is. The map shown here portrays the movement of enslaved people from Africa to the Americas.

THINK LIKE A GEOGRAPHER

- How do the title and legend of the map identify the data being presented?

- What does the width of the arrows on the map represent?

- What does the direction of the arrows represent?

Map Practice

Use pages A4–A7 to help you answer these questions.

MAIN IDEA

1. In what country is the Mato Grosso Plateau located?

2. Georgetown is the capital of which South American country?

CRITICAL THINKING

3. In 1795, which country received the largest area of Poland?

4. How are thematic maps an effective way of presenting information?

Geographic Dictionary

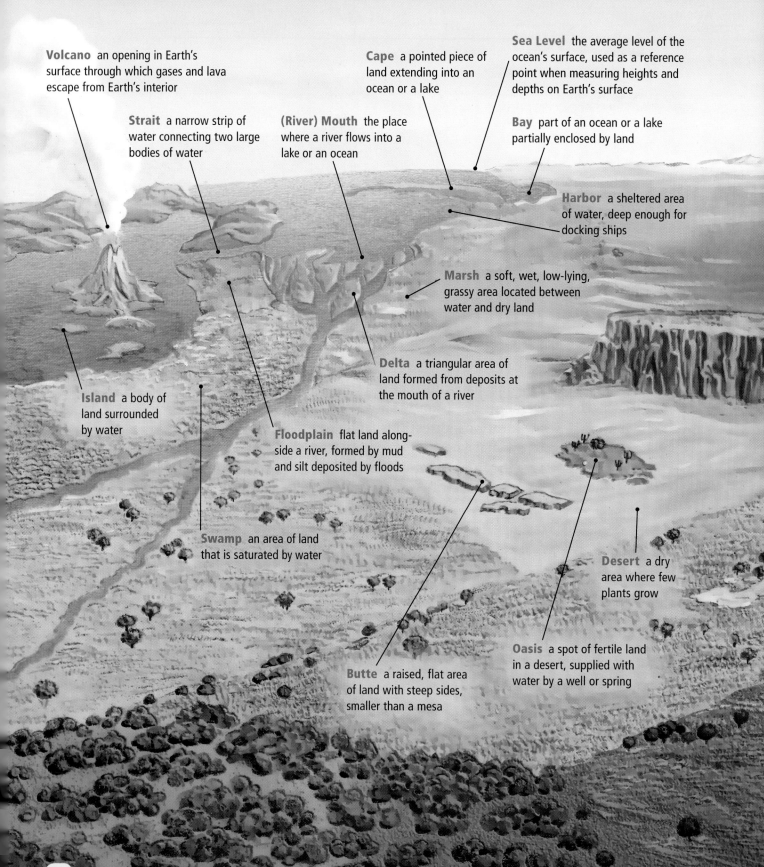

Volcano an opening in Earth's surface through which gases and lava escape from Earth's interior

Strait a narrow strip of water connecting two large bodies of water

(River) Mouth the place where a river flows into a lake or an ocean

Cape a pointed piece of land extending into an ocean or a lake

Sea Level the average level of the ocean's surface, used as a reference point when measuring heights and depths on Earth's surface

Bay part of an ocean or a lake partially enclosed by land

Harbor a sheltered area of water, deep enough for docking ships

Marsh a soft, wet, low-lying, grassy area located between water and dry land

Island a body of land surrounded by water

Delta a triangular area of land formed from deposits at the mouth of a river

Floodplain flat land alongside a river, formed by mud and silt deposited by floods

Swamp an area of land that is saturated by water

Desert a dry area where few plants grow

Butte a raised, flat area of land with steep sides, smaller than a mesa

Oasis a spot of fertile land in a desert, supplied with water by a well or spring

Mountain a natural elevation of Earth's surface with steep sides, higher than a hill

Glacier a large ice mass that moves slowly down a mountain or over land

Prairie a large, level area of grassland with few or no trees

Steppe a wide, treeless plain

Valley low land between hills or mountains

Mesa a wide, flat-topped mountain with steep sides, larger than a butte

Cataract a large, powerful waterfall

Plateau a broad, flat area of land higher than the surrounding land

Canyon a deep, narrow valley with steep sides

Cliff the steep, almost vertical edge of a hill, mountain, or plain

Graphs

Graphs are often used to show numbers in visual form. Bar graphs make it easy to compare numbers. Line graphs show changes over time. Pie graphs show the relationship among parts of a whole. Climographs show the monthly average temperature and precipitation in a place.

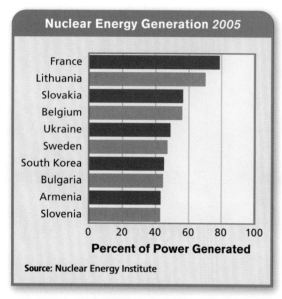

Bar Graph This bar graph compares ten countries' use of nuclear power to produce energy. The graph shows what percent of the energy each country used was from nuclear power.

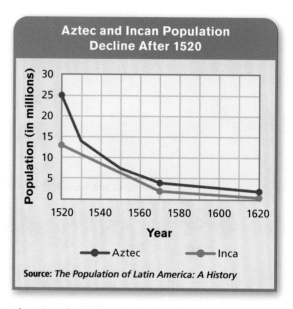

Line Graph This line graph shows how the population of the Aztec and Inca changed between 1520 and 1620.

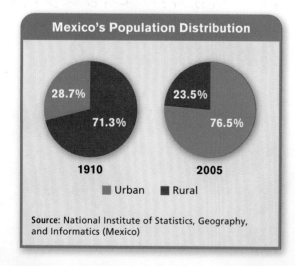

Pie Graph This pie graph shows the percentage of Mexico's population that was urban and rural in two different years.

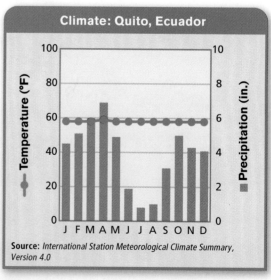

Climograph This climograph shows the climate of Quito, Equador. Bars represent the average monthly precipitation, and a line represents the average monthly temperature in the city.

Geography Standards

To help you study the world, geographers have set up 18 geography standards. These standards provide guidelines for what you will need to be informed about the people, places, and environments of Earth.

THE WORLD IN SPATIAL TERMS

1. How to use maps and other tools
2. How to use mental maps to organize information
3. How to analyze the spatial organization of people, places, and environments

PLACES AND REGIONS

4. The physical and human characteristics of places
5. How people create regions to interpret Earth
6. How culture and experience influence people's perceptions of places and regions

PHYSICAL SYSTEMS

7. The physical processes that shape Earth's surface
8. The distribution of ecosystems on Earth

HUMAN SYSTEMS

9. The characteristics, distribution, and migration of human populations
10. The complexity of Earth's cultural mosaics
11. The patterns and networks of economic interdependence on Earth
12. The patterns of human settlement
13. The forces of cooperation and conflict

ENVIRONMENT AND SOCIETY

14. How human actions modify the physical environment
15. How physical systems affect human systems
16. The distribution and meaning of resources

THE USES OF GEOGRAPHY

17. How to apply geography to interpret the past
18. How to apply geography to interpret the present and plan for the future

RAND M^{c}NALLY
World Atlas

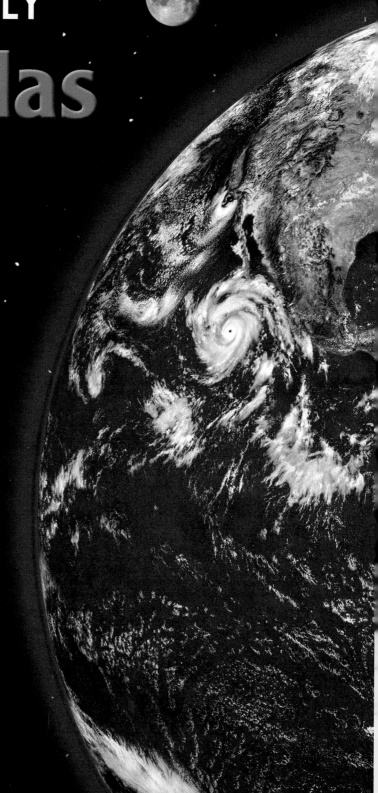

CONTENTS

Legend

Complete Legend for Physical and Political Maps

Water Features

ATLANTIC OCEAN — Ocean or sea

 Lake

 Salt lake

 Seasonal lake

 Mississippi — River

 Niagara Falls — Waterfall

 Ice pack

Land Features

Mt. Mitchell 6,684 ft. 2,037 m. △ Mountain peak

Mt. McKinley 20,320 ft. 6,194 m. ▲ Highest mountain peak

Great Basin — Physical feature (mountain range, desert, plateau, etc.)

Nantucket Island — Island

Cultural Features

——— International boundary

——— State boundary

CANADA — Country

KANSAS — State

Population Centers

National capital	State capital	Town	Population
✪	✪	■	Over 1,000,000
✪	✪	▣	250,000 – 1,000,000
✪	✪	•	Under 250,000

Land Elevations and Ocean Depths

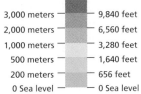

Land elevation

3,000 meters	9,840 feet
2,000 meters	6,560 feet
1,000 meters	3,280 feet
500 meters	1,640 feet
200 meters	656 feet
0 Sea level	0 Sea level

Water depth

0 Sea level	0 Sea level
200 meters	656 feet
2,000 meters	6,560 feet

RAND MᶜNALLY

A13

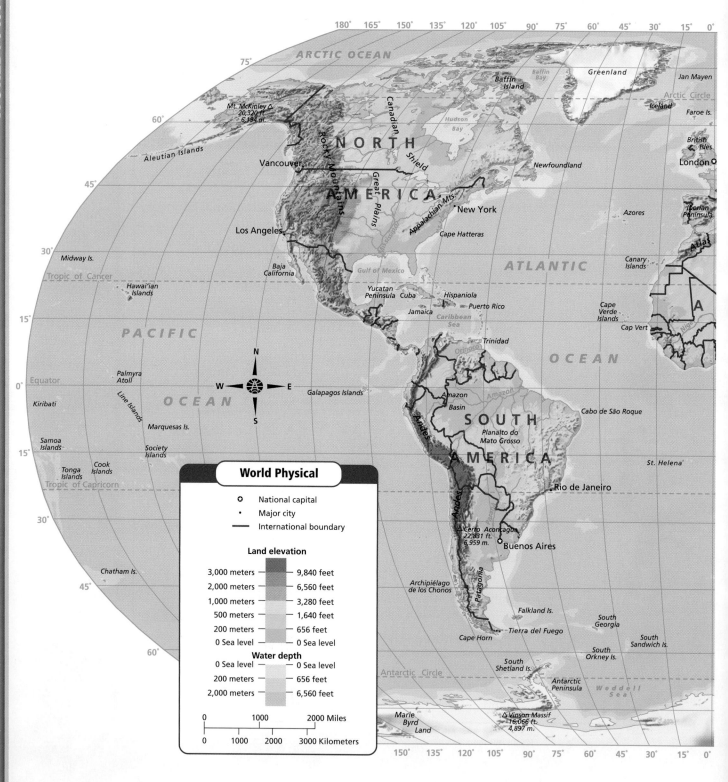

World Physical

⊙ National capital

• Major city

— International boundary

Land elevation

3,000 meters	9,840 feet
2,000 meters	6,560 feet
1,000 meters	3,280 feet
500 meters	1,640 feet
200 meters	656 feet
0 Sea level	0 Sea level

Water depth

0 Sea level	0 Sea level
200 meters	656 feet
2,000 meters	6,560 feet

0   1000   2000 Miles

0   1000   2000   3000 Kilometers

ARCTIC OCEAN

Greenland

Baffin Island

Baffin Bay

Jan Mayen

Arctic Circle

Iceland

Faroe Is.

Mt. McKinley △ 20,320 ft 6,194 m.

Hudson Bay

Canadian Shield

British Isles

London ⊙

Aleutian Islands

Vancouver

NORTH AMERICA

Rocky Mountains

Great Plains

St. Lawrence

Newfoundland

Azores

Iberian Peninsula

Los Angeles

Appalachian Mts.

New York

Cape Hatteras

ATLANTIC

Canary Islands

Atlas

Midway Is.

Tropic of Cancer

Baja California

Gulf of Mexico

Yucatan Peninsula

Cuba

Hispaniola

Puerto Rico

Cape Verde Islands

Cap Vert

A

Hawai'ian Islands

Jamaica

Caribbean Sea

Niger

PACIFIC

Trinidad

Orinoco

OCEAN

Kiribati

Palmyra Atoll

Equator

Line Islands

OCEAN

Galapagos Islands

Amazon Basin

Amazon

Cabo de São Roque

SOUTH

Andes

Planalto do Mato Grosso

Marquesas Is.

Samoa Islands

Society Islands

AMERICA

St. Helena

Tonga Islands

Cook Islands

Tropic of Capricorn

Andes

Rio de Janeiro

Chatham Is.

△ Cerro Aconcagua 22,831 ft. 6,959 m.

Buenos Aires ⊙

Archipiélago de los Chonos

Patagonia

Falkland Is.

South Georgia

Tierra del Fuego

South Sandwich Is.

Cape Horn

South Orkney Is.

South Shetland Is.

Antarctic Circle

Marie Byrd Land

△ Vinson Massif 16,066 ft. 4,897 m.

Antarctic Peninsula

Weddell Sea

N W E S

ARCTIC OCEAN

75°

Spitsbergen
Franz
Josef Land
Nordkapp
Novaya
Zemlya
Scandinavia
Siberia
60°
North
Sea
Bering
Sea
◇ Moscow
Volga
Ural Mts.
Sea of Okhotsk
Kamchatka
Peninsula
Sakhalin
45°
Alps
Balkan
Peninsula
Caucasus
Black Sea
Gora El'brus
18,510 ft.
5,642 m.
Pamir
Gobi Desert
Hokkaidō
Honshū
Sardinia
Sicily
Creté Cyprus
Mediterranean Sea
A S I A
Beijing ◇
Sea of Japan
Mts.
Cairo
Zagros Mts.
Plateau
of
Tibet
Himalayas
East
China
Sea
Kyūshū
30°
Sahara
Nile
Arabian
Peninsula
△ Mt. Everest
29,028 ft.
8,848 m.
Taiwan
PACIFIC
Tropic of Cancer
F R I C A
Mumbai
(Bombay)
Deccan
Hainan Dao
South China
Sea
Mariana
Islands
Wake
Island
15°
Sahel
Arabian
Sea
Socotra
Luzon
Guam
O C E A N
Ethiopian
Plateau
Lakshadweep
Bay of
Bengal
Mindanao
Palau
Islands
Caroline
Islands
Marshall
Islands
Gulf of
Guinea
Sri Lanka
Malay
Peninsula
0°
Congo
Basin
Maldive
Islands
Borneo
Celebes
Equator
△Kilimanjaro
19,340 ft.
5,895 m.
Sumatra
New Guinea
Solomon
Islands
Seychelles
Java
I N D I A N
Madagascar
Mauritius
Reunion
Cocos
Islands
Coral Sea
New
Hebrides
15°
Great
Sandy
Desert
New Caledonia
Fiji
Is.
O C E A N
A U S T R A L I A
Tropic of Capricorn
Kalahari
Desert
Johannesburg
Darling
Great Dividing Range
Sydney
30°
Cape of Good Hope
Cape Leeuwin
North Island
Aoraki
(Mt. Cook)
12,316 ft.
3,754 m. △
Tasmania
South Island
45°
Îles Kerguélen
60°
SOUTHERN
OCEAN
Antarctic Circle
Queen Maud
Land
Enderby
Land
Wilkes Land
Victoria Land
75°
A N T A R C T I C A

© Rand McNally & Co.
Made in U.S.A.
N-MDG10000-A1·-·1·-1

15° 30° 45° 60° 75° 90° 105° 120° 135° 150° 165° 180°

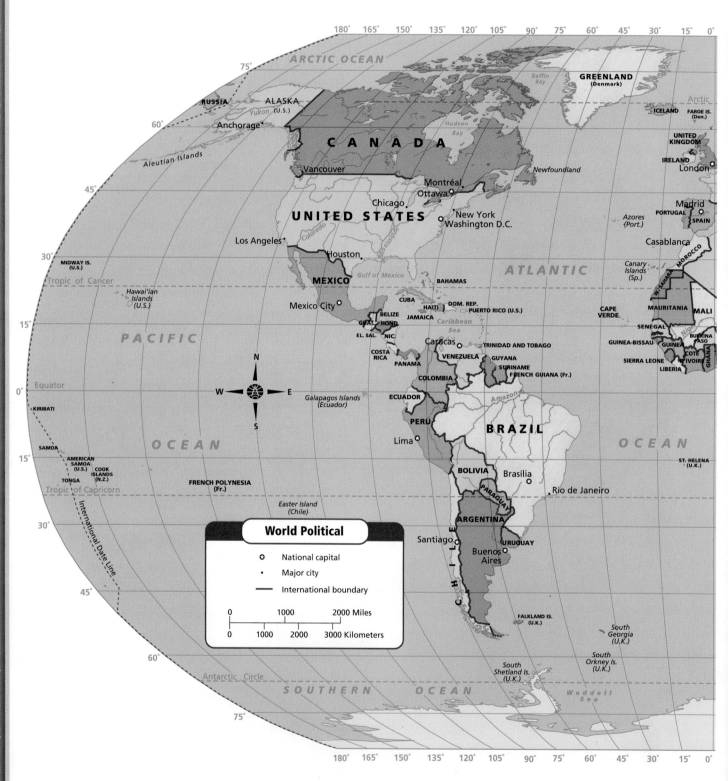

ARCTIC OCEAN

RUSSIA
ALASKA (U.S.)
Anchorage
Aleutian Islands

Yukon

Baffin Bay

GREENLAND (Denmark)

Arctic

ICELAND   FAROE IS. (Den.)

UNITED KINGDOM

IRELAND
London

C A N A D A

Hudson Bay

Newfoundland

Vancouver

Montréal
Ottawa
Chicago
UNITED STATES
New York
Washington D.C.

Madrid
PORTUGAL   SPAIN
Azores (Port.)

Los Angeles
Houston
Colorado
Mississippi

Casablanca

Canary Islands (Sp.)

MOROCCO
W. SAHARA

ATLANTIC

MIDWAY IS. (U.S.)
Tropic of Cancer
Hawai'ian Islands (U.S.)

MEXICO
Gulf of Mexico
Mexico City

BAHAMAS
CUBA
BELIZE
GUAT. HOND.
EL. SAL. NIC.
HAITI DOM. REP.
JAMAICA
PUERTO RICO (U.S.)
Caribbean Sea

CAPE VERDE
MAURITANIA
MALI
SENEGAL
GUINEA-BISSAU GUINEA
SIERRA LEONE
LIBERIA
BURKINA FASO
COTE D'IVOIRE GHANA
Niger

P A C I F I C

COSTA RICA
PANAMA
Caracas
TRINIDAD AND TOBAGO
VENEZUELA   GUYANA
COLOMBIA   SURINAME
        FRENCH GUIANA (Fr.)

KIRIBATI

Equator

Galapagos Islands (Ecuador)

ECUADOR

Amazon

BRAZIL

O C E A N

SAMOA

O C E A N

PERU
Lima

ST. HELENA (U.K.)

N
W   E
S

AMERICAN SAMOA (U.S.)
COOK ISLANDS (N.Z.)
TONGA

FRENCH POLYNESIA (Fr.)

Tropic of Capricorn

BOLIVIA
Brasília

Rio de Janeiro

Easter Island (Chile)

PARAGUAY

International Date Line

World Political

⊙ National capital
• Major city
— International boundary

0   1000   2000 Miles
0   1000   2000   3000 Kilometers

ARGENTINA
URUGUAY
Santiago
Buenos Aires

CHILE

FALKLAND IS. (U.K.)

South Georgia (U.K.)

South Orkney Is. (U.K.)

Antarctic Circle

South Shetland Is. (U.K.)

S O U T H E R N   O C E A N

Weddell Sea

ARCTIC OCEAN

Franz Josef Land

Spitsbergen
(Nor.)

Novaya
Zemlya

Circle

NORWAY   FINLAND

North   SWEDEN   EST.
Sea   LAT.
          DEN.   LITH.   ☆ Moscow
NETH.   BELARUS
  GERMANY   POLAND
FRANCE   UKRAINE
                         MOLD.
     ITALY   Black Sea
          ALB. BUL.   GEO.
Rome   GREECE TURKEY   ARM. AZER.
                          TURKMENISTAN
TUNISIA   Mediterranean Sea   CYPRUS SYRIA
          Crete   LEB. IRAQ
                            ISRAEL
ALGERIA   JORDAN
                                  KUWAIT
          Cairo
LIBYA   EGYPT   SAUDI   QATAR
                        ARABIA   U.A.E.
NIGER   Karachi
          CHAD   SUDAN   YEMEN
NIGERIA   ERITREA
Lagos   CENTRAL   Addis   DJIBOUTI
         AFRICAN   Ababa
         REPUBLIC   ETHIOPIA
CAMEROON
EQUATORIAL   UGANDA
GUINEA   Congo
GABON   DEM. REP. KENYA   SOMALIA
               OF THE CONGO
               RWANDA
               BURUNDI
                       TANZANIA
ANGOLA   COMOROS
         ZAMBIA
                                 MADAGASCAR
ZIMBABWE   MAURITIUS
NAMIBIA MOZAMBIQUE   REUNION
         BOTSWANA   (Fr.)
Johannesburg   SWAZILAND
SOUTH   LESOTHO
AFRICA

RUSSIA

· Novosibirsk

Volga   Ob'   Yenisey   Lena

KAZAKHSTAN   MONGOLIA

UZBEKISTAN   KYRG.
              TAJIK.
☆ Tehrān   AFGHANISTAN   CHINA   Beijing ☆

IRAN   PAKISTAN   NEPAL   Yangtze
                                 BHU.

          Ganges   Kolkata
                        (Calcutta) BNG.
Mumbai   INDIA   MYANMAR LAOS
(Bombay)   Bay of   THAILAND
          Arabian   Bengal   Bangkok ☆ CAMBODIA
          Sea   VIETNAM

                    SRI LANKA

          MALDIVES

                    SEYCHELLES

INDIAN

          Îles Kerguélen
          (Fr.)

NORTH
KOREA   Sea of Japan
SOUTH   JAPAN
Seoul ☆ KOREA   Tōkyō

Shanghai ·

TAIWAN   PACIFIC
Hong Kong

South China   NORTHERN
Sea   MARIANA ISLANDS
                (U.S.)
PHILIPPINES   GUAM
       Manila ☆ (U.S.)
BRUNEI   PALAU
MALAYSIA
SINGAPORE   Borneo
                         New Guinea
          Sumatra   PAPUA
                    Jakarta · INDONESIA NEW GUINEA
          Java   EAST TIMOR

Tropic of Cancer

WAKE ISLAND
(U.S.)

OCEAN

15°

FED. STATES OF
MICRONESIA   MARSHALL
                ISLANDS

Equator   0°

SOLOMON
ISLANDS

Coral Sea   VANUATU

NEW CALEDONIA   FIJI
(Fr.)

AUSTRALIA   Tropic of Capricorn

Perth ·   Darling   · Brisbane
                · Sydney
                           Auckland ·
Melbourne ·
                NEW ZEALAND
Tasmania

OCEAN

SOUTHERN   OCEAN

Antarctic Circle

ANTARCTICA   © Rand McNally & Co.
                Made in U.S.A.
                N-MDG10000-P1- -:-1-1-1

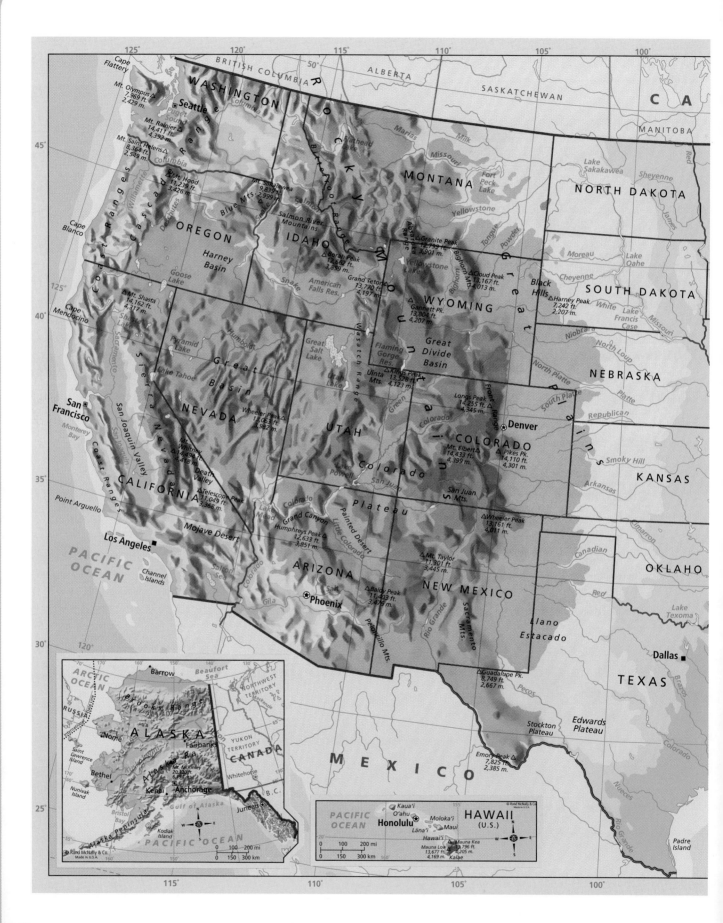

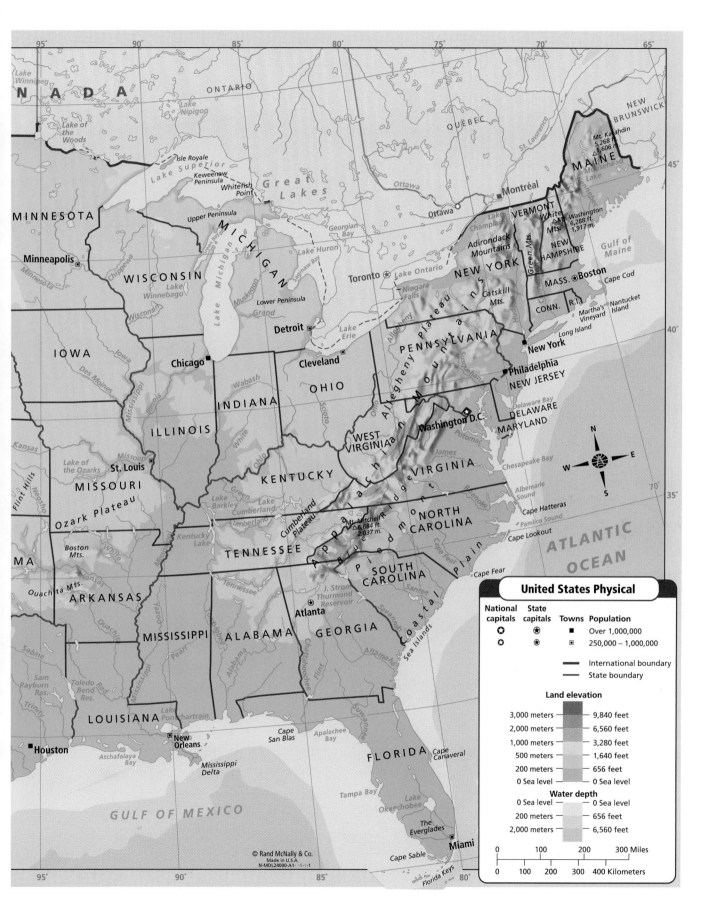

RAND McNALLY

United States Physical

National capitals	State capitals	Towns	Population
✪	✪	■	Over 1,000,000
✪	✪	▣	250,000 – 1,000,000

International boundary
State boundary

Land elevation

3,000 meters	9,840 feet
2,000 meters	6,560 feet
1,000 meters	3,280 feet
500 meters	1,640 feet
200 meters	656 feet
0 Sea level	0 Sea level

Water depth

0 Sea level	0 Sea level
200 meters	656 feet
2,000 meters	6,560 feet

0   100   200   300 Miles
0 100 200 300 400 Kilometers

© Rand McNally & Co.
Made in U.S.A.
N-MDL24000-A1- -1-1-1

A19

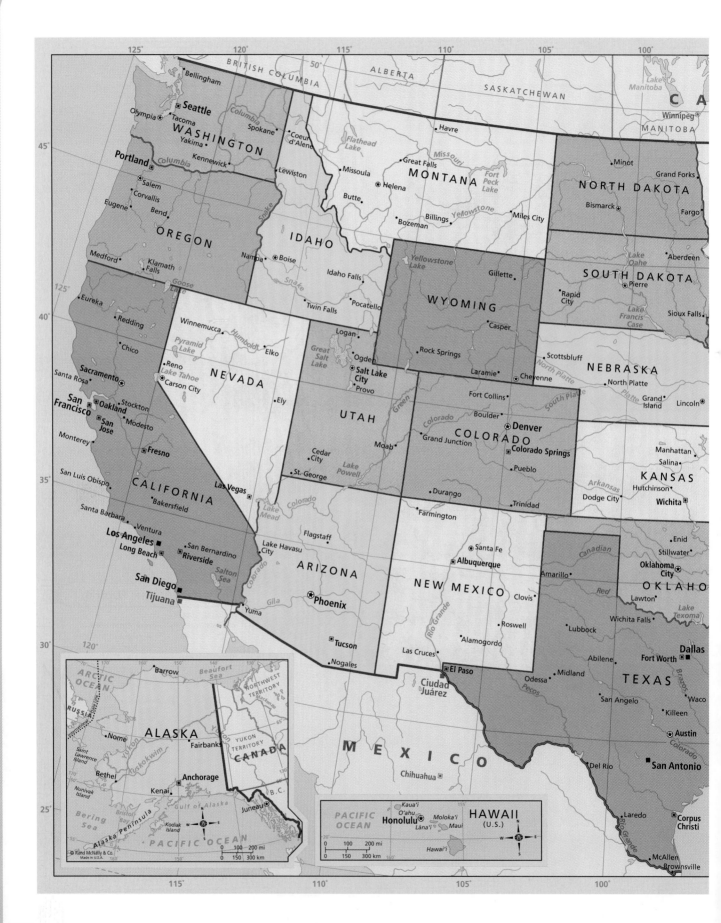

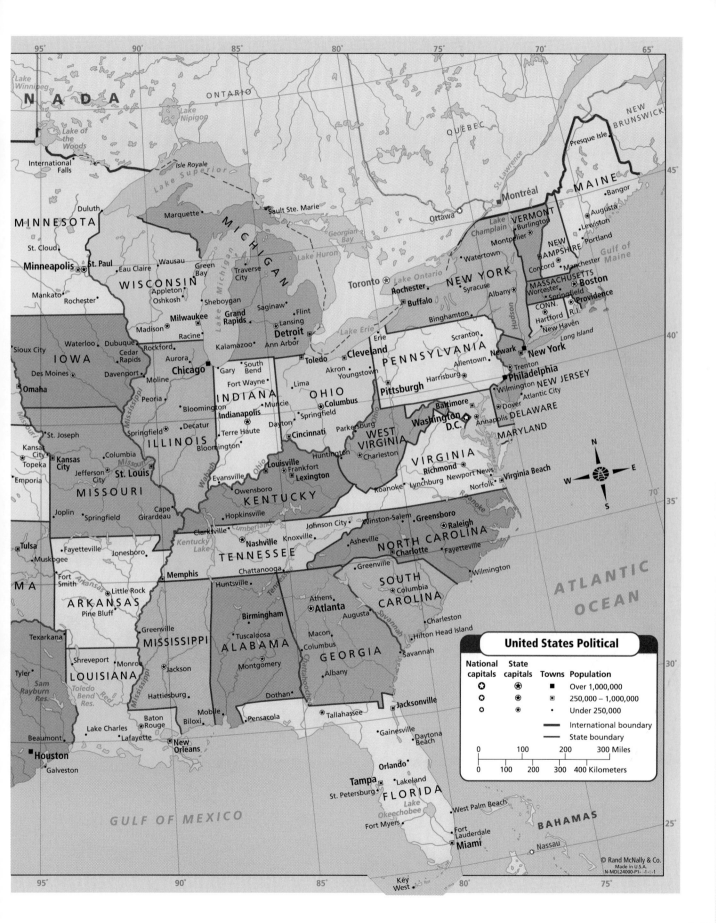

RAND M?NALLY

United States Political

National capitals	State capitals	Towns	Population
✪	✪	■	Over 1,000,000
✪	✪	◙	250,000 – 1,000,000
✪	✪	•	Under 250,000

International boundary

State boundary

0   100   200   300 Miles

0   100   200   300   400 Kilometers

© Rand McNally & Co.
Made in U.S.A.
N-MDL24000-P1- -1-|-1

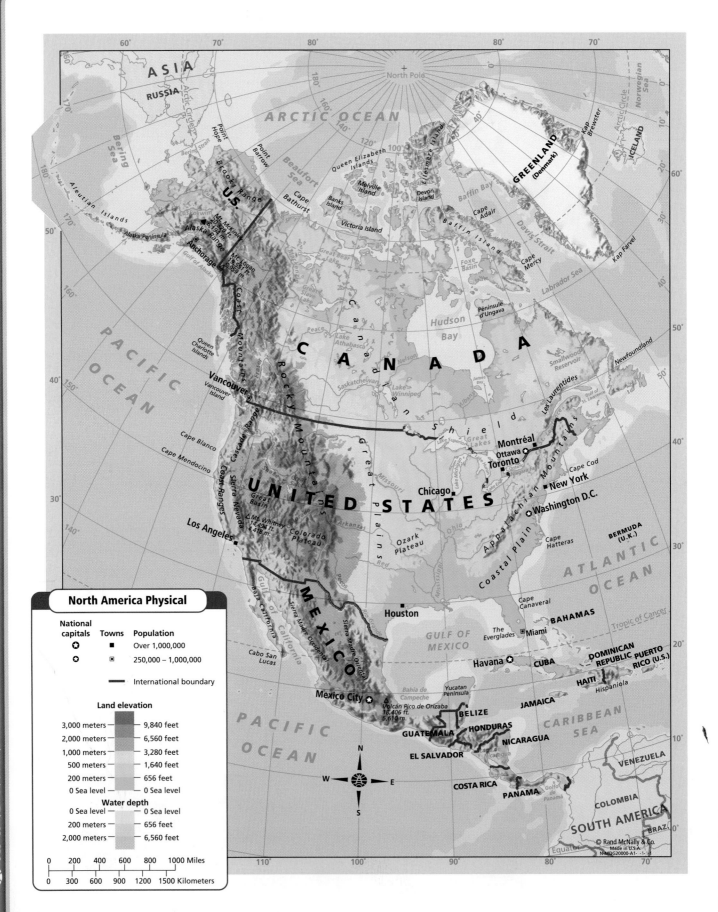

North America Physical

National capitals
⊕ Over 1,000,000
⊕ 250,000 – 1,000,000

Towns
■
▫

Population
Over 1,000,000
250,000 – 1,000,000

International boundary

Land elevation

3,000 meters	9,840 feet
2,000 meters	6,560 feet
1,000 meters	3,280 feet
500 meters	1,640 feet
200 meters	656 feet
0 Sea level	0 Sea level

Water depth

0 Sea level	0 Sea level
200 meters	656 feet
2,000 meters	6,560 feet

0   200   400   600   800   1000 Miles
0   300   600   900   1200   1500 Kilometers

RAND McNALLY

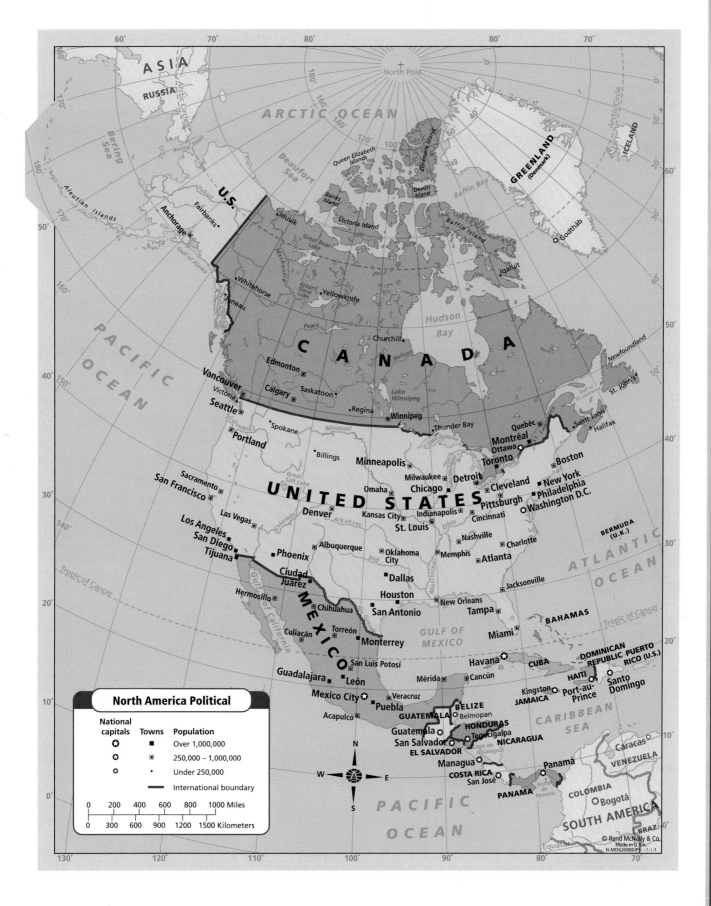

North America Political

National capitals
- ✪ (capital symbol)

Towns
- ■ Population Over 1,000,000
- ▣ 250,000 – 1,000,000
- ▪ Under 250,000

Population
- ─── International boundary

| 0 | 200 | 400 | 600 | 800 | 1000 Miles |

| 0 | 300 | 600 | 900 | 1200 | 1500 Kilometers |

ASIA
RUSSIA
ARCTIC OCEAN
North Pole
Queen Elizabeth Islands
Ellesmere Island
GREENLAND (Denmark)
ICELAND
Bering Strait
Beaufort Sea
Banks Island
Devon Island
Baffin Bay
Godthåb
Bering Sea
Aleutian Islands
U.S.
Anchorage
Fairbanks
Inuvik
Victoria Island
Great Bear Lake
Baffin Island
Iqaluit
PACIFIC OCEAN
Whitehorse
Juneau
Yellowknife
Great Slave Lake
Mackenzie
Peace
C A N A D A
Hudson Bay
Churchill
Nelson
Newfoundland
Edmonton
Calgary
Saskatoon
Lake Winnipeg
St. John's
Vancouver
Victoria
Regina
Winnipeg
Thunder Bay
Gulf of St. Lawrence
Saint John
Halifax
Seattle
Spokane
Missouri
Lake Superior
Québec
Montréal
Portland
Billings
Minneapolis
Ottawa
Toronto
Boston
Great Salt Lake
Milwaukee
Detroit
Cleveland
New York
Sacramento
Omaha
Chicago
Pittsburgh
Philadelphia
San Francisco
UNITED STATES
Indianapolis
Washington D.C.
BERMUDA (U.K.)
Las Vegas
Denver
Colorado
Kansas City
Ohio
Cincinnati
Arkansas
St. Louis
Nashville
Los Angeles
San Diego
Albuquerque
Oklahoma City
Memphis
Charlotte
ATLANTIC OCEAN
Tijuana
Phoenix
Red
Dallas
Atlanta
Ciudad Juárez
Houston
Jacksonville
Hermosillo
MEXICO
San Antonio
New Orleans
Tampa
Tropic of Cancer
Gulf of California
Chihuahua
Tropic of Cancer
Culiacán
Torreón
Monterrey
GULF OF MEXICO
Miami
BAHAMAS
San Luis Potosí
Havana
DOMINICAN REPUBLIC
PUERTO RICO (U.S.)
Guadalajara
León
Mérida
Cancún
CUBA
HAITI
Santo Domingo
Mexico City
Veracruz
Kingston
Port-au-Prince
Puebla
BELIZE
JAMAICA
Acapulco
GUATEMALA
Belmopan
CARIBBEAN SEA
Guatemala
HONDURAS
Tegucigalpa
San Salvador
NICARAGUA
EL SALVADOR
Managua
Caracas
Lago de Nicaragua
Panamá
VENEZUELA
N
W   E
S
COSTA RICA
San José
PANAMA
Golfo de Panamá
COLOMBIA
Bogotá
PACIFIC OCEAN
SOUTH AMERICA
Equator
BRAZ.

© Rand McNally & Co.
Made in U.S.A.
N-MDG20000-PS -1-1-1

RAND M℃NALLY

North America

GULF OF MEXICO

CUBA

HAITI

DOMINICAN REPUBLIC

JAMAICA

PUERTO RICO (U.S.)

CARIBBEAN SEA

MEXICO

BELIZE

GUATEMALA

HONDURAS

EL SALVADOR

NICARAGUA

COSTA RICA

PANAMA

Greater Antilles

Lesser Antilles

TRINIDAD AND TOBAGO

ATLANTIC OCEAN

Tropic of Cancer

Punta Gallinas

Pico Cristóbal Colón 18,947 ft. 5,775 m.

◉ Caracas

Boca Grande

Orinoco

VENEZUELA

Llanos

Roraima

GUYANA

SURINAME

FRENCH GUIANA (FR.)

Cabo Orange

Golfo de Panamá

✪ Bogotá

COLOMBIA

Nev. del Huila 18,865 ft. 5,750 m.

Putumayo

Japurá

Negro

Amazon

Manaus

Ilha de Marajó

Amazon

Equator

Punta Galera

Galapagos Islands (Ec.)

ECUADOR

Chimborazo 20,702 ft. 6,310 m.

Punta Pariñas

Marañón

Amazon

Juruá

Selvas

Amazon Basin

BRAZIL

Xingu

Tapajós

Tocantins

Cabo de São Roque

São Francisco

Recife

PERU

Andes

Nev. Huascarán 22,133 ft. 6,746 m.

Lima ✪

Purus

Madeira

Planalto do Mato Grosso

Serra do Espinhaço

Punta Carreta

Lago Titicaca

Nev. Illampu 21,066 ft. 6,421 m.

La Paz ✪

BOLIVIA

Cordillera Real

Brasília ◉

Nev. Sajama 21,463 ft. 6,542 m.

Gran Chaco

PARAGUAY

São Paulo ■

Rio de Janeiro ■

Cabo de São Tomé

Tropic of Capricorn

Isla San Ambrosio (Chile)

Atacama Desert

Nev. Ojos del Salado 22,615 ft. 6,893 m.

Paraná

Isla San Felix (Chile)

CHILE

Andes

ARGENTINA

Uruguay

Paraná

Lagoa dos Patos

URUGUAY

Lagoa Mirim

Archipiélago Juan Fernández (Chile)

Cerro Aconcagua 22,831 ft. 6,959 m.

Santiago ◉

Buenos Aires ◉

Río de la Plata

Pampas

Punta Lavapié

Golfo San Matías

Península Valdés

N

W E

S

ATLANTIC OCEAN

Isla Grande de Chiloé

Patagonia

Cabo Dos Bahías

Golfo San Jorge

Cabo Tres Puntas

Archipiélago de los Chonos

Isla Wellington

PACIFIC OCEAN

Bahía Grande

FALKLAND ISLANDS (U.K.)

West Falkland

East Falkland

Isla Santa Inés

Strait of Magellan

Tierra del Fuego

Cape Horn

South Georgia (U.K.)

Drake Passage

South Shetland Islands (U.K.)

South Orkney Islands (U.K.)

South Sandwich Islands (U.K.)

© Rand McNally & Co.
N-MDG40000-A1- -1-1-1

South America Physical

National capitals		
◉		Towns
✪		

Towns	Population
■	Over 1,000,000
▣	250,000 – 1,000,000

—— International boundary

Land elevation

3,000 meters	9,840 feet
2,000 meters	6,560 feet
1,000 meters	3,280 feet
500 meters	1,640 feet
200 meters	656 feet
0 Sea level	0 Sea level

Water depth

0 Sea level	0 Sea level
200 meters	656 feet
2,000 meters	6,560 feet

0   200   400   600   800   1000 Miles

0   300   600   900   1200   1500 Kilometers

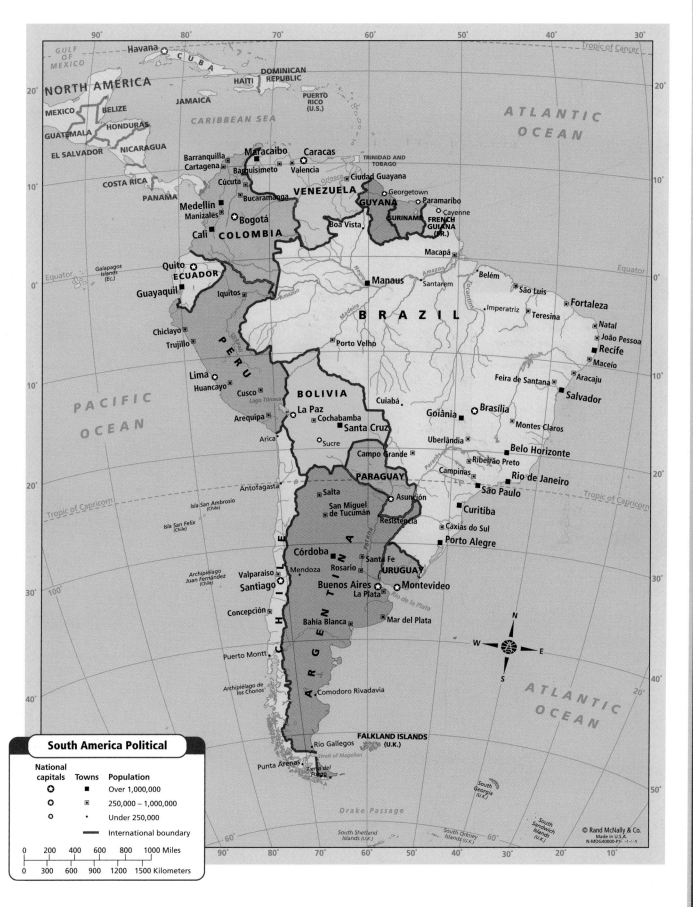

90° 80° 70° 60° 50° 40° 30°

Tropic of Cancer

GULF OF MEXICO
Havana
CUBA
NORTH AMERICA
HAITI DOMINICAN REPUBLIC
20°
JAMAICA PUERTO RICO (U.S.)
MEXICO BELIZE
GUATEMALA HONDURAS
EL SALVADOR NICARAGUA
CARIBBEAN SEA
ATLANTIC OCEAN

COSTA RICA
PANAMA
Barranquilla
Cartagena
Maracaibo Caracas
Barquisimeto Valencia
TRINIDAD AND TOBAGO
Cúcuta
Ciudad Guayana
VENEZUELA
Orinoco
10°
Bucaramanga
Georgetown
Medellín **GUYANA**
Manizales Paramaribo
Bogotá **SURINAME** Cayenne
Cali **COLOMBIA** Boa Vista **FRENCH GUIANA (FR.)**
Macapá

Galapagos Islands (Ec.)
Quito Equator
ECUADOR
Amazon
Belém
São Luís
0° Equator
Guayaquil
Iquitos
Manaus Santarem Fortaleza
Amazon Imperatriz Teresina
Natal
P E R U Madeira **B R A Z I L** João Pessoa
Chiclayo Porto Velho Recife
Trujillo Maceió

Lima Feira de Santana Aracaju
Huancayo Cusco Salvador
10°
Lago Titicaca **BOLIVIA** Cuiabá Goiânia Brasília
Arequipa La Paz Cochabamba Montes Claros
Arica Santa Cruz Uberlândia
Sucre Belo Horizonte
Campo Grande Ribeirão Preto
Antofagasta **PARAGUAY** Campinas Rio de Janeiro
20° Paraná São Paulo
Tropic of Capricorn
Isla San Ambrosio (Chile) Salta Asunción Curitiba
Isla San Felix (Chile) San Miguel de Tucumán Resistencia Caxias do Sul
Porto Alegre
Archipiélago Juan Fernández (Chile) Córdoba Santa Fe
Valparaíso Mendoza Rosario **URUGUAY**
Santiago Buenos Aires Montevideo
La Plata Río de la Plata
Concepción Mar del Plata
30°
A R G E N T I N A Bahía Blanca
C H I L E

Puerto Montt

Archipiélago de los Chonos Comodoro Rivadavia

N
W E
S

ATLANTIC OCEAN
40°

FALKLAND ISLANDS (U.K.)
Río Gallegos
Strait of Magellan
Punta Arenas Tierra del Fuego

South Georgia (U.K.)
South Shetland Islands (U.K.) South Orkney Islands (U.K.)
Drake Passage © Rand McNally & Co.
Made in U.S.A.
N-MDG40000-P1- -1-1-1
South Sandwich Islands (U.K.)

PACIFIC OCEAN

South America Political

National capitals	Towns	Population
⊛	■	Over 1,000,000
⊛	▫	250,000 – 1,000,000
○	•	Under 250,000
—		International boundary

0 200 400 600 800 1000 Miles
0 300 600 900 1200 1500 Kilometers

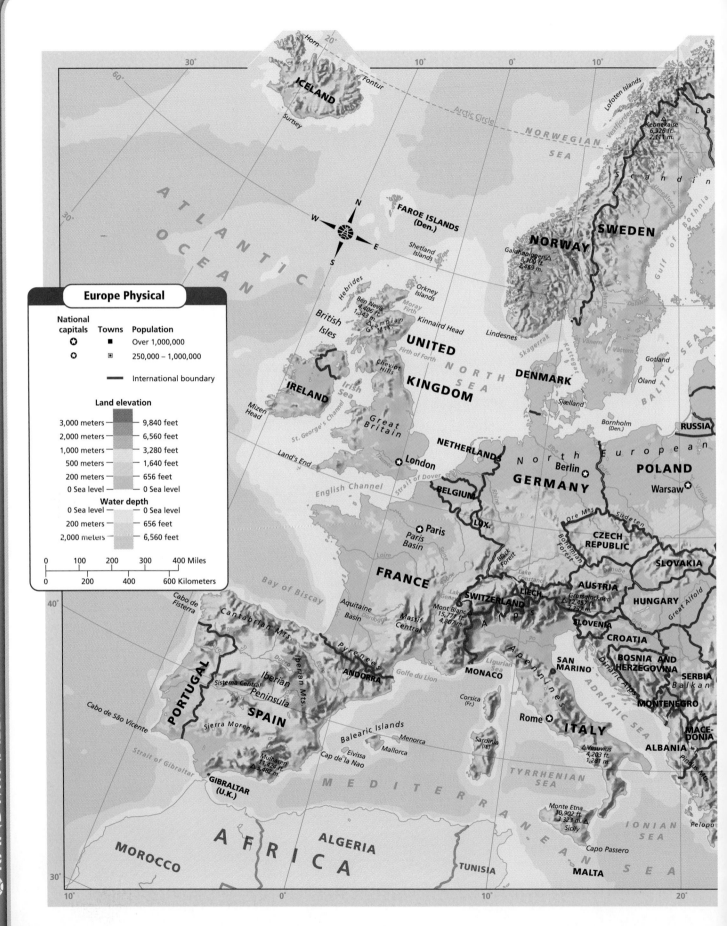

Europe Physical

National capitals
⊕ Over 1,000,000
○

Towns
■ Over 1,000,000
▣ 250,000 – 1,000,000

Population

International boundary

Land elevation

3,000 meters	9,840 feet
2,000 meters	6,560 feet
1,000 meters	3,280 feet
500 meters	1,640 feet
200 meters	656 feet
0 Sea level	0 Sea level

Water depth

0 Sea level	0 Sea level
200 meters	656 feet
2,000 meters	6,560 feet

0 100 200 300 400 Miles
0 200 400 600 Kilometers

ICELAND
Horn
Fontur
Surtsey

Arctic Circle

NORWEGIAN SEA

Lofoten Islands
Vestfjorden
Kebnekaise
6,926 ft.
2,111 m.

FAROE ISLANDS (Den.)

Shetland Islands

SWEDEN

NORWAY
Galdhøpiggen
8,100 ft.
2,469 m.

Scandinavia

Gulf of Bothnia

Hebrides

Orkney Islands

Moray Firth
Kinnaird Head

Lindesnes

Skagerrak

Umealven

British Isles

Ben Nevis
4,406 m.
1,343 m.
Grampian Mts.

UNITED KINGDOM

Firth of Forth

Kattegat

Vänern

Vättern

BALTIC SEA

Gotland

Öland

ATLANTIC OCEAN

IRELAND

Mizen Head

Cheviot Hills

Irish Sea

Great Britain

St. George's Channel

NORTH SEA

DENMARK

Sjælland

Bornholm (Den.)

RUSSIA

Land's End

London

NETHERLANDS

Elbe

North European

POLAND

Berlin

Warsaw

Vistula

English Channel

Strait of Dover

BELGIUM

GERMANY

Rhine

Ore Mts.

Sudeten

Bohemian Forest

CZECH REPUBLIC

SLOVAKIA

Paris
Paris Basin

LUX.

Seine

Loire

FRANCE

Black Forest

Lake Constance

Bohemian Forest

Danube

AUSTRIA

Grossglockner
12,457 ft.
3,792 m.

HUNGARY

Great Alföld

Bay of Biscay

Aquitaine Basin

Dordogne

Massif Central

SWITZERLAND

LIECH.

Alps

Lake Geneva

SLOVENIA

CROATIA

Po

Dinaric Alps

Cabo de Fisterra

Cantabrian Mts.

Pyrenees

ANDORRA

Golfe du Lion

MONACO

Ligurian Sea

SAN MARINO

Apennines

BOSNIA AND HERZEGOVINA

SERBIA

Balkan

ADRIATIC SEA

MONTENEGRO

MACE-DONIA

PORTUGAL

Duero

Ebro

Iberian Mts.

Sistema Central

Iberian Peninsula

SPAIN

Corsica (Fr.)

Rome

ITALY

Vesuvius
4,203 ft.
1,281 m.

ALBANIA

Pindus Mts.

Cabo de São Vicente

Sierra Morena

Balearic Islands

Menorca

Eivissa

Mallorca

Cap de la Nao

Sardinia (It.)

TYRRHENIAN SEA

IONIAN SEA

Pelopo

Strait of Gibraltar

Mulhacén
11,424 ft.
3,482 m.

GIBRALTAR (U.K.)

MEDITERRANEAN

Monte Etna
10,902 ft.
3,323 m.
Sicily

Capo Passero

SEA

MOROCCO

AFRICA

ALGERIA

TUNISIA

MALTA

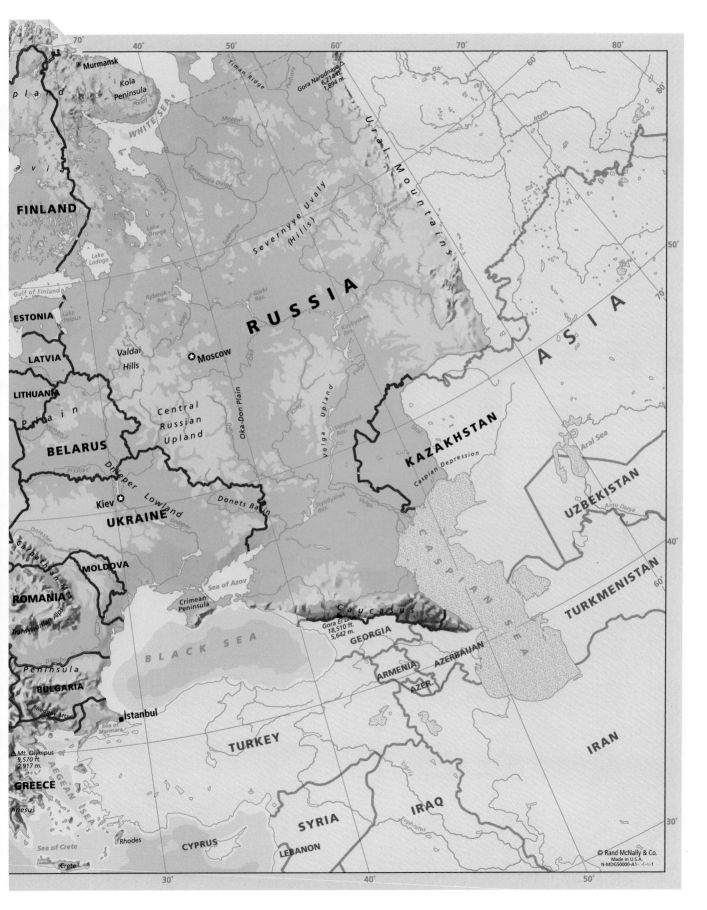

Murmansk

Kola
Peninsula

WHITE SEA

Timan Ridge

Gora Narodnaya △
6,214 m.
1,894 m.

FINLAND

pland

avia

Mezen

Severnaya Dvina

Onega

Sukhona

Severnyye Uvaly
(Hills)

Ural Mountains

Ob'

Irtysh

ASIA

Lake
Onega

Gulf of Finland

ESTONIA

Lake
Ladoga

Lake
Peipus

Rybinsk
Res.

Volga

Gorki
Res.

Kama

Kama
Resevoir

RUSSIA

Moscow

Oka

Volga

Kuybyshev
Res.

Valdai
Hills

LATVIA

LITHUANIA

P l a i n

Nemnas

Central
Russian
Upland

Oka-Don Plain

Don

Khopr

Volga Upland

Volgograd
Res.

Ural

KAZAKHSTAN

Aral Sea

Caspian Depression

UZBEKISTAN

Amu Darya

BELARUS

Prypiac'

Dnieper Lowland

Dnieper

Kiev

UKRAINE

Donets Basin

Dnieper

Tsymlyansk
Res.

Volga

TURKMENISTAN

Dniester

MOLDOVA

Carpathian Mts.

ROMANIA

Transylvanian Alps

Sea of Azov

Crimean
Peninsula

Caucasus

Gora El'brus
18,510 ft.
5,642 m.

GEORGIA

CASPIAN SEA

IRAN

Danube

Peninsula

BULGARIA

Rhodope Mts.

BLACK SEA

ARMENIA

AZERBAIJAN

AZER.

İstanbul

Sea of
Marmara

△ Mt. Olympus
9,570 ft.
2,917 m.

GREECE

nnesus

AEGEAN SEA

TURKEY

SYRIA

IRAQ

Tigris

Euphrates

Sea of Crete

Rhodes

CYPRUS

LEBANON

Crete

© Rand McNally & Co.
N-MDG50000-A1- -1-1-1

70°   40°   50°   60°   70°   80°

60°

80°

50°

70°

40°

60°

40°

30°

30°   40°   50°

A27

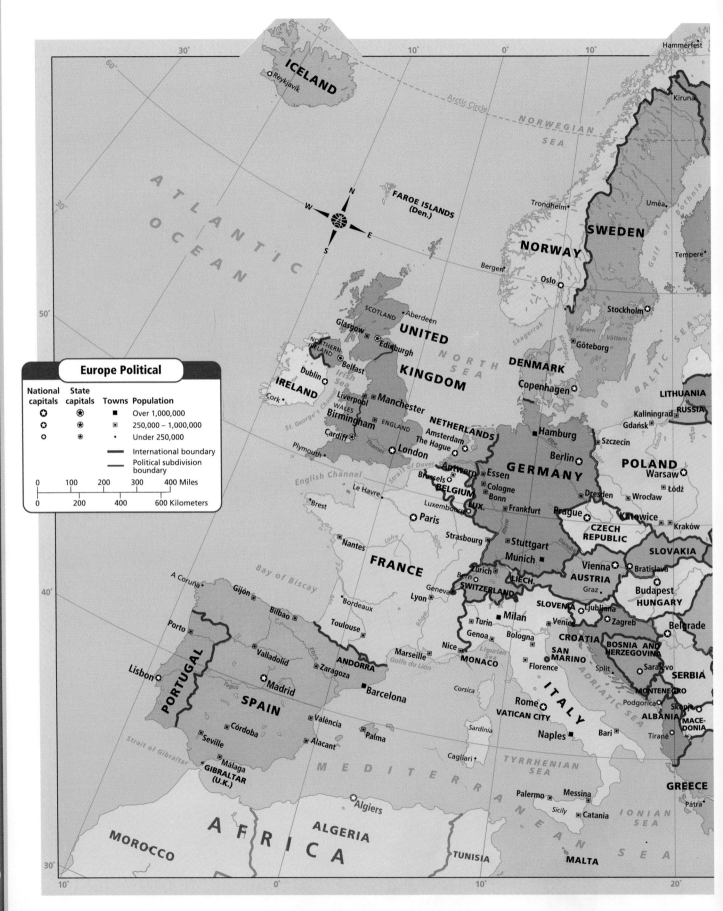

Europe Political

National capitals
⊛ ⊛ ⊛

State capitals
★ ★ ★

Towns
■ Population
■ Over 1,000,000
▣ 250,000 – 1,000,000
• Under 250,000

━━ International boundary
── Political subdivision boundary

0   100   200   300   400 Miles
0   200   400   600 Kilometers

ICELAND
Reykjavík

Arctic Circle

NORWEGIAN SEA

Hammerfest
Kiruna

FAROE ISLANDS (Den.)

Trondheim
Umeå

SWEDEN
NORWAY

Bergen
Oslo
Göteborg
Stockholm
Tempere

ATLANTIC OCEAN

SCOTLAND
Aberdeen
Glasgow
Edinburgh
UNITED KINGDOM

NORTHERN IRELAND
Belfast
Dublin
IRELAND
Cork

Liverpool
Manchester
WALES
Birmingham
ENGLAND
Cardiff
Plymouth
London

NORTH SEA

Skagerrak
DENMARK
Kattegat
Copenhagen

Vänern
Vättern

Gulf of Bothnia

BALTIC SEA

LITHUANIA
Kaliningrad
RUSSIA
Gdańsk

NETHERLANDS
Amsterdam
The Hague
Antwerp
BELGIUM
Brussels
LUX.
Luxembourg

Hamburg
Berlin
Szczecin

GERMANY

POLAND
Warsaw
Łódź

Essen
Cologne
Bonn
Frankfurt

Dresden
Wrocław
Katowice
Kraków

Prague
CZECH REPUBLIC

SLOVAKIA

English Channel
Strait of Dover

Le Havre
Brest
Nantes

Paris

Strasbourg
Stuttgart
Munich
Zürich
Bern
SWITZERLAND
LIECH.

Vienna
AUSTRIA
Graz

Bratislava

Budapest
HUNGARY

FRANCE

Lyon
Geneva

Bordeaux
Toulouse

Bay of Biscay

A Coruña
Gijón
Bilbao

Porto

Valladolid
Zaragoza
ANDORRA

PORTUGAL
Lisbon
Madrid
SPAIN

Córdoba
València
Alacant
Palma

Seville
Málaga
GIBRALTAR (U.K.)
Strait of Gibraltar

Marseille
Golfe du Lion
MONACO

Turin
Milan
Genoa
Nice
Venice
Bologna
SLOVENIA
Ljubljana
Zagreb
CROATIA
SAN MARINO
Florence
Split

Barcelona

Corsica

Sardinia

Rome
VATICAN CITY
ITALY
Naples
Bari

Ligurian Sea
ADRIATIC SEA

BOSNIA AND HERZEGOVINA
Sarajevo
SERBIA
Belgrade
MONTENEGRO
Podgorica
Skopje
ALBANIA
MACEDONIA
Tiranë

Cagliari

TYRRHENIAN SEA

MEDITERRANEAN SEA

Palermo
Messina
Sicily
Catania

GREECE
Pátra

IONIAN SEA

MOROCCO
AFRICA
ALGERIA
Algiers
TUNISIA
MALTA

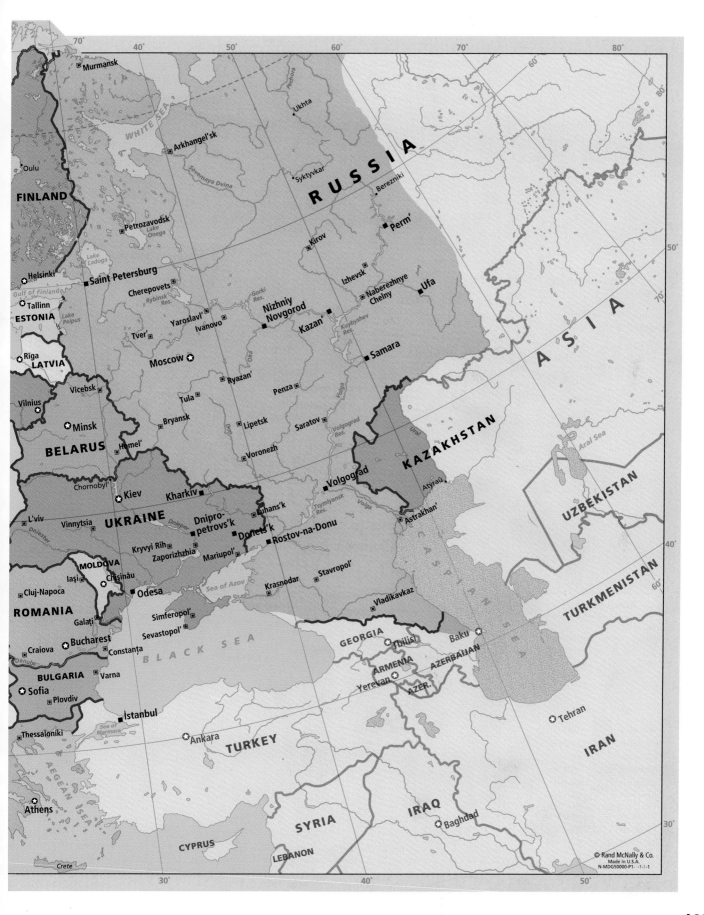

70° 40° 50° 60° 70° 80°

Murmansk

FINLAND

Oulu

WHITE SEA

Arkhangel'sk

Severnaya Dvina

Ukhta

RUSSIA

Syktyvkar

Berezniki

Petrozavodsk
Lake Onega

Kirov

Perm'

Helsinki

Saint Petersburg

Tallinn

ESTONIA

Lake Ladoga

Cherepovets
Rybinsk Res.

Gorki Res.

Izhevsk

Naberezhnye Chelny

Ufa

ASIA

Gulf of Finland

Lake Peipus

Yaroslavl'

Ivanovo

Nizhniy Novgorod

Kazan'

Kuybyshev Res.

Rīga

LATVIA

Tver'

Moscow

Samara

Vicebsk

Vilnius

Ryazan'

Oka

Volga

Minsk

Tula

Penza

BELARUS

Homel'

Bryansk

Lipetsk

Saratov

Volgograd Res.

Ural

KAZAKHSTAN

Aral Sea

Chornobyl'

Voronezh

Atyraū

UZBEKISTAN

L'viv

Kiev

Kharkiv

Volgograd

Vinnytsia

UKRAINE

Dnipro-petrovs'k

Luhans'k

Tsymlyansk Res.

Volga

Dnieper

Donets'k

Astrakhan'

Dniester

Kryvyi Rih

Zaporizhzhia

Mariupol'

Rostov-na-Donu

MOLDOVA

Iași

Chișinău

Sea of Azov

Krasnodar

Stavropol'

CASPIAN SEA

TURKMENISTAN

Cluj-Napoca

Odesa

ROMANIA

Galați

Simferopol'

Vladikavkaz

Craiova

Bucharest

Constanța

Sevastopol'

BLACK SEA

GEORGIA

Tbilisi

Baku

AZERBAIJAN

Danube

BULGARIA

Varna

ARMENIA

AZER.

Sofia

Plovdiv

Yerevan

Thessaloníki

İstanbul

Sea of Marmara

Tehran

AEGEAN SEA

Ankara

TURKEY

IRAN

Athens

CYPRUS

SYRIA

IRAQ

Baghdad

LEBANON

Crete

© Rand McNally & Co.
Made in U.S.A.
N-MDG50000-P1- -1-1-1

30° 40° 50°

60° 70°

50°

40°

30°

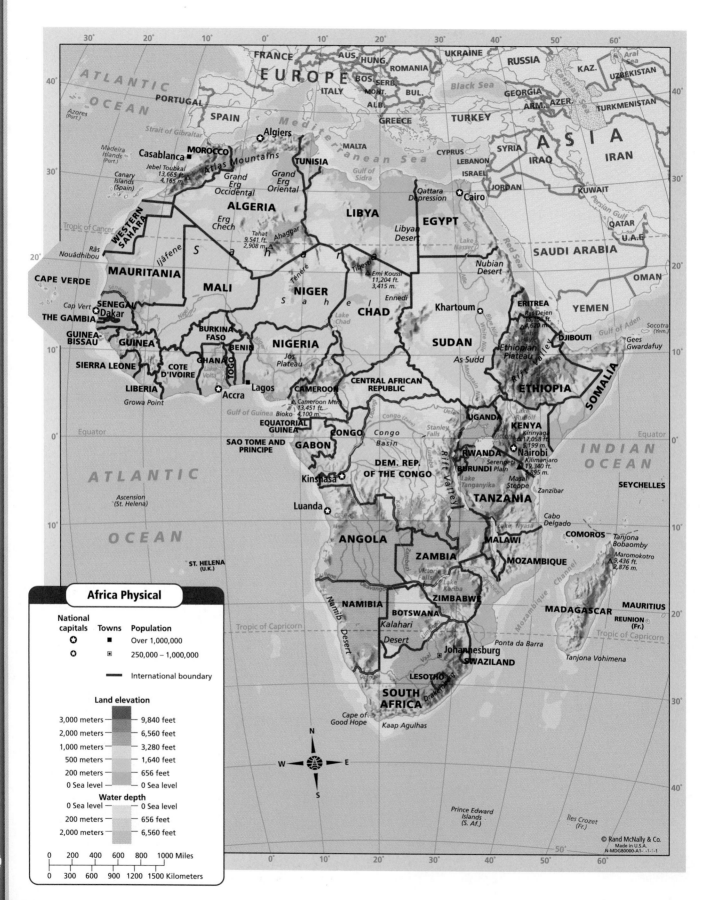

Africa Physical

National capitals
- ✪ Over 1,000,000 (National capitals)
- ✪ 250,000 – 1,000,000 (National capitals)

Towns
- ■ Over 1,000,000
- ▣ 250,000 – 1,000,000

— International boundary

Land elevation

3,000 meters	9,840 feet
2,000 meters	6,560 feet
1,000 meters	3,280 feet
500 meters	1,640 feet
200 meters	656 feet
0 Sea level	0 Sea level

Water depth

0 Sea level	0 Sea level
200 meters	656 feet
2,000 meters	6,560 feet

0   200   400   600   800   1000 Miles
0   300   600   900   1200   1500 Kilometers

© Rand McNally & Co.
Made in U.S.A.
N-MDG80000-A1- -1- -1-1

RAND MCNALLY

A30

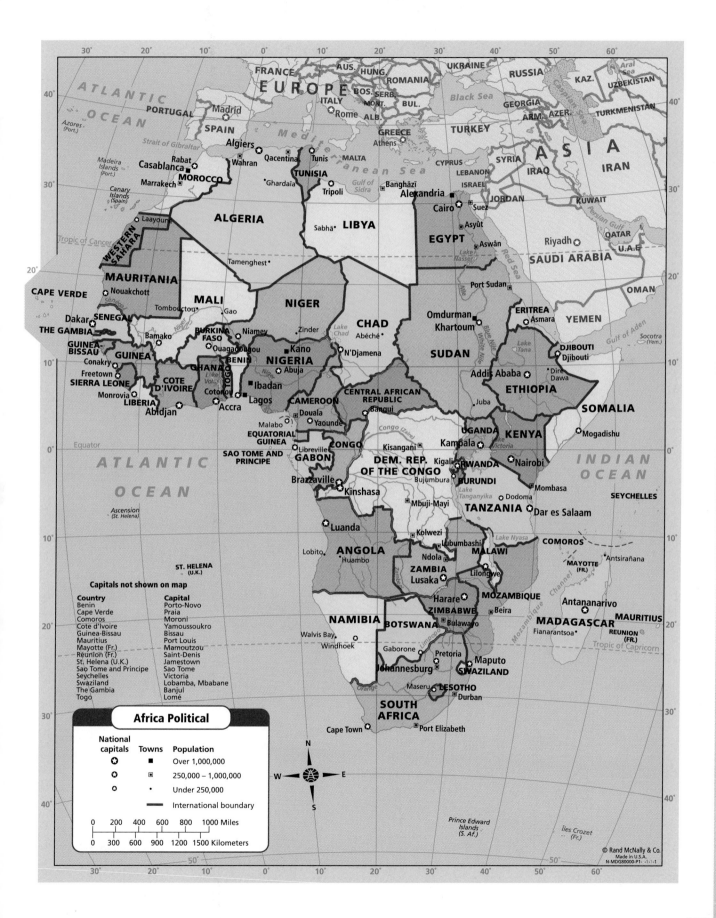

ATLANTIC OCEAN

EUROPE

FRANCE
AUS. HUNG.
ROMANIA
UKRAINE
RUSSIA
KAZ.
UZBEKISTAN
Aral Sea
PORTUGAL
Madrid
SPAIN
ITALY
Rome
BOS. SERB.
MONT.
ALB.
BUL.
Black Sea
GEORGIA
ARM. AZER.
TURKMENISTAN
Mediterranean Sea
GREECE
Athens
TURKEY
CYPRUS
SYRIA
LEBANON
ISRAEL
ASIA
IRAN
IRAQ

Azores (Port.)
Strait of Gibraltar
Algiers
Qacentina
Tunis
MALTA
Gulf of Sidra
Banghāzī
Tripoli

Madeira Islands (Port.)
Rabat
Casablanca
MOROCCO
Marrakech
Wahran
TUNISIA
Ghardaïa

Canary Islands (Spain)
Laayoune
WESTERN SAHARA
ALGERIA
Sabhā
LIBYA
Alexandria
Cairo
Suez
JORDAN
KUWAIT
QATAR
U.A.E.
Riyadh
SAUDI ARABIA
OMAN

Tropic of Cancer
Tamenghest
EGYPT
Asyût
Aswân
Lake Nasser

CAPE VERDE
Nouakchott
MAURITANIA
MALI
NIGER
CHAD
Abéché
N'Djamena
Port Sudan
Red Sea
Omdurman
Khartoum
SUDAN
Blue Nile
ERITREA
Asmara
Lake Tana
YEMEN
Gulf of Aden
Socotra (Yem.)
DJIBOUTI
Djibouti

Tombouctou
Gao
Niger
Niamey
Zinder
Lake Chad

Dakar
SENEGAL
THE GAMBIA
GUINEA-BISSAU
GUINEA
Conakry
Freetown
SIERRA LEONE
Monrovia
LIBERIA
Bamako
BURKINA FASO
Ouagadougou
BENIN
GHANA
Lake Volta
TOGO
COTE D'IVOIRE
Cotonou
Accra
Abidjan
NIGERIA
Kano
Abuja
Ibadan
Lagos
CAMEROON
Douala
Yaoundé
CENTRAL AFRICAN REPUBLIC
Bangui
Addis Ababa
ETHIOPIA
Dire Dawa
Juba
SOMALIA
Mogadishu

Equator
ATLANTIC OCEAN
Ascension (St. Helena)
Malabo
EQUATORIAL GUINEA
SAO TOME AND PRINCIPE
Libreville
GABON
CONGO
Brazzaville
Kinshasa
Congo (Zaïre)
Kisangani
DEM. REP. OF THE CONGO
Mbuji-Mayi
UGANDA
Kampala
Lake Victoria
RWANDA
Kigali
Bujumbura
BURUNDI
Lake Tanganyika
KENYA
Nairobi
Mombasa
Dodoma
TANZANIA
Dar es Salaam
INDIAN OCEAN
SEYCHELLES

ST. HELENA (U.K.)
Luanda
Lobito
ANGOLA
Huambo
Kolwezi
Lubumbashi
Ndola
ZAMBIA
Lusaka
Lake Nyasa
MALAWI
Lilongwe
COMOROS
MAYOTTE (FR.)
Antsiranana

Capitals not shown on map

Country	Capital
Benin	Porto-Novo
Cape Verde	Praia
Comoros	Moroni
Cote d'Ivoire	Yamoussoukro
Guinea-Bissau	Bissau
Mauritius	Port Louis
Mayotte (Fr.)	Mamoutzou
Réunion (Fr.)	Saint-Denis
St. Helena (U.K.)	Jamestown
Sao Tome and Principe	Sao Tome
Seychelles	Victoria
Swaziland	Lobamba, Mbabane
The Gambia	Banjul
Togo	Lomé

Harare
ZIMBABWE
Bulawayo
Beira
MOZAMBIQUE
Mozambique Channel
Antananarivo
MADAGASCAR
Fianarantsoa
MAURITIUS
REUNION (FR.)
Tropic of Capricorn

NAMIBIA
BOTSWANA
Walvis Bay
Windhoek
Gaborone
Pretoria
Maputo
Johannesburg
SWAZILAND
Maseru
LESOTHO
Durban
Limpopo
Orange
SOUTH AFRICA
Cape Town
Port Elizabeth

Africa Political

National capitals · **Towns** · **Population**

⊛	■	Over 1,000,000
⊙	▣	250,000 – 1,000,000
○	•	Under 250,000
	—	International boundary

N
W — ⊛ — E
S

0   200   400   600   800   1000 Miles
0   300   600   900   1200 1500 Kilometers

Prince Edward Islands (S. Af.)
Îles Crozet (Fr.)

© Rand McNally & Co.
Made in U.S.A.
N-MDG80000-P1- -1-1-1

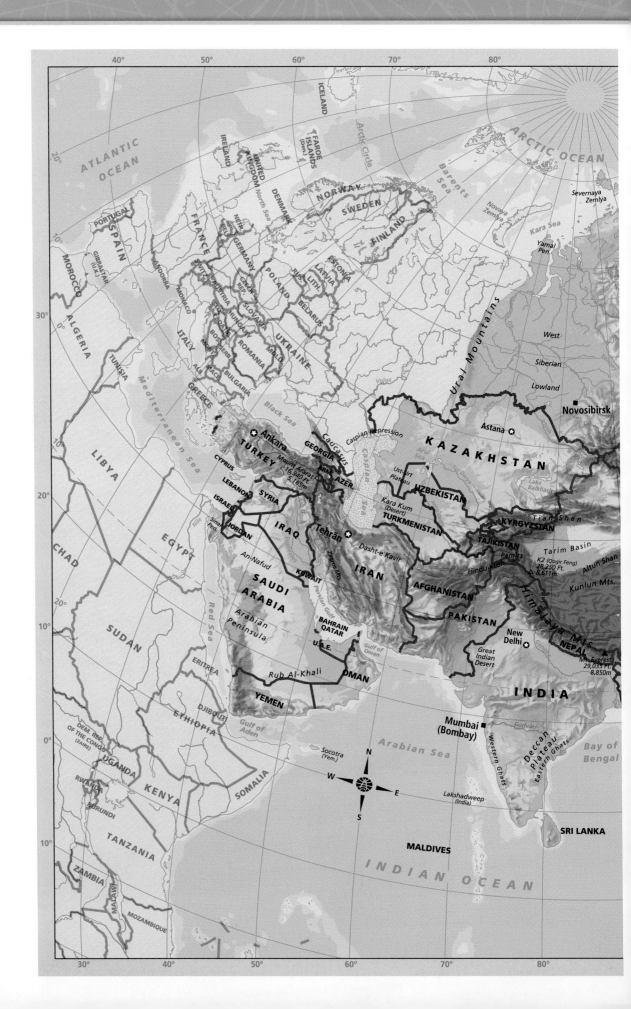

ATLANTIC
OCEAN

ICELAND

ARCTIC OCEAN

Arctic Circle

Severnaya
Zemlya

Barents
Sea

Novaya
Zemlya

Kara Sea

Yamal
Pen.

IRELAND

UNITED
KINGDOM

FAROE
ISLANDS
(Den.)

North Sea

NORWAY

SWEDEN

FINLAND

DENMARK

PORTUGAL

SPAIN

GIBRALTAR
(U.K.)

ANDORRA

FRANCE

BELG.
NETH.
SWITZ.
AUSTRIA
MONACO
ITALY
CZECH
REP.
SLOVAKIA
HUNGARY
SLOVENIA
BOSNIA
MAC.
GREECE

GERMANY

POLAND

RUS.
LITH.
LATVIA
ESTONIA

BELARUS

UKRAINE

ROMANIA

BULGARIA

ALB.
MALTA

Ural Mountains

West
Siberian
Lowland

Novosibirsk

MOROCCO

ALGERIA

TUNISIA

Mediterranean Sea

Black Sea

Volga

Caspian Depression

Caspian Sea

Aral
Sea

Ust-Urt
Plateau

KAZAKHSTAN

Astana

Syr Darya

Lake
Balkhash

LIBYA

EGYPT

CHAD

SUDAN

Nile

Sinai
Pen.

CYPRUS

LEBANON

ISRAEL
JORDAN

SYRIA

TURKEY

Ankara

Mount Ararat
16,940 Ft.
5,165m

GEORGIA

ARM.
AZER.

IRAQ

Euphrates

An-Nafud

KUWAIT

SAUDI
ARABIA

Arabian
Peninsula

Tehrān

Dasht-e Kavir

IRAN

Zagros Mts.

Persian Gulf

BAHRAIN
QATAR

U.A.E.

Gulf of
Oman

Kara Kum
(Desert)

TURKMENISTAN

UZBEKISTAN

Amu Darya

Tian Shan

KYRGYZSTAN

TAJIKISTAN

Pamirs

AFGHANISTAN

Hindu Kush

K2 (Qogir Feng)
28,250 Ft.
△ 8,611m

Tarim Basin

Altun Shan

Kunlun Mts.

PAKISTAN

Himalaya Mts.

Great
Indian
Desert

New
Delhi

NEPAL

Mt. Everest
29,035 Ft.
8,850m

ERITREA

DJIBOUTI

ETHIOPIA

Red Sea

Rub Al-Khali

OMAN

YEMEN

Gulf of
Aden

SOMALIA

DEM. REP.
OF THE CONGO
(ZAIRE)

UGANDA

RWANDA
BURUNDI

KENYA

Socotra
(Yem.)

Arabian Sea

N
W   E
S

INDIA

Mumbai
(Bombay)

Godāvari

Deccan
Plateau

Western Ghats

Eastern Ghats

Bay of
Bengal

Lakshadweep
(India)

SRI LANKA

TANZANIA

ZAMBIA

MALAWI

MOZAMBIQUE

MALDIVES

INDIAN OCEAN

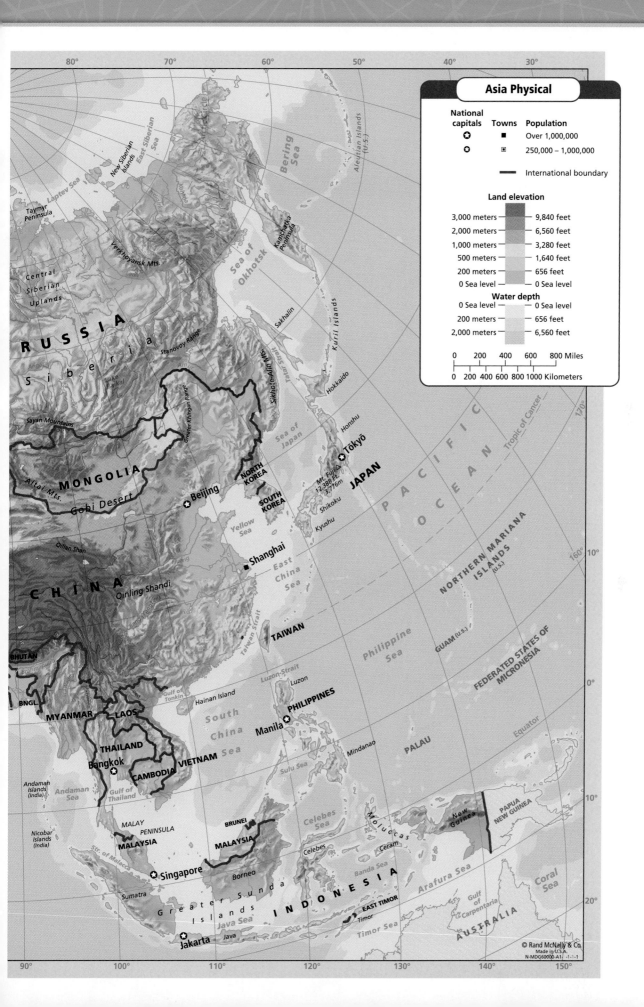

RAND M:NALLY

A33

Asia Physical

National capitals	Towns	Population
⊕	■	Over 1,000,000
⊙	▣	250,000 – 1,000,000

── International boundary

Land elevation

3,000 meters	9,840 feet
2,000 meters	6,560 feet
1,000 meters	3,280 feet
500 meters	1,640 feet
200 meters	656 feet
0 Sea level	0 Sea level

Water depth

0 Sea level	0 Sea level
200 meters	656 feet
2,000 meters	6,560 feet

0 200 400 600 800 Miles

0 200 400 600 800 1000 Kilometers

© Rand McNally & Co.
Made in U.S.A.
N-MDG60000-A1 -1-1-1

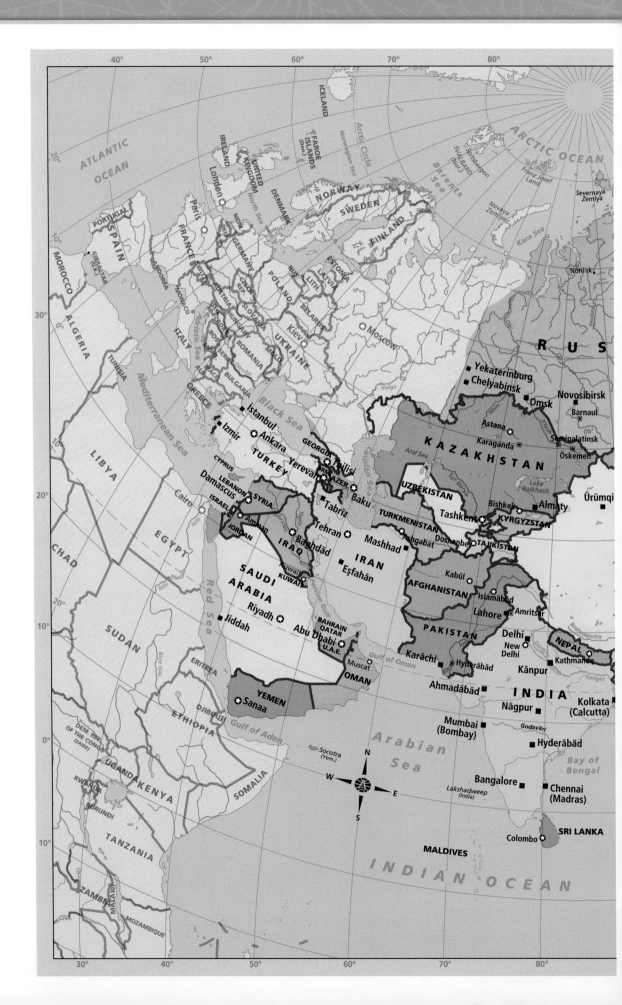

ATLANTIC
OCEAN

ICELAND

Arctic Circle

Norwegian Sea

ARCTIC OCEAN

FAROE
ISLANDS
(Den.)

SVALBARD
(Nor.)

Spitsbergen

Franz Josef
Land

Barents
Sea

Severnaya
Zemlya

IRELAND

UNITED
KINGDOM

London

North Sea

NORWAY

SWEDEN

FINLAND

DENMARK

Novaya
Zemlya

Kara Sea

Noril'sk

PORTUGAL

Paris

SPAIN

FRANCE

BEL.

NETH.

GERMANY

ESTONIA

LATVIA

LITH.

BELARUS

POLAND

RUS.

Moscow

Volga

RUSS

Yekaterinburg

Chelyabinsk

Novosibirsk

Omsk

Barnaul

MOROCCO

GIBRALTAR
(U.K.)

ANDORRA

MONACO

SWITZ.

AUSTRIA

CZECH

SLOVAKIA

HUNGARY

ROMANIA

MOLD.

UKRAINE

Kiev

Astana

Karaganda

Semipalatinsk

KAZAKHSTAN

Öskemen

ALGERIA

TUNISIA

ITALY

SLOV.

CRO.

BOS.

SERB.

MONT.

ALB.

MAC.

BULGARIA

Danube

Black Sea

GREECE

Istanbul

Izmir

Ankara

TURKEY

Yerevan

GEORGIA

ARM.

Tbilisi

AZER.

Baku

Caspian Sea

Aral Sea

Syr Dar'ya

UZBEKISTAN

Tashkent

Lake
Balkhash

Bishkek

Almaty

KYRGYZSTAN

Ürümqi

CYPRUS

LEBANON

Damascus

SYRIA

ISRAEL

Amman

JORDAN

Tabriz

Euphrates

Tigris

Baghdād

IRAQ

Tehran

Mashhad

TURKMENISTAN

Ashgabat

Dushanbe

TAJIKISTAN

LIBYA

Mediterranean Sea

EGYPT

Cairo

Nile

SAUDI
ARABIA

Kuwait

KUWAIT

IRAN

Eşfahān

AFGHANISTAN

Kabūl

Islāmābād

Lahore

Amritsar

PAKISTAN

Delhi

New
Delhi

NEPAL

Kathmandu

Brahmaputra

CHAD

Red Sea

Riyadh

Jiddah

Abu Dhabi

BAHRAIN

QATAR

U.A.E.

Persian Gulf

Muscat

Gulf of Oman

OMAN

Karāchi

Hyderābād

Ahmadābād

INDIA

Kānpur

Ganges

SUDAN

Blue Nile

Nile

ERITREA

DJIBOUTI

YEMEN

Sanaa

Gulf of Aden

Socotra
(Yem.)

Arabian
Sea

Nāgpur

Kolkata
(Calcutta)

Mumbai
(Bombay)

Godāvari

Hyderābād

Bay of
Bengal

ETHIOPIA

DEM. REP.
OF THE CONGO
(ZAIRE)

UGANDA

KENYA

SOMALIA

N

W

E

S

Bangalore

Lakshadweep
(India)

Chennai
(Madras)

RWANDA

BURUNDI

TANZANIA

Colombo

SRI LANKA

MALDIVES

INDIAN OCEAN

ZAMBIA

MALAWI

MOZAMBIQUE

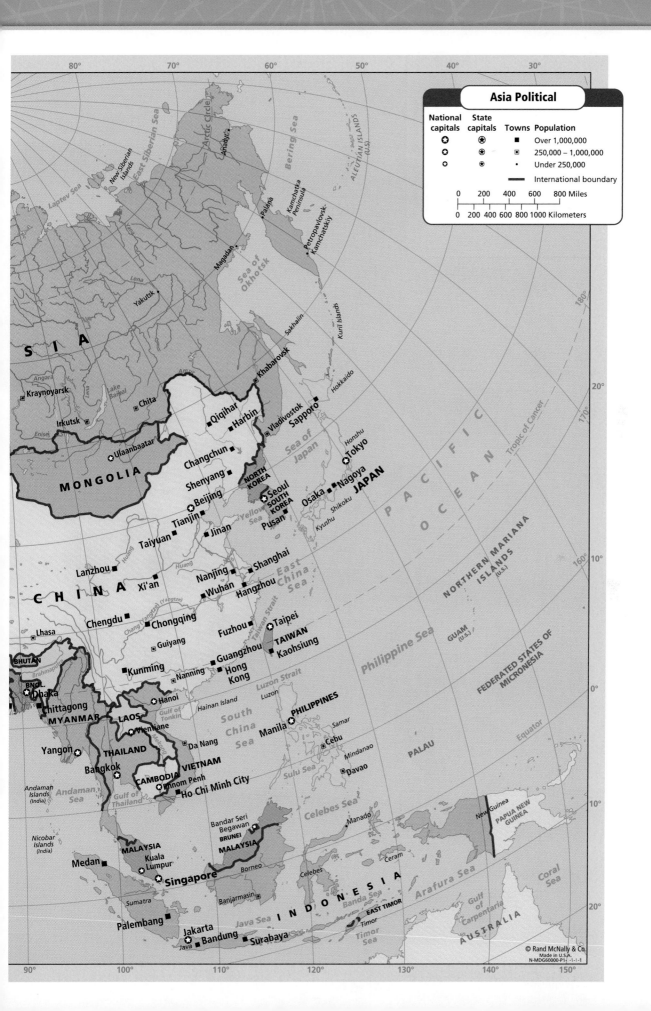

Asia Political

National capitals	State capitals	Towns	Population
✪	✸	■	Over 1,000,000
✪	✸	▣	250,000 – 1,000,000
✪	✸	•	Under 250,000
		▬	International boundary

0 200 400 600 800 Miles

0 200 400 600 800 1000 Kilometers

80° 70° 60° 50° 40° 30°

Arctic Circle

New Siberian Islands

East Siberian Sea

Laptev Sea

Bering Sea

ALEUTIAN ISLANDS (U.S.)

Anadyr

Palana

Kamchatka Peninsula

Magadan

Petropavlovsk-Kamchatskiy

Sea of Okhotsk

180°

A S I A

Angara

Kraynoyarsk

Irkutsk

Lena

Lake Baikal

Yakutsk

Chita

Enisei

Khabarovsk

Sakhalin

Kuril Islands

170°

20°

Qiqihar

Harbin

Vladivostok

Sapporo

Hokkaido

Ulaanbaatar

Changchun

Sea of Japan

MONGOLIA

Shenyang

NORTH KOREA

Honshu

Tokyo

P A C I F I C

Beijing

SOUTH KOREA

Seoul

Osaka

Nagoya

JAPAN

Tianjin

Pusan

Shikoku

10°

Taiyuan

Jinan

Yellow Sea

Kyushu

O C E A N

Tropic of Cancer

160°

Lanzhou

Huang

NORTHERN MARIANA ISLANDS (U.S.)

C H I N A

Xi'an

Nanjing

Shanghai

East China Sea

Chengdu

Chang (Yangtze)

Chongqing

Hangzhou

GUAM (U.S.)

Lhasa

Guiyang

Fuzhou

Taipei

Taiwan Strait

FEDERATED STATES OF MICRONESIA

BHUTAN

Kunming

Guangzhou

TAIWAN

Kaohsiung

Philippine Sea

Brahmaputra

Nanning

Hong Kong

Luzon Strait

BNGL.

Dhaka

Hanoi

Luzon

PHILIPPINES

Chittagong

Gulf of Tonkin

Hainan Island

MYANMAR

LAOS

Da Nang

South China Sea

Manila

Samar

PALAU

Yangon

Vientiane

Cebu

THAILAND

VIETNAM

Mindanao

Bangkok

CAMBODIA

Phnom Penh

Ho Chi Minh City

Davao

Andaman Islands (India)

Andaman Sea

Mekong

Gulf of Thailand

Sulu Sea

Celebes Sea

Manado

New Guinea

PAPUA NEW GUINEA

Nicobar Islands (India)

Bandar Seri Begawan

BRUNEI

MALAYSIA

MALAYSIA

Ceram

10°

Medan

Kuala Lumpur

Borneo

Celebes

Banda Sea

Arafura Sea

Gulf of Carpentaria

Coral Sea

Singapore

Sumatra

I N D O N E S I A

Palembang

Banjarmasin

Java Sea

EAST TIMOR

Jakarta

Bandung

Surabaya

Timor

Timor Sea

AUSTRALIA

20°

Java

90° 100° 110° 120° 130° 140° 150°

© Rand McNally & Co.
Made in U.S.A.
N-MDG60000-P1- -1-1-1

RAND McNALLY

A35

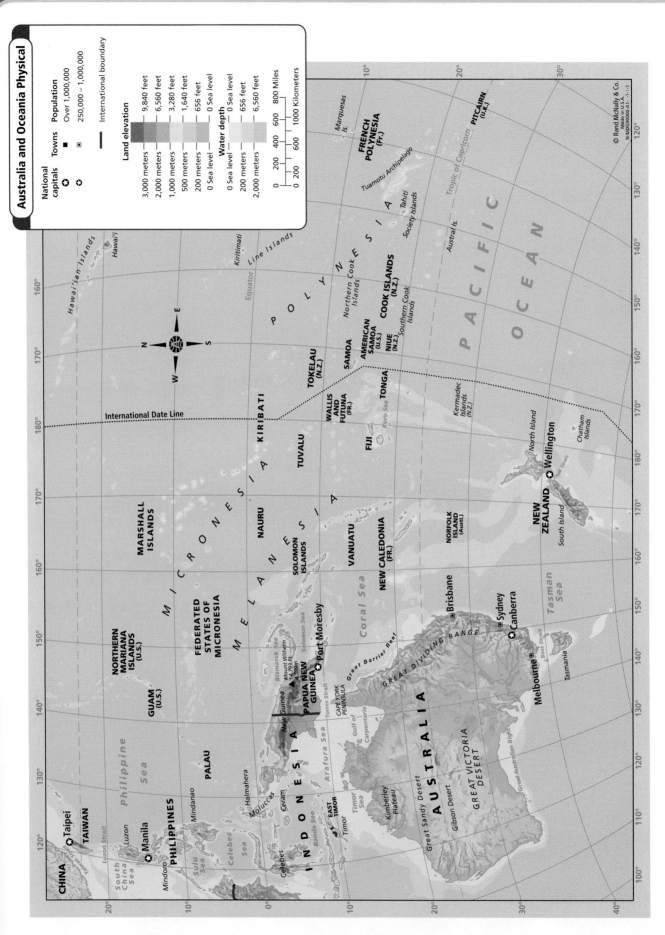

Australia and Oceania Physical

National capitals
⊕ Over 1,000,000
⊕ 250,000 – 1,000,000

Towns
■ Over 1,000,000
⊡ 250,000 – 1,000,000

— International boundary

Land elevation
9,840 feet — 3,000 meters
6,560 feet — 2,000 meters
3,280 feet — 1,000 meters
1,640 feet — 500 meters
656 feet — 200 meters
0 Sea level — 0 Sea level

Water depth
0 Sea level — 0 Sea level
656 feet — 200 meters
6,560 feet — 2,000 meters

0   200   400   600   800 Miles
0   200   400   600   800   1000 Kilometers

CHINA
Taipei
TAIWAN

PHILIPPINES
Manila
Luzon
Mindoro
Mindanao
Philippine Sea
South China Sea
Sulu Sea
Celebes Sea
Luzon Strait
Taiwan Strait

PALAU
Halmahera
Ceram
Moluccas
Celebes
Banda Sea
INDONESIA
EAST TIMOR
Timor
Timor Sea
Arafura Sea

GUAM (U.S.)
NORTHERN MARIANA ISLANDS (U.S.)

FEDERATED STATES OF MICRONESIA

MICRONESIA

MARSHALL ISLANDS

KIRIBATI

NAURU

TUVALU

SOLOMON ISLANDS

PAPUA NEW GUINEA
Port Moresby
New Guinea
Mount Wilhelm 14,793 ft. 4,509m
Bismarck Sea
Solomon Sea
CAPE YORK PENINSULA
Torres Strait

MELANESIA

VANUATU

NEW CALEDONIA (Fr.)

Coral Sea
Great Barrier Reef

AUSTRALIA
Great Sandy Desert
Gibson Desert
Kimberley Plateau
GREAT VICTORIA DESERT
Great Australian Bight
GREAT DIVIDING RANGE
Murray

Gulf of Carpentaria

Brisbane
Sydney
Canberra
Melbourne
Tasmania
Bass Strait
Tasman Sea

POLYNESIA

Line Islands
Kiritimati
Equator

TOKELAU (N.Z.)

WALLIS AND FUTUNA (FR.)

SAMOA
AMERICAN SAMOA (U.S.)
NIUE (N.Z.)

TONGA
FIJI
Koro Sea

Northern Cook Islands
COOK ISLANDS (N.Z.)
Southern Cook Islands

FRENCH POLYNESIA (Fr.)
Marquesas Is.
Tahiti
Society Islands
Tuamotu Archipelago
Austral Is.

PITCAIRN (U.K.)

Tropic of Capricorn

PACIFIC OCEAN

Kermadec Islands (N.Z.)

NEW ZEALAND
Wellington
North Island
Cook Strait
South Island
Chatham Islands

Hawaiian Islands
Hawai'i

International Date Line

N E S W

A36

North Pole

⊛ National capital
● Town
— International boundary

| 0 | 200 | 400 | 600 | 800 | 1000 Miles |
| 0 | 400 | 800 | 1200 | 1600 Kilometers |

© Rand McNally & Co.
Made in U.S.A.
N-MDG10091-P1-·-1-1-1

South Pole

| 0 | 200 | 400 | 600 | 800 | 1000 Miles |
| 0 | 400 | 800 | 1200 | 1600 Kilometers |

© Rand McNally & Co.
Made in U.S.A.
N-MDG94000-P1-·-1-1-1

❀ RAND McNALLY

UNIT 1

Introduction to World Geography

Why It Matters:

You live on a unique planet in the Sun's planetary system. It is the only planet capable of supporting a wide variety of life forms. As human beings we adapt and alter the environments on Earth.

Landsat satellite

CHAPTER 1
Understanding the Earth and Its Peoples

Fiery volcanic eruption

CHAPTER 2
Earth's Interlocking Systems

Indonesian rice fields

CHAPTER 3
Human Geography

Cave of Hands, Santa Cruz, Argentina

CHAPTER 4
People and Culture

1 Understanding the Earth and Its Peoples

 ESSENTIAL QUESTION

In what ways does geography help us understand our world?

CONNECT ↻ Geography & History

Use the satellite image and the time line to answer the following questions.

1. The large continent in the center of the image is Africa. How would you describe the land?

2. Which of the events listed on the time line made this image possible?

Culture

◄ c. A.D. 1st century
Strabo describes the world known to the Greeks and Romans in his 17-volume *Geography*.

A.D. 1

Geography
c. A.D. 2nd century
Greek geographer Ptolemy writes his 8-volume *Geography* on mapmaking.

Geography
▲ 1100 Chinese begin using the magnetic compass.

Click here to explore Earth and its people @ ClassZone.com

Ⓐ

Ⓑ

Ⓐ
Amazon Rain Forest The Amazon rain forest in South America is the largest rain forest in the world.

Ⓑ
Sahara Desert The Sahara is the largest desert in the world.

History
1730 John Hadley creates the basic design for a sextant. ▼

History
1972 First Landsat satellite is launched.

History
1960s Geographic Information Systems (GIS) development begins.

Geography
1983 The Global Positioning System (GPS) becomes operational. ▶

Today

Reading for Understanding

▶ Key Ideas

BEFORE YOU READ

Think about what you already know about the Earth's physical geography.

NOW YOU WILL LEARN

Geographers have specialized ways to view and interpret information about the world.

▶ Vocabulary

TERMS & NAMES

geography the study of people, places, and environments

environment the physical surroundings of a location

spatial where a place is located and its physical relationship to other places, people, or environments

location an exact position using latitude and longitude, or a description of a place in relation to places around it

place a geographical term that describes the physical and human characteristics of a location

region an area that has one or more common characteristics that unite or connect it with other areas

BACKGROUND VOCABULARY

three-dimensional an image in which there is a sense of depth and perspective

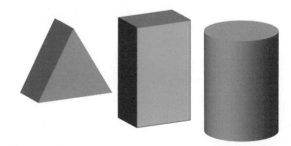

Visual Vocabulary Three-dimensional shapes

▶ Reading Strategy

Re-create the web diagram shown at right. As you read and respond to the **KEY QUESTIONS**, use the diagram to help you find main ideas about the themes and elements of geography.

 Skillbuilder Handbook, page R4

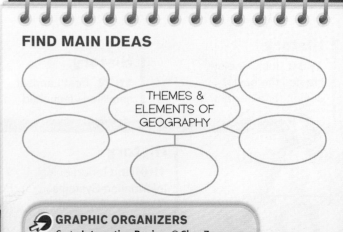

FIND MAIN IDEAS

THEMES & ELEMENTS OF GEOGRAPHY

GRAPHIC ORGANIZERS
Go to **Interactive Review** @ClassZone.com

Themes and Elements of Geography

1.02 Generate, interpret, and manipulate information from tools such as maps, globes, charts, graphs, databases, and models to pose and answer questions about space and place, environment and society, and spatial dynamics and connections.
3.04 Describe how physical processes such as erosion, earthquakes, and volcanoes have resulted in physical patterns on the earth's surface and analyze their effects on human activities.

Connecting to Your World

Have you ever drawn a map to show someone how to get to your house? Or have you described your hometown to someone who doesn't live there? If you answered yes to these questions, you were doing what geographers do. Geographers try to answer the questions, "Where are things located?" and "Why are they there?" Basic questions like these form the framework for the subject called geography. **Geography** is the study of people, places, and environments. An **environment** is the physical surroundings of a location.

Ways of Thinking About Geography

▼ **KEY QUESTION** What are the themes and elements of geography?

Geographers study the world in **spatial** terms. This means they look at the space where a place is located and its physical relationship to other places, people, and environments. Geographers—and students of geography— use two different methods to organize geographic information: the five themes and the six essential elements of geography. The categories vary slightly, but the graphic on the next two pages will help you learn how to apply these ideas as you read this text.

Three-Dimensional Model This computer-generated model is used to study geographic conditions in the Los Angeles region.

The Five Themes of Geography

The world is a big place and studying it is a complicated task. You can make that job easier by learning five core themes of geography. These themes can help you answer geographic questions.

1 LOCATION

Where are things located?

Location means either an exact position using latitude or longitude, or a description of a place in relation to places around it.

Rio de Janeiro, Brazil

2 PLACE

What is a particular location like?

Place describes physical characteristics such as mountains or rivers, as well as human characteristics such as the people who live there.

Beijing, China

3 REGION

How are places similar or different?

Regions have physical or human characteristics that unite them and make them different from or similar to other regions.

Gobi Desert

4 MOVEMENT

How do people, goods, and ideas move from one location to another?

Movement of people, goods, and ideas changes places and regions and the people who live there.

Interstate Cloverleaf

5 HUMAN–ENVIRONMENT INTERACTION

How do people relate to the physical world?

Humans adapt to their environment and change elements of it.

Pacific Ocean Windsurfing

Six Essential Elements

Geographers use six key ideas or elements to help them understand people, places, and environments on the Earth.

1 THE WORLD IN SPATIAL TERMS

Geographers study the locations of places and distributions or patterns of features by using maps, data, and other geographic tools. Knowing about the world in spatial terms helps geographers understand physical and human patterns.

2 PLACES AND REGIONS

Geographers look for characteristics of places and then compare their similarities and differences.

Mount Everest

3 PHYSICAL SYSTEMS

Geographers study changes in the Earth's surface. Where and why people choose to live in certain locations may depend on Earth's surface conditions.

4 HUMAN SYSTEMS

Geographers study human settlement patterns and use of resources. This information helps explain human interactions and lifestyles.

5 ENVIRONMENT AND SOCIETY

Geographers study how people interact with the environment and how they use resources.

6 THE USES OF GEOGRAPHY

Geographers study patterns and processes in the world. This information helps people understand the past and plan for the future.

Washington, D.C.

Volcano Specialist

South Asian Teapickers

Surveyor

Understanding the Earth and Its Peoples **7**

Five Themes of Geography Now that you have seen the geographic themes and elements side by side, let's look more closely at an example of one of the themes and elements as it applies to a particular place.

The theme of human-environment interaction is a good place to get an idea of how a geographer thinks. For thousands of years, people have found it valuable to settle by rivers. A river can provide food, water, transportation, and other needs of daily life. However, rivers can flood, destroying homes and villages, and taking human life. So, humans began to alter their environment by building walls called levees to protect the land from floods. Sometimes they created dams to control the flow of water and to save some water for times when they needed it. A geographer who asks the questions "Where do people choose to live?" and "Why here?" will answer that the river provides many needs for a group of people. So, people will likely be found in areas that have rivers as a resource. As it turns out, we know that early civilizations such as those in Egypt, Southwest Asia, India, and China began in river valleys.

Six Essential Elements Using the six elements helps geographers make sense both of physical processes on the Earth and of human systems devised by the people who live there.

Let's look at the element of physical systems. Geographers want to know how these systems work to reshape the Earth's surface and what impact these changes have on plants, animals, and people. Volcanoes

CONNECT to Geography

Chicago The skyline of Chicago towers over the shore of Lake Michigan. One of the largest cities in the United States, Chicago has long been the economic and cultural center of the region.

CRITICAL THINKING

Find Main Ideas Look at the image of Chicago at right. Which of the five themes and six elements of geography do the captions reflect?

High-rise buildings maximize the use of valuable land.

Chicago is a major hub for Great Lakes water transportation and a main railroad headquarters.

Chicago is located in the upper Midwest of the United States.

are an example of a physical force that changes the shape of the Earth's surface and may have a dramatic effect on human populations. A volcanic eruption may kill people, plants, and animals living in the area. Flows of lava may change the landscape, burn forests or crops, and possibly alter the course of rivers. Islands in the Pacific Ocean have been created by volcanic eruptions, and still others have disappeared between the waves when they were blown apart by eruptions. Volcanoes can also trigger earthquakes. Geographers studying physical systems point out that many volcanoes take place in certain areas of the world. Studying this pattern of volcanic action helps explain where and why people live in certain locations.

Using the five themes of geography and the six essential elements will help you to think like a geographer. The themes and elements will help you to think about particular places and the physical processes and human activities that shaped those places in the past—and continue to do so. They will also enable you to look for patterns and connections in geographic information. You will be better able to answer the two main geographic questions, "Where are things located?" and "Why are they there?" You will learn about the tools used to record and analyze geographic information in the next section.

 FIND MAIN IDEAS Identify the five themes and six essential elements of geography.

 **ONLINE QUIZ**
For test practice, go to
Interactive Review
@ ClassZone.com

Section 1 Assessment

TERMS & NAMES

1. Explain the importance of
- geography
- environment
- spatial

USE YOUR READING NOTES

2. Find Main Ideas Use your completed web diagram to answer the following question:

What are the five themes of geography?

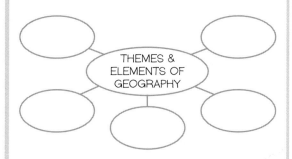

KEY IDEAS

3. What two questions do geographers try to answer?

4. How do geographers use the five themes?

5. What are the six elements that geographers use to look at the world?

CRITICAL THINKING

6. Summarize What does it mean to study the world in spatial terms?

7. Compare and Contrast How do you think the study of geography differs from that of history?

8. CONNECT to Today How does studying geography help you understand the world in which you live?

9. ART **Make a Poster** Create a poster that lists the five themes and six elements of geography. For each theme or element, include the definition and a photograph or drawing to illustrate it.

Reading for Understanding

▶ Key Ideas

BEFORE, YOU LEARNED

Geography is the study of Earth's physical features and the interaction of people with the environment and with each other.

NOW YOU WILL LEARN

Geographers use technological tools to help them understand both Earth's physical processes and the activities of people on Earth.

▶ Vocabulary

TERMS & NAMES

globe a model of the earth in the shape of a sphere

map a representation of a part of the Earth

cartographer (kahr•TAHG•ruh•fur) a geographer who creates maps

surveyor a person who measures the land

remote sensing obtaining information about a site by using an instrument that is not physically in contact with the site

Landsat a series of information-gathering satellites that orbit above Earth

Global Positioning System (GPS) a system that uses a network of earth-orbiting satellites to pinpoint location

Geographic Information Systems (GIS) a computer or Internet-based mapping technology

BACKGROUND VOCABULARY

database a collection of information that can be analyzed

debris (duh•BREE) the scattered remains of something broken or destroyed

▶ Reading Strategy

Re-create the web diagram shown at right. As you read and respond to the **KEY QUESTIONS**, use the diagram to summarize ideas about geographers' technological tools.

 Skillbuilder Handbook, page R5

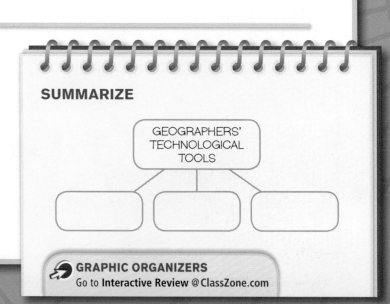

SUMMARIZE

GEOGRAPHERS' TECHNOLOGICAL TOOLS

GRAPHIC ORGANIZERS
Go to **Interactive Review** @ ClassZone.com

Technology Tools for Geographers

1.02 Generate, interpret, and manipulate information from tools such as maps, globes, charts, graphs, databases, and models to pose and answer questions about space and place, environment and society, and spatial dynamics and connections.
3.03 Examine the development and use of tools and technologies and assess their influence on the human ability to use, modify, or adapt to their environment.

Connecting to Your World

When you were a much younger student, you probably used paper and pencil to do your schoolwork. Now, when you have an assignment to complete, you most likely use a computer and the Internet. Today's geographers and other scientists use high-tech instruments and advanced computer software to create maps and databases. A **database** is a collection of information that can be analyzed. Geographers use these tools and their analysis to answer geographic questions.

Gerardus Mercator
A Flemish cartographer, Mercator developed a type of map still used today.

The Science of Mapmaking

▼ **KEY QUESTION** How has technology changed mapmaking?

In their work, geographers use photographs, graphs, globes, and maps. A **globe** is a model of the Earth in the shape of a sphere. It shows the actual shape of the Earth. But you can only see half at any one time, and it is not easy to carry around. So, geographers use maps. A **map** is a representation of a part of the Earth. Maps can help geographers see patterns in the way human or physical processes occur. **Cartographers** (kahr•TAGH•ruh•furs) are geographers who create maps.

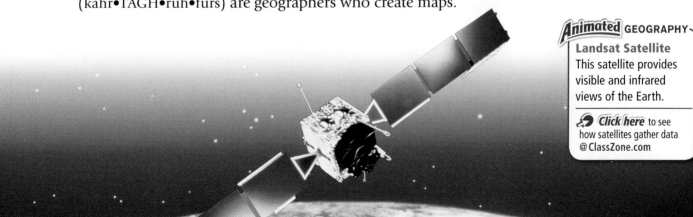

Animated GEOGRAPHY
Landsat Satellite
This satellite provides visible and infrared views of the Earth.

↪ **Click here** to see how satellites gather data @ClassZone.com

Cartographers create maps from data collected in surveys. **Surveyors** are people who map and measure the land. They go out to a location and mark down the physical features they see, such as rivers, mountains, or towns. Today, cartographers use technologically advanced tools that provide a much more detailed and accurate picture of the world.

To create modern maps, geographers often use remote sensing equipment. **Remote sensing** means obtaining information about a site by using an instrument that is not physically in contact with the site. Generally, these instruments are cameras mounted on airplanes or Earth-orbiting satellites.

Satellites Two of the best-known satellites are Landsat and GOES. **Landsat** is actually a series of information-gathering satellites that orbit more than 100 miles above the Earth. Each has a variety of sensing devices to collect images and data. Each time a satellite makes an orbit, it gathers information from an area about 115 miles wide. Landsat can scan the entire Earth in 18 days.

GOES, or Geostationary Operational Environmental Satellite, is a weather satellite. This satellite flies in an orbit at the same speed as the

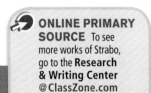
ONLINE PRIMARY SOURCE To see more works of Strabo, go to the **Research & Writing Center** @ClassZone.com

ANALYZING Primary Sources

Strabo (c. 64 B.C.–A.D. 23) was a Greek who wrote books about geography and history. His 17-volume *Geography* is the main source for information about the world known to the ancient Greeks and Romans. Strabo drew the map below for his geography book.

Strabo

DOCUMENT–BASED QUESTION
Which two continents labeled on the map were known to the ancient Greeks and Romans?

Earth's rotation. In this way it remains "stationary" above a fixed area. It gathers images of conditions that are used to forecast the weather. In 2006, there were two GOES satellites. One provided images from the eastern United States and the other from the west. You see GOES images when you watch a TV weather forecast.

Global Positioning System The U.S. Department of Defense developed technology to help American military forces know exactly where they were. The **Global Positioning System (GPS)** employs a network of Earth-orbiting satellites to collect information about the location of a receiver. The satellites beam the receiver's exact position—latitude, longitude, elevation, and time—to Earth. This information is displayed on the receiver.

A GPS receiver can be small enough to fit in your hand. It has an electronic position locator that sends a beam from where you and the device are to an orbiting satellite. The satellite measures where the GPS device is and beams back your exact position.

GPS can be used from any point on the Earth and in any type of weather. You can use its data to help you figure out "Where am I?" and "Where am I going?" GPS data can be used to determine location, aid in navigating from place to place, create maps, and track the movement of people and things. Animal biologists, for example, use GPS devices to track animals and learn about their habits.

▲ **DRAW CONCLUSIONS** Explain how technology has changed mapmaking.

◀ COMPARING ▶ Mapping Styles: Washington, D.C.

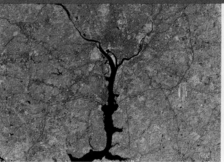

Road Maps Road maps are created from information including aerial photographs, road surveys made with hand-held digitizers, and maps showing the positions of such features as lakes and mountains.

Satellite Images Satellite images are produced by equipment that records information in a digital format. The information is then converted to images that look like photographs.

Infrared Images Infrared images measure the radiation emitted by water bodies, vegetation, and buildings. In this type of image, the warm areas appear in light blue, areas with vegetation appear red, and water is black.

CRITICAL THINKING

Evaluate Which of these mapping styles would be the most valuable for determining where earthquake damage has occurred?

Geographic Information Systems

▼ **KEY QUESTION** How do Geographic Information Systems work?

A very technologically advanced tool geographers use is the **Geographic Information Systems (GIS)**. GIS is a computer-based mapping technology. The complete system is able to gather, store, analyze, and display spatial information about places. It combines information from a variety of sources into digital databases.

GIS can integrate geographic information, such as maps, aerial photographs, and satellite images. It can also include information such as population figures, economic statistics, or temperature readings. Someone using GIS selects the information needed to answer a geographic question. Then GIS combines layers of information to give the user a better understanding of how the data works together. It can display the information in different ways, such as on a map, design, chart, or graph. The diagram below shows how GIS works.

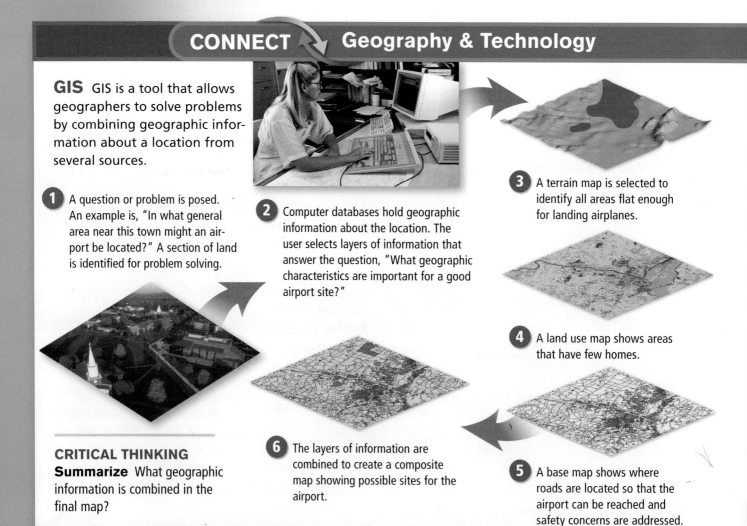

CONNECT **Geography & Technology**

GIS GIS is a tool that allows geographers to solve problems by combining geographic information about a location from several sources.

1 A question or problem is posed. An example is, "In what general area near this town might an airport be located?" A section of land is identified for problem solving.

2 Computer databases hold geographic information about the location. The user selects layers of information that answer the question, "What geographic characteristics are important for a good airport site?"

3 A terrain map is selected to identify all areas flat enough for landing airplanes.

4 A land use map shows areas that have few homes.

5 A base map shows where roads are located so that the airport can be reached and safety concerns are addressed.

6 The layers of information are combined to create a composite map showing possible sites for the airport.

CRITICAL THINKING
Summarize What geographic information is combined in the final map?

GIS projects can range from simple, specific site questions to more complex global problems. For example, you could use GIS to determine the quickest and safest path to walk to your school. The federal government was able to use GIS to predict the location of **debris** (duh•BREE) from the space shuttle *Columbia*, which broke up upon reentry into the Earth's atmosphere in 2003. GIS can be used to plan for hurricane evacuations or to monitor the possible spread of avian flu. Urban planners use GIS to determine where to place a park or where to relocate a dangerous highway intersection. Private companies use GIS to decide where to drill for oil or even where to place a new fast-food restaurant.

GIS makes it possible for geographers to answer geographic questions quickly and accurately. They are better able to see relationships between data, to understand the past and present, and to predict future situations.

In the next section, you will learn about the many different kinds of jobs geographers perform.

 SUMMARIZE Explain how GIS works.

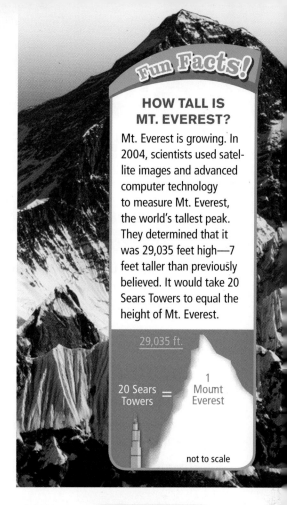

Fun Facts!

HOW TALL IS MT. EVEREST?

Mt. Everest is growing. In 2004, scientists used satellite images and advanced computer technology to measure Mt. Everest, the world's tallest peak. They determined that it was 29,035 feet high—7 feet taller than previously believed. It would take 20 Sears Towers to equal the height of Mt. Everest.

29,035 ft.

20 Sears Towers = 1 Mount Everest

not to scale

Section 2 Assessment

ONLINE QUIZ
For test practice, go to
Interactive Review
@ ClassZone.com

TERMS & NAMES

1. **Explain the importance of**
   • map
   • cartographer
   • Geographic Information Systems (GIS)

USE YOUR READING NOTES

2. **Summarize** Use your completed web diagram to answer the following question:

   What are some geographers' tools besides maps and globes?

GEOGRAPHERS' TECHNOLOGICAL TOOLS

KEY IDEAS

3. What were two early means of showing the Earth's surface?

4. How did remote sensing change the way geographic data were obtained?

5. What are some ways GIS can be used?

CRITICAL THINKING

6. **Make Inferences** How were early geographers limited in gathering geographic information?

7. **Draw Conclusions** How does technology help geographers?

8. **CONNECT to Today** In what ways do you think that new geography technology might aid military forces in modern warfare?

9. **TECHNOLOGY Make a Multimedia Presentation** Use an Internet-based GIS to demonstrate the uses of this geographic tool. Give examples of the different tasks a GIS can do.

Reading for Understanding

SECTION 3

▶ Key Ideas

BEFORE, YOU LEARNED

Geographers use technology to help them do their jobs of finding information about selected areas.

NOW YOU WILL LEARN

Geographers do many different kinds of jobs as they gather data and analyze and interpret it.

▶ Vocabulary

TERMS & NAMES

location analyst a person who studies an area to find the best location for a client

climatologist a geographer who studies climates

Visual Vocabulary Climatologist

urban planner a person who creates plans for developing and improving parts of a city

geomorphology (JEE•oh•mawr•FAHL•uh•jee) the study of how the shape of the Earth changes

REVIEW VOCABULARY

surveyor a person who maps and measures the land

Geographic Information Systems (GIS) a computer-based mapping technology

urban having to do with a city

▶ Reading Strategy

Re-create the web diagram shown at right. As you read and respond to the **KEY QUESTIONS**, use the web diagram to categorize details about careers in geography.

 Skillbuilder Handbook, page R7

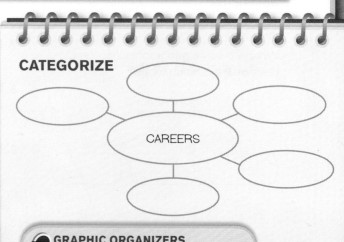

CATEGORIZE

CAREERS

GRAPHIC ORGANIZERS
Go to **Interactive Review** @ ClassZone.com

Careers in Geography

1.02 Generate, interpret, and manipulate information from tools such as maps, globes, charts, graphs, databases, and models to pose and answer questions about space and place, environment and society, and spatial dynamics and connections.

3.03 Examine the development and use of tools and technologies and assess their influence on the human ability to use, modify, or adapt to their environment.

Connecting to Your World

"What are you going to be when you grow up?" is a question that you may have been asked. You may not even know there are a variety of geography-related jobs. The Association of American Geographers lists nearly 150 different geography jobs. So, if you are interested in people, places, and environments, consider a job in geography. Your work will not be limited to maps—it might range from analyzing data to planning projects, or making decisions about the environment.

Modern Cartographer A cartographer works at updating a street map.

Processing Geographic Data

🔻 **KEY QUESTION** What is a geographer's main activity?

A geographer's main activity is analyzing geographic information to answer geographic questions. Jobs processing geographic data begin, of course, with collecting the information. One on-the-ground job in data collection is that of a **surveyor**. Surveyors map and measure the land directly. They may mark boundaries, study the shape of the land, or even help find sewer and water systems beneath the Earth.

Surveyor A surveyor in Dhaka, Bangladesh, gathers data for a project.

High-tech information-gathering jobs include working with **Geographic Information Systems (GIS)** data. Some examples of these jobs include remote sensing specialists and GIS analysts. Take a look back at the GIS feature in Section 2 to get an idea of what a job using GIS would be like. Data analysis jobs require the ability to think critically, high-level computer skills, and a college education.

Once data have been processed, a geographer may study the information to use in planning projects such as a new urban area, a disaster evacuation plan, or the placement of a new highway. Planners can also help determine how to make a neighborhood a better place to live. These jobs, too, require good critical thinking, writing, and computer skills, as well as a college education. Planners are valuable to the success of a community.

▲ **FIND MAIN IDEAS** Explain the main job of a geographer.

Advising Businesses and Government

▼ **KEY QUESTION** How do geographers help businesses and government?

About half of jobs using geography are in business and government. All kinds of businesses use geographic information to help build and expand their operations. A **location analyst** studies an area to find the best location for a client. The client might be a large retail store chain that wants to know which location would be best for opening a new store. The location analyst can study GIS reports on such elements as transportation networks or population in an area and give the business owners the positive and negative points about a location being considered.

In 1967, the Mexican government was looking for a location to create a new international tourist resort. They used location analysts to find an area that had good beaches and was easy to reach from the United States. The result was Cancún, today one of the world's most desirable vacation sites.

Businesses connected with natural resources such as forests also rely on geographers. Geographers help them understand the relationship between their business and the environment where their business is located. **Climatologists** are geographers who study

CONNECT **Geography & Culture**

Cancún Then and Now

In 1967, Cancún was a small, swampy island on Mexico's Caribbean coast. It had white sand beaches, many birds and mangrove trees, but few people. After it was selected as a resort site, it was quickly transformed. Today, Cancún has more than 100 hotels and 500,000 permanent residents. Many work in the tourist industry that serves the millions of visitors who come each year from all over the world.

climates. They are used by businesses that need information about climate to conduct their operations. For example, coffee-growers in Brazil must have an idea if the weather during the next year will be helpful or harmful to their crop. To determine this, a climatologist might study the long-term climate data about the region to project future weather patterns.

City governments often use an **urban planner** to create plans for improving parts of the city. Planners may help locate and design residential or business areas, or parks and recreational spaces. They may find a location for an airport, mass transit routes, or sewer and water lines.

 **FIND MAIN IDEAS** Explain how geographers help business and government.

Urban Planners Planners help city governments locate projects being built in a city. **What questions might a planner ask to help a city find the right location for a project?**

CONNECT to Your World

Geography Competitions

Across the United States and in foreign countries, students in grades four through eight compete in geography contests. Students are quizzed on all types of geography, including physical geography—such as locations of places and land and water features—and human geography.

Students compete in Washington, D.C., for the right to represent the United States in international competition for the world championship.

CRITICAL THINKING

Journal Entry Start a page in your journal with questions you could use in a geography contest at your school.

Physical and Human Geography

▼ **KEY QUESTION** What jobs are available related to physical and human geography?

Physical geographers are sometimes called earth scientists. Some study such topics as **geomorphology** (JEE•oh•mawr•FAHL•uh•jee), that is, the study of how the shape of the Earth changes. Others study weather and climate. Still others study water, the oceans, soils, or ecology. Jobs in these fields require special scientific training.

Some geographers study social, political, and economic issues as they relate to place or region. Human geographers are usually hired by government agencies to analyze a specific problem. These geographers work closely with political scientists, economists, and sociologists. Together, they provide possible solutions to problems from many different aspects of life in an area. And, of course, geographers teach the subject at all levels of education, from elementary schools to universities.

But no matter what geography jobs people might hold, they are always trying to answer the basic geographic questions: "Where are things located?" and "Why are they there?"

Surveying the Public
Human geographers ask residents about problems in the neighborhood. **Why would geographers ask residents questions about their neighborhood?**

▲ **SUMMARIZE** Name some physical and human geography jobs.

Section ③ Assessment

ONLINE QUIZ
For test practice, go to
Interactive Review
@ ClassZone.com

TERMS & NAMES

1. Explain the importance of
- location analyst
- climatologist
- urban planner

USE YOUR READING NOTES

2. Categorize Use your completed web diagram to answer the following question:

In what ways could a business use the skills of a geographer?

KEY IDEAS

3. What are three requirements for most careers in geography?

4. Who are the two major employers of geographers?

5. What questions do all types of geographers ask?

CRITICAL THINKING

6. Find Main Ideas How important are geographers to businesses?

7 Summarize How do you train for a geographer's job in business and government?

8. CONNECT to Today How do planners help governments with public projects?

9. WRITING **Write a Job Description** Select a specific job in the field of geography and research it on the Internet. Then write a description of the job's skill requirements and its responsibilities. If possible find a person doing that job and do an interview or have that person speak to the class.

Interactive ← Review

Click here to complete these and other activities online @ ClassZone.com

CHAPTER SUMMARY

Key Idea 1
Geographers have specialized ways to view and interpret information about the world.

Key Idea 2
Geographers use technical tools to help them understand both the Earth's physical processes and the activities of people on Earth.

Key Idea 3
Geographers do many different kinds of jobs as they gather data and analyze and interpret it.

For **Review and Study Notes**, go to **Interactive Review** @ ClassZone.com

NAME GAME

Use the Terms & Names list to complete each sentence on paper or online.

1. I am a model of the Earth.
   _____ globe _____

2. I am in orbit 100 miles above the Earth.
   _____

3. I am the study of people, places, and things. _____

4. I create plans for improving parts of a city.
   _____

5. I am an advanced technology tool used by geographers. _____

6. I am a representation of a part of the Earth.
   _____

7. I am a person who creates maps. _____

8. I am a group of places that have something in common. _____

9. I am a description of the physical and human characteristics of a location.
   _____

10. I am a person who maps and measures the land. _____

cartographer
climatologist
environment
Geographic Information Systems
geography
globe
Global Positioning System
Landsat
location analyst
map
spatial
surveyor
place
region
urban planner

Activities

Flip Cards

Use the online flip cards to quiz yourself on terms and names introduced in this chapter.

map

? a representation of a part of the Earth

Crossword Puzzle

Complete an online crossword puzzle to test your knowledge of basic geographic terms.

ACROSS
1. a model of the Earth

Assessment

CHAPTER 1

VOCABULARY

Explain the significance of each of the following.

1. spatial
2. remote sensing
3. environment
4. database
5. geography

Explain how the terms and names in each group are related.

6. map, globe
7. map, cartographer
8. place, region
9. remote sensing, Landsat, Global Positioning System, Geographic Information System
10. cartographer, surveyor, climatologist, urban planner

KEY IDEAS

① Themes and Elements of Geography

11. What are the three topics you study in geography?
12. Why is geography considered both science and social studies?
13. What is the difference between location and place?
14. What forces continually change Earth's surface?

② Technology Tools for Geographers

15. What is remote sensing?
16. How do satellites aid in mapmaking?
17. What two basic geography questions does the Global Positioning System help you answer?
18. What is an example of a technologically advanced geographer's tool?

③ Careers in Geography

19. What is the main activity of a geographer's job?
20. What does a location analyst do?
21. What does an urban planner do?
22. What types of geography are included in physical geography?

CRITICAL THINKING

23. **Categorize** Create a table that lists the five themes of geography and shows two examples of geographic information that would be included in each theme's description.

FIVE THEMES	GEOGRAPHIC INFORMATION

24. **Find Main Ideas** How do people adapt to their physical world?
25. **Summarize** How does modern technology help geographers?
26. **Connect to Economics** What role do geographers play in business operations?
27. **Connect Geography & History** How does the study of geographic patterns help us to understand past events?
28. **Five Themes: Human-Environment Interaction** What can be learned about people by studying their interaction with the environment?

Answer the
ESSENTIAL QUESTION

In what ways does geography help us understand our world?

Written Response Write a two- or three-paragraph response to the Essential Question. Be sure to consider the key ideas of each section as well as specific ideas about how geographers answer geographic questions. Use the rubric below to guide your thinking.

Response Rubric
A strong response will:

- discuss the two basic geographic questions
- identify and describe the five themes and six essential elements of geography

POLITICAL MAP

Use the map to answer questions 1 and 2 on your paper.

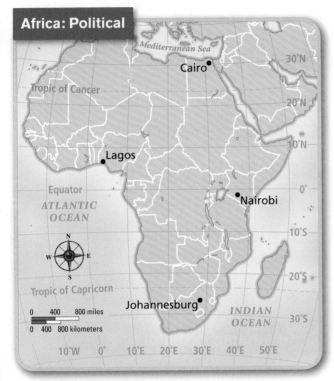

Africa: Political

1. **Which of the cities shown on the map is located south of the Tropic of Capricorn?**

   A. Cairo
   B. Johannesburg
   C. Nairobi
   D. Lagos

2. **Which of the cities shown on the map is located at approximately 30° N and 31° E?**

   A. Cairo
   B. Johannesburg
   C. Nairobi
   D. Lagos

CLIMATE GRAPH

Examine the climate graph below. Use the information in the graph to answer question 3 on your paper.

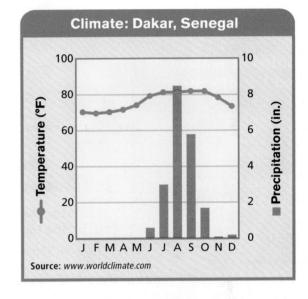

Climate: Dakar, Senegal

Source: www.worldclimate.com

3. **In which months does Dakar get the most rainfall?**

GeoActivity

1. INTERDISCIPLINARY ACTIVITY–TECHNOLOGY

With a small group, review new geographic technology. Choose one new tool to research further and create a museum-style display. Be sure your display shows the tool and how it works. Also, explain how the tool has changed the way geographic information is gathered.

2. WRITING FOR SOCIAL STUDIES

Imagine that you are an urban planner and have been asked to develop a plan for placement of a park in your city. Write one paragraph describing the location you chose and the reasons you selected it.

3. MENTAL MAPPING

Create an outline map of your neighborhood, city, or town and locate and label any of the following that are present in the area you map:

- physical features
- your home
- your school
- fire station
- hospital
- shopping area

Earth's Interlocking Systems

 ESSENTIAL QUESTION

How do Earth's physical systems make life on Earth possible?

CONNECT **Geography & History**

Use the map and the time line to answer the following questions.

1. On which plate does most of the United States sit?

2. Which event on the time line is supported by the evidence on this map?

1500

Geography

1620 English philosopher Francis Bacon suggests the continents were once a supercontinent. ▶

Geography

1883 Volcanic eruption destroys two-thirds of Krakatoa Island, Indonesia.

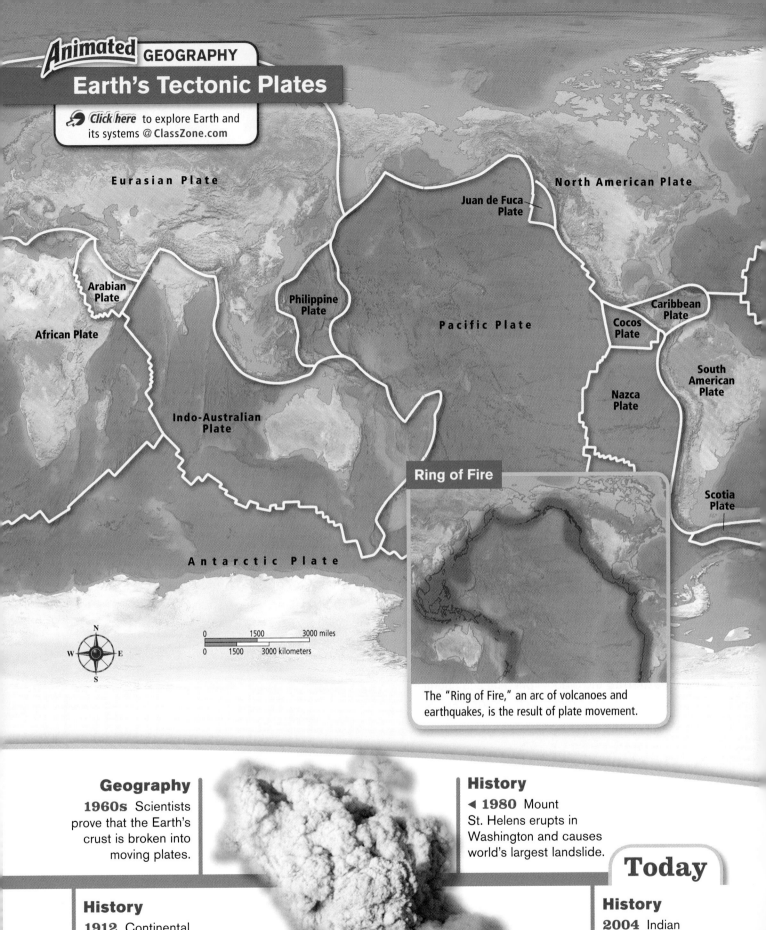

Earth's Tectonic Plates

Click here to explore Earth and its systems @ ClassZone.com

Eurasian Plate

North American Plate

Juan de Fuca Plate

Arabian Plate

African Plate

Philippine Plate

Pacific Plate

Caribbean Plate

Cocos Plate

South American Plate

Nazca Plate

Indo-Australian Plate

Scotia Plate

Antarctic Plate

N
W E
S

| 0 | 1500 | 3000 miles |
| 0 | 1500 | 3000 kilometers |

Ring of Fire

The "Ring of Fire," an arc of volcanoes and earthquakes, is the result of plate movement.

Geography

1960s Scientists prove that the Earth's crust is broken into moving plates.

History

1912 Continental drift theory proposed

History

◄ **1980** Mount St. Helens erupts in Washington and causes world's largest landslide.

Today

History

2004 Indian Ocean earthquake and tsunami kill more than 280,000.

25

SECTION 1

Reading for Understanding

▶ Key Ideas

BEFORE, YOU LEARNED

Geographers use technology to learn about physical processes on Earth.

NOW YOU WILL LEARN

The Earth is composed of many layers. Its surface continually changes because of the drifting of its plates.

▶ Vocabulary

TERMS & NAMES

magma molten rock

continent one of seven large landmasses on the Earth's surface

tectonic plate a large rigid section of the Earth's crust that is in constant motion

earthquake a sudden movement of the Earth's crust followed by a series of shocks

Ring of Fire a zone of volcanoes around the Pacific Ocean

volcano an opening in the Earth's crust from which molten rock, ash, and hot gases flow or are thrown out

weathering the gradual physical and chemical breakdown of rocks on the Earth's surface

erosion the wearing away and movement of weathered materials by water, wind, or ice

sediment pieces of rock in the form of sand, stone, or silt deposited by wind, water, or ice

glacier a large, slow-moving mass of ice

Visual Vocabulary glacier

▶ Reading Strategy

Re-create the chart shown at right. As you read and respond to the **KEY QUESTIONS**, use the chart to organize important details about the external and internal forces shaping the Earth.

 Skillbuilder Handbook, page R7

CATEGORIZE

INTERNAL FORCES	EXTERNAL FORCES
1.	1.
2.	2.
3.	3.
4.	4.

 GRAPHIC ORGANIZERS
Go to **Interactive Review** @ ClassZone.com

The Earth and Its Forces

1.02 Generate, interpret, and manipulate information from tools such as maps, globes, charts, graphs, databases, and models to pose and answer questions about space and place, environment and society, and spatial dynamics and connections.

3.04 Describe how physical processes such as erosion, earthquakes, and volcanoes have resulted in physical patterns on the earth's surface and analyze their effects on human activities.

Connecting to Your World

Have you ever experienced an earthquake or the eruption of a volcano? Probably not. But you may have seen these events on television. Perhaps you saw the coverage of the great earthquake in Indonesia on December 26, 2004. Hundreds of thousands of people were killed or displaced by this earthquake and the tsunami, or great wave, it caused. Earthquakes and volcanoes are just two of the many forces that change the Earth's surface.

Internal Forces Shaping the Earth

▼ **KEY QUESTION** How is the Earth's surface shaped by internal forces?

The Earth is one of eight planets that orbit the sun. It is located about 93 million miles from the sun. The Earth's circumference, or distance around, is 24,900 miles. Its diameter, or distance through the center of Earth, is about 7,900 miles. Earth is unique in the solar system—the sun and its planets—because it supports life. This is because the Earth has lots of breathable air and usable water. In fact, the Earth's surface is about three-fourths water and one-fourth land. The Earth appears to be a solid ball, but it is actually made of different layers that are like shells set inside each other.

San Francisco Earthquake The earthquake in 1989 was the worst quake since 1906.

It is about 3,900 miles to the center of the Earth. The Earth has five different layers.

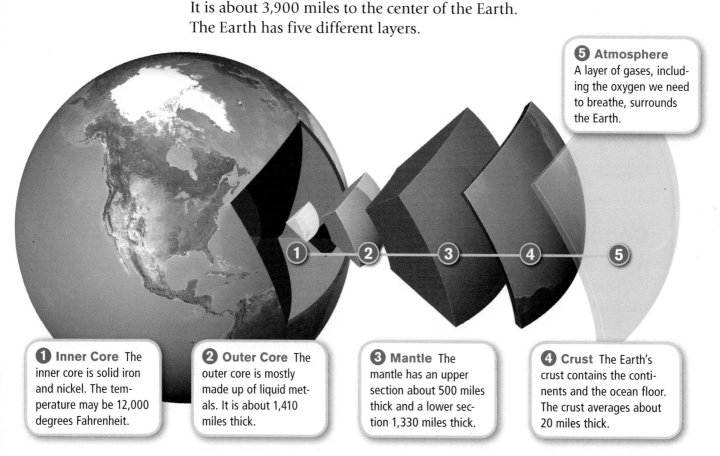

5 Atmosphere A layer of gases, including the oxygen we need to breathe, surrounds the Earth.

1 Inner Core The inner core is solid iron and nickel. The temperature may be 12,000 degrees Fahrenheit.

2 Outer Core The outer core is mostly made up of liquid metals. It is about 1,410 miles thick.

3 Mantle The mantle has an upper section about 500 miles thick and a lower section 1,330 miles thick.

4 Crust The Earth's crust contains the continents and the ocean floor. The crust averages about 20 miles thick.

Earth's Molten Interior The center of the Earth's interior is a hot metal core made up of one layer of iron and one of nickel. The inner core is solid. The outer core is liquid, because the metal has melted. Lying just above the core is the mantle. The mantle is a soft layer of hot rock, some of which is molten, or melted. It is the largest of the Earth's layers. The molten rock of the mantle is called **magma**.

The crust is the Earth's thin outer layer, or shell. It is the solid, rocky surface of the Earth that forms the ocean floors and the large landmasses called **continents**. The crust is the part of the Earth on which we live. It floats on top of the mantle. The crust is only about five miles thick under the oceans but averages about 22 miles thick under the continents. The Earth's layers are illustrated above.

Geographers have identified seven continents on the Earth's surface. The continents, in order of their size, are Asia, Africa, North America, South America, Antarctica, Europe, and Australia. Europe and Asia are actually one great landmass that is sometimes referred to as Eurasia or the Eurasian continent. Antarctica is a continent because it has a landmass beneath its icy surface. The Arctic does not, and so it is not a continent.

Tectonic Plates The surface of the Earth is constantly moving and changing, even as you read this sentence. Geographers use technological tools to observe and measure forces deep inside the Earth and on the surface that reshape the Earth's crust.

Plate movement, earthquakes, and the activity of volcanoes are all internal forces that change the landscape. The Earth's crust is divided into a number of large rigid pieces called **tectonic plates**. These plates are shown on the map at the beginning of the chapter. The continents and oceans are located on these plates, which float on the magma of the Earth's mantle. Heated magma cools as it reaches the crust and then sinks downward. This process causes the magma to act like a conveyor belt under the plates. The plates move slowly against each other, at a rate of up to four inches a year. The plate movement can cause earthquakes and volcanic eruptions. There are four types of tectonic plate movements that are shown in the diagrams below. Each of the movements causes changes in the shape of Earth's crust.

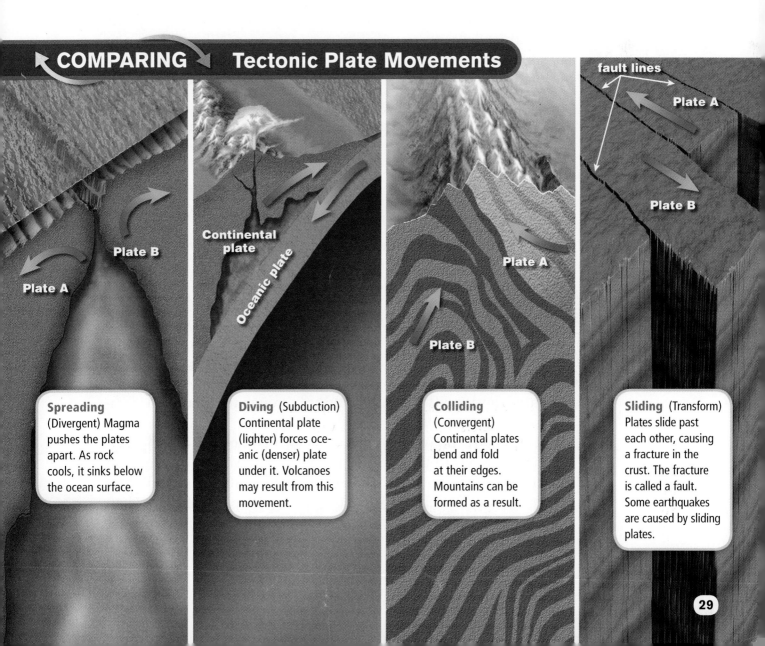

COMPARING Tectonic Plate Movements

fault lines
Plate A
Plate B

Plate B
Plate A

Continental plate
Oceanic plate

Plate A
Plate B

Spreading (Divergent) Magma pushes the plates apart. As rock cools, it sinks below the ocean surface.

Diving (Subduction) Continental plate (lighter) forces oceanic (denser) plate under it. Volcanoes may result from this movement.

Colliding (Convergent) Continental plates bend and fold at their edges. Mountains can be formed as a result.

Sliding (Transform) Plates slide past each other, causing a fracture in the crust. The fracture is called a fault. Some earthquakes are caused by sliding plates.

Animated GEOGRAPHY
Continental Drift Theory

Click here to see the movement of the continents @ ClassZone.com

1 The world map at left shows the supercontinent of Pangaea about 200 million years ago as it begins to break apart.

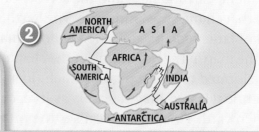

2 This world map shows the Earth about 65 million years ago. Some of the modern-day continents are visible.

CONNECT Geography & History
Draw Conclusions Which continents were connected 65 million years ago?

Continental Drift If you look at the continents, they look like giant pieces of a jigsaw puzzle waiting to be fit together. Alfred Wegener, a German meteorologist, noticed this pattern. He believed that the continents were once part of a supercontinent called Pangaea (pan•JEE•uh). He suggested that Pangaea divided and drifted apart about 200 million years ago. It contained almost all of the landmasses on Earth and was surrounded by one vast ocean. When it began to break apart, its pieces slowly moved in different directions, and some formed the continents we now know. To this day, the continents continue to move.

▲ **SUMMARIZE** Explain how internal forces shape the Earth's surface.

Extreme Events

▼ **KEY QUESTION** How are earthquakes and volcanoes connected?

Two events caused by internal forces may dramatically reshape the Earth's surface—earthquakes and volcanic eruptions. Both can be deadly, and both have powerful effects on human life.

Earthquakes An **earthquake** is a sudden movement of the Earth's crust that is followed by a series of shocks. Huge rocks along a line where faults are located slide apart and break up, causing that area of the Earth's surface to shake. The stress in the rocks builds for years. Then, energy is swiftly released outward through the ground in vibrations called shock waves.

Earthquakes occur constantly. Some we may not feel, but scientific instruments record them. Some produce slight shock waves. Other earthquakes and their aftershocks cause major disasters. Buildings collapse, cities are destroyed, and thousands of lives may be lost. Fires, floods, landslides, and avalanches can also follow earthquakes.

Earthquakes may also be triggered by the explosive action of a volcano. Most of Earth's active volcanoes are located in a zone around the rim of the Pacific Ocean called the **Ring of Fire**. A number of tectonic plates meet in this zone, and many of the largest earthquakes in the world have occurred there.

One of the biggest earthquakes ever recorded took place near the coast of Indonesia in 2004. It occurred on the floor of the Indian Ocean where two tectonic plates meet. The quake produced a giant ocean wave called a tsunami (tsu•NAH•mee). Within hours, the tsunami had devastated the coasts of 12 countries in southern Asia and eastern Africa. Whole villages were swept away, and more than 280,000 people were killed.

Volcanoes A **volcano** is an opening in the Earth's crust from which molten rock, ash, and hot gases flow. Molten rock rises from the Earth's mantle and is stored in a chamber beneath the crust. Pressure builds and forces the molten rock, or lava, to erupt onto the Earth's surface, burning or burying anything it touches. The eruption may also throw large clouds of gases and ash into the atmosphere.

Some volcanoes erupt constantly. Others are inactive, but could erupt at some future time. The most destructive eruption in recorded history happened in 1883, when two-thirds of the Indonesian island of Krakatoa (KRAK•uh•TOH•uh) was blown apart. The most active volcano in the United States is Mount St. Helens in Washington. It blew its top off in 1980. Activity occurred again in 2005.

▲ **UNDERSTAND CAUSES** Explain how earthquakes and volcanoes are connected.

CONNECT ↘ to Science

In a volcanic eruption, red-hot magma rises through cracks in the Earth's crust. Gases are released, causing a violent explosion of liquid rock, hot ash, and fiery gases into the air.

Kilauea, Hawaii

Activity
Make a Model of a Volcano
Materials
- small drink bottle (1/2 pint or 12 oz.)
- 1/4 cup of water
- a few drops of dishwashing detergent
- orange food coloring
- 1/4 cup vinegar
- 1 tablespoon baking soda
- a small square of tissue

1. Place the water, soap, food coloring, and vinegar in the bottle.

2. Wrap the baking soda in the tissue and drop the baking soda packet in the bottle. Watch the eruption.

External Forces Shaping the Earth

▼ **KEY QUESTION** What external forces shape the Earth?

External forces also reshape the Earth's surface. The two main external forces are weathering and erosion. **Weathering** is the gradual physical and chemical breakdown of rocks near or on the Earth's surface. **Erosion** is the wearing away and movement of weathered materials from one place to another by the action of water, wind, or ice. As you can see, weathering and erosion work together to shape the Earth.

Weathering Weathering occurs slowly, over many years or even centuries. The two types of weathering are mechanical weathering and chemical weathering. Mechanical weathering is a process in which rocks are broken down into smaller pieces by physical means. It takes place when ice, extremes of hot and cold, or even tree roots cause rocks to split apart. It also occurs when hard objects, such as other rocks or sand, scrape or rub against a rock, and pieces of the rock break off.

Chemical weathering is caused by chemical reactions between the minerals in the rock and elements in the air or water. This process changes the make-up of the rock itself. For example, most rocks contain iron. When iron comes in contact with water, it rusts, which helps to break down the rock. Water and elements in the air can cause other minerals in rocks to dissolve.

The Grand Canyon The Grand Canyon is located on the Colorado River in Arizona. It is an example of both weathering and erosion caused by wind and water.

UNITED STATES

O Grand Canyon

ARIZONA

MEXICO

Erosion New landforms and new soil are formed by erosion. It occurs when materials loosened by weathering are moved by water, wind, or ice to new locations. Currents in streams and rivers pick up loose materials and deposit them downstream or carry them out to sea. These tiny pieces of rock, deposited by water, wind, or ice are called **sediment**. Sediment can be sand, stone, or finely ground particles called silt.

Wave action along coastlines carries rocks and sand from one place to another. Waves also pound boulders into smaller rocks. Wind erosion lifts particles from the Earth's surface and blows them great distances. The wind's actions can reshape rock surfaces. Arizona's Grand Canyon is a result of both wind and water erosion.

Another type of erosion is caused by glaciers. **Glaciers** are large, slow-moving masses of ice. They grind rocks and boulders underneath the ice and leave behind the rock when the ice melts. Parts of the central United States have been shaped by glacial erosion.

Beach Erosion Ocean waves and tides eroded this section of beach in California.

 SYNTHESIZE Explain how external forces shape the Earth's surface.

Section ① Assessment

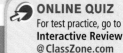 **ONLINE QUIZ**
For test practice, go to **Interactive Review** @ ClassZone.com

TERMS & NAMES

1. Explain the importance of
- continent
- tectonic plate
- weathering
- erosion

USE YOUR READING NOTES

2. Categorize Use your completed chart to answer the following question:

Are external or internal forces responsible for volcanoes? Explain your answer.

INTERNAL FORCES	EXTERNAL FORCES
1.	1.
2.	2.
3.	3.
4.	4.

KEY IDEAS

3. What are the five layers that make up the Earth's interior and exterior?

4. How were the continents formed?

5. What are the two major external forces reshaping the Earth?

CRITICAL THINKING

6. Draw Conclusions How does the movement of wind, water, or ice reshape the Earth's surface?

7. Analyze Causes and Effects What is the relationship between plate movement, volcanoes, and earthquakes?

8. CONNECT to Today In which parts of the United States are external forces shaping the landscape?

9. ART Create a Puzzle Make a copy of a map of the world. Cut out the continents. Use the continents as puzzle pieces to form the continent of Pangaea. When you have finished putting the pieces together, draw an outline around the entire supercontinent.

Reading for Understanding

▶ Key Ideas

BEFORE, YOU LEARNED

Internal and external forces shape the surface of the Earth.

NOW YOU WILL LEARN

Interaction between landforms and bodies of water makes life on Earth possible.

▶ Vocabulary

TERMS & NAMES

drainage basin the area drained by a major river

ground water water found beneath the Earth's surface

hydrologic cycle the circulation of water between the Earth, the oceans, and the atmosphere

landform a feature on the Earth's surface formed by physical force

plateau a broad, flat area of land higher than the surrounding land

relief the difference in the elevation of a landform from its lowest point to its highest point

continental shelf the submerged land at the edge of a continent

BACKGROUND VOCABULARY

atmosphere the layer of gases that surround the Earth

Visual Vocabulary landform

▶ Reading Strategy

Re-create the web diagram shown at right. As you read and respond to the **KEY QUESTIONS**, use the diagram to organize important details about the Earth's landforms and bodies of water.

 See Skillbuilder Handbook, page R4

FIND MAIN IDEAS

WATER BODIES   LANDFORMS

GRAPHIC ORGANIZERS
Go to **Interactive Review** @ ClassZone.com

SECTION

2

GEOGRAPHY

Bodies of Water and Landforms

2.01 Identify key physical characteristics such as landforms, water forms, and climate, and evaluate their influence on the development of cultures in selected African, Asian and Australian regions.
3.04 Describe how physical processes such as erosion, earthquakes, and volcanoes have resulted in physical patterns on the earth's surface and analyze their effects on human activities.

Connecting to Your World

How important is water to your life and to life on Earth? Without enough usable water, there would be no life. The Earth is able to support plant and animal life because of its abundance of water. It appears to be the only planet in our solar system able to do so. The Earth is sometimes called the "blue planet" because bodies of water cover so much of its surface.

The Earth from Space

Bodies of Water

▼ **KEY QUESTION** What are the two types of water found on Earth?

Almost three-fourths of the surface of the Earth is covered by water. Most of the water—more than 97 percent of it—is salt water. This is the water in the oceans and seas. Only about 2.5 percent of the Earth's water is fresh water—that is, water containing little or no salt.

Fresh Water Most fresh water is locked in frozen form in ice caps or glaciers. Much of the rest is found in rivers, streams, and lakes.

Iguacu Falls This series of 275 falls is located between Brazil and Argentina.

BRAZIL
Iguacu Falls
ARGENTINA

The Great Salt Lake This huge lake in northern Utah covers about 1,700 square miles. It is a remnant, or remainder, of a huge ancient fresh water lake called Lake Bonneville. That lake existed around 14,000 years ago and was about ten times as large as the Great Salt Lake. As the climate became drier and warmer over the centuries, Lake Bonneville's waters began to evaporate. But the salt it contained did not. That's why the Great Salt Lake is one of the saltiest bodies of water in the world.

CRITICAL THINKING

Summarize How did freshwater Lake Bonneville become the Great Salt Lake?

Russia's Lake Baikal, for example, is the world's largest lake and contains 20 percent of all Earth's fresh water. Rivers and streams move water downhill to or from larger bodies of water. Smaller streams and rivers that flow into a major river are called tributaries. The region drained by a river and its tributaries is called a **drainage basin**. The Amazon River system in South America is the world's largest drainage basin.

Some fresh water, called **ground water**, is found beneath the Earth's surface. This water is held in the pores and cracks of rocks and can be pumped from the ground.

Salt Water The water in the Earth's oceans and seas is called salt water because it contains a small percentage of dissolved minerals and chemical compounds called salts. Actually, all of the oceans and seas are part of the same body of water, which is divided by the continents. Geographers gave names to the different areas of the oceans.

The Earth's oceans are the Pacific, Atlantic, Indian, and Arctic, and the Southern Ocean, which is the body of water around Antarctica. The Pacific Ocean is the largest and covers almost one-third of the Earth. A body of salt water that is completely or partly enclosed by land is called a sea. An example is the Mediterranean Sea. Oceans and seas are sources of food, energy, and minerals and are used for transportation and recreation. They also help to distribute Earth's heat.

▲ **COMPARE** Compare the two types of water on the Earth.

Hydrologic Cycle

The Earth's water is renewed by a never-ending process called the hydrologic cycle, or water cycle. The **hydrologic cycle** is the circulation of water between the Earth, the oceans, and the atmosphere. Approximately 119,000 cubic miles of water evaporates into the atmosphere each year. The **atmosphere** is the layer of gases that surround the Earth.

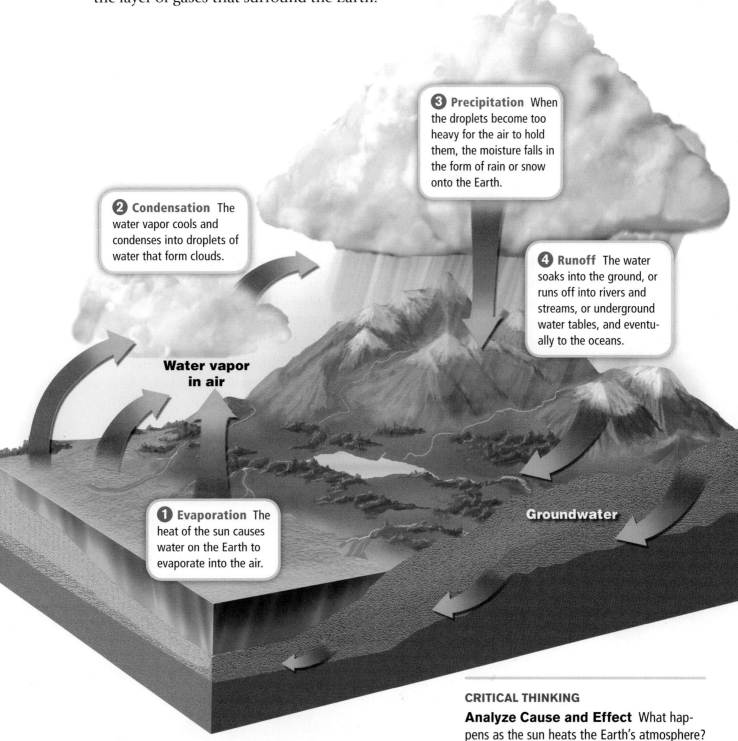

3 Precipitation When the droplets become too heavy for the air to hold them, the moisture falls in the form of rain or snow onto the Earth.

2 Condensation The water vapor cools and condenses into droplets of water that form clouds.

4 Runoff The water soaks into the ground, or runs off into rivers and streams, or underground water tables, and eventually to the oceans.

Water vapor in air

1 Evaporation The heat of the sun causes water on the Earth to evaporate into the air.

Groundwater

CRITICAL THINKING

Analyze Cause and Effect What happens as the sun heats the Earth's atmosphere?

Landforms

▼ KEY QUESTION How are landforms created?

Features on the Earth's surface formed by physical forces are called **landforms**. Landforms are produced by the internal and external forces that reshape the Earth. Internal forces push, move, and raise up parts of the Earth's crust. The result is the creation of new rock formations, such as mountains. External forces wear down these formations and transport the eroded materials to other locations. The eroded materials then become new landforms. These processes take a long time, but they are constantly at work. The location and size of landforms often affect where people choose to live.

Many of the same landforms found on dry land are also found under water. Those on the land are called continental landforms. Those on the sea floor are called oceanic landforms.

Continental Landforms The major continental landforms are mountains, hills, plains, and plateaus. A **plateau** is a broad area of land higher than the surrounding land. The same landforms are found on all of the continents. In fact, satellite photographs show a pattern on most continents: wide plains in the center and a narrow belt of mountains near the edge of the continent, where tectonic plates collide. For example, the landscape of the United States has the Rocky Mountains and coastal mountains in the west, the Appalachian Mountains in the east, and the Great Plains in the center.

The difference in the elevation of a landform from its lowest point to its highest point is called **relief**. Mountains show great relief compared to plains and plateaus. Many of the maps in this book have a relief indicator to show these differences in elevation.

Oceanic Landforms The landforms on the ocean floor are like an invisible landscape. Most cannot be seen from the surface of the water. But high mountains, vast plains, deep valleys, and coral reefs are present under the water's surface. Some are the result of the same tectonic forces that shape the continental landforms. The submerged

Monument Valley, Arizona In this photograph, you can see dramatic examples of relief between the floor of the valley and the tops of the landforms.

UTAH

○ Monument
  Valley

ARIZ.

land at the edge of a continent is called the **continental shelf**. It slopes downward and then descends to the deep part of the ocean. On the deep ocean floor are volcanoes, mountain chains, plains, and trenches. These landforms are created by the movement of tectonic plates, the same forces as those on the continent.

Some of the oceanic landforms are pushed up above the water and become islands. Many islands, such as the Hawaiian Islands, are formed by volcanic action. Other islands are formed from coral reefs. However, all islands are subject to the same external forces that wear down landforms on the continent. These forces include the weathering and erosion caused by wind, water, and ice.

Indian Ocean Reef
A diver views plant and animal life on a coral reef.

 SUMMARIZE Explain how landforms are created.

Section 2 Assessment

ONLINE QUIZ
For test practice, go to **Interactive Review** @ClassZone.com

TERMS & NAMES

1. Explain the importance of
- hydrologic cycle
- landform
- relief
- continental shelf

USE YOUR READING NOTES

2. Find Main Ideas Use your completed web diagram to answer the following question:

How is it possible for the oceans to have landforms?

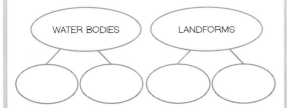

WATER BODIES   LANDFORMS

KEY IDEAS

3. How much water on the Earth's surface is fresh water?

4. What are the four components that keep the hydrologic cycle going?

5. What are the major continental landforms?

CRITICAL THINKING

6. Find Main Ideas Why are oceans important to life on Earth?

7. Compare and Contrast How are continental and oceanic landforms the same? different?

8. CONNECT to Today In what ways does water affect your daily life?

9. TECHNOLOGY **Make a Multimedia Presentation** Plan a slide show about the hydrologic cycle. Sketch each step in the cycle and explain what is happening.

Reading for Understanding

▶ Key Ideas

BEFORE, YOU LEARNED

The Earth's surface is covered with both continental and oceanic landforms. The hydrologic cycle circulates the water.

NOW YOU WILL LEARN

The Earth's rotation and revolution influence weather, climate, and living conditions on Earth.

▶ Vocabulary

TERMS & NAMES

solstice the time during the year when the sun reaches the farthest northern or southern point in the sky

equinox one of the two times a year when the sun's rays are over the equator and days and night around the world are equal in length

weather the condition of the Earth's atmosphere at a given time and place

climate the typical weather conditions of a region over a long period of time

precipitation falling water droplets in the form of rain, snow, sleet, or hail

vegetation region an area that has similar plants

savanna a vegetation region with a mix of grassland and scattered trees

desert a region with plants specially adapted to dry conditions

Visual Vocabulary desert

▶ Reading Strategy

Re-create the diagram shown at right. As you read and respond to the **KEY QUESTONS**, use the diagram to help you summarize information about the world's climate and vegetation.

 See Skillbuilder Handbook, page R5

SUMMARIZE

CLIMATE

VEGETATION

GRAPHIC ORGANIZERS
Go to **Interactive Review** @ ClassZone.com

Climate and Vegetation

1.02 Generate, interpret, and manipulate information from tools such as maps, globes, charts, graphs, databases, and models to pose and answer questions about space and place, environment and society, and spatial dynamics and connections.
1.03 Use tools such as maps, globes, graphs, charts, databases, models, and artifacts to compare data on different countries of Africa, Asia, and Australia and to identify patterns as well as similarities and differences.

Connecting to Your World

Every moment in the day, weather and climate are a part of your life. They affect what clothes you wear and how you get to school. You might walk or ride your bike if it is not too cold or too wet. But if it's raining or snowing you may go in a car or by bus. Some school activities, like sports, depend on weather and climate, too. In fact, weather and climate affect plant and animal life and nearly every human activity.

The Earth's Rotation and Revolution

▼ **KEY QUESTION** How does Earth's revolution affect seasons?

The Earth rotates as it revolves around the sun. Rotation is the motion of the Earth as it spins on its axis once every 24 hours. Revolution is the motion of the Earth as it circles, or makes a year-long orbit, of the sun.

Earth's Movement The Earth is tilted at a 23.5° angle. The Earth's revolution around the sun affects patterns of Earth's weather and climate. The Earth's tilt stays the same as it revolves around the sun. As a result, different parts of the Earth get direct rays from the sun for more hours of the day at certain times of the year. This causes the changing seasons.

Inupiat Woman The harsh climate of the Arctic makes wearing a fur parka necessary.

Midnight Sun in the Arctic Multiple exposures show the position of the sun over a 24-hour period in the Arctic summer.

ARCTIC OCEAN

ARCTIC CIRCLE

ALASKA

Earth's Revolution
The seasons are related to the Earth's tilt and revolution around the sun.

CRITICAL THINKING

Compare and Contrast Which part of the Earth's surface doesn't experience seasons?

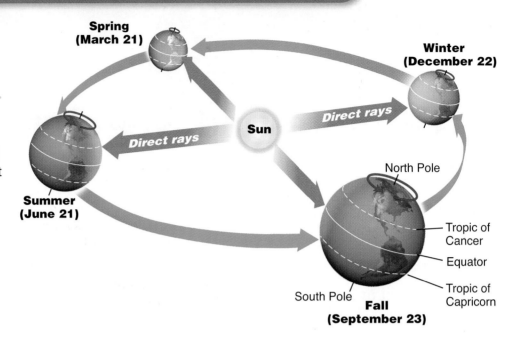

Seasons The term **solstice** is used to describe the time during the year when the sun reaches the farthest northern or southern point in the sky. In the Northern Hemisphere, the summer solstice is the longest day of the year and begins summer. The winter solstice is the shortest day of the year and begins winter. These dates are reversed in the Southern Hemisphere. The beginning of spring and autumn start on the **equinox**. On these two days, the sun's rays are directly over the equator, and days and nights around the world are equal in length. The Earth's revolution brings the temperature and weather changes we call seasons to many parts of the Earth. But in some regions there is little change. The illustration above shows the position of the Earth at the start of the four seasons in the Northern Hemisphere.

▲ **SUMMARIZE** What causes seasons on Earth?

Weather and Climate

▼ **KEY QUESTION** What is the difference between weather and climate?

People often confuse weather and climate. **Weather** is the condition of the Earth's atmosphere at a given time and place. For example, today may be sunny and warm. **Climate** is the term for the typical weather conditions of a certain region over a long period of time.

Causes of Weather Several factors interact to cause weather at a particular location. They include solar energy, wind, landforms,

Climate Regions As you can see on the map on the opposite page, the Earth has five general climate regions: tropical, mid-latitude, high latitude, dry, and highland. Tropical climates are always hot and can be rainy most of the year or only during one season. The middle latitudes have the greatest variety of climates, ranging from hot and humid to cool and fairly dry. Climates along the oceans are also included in this category. High latitude climates are cool to cold all year long. Dry climates can be found in every latitude region. Highland climates are based on the elevation of a particular place. So, for example, as you go up a mountain, the climate may change from warm to cooler to cold.

Vegetation Regions The term **vegetation region** refers to an area that has similar plants. A vegetation region is named for the types of trees, grasslands, and specially adapted plants found there. The four basic types of vegetation are: forest, savanna, grasslands, and desert. Forests can be cold, tropical, or temperate. **Savanna** is a mix of grasslands and trees. Grasslands can have short or tall grasses, depending on the amount of rain. Finally, a **desert**—which can be hot or cold—has plants specially adapted to very dry conditions.

SUMMARIZE Identify the five main climate regions.

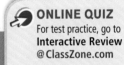

ONLINE QUIZ
For test practice, go to
Interactive Review
@ ClassZone.com

Section 3 Assessment

TERMS & NAMES

1. Explain the importance of
- weather
- climate
- precipitation
- vegetation region

USE YOUR READING NOTES

2. Summarize Use your completed chart to answer the following question:

What are the basic causes of weather and which factor is the most important?

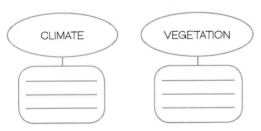

KEY IDEAS

3. What causes the changing seasons?

4. What are the causes of climate?

5. How are vegetation regions named?

CRITICAL THINKING

6. Analyze Causes and Effects Why are the seasons reversed in the Northern and Southern Hemispheres?

7. Draw Conclusions How does location affect climate and vegetation?

8. CONNECT to Today What weather conditions have caused problems in the United States recently?

9. WRITING Write a Description Determine what climate and vegetation region you live in. Then write a paragraph describing the climate features and types of vegetation.

Amazon Rain Forest

Click here to enter the rain forest @ ClassZone.com

AMAZON RAIN FOREST

The Amazon rain forest is one of the world's most important physical features. It acts as the "lungs of the planet" by producing oxygen, and is the home of millions of plants and animals.

Click here to learn more about this frog and the amazing diversity of plants and animals in the forest.

Click here to see Yanamamö village life in the rain forest and learn about how the Yanamamö interact with the forest.

Click here to see the methods scientists are using to study plants and animals in the rain forest.

The Disappearing Amazon Rain Forest

Remaining Area of Rain Forest

89% 88% 86% 84% 81%

1980 1990 1995 2000 2005

Source: Brazilian National Institute of Space Research

GeoActivity

Plan a Scientific Study
With a small group, plan the scientific study of one of the plants or animals in the picture. Identify the subject you wish to study. Talk about what information you want to find. Then write questions that would help you track down that information.

Reading for Understanding

▶ Key Ideas

BEFORE, YOU LEARNED

Many different physical systems influence the way we live on Earth.

NOW YOU WILL LEARN

Human interference with physical systems can cause problems with the environment.

▶ Vocabulary

TERMS & NAMES

global warming an increase in the average temperature of the Earth's atmosphere

greenhouse effect the trapping of the sun's heat by gases in the Earth's atmosphere

greenhouse gas any gas in the atmosphere that contributes to the greenhouse effect

fossil fuels fuels such as coal, oil, and natural gas

desertification the process in which farmland becomes less productive because the land is degraded

sustainable using natural resources in a way that they exist for future generations

BACKGROUND VOCABULARY

carbon dioxide a gas composed of carbon and oxygen

emissions substances discharged into the air

degraded of lower quality

Visual Vocabulary desertification

▶ Reading Strategy

Re-create the chart shown at right. As you read and respond to the **KEY QUESTIONS**, use the chart to compare and contrast details about environmental challenges the world faces.

 Skillbuilder Handbook, page R9

COMPARE AND CONTRAST

GLOBAL WARMING	DESERTIFICATION

 GRAPHIC ORGANIZERS
Go to **Interactive Review** @ ClassZone.com

Environmental Challenges

3.01 Identify ways in which people of selected areas in Africa, Asia, and Australia have used, altered, and adapted to their environments in order to meet their needs, and evaluate the impact of their actions on the development of cultures and regions.

3.02 Describe the environmental impact of regional activities such as deforestation, urbanization, and industrialization and evaluate their significance to the global community.

Connecting to Your World

Have your parents or other adults ever told you that the climate seems to be changing? Maybe they said something like, "We never had hurricanes or tornados like these when I was a kid." They could be right—climates do change. Some changes take place naturally over many years, such as the build-up of ice during ice ages. But recently, scientists have noticed rapid climate changes that some believe is the result of human activity.

Global Warming

🔻 **KEY QUESTION** How are global warming and the greenhouse effect related?

Global warming and desertification are two possible threats to the environment. **Global warming** is an increase in the average temperature of the Earth's atmosphere. It refers to an increase large enough to cause changes in the Earth's overall climate. The Earth's average temperature has risen between 0.9 and 1.3°F since the late 1800s. Many scientists think that temperatures may rise another 2.5 to 10.4°F by the end of the century. Some scientists believe that this warming is part of the larger cycle of warm and cold periods in the Earth's history. Others suspect that it is caused by humans.

Dori, Burkina Faso Changes in the climate have caused drought in this region, leading to fewer crops.

AFRICA

BURKINA FASO

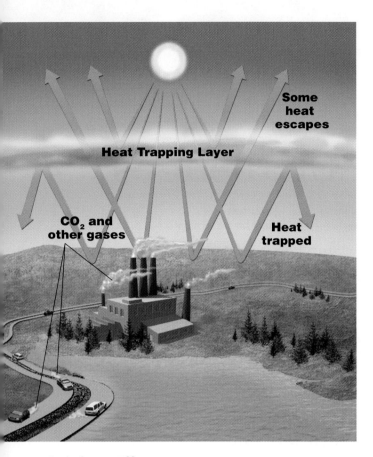

The Greenhouse Effect The trapping of the sun's heat by gases in the Earth's atmosphere is called the **greenhouse effect**. These gases act like the glass roof of a greenhouse. They let in solar energy, which heats up the planet, but they trap much of the heat that rises from the Earth's surface. So, the Earth becomes warmer. Some greenhouse effect is necessary. Without it, you would be living on a freezing cold planet. The temperature would be about zero degrees Fahenheit.

Any gas in the atmosphere that contributes to the greenhouse effect is called a **greenhouse gas**. Greenhouse gases include water vapor and **carbon dioxide**, a gas composed of carbon and oxygen. The burning of **fossil fuels**, such as coal, oil, and natural gas, has caused an increase in carbon dioxide in the atmosphere. As this gas builds in the atmosphere, the atmosphere becomes warmer and speeds up the heating effect.

Greenhouse Effect
Trapped gases and heat combine to change the Earth's temperature. **How do humans add to the greenhouse effect?**

The Impact on the Climate In theory, a more intense greenhouse effect could change the Earth's climate. Warmer temperatures could cause the ice caps and glaciers around the world to melt and sea levels to rise. Flooding could occur along coastal regions. Global land-use patterns would change. Some crops would no longer grow in certain areas. Some areas would become hotter and drier, with extreme heat waves, droughts, and more forest fires. These changes would alter the fragile relationships between living things and the environment.

Solutions Lowering the levels of greenhouse gases is a complex, worldwide goal. Some nations generate huge amounts of greenhouse gases. These gases affect not only those nations, but also the whole planet. So, humans need to take steps to reduce the levels of greenhouse gases. One solution might be to build more energy-efficient cars and factories. Another could be to use alternative energy sources such as energy produced by the sun, or the internal heat of the Earth.

In 1997, nations from around the world gathered at Kyoto, Japan, to discuss plans to reduce greenhouse gases. The result of their meeting was an agreement to cut emissions of carbon dioxide and other greenhouse gases. (**Emissions** are substances discharged into the air.) The agreement, called the Kyoto Protocol, went into effect in 2005.

▲ **SUMMARIZE** Explain how global warming takes place.

Desertification

▼ **KEY QUESTION** What causes desertification?

Desertification is the process in which farmland becomes less productive because the land is **degraded**. The land becomes more desert-like, that is, dry and unproductive. Desertification is a serious problem because it turns arid and semiarid areas into nonproductive wasteland. Each year, about 25,000 square miles of land—an area the size of West Virginia—is degraded. This process is happening in many parts of the world, including Africa, China, and the American West.

Causes and Effects In desertification, natural vegetation is removed or destroyed, and soil is exposed to wind. Without shade from the sun, the moisture in the soil evaporates more quickly. The dry top layers of soil particles then blow away. The soil becomes less able to support plant life. The loss of moisture and plants may in itself cause more desertification. But destructive practices in arid and semiarid regions have speeded up the process. Some of these practices are

- **overgrazing** allowing animals to graze so much that plants are unable to grow back
- **cultivation of marginal land** planting crops on fragile soil
- **deforestation** cutting down trees and not replanting new trees

⌕ **ONLINE PRIMARY SOURCE** To read more of Wangari Maathai's writing, go to the **Research & Writing Center** @ClassZone.com

ANALYZING Primary Sources

Wangari Maathai (born 1940) won the 2004 Nobel Peace Prize for her work fighting deforestation in Africa. To combat desertification, she founded the Green Belt Movement, which has planted 30 million trees across Africa, including her native Kenya.

> [The Green Belt Movement] encourages women to create jobs, prevent soil loss, slow the process of desertification and [to] plant and to eat indigenous [local] food crops.
>
> Source: Speech to the 4th United Nations World Women's Conference, Beijing, China, 1995

DOCUMENT–BASED QUESTION
What is the goal of the Green Belt Movement?

Green Belt Movement

The Green Belt Movement, founded by Wangari Maathai in Kenya in 1977, is an example of a program of sustainable development. It started out as a jobs program to pay rural and urban women to plant trees. But it soon became a movement to improve the environment, slow deforestation, and halt desertification.

Solutions There are different solutions to the growing problem of desertification. Each depends on the underlying cause. Some simple solutions are to build sand fences that interrupt the wind, or to use straw mats to reduce evaporation so young plants can take root. Still another is to use solar ovens in place of open fires that require firewood. Planting tree fences and grass belts also reduces the spread of sandy areas. This practice is being used in China and Africa today.

Solutions like the ones above are examples of sustainable practices. **Sustainable** means that these practices use natural resources in such a way as to ensure that they exist for future generations. Sustainable practices work with the environment to protect the land, preserve wildlife, and repair the damage that has been done to it. The practices allow people to live a better life and ensure that resources will be available both now and in the future.

 DRAW CONCLUSIONS Explain what causes desertification.

Section 4 Assessment

ONLINE QUIZ
For test practice, go to **Interactive Review** @ ClassZone.com

TERMS & NAMES

1. Explain the importance of
• global warming
• greenhouse effect
• desertification
• sustainable

USE YOUR READING NOTES

2. Compare and Contrast Use your completed chart to answer the following question:

How does the greenhouse effect contribute to global warming?

GLOBAL WARMING	DESERTIFICATION

KEY IDEAS

3. Why is global warming a problem?

4. What are greenhouse gases?

5. What are three simple solutions to controlling desertification?

CRITICAL THINKING

6. Evaluate Which environmental problem, global warming or desertification, is a greater threat to the Earth? Why?

7. Summarize How does deforestation cause desertification?

8. CONNECT to Today What might happen if more gasoline-powered motor vehicles were used around the world?

9. MATH **Make a Chart** Use the Internet to find information about desertification. Then make a chart that shows locations and the percentage of land that has been degraded.

Interactive ⟲ Review

Click here to complete these and other activities online @ ClassZone.com

CHAPTER SUMMARY

Key Idea 1
The Earth is composed of many layers, and its surface continually changes because of the drifting of the continents.

Key Idea 2
Interaction between landforms and bodies of water makes life on Earth possible.

Key Idea 3
The Earth's rotation and revolution influence weather, climate, and living conditions on Earth.

Key Idea 4
Human interference with physical systems causes problems with the environment.

For **Review and Study Notes**, go to **Interactive Review** @ ClassZone.com

NAME GAME

Use the Terms & Names list to complete each sentence on paper or online.

1. I am the hot metal center of the Earth. ____core____

2. I am a naturally formed feature on the Earth's surface. _____

3. I fall in the form of rain, snow, sleet, or hail. _____

4. I am an increase in the Earth's temperature. _____

5. I move weathered materials from one place to another. _____

6. I am the trapping of the sun's heat by gases in the atmosphere. _____

7. I am a large rigid piece of the Earth's crust that is in motion. _____

8. I am typical weather conditions over a period of time. _____

9. I circulate water between the Earth, oceans, and atmosphere. _____

10. I am plants that grow in a region. _____

climate
core
desertification
erosion
global warming
greenhouse effect
hydrologic cycle
landform
magma
precipitation
relief
sediment
tectonic plate
vegetation
weather

Activities

Flip Cards

Use the online flip cards to quiz yourself on terms and names introduced in this chapter.

magma

?

melted or liquid rock

Crossword Puzzle

Complete an online crosword puzzle to test your knowledge of Earth's physical systems.

ACROSS

1. a naturally formed feature on the Earth's surface

VOCABULARY

Explain the significance of each of the following.

1. tectonic plate
2. greenhouse effect
3. hydrologic cycle
4. global warming
5. desertification

Explain how the terms and names in each group are related.

6. magma, crust, and continent
7. weathering, erosion, and desertification
8. hydrologic cycle, precipitation, and atmosphere
9. greenhouse gas and global warming
10. vegetation and climate

KEY IDEAS

❶ The Earth and Its Forces

11. What is the continental drift theory?
12. What are the four types of tectonic plate movements?
13. How do weathering and erosion reshape the Earth's surface?

❷ Bodies of Water and Landforms

14. Why is the Earth sometimes called the "blue planet"?
15. What are the names of the world's five oceans?
16. What two general features do most continents have in common?

❸ Climate and Vegetation

17. What are the two motions of the Earth in relation to the sun?
18. What are the four factors that influence climate?
19. What are the basic types of vegetation?

❹ Environmental Challenges

20. What happens to the sun's heat in the greenhouse effect?
21. What are two alternative energy sources?
22. What are three areas of the world that have a serious problem with desertification?

CRITICAL THINKING

23. **Analyze Cause and Effect** Create a web diagram to show the effects of global warming. List at least five effects caused by a more intense greenhouse effect.

```
         ⬭        ⬭
    ⬭  EFFECTS OF
       GLOBAL WARMING
    ⬭       ⬭        ⬭
```

24. **Summarize** Why are so many earthquakes and volcanoes found near the Ring of Fire?
25. **Draw Conclusions** Why is the surface of the Earth constantly changing?
26. **Connect to Economics** What are the economic costs of earthquakes or volcanoes?
27. **Five Themes: Human-Environment Interaction** What steps have been taken to control global warming?
28. **Connect Geography & Culture** Why might the location and size of landforms affect where people live?

Answer the ESSENTIAL QUESTION

How do Earth's physical systems make life on Earth possible?

Written Response Write a two- or three-paragraph response to the Essential Question. Be sure to consider the key ideas of each section as well as ways in which the systems interlock. Use the rubric below to guide your thinking.

Response Rubric

A strong response will:

- discuss how the hydrologic cycle makes human occupation of the Earth possible
- describe the causes of weather and climate
- explain how the above systems affect humans

THEMATIC MAP

Use the map to answer questions 1 and 2 on your paper.

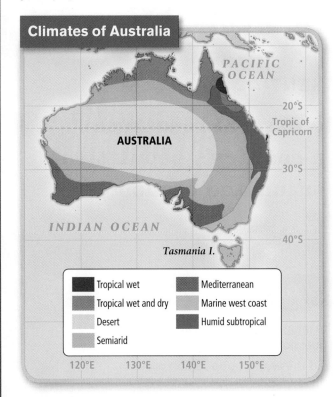

Climates of Australia

PACIFIC OCEAN

AUSTRALIA

20°S
Tropic of Capricorn

30°S

INDIAN OCEAN

40°S

Tasmania I.

- Tropical wet
- Tropical wet and dry
- Desert
- Semiarid
- Mediterranean
- Marine west coast
- Humid subtropical

120°E   130°E   140°E   150°E

1. Which climate takes up the largest portion of Australia?

A. Desert

B. Mediterranean

C. Semiarid

D. Tropical wet and dry

2. In which part of Australia would you find a tropical wet climate?

A. northwestern   **C.** southwestern

B. northeastern   **D.** southeastern

CHART

Study the chart below. Use the information in the chart to answer questions 3 and 4.

Deadliest Earthquakes *1975* to *2005*		
Country	**Year**	**Deaths**
Indonesia	2004	283,106
China	1976	255,000
Pakistan	2005	80,361
Iran	1990	40,000
Iran	2003	26,200
Armenia	1988	25,000
Guatemala	1976	23,000
India	2001	20,230
Turkey	1999	17,119

Source: USGS Earthquake Hazards Program

3. Which country has experienced the greatest number of deadly earthquakes?

4. In what year did the single most deadly earthquake strike?

GeoActivity

1. INTERDISCIPLINARY ACTIVITY–SCIENCE

Select one of the Earth's major mountain chains and illustrate its creation on a poster. Be sure the poster shows the plates involved, the direction of the collision, and the name of the mountains that were formed.

2. WRITING FOR SOCIAL STUDIES

Review the illustration of the Earth's interior in Section 1. Write a one-paragraph description that would help a younger student understand the layers of the Earth's interior.

3. MENTAL MAPPING

Create an outline map of the world and label the following:

• the seven continents
• the five oceans

Human Geography

 ESSENTIAL QUESTION

**How do natural resources
affect a country's population
distribution and economy?**

CONNECT ⟳ **Geography & History**

Use the satellite image and the time line to answer
the following questions.

1. How much did the world's population grow
between 1 A.D. and 2000?

2. How different would this image have appeared
when the population of the world hit one billion?

1000 B.C.

History
◄ **1000 B.C.** Bantu
migrations in Africa

Geography
1 A.D. Total world
population hits 300 million.

History
180 Roman
Empire at its peak ►

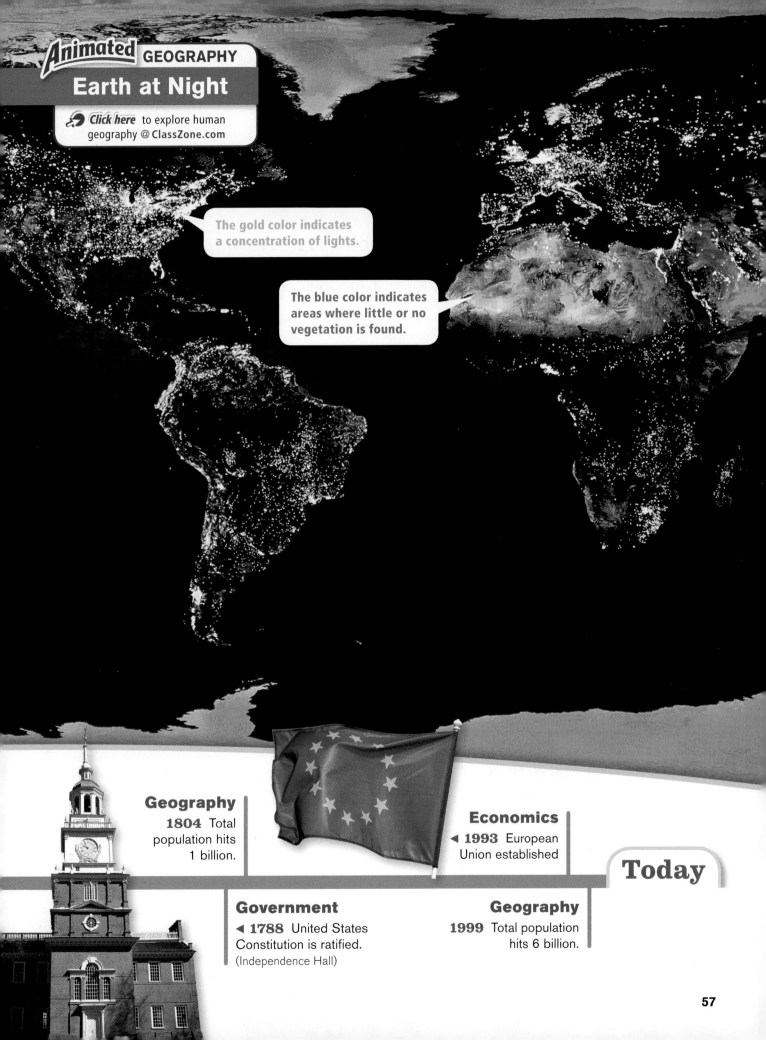

The gold color indicates
a concentration of lights.

The blue color indicates
areas where little or no
vegetation is found.

Geography
1804 Total
population hits
1 billion.

Economics
◀ **1993** European
Union established

Today

Government
◀ **1788** United States
Constitution is ratified.
(Independence Hall)

Geography
1999 Total population
hits 6 billion.

57

Reading for Understanding

▶ Key Ideas

BEFORE, YOU LEARNED

The interlocking physical systems of the Earth make life on the planet possible.

NOW YOU WILL LEARN

People are not equally distributed on the Earth's surface.

▶ Vocabulary

TERMS & NAMES

population the number of people who live in a specified area

birth rate the number of births per 1,000 people per year

death rate the number of deaths per 1,000 people per year

rate of natural increase the death rate subtracted from the birth rate

population density the average number of people who live in a certain area

urbanization the process of city development

demographer a geographer who studies the characteristics of human populations

BACKGROUND VOCABULARY

habitable lands lands suitable for human living

urban relating to, or located in, a city

rural relating to the country or farming

Visual Vocabulary Urbanization (Los Angeles, California)

▶ Reading Strategy

Re-create the web diagram shown at right. As you read and respond to the **KEY QUESTIONS**, use the diagram to help you identify important details to compare and contrast population growth, distribution, and density.

 See Skillbuilder Handbook, page R9

COMPARE AND CONTRAST

```
                POPULATION
               /     |      \
     Population   Population   Population
       Growth    Distribution   Density
```

 **GRAPHIC ORGANIZERS**
Go to **Interactive Review** @ClassZone.com

The Geography of Population

1.02 Generate, interpret, and manipulate information from tools such as maps, globes, charts, graphs, databases, and models to pose and answer questions about space and place, environment and society, and spatial dynamics and connections.

2.02 Describe factors that influence changes in distribution patterns of population, resources, and climate in selected regions of Africa, Asia, and Australia and evaluate their impact on the environment.

Connecting to Your World

Do you know how many people there are in the world? About 6.5 billion! In the time it takes you to read this paragraph, another 140 people will be born somewhere in the world. Where do the 6.5 billion people live? More than half of them live in Asia. In fact, over 2 billion are located in just two countries—China and India. The world's third most populous country is the United States, which has over 300 million people.

Population Growth

▼ **KEY QUESTION** What challenges does rapid population growth cause?

Geographers use the term **population** to mean the total number of people who live in a specified area. The population of the world today is more than 6 billion. It did not reach one billion until about 1804. Yet, over the last 200 years, the number has jumped by some 5 billion. What factors are responsible? The most important factors were increases in food production, discoveries in medical science, and improvements in sanitation. As a result, more babies survived and people lived longer, healthier lives.

Shanghai, China
China's largest city is home to more than 12 million people.

CHINA
Shanghai
East China Sea

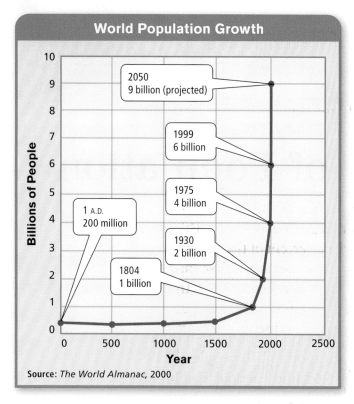

World Population Growth

Billions of People (y-axis): 0 to 10
Year (x-axis): 0 to 2500

- 2050 9 billion (projected)
- 1999 6 billion
- 1975 4 billion
- 1 A.D. 200 million
- 1930 2 billion
- 1804 1 billion

Source: *The World Almanac*, 2000

Measuring Growth Geographers measure population growth by figuring out how many people have been born and how many have died, how many have moved into and how many have moved out of a specific area. The **birth rate** measures the number of births per 1,000 people per year. The **death rate** measures the number of deaths per 1,000 people per year. To find out the **rate of natural increase**, the death rate is subtracted from the birth rate. This is the population growth that results from natural processes of birth and death.

Today, in most of Asia, Africa, and South America, the rate of natural increase is very high. Farming is a major way of life in these regions, and families need many children to help with the farm work. In most countries of Europe and North America, and also in Japan, the population growth rate is much lower. In these countries, most people live in cities and have few children, making their rate of natural increase much lower than in regions with a higher rural population.

Growth Challenges The expanding population creates serious challenges. The Earth's resources are limited and not evenly distributed throughout the world. In many countries, it is difficult just to provide the basic needs such as food, clean water, and housing. Many people move from rural areas to cities to make a better life for themselves and their families. If they cannot find housing, they often build houses on the outskirts of cities with whatever materials they can find. Some of these squatter settlements become very large, even as large as the city itself, but they often lack clean water, sewers, or paved roads.

▲ **SUMMARIZE** Explain the challenges of rapid population growth.

Rio de Janeiro, Brazil
These houses are part of squatter settlements on the outskirts of the main city.

BRAZIL

Rio de Janeiro

Population Distribution and Density

▼ **KEY QUESTION** What are the factors that influence where people choose to live?

As you read earlier, people are not distributed equally around the world. Where they choose to live is partly affected by climate, elevation, and resources such as fertile soil and fresh water. Today, the largest populations are found in what are called **habitable lands**.

Population Distribution Only a small portion of the Earth's surface is suitable for humans to settle. Almost 75 percent of the Earth's surface is water. In addition, between 35 and 40 percent of the Earth's land is too hot, too cold, too wet, or too dry for large-scale settlement. Most people live in the Northern Hemisphere, between 20° North and 60° North latitude. Fewer people live in the Southern Hemisphere because there is less land available. The edges of continents are more heavily populated than interior lands. Many people choose to live in coastal lands and in river valleys because these locations offer people opportunities to earn a living. About two-thirds of the world's population is found within 300 miles of ocean waters.

◄ COMPARING ► Urban Populations

More than 400 cities have populations of one million or more. Many cities in Africa and Asia, such as Lagos, Nigeria, and Mumbai, India, are expected to grow rapidly in the 21st century.

Mumbai, India

Top 7 Most Populous Cities	Population (in millions*)
Tokyo, Japan	34.45
Mexico City, Mexico	18.07
New York City, U.S.A.	17.85
São Paulo, Brazil	17.10
Mumbai, India	16.09
Kolkata, India	13.06
Shanghai, China	12.89

CRITICAL THINKING

Compare and Contrast What is the total population of the Indian cities listed? How does that compare with the population of Tokyo?

* Population shown is for an entire urban area, not just the city itself.

Source: *The World Almanac and Book of Facts, 2006*

CONNECT to Math

Population density is different from population distribution. Population distribution shows where people live. **Population density** shows on average how many people are living in a specific size area such as a square mile or square kilometer. The density number helps explain how crowded an area is.

To find the population density number, add up the total number of people living in an area and divide by the total amount of land they occupy. Some areas of Earth are very lightly populated and others are quite densely populated.

World Population Density

Persons per square mile
- Over 520
- 260–519
- 130–259
- 25–129
- 1–24
- 0

Activity

Calculating Population Density

Materials
- a calculator
- paper and pencil

1. Review the paragraph at left to see how population density is calculated.

2. Use the information below to calculate the population density for eight countries.

3. After you have completed your calculations, create a bar graph showing the population densities of the eight nations.

Country	Area (km²)	Population
Afghanistan	647,500	31,056,997
Brazil	8,511,965	188,078,227
Chad	1,284,000	9,944,200
Finland	338,145	5,231,372
France	547,030	60,876,136
Iraq	437,072	26,783,383
Thailand	514,000	64,631,595
United States	9,631,420	298,444,215

Source: *CIA World Factbook*, 2006

Rural vs. Urban Today, about half the world's population lives in **urban** areas, such as cities and their suburbs. This is a big change from a hundred years ago. Then, most people lived in **rural** areas, on farms and in small villages. Only about 14 percent lived in cities. By 2030, population experts believe that 60 percent of all people will live in urban areas. This process of development from small settlements to large ones is called **urbanization**.

Population Density Geographers who study the characteristics of human populations are called **demographers**. They use population density to find out how heavily populated an area is. One of the most densely populated countries is Bangladesh in South Asia, with over 1,900 people per square mile. The average population density of the entire planet is 113 people per square mile.

Statistics can be deceiving because the number is an average. Some areas of a country might be lightly populated, while others are heavily populated. In the United States, the population density is about 80 people per square mile. However, New Jersey has 1,134 people per square mile and Alaska has only 1.1 people per square mile.

 UNDERSTAND CAUSES Identify the factors that influence where people choose to live.

Section 1 Assessment

ONLINE QUIZ
For test practice, go to
Interactive Review
@ ClassZone.com

TERMS & NAMES

1. **Explain the importance of**
   • birth rate
   • death rate
   • population density
   • urbanization

USE YOUR READING NOTES

2. **Compare and Contrast** Use your completed web diagram to answer the following question:

   How is population density different from population distribution?

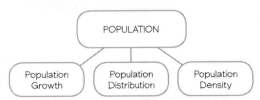

POPULATION

Population Growth | Population Distribution | Population Density

KEY IDEAS

3. What are three factors that have caused the world's population to grow so rapidly?

4. What is urbanization?

5. How is population density determined?

CRITICAL THINKING

6. **Make Inferences** Why are people unevenly distributed on the Earth's surface?

7. **Compare and Contrast** Why do some countries have much lower growth rates than others?

8. **CONNECT to Today** What do you think are the major problems that the world faces as the population continues to grow?

9. **MATH** **Create a Population Density Table** Use the Internet to find statistics for population and an average population density for each continent. Create a table and a bar chart showing these statistics. Continents should be listed in order from highest density to lowest density.

Population density is an average figure for a specific area. However, it does not account for the distribution of population in an area. Notice in these two examples how the pattern of population density varies even within a country.

Australia

Australia is ranked 54th in the world for total population, but 191st in population density. This is because Australia has a great deal of land but a small population. It has a lot of open space sometimes called the Outback, shown below. The heaviest population is found in the coastal cities.

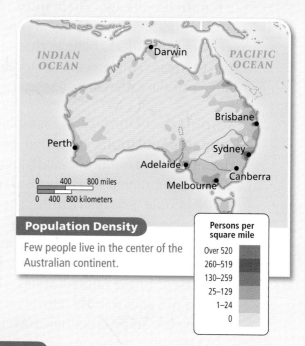

Population Density

Few people live in the center of the Australian continent.

Persons per square mile
Over 520
260–519
130–259
25–129
1–24
0

Work

Australia's wide open spaces makes cattle ranching one of the biggest businesses.

Transportation

A lone vehicle travels a dusty Outback road.

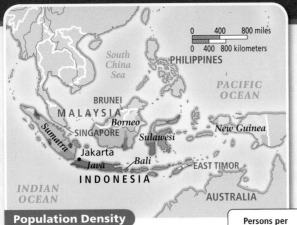

Population Density

The islands of Indonesia have a greater population density than Australia.

Persons per square mile

Over 520
260–519
130–259
25–129
1–24
0

Transportation

Thousands of buses and cars are needed to move Jakarta's population.

Indonesia

Indonesia is ranked 4th in the world for total population, but 60th in population density. This is because two Indonesian islands, Bali and Java, and the capital, Jakarta, are heavily populated. Other parts of the island nation are not as densely populated. Jakarta is pictured below.

Work

Manufacturing takes place in the larger cities of Indonesia.

CRITICAL THINKING

1. **Compare and Contrast** How are the patterns of density different in the two countries?

2. **Draw Conclusions** In what ways do the images illustrate how density may affect ways of living in the two countries?

Reading for Understanding

▶ Key Ideas

BEFORE, YOU LEARNED

Population patterns differ by place and region and may change over time.

NOW YOU WILL LEARN

People move from one place to another to meet their needs.

▶ Vocabulary

TERMS & NAMES

migration the process of relocating to a new region

immigrant a person who leaves one area to settle in another

push factor a reason that causes people to leave an area

pull factor a reason that attracts people to another area

culture the shared attitudes, knowledge, and behaviors of a group

diversity having many different ways to think or to do something, or a variety of people

discrimination actions that might be hurtful to an individual or a group

BACKGROUND VOCABULARY

refugee a person who flees a place to find safety

persecution cruel treatment on the basis of religion, race, ethnic group, nationality, political views, gender, or class

Visual Vocabulary diversity

▶ Reading Strategy

Re-create the chart shown at right. As you read and respond to the **KEY QUESTIONS**, use the chart to compare and contrast important details about the reasons people move.

 See Skillbuilder Handbook, page R9

COMPARE AND CONTRAST

PUSH FACTORS	PULL FACTORS
1.	1.
2.	2.

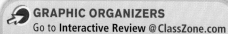

GRAPHIC ORGANIZERS
Go to **Interactive Review** @ ClassZone.com

Why People Move

4.01 Describe the patterns of and motives for the migrations of people, and evaluate their impact on the political, economic, and social development of selected societies and regions.
13.01 Identify historical movements such as colonization, revolution, emerging democracies, migration, and immigration that link North Carolina and the United States to selected societies of Africa, Asia, and Australia, and evaluate their influence on local, state, regional, national, and international communities.

Connecting to Your World

Have you ever moved from one part of the city or town where you live to another? Maybe you moved to be closer to your school or to where a parent works. It may be that one of your parents took a job in a different city. Perhaps your family had to move to a different climate for health reasons. Whatever the reason, moving to a new, unfamiliar area could change your life in many ways.

Moving Day About 112 million Americans relocate every year.

Causes of Migration

🔻 **KEY QUESTION** Why do people move from place to place?

From earliest times, people have moved to new locations. This process of relocating to a new region is called **migration**. A person who leaves one country to settle in another is called an **immigrant**. Population geographers often talk about push-pull factors when they study migration. The **push factors** are the reasons that cause people to leave an area. **Pull factors** are the reasons that attract people to another area. For example, a group may decide to move to a better location after their crops fail for several years. The crop failure is the "push" factor, and the better location is the "pull" factor. Together, they give the group a reason for migrating. Generally, the causes of migration are environmental, economic, cultural, or political.

Ellis Island, New York Millions of people entered the United States here between 1892 and 1954.

NEW YORK
Ellis Island ○
ATLANTIC OCEAN

Push Factors In early times, a change in environment was a major cause of migration. For example, climate changes thousands of years ago brought on an ice age. People in northern Europe moved south in order to survive. Sometimes, an environment is unable to support growing numbers of people. So some part of the group needs to move to a place that would better support them.

Political actions may push a person or group to migrate to a new area. **Refugees** might flee a place to find safety from war. For example, beginning in 2003, an ethnic war in the Darfur region of Sudan caused about 2 million people to flee to refugee camps. Governments can force people to relocate even if they do not want to go. Cruel treatment, or **persecution**, of a particular group could also cause people to leave. People have sometimes been persecuted for their religion, race, nationality, political views, or membership in an ethnic group.

Pull Factors The desire for land has pulled people to new regions for thousands of years. During the 1800s, millions immigrated to the United States in search of land to farm or ranch. Economic opportunities are still a major reason for migration. Today, people move to find a job or to get a better job.

Sometimes people move for cultural reasons. For example, they may want to return to an area they consider the homeland of their people. Another pull factor may be that the land or the region has religious significance. Israel is an example of both reasons. Jews from all over the world immigrate to Israel because they consider it their homeland, and because it also contains many Jewish holy sites.

▲ **SUMMARIZE** What are the push-pull factors of migration?

◄ **COMPARING** ► **Migration Factors**

PUSH FACTORS	PULL FACTORS
Environmental • lack of resources to support an entire group • change in climate or vegetation	**Economic** • availability of land • job opportunities
Political • escape from war or persecution • forced removal	**Cultural** • return to a homeland • desire to live near a holy site

CRITICAL THINKING

Make Inferences Which factor do you think is most often the cause of migration?

Where People Migrate

▼ **KEY QUESTION** What are the two kinds of migration?

Geographers identify two different types of migration. Internal migration occurs when people move within a country. Moving across a continent or even to another continent is called external migration.

Internal Migration Internal migration happens when people move from one place to another but stay within the same country. Someone who does this is called a migrant. If you move from Pennsylvania to California, you have moved a very long distance, but you have stayed within the United States, so you are an internal migrant. Two of the most common forms of internal migration are moving from rural areas or small towns to cities, and from cities to suburbs.

The world is becoming more urban. In many countries, more than 70 percent of the population lives in urban areas. Pull factors attract people to cities. If migrants can't find affordable housing in the city, they often build houses on the outskirts. This kind of growth on the outskirts of a city is sometimes called urban sprawl. In developed countries such as the United States, sprawl happens as new suburbs are built around the edges of a city.

External Migration Migration across parts of a continent may take place quickly, but sometimes it takes hundreds or even thousands of years. For example, Bantu-speaking people of Africa slowly spread across the southern half of the continent from 1000 B.C. to A.D. 1100. The push factor was environmental. The numbers of Bantu people were increasing, and they needed more land for farming and herding.

Migration also takes place from one continent to another continent. The countries of the Western Hemisphere as well as Australia and New Zealand, are filled with immigrants from Europe, Africa, and Asia.

▲ **COMPARE** Explain the difference between internal and external migration.

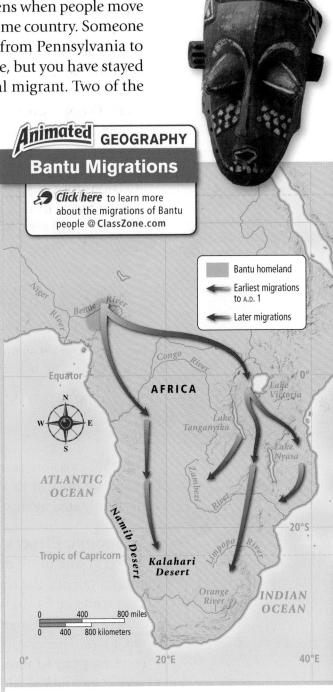

Kuba Mask The Kuba are a Bantu-speaking people.

Animated GEOGRAPHY

Bantu Migrations

🖰 *Click here* to learn more about the migrations of Bantu people @ ClassZone.com

- Bantu homeland
- ← Earliest migrations to A.D. 1
- ← Later migrations

Niger River · Benue River · Congo River · Equator · AFRICA · Lake Victoria · 0° · Lake Tanganyika · Lake Nyasa · Zambezi River · ATLANTIC OCEAN · Namib Desert · 20°S · Tropic of Capricorn · Kalahari Desert · Limpopo River · Orange River · INDIAN OCEAN

N · W · E · S

0   400   800 miles
0   400   800 kilometers

0° · 20°E · 40°E

CONNECT Geography & Culture

Movement Toward which body of water did the eastern branch of the early migrations move?

The Effects of Migration

🔻 **KEY QUESTION** How does migration affect people and lands?

People bring the customs and traditions of their culture with them when they relocate. **Culture** is the shared attitudes, knowledge, and behaviors of a group. As a result of migration, the cultures of both the immigrants and the people living in an area may change. Migration also has economic and political effects, both positive and negative.

Cultural Effects When different groups in an area interact, they learn about each other—what they eat, wear, and believe. If people accept these different ideas and behaviors, it adds to the diversity of the group. **Diversity** means having many different ways to think about or to do something, or it may refer to a variety of people. Many people believe that having diversity in a group makes it stronger.

Earlier you learned about the Bantu-speaking people and how they spread across southern Africa. Wherever they settled, the Bantu brought their language and iron-making skills to the people in the region. Even if the Bantu moved on, their language and iron-working techniques remained. So migration changed the existing culture in several ways.

Migration does not always benefit the people who move. This is especially true if a group did not want to move. For example, refugees who flee war may be forced into overcrowded camps with little hope of returning home. Another possible result of migration is **discrimination**, actions that might be hurtful to an individual or group. For example, the group discriminated against may not be able to get jobs or housing.

CONNECT ➤ **Geography & Culture**

Bantu Languages

The Bantu spread their languages when they migrated across Africa. Today, about 240 million Africans speak one of the hundreds of Bantu languages as their first language. Some 50 million of them in central and east Africa speak Swahili (swah•HEE•lee), also known as Kiswahili (KEY•swah•HEE•lee).

Economic Effects The arrival of a new group can help or hurt a region's economy. If more workers are needed or the new workers have special talents, the region's economy may be improved. This was the case with the Bantu who brought iron-making skills with them.

The arrival of large numbers of people sometimes strains a region's resources. This occurs when, for example, war refugees with limited resources crowd into refugee camps. The living conditions may be very poor and the additional numbers make life in the camps miserable. In 2005, many thousands of people fled their homes as warfare swept Sudan in Africa. The refugees found little shelter, water, or firewood in the camps. In fact, violence often broke out over the available water. Security and protection for the people in the camps can also become a problem. Governments may not be able to adequately provide for the refugees or may need to ask other nations to help care for the people.

Political Effects The policies of a country or region can be affected by the arrival of immigrants. Sometimes immigrants may be viewed as unwanted or dangerous. The government of a country might then support actions to remove the immigrants or allow them to be treated badly in hopes that they will leave. The immigrants may worry about their personal safety and ability to provide for themselves and their families.

In the best of times, the new immigrants make contributions to the country and are viewed as assets. For example, many immigrant groups brought valuable skills to the United States and were given the opportunity to become citizens.

 DRAW CONCLUSIONS Identify positive and negative effects of migration.

Water Cans at a Refugee Camp Water is scarce in this African refugee camp. Each day people line up in hopes of getting a supply of water.

Section 2 Assessment

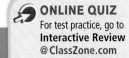 **ONLINE QUIZ**
For test practice, go to
Interactive Review
@ ClassZone.com

TERMS & NAMES

1. Explain the importance of
- migration
- push factor
- pull factor
- culture

USE YOUR READING NOTES

2. Compare and Contrast Use your completed chart to answer the following question:

Which factors do you think are more powerful in encouraging migration?

PUSH FACTORS	PULL FACTORS
1.	1.
2.	2.

KEY IDEAS

3. What has been a major push factor in migration since earliest times?

4. Which form of internal migration has affected most countries?

5. What are the three ways that migration affects people and lands?

CRITICAL THINKING

6. Analyze Causes and Effects How do push-pull factors work together?

7. Summarize How is a culture affected by migration?

8. CONNECT to Today What are the pull factors that would attract people to move to your community?

9. HISTORY **Create a Push-Pull Poster** Choose two immigrant groups that came to the United States at any time in its history. Create a poster with images to show where they came from, what pushed them from their homeland, and what pulled them to the United States.

SECTION 3 Reading for Understanding

▶ Key Ideas

BEFORE, YOU LEARNED

Migration changes places and regions by introducing new people and cultures.

NOW YOU WILL LEARN

Economic activities in an area depend on the presence of natural resources.

▶ Vocabulary

TERMS & NAMES

natural resource something that is found in nature that is necessary or useful to humans

economy a system for producing and exchanging goods and services among a group of people

economic system a way people use resources to make and exchange goods

command economy an economic system in which the production of goods and services is decided by a central government

market economy an economic system in which the production of goods and services is decided by supply and the demand of consumers

Gross Domestic Product (GDP) the total value of all the goods and services produced in a country in a year

export a product or resource sold to another country

import a product or resource that comes into a country

specialization a focus on producing a limited number of a specific products

BACKGROUND VOCABULARY

raw material an unprocessed natural resource that will be converted to a finished product

▶ Reading Strategy

Re-create the chart shown at right. As you read and respond to the **KEY QUESTIONS**, use the chart to categorize important details about types of economic systems.

 Skillbuilder Handbook, page R7

CATEGORIZE

ECONOMIC SYSTEMS			
Traditional	Market	Command	Mixed
1.	1.	1.	1.
2.	2.	2.	2.
3.	3.	3.	3.

 GRAPHIC ORGANIZERS
Go to **Interactive Review** @ ClassZone.com

Resources and Economics

5.04 Describe the relationship between specialization and interdependence, and analyze its influence on the development of regional and global trade patterns.
6.01 Describe different levels of economic development and assess their connections to standard of living indicators such as purchasing power, literacy rate, and life expectancy.

Connecting to Your World

What natural resources are found in your area? A **natural resource** is something found in nature that is necessary or useful to humans. Forests, mineral deposits, and fresh water are examples of natural resources. Often, the presence of natural resources attracts people to a particular area. Think about how important natural resources are to your life, to your community, and to your country. How are they being used, and how long will they last?

Natural Resources

▼ **KEY QUESTION** What are the different types of natural resources?

Natural resources are essential for economic development, but resources are not equally distributed around the world. People learn to use the resources in their own areas to their best advantage. However, just because a natural resource is present does not mean it can or will be used. People in some countries may not have the technology to take the resource and turn it into usable products. For example, iron ore is useless until technology turns it into iron and steel products. Technology changes over time, making the value of resources change as well.

Copper Mine
This copper mine in Spain has been producing copper since Roman times.

SPAIN

Geographers divide natural resources into three main categories: renewable, non-renewable, and unlimited. Renewable resources are those that nature can replace, such as trees or plants. Unlimited resources are things such as sunlight and wind—these never run out and often are used to produce energy. Non-renewable resources can't be easily replaced, so when they are used up, there aren't additional resources. Minerals and fuels like coal and oil fall into this category.

▲ **CATEGORIZE** Identify three basic types of resources.

CONNECT → Geography & Economics

Natural Resources The map below shows the location of some major non-renewable resources. When supplies of these resources are gone, countries relying on them for their economies will have to change their economic focus.

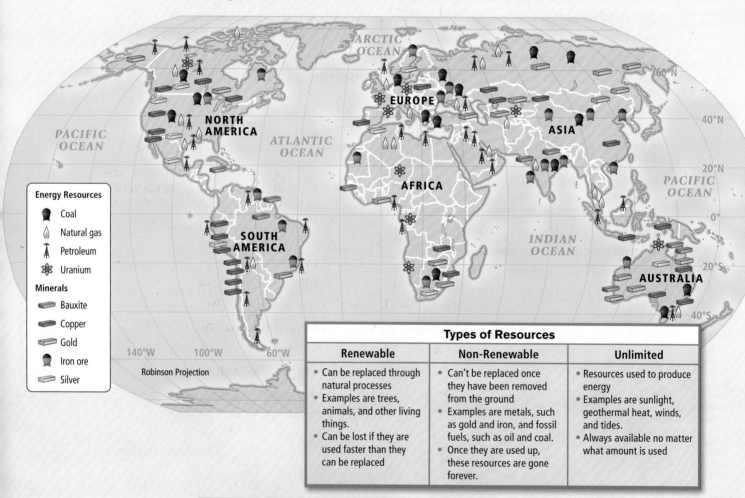

Energy Resources
- Coal
- Natural gas
- Petroleum
- Uranium

Minerals
- Bauxite
- Copper
- Gold
- Iron ore
- Silver

Robinson Projection

Types of Resources		
Renewable	**Non-Renewable**	**Unlimited**
• Can be replaced through natural processes • Examples are trees, animals, and other living things. • Can be lost if they are used faster than they can be replaced	• Can't be replaced once they have been removed from the ground • Examples are metals, such as gold and iron, and fossil fuels, such as oil and coal. • Once they are used up, these resources are gone forever.	• Resources used to produce energy • Examples are sunlight, geothermal heat, winds, and tides. • Always available no matter what amount is used

CRITICAL THINKING

Draw Conclusions Which of the three categories of natural resources are likely to be most desirable?

Economic Systems

▼ **KEY QUESTION** What are the four basic economic systems?

An **economy** consists of the production and exchange of goods and services among a group of people. Economies exist at the local, regional, national, and international levels. **Economic systems** are different ways that people use resources to make and exchange goods and services.

Four basic economic systems are traditional, command, market, and mixed.

Traditional economy Goods and services are traded, but money is rarely exchanged. This process is called "barter" and is the oldest economic system. It is not used much today.

Command economy A **command economy** is one in which production of goods and services is decided by a central government. The government usually owns most of the resources and businesses that make the products or provide the services. This type of economy is also called a planned economy.

Food Market in Vietnam Supply and demand help determine which products will be sold. **How is this market different from most food markets in the United States?**

Market economy When the production of goods and services is determined by the supply and the demand of consumers it is called a **market economy**. It is also known as a demand economy, or capitalism. This is the type of economy found in the United States.

Mixed economy In this economy, a combination of command and market economies provides goods and services.

Economic activities are all the different ways that people make a living under these economic systems, including manufacturing, agriculture, fishing, and providing services. Some countries have a wide mix of economic activities while others may have only one or two main economic activities.

▲ **SUMMARIZE** Name the four basic types of economic systems.

Measuring Economic Development

🔻 **KEY QUESTION** How is economic development measured?

To measure economic development, geographers may look at such figures as literacy, health information, life expectancy, or the value of a country's economy. One of the most important measures used is Gross Domestic Product (GDP). The **Gross Domestic Product (GDP)** measures the total value of all the goods and services produced in a country in a year. Countries are divided into two categories based on economic development: developing or developed nations.

Developing Nations These nations have low GDP and few economic activities. Many people raise food or animals to survive and have little or no machinery or advanced technology to do the work.

Developed Nations These nations have high GDP and many economic activities, especially business and information processing, and a lot of high-level technology. Food is grown on commercial farms, and most people work in offices and factories.

🔺 **COMPARE** Identify information used to measure development.

COMPARING Economic Development

Geographers use many different measurements to look at the development level of a country's economy. Here is a comparison of some developing nations and some developed nations.

◀ *Brazilian coffee bean worker*

	Status	GDP	GDP/ Person In US Dollars*	Infant Mortality (1000 Live Births)	Life Expectancy (At Birth)	Literacy Rate (Percent)
Burkina Faso	developing	5.4 billion	1,300	91.4	48.9	26.6
India	developing	719.8 billion	3,400	54.6	64.7	59.5
Uruguay	developing	13.2 billion	9,600	11.6	76.3	98.0
Germany	developed	2.8 trillion	30,400	4.1	78.8	99.0
Japan	developed	4.9 trillion	31,500	3.2	81.3	99.0
United States	developed	12.5 trillion	42,000	6.4	77.9	99.0

* official exchange rate   Source: *CIA World Factbook, 2006*

CRITICAL THINKING

Compare and Contrast How can you tell Uruguay has developed more than Burkina Faso?

World Trade

▼ **KEY QUESTION** Why do countries trade with one another?

Early trade networks started because people who did not have certain resources, such as salt, wanted them. For trade to happen, nations usually have to give up some of their resources in exchange. Products or resources sold to other countries are called **exports**. Products or resources that come into a country are called **imports**. For example, U.S.-made mining equipment sold to Brazil is an export of the United States. Brazilian coffee sold to the United States is a U.S. import.

A country may choose to focus on producing only one or two products or resources and exclude other economic activities. This practice is called **specialization**. Countries specialize because it allows them to trade for products they can't produce themselves. For example, a country may sell cocoa beans or wheat or iron ore in exchange for machinery, or chemicals, or electronic goods. In general, developing nations specialize in **raw materials** or low-cost items, while developed nations sell high-level technology goods or services. This focus leads to interdependence between countries. When countries produce the same trade items, competition results.

▲ **FIND MAIN IDEAS** Explain why nations trade.

Fun Facts!

OSTRICH MEAT EXPORTS

Chile is known for its major exports of copper, fruit, and paper. But it has added a new export—ostrich meat—that is bringing in more than 17 billion dollars per year. This nontraditional export is bringing money and jobs to Chile.

Section ③ Assessment

🔖 **ONLINE QUIZ**
For test practice, go to
Interactive Review
@ ClassZone.com

TERMS & NAMES

1. Explain the importance of
- economic system
- Gross Domestic Product (GDP)
- export
- import

USE YOUR READING NOTES

2. Categorize Use your completed chart to answer the following question:

In which economic system are the production of goods and services determined by consumer demand?

ECONOMIC SYSTEMS			
Traditional	Market	Command	Mixed
1.	1.	1.	1.
2.	2.	2.	2.
3.	3.	3.	3.

KEY IDEAS

3. What is a natural resource?

4. What are the four basic economic systems?

5. What is the difference between an export and an import?

CRITICAL THINKING

6. Summarize How do geographers divide countries into developed and developing nations?

7. Compare and Contrast How are command and market economic systems different?

8. CONNECT to Today What natural resources are located in your area and how are they used?

9. TECHNOLOGY Create a Multimedia Presentation Use the Internet to study the imports and exports of the United States or another country. Plan a slide show about major exports and what countries buy them and major imports and what countries sell them.

Reading for Understanding

▶ Key Ideas

BEFORE, YOU LEARNED

People have different ways to use and trade the Earth's natural resources.

NOW YOU WILL LEARN

The world is divided into many political regions and organizations.

▶ Vocabulary

TERMS & NAMES

government an organization set up to make and enforce rules for a society

citizen a person who owes loyalty to a country and receives its protection

representative democracy a type of government in which citizens hold political power through elected representatives

monarchy a type of government in which a ruling family headed by a king or queen holds political power

oligarchy (AHL•ih•GAHR•kee) a type of government in which a small group of people holds power

dictatorship a type of government in which an individual holds complete political power

communism a type of government in which the Communist Party holds all political power and controls the economy

Visual Vocabulary monarchy (The queen of Denmark)

▶ Reading Strategy

Re-create the chart shown at right. As you read and respond to the **KEY QUESTIONS**, use the chart to categorize important details about types of government.

 See Skillbuilder Handbook, page R7

CATEGORIZE

	RULER	BASIS OF RULE
Democracy		
Monarchy		
Dictatorship		
Oligarchy		
Communism		

 GRAPHIC ORGANIZERS
Go to **Interactive Review** @ClassZone.com

Why We Need Government

9.02 Describe how different types of governments such as democracies, dictatorships, monarchies, and oligarchies in Africa, Asia, and Australia carry out legislative, executive, and judicial functions, and evaluate the effectiveness of each.

11.03 Compare characteristics of political, economic, religious, and social institutions of selected cultures, and evaluate their similarities and differences.

Connecting to Your World

You live in one of nearly 200 countries in the world. Some countries are tiny when compared to the United States; others are larger in physical size or in population. All countries have one thing in common—a government. A **government** is an organization set up to make and enforce rules for a group of people. It has authority over the land within its boundaries.

Passport An official document that allows a person to travel abroad.

Types of Government

▼ **KEY QUESTION** What types of government operate around the world?

Government is needed to provide security, make and enforce the laws, furnish the services that keep a country running, and protect the rights of citizens. A **citizen** is a person who owes loyalty to a country and receives its protection. The government also acts on behalf of the people in the country when it deals with other countries. As you have read, all countries have some type of government. The types differ mainly over how much power the people have. Some countries are ruled by a single person, others by a small group, and still others are ruled by many people.

U.S. Capitol Building This is the official seat of government for the country.

Washington, D.C.
UNITED STATES

COMPARING Governments

TYPES OF GOVERNMENT

DEMOCRACY
- Rule by citizens through elected officials
- Rule is based on citizenship.
- Majority rules

DICTATORSHIP
- Rule by a single individual
- Ruler controls military.
- Citizens have little power to change government.

OLIGARCHY
- Rule by a small group of citizens
- Rule is based on wealth or privilege.
- Ruling group controls military.

MONARCHY
- Rule by a king or queen
- Rule is hereditary.
- May share power through a constitution

COMMUNISM
- Rule by the Communist Party on behalf of the people
- Government owns all economic goods and services.
- Citizens have little power to change government.

CRITICAL THINKING
Evaluate In which type of government do citizens have the most power?

Generally, the type of government a country has falls into one of the following categories:

Representative Democracy Citizens hold political power and rule through elected representatives. In a **representative democracy**, such as the United States, representatives create laws for all the people. If the people object to the laws, they can work to change the laws or change the representatives through elections.

Monarchy In a **monarchy**, a ruling family headed by a king, queen, emperor, or sultan holds political power. Power may or may not be shared with citizens. Saudi Arabia is an example of a traditional monarchy, in which the monarch has complete power. The United Kingdom is a constitutional monarchy, in which the monarch's power is limited by a constitution.

Oligarchy A government where a small group of people holds power, usually because of their wealth, military strength, family connections, political influence, or privilege, is called an **oligarchy**. The military government of the country of Burma is an oligarchy.

Dictatorship In a **dictatorship**, an individual holds complete political power. North Korea is an example.

Communism In **communism**, all political power and control of the economy is held by the government, which is controlled by the Communist Party. The government controls all economic goods and services. Cuba is an example.

There are also different levels of government. The national government oversees the entire country. Countries often have smaller governmental units like state or provincial governments and local governments. Each of these political units deals with specific aspects of life at the state or local level.

▲ **DRAW CONCLUSIONS** What are the major types of government?

Being an Active Citizen

▼ **KEY QUESTION** What are your most important responsibilities as a citizen?

As a citizen in a democracy, you have important responsibilities. These responsibilities fall into two categories—personal and community. Personal responsibilities involve your personal behavior and relationships with others. They include taking care of yourself, helping your family, knowing right from wrong, and behaving in a respectful way. Community responsibilities involve the government and your community. They include obeying the law, voting, paying taxes, serving on a jury, and defending your country.

Being an informed citizen means you need to make yourself aware of the issues in an election and the positions held by the candidates running for office. You can also make elected officials aware of your concerns.

▲ **EVALUATE** Which responsibilities of a citizen apply to you?

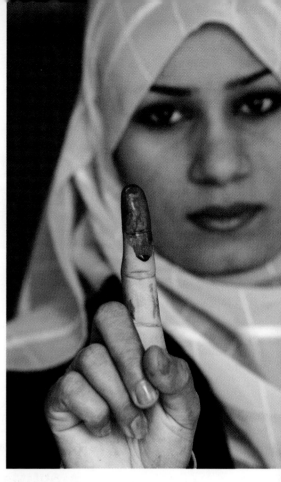

Iraqi Woman Voter This woman shows a purple finger, the sign she has voted. The 2005 election was the first free election in Iraq in 50 years. **How might having a democratic government change this woman's life?**

Responsibilities of a U.S. Citizen

As a young person, you can be a good citizen in a number of ways. Notice that some responsibilities are especially for people under 18, and some are specifically for those over 18. And all citizens have some responsibilities in common.

CRITICAL THINKING
Draw Conclusions
Which of the responsibilities shown are community responsibilities?

UNDER 18
- Attend and do well in school
- Take responsibility for one's behavior
- Help one's family

ALL AGES
- Obey rules and laws
- Be tolerant of others
- Pay taxes
- Volunteer for a cause
- Stay informed about issues

OVER 18
- Vote
- Serve on a jury
- Defend the country

International Organizations

▼ **KEY QUESTION** Why are international organizations formed?

Countries may join with other nations to form organizations to promote common goals. These organizations might have military, economic, or political goals. Sometimes, countries in a region will form an organization. One example, the Tsunami Warning System (TWS), is a group of 26 nations with coasts or territories on the Pacific Ocean. The TWS was organized to gather information about and send out warnings of these dangerous oceanic events. Other groups are organized to promote economic development, such as the Economic Community of West African States (ECOWAS).

The largest international organization in the world is the United Nations (UN). Nearly 200 countries belong to this organization. Its members work to improve political, cultural, educational, health, and economic conditions around the world.

▲ **SUMMARIZE** Explain why nations form international organizations.

United Nations Security Council This part of the UN deals with political situations that pose a threat to its members. **Why might a nation want to join an organization like the UN?**

Section 4 Assessment

ONLINE QUIZ
For test practice, go to
Interactive Review
@ ClassZone.com

TERMS & NAMES
1. Explain the importance of
- government
- citizen
- representative democracy
- dictatorship

USE YOUR READING NOTES
2. Compare and Contrast Use your completed chart to answer the following question:

In which form of government is power held by a small group of people?

	RULER	BASIS OF RULE
Democracy		
Monarchy		
Dictatorship		
Oligarchy		
Communism		

KEY IDEAS
3. What are the five types of government?

4. What civic responsibilities does a citizen have?

5. What is the main reason for creating a regional or international organization?

CRITICAL THINKING
6. Draw Conclusions Why do people form governments?

7. Make Inferences Why do local governments exist?

8. **CONNECT to Today** Identify the name of your state and local governments, and explain what each does.

9. **WRITING** **Write a Web Log Entry** Imagine that someone living under a different system of government has been critical of democracy on a web log. Write a response telling the reasons why you support your form of government.

Interactive ⬅ Review

Click here to complete these and other activities online @ ClassZone.com

CHAPTER SUMMARY

Key Idea 1
People are not equally distributed on the Earth's surface.

Key Idea 2
People move from one place to another to meet their needs for certain resources.

Key Idea 3
Economic activities in an area depend on the presence of natural resources.

Key Idea 4
The world is divided into many political regions and organizations.

For **Review and Study Notes**, go to **Interactive Review** @ ClassZone.com

NAME GAME

Use the Terms & Names list to complete each sentence on paper or online.

1. I am the average number of people who live in a specific area.
   _____ population density _____

2. I am something that is found in nature that is necessary or useful to humans. _____

3. I am the process of relocating to a new region. _____

4. I am an organization set up to make and enforce rules for society. _____

5. I am the growth in the number of people living in urban areas. _____

6. I am the way people use resources to make and exchange goods. _____

7. I am a reason that attracts people to another area. _____

8. I am a type of government in which citizens hold political power. _____

9. I am a product or resource sold to another country. _____

10. I am a person who owes loyalty to a country and receives its protection. _____

citizen
democracy
export
economic system
government
Gross Domestic Product
immigrant
import
migration
natural resource
population
population density
pull factor
push factor
urbanization

Activities

Flip Cards

Use the online flip cards to quiz yourself on the terms and names introduced in this chapter.

Monarchy

?

a type of government in which a ruling family headed by a king or queen holds political power

Crossword Puzzle

Complete an online crossword puzzle to test your knowledge of human geography.

ACROSS
1. something found in nature that is useful to humans

VOCABULARY

Explain the significance of each of the following.

1. urbanization
2. population density
3. economic system
4. Gross Domestic Product (GDP)

Explain how the terms and names in each group are related.

5. immigrant, push factor, and pull factor
6. democracy, dictatorship, and communism
7. government and citizen

KEY IDEAS

① The Geography of Population

8. Where do most of the world's people live?
9. What are three factors that influence where people choose to live?
10. How does urbanization occur?

② Why People Move

11. What are two main push factors and two main pull factors of migration?
12. How do internal and external migrations differ?
13. What are two cultural effects of migration?

③ Resources and Economics

14. What types of resources are renewable? Non-renewable?
15. In what ways is a mixed economy like both market and command economies?
16. What two categories do geographers use to refer to a country's level of economic development?

④ How Governments Work

17. What is a government?
18. What are three characteristics of a democracy?
19. What is the largest international organization in the world, and why was it formed?

CRITICAL THINKING

20. **Compare and Contrast** Create a table to compare and contrast who holds political power in the five systems of government.

TYPE OF GOVERNMENT	WHO HOLDS POWER

21. **Analyze Causes and Effects** How might migration affect population density?
22. **Compare and Contrast** What is the difference between a democracy and a dictatorship?
23. **Connect to Economics** Why do countries need to engage in trade?
24. **Connect Geography & History** Why have people needed to form governments?
25. **Five Themes: Movement** What might happen when a group of people brings their culture to a new area?

Answer the ESSENTIAL QUESTION

How do natural resources affect a country's population distribution and economy?

Written Response Write a two- or three-paragraph response to the Essential Question. Be sure to consider the key ideas of each section as well as specific ideas about population distribution and economics. Use the rubric below to guide your thinking.

Response Rubric
A strong response will:
- explain why natural resources influence population distribution
- discuss how natural resources impact an economy

THEMATIC MAP

Use the map to answer questions 1 and 2 on your paper.

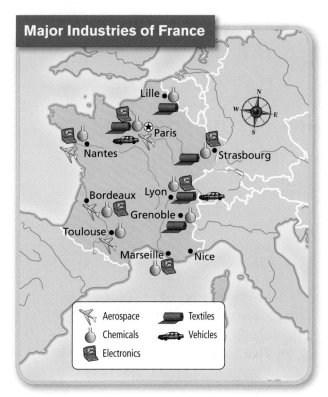

Major Industries of France

Lille
Paris
Nantes
Strasbourg
Bordeaux
Lyon
Grenoble
Toulouse
Marseille
Nice

Aerospace   Textiles
Chemicals   Vehicles
Electronics

1. Which of the industries shown on the map is not present at Lyon?

  A. aerospace
  B. chemicals
  C. electronics
  D. vehicles

2. In which part of France are the fewest industries located?

  A. northern
  B. central
  C. eastern
  D. southern

CHART

Use the information in the chart to briefly answer questions 3 and 4 on your paper.

Birth Rates		
Country	**Rank Out of 226**	**Birth Rate per 1000**
Niger	1	50.73
Tajikistan	49	32.65
Ecuador	90	22.29
Vietnam	131	16.86
United States	155	14.14
Italy	222	8.72
Source: *CIA World Factbook*, 2006		

3. How does the birth rate of Niger compare with that of Italy?

4. How does the United States' rate compare with that of Vietnam?

GeoActivity

1. INTERDISCIPLINARY ACTIVITY–ECONOMICS

With a small group, come up with a list of 10 products that you use daily, such as a computer. Research these products to find out where they are produced. Create a slide show that displays the product and the country or countries that produce it.

2. WRITING FOR SOCIAL STUDIES

Reread the part of Section 1 that discusses population geography. Write a series of newspaper headlines that tell the story of the growth of the world's population. Arrange them in chronological order on a poster.

3. MENTAL MAPPING

Create an outline map of your state. Label the sites of the following:

• the state government
• your county government
• your community government

CHAPTER 4 People and Culture

1 CULTURE

What Is Culture?

2 CULTURE

How Does Culture Change?

 ESSENTIAL QUESTION

How does culture develop and how does it shape our lives?

CONNECT Geography & History

Use the map and the time line to answer the following questions.

1. Which early cultural centers are found in Africa?

2. One of the world's oldest religions developed in the Indus River valley. What is the religion?

9000 B.C.

Economics
8000 B.C.
Development of agriculture
(Early farm tools) ▶

Economics
9000 B.C.
Domestication of animals begins.

Culture
5000 B.C.
First cities develop.
(Home in early city) ▶

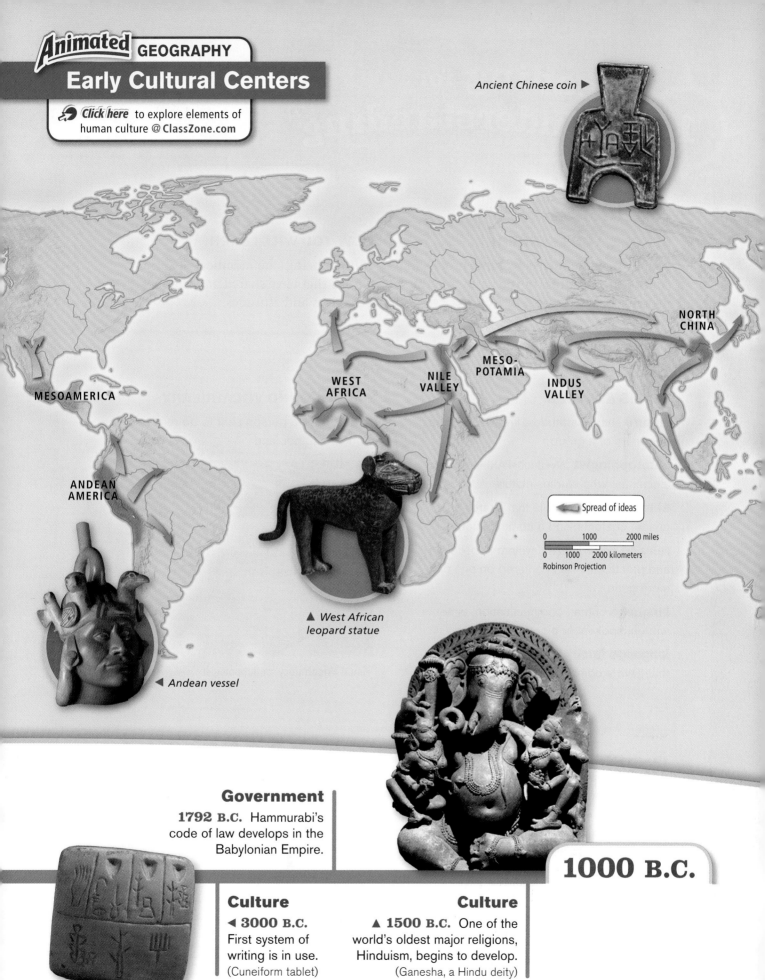

Ancient Chinese coin ▶

NORTH
CHINA

WEST
AFRICA

NILE
VALLEY

MESO-
POTAMIA

INDUS
VALLEY

MESOAMERICA

ANDEAN
AMERICA

◀ Spread of ideas

0   1000   2000 miles
0   1000   2000 kilometers
Robinson Projection

▲ *West African
leopard statue*

◀ *Andean vessel*

Government

1792 B.C. Hammurabi's
code of law develops in the
Babylonian Empire.

1000 B.C.

Culture

◀ **3000 B.C.**
First system of
writing is in use.
(Cuneiform tablet)

Culture

▲ **1500 B.C.** One of the
world's oldest major religions,
Hinduism, begins to develop.
(Ganesha, a Hindu deity)

Reading for Understanding

▶ Key Ideas

BEFORE, YOU LEARNED

People organize themselves into groups to control specific areas of the Earth and the people who live there.

NOW YOU WILL LEARN

Human beings are members of social groups that have shared and unique behaviors and attitudes.

▶ Vocabulary

TERMS & NAMES

culture shared attitudes, knowledge, and behaviors of a group

anthropologist (AN•thruh•PAHL•uh•jihst) a scientist who studies culture

ethnic group a people that shares a language, customs, and a common heritage

religion an organized system of beliefs and practices, often centered on one or more gods

language human communication, either written, spoken, or signed

language family a group of languages that have a common origin

BACKGROUND VOCABULARY

missionary a person sent to do religious work in another land

Visual Vocabulary anthropologist

▶ Reading Strategy

Re-create the web diagram shown at right. As you read and respond to the **KEY QUESTIONS**, use the diagram to find main ideas about culture.

 See Skillbuilder Handbook, page R4

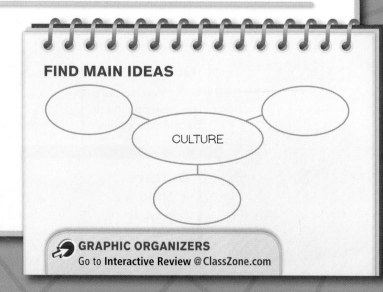

FIND MAIN IDEAS

CULTURE

GRAPHIC ORGANIZERS
Go to **Interactive Review** @ ClassZone.com

What Is Culture?

1.02 Generate, interpret, and manipulate information from tools such as maps, globes, charts, graphs, databases, and models to pose and answer questions about space and place, environment and society, and spatial dynamics and connections.
11.01 Identify the concepts associated with culture such as language, religion, family, and ethnic identity, and analyze how they can link and separate societies.

Connecting to Your World

How does your daily life compare to the lives of students in other parts of the world? Maybe you get up, have cereal for breakfast, and then walk to school. A young person your age in a rural area in Africa may have to work in the fields. When your school day ends, you may have sports or club activities before you go home. If you lived in China's crowded capital of Beijing, you might go home to your family's one-room apartment, where you would study or watch television.

Culture: A Way of Life

▼ **KEY QUESTION** What is culture?

People meet their basic needs in many different ways. This is because each society has its own culture. **Culture** is the shared attitudes, knowledge, and behaviors of a group. It is the total way of life held in common by a specific group of people. Culture includes language, religion, art, and music. It also includes how a group of people live, what work they do, what food they eat, what beliefs they hold, and how they use the environment to meet their needs. Cultures also create social customs and technologies to solve problems. A culture unites people by helping them to understand their world and to relate to others in the group or those outside the group. Culture is passed from generation to generation.

Newspaper Rock, Utah For perhaps 2,000 years, native peoples and passersby have carved symbols into this sandstone rock.

UTAH
Newspaper Rock

Elements of Culture Scientists called **anthropologists** study culture. They have found that there are basic elements for all cultures. These include language, religion, certain foods and clothing, arts and crafts, technology, and government. Cultural elements also include a group's common practices, its shared understandings, and its social organization. The way a group uses these elements is what makes its culture unique, or one of a kind. Geographers study where different cultures are located and how they interact with their environment.

Every culture contains smaller social groups. The family is the smallest and most basic unit of a culture. Sometimes a culture includes ethnic groups. An **ethnic group** is a people that shares a language, customs, and a common heritage. Mexican Americans and Korean Americans are examples of ethnic groups that are part of the larger culture region that is the United States.

Learning Culture People are not born with cultural knowledge— they learn it from family, friends, and others. Generally, people learn culture in two ways: by observing others in their culture, and from direct teaching. Think about how you learned to speak. At first, you learned from listening to others and by imitating them. Later, when you went to school, you were directly taught the language, so that you could not only speak it, but write and read it too.

▲ **FIND MAIN IDEAS** Identify the elements of culture.

ANALYZING Primary Sources

Aimé Césaire (born 1913), a poet and political leader, was born in Martinique, a French island in the West Indies. He helped to found the Negritude movement. Its purpose was to glorify traditional African culture and identity.

> Culture is everything. Culture is the way we dress, the way we carry our heads, the way we walk, the way we tie our ties—it is not only the fact of writing books or building houses.

Source: Aimé Césaire, speech to the World Congress of Black Writers and Artists, Paris, France, 1956

DOCUMENT-BASED QUESTION
What point is Césaire making about the role of culture in life?

To learn more about how culture is learned, go to the **Activity Center** @ ClassZone.com

How Culture Is Learned

We learn about common practices, shared understandings, and social organization from direct teaching and from observing cultural practices. Family and friends, school, the media, the government, and religious institutions all help us learn our culture.

Family, Friends, and School Family and friends teach us social customs, values, religious and political beliefs, and the basics of living with others. At school, students learn about their culture and the cultures of others.

Media Media, such as television, the Internet, music, books, magazines, and newspapers, help communicate what is happening in our society and in the world around us.

Government Some of the most directed cultural learning comes from the government. It provides schools to instruct young people in the customs and traditions of their culture.

Religious Institutions Personal values and religious beliefs help people learn to live with others.

CONNECT to Your Life

Journal Entry Think about the culture in which you live. What objects might best represent parts of your culture? Record your ideas in your journal.

World Religions and Culture

▼ **KEY QUESTION** What role does religion have in a culture?

Because religion has such an influence on people's lives, it is an important element in most cultures. **Religion** is an organized system of beliefs and practices, often centered on one or more gods. Religion establishes beliefs and values. These beliefs and values guide people's behaviors toward each other and toward the environment.

Types of Religions There are thousands of religions in the world, but many religions have common elements. These elements may include specific behaviors to be practiced, important dates and rituals, holy books, and standards of proper behavior. Religions are often divided into three types—those with a belief in one god, those with a belief in more than one god, and those with a belief in divine forces in nature. The five major world religions are Buddhism, Christianity, Hinduism, Islam, and Judaism, as described in the chart below. You will learn more about them in other chapters of this book and in the World Religions handbook at the back of this text.

◀ COMPARING ▶ World Religions

RELIGION	BASIC BELIEFS	TEACHER OR LEADER	FOLLOWERS
Buddhism	Followers can achieve enlightenment by understanding the Four Noble Truths and following the Eightfold Path.	Siddhartha Gautama, the Buddha	379 million
Christianity	There is only one God. Jesus is the Son of God. Jesus' death and resurrection made eternal life possible.	Jesus of Nazareth	2.1 billion
Hinduism	The soul never dies but is continually reborn until it becomes enlightened. Enlightenment comes after people free themselves from earthly desires.	no one leader	860 million
Islam	There is only one God. Persons achieve salvation by following the Five Pillars of Islam and living a just life.	Muhammad	1.3 billion
Judaism	There is only one God. According to believers, God loves and protects his people, but then holds them accountable for their sins.	Abraham	15.1 million

◀ *A Chinese-Buddhist Enlightened Being*

Spread of Religion Over the centuries, religions have spread from their points of origin to the rest of the world. All of the world's major religions began in Asia and moved to other continents. At first, religious beliefs were carried to different places by followers of the religion or traders. Later, **missionaries**, people sent to do religious work in other lands, spread their faiths. For example, Christianity began in Southwest Asia and was spread throughout the world by missionaries. Still later, immigrants brought their religious beliefs with them as they moved to other countries.

In some lands, traditional religions have been practiced for as long as people have lived in a culture group. In areas where there has been little immigration, most of the people have the same religion. In countries where there has been much immigration, several religions might be practiced. This is the case in the United States, where all the world's major religions and many others are practiced. In fact, the United States has more religious groups than any other country in the world, although the two largest groups are Protestant and Roman Catholic.

▲ **SUMMARIZE** Explain the role religion has in culture.

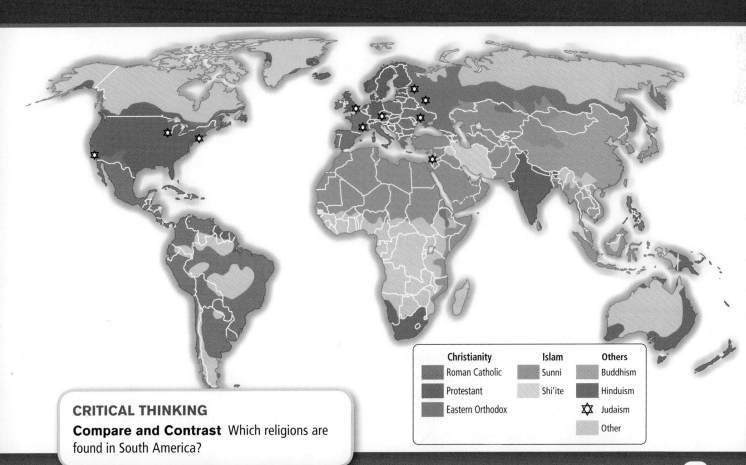

Christianity
- Roman Catholic
- Protestant
- Eastern Orthodox

Islam
- Sunni
- Shi'ite

Others
- Buddhism
- Hinduism
- ✡ Judaism
- Other

CRITICAL THINKING

Compare and Contrast Which religions are found in South America?

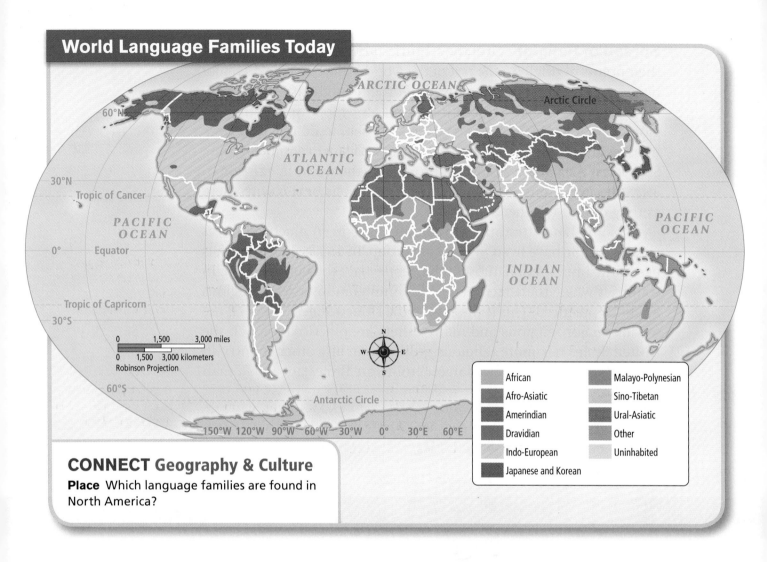

African		Malayo-Polynesian	
Afro-Asiatic		Sino-Tibetan	
Amerindian		Ural-Asiatic	
Dravidian		Other	
Indo-European		Uninhabited	
Japanese and Korean			

CONNECT Geography & Culture

Place Which language families are found in North America?

World Languages and Culture

▼ **KEY QUESTION** Why is language important?

Language is the way cultural values and traditions are passed from one generation to another. **Language** is human communication either written, spoken, or signed, such as American Sign Language. Your family and teachers use language to help you understand your world and how to live in it. Because language relates to all aspects of life, it helps a people to establish a cultural identity.

Sharing the same language is also important to a culture's sense of unity. Sometimes, if more than one language is spoken in an area, people don't feel connected to each other. In Canada, for example, both English and French are spoken. As a result, at times English- and French-speaking Canadians experience conflict.

Language Families Geographers believe that there are between 3,000 and 6,500 languages in the world today. India, for example, has 18 official languages, and more than 800 other languages are spoken there. Some of the world's languages are spoken by only a few thousand people. Other languages have millions of speakers. The language with the largest number of native speakers is Mandarin Chinese, spoken by an estimated 885 million people, mostly in China. English is the most widespread language in the world.

Scholars have arranged the world's languages into 11 main language families. A **language family** is a group of languages that have a common origin. English is in the Indo-European language family, the most widespread language family. An estimated one-half of the world's population speaks an Indo-European language.

Spread and Change of Language Geographers study how languages are distributed throughout the world as a way to learn more about cultures. Like religion and other elements of culture, language spreads in many ways. People bring their language and their culture with them when they move from place to place. Indo-European languages, such as English, Dutch, Portuguese, Spanish, and French, were carried to all parts of the world by European explorers and colonists.

Language not only spreads, it also changes. Language changes when people interact and borrow words from one another. Change also happens when people need new words to express new ideas or to represent new objects or activities, such as *weblog*, or *blog*.

 FIND MAIN IDEAS Explain why language is important to culture.

Hello
Buon Giorno
Zdravstvui
Dzien Dobry Dia Dhuit
Namasté
Gei Sou

Fun Facts!

INDO-EUROPEAN LANGUAGES

All of the above greetings come to you from the same language family—Indo-European. These words are variations of *hello* in English, Italian, Russian, Polish, Hindi, Greek, and Irish. These seven languages are a part of more than 400 in this language family.

ONLINE QUIZ
For test practice, go to
Interactive Review
@ ClassZone.com

Section ① Assessment

TERMS & NAMES

1. Explain the importance of
- culture
- ethnic group
- religion
- language

USE YOUR READING NOTES

2. Summarize Use your completed chart to answer the following question:

Why is language important in a culture?

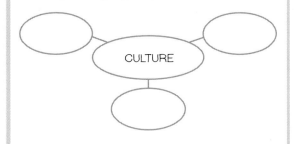

CULTURE

KEY IDEAS

3. What are the basic elements of culture?

4. What are the five major religions of the world?

5. How are the world's languages organized?

CRITICAL THINKING

6. Draw Conclusions Why is religion an important part of a group's culture?

7. Sequence Events How does culture pass from one generation to the next?

8. CONNECT to Today What are the most influential elements in the culture of the United States?

9. WRITING **Write a Brief Description** Choose a cultural group. Write a description that includes information on cultural elements, such as religion, language, government, technology, arts and crafts, and food and clothing.

Reading for Understanding

▶ Key Ideas

BEFORE, YOU LEARNED

People belong to specific groups that share a common culture.

NOW YOU WILL LEARN

Cultures do not remain the same but change over time.

▶ Vocabulary

TERMS & NAMES

agricultural revolution the shift from gathering food to raising food

innovation something new that is introduced for the first time

technology people's application of knowledge, tools, and inventions to meet their needs

diffusion the spread of ideas, inventions, and patterns of behavior from one group to another

cultural hearth an area where a culture originated and spread to other areas

BACKGROUND VOCABULARY

domestication the raising and tending of a plant or animal to be of use to humans

nomad a person who has no set home but moves from place to place in search of food for animals

Visual Vocabulary nomad group

▶ Reading Strategy

Re-create the diagram at right. As you read and respond to the **KEY QUESTIONS**, use the diagram to analyze the causes and effects of cultural change.

 Skillbuilder Handbook, page R8

ANALYZE CAUSE AND EFFECT

Innovation
1._____
2._____

Diffusion
1._____
2._____

CULTURAL CHANGE

GRAPHIC ORGANIZERS
Go to **Interactive Review** @ ClassZone.com

How Does Culture Change?

1.02 Generate, interpret, and manipulate information from tools such as maps, globes, charts, graphs, databases, and models to pose and answer questions about space and place, environment and society, and spatial dynamics and connections.
3.03 Examine the development and use of tools and technologies and assess their influence on the human ability to use, modify, or adapt to their environment.

Connecting to Your World

Think about all the information and communication tools you have in your daily life. Did you include cell phones, mp3 players, DVDs, digital cameras, or laptop computers? When your parents were your age, none of these devices were available to them. These improvements in technology have changed the ways many people live their lives—and this change has taken place in only one generation. Cultural change happens much more rapidly now than it did in the past.

Zulu Girl, South Africa, with Cell Phone

Culture Change and Exchange

▼ **KEY QUESTION** How does culture change?

Culture changes over time. The changes may be very slow or quite rapid. Some changes are simple, such as changes in clothing styles. Other changes are more complex, such as the agricultural revolution. In the **agricultural revolution**, which happened thousands of years ago, humans shifted from gathering food to raising food. Because the food source was more reliable, fewer people were needed for raising food, and ways of life changed. Two ways that culture changes are through innovation and diffusion.

Camels Go to Pasture Traditional ways are replaced by modern ones.

Innovation Something new that is introduced for the first time is called an **innovation**. New ideas, inventions, and patterns of behavior are types of innovations that change a culture. The computer is an example of an invention that changed cultures in the United States and around the world. Innovation may take place by accident, or it may be deliberate. The prehistoric control of fire was probably an accident, but it forever changed the way people lived. However, the use of existing resources and technology to solve an old or a new problem is a deliberate innovation. **Technology** refers to people's application of knowledge, tools, and inventions to meet their needs.

Some innovations can dramatically change the way people live. The domestication of wild plants thousands of years ago was such a change. **Domestication** means to raise or to tend plants or animals to be of use to humans. Dependence on agriculture resulted in more densely populated settlements.

Like most cultural changes, the agricultural revolution led to other changes. These settled societies needed to be organized differently from groups of **nomads**, who had no set home but moved from place to place to find food for their animals. This led to more innovations. For example, people needed to find ways to water crops in the field and to store the food once harvested. Look at the pictures below to see how different cultures used the resources and technology available to them to solve a storage problem. New or different tools were also needed to farm the land.

◄ COMPARING ► Storage Unit Innovations

Clay Pot Where clay was plentiful, clay pots served as storage units. **1. What would be the advantage of a clay pot for storage?**

Basket Woven grass or reeds created light, portable storage units. **2. Why would this material be used for storage?**

Leather Bag Hides made into bags made storage units easy to transport. **3. What would be a disadvantage of this type of storage?**

The Spread of Agriculture

The spread of agriculture is the most significant change in human history. Having available food year-round allowed people to settle and eventually to develop specialized labor and cities.

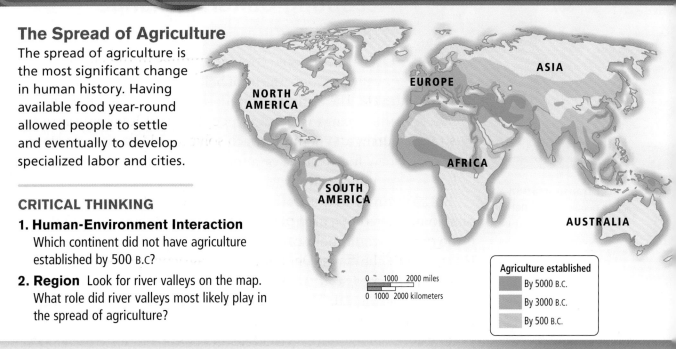

Agriculture established
- By 5000 B.C.
- By 3000 B.C.
- By 500 B.C.

0   1000   2000 miles
0 1000 2000 kilometers

CRITICAL THINKING

1. **Human-Environment Interaction** Which continent did not have agriculture established by 500 B.C?

2. **Region** Look for river valleys on the map. What role did river valleys most likely play in the spread of agriculture?

Diffusion The spread of ideas, inventions, and patterns of behavior from one group to another is called **diffusion**. Whenever a group of people comes in contact with another group, diffusion is possible.

The spread of agriculture is an early example of diffusion. The spread of U.S. fast-food restaurants around the world is a modern example. In early times, traders often brought new ideas and inventions to other cultures. Written language, the use of coins, and religious beliefs all moved along ancient trade routes. Missionaries and invaders also carried cultural elements with them.

Geographers study diffusion to see patterns in the development of cultures across the Earth's surface. One pattern they have observed is diffusion from cultural hearths. A **cultural hearth** is an area with an advanced culture from which ideas or technology spread. The map above shows where early cultural hearths existed.

In the past, the spread of culture was usually slow because of geographic barriers. Large bodies of water, mountains, or deserts often made it difficult for people to interact with others. Sometimes political boundaries limited contact between peoples. In today's world, it's almost impossible to avoid some kind of interaction with other groups of people. Satellite television, the Internet, and other forms of mass communication speed new ideas, practices, and inventions around the globe.

▲ **FIND MAIN IDEAS** Identify the ways that culture changes.

Amish Transportation
Amish people choose not to drive automobiles, but use horse-drawn vehicles.

Accepting Cultural Change

 KEY QUESTION Is cultural change always accepted?

Over time, people come in contact with different ideas, inventions, or patterns of behavior. If a cultural exchange takes place, the culture begins to change. Sometimes this change is slow, and people just become used to the change. When the effects of cultural change— such as a new food source or a tool—are positive, the lives of the group may improve.

But sometimes an innovation is unacceptable, such as use of lands or animals sacred to a group. Sometimes a group may need to decide if the change would help or harm their society. For example, in the United States, the Amish choose not to drive cars, not to have electricity in their homes, and to send their children to private, one-room schoolhouses. They do this because they reject the impact of modern life on their way of life.

Change may sometimes be forced on a group. This often happens when a region is invaded. For example, Spanish conquerors pressed their culture on the native peoples of the Americas in the 1500s.

▲ **MAKE GENERALIZATIONS** Explain why some cultural changes might be rejected.

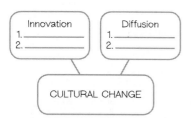
Section 2 Assessment

ONLINE QUIZ
For test practice, go to **Interactive Review** @ ClassZone.com

TERMS & NAMES

1. Explain the importance of
- innovation
- technology
- diffusion
- cultural hearth

USE YOUR READING NOTES

2. Analyze Cause and Effect Use your completed web diagram to answer the following question:

What role do cultural hearths play in changing cultures?

Innovation
1. _____
2. _____

Diffusion
1. _____
2. _____

CULTURAL CHANGE

KEY IDEAS

3. What are two ways that bring about cultural change?

4. How does deliberate innovation take place?

5. What three groups helped to spread culture in earlier times?

CRITICAL THINKING

6. Make Inferences What are some reasons why a group may accept cultural change?

7. Draw Conclusions How has mass communication changed the way culture spreads?

8. CONNECT to Today How has the United States been affected by cultural exchange in recent times?

9. TECHNOLOGY **Make a Multimedia Presentation** Plan a power presentation slide show illustrating three inventions in transportation and three in communication that brought cultural change. Each slide should have a visual of the invention and a description of the change.

Interactive ← Review

Click here to complete these and other activities online @ ClassZone.com

CHAPTER SUMMARY

Key Idea 1
Human beings are members of social groups that have shared and unique behaviors and attitudes.

Key Idea 2
Cultures do not remain the same but change over time.

For **Review and Study Notes**, go to **Interactive Review @ ClassZone.com**

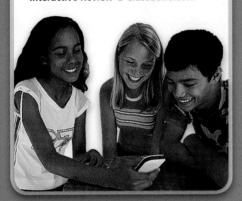

NAME GAME

Use the Terms & Names list to complete each sentence on paper or online.

1. I am the spread of ideas, inventions, and patterns of behavior from one group to another. ___diffusion___

2. I am a scientist who studies culture. _____

3. I am a people that shares a language, customs, and a common heritage. _____

4. I am the methods, materials, or tools available to complete a task. _____

5. I am the total way of life held in common by a specific group of people. _____

6. I am something new that is introduced for the first time. _____

7. I am a group of languages that have a common origin. _____

8. I am an area where the transfer of elements of culture between two groups occurs. _____

9. I am human communication, either written, spoken, or signed. _____

10. I am an organized system of beliefs in a god or gods and a set of practices. _____

agricultural revolution
anthropologist
culture
cultural hearth
diffusion
domestication
ethnic group
innovation
language
language family
missionary
nomad
religion
technology

Activities

Flip Cards

Use the online flip cards to quiz yourself on terms and names introduced in this chapter.

anthropologist

? a scientist who studies culture

Crossword Puzzle

Complete an online crossword puzzle to test your knowledge of culture.

ACROSS
1. human communication, either written, spoken, or signed

VOCABULARY

Explain the significance of each of the following.

1. culture
2. ethnic group
3. religion
4. language
5. technology

Explain how the terms and names in each group are related.

6. culture, religion, and language
7. innovation, diffusion, and cultural hearth
8. domestication and agricultural revolution

KEY IDEAS

1 What Is Culture?

9. Why are there different cultures?
10. How do people learn about their culture?
11. What are two of the most important elements of culture?
12. What are the three types of religious beliefs?
13. Why is language important to a culture?
14. How does language change?

2 How Does Culture Change?

15. How does innovation change culture?
16. How does diffusion change culture?
17. What is a cultural hearth?
18. Why was culture change a slow process in earlier times?
19. Why might a people accept a cultural change?
20. In what way is cultural change forced upon a people?

CRITICAL THINKING

21. **Categorize** Create a table to list the factors that have helped or limited cultural change over the years.

HELP	LIMIT

22. **Make Generalizations** What makes each culture unique?
23. **Make Inferences** Why are families important in a culture?
24. **Connect to Economics** Why was the agricultural revolution such a dramatic cultural change?
25. **Five Themes: Movement** How have aspects of culture been spread throughout history?
26. **Connect Geography & Culture** How important is culture to a person's sense of identity?

Answer the ESSENTIAL QUESTION

How does culture develop, and how does it shape our lives?

Written Response Write a two- or three-paragraph response to the Essential Question. Be sure to consider the key ideas of each section and the fact that all human beings are a part of a culture.

Response Rubric
A strong response will:
- explain the nature of culture and its elements
- discuss how culture shapes the lives of individuals

THEMATIC MAP

Use the map and your knowledge of geography to answer questions 1 and 2 on your paper.

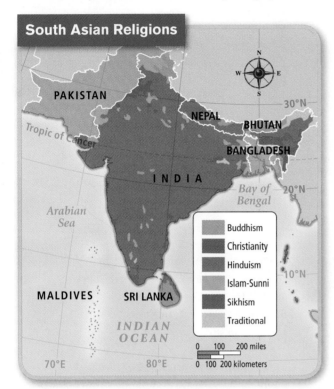

South Asian Religions

Legend:
- Buddhism
- Christianity
- Hinduism
- Islam-Sunni
- Sikhism
- Traditional

0 100 200 miles
0 100 200 kilometers

1. Which of the following countries has a large Buddhist population?

A. India
B. Sri Lanka
C. Bangladesh
D. Nepal

2. Which of the following countries has a large population of Muslims?

A. Bhutan
B. Sri Lanka
C. Bangladesh
D. India

CHART

Study the chart below. Use the information in the chart to answer questions 3 and 4.

Languages of Europe	
Country	**Languages Spoken**
Austria	German, Slovene, Croatian, Hungarian
Belgium	Flemish, French, German
France	French
Germany	German
Netherlands	Dutch, Frisian
Switzerland	German, French, Italian, Romansch

Source: *Infoplease database 2006*

3. In which countries is a single language spoken?

4. If you only spoke German, in which countries would you need a translator?

GeoActivity

1. INTERDISCIPLINARY ACTIVITY–MATHEMATICS

With a small group, research world religions on the Internet. Use a computer program to create a database and a graph showing the three countries with the largest number of members for each of the major religions, and the total population of those countries.

2. WRITING FOR SOCIAL STUDIES

Reread the paragraphs on the elements of culture. Then write a paragraph describing the culture of your community. Discuss such elements as religion, language, government, and economic activities.

3. MENTAL MAPPING

Create a map of your town or neighborhood showing schools and places of worship. Be sure to include

- elementary, middle, and high schools, public and private
- any places of worship

UNIT 2

Latin America

Why It Matters:

Latin America is a region of many countries. The region spans a large area north and south of the equator. The region faces political and economic challenges. How it meets these challenges will have an impact on other parts of the world.

CHAPTER 5
The Andes Mountains, Chile
Latin America
Physical Geography & History

CHAPTER 6
Paseo de la Reforma, Mexico City
Mexico

CHAPTER 7
Marketplace in Guatemala
Middle America and Spanish-Speaking South America

CHAPTER 8
Amazon River
Brazil

UNIT 2 ATLAS

The region of Latin America stretches from Mexico to the tip of South America. As you study the maps, notice geographic patterns and specific details about the region. Answer the GeoActivity questions on each map in your notebook.

As you study the graphs on this page, compare the landmass, population, rivers, and mountains of Latin America with those of the United States. Then jot down the answers to the following questions in your notebook.

Comparing Data

1. Compare the population of Latin America with that of the United States. How many more people live in Latin America than in the United States?

2. The discharge rate of a river measures how much water moves through a certain location in a certain amount of time. The rate in this graph is measured in cubic feet per second. How much greater is the discharge rate of the Amazon River than that of the Mississippi River?

Comparing Data

Landmass

Latin America
7,888,955 sq. mi.

Continental United States
3,165,630 sq. mi.

Population

Latin America 561,346,000

United States 296,410,404

0   100   200   300   400   500   600
Population (in millions)

Rivers

Discharge Rate (in cubic feet per second)

Amazon 6,356,000   Paraná 777,000   Mississippi 636,000   Nile 106,000

Mountains

Andes 5,500 mi.
Himalayas 1,550 mi.
Atlas 1,200 mi.
Alps 750 mi.

0   1000   2000   3000   4000   5000   6000
Length of Mountain Chains (in miles)

Population Density

Gulf of
Mexico

Tropic of Cancer

20°N

ATLANTIC
OCEAN

Caribbean Sea

Mexico
City

PACIFIC
OCEAN

Caracas

Equator

0°

**Persons per
square mile**

Over 520
260–519
130–259
25–129
1–24
0

Belo Horizonte

20°S

Rio de Janeiro

Tropic of Capricorn

São Paulo

Santiago

Buenos Aires

ATLANTIC
OCEAN

THINK LIKE A GEOGRAPHER

1. **Place** Where is the population of
Mexico most dense?

2. **Region** Where do most people live in
Latin America?

0   500   1,000 miles
0   500   1,000 kilometers

40°S

120°W   100°W   80°W   60°W   40°W

MEXICO

Gulf of Mexico

BAHAMAS

Tropic of Cancer

20°N

CUBA

DOMINICAN REPUBLIC

BELIZE

JAMAICA

HAITI

ATLANTIC OCEAN

HONDURAS

Caribbean Sea

GUATEMALA

EL SALVADOR

NICARAGUA

COSTA RICA

PANAMA

PACIFIC OCEAN

VENEZUELA

GUYANA

SURINAME

FRENCH GUIANA

COLOMBIA

Equator

0°

ECUADOR

PERU

BRAZIL

BOLIVIA

Tropic of Capricorn

20°S

PARAGUAY

CHILE

ARGENTINA

URUGUAY

ATLANTIC OCEAN

40°S

Tropical
Tropical wet
Tropical wet and dry

Dry
Desert
Semiarid

Mid-Latitude
Mediterranean
Marine west coast
Humid subtropical

Highland

N
W   E
S

| 0 | 500 | 1,000 miles |
| 0 | 500 | 1,000 kilometers |

THINK LIKE A GEOGRAPHER

1. **Place** What is the climate of the southernmost tip of South America?

2. **Region** In what parts of Latin America can you find a highland climate?

100°W   80°W   60°W   40°W   20°W

Gulf of Mexico

BAHAMAS

Tropic of Cancer

20°N

Monterrey
MEXICO

Mexico City

DOMINICAN
REPUBLIC

CUBA

BELIZE

JAMAICA

HONDURAS

HAITI

ATLANTIC
OCEAN

Caribbean Sea

GUATEMALA

EL SALVADOR

NICARAGUA

COSTA RICA

PANAMA

PACIFIC
OCEAN

COLOMBIA

Caracas

VENEZUELA

GUYANA

SURINAME

FRENCH
GUIANA

Equator

0°

ECUADOR

PERU

BRAZIL

Land use

- Commercial agriculture
- Livestock raising
- Subsistence agriculture
- Forestland
- Limited agriculture

Major resources

- Bauxite
- Copper
- Fish
- Gold
- Iron ore
- Natural gas
- Oil
- Silver
- Timber
- Tin
- Other minerals
- ● Manufacturing center

BOLIVIA

Belo Horizonte

Tropic of Capricorn

20°S

PARAGUAY

Rio de Janeiro

São Paulo

CHILE

ARGENTINA

Santiago

Buenos Aires

URUGUAY

ATLANTIC
OCEAN

40°S

N
W   E
S

0   500   1,000 miles
0   500   1,000 kilometers

THINK LIKE A GEOGRAPHER

1. **Place** What do the colors on the economic activity map represent?

2. **Human-Environment Interaction** What are the main economic activities of Mexico?

120°W   100°W   80°W   60°W   40°W

Regional Overview

Latin America

Latin America is a far-reaching region of many countries. The region spans a great distance both north and south of the equator. Latin America is diverse in its land, climate, and people.

GEOGRAPHY

Mountain ranges and highlands make up a large part of Latin America. The Andes Mountains, along the western coast of South America, are the largest and the longest mountain range above sea level in the world. Volcanoes, some of them active, extend through parts of Mexico, Central America, and South America. Large plateaus and vast plains provide lands for grazing and farming.

Latin America's climate is as varied as its landscape. The climate ranges from dry deserts to hot, tropical regions to cold highlands. Vegetation in Latin America varies based on the climate.

HISTORY

The Maya, Aztec, and Inca developed advanced civilizations in Latin America before the arrival of the Spanish in the 15th century. They built complex cities and structures and changed their environment to meet their needs.

After the voyages of Columbus, Spanish *conquistadors* destroyed these civilizations. Spain and Portugal set up colonies in the region and controlled most of it for the next 300 years. By the early 1800s, most Latin American countries had gained their independence.

Machu Picchu
This ancient Inca city is located near present-day Cuzco, Peru.

CULTURE

Latin American culture today is a blend of several cultures—Indian, European, African, Asian, and people of mixed ancestry. This blend is evident in the music, art, foods, and languages of the region. The majority of Latin Americans speak Spanish, but others speak Portuguese, French, English, and Dutch. Some Indian groups continue to speak their traditional languages.

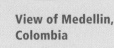

View of Medellin, Colombia

GOVERNMENT

As colonies, Latin Americans had little or no say in how they were governed. This inexperience made it difficult to establish stable governments after gaining independence. As a result, the governments of many Latin American countries came under the rule of wealthy landowners or military dictators. By the 1980s, widespread protests against these governments occurred in several countries. Today more Latin American countries have democratic governments.

ECONOMICS

Since the 1800s, many Latin American countries have depended on one or two products for export, particularly agricultural products, and have imported most of their manufactured goods. Recently, however, many Latin American countries began to develop other industries. Some Latin American countries have become major exporters of manufactured goods. Latin American countries have also established organizations to promote trade among countries in the region.

Country Almanac

 Click here to compare the most recent data on countries @ ClassZone.com

Unit Writing Project

As you read this unit, choose a country or an area of Latin America that interests you. Imagine that you are on a week's vacation there. Write a daily journal entry describing what you've seen and learned about the area and your reactions to it.

Think About:

- an area that you find interesting
- what you learned about the area that makes it interesting to you

Latin America

The Almanac provides information about the geography, economy, and culture of the countries of Latin America.

Antigua and Barbuda

GEOGRAPHY
Capital: St. John's
Total Area: 171 sq. mi.
Population: 68,722

ECONOMY
Imports: machinery; agricultural products
Exports: petroleum products

CULTURE
Language: English
Religion: Anglican 32%; Moravian 12%; Catholic 11%

Argentina

GEOGRAPHY
Capital: Buenos Aires
Total Area: 1,068,302 sq. mi.
Population: 38,747,000

ECONOMY
Imports: chemicals; machinery
Exports: food and livestock

CULTURE
Language: Spanish
Religion: Catholic 80%; Protestant 5%

Bahamas

GEOGRAPHY
Capital: Nassau
Total Area: 5,382 sq. mi.
Population: 323,000

ECONOMY
Imports: machinery; food products
Exports: crustaceans and mollusks

CULTURE
Language: English
Religion: Baptist 18%; Catholic 17%; Anglican 11%

Barbados

GEOGRAPHY
Capital: Bridgetown
Total Area: 166 sq. mi.
Population: 270,000

ECONOMY
Imports: capital goods; food
Exports: food; sugar and molasses; rum

CULTURE
Language: English
Religion: Anglican 26%; Pentecostal 11%

Belize

GEOGRAPHY
Capital: Belmopan
Total Area: 8,867 sq. mi.
Population: 270,000

ECONOMY
Imports: machinery; mineral fuels; food
Exports: seafood; sugar; bananas

CULTURE
Language: English
Religion: Catholic 50%; Protestant 32%; nonreligious 9%

Bolivia

GEOGRAPHY
Capital: Sucre
Total Area: 424,164 sq. mi.
Population: 9,182,000

ECONOMY
Imports: machinery; chemicals; food
Exports: soybean products; natural gas

CULTURE
Language: Spanish; Aymara; Quechua
Religion: Catholic 89%; Protestant 9%

Brazil

GEOGRAPHY
Capital: Brasília
Total Area: 3,286,488 sq. mi.
Population: 186,405,000

ECONOMY
Imports: machinery; chemicals
Exports: meat; sugar; coffee; soybeans

CULTURE
Language: Portuguese
Religion: Catholic 72%; Protestant 23%

Chile

GEOGRAPHY
Capital: Santiago
Total Area: 292,260 sq. mi.
Population: 16,295,000

ECONOMY
Imports: machinery; metals; copper
Exports: copper; food products; fruit

CULTURE
Language: Spanish
Religion: Catholic 70%; Protestant 15%

Colombia

GEOGRAPHY
Capital: Bogotá
Total Area: 439,736 sq. mi.
Population: 45,600,000

ECONOMY
Imports: capital goods; consumer goods
Exports: petroleum; chemicals; coal; food; machinery; coffee

CULTURE
Language: Spanish
Religion: Catholic 92%

Costa Rica

GEOGRAPHY
Capital: San José
Total Area: 19,730 sq. mi.
Population: 4,327,000

ECONOMY
Imports: general merchandise
Exports: bananas; coffee; tropical fruit

CULTURE
Language: Spanish
Religion: Catholic 86%; Protestant 9%; other Christian 2%

Cuba

GEOGRAPHY
Capital: Havana
Total Area: 42,803 sq. mi.
Population: 11,269,000

ECONOMY
Imports: food and livestock; cereals
Exports: raw sugar; nickel; seafood; medicines

CULTURE
Language: Spanish
Religion: Catholic 39%

Dominica

GEOGRAPHY
Capital: Roseau
Total Area: 291 sq. mi.
Population: 69,029

ECONOMY
Imports: food; machinery
Exports: coconut-based soaps; cosmetics

CULTURE
Language: English
Religion: Catholic 70%; six largest Protestant groups 17%

Dominican Republic

GEOGRAPHY
Capital: Santo Domingo
Total Area: 18,815 sq. mi.
Population: 8,895,000

ECONOMY
Imports: refined petroleum; food
Exports: ferronickel; ships' stores; raw sugar; cocoa

CULTURE
Language: Spanish
Religion: Catholic 82%; Protestant 6%

Ecuador

GEOGRAPHY
Capital: Quito
Total Area: 109,483 sq. mi.
Population: 13,228,000

ECONOMY
Imports: chemicals; food and live animals
Exports: fish and crustaceans; cut flowers

CULTURE
Language: Spanish; Quechua; Shuar
Religion: Catholic 94%; Protestant 2%

El Salvador

GEOGRAPHY
Capital: San Salvador
Total Area: 8,124 sq. mi.
Population: 6,881,000

ECONOMY
Imports: machinery; chemicals and chemical products; food; petroleum
Exports: clothing; coffee; paper; yarn

CULTURE
Language: Spanish
Religion: Catholic 78%; Protestant 17%

Grenada

GEOGRAPHY
Capital: St. George's
Total Area: 133 sq. mi.
Population: 89,502

ECONOMY
Imports: machinery; food; chemicals
Exports: electronic components; nutmeg; fish; paper products; cocoa beans

CULTURE
Language: English
Religion: Catholic 58%; Protestant 38%

Guatemala

GEOGRAPHY
Capital: Guatemala City
Total Area: 42,043 sq. mi.
Population: 12,599,000

ECONOMY
Imports: machinery; chemicals; crude and refined petroleum; road vehicles
Exports: coffee; sugar; bananas; spices

CULTURE
Language: Spanish
Religion: Catholic 76%; Protestant 22%

Rio de Janeiro Located on Brazil's southeast coast, Rio de Janeiro is Brazil's second-largest city.

Guyana

GEOGRAPHY
Capital: Georgetown
Total Area: 83,000 sq. mi.
Population: 751,000

ECONOMY
Imports: consumer goods; fuels
Exports: gold; sugar; shrimp; rice; timber

CULTURE
Language: English
Religion: Hindu 34%; Protestant 28%; Catholic 12%; Muslim 9%

Jamaica

GEOGRAPHY
Capital: Kingston
Total Area: 4,244 sq. mi.
Population: 2,651,000

ECONOMY
Imports: consumer goods; petroleum
Exports: alumina; bauxite; clothing; sugar; coffee; rum

CULTURE
Language: English
Religion: Protestant 61%; Catholic 3%

Panama

GEOGRAPHY
Capital: Panama City
Total Area: 30,193 sq. mi.
Population: 3,232,000

ECONOMY
Imports: mineral fuels; petroleum; machinery; transport equipment
Exports: bananas; seafoods

CULTURE
Language: Spanish
Religion: Catholic 82%; Christian 13%

Haiti

GEOGRAPHY
Capital: Port-au-Prince
Total Area: 10,714 sq. mi.
Population: 8,528,000

ECONOMY
Imports: food and livestock; machinery
Exports: clothing; mangoes; cacao; essential oils; leather goods

CULTURE
Language: Haitian Creole; French
Religion: Catholic 69%; Protestant 24%

Mexico

GEOGRAPHY
Capital: Mexico City
Total Area: 761,606 sq. mi.
Population: 107,029,000

ECONOMY
Imports: electronics; clothing; rubber and plastic products
Exports: road vehicles; machinery; textiles

CULTURE
Language: Spanish
Religion: Catholic 90%; Protestant 4%;

Honduras

GEOGRAPHY
Capital: Tegucigalpa
Total Area: 43,278 sq. mi.
Population: 7,205,000

ECONOMY
Imports: food and livestock; machinery
Exports: shrimp; coffee; palm oil

CULTURE
Language: Spanish
Religion: Catholic 87%; Protestant 10%

Nicaragua

GEOGRAPHY
Capital: Managua
Total Area: 49,998 sq. mi.
Population: 5,487,000

ECONOMY
Imports: consumer goods; fuels
Exports: food products; coffee

CULTURE
Language: Spanish
Religion: Catholic 85%; Protestant 12%

Paraguay

GEOGRAPHY
Capital: Asunción
Total Area: 157,047 sq. mi.
Population: 6,158,000

ECONOMY
Imports: machinery; chemicals; food
Exports: soybean products; meats

CULTURE
Language: Spanish; Guaraní
Religion: Catholic 90%; Protestant 5%

Green Crested Basilisk This lizard is one of many species of animals found in the rain forests of Latin America.

Peru

GEOGRAPHY
Capital: Lima
Total Area: 496,226 sq. mi.
Population: 27,968,000

ECONOMY
Imports: machinery; chemicals and chemical products; petroleum; food
Exports: gold; animal feed; copper

CULTURE
Language: Spanish; Quechua; Aymara
Religion: Catholic 96%

St. Kitts and Nevis

GEOGRAPHY
Capital: Basseterre
Total Area: 101 sq. mi.
Population: 38,958

ECONOMY
Imports: machinery; food; metals
Exports: raw sugar; telecommunications equipment

CULTURE
Language: English
Religion: Protestant 85%; Catholic 7%

St. Lucia

GEOGRAPHY
Capital: Castries
Total Area: 238 sq. mi.
Population: 161,000

ECONOMY
Imports: food; machinery; manufactured goods
Exports: bananas; beer and ale; clothing

CULTURE
Language: English
Religion: Catholic 69%; Protestant 22%

St. Vincent and the Grenadines

GEOGRAPHY
Capital: Kingstown
Total Area: 150 sq. mi.
Population: 119,000

ECONOMY
Imports: food products; machinery
Exports: bananas; packaged flour; packaged rice; eddoes and dasheens

CULTURE
Language: English
Religion: Protestant 58%; Catholic 11%

Suriname

GEOGRAPHY
Capital: Paramaribo
Total Area: 63,039 sq. mi.
Population: 449,000

ECONOMY
Imports: machinery; food; road vehicles
Exports: alumina; gold; petroleum; rice

CULTURE
Language: Dutch
Religion: Christian 50%; Hindu 18%; Muslim 14%

Trinidad and Tobago

GEOGRAPHY
Capital: Port of Spain
Total Area: 1,980 sq. mi.
Population: 1,305,000

ECONOMY
Imports: petroleum; industrial machinery
Exports: floating docks; iron and steel

CULTURE
Language: English
Religion: six largest Protestant bodies 30%; Catholic 29%; Hindu 24%

Uruguay

GEOGRAPHY
Capital: Montevideo
Total Area: 68,039 sq. mi.
Population: 3,463,000

ECONOMY
Imports: chemicals; food and tobacco
Exports: leather goods; beef

CULTURE
Language: Spanish
Religion: Catholic 78%; atheist 6%

Venezuela

GEOGRAPHY
Capital: Caracas
Total Area: 352,144 sq. mi.
Population: 26,749,000

ECONOMY
Imports: machinery; chemicals; vehicles
Exports: petroleum products; aluminum

CULTURE
Language: Spanish; 31 indigenous Indian Languages
Religion: Catholic 90%; Protestant 2%

Caribbean Islands The islands of the Caribbean are among the world's most popular tourist destinations.

CHAPTER **5**

Latin America

Physical Geography and History

1 GEOGRAPHY
Physical Geography of Mexico, Central America, and the Caribbean

2 GEOGRAPHY
Physical Geography of South America

3 HISTORY
Ancient Civilizations

4 HISTORY
From Colonization to Independence

ESSENTIAL QUESTION

How have Latin America's geography and resources helped shape its history?

CONNECT ➤ **Geography & History**

Use the map and the time line to answer the following questions.

1. What is the largest country in Latin America?
2. What country is named after Simón Bolívar, one of the leaders for South American independence?

Culture
◄ **1200 B.C.** Olmec build the first known civilization in southeastern Mexico.

Geography
1200s Inca settle in Cuzco Valley.

1200 B.C.

History
A.D. 900 Classic period of Mayan civilization ends.

Geography
1325 Aztecs establish their capital city, Tenochtitlán. ►

120°W 110°W 100°W 90°W 80°W 70°W 60°W 50°W 40°W 30°W 20°W

30°N
Tropic of Cancer
20°N
10°N
Equator 0°
10°S
Tropic of Capricorn 20°S
30°S
40°S

Tijuana

UNITED STATES

Gulf of Mexico

Monterrey

MEXICO
Guadalajara
México City

BAHAMAS
Havana   Nassau
CUBA
BELIZE   JAMAICA   HAITI   Santo Domingo
Belmopan Kingston Port-au-Prince   DOMINICAN REPUBLIC
Guatemala City
GUATEMALA   HONDURAS
EL SALVADOR Tegucigalpa   Caribbean Sea
San Salvador NICARAGUA
Managua   Panamá City
San José   Caracas
COSTA RICA PANAMA   Mérida   VENEZUELA   GUYANA
Bogotá   Georgetown   SURINAME
COLOMBIA   Paramaribo   Cayenne
                                   FRENCH GUIANA (FRANCE)
Orinoco R.
Galápagos Is. (ECUADOR)
Quito
Guayaquil ECUADOR   Negro R.   Manaus   Amazon R.   Fortaleza
PERU   BRAZIL
Lima
                    BOLIVIA   Salvador
                    La Paz   Brasília
                    Sucre   Belo Horizonte
PACIFIC OCEAN   Madeira R. Araguaia R. Paraguay R.
                    PARAGUAY   Rio de Janeiro
                    Asunción   Paraná R. São Paulo
Juan Fernández Is. (CHILE)
            Santiago   ARGENTINA   URUGUAY
                                   Montevideo
            Buenos Aires
CHILE

ATLANTIC OCEAN

ATLANTIC OCEAN

Falkland Is. (U.K.)

Legend
(★) National capital
(•) Other city

0   500   1,000 miles
0   500   1,000 kilometers

History
◄ **1532** Francisco Pizarro conquers the Inca.

History
1810–1825 Simón Bolívar leads South American countries in their fight for independence from Spain. ►

1850

History
1521 Hernán Cortés conquers the Aztecs.

History
1810 Father Hidalgo calls for Mexico's independence from Spain.

Reading for Understanding

▶ Key Ideas

BEFORE, YOU LEARNED

The United States and Canada share many cultural and geographic similarities.

NOW YOU WILL LEARN

The geography of Mexico, Central America, and the Caribbean Islands, south of the United States, contains mountains, highlands, and plains.

▶ Vocabulary

TERMS & NAMES

Latin America the region that includes Mexico, Central America, the Caribbean Islands, and South America

Sierra Madre Occidental mountain range that runs from north to south down the western part of Mexico

Sierra Madre Oriental mountain range that runs from north to south down the eastern part of Mexico

isthmus strip of land that connects two landmasses

highlands mountainous and hilly sections of a country

archipelago a chain of islands

Greater Antilles the northern largest Caribbean islands that include Cuba, Jamaica, Hispaniola (which includes Haiti and the Dominican Republic), and Puerto Rico

Lesser Antilles the smaller Caribbean islands southeast of the Greater Antilles

REVIEW

plateau a broad, flat area of land higher than the surrounding land

tectonic plate a large rigid section of the Earth's crust that is in constant motion

▶ Reading Strategy

Re-create the chart shown at right. As you read and respond to the **KEY QUESTIONS**, use the chart to organize details about the geography of Mexico, Central America, and the Caribbean Islands.

 See Skillbuilder Handbook, page R7

CATEGORIZE

LANDFORMS	INFLUENCES ON CLIMATE	VEGETATION
1.	1.	1.
2.	2.	2.
3.	3.	3.

GRAPHIC ORGANIZERS
Go to **Interactive Review** @ ClassZone.com

Physical Geography of Mexico, Central America, and the Caribbean

2.01 Identify key physical characteristics such as landforms, water forms, and climate, and evaluate their influence on the development of cultures in selected South American and European regions.

3.01 Identify ways in which people of selected areas in South America and Europe have used, altered, and adapted to their environments in order to meet their needs, and evaluate the impact of their actions on the development of cultures and regions.

Connecting to Your World

What would you do if the ground started to open up as you were walking? That is what happened to a Mexican farmer in February 1943. The farmer watched in amazement as the ground rumbled and split open while he worked. Within 24 hours, a small smoking cone had appeared. The cone was the beginning of the volcano Paricutín (pah•REE•koo•TEEN).

Volcanoes are just one feature of Latin America's geography. Let's take a look at some other geographic features.

Mountains and Islands

▼ **KEY QUESTION** How is the geography of Mexico, Central America, and the Caribbean Islands alike?

The region of **Latin America** includes Mexico, Central America, the Caribbean Islands, which together make up Middle America, and South America. The Spanish and Portuguese colonized much of the region. Their languages derived from Latin, so they called the region *Latin America*. In this section, you will learn about the geography of Middle America.

Montserrat This Caribbean volcano lay dormant for 500 years, then erupted from 1995 through 1997.

Montserrat

Mexico Mexico's landforms include mountains, **plateaus**, and plains. You can see these on the map opposite. Two major mountain ranges are the **Sierra Madre Occidental Ⓐ**, located in western Mexico, and the **Sierra Madre Oriental Ⓑ**, located in eastern Mexico. Mexico sits on three large **tectonic plates**, and the movement of these plates causes earthquakes and volcanic activity.

Between the two mountain ranges lies the vast Mexican Plateau, making up about 40 percent of Mexico's land regions. Most of Mexico's people live in this area. The plateau rises about 4,000 feet above sea level in the northern part to about 8,000 feet in the southern part. Several volcanoes frame the southern edge of the plateau. East and west of the plateau, along the Gulf of Mexico and the Pacific Ocean, lie the coastal plains.

Mexico has few major rivers. Most of the rivers are not deep enough or wide enough for large boats to move through. Mexico's largest river is the Rio Grande, which is the northern border with Texas.

Sea Turtles These hawksbill sea turtles are swimming over reefs in the Caribbean Sea off the coast of the Cayman Islands.

Central America South of Mexico are the countries of Central America. Central America is an **isthmus**, a strip of land that connects two large landmasses. It connects the North and South American continents.

Highlands, the hilly sections of a country, make up most of Central America. Like Mexico, Central America lies at the edge of tectonic plates, so earthquakes occur often. A string of volcanoes, some of which are active, lines the Pacific Coast. Plains lie along both the Pacific and Caribbean coasts.

The Caribbean Islands East of Central America lie the Caribbean Islands. The islands are made up of three main parts. The Bahamas are an **archipelago**, a chain of nearly 700 islands. The **Greater Antilles Ⓒ** include the largest islands of Cuba, Jamaica, Hispaniola (which includes Haiti and the Dominican Republic), and Puerto Rico. The **Lesser Antilles Ⓓ** include the remaining smaller islands. Many of the Caribbean Islands are actually the exposed tops of underwater mountains. Mountains and highlands make up the interior of most Caribbean Islands, and plains circle the highlands.

▲ **COMPARE AND CONTRAST** Describe how the geography of Mexico, Central America, and the Caribbean Islands is alike.

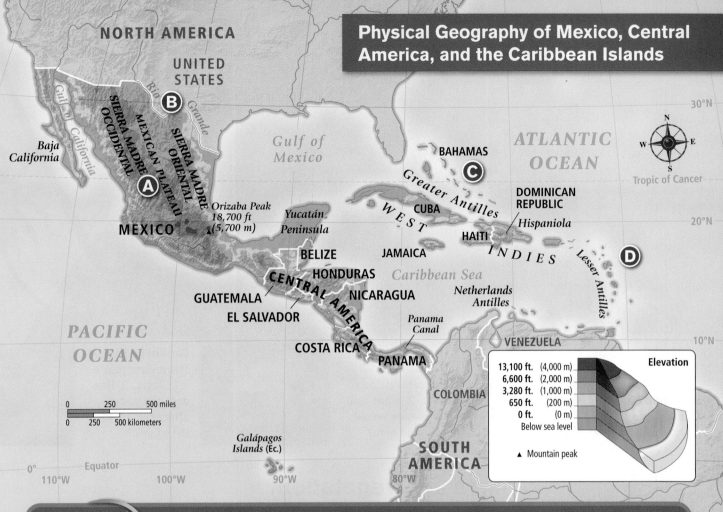

Physical Geography of Mexico, Central America, and the Caribbean Islands

NORTH AMERICA

UNITED STATES

Rio Grande

B

Baja California

SIERRA MADRE OCCIDENTAL

MEXICAN PLATEAU

SIERRA MADRE ORIENTAL

A

Gulf of California

Gulf of Mexico

BAHAMAS

C

ATLANTIC OCEAN

Greater Antilles

DOMINICAN REPUBLIC

CUBA

Hispaniola

HAITI

WEST

MEXICO

Orizaba Peak 18,700 ft (5,700 m)

Yucatán Peninsula

BELIZE

JAMAICA

INDIES

Lesser Antilles

D

HONDURAS

Caribbean Sea

GUATEMALA

CENTRAL AMERICA

NICARAGUA

Netherlands Antilles

EL SALVADOR

Panama Canal

PACIFIC OCEAN

COSTA RICA

PANAMA

VENEZUELA

COLOMBIA

Tropic of Cancer

30°N

20°N

10°N

Elevation

13,100 ft. (4,000 m)
6,600 ft. (2,000 m)
3,280 ft. (1,000 m)
650 ft. (200 m)
0 ft. (0 m)
Below sea level

▲ Mountain peak

0   250   500 miles
0   250   500 kilometers

Galápagos Islands (Ec.)

Equator

0°

110°W   100°W   90°W   80°W

SOUTH AMERICA

CONNECT ➤ Geography & Economics

Panama Canal
The Panama Canal was built by cutting through the Central American land bridge, which connected the Atlantic and Pacific oceans. Before the canal was opened in 1914, a ship bringing copper from Peru to Florida had to sail south around South America and then north. Using the canal shortened the distance and time.

- - - Route before canal (almost 14,000 mi.)
——— Route after canal (roughly 4,000 mi.)

UNITED STATES
FLORIDA
Panama Canal
PERU
SOUTH AMERICA

CRITICAL THINKING
1. **Movement** By how many miles did the canal shorten a ship's journey?
2. **Make Inferences** Why was Panama a good choice for building a canal?

COMPARING Climates

Desert Barrel cacti grow in Mexico's deserts. **1. How are these plants able to thrive in this dry climate?**

Rain Forest La Fortuna Waterfall is located in Costa Rica. **2. What kind of climate would you find here?**

Caribbean Islands This volcanic peak is in St. Lucia. **3. How does the water affect climate in the islands?**

Climate and Vegetation

▼ **KEY QUESTION** What is a major influence on the climate of the Caribbean Islands?

Latin America stretches across more than one-half of the Western Hemisphere. It has a wide variety of climates and vegetation.

Mexico About half of Mexico lies south of the tropic of Cancer. The temperatures in this part of Mexico are generally warm and constant year-round, with abundant rainfall. Tropical rain forests thrive here.

A greater variation in temperatures exists in places located north of the tropic of Cancer. The driest areas are in the deserts of northwestern Mexico, as well as in the northern part of the Mexican Plateau. Desert shrubs grow in this climate. In Mexico's mountains and highlands, average temperatures vary with increases in elevation. The vegetation here consists mostly of coniferous and deciduous forests.

Central America All of Central America is located in the tropical zone, so temperatures are generally warm year-round. The plains along the Caribbean coast receive the greatest amount of precipitation. The climate is perfect for the lush rain forests that grow there.

As in Mexico, places at higher elevations in Central America experience cooler average temperatures than those at lower elevations. Winds that blow inland from the warm Caribbean Sea bring heavy rains on the eastern side of the mountains. Places on the westward side and in the interior highlands receive the least amount of precipitation. Forests of oak and pine grow at higher elevations, while desert shrubs grow in the drier areas on the Pacific side.

The Caribbean Islands Winds play a big role in the climate of the Caribbean Islands. The waters in the Caribbean Sea stay warm most of the year and heat the air over them. Warm winds blow across the islands, keeping the temperatures warm and constant year-round. The Lesser Antilles are divided into islands that face the wind and those that are protected from the wind. Those protected from the wind receive less rain than those facing the wind.

As in Mexico and Central America, elevation influences climate in the islands' mountains. The islands' climates allow diverse vegetation, including rain forests, deciduous forests, and desert shrubs, to grow there.

 SUMMARIZE Describe the major influence on the climate of the Caribbean Islands.

Tree Frog A red-eyed tree frog, a unique animal found in Costa Rica's rain forest, hops a ride on a caiman, an alligator-like reptile.

 **ONLINE QUIZ**
For test practice, go to
Interactive Review
@ ClassZone.com

Section ① Assessment

TERMS & NAMES

1. Explain the importance of
- isthmus
- archipelago
- Greater Antilles
- Lesser Antilles

USE YOUR READING NOTES

2. Categorize Use your completed chart to answer the following question:

How does climate influence the location of rain forests in Central America?

LANDFORMS	INFLUENCES ON CLIMATE	VEGETATION
1.	1.	1.
2.	2.	2.
3.	3.	3.

KEY IDEAS

3. How did Latin America get its name?

4. Where do most people in Mexico live?

5. What affects climate in the mountains and highlands of Mexico and Central America?

CRITICAL THINKING

6. Analyze Causes and Effects How did the Panama Canal help trade in Latin America?

7. Make Generalizations What generalization can you make about climate in Mexico, Central America, and the Caribbean Islands?

8. CONNECT to Today In 1999, the United States gave control of the Panama Canal to Panama. How do you think the country of Panama will benefit from the canal?

9. WRITING Create a Poster Choose a country in Central America or one of the Caribbean Islands and prepare a captioned poster for a geography fair. Include information about the country's land, climate, and vegetation.

Reading for Understanding

▶ Key Ideas

BEFORE, YOU LEARNED

The physical geography of much of Mexico, Central America, and the Caribbean Islands consists of mountains and highlands.

NOW YOU WILL LEARN

The physical geography of South America consists of a wide variety of landforms and climates.

▶ Vocabulary

TERMS & NAMES

Andes Mountains a mountain range located on South America's west coast and extending the full length of the continent

altiplano a high plateau

llanos (YAH•nohs) grasslands of western Venezuela and northeastern Colombia

Pampas grassy plains in south-central South America

Amazon River South America's longest river (about 4,000 miles, or 6,400 kilometers) and the second-longest river in the world

REVIEW

highlands mountainous or hilly sections of a country

rain forest a broadleaf tree region in a tropical climate

Visual Vocabulary *altiplano*

▶ Reading Strategy

Re-create the diagram shown at right. As you read and respond to the **KEY QUESTIONS**, use the diagram to summarize each of the main parts of Section 2.

 See Skillbuilder Handbook, page R5

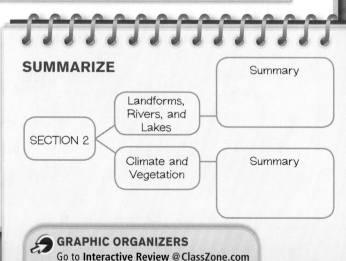

SUMMARIZE

SECTION 2

Landforms, Rivers, and Lakes → Summary

Climate and Vegetation → Summary

GRAPHIC ORGANIZERS
Go to **Interactive Review** @ ClassZone.com

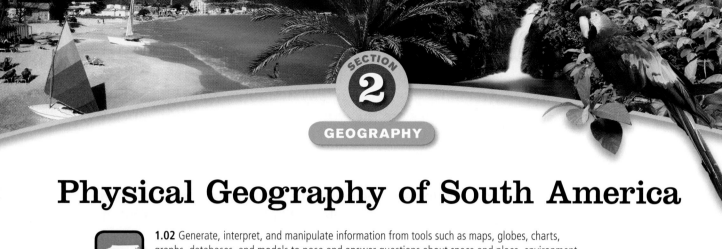

Physical Geography of South America

1.02 Generate, interpret, and manipulate information from tools such as maps, globes, charts, graphs, databases, and models to pose and answer questions about space and place, environment and society, and spatial dynamics and connections.

2.01 Identify key physical characteristics such as landforms, water forms, and climate, and evaluate their influence on the development of cultures in selected South American and European regions.

Connecting to Your World

Look carefully at a map of South America, and you will see many physical features similar to those that define North America, particularly the United States. Just as the Rocky Mountains rise in western North America, the Andes Mountains stretch the entire length of western South America. Great river systems drain both continents, and large plains are central to both North and South America. Of course, as you will soon learn, there are important differences as well.

Landforms, Rivers, and Lakes

▼ **KEY QUESTION** What are the main features of South America's landscape?

South America has nearly every type of physical feature, including mountains, grasslands, plains, and **highlands**. The continent has few large lakes but is drained by five major river systems, including the Amazon River, one of the largest rivers in the world.

Patagonia Deserts, plateaus, and highlands make up this area.

PATAGONIA

The Andes As the map on the opposite page shows, the **Andes Mountains** Ⓐ stretch along western South America for a distance of about 5,500 miles. Longer than any other mountain range above sea level, the Andes are the world's second-highest range. Only the Himalayas in Asia are higher. The tallest Andean peak, Mount Aconcagua, is the Western Hemisphere's tallest mountain. People living in the Andes grow crops on terraces cut into the mountains.

The Andes region also includes valleys and the *altiplano*, or "high plateau," shared by Peru and Bolivia. Made up of a series of basins between mountains, the *altiplano* is one of the world's highest inhabited regions. Its southern half contains important deposits of copper, silver, tungsten, and tin.

Plains and Highlands The Central Plains extend eastward from the Andes and cover about three-fifths of South America. The *llanos*, Gran Chaco, Amazon rain forest, and Pampas make up the Central Plains. The ***llanos*** (YAH•nohs) are wide grasslands that stretch across northeastern Colombia and western Venezuela. There, cattle ranches and small farms are common.

A tropical **rain forest** in the Amazon Basin Ⓑ covers about 40 percent of Brazil. The Gran Chaco is a largely uninhabited area consisting of subtropical grasslands and low forests. Nearly half of this region is located in Argentina. The remainder extends into Paraguay and Bolivia. Just south of the Gran Chaco lies a large grassy plain called the **Pampas**, Argentina's most populated area.

The Eastern Highlands are two separate regions. The Guiana Highlands Ⓒ to the north of the Amazon Basin consist of tropical forests and grasslands. The Brazilian Highlands Ⓓ to the south cover about one-fourth of South America and consist mostly of hills and plateaus.

Fun Facts!

ANGEL FALLS
Angel Falls in the Guiana Highlands of southeastern Venezuela, the world's tallest waterfall, drops 3,212 feet. The waterfall was named for Jimmy Angel, an American pilot who spotted it from his airplane in 1935.

3,000 ft.

2,000 ft.

1,000 ft.

3,212 ft.

1,450 ft.

176 ft.

Niagara Falls   Sears Tower   Angel Falls

Physical Geography of South America

Caribbean Sea

Netherlands Antilles

CENTRAL AMERICA

VENEZUELA

ATLANTIC OCEAN

Elevation

13,100 ft.	(4,000 m)
6,600 ft.	(2,000 m)
3,280 ft.	(500 m)
650 ft.	(200 m)
0 ft.	(0 m)
Below sea level	

▲ Mountain peak

Orinoco River

Ⓒ

GUYANA

GUIANA HIGHLANDS

SURINAME

FRENCH GUIANA

COLOMBIA

Llanos

Negro River

ECUADOR

AMAZON

Amazon River

Equator 0°

BASIN

Ⓑ

SOUTH

PERU

Amazon River

Madeira River

AMERICA

BRAZIL

ANDES

Mato Grosso Plateau

Araguaia River

BRAZILIAN

Ⓓ

10°S

HIGHLANDS

Ⓐ

Lake Titicaca

Altiplano

BOLIVIA

Gran Chaco

N

W E

S

Atacama Desert

PARAGUAY

Paraguay River

Tropic of Capricorn

20°S

ANDES

Paraná River

Uruguay River

PACIFIC OCEAN

ATLANTIC OCEAN

Mount Aconcagua 22,834 ft (6,960 m)

Pampas

URUGUAY

30°S

CHILE

Río de la Plata

ARGENTINA

Patagonia

0   250   500 miles

0   250   500 kilometers

Falkland Islands

CONNECT Geography & History

READING A PHYSICAL MAP

Use the key in this physical map to identify the elevations of Patagonia and the Amazon Basin.

1. **Place** What two oceans border South America?

2. **Region** Where are large areas of highlands found in South America?

Tierra del Fuego Cape Horn

Drake Passage

127

90°W   80°W   70°W   60°W   50°W   40°W   30°W   20°W   50°S

Rivers and Lakes South America has five large river systems. The largest is the Amazon river system, which carries about one-fifth of the Earth's river water. The **Amazon River** flows from the Andes to the Atlantic Ocean and is about 4,000 miles long. The river and its tributaries drain much of Brazil and Peru, as well as parts of Colombia, Ecuador, Bolivia, and Venezuela. South America's other river systems are the Rio de la Plata, the Magdalena-Cauca, the Orinoco, and the São Francisco.

South America has few large natural lakes. The largest, Lake Maracaibo in northwestern Venezuela, covers an area of more than 5,000 square miles. About two-thirds of Venezuela's total petroleum output comes from the Lake Maracaibo region. Lake Titicaca is the second largest lake in South America. Located in the altiplano at an elevation of 12,500 feet, Lake Titicaca is the world's highest navigable lake.

▲ **SUMMARIZE** List the main geographic features of South America.

Lake Maracaibo A girl uses a pole to move her boat between houses on Lake Maracaibo. **How have people living on Lake Maracaibo adapted to their environment?**

Climate and Vegetation

▼ **KEY QUESTION** What kinds of vegetation are found in the tropical and desert climates of South America?

South America has a wide range of climates—from the steamy rain forest of the Amazon Basin to the icy cold of the upper Andes. Because climate largely determines the vegetation of a region, South America has a great variety of plant life as well.

Mountain Climates The climate of the Andes Mountains changes with elevation. For example, near the equator, the climate at the lowest elevations is tropical. However, if you were to climb midway up the mountains, you would most likely find a more temperate, or mild, climate. At an elevation of more than 15,000 feet, you would encounter extremely low temperatures and icy winds. The only vegetation would be a sparse assortment of mosses, lichens, and dwarf shrubs. Climate zones at various elevations in the Andes are compared on the opposite page.

Ⓐ Guanaco (a kind of llama) in the Chilean Andes

Ⓑ Potato fields in Peru

Ⓐ **Tierra Helada (Frozen Land)**
• Above 10,000 feet
• Livestock: llamas, sheep

Ⓒ **Tierra Templada (Temperate Land)**
• 3,000–6,000 feet
• Crops: corn, cotton, coffee, citrus fruits

Ⓑ **Tierra Fría (Cold Land)**
• 6,000–10,000 feet
• Crops: wheat, apples, potatoes, barley

Ⓓ **Tierra Caliente (Hot Land)**
• Sea level–3,000 feet
• Crops: bananas, cacao, sugar cane, rice

CRITICAL THINKING
Draw Conclusions What zones are most productive for growing crops?

Ⓒ Corn fields in Ecuador

Ⓓ Sugar cane fields in Colombia

Tropical Rain Forests Much of South America lies in the low latitudes, which are tropical. There, the Amazon rain forest covers more than 2 million square miles. Located primarily in Brazil, the rain forest is bounded to the north by the Guiana Highlands, to the south by Brazil's central plateau, to the west by the Andes, and to the east by the Atlantic Ocean. The rain forest climate is hot and wet. Although the average temperature remains a fairly constant 80°F, high humidity makes it seem hotter. Rain falls throughout the year, for a yearly average of between 50 to 175 inches.

The Amazon rain forest has the world's richest collection of life forms. In fact, many of its insects, birds, and plants have yet to be named. Wildlife includes jaguars, monkeys, and manatees. Plant life is abundant. The rain forest's many varieties of trees include rosewood, Brazil nut, rubber, mahogany, and cedar.

Grasslands Located in Venezuela and Colombia, the *llanos* cover an area of about 220,000 square miles. They extend north and west to the Andes and south to the Amazon Basin. The *llanos* have a warm climate, and their rainfall averages between 45 and 180 inches.

The Pampas cover an area of about 295,000 square miles in central Argentina, and they extend into Uruguay. The grasslands are good for raising cattle, and the rich soil produces a variety of crops, particularly soybeans and wheat. In addition to being an important agricultural area, the Pampas are also home to most of Argentina's cities.

The *Llanos* Cattle graze on the *llanos* in Venezuela. **Why is this area a good place to raise cattle?**

Deserts Desert climates occur along much of Peru's coast, as well as in northern Chile's Atacama Desert and southern Argentina's Patagonian desert. Desert climates are dry, and temperatures may be hot or cold. The desert in southern Patagonia is an example of a cold desert, with temperatures averaging only about 44°F.

The Atacama Desert is warmer, with summer temperatures averaging in the mid-60s°F. Although an ocean current from the Antarctic mixes with warm air to produce clouds and fog in the Atacama Desert, there is little rain. In fact, in the center of the Atacama, no rainfall has ever been recorded. There, nothing grows. Yet in the desert's fog zones, cacti, ferns, and many other types of vegetation grow.

 CATEGORIZE Identify the kinds of vegetation found in South America's tropical and desert climates.

Jujuy Desert The Jujuy Desert is located in northwestern Argentina.

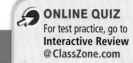 **ONLINE QUIZ**
For test practice, go to
Interactive Review
@ ClassZone.com

Section ② Assessment

TERMS & NAMES
1. Explain the importance of
- *altiplano*
- *llanos*
- Pampas
- Amazon River

USE YOUR READING NOTES
2. Summarize Use your completed chart to answer the following question:

How is Lake Maracaibo important to South America?

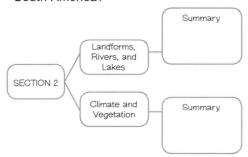

KEY IDEAS
3. What are the main river systems of South America?

4. Where are the Guiana and Brazilian Highlands located?

5. What relationship exists between elevation and climates of the Andes?

CRITICAL THINKING
6. Compare and Contrast How are the four main regions of the Central Plains different from one another?

7. Analyze Causes and Effects Why is a variety of plant life able to grow in the Atacama Desert?

8. CONNECT to Today The Amazon rain forest is a popular destination for tourists today. What features do you think attract tourists to this area?

9. ART **Create a Mural** Draw a panoramic mural of the geographic features of South America. Include the continent's landforms and waterways.

Reading for Understanding

▶ Key Ideas

BEFORE, YOU LEARNED

Latin America contains a wide variety of landforms, climates, and vegetation.

NOW YOU WILL LEARN

People adapted to these challenging geographic and climatic conditions and developed great civilizations.

▶ Vocabulary

TERMS & NAMES

Olmec an early civilization along the Gulf Coast of what is now southern Mexico

Maya an early civilization located in what is now the Yucatán Peninsula, Guatemala, and northern Belize

cultural hearth the heartland, or place of origin, of a major culture

glyph a carved or engraved symbol that stands for a syllable or a word

empire a political system in which people or lands are controlled by one ruler

Aztec an early civilization in the Valley of Mexico

chinampas artificial islands used for farming

Inca an early civilization in the Andes Mountains of Peru

REVIEW

culture the shared attitudes, knowledge, and behaviors of a group

BACKGROUND VOCABULARY

jaguar a large cat mainly found in Central and South America

Visual Vocabulary glyph

▶ Reading Strategy

Re-create the Venn diagram shown at right. As you read and respond to the **KEY QUESTIONS**, use the diagram to show how the Aztec and Inca empires were alike and different.

 Skillbuilder Handbook, page R9

COMPARE AND CONTRAST

AZTEC EMPIRE   BOTH   INCA EMPIRE

 GRAPHIC ORGANIZERS
Go to **Interactive Review** @ ClassZone.com

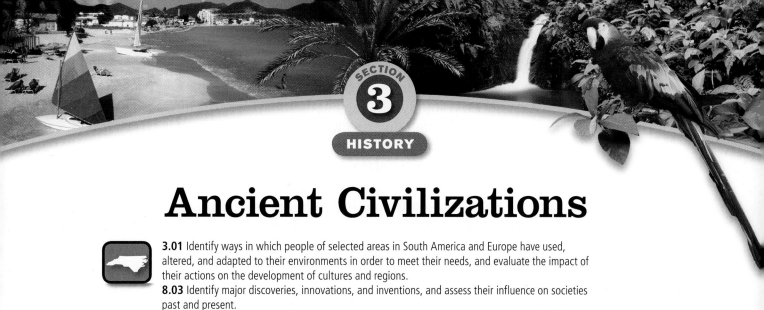

Ancient Civilizations

3.01 Identify ways in which people of selected areas in South America and Europe have used, altered, and adapted to their environments in order to meet their needs, and evaluate the impact of their actions on the development of cultures and regions.
8.03 Identify major discoveries, innovations, and inventions, and assess their influence on societies past and present.

Connecting to Your World

How do you think the stone head pictured here was made? An ancient civilization in Latin America carved these heads about 3,000 years ago. What do you think of when you hear the word *pyramid*? Most likely, you think of the pyramids built about 4,500 years ago by the ancient Egyptians. Did you know that ancient civilizations in Latin America, such as the Maya, constructed these huge structures too? As you read this section, you will find out more about the Maya and other early civilizations that thrived in what is now Latin America.

Olmec Head The Olmec carved these large heads from a stone called basalt.

The Olmec and the Maya

🔻 **KEY QUESTION** How were the Olmec and Mayan civilizations alike?

The first known civilization to develop in Latin America were the **Olmec**. They lived along the Gulf Coast of what is now southern Mexico about 3,200 years ago. Another civilization, the **Maya**, developed in the highlands and flatlands of what is now the Yucatán Peninsula, Guatemala, and northern Belize. Archaeological evidence shows that these two cultures built well-laid-out cities and complex civilizations. They were farmers, artists, and architects.

The Tikal Pyramid
The Maya built this pyramid in the rain forest of what is now Guatemala.

The Olmec, a Cultural Hearth The Olmec were traders and skilled farmers. As farming began to thrive, the Olmec could count on a steady food supply. Having enough food led to a larger population and allowed the Olmec to focus on tasks other than farming. An adequate food supply also led to the growth of cities.

Olmec cities included plazas, housing areas, and ceremonial centers. Their oldest known city is San Lorenzo. The Olmec are known for their huge stone sculptures of heads. Some sculptures show a half-human, half-animal **jaguar**, the Olmec's chief god.

The Olmec began to abandon their cities beginning around 600 B.C. for unknown reasons. However, historians consider the Olmec civilization a **cultural hearth**, the place of origin of a major **culture**. The Olmec culture shaped other cultures in the region, particularly the Maya.

CONNECT ➤ **History to Today**

A Recent Maya Discovery

In 2005, archaeologists working in Guatemala at the site of an ancient Mayan city made an exciting discovery—a stone monument with the carving of a woman's face. The carving dates back to around the A.D. 500s, making it the earliest known likeness of a woman that the Maya carved in stone. This is significant because it suggests that women had important leadership roles in Mayan society early on in Mayan history.

An archaeology student wraps the Mayan stone monument to take for further study.

The Maya, Masters of the City The Maya lived in villages in southern Mexico and northern Central America as early as 1500 B.C. At the height of their civilization, around A.D. 250, the Maya built impressive cities with stone temples, pyramids, plazas, palaces, and ball courts. They were farmers and traders. Corn, beans, and squash were important crops. The Maya also traded salt, chocolate, and cotton with other cultures.

The Maya were advanced in their knowledge of science and technology. They created a 365-day calendar by watching the stars. The calendar identified events throughout the year, such as planting times and holidays. The Maya used a mathematical system based on the number 20 and were the first people to use the zero. They also developed **glyph** writing, carved symbols that stood for a syllable or a word.

In about A.D. 900, the Maya started abandoning their cities, like the Olmec had done earlier. The reasons remain unclear. However, descendants of the Maya still live in the region today.

🔺 **COMPARE AND CONTRAST**
Explain how the Olmec and Mayan civilizations were alike and different.

Stone Carving
The drawing (right) helps to more clearly see what is carved in part of the stone monument.

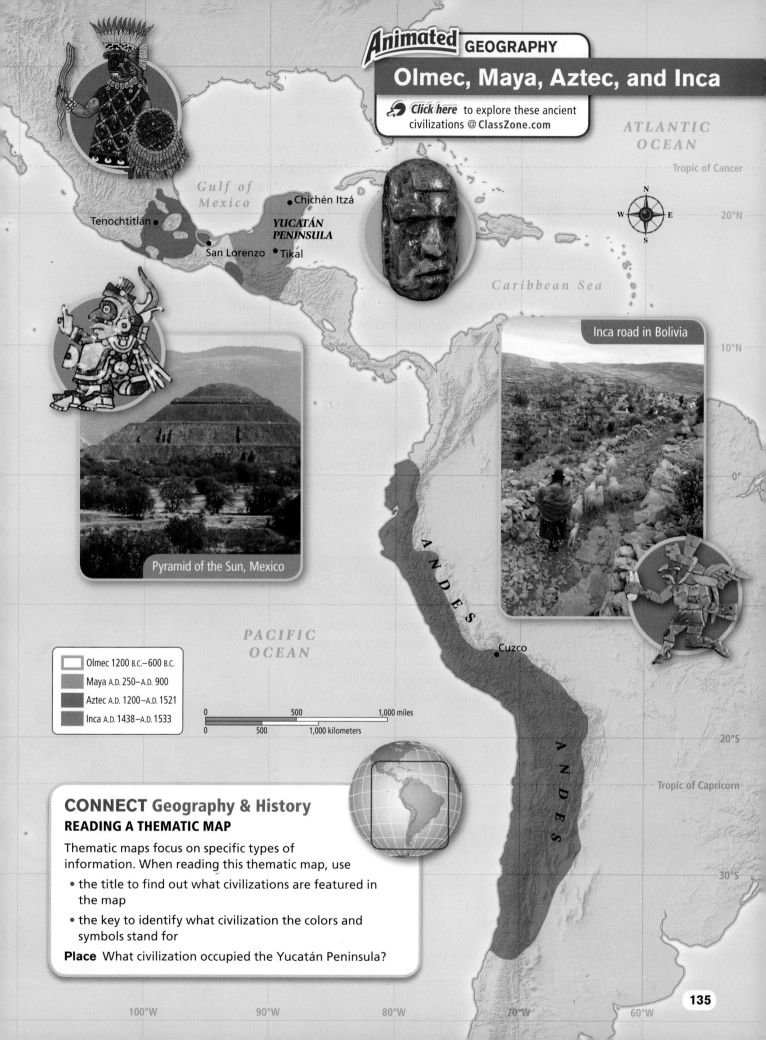

Animated GEOGRAPHY

Olmec, Maya, Aztec, and Inca

Click here to explore these ancient civilizations @ ClassZone.com

ATLANTIC OCEAN

Tropic of Cancer

20°N

Gulf of Mexico

Tenochtitlán •

• Chichén Itzá

YUCATÁN PENINSULA

San Lorenzo • • Tikál

Caribbean Sea

10°N

Inca road in Bolivia

0°

PACIFIC OCEAN

ANDES

• Cuzco

Pyramid of the Sun, Mexico

	Olmec 1200 B.C.–600 B.C.
	Maya A.D. 250–A.D. 900
	Aztec A.D. 1200–A.D. 1521
	Inca A.D. 1438–A.D. 1533

0   500   1,000 miles
0   500   1,000 kilometers

20°S

ANDES

Tropic of Capricorn

CONNECT Geography & History
READING A THEMATIC MAP

Thematic maps focus on specific types of information. When reading this thematic map, use

- the title to find out what civilizations are featured in the map
- the key to identify what civilization the colors and symbols stand for

Place What civilization occupied the Yucatán Peninsula?

30°S

100°W   90°W   80°W   70°W   60°W

135

The Aztec and the Inca

▼ **KEY QUESTION** How did the Aztec and the Inca use their environments to develop their empires?

Two great civilizations, the Aztec and the Inca, developed vast **empires**, political systems in which people or lands are controlled by one ruler. Both civilizations were very powerful in their regions until the Spanish conquered them in the 1500s.

The Aztec, a Military Culture The **Aztec** moved from northern Mexico into the Valley of Mexico and what is now Mexico City in about the A.D. 1300s. They took control of the valley in about 1428 and ruled their empire until 1521. The Aztec built a strong military empire through warfare and by collecting tribute—money, goods, or crops—from the people they defeated.

The Aztec built Tenochtitlán (teh•NOHCH•tee•TLAHN), their capital city, on an island in Lake Texcoco. The city included houses and causeways, or roads made of earth. At its height, the population reached around 300,000. A great pyramid dedicated to Huitzilopochtli, the sun and war god, stood in the center of the city. The Aztec used the watery environment around Tenochtitlán to create **chinampas**, or island gardens, to grow food and flowers.

ONLINE PRIMARY SOURCE To read more legends of the Aztec and Inca, go to **Research & Writing Center** @ ClassZone.com

ANALYZING Primary Sources

The Eagle on the Prickly Pear Why would the Aztec build a city in the middle of a swampy lake? According to legend, one of their gods predicted that they would see a prickly pear cactus with an eagle sitting on top of it. The Aztec wandered until they saw this sign. There they built Tenochtitlán, which is now Mexico City.

[A]s they passed through the reeds, there in front of them was the prickly pear with the eagle perched on top, . . . his claws punching holes in his prey. When he saw the Mexicans in the distance, he bowed to them. . . . The . . . spirit said, 'Mexicans, this is the place.' And with that they all wept. 'We are favored,' they said. 'We are blessed. We have seen where our city will be. Now let us go rest.'

Source: *The Eagle on the Prickly Pear*, retold by John Bierhorst

DOCUMENT-BASED QUESTION
How did the Aztec know where to stop to build their capital city?

Inca, Mountain Empire The **Inca** lived in the Andes Mountains in what is now Peru. They controlled a large empire from the early 1400s until 1533. The empire centered around Cuzco (KOOZ•koh), the Inca's mountain capital city. By 1500, the empire extended about 2,500 miles along the west coast of South America. The Inca built complex cities such as Machu Picchu. To farm the steep land, they cut terraces into the mountainsides, where they grew corn and potatoes. They built aqueducts, or canals, to irrigate the land. On higher areas, the Inca grazed llamas.

The Inca adapted to difficult conditions. They built 14,000 miles of roads on which runners carried messages. To keep records, they used *quipus* (KEE•poos), counting tools of knotted cords. Today's descendants of the Inca, the Quechua (KEHCH•wuh), make up about 45 percent of Peru's population. They still use terraces and aqueducts, raise corn and potatoes, and graze llamas.

 SYNTHESIZE Describe how the Inca changed their environment to develop an empire.

Machu Picchu Flowers grow on the slopes of Machu Picchu today.

Section ❸ Assessment

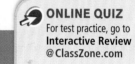 **ONLINE QUIZ**
For test practice, go to
Interactive Review
@ ClassZone.com

TERMS & NAMES

1. Explain the importance of
- Olmec
- Maya
- Aztec
- Inca

USE YOUR READING NOTES

2. Compare and Contrast Use your completed Venn diagram to answer the following question:

How were the ways the Aztec and Inca modified their environments similar?

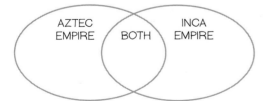

KEY IDEAS

3. What are the earliest known civilizations in what is now southern Mexico?

4. How did the Aztec build their large empire?

5. How were the Inca able to communicate throughout their large empire?

CRITICAL THINKING

6. Compare and Contrast How was the decline of the Mayan and Olmec civilizations different from the decline of the Aztec and Inca civilizations?

7. Identify Problems and Solutions What problems might an empire have in ruling millions of people?

8. CONNECT to Today Each year, around 300,000 people visit Machu Picchu. What problems do you think this presents for this archaeological site? Explain.

9. WRITING **Write a Newspaper Article** Imagine that you are a reporter visiting a city in one of the early Latin American civilizations. Write a short article that describes the city's architecture.

Latin America: Physical Geography and History **137**

Click here to enter the *chinampas* @ ClassZone.com

ISLAND GARDENS

Much of the land around Tenochtitlán, where the Aztec settled, was swampy, posing a challenge for farming. The Aztec were resourceful at adapting to their environment. They built *chinampas*, human-made islands created for planting. The rich soil allowed the Aztec to grow crops and flowers.

Click here to see how the Aztec built the *chinampas*. Learn how the Aztec used woven mats and mud from the lake to build the chinampas.

Click here to see how the Aztec lived on the *chinampas*. Learn where they lived, what they wore, and what they ate.

Click here to see how *chinampas* are used today and the problems they face.

MEXICO

Tenochtitlán

Valley
of
Mexico

Lake
Texcoco

Tenochtitlán

—— Causeways

▬ Chinampas

GeoActivity

Make a Model Work with a partner to create a small model of a *chinampa*. Apply what you have learned about how the Aztec built *chinampas* to make a model using materials similar to those the Aztec used.

Reading for Understanding

▶ Key Ideas

BEFORE, YOU LEARNED

Powerful civilizations arose in Latin America but eventually fell.

NOW YOU WILL LEARN

Life was hard, as the people of Latin America struggled to gain their independence.

▶ Vocabulary

TERMS & NAMES

Columbian Exchange the movement of plants and animals between Latin America and Europe after Columbus' voyage to the Americas in A.D. 1492

conquistador (kahn•KWIHS•tuh•DAWR) Spanish word for "conqueror"

colony overseas territory ruled by a nation

mestizo (mehs•TEE•zoh) person with mixed European and Indian ancestry

Father Hidalgo father of Mexican independence

Simón Bolívar leader for independence in northern South America

José de San Martín leader for independence in southern South America

REVIEW

empire a political system in which people or lands are controlled by one ruler

Visual Vocabulary *conquistador*

▶ Reading Strategy

Re-create the time line shown at right. As you read and respond to the **KEY QUESTIONS**, use the time line to show the events that led to independence in Mexico and countries in South America.

 See Skillbuilder Handbook, page R6

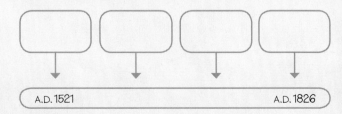

SEQUENCE EVENTS

A.D. 1521   A.D. 1826

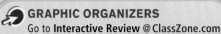

GRAPHIC ORGANIZERS
Go to **Interactive Review** @ ClassZone.com

From Colonization to Independence

7.01 Identify historical events such as invasions, conquests, and migrations and evaluate their relationship to current issues.
7.02 Examine the causes of key historical events in selected areas of South America and Europe and analyze the short- and long-range effects on political, economic, and social institutions.

Connecting to Your World

If you had lived in Europe before Christopher Columbus arrived in the Americas, you would have never enjoyed chocolate, corn, turkey, peppers, potatoes, or tomatoes. And if you had lived in the Americas, you would never have eaten oranges, bananas, beef, or pork. After the Spanish came to America, plants and animals were exchanged, or traded, between America and Europe. This came to be known as the **Columbian Exchange**.

Conquered Lands

▼ **KEY QUESTION** How did Spanish rule affect life in Latin America?

After Columbus arrived in 1492, life for the Indians changed dramatically. In 1521, a Spanish *conquistador* (kahn•KWIHS•tuh•DAWR), or conqueror, Hernán Cortés, defeated the Aztec. And in 1533 Francisco Pizarro, another Spanish *conquistador*, defeated the Inca.

The Exchange
The graphic shows the goods and diseases transferred between the two hemispheres. **What vegetables did Europeans bring to the Americas?**

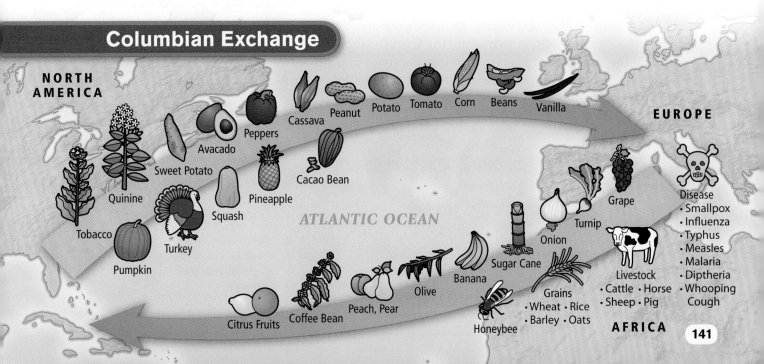

Columbian Exchange

NORTH AMERICA

EUROPE

ATLANTIC OCEAN

AFRICA

Peanut · Potato · Tomato · Corn · Beans · Vanilla
Cassava
Peppers
Avacado
Sweet Potato
Cacao Bean
Pineapple
Quinine
Squash
Turkey
Tobacco
Pumpkin

Grape
Turnip
Onion
Sugar Cane
Banana
Olive
Grains
· Wheat · Rice
· Barley · Oats
Honeybee
Coffee Bean
Peach, Pear
Citrus Fruits
Livestock
· Cattle · Horse
· Sheep · Pig

Disease
· Smallpox
· Influenza
· Typhus
· Measles
· Malaria
· Diptheria
· Whooping Cough

Colonial Rule By the mid-1500s, the Spanish had set up **colonies**, or overseas territories ruled by a nation, in various parts of Latin America. Spain's goal was to take advantage of the resources and vast lands in its new **empire**.

To rule the empire, Spain set up a class society. At the top were the *peninsulares* (peh•neen•soo•LAHR•ehs), people born in Spain. They held the high government positions. Below them were the *criollos* (kree•OH•lohs), Spaniards born in Latin America. They were often wealthy, but could not hold high government offices. These two groups controlled land, wealth, and power in the colonies.

Below the *criollos* were the **mestizos** (mehs•TEE•zohs), people of Spanish and Indian ancestry. They had little power. Finally, African enslaved persons and Indians were at the bottom and had no power.

Colonial Economy One of Spain's main purposes in creating colonies was to make Spain wealthy. To do so, Spain set up a system known as *encomienda* (ehn•koh•mee•EHN•duh). Under this system, Indians mined, ranched, and farmed for Spanish landlords. The Indians lived in poverty and hardship, essentially enslaved.

Spain, however, grew wealthy. The Spanish established huge ranches to raise cattle and sheep and large plantations to grow sugar cane, coffee, and cacao in various parts of Latin America. Spain made huge profits from the gold and silver extracted from Mexican mines.

▲ **SYNTHESIZE** Explain how life changed for people in Latin America under Spanish rule.

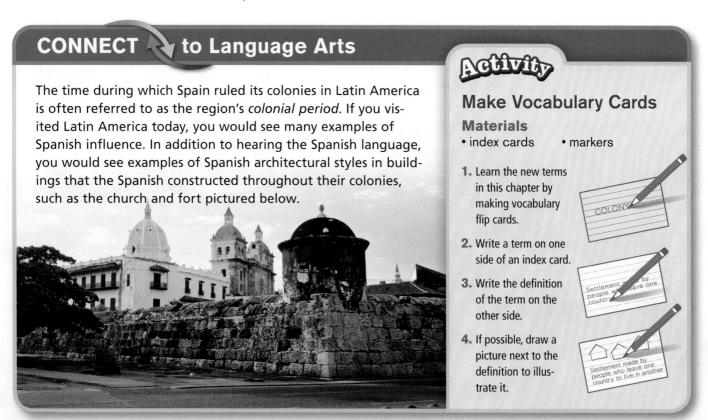

CONNECT to Language Arts

The time during which Spain ruled its colonies in Latin America is often referred to as the region's *colonial period*. If you visited Latin America today, you would see many examples of Spanish influence. In addition to hearing the Spanish language, you would see examples of Spanish architectural styles in buildings that the Spanish constructed throughout their colonies, such as the church and fort pictured below.

Activity

Make Vocabulary Cards

Materials
• index cards   • markers

1. Learn the new terms in this chapter by making vocabulary flip cards.

2. Write a term on one side of an index card.

3. Write the definition of the term on the other side.

4. If possible, draw a picture next to the definition to illustrate it.

COLONY

Settlement made by people who leave one country

Settlement made by people who leave one country to live in another

Independence from the Spanish

▼ **KEY QUESTION** What events led to independence in Mexico and South America?

In the 1800s, Spain began paying less attention to its Latin American colonies because it was fighting a war in Europe against Napoleon. Various groups in Latin America saw a chance to gain their freedom. The *criollos* and *mestizos* began to organize an independence movement. They called upon the Indians and enslaved persons to join their rebellion. By 1826, all of Latin America, except Cuba and Puerto Rico, became independent.

Mexico's Path to Independence In the late 1700s and early 1800s, freedom was in the air. The people of Mexico had heard about the American Revolution of 1776 and the French Revolution of 1789. The rights of all people were being talked about around the world. Many people in Mexico became excited by these ideas. They wanted their independence from Spain.

The first step toward independence happened in 1810 in a small village in north central Mexico. **Father Hidalgo**, a priest in the village, called on the people to rebel against Spain. The rebellion failed, however, and Father Hidalgo was captured and executed by the Spanish.

A new leader took Father Hidalgo's place. José María Morelos y Pavón also organized an army to fight the Spanish. He and other revolutionaries declared Mexico's independence in 1813. However, the Spanish defeated Morelos, and he was executed in 1815.

In 1821, the revolutionaries made a plan to win the support of all the groups in Mexico. The plan guaranteed independence, freedom of religion, and equality. Spain then declared Mexico independent with the Treaty of Cordoba in August 1821.

Mexico's struggle for independence lasted 11 years. But Mexico still had hard times ahead. You will learn more about Mexico's struggle toward democracy in the next chapter.

HISTORY MAKERS

Father Miguel Hidalgo
1753–1811

Father Hidalgo, a priest in the village of Dolores, sympathized with the Indians and *mestizos* and joined a secret society to work for Mexican independence. On September 16, 1810, Father Hidalgo rang the church bell in Dolores and urged his parishioners to fight for freedom. Thousands joined his army, but with clubs and farm tools as weapons, they were no match against the Spanish soldiers.

Today, Father Hidalgo is known as the father of Mexican independence. To honor him, Mexican Independence Day is celebrated on September 16.

 ONLINE BIOGRAPHY
For more on the life of Father Hidalgo, go to the **Research & Writing Center @ ClassZone.com**

Independence for South America Just as they did in Mexico, the American and French revolutions had inspired dreams of freedom among people throughout South America. Beginning in 1810, two leaders led the fight for independence from Spain.

Simón Bolívar, a Venezuelan general, led the fight in the northern part of South America. To honor his efforts, South Americans call him "the Liberator." **José de San Martín**, an Argentine general, led the fight for independence in the southern part of South America. By 1825, nearly all of South America was free from Spanish rule.

Brazil, a Portuguese colony, also gained independence at this time. When Brazilians demanded independence in 1822, Dom Pedro, the son of the Portuguese king, declared Brazil independent and made himself emperor. You will read more about Brazil in a later chapter.

 SUMMARIZE Discuss the events that led to independence in Mexico and South America.

CONNECT History & Economics

Coffee

Coffee was first grown in Africa. European colonists brought coffee trees, like those shown in the illustration below, to the Americas in the Columbian Exchange. Brazil and Colombia, along with the rest of Latin America, produce two-thirds of the world's coffee.

 **ONLINE QUIZ** For test practice, go to **Interactive Review** @ ClassZone.com

Section 4 Assessment

TERMS & NAMES

1. Explain the importance of
- Columbian Exchange
- *conquistador*
- colony
- *mestizo*

USE YOUR READING NOTES

2. Sequence Events Use your time line to answer the following question:

How long was much of Latin America under Spanish rule?

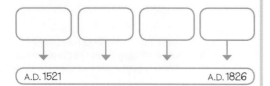

A.D. 1521   A.D. 1826

KEY IDEAS

3. Why were the *mestizos* important in Mexico's fight for independence?

4. Who was Father Hidalgo and why was he important?

5. How did most of South America gain its independence?

CRITICAL THINKING

6. Analyze Causes and Effects Why did Mexicans decide to fight for independence from Spain?

7. Evaluate What geographical challenges did South Americans have in their fight for independence?

8. (CONNECT to Today) What problems from the colonial days might still affect people in Latin America today?

9. (TECHNOLOGY) Write a Biography Use the Internet to find more information about one of the leaders for independence in Latin America discussed in this section. Then use a word processor to write a brief biography of that individual.

Click here to complete these and other activities online @ ClassZone.com

CHAPTER SUMMARY

Key Idea 1
The geography of Mexico, Central America, and the Caribbean Islands contains mountains, highlands, and plains.

Key Idea 2
The physical geography of South America consists of a wide variety of landforms and climates.

Key Idea 3
People adapted to these challenging geographic and climatic conditions and developed great civilizations.

Key Idea 4
Life under the conquerors was hard, as the people of Latin America struggled to gain their independence.

For **Review and Study Notes**, go to **Interactive Review** @ ClassZone.com

NAME GAME

Use the Terms & Names list to complete each sentence on paper or online.

1. I am built to make farming on mountainsides easier. **terrace** _____
2. I am the civilization that built a vast empire in Peru. _____
3. I am a large plain in Argentina. _____
4. I am the civilization that is considered the cultural hearth of southern Mexico. _____
5. I am the father of Mexican independence. _____
6. I am a large region that includes Mexico, Central and South America, and the Caribbean Islands. _____
7. I allowed plants, animals, and ideas to be traded between Europe and the Americas. _____
8. I am the large islands in the Caribbean Sea. _____
9. I am a landform on which the Panama Canal is located. _____
10. I am the place on which the Aztec grew food and flowers. _____

chinampas
Columbian Exchange
Father Hidalgo
Greater Antilles
Inca
isthmus
Latin America
Lesser Antilles
Olmec
Pampas
Simón Bolívar
terrace

Activities

GeoGame

Use this online map to show what you know about present-day Latin America. Click and drag each place name to its location on the map.

To play the complete game, go to **Interactive Review** @ClassZone.com

Crossword Puzzle

Complete an online crossword puzzle to test your knowledge of the geography and history of Latin America.

ACROSS
1. Mayan writing—a carved symbol that stands for a syllable or word

VOCABULARY

Explain the significance of each of the following.

1. Latin America
2. isthmus
3. Andes Mountains
4. Pampas
5. Amazon River
6. Aztec
7. Inca
8. *chinampas*
9. *mestizo*
10. Simón Bolívar

Explain how the terms and names in each group are related.

11. Olmec, Maya, and Aztec
12. Pampas, Andes Mountains, and Amazon River

KEY IDEAS

1 **Physical Geography of Mexico, Central America, and the Caribbean**

13. Why are Mexico, Central and South America, and the Caribbean Islands called Latin America?
14. What are two mountain ranges in Mexico?
15. Why is Central America's climate warm year-round?

2 **Physical Geography of South America**

16. Where is the world's largest tropical rain forest?
17. What is the largest river system in South America?
18. What affects climate in the Andes Mountains?

3 **Ancient Civilizations**

19. Where was the Mayan civilization located?
20. What features did Tenochtitlán have?
21. How did the Inca keep records?

4 **From Colonization to Independence**

22. Who defeated the Aztec and Inca empires?
23. Who were the *mestizos* and why are they important?
24. How did most South American countries become independent?

CRITICAL THINKING

25. **Compare and Contrast** Create a table to compare and contrast the landforms, farming methods, and building methods in the Aztec and Inca empires.

AZTEC	INCA

26. **Analyze Causes and Effects** How did the lives of Indians change after the Spanish conquered them?
27. **Identify Problems and Solutions** How might the Spanish have prevented rebellion?
28. **Connect to Economics** How did the *encomienda* system prevent the Mexican economy from being open to all people?
29. **Five Themes: Human-Environment Interaction** How did the Aztec and Inca use technology to change the environment?
30. **Make Inferences** What problems did Latin Americans likely face after independence?

Answer the ESSENTIAL QUESTION

How have Latin America's geography and resources helped shape its history?

Written response Write a two- or three-paragraph response to the Essential Question. Be sure to consider the key ideas of each section as well as specific details about how geography affected ancient civilizations. Use the rubric to guide your thinking.

Response Rubric
A strong response will:
- discuss the geographic features in one region
- summarize how the geography affected the history of the region's people

STANDARDS-BASED ASSESSMENT

SECONDARY SOURCE

Use context clues in the paragraph below to answer questions 1 and 2.

> The full knowledge of the Maya calendar must have been guarded . . . by the ruling elite, since it was undoubtedly a source of great power. . . . One might assume, however, that even the poorest farmer had some knowledge of the basic system, by which to guide his family's daily life.
>
> Source: *The Ancient Maya*, by Robert J. Sharer

1. What is the most likely reason that the ruling elite guarded knowledge of the calendar?

A. They did not want the farmers to be confused.

B. They wanted to stop other people from stealing the calendar.

C. They believed the knowledge gave them power over others.

D. They didn't want others to use the knowledge against them.

2. What statement does the paragraph support?

A. The Maya did not know about the calendar.

B. Most Maya had some knowledge of the calendar.

C. Most Maya did not care about the calendar.

D. The ruling elite wanted everyone to know about the calendar.

LINE GRAPH

Use the line graph below to answer questions 3 and 4 on your paper.

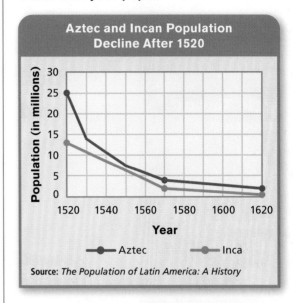

Aztec and Incan Population Decline After 1520

Source: *The Population of Latin America: A History*

3. Between what years did the Aztec population show the sharpest decline?

4. What was the Inca population in 1520? In 1620?

1. INTERDISCIPLINARY ACTIVITY–DRAMA

With a small group, find another legend from the ancient civilizations of Latin America, such as the Aztec legend about the volcano Popocatépetl. Create a skit of the legend to present to the class.

2. WRITING FOR SOCIAL STUDIES

Reread the part of Section 2 about Tenochtitlán. Imagine that you are visiting the city. Write a letter to a friend telling about your visit. Describe the features of the city and give your impression of it.

3. MENTAL MAPPING

Create an outline map of Latin America and label the following:

• Mexico
• Mexico City
• Central America
• Panama Canal
• Greater Antilles
• Lesser Antilles
• South America
• Amazon River

CHAPTER 6 Mexico

ESSENTIAL QUESTION

How does Mexico reflect both ancient traditions and the challenges of the modern world?

① HISTORY & GOVERNMENT

A Struggle Toward Democracy

② CULTURE

A Blend of Traditions

③ GOVERNMENT & ECONOMICS

Creating a New Economy

CONNECT → **Geography & History**

Use the map and the time line to answer the following questions.

1. What Mexican states are located on a peninsula on the Pacific Coast?
2. What was one result of the Mexican Revolution?

1848

History
◄ **1864** Napoleon appoints Maximilian as Emperor of Mexico.
(Maximilian)

Geography
1848 Mexico signs treaty of Guadalupe Hidalgo and loses territory to the United States.

Economics
1917 New constitution redistributes land more equally among the people.

History
◄ **1910** Mexican Revolution begins.

Animated GEOGRAPHY
Present-Day Mexico

Click here to explore Mexico
@ ClassZone.com

UNITED STATES

Tijuana

BAJA CALIFORNIA

Ciudad Juárez

SONORA

CHIHUAHUA

Rio Grande

COAHUILA

BAJA CALIFORNIA SUR

Gulf of California (Sea of Cortez)

NUEVO LEÓN

Monterrey

Gulf of Mexico

DURANGO

SINALOA

ZACATECAS

TAMAULIPAS

Tropic of Cancer

AGUASCALIENTES

SAN LUIS POTOSÍ

QUERÉTARO

NAYARIT

León

TLAXCALA

YUCATÁN

Guadalajara

GUANAJUATO

HIDALGO

JALISCO

Mexico City
MÉXICO

VERACRUZ

QUINTANA ROO

Bay of Campeche

CAMPECHE

COLIMA

Puebla

MICHOACÁN

PUEBLA

TABASCO

BELIZE

PACIFIC OCEAN

DISTRITO FEDERAL

GUERRERO

OAXACA

CHIAPAS

MORELOS

Gulf of Tehuantepec

GUATEMALA

HONDURAS

★ National capital
• Other city

0   150   300 miles
0   150   300 kilometers

N W E S

Government

▲ **1929** The Institutional Revolutionary Party (Partido Revolucionario Institucional, or PRI) comes to power.

Culture

1990 Octavio Paz wins Nobel Prize for Literature.

Economics

1992 Mexico signs the North American Free Trade Agreement (NAFTA).

Today

Government

◀ **2000** Vicente Fox is elected president of Mexico.

149

Reading for Understanding

▶ Key Ideas

BEFORE, YOU LEARNED

Mexico rebelled against colonial rule and gained its independence from Spain in 1821.

NOW YOU WILL LEARN

Mexico had to overcome many obstacles as the country moved toward establishing a democracy.

▶ Vocabulary

TERMS & NAMES

Antonio López de Santa Anna (1794–1876) Mexican general, president, and leader of Mexican independence from Spain

Republic of Texas constitutional government of Texas after independence from Mexico

annex to add to an existing territory

cession surrendered territory

Benito Juárez (1806–1872) Indian who became president and a Mexican national hero

Mexican Revolution a fight for reforms in Mexico from 1910 to 1920

Constitution of 1917 Mexican constitution written during the revolution that is still in effect today

Vicente Fox Mexican president from the National Action Party who was elected in 2000

REVIEW

constitution a formal plan of government

revolution the overthrow of a ruler or government; a major change in ideas

▶ Reading Strategy

Re-create the chart shown at right. As you read and respond to the **KEY QUESTIONS**, look for the effects of the causes that are listed.

 See Skillbuilder Handbook, page R8

ANALYZE CAUSES AND EFFECTS

CAUSES	EFFECTS
Mexico and the United States could not agree on the border of Texas.	
Benito Juárez instituted a new constitution in 1857.	
Huge gap existed between rich and poor; most Mexicans did not own land.	
The Constitution of 1917 was created.	

 GRAPHIC ORGANIZERS
Go to **Interactive Review** @ClassZone.com

SECTION

1

HISTORY & GOVERNMENT

A Struggle Toward Democracy

1.02 Generate, interpret, and manipulate information from tools such as maps, globes, charts, graphs, databases, and models to pose and answer questions about space and place, environment and society, and spatial dynamics and connections.

8.01 Describe the role of key historical figures and evaluate their impact on past and present societies in South America and Europe.

Connecting to Your World

Think what an important part George Washington played in the U.S. fight for independence from Britain. In Mexican history, General **Antonio López de Santa Anna** played a key role in Mexico's fight for independence from Spain. He served as both a soldier and a president. As president, however, Santa Anna was not able to establish a secure government. Several factors made it difficult for the Mexican people to create a stable government.

Santa Anna

War and Reform

🔻 **KEY QUESTION** What challenges did Mexico have in establishing a stable government?

During Spanish rule, Mexicans had little control over their lives. Spain made many decisions for Mexico. As a result, after gaining independence in 1821, Mexico had trouble establishing a stable government. The Mexican people had no experience in governing themselves, and the nation had a weak economy. Invasion by foreign countries also prevented Mexico from establishing a strong government.

Reform Demands Protests, pictured in this mural by David Siquieros, led to the Mexican Revolution.

The Mexican War Until 1848, Mexican territory included what is now the southwestern part of the United States. In the early 1800s, few Mexicans lived there. To increase the population, Mexico encouraged settlers from the United States to move to Texas. To get land, the settlers had to follow Mexican law and pay a small fee.

Soon, the American settlers wanted more independence. When the Mexican government refused to grant independence, Texans revolted and broke away from Mexico. Santa Anna and his troops won early victories against the Texans, including the Battle of the Alamo in San Antonio, but eventually they were defeated at the Battle of San Jacinto in 1836. That same year, Santa Anna signed a treaty granting Texas independence, and the **Republic of Texas** was established.

Mexico faced another problem when the United States **annexed**, or added, Texas in 1845. The United States and Mexico could not agree on the southern boundary of Texas. By 1846, the dispute led to a war that lasted two years. Then in 1848, Mexico and the United States signed the Treaty of Guadalupe Hidalgo. As a result of this treaty, Mexico's surrendered territory, or **cession**, included the northern half of what was once Mexico.

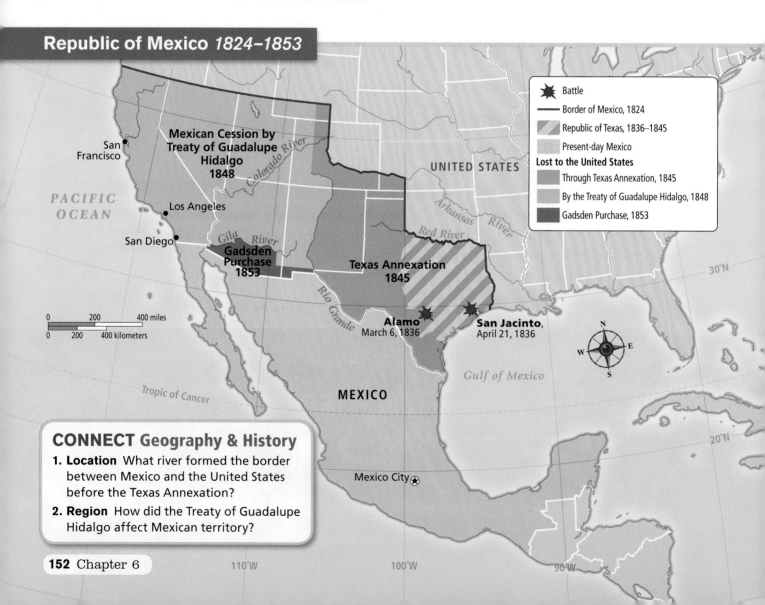

Republic of Mexico *1824–1853*

Legend:
- ✴ Battle
- — Border of Mexico, 1824
- Republic of Texas, 1836–1845
- Present-day Mexico
- **Lost to the United States**
- Through Texas Annexation, 1845
- By the Treaty of Guadalupe Hidalgo, 1848
- Gadsden Purchase, 1853

Mexican Cession by Treaty of Guadalupe Hidalgo 1848

San Francisco

PACIFIC OCEAN

Los Angeles

San Diego

Gila River

Gadsden Purchase 1853

Colorado River

UNITED STATES

Arkansas River

Red River

Texas Annexation 1845

Rio Grande

Alamo, March 6, 1836

San Jacinto, April 21, 1836

30°N

Gulf of Mexico

20°N

Tropic of Cancer

MEXICO

0   200   400 miles
0   200   400 kilometers

Mexico City ✪

CONNECT Geography & History

1. **Location** What river formed the border between Mexico and the United States before the Texas Annexation?

2. **Region** How did the Treaty of Guadalupe Hidalgo affect Mexican territory?

110°W   100°W   90°W

Fight for Reforms The Mexican War drained Mexico's economy and left the government in disorder. After the war, two groups within the country, the liberals and conservatives, struggled for power.

Conservatives consisted of Mexico's rich landowners and military leaders. The liberals generally consisted of the nation's poor, landless people. A liberal leader, **Benito Juárez**, greatly influenced Mexican politics at this time. He led a reform movement that resulted in a new **constitution** in 1857. Among other things, the constitution guaranteed freedom of speech and called for a federal system of government. But it did not make Catholicism the official religion, as many church officials wanted. Juárez and other reformers fought against the opponents of the constitution. This struggle left Mexico weak and open to foreign invasion.

France, Spain, and Britain sent forces to Mexico in 1861. France captured Mexico City in 1863 and named Maximilian, a European nobleman, as emperor of Mexico. His rule ended when the Mexican people overthrew and executed him. Juárez, who had been elected president in 1861, returned to that office until his death in 1872.

 ANALYZE CAUSES AND EFFECTS Explain why establishing a stable government was difficult in Mexico.

HISTORY MAKERS

Benito Juárez 1806–1872

Benito Juárez, an Indian, was born in Oaxaca (wuh•HAH•kuh), where he received a law degree in 1831. Politics became Juárez's life, and he served in many capacities, including governor of Oaxaca and president of Mexico. His work for fairness and equality made Juárez a hero in the eyes of many Mexican people.

ONLINE BIOGRAPHY
For more on the life of Benito Juárez, go to the **Research & Writing Center** @ ClassZone.com

Revolution and Constitutional Change

▼ **KEY QUESTION** Why was the election of President Vicente Fox significant?

After Juárez's death, the reform movement weakened. Juárez's successors were more interested in developing the economy than in reform. They believed in government controlled by a small group.

In 1876, General Porfirio Díaz became dictator. Unlike Juárez, he gave land, power, or favors to anyone who supported him. Those who did not support him were shut out of power. By 1910, the gap between the rich and poor had grown huge. Just one percent of landowners controlled more than 90 percent of the land. Most Mexicans owned no land at all. This gap set the stage for the Mexican Revolution.

The Mexican Revolution By 1910, Mexicans from various walks of life were protesting Díaz's rule and calling for reforms. Farmers wanted land, and workers wanted fair wages and better working conditions.

The **Mexican Revolution** began when Francisco Madero, a wealthy rancher, called for a **revolution** to defeat Díaz. Leaders arose in different parts of Mexico and gathered their own armies. Emiliano Zapata led an army in southern Mexico and fought for land ownership for poor farmers. Pancho Villa led forces in northern Mexico. He became popular for his policy of stealing from the rich to give to the poor. Madero became president, but was soon overthrown. The fighting among the various Mexican groups for control of the government continued, turning the Revolution into a civil war. By the time it was over in 1920, more than one million Mexicans had been killed.

CONNECT — Geography & History

Pancho Villa: Knowing the Land

Pancho Villa's knowledge of northern Mexico's geography helped him to avoid being captured by the U.S. army. In 1916, Villa, angry over U.S. involvement in the Mexican Revolution, led an attack in Columbus, New Mexico, in which 18 U.S. citizens were killed. The United States sent soldiers to capture Villa, but Villa's knowledge of the land and his popularity helped him elude the U.S. army.

New Constitution The **Constitution of 1917** was adopted during the revolution to meet the demands of Mexico's various groups and regions. Land reform was the central issue. Eventually, the government redistributed nearly half of Mexico's farmland to poor people. Millions of acres of farmland were divided into *ejidos* (eh•HEE•thaws), community farms owned by villagers. The constitution also brought about changes regarding workers' rights and the relationship of the government and the Church. The Constitution of 1917 is still in effect in Mexico today.

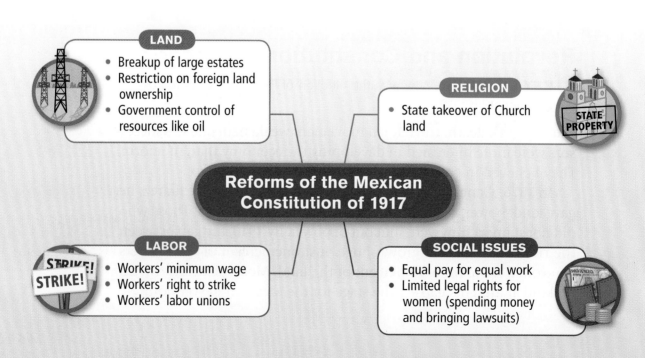

LAND
- Breakup of large estates
- Restriction on foreign land ownership
- Government control of resources like oil

RELIGION
- State takeover of Church land

STATE PROPERTY

Reforms of the Mexican Constitution of 1917

LABOR
STRIKE! STRIKE!
- Workers' minimum wage
- Workers' right to strike
- Workers' labor unions

SOCIAL ISSUES
- Equal pay for equal work
- Limited legal rights for women (spending money and bringing lawsuits)

Democratic Rule In the 1920s, one political party came to power by making peace among the various armies. Today it is called the Institutional Revolutionary Party (Partido Revolucionario Institucional, or PRI). The party controlled the government from 1929 until 2000. It helped introduce elements of democracy and stability to Mexico. But the party often blocked opposition to its policies and was accused of corruption.

In 2000, **Vicente Fox**, a member of the National Action Party (Partido Acción Nacional, or PAN), was elected president. His election signaled Mexico's move toward a multiparty democracy. In 2006, Felipe Calderon, also a member of PAN, won the presidential election. Today, besides PRI and PAN, there are at least five other political parties in Mexico.

Today, Mexico is a democracy organized much like the U.S. government. Mexico is a federal republic made up of 31 states and a federal district. Mexico also has three branches of government. But the Mexican president has more control than the U.S. president.

Campaign Rally Supporters take part in an election rally for PAN in June 2000.

 MAKE INFERENCES Explain the significance of the election of Vicente Fox as Mexico's president.

Section 1 Assessment

ONLINE QUIZ
For test practice, go to
Interactive Review
@ ClassZone.com

TERMS & NAMES

1. Explain the importance of
- Antonio López de Santa Anna
- Benito Juárez
- Constitution of 1917
- Vicente Fox

USE YOUR READING NOTES

2. Analyze Causes and Effects Use your completed chart to answer the following question:

What effect did the Constitution of 1857 have on Mexico?

CAUSES	EFFECTS
Mexico and the United States could not agree on the border of Texas.	
Benito Juárez instituted a new constitution in 1857.	
Huge gap existed between rich and poor; most Mexicans did not own land.	
The Constitution of 1917 is created.	

KEY IDEAS

3. What dispute led to war between Mexico and the United States?

4. Why was the Mexican Revolution fought among different groups?

5. How did the Constitution of 1917 help farmers?

CRITICAL THINKING

6. Analyze Points of View Before 1910, how did different groups in Mexico view the need for reform?

7. Make Inferences Why do you think that Benito Juárez's background might have led him to support reform in Mexico?

8. CONNECT to Today How might having more than one political party benefit Mexico today?

9. TECHNOLOGY Use the Internet Find out more about a political leader mentioned in this lesson by using the Internet. Then prepare a bulleted list of the top five most interesting facts about the person.

Reading for Understanding

SECTION 2

▶ Key Ideas

BEFORE, YOU LEARNED

Mexico's history reflects the impact of ancient civilizations, colonial powers, and the modern world.

NOW YOU WILL LEARN

These three influences affect the culture and daily lives of the Mexican people.

▶ Vocabulary

TERMS & NAMES

Plaza of the Three Cultures plaza in Mexico City that shows parts of Aztec, Spanish, and modern influences in Mexico

colonia a neighborhood in Mexico

squatter person who settles on unoccupied land without having legal claim to it

mural a wall painting

Diego Rivera famous muralist who painted the history of Mexico on the walls of the National Palace

fiesta a holiday celebrated with parades, games, and food

Day of the Dead holiday to remember loved ones who have died

REVIEW

urban having to do with a city

rural having to do with the countryside

push factor a reason that causes people to leave an area

Visual Vocabulary fiesta

▶ Reading Strategy

Re-create the chart shown at right. As you read and respond to the **KEY QUESTIONS**, use the chart to summarize each of the main sections of Section 2.

 See Skillbuilder Handbook, page R5

SUMMARIZE

SECTION	SUMMARY
People and Lifestyle	
Mexico's Great Murals	
Celebrations and Sports	

 GRAPHIC ORGANIZERS
Go to **Interactive Review** @ ClassZone.com

A Blend of Traditions

4.01 Describe the patterns of and motives for the migrations of people, and evaluate their impact on the political, economic, and social development of selected societies and regions.
12.02 Describe the relationship between cultural values of selected societies of South America and Europe and their art, architecture, music and literature, and assess their significance in contemporary culture.

Connecting to Your World

When you look around your community, do you see the influences of different cultures? Are there places that date back many years and places that are modern? Mexico today reflects a blend of different cultures, both traditional and modern. The **Plaza of the Three Cultures** in Mexico City displays this blend. The plaza contains the ruins of an Aztec city, a Spanish colonial church, and modern government buildings. Other parts of life in Mexico also reflect these influences.

People and Lifestyle

▼ **KEY QUESTION** How do urban and rural life in Mexico differ?

Mexico today is a living blend of Indian, Spanish, and modern influences. The majority of Mexican people are *mestizos*. Almost all Mexicans speak Spanish, the nation's official language. Many Mexican Indians also speak their Indian languages, such as Maya and Náhuatl. Most Mexicans are Roman Catholics, but some belong to other religions.

The Plaza of the Three Cultures This plaza in Mexico City reflects the influences of the Aztec, Spanish, and modern cultures.

Spanish colonial cathedral

Modern-day apartments

Ruins of Aztec temple

City and Country Life Today, over three-fourths of Mexico's people live in **urban** areas. More than 22 million people live in and around Mexico City, making it one of the largest cities in the world. Mexican cities include high-rise office buildings and modern apartment buildings, as well as older houses built in the Spanish colonial style.

The cities' neighborhoods are called *colonias*. Wealthy people generally live in prosperous neighborhoods, away from the city center. Poorer people live closer to the center of the city, sometimes in neighborhoods with unpaved streets and no running water. Some people work in factories or as street vendors, but many are unemployed.

In contrast to city life, people in Mexico's **rural** areas live in villages or on farms, near their fields. Homes are small, often having only one room and a dirt floor. Rural areas have few health-care services, roads, and schools. The Mexican government is working to improve the public services in rural areas.

The poor conditions in the rural areas are the **push factors** that cause people to move to cities. But once there, they become **squatters**, people who settle on unoccupied land without having legal claim to it. Over time, these areas develop into new *colonias*. Some rural Mexicans migrate to other countries, including the United States.

◄ COMPARING ► Urban and Rural Life

URBAN

- Densely populated; about 75% of the population
- Primary schools, secondary schools, and universities
- Major source of energy is electricity
- Clothes similar to those worn in the United States; bought in stores

RURAL

- Less densely populated; about 25% of the population
- Primary schools; almost no secondary schools; no universities
- Major source of energy is firewood
- Clothes often traditional; sometimes homemade

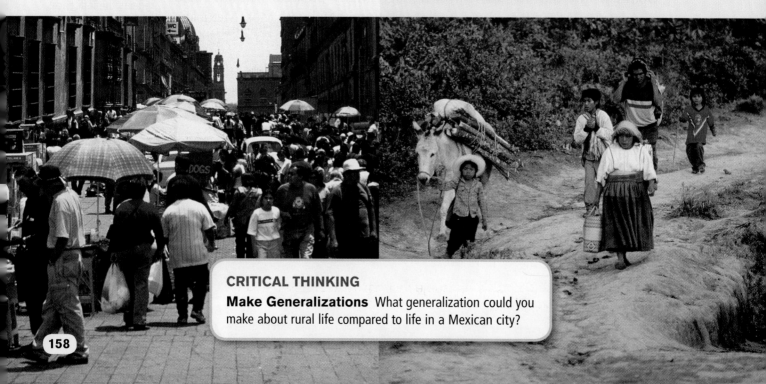

CRITICAL THINKING

Make Generalizations What generalization could you make about rural life compared to life in a Mexican city?

Family Life Family life is important in Mexico. In some families, several generations of family members may live together. Older members of the family are honored. Children are taught to respect adults.

The social life of many Mexicans centers on the family. Families gather together to celebrate birthdays and other kinds of holidays.

Mexican children are required to attend school for nine years—six years of primary school and three years of middle school. Some continue their education in a three-year high school and then a university. In some rural areas, students attend classes in one-room schools. They often travel to nearby towns to go to middle school or high school.

▲ **COMPARE AND CONTRAST** Describe the differences between urban and rural life in Mexico.

Mexico's Great Murals

▼ **KEY QUESTION** What common subjects do Mexican artists and writers focus on in their works?

Creating art has a long history in Mexico. The Olmec carved sculptures. The Aztec wrote music and poetry. The Maya created paintings in their pyramids and the Spanish in their colonial churches. Mexican art today blends these influences.

After the Mexican Revolution, Mexican art experienced a great awakening. Just as ancient artists had created paintings on their pyramids, Mexican artists created **murals**, or wall paintings, that often depicted scenes from Mexico's history. Many important painters portrayed such scenes on murals in Mexico's public buildings. The most famous Mexican muralists are José Orozco, David Siquieros, and **Diego Rivera**. Frida Kahlo, another important Mexican painter, is known for paintings that show her personal feelings about events in her life.

Self-portrait with Monkey Frida Kahlo is known for her self-portraits. Monkeys and other animals roamed the gardens around her home and were often included in her artwork.

Mexican writers have often written about Mexico's social and political problems. Octavio Paz, Carlos Fuentes, and Laura Esquivel are three well-known Mexican writers. Paz won the 1990 Nobel Prize for Literature; he was the first Mexican to win this award. Fuentes writes novels about Mexican history. In one popular novel, Esquivel described life for rural Mexican women during the Mexican Revolution.

▲ **SUMMARIZE** Describe the subjects that Mexican artists and writers focus on in their works.

Celebrations and Sports

🔻 **KEY QUESTION** What kinds of holidays do Mexicans celebrate?

Mexicans celebrate many holidays and events with a fiesta. A **fiesta** is a celebration with fireworks, parades, music, dancing, and foods. At some fiestas, children enjoy themselves by trying to break open a piñata. A piñata is a decorated container filled with candy and toys, usually hung from the ceiling. Children are blindfolded and given a stick to break open the piñata and gather its treats. Fiestas bring people together to have fun.

Celebrations Mexicans celebrate Mexico's Independence Day on September 16. Mexicans also celebrate *Cinco de Mayo* (May 5), which is the day in 1862 when the Mexican army defeated the French.

Mexicans celebrate religious holidays such as Easter with church services and processions. They celebrate the **Day of the Dead** on November 1 and 2 to honor family members who have died.

La Quinceañera is a celebration of a Mexican girl's 15th birthday. The girl dresses in a full-length gown. She first takes part in church services with family and friends. After church, everyone goes to a reception where a huge fiesta takes place.

Fun Facts!

PIÑATAS

Piñatas are part of many Mexican fiestas. But where did piñatas come from? Some historians believe Marco Polo brought them from China to Italy in the 1200s. The Spanish brought them to Spain and then introduced them to Mexico.

CONNECT ▶ History & Culture

Day of the Dead This holiday has its roots in an ancient Aztec celebration, in which people remembered dead ancestors. Today, particularly in rural areas, relatives celebrate the Day of the Dead by gathering in cemeteries to decorate family graves with candles and flowers and to share stories about loved ones who have died.

CRITICAL THINKING
Make Inferences How does this holiday show the importance of family to Mexican people?

Sports The number one sport in Mexico is *fútbol*, or soccer. Mexicans enjoy playing it and watching it. Fans cheer on their favorite teams in stadiums located in several Mexican cities. Aztec Stadium in Mexico City holds 114,000 fans! Mexicans also enjoy playing baseball and watching their professional baseball teams.

Many Mexicans enjoy bullfighting, a sport brought to Mexico by the Spanish. The number of bullfights has decreased in recent years because some people have led campaigns to ban them. However, people still attend bullfights in the bullrings found in many Mexican cities.

A sport growing in popularity in Mexico is jai alai, a fast-paced ball game played in a three-walled court. The equipment includes a hard rubber ball and wicker-basket scoops, which players use to catch and throw the ball.

 FIND MAIN IDEAS Identify the kinds of holidays that Mexican people celebrate today.

Soccer in Aztec Stadium Fans watch as a player from the Mexican team (left) battles for the ball in a game with a player from Argentina.

Section 2 Assessment

 **ONLINE QUIZ**
For test practice, go to
Interactive Review
@ ClassZone.com

TERMS & NAMES
1. Explain the importance of
- Plaza of the Three Cultures
- *colonia*
- mural
- fiesta

USE YOUR READING NOTES
2. Summarize Use your completed chart to answer the following question:

What are some ways Mexicans spend their leisure time?

SECTION	SUMMARY
People and Lifestyle	
Mexico's Great Murals	
Celebrations and Sports	

KEY IDEAS
3. What two cultures have influenced modern Mexico?

4. Where do most Mexican people live today?

5. What is the subject of many Mexican murals?

CRITICAL THINKING
6. Draw Conclusions Why do many people in Mexico's rural areas move to cities?

7. Form and Support Opinions What problems of urban and rural life do you think are most important for Mexico to address?

8. CONNECT to Today Some people have led campaigns to ban bullfighting. What kinds of campaigns does your area have on behalf of animals?

9. ART **Create a Mural Panel** Work with a group to research an important event in the history of your community. Decide what aspect of the event you want to illustrate. Then create a mural panel to depict the scene you have chosen.

Mexican culture is a blend of both Indian and Spanish traditions. The influences of both cultures are evident in Mexico today.

Indian Traditions

Before the Spanish conquest in 1521, Mexico's Indian groups had well-established, unique cultures. Indian groups created cities with huge structures. They held celebrations, such as festivals to remember those who died. Crops such as corn, chilies, and tomatoes contributed to their flavorful diet.

Food

Tortillas, a popular Mexican food made from corn, date back to the ancient Aztecs.

Clothing

These girls wear handmade, colorful dresses.

▲ *Ruins of Mayan temple at Palenque, Mexico*

Festivals

Mexican children of Indian ancestry dressed in traditional clothing participate in a local festival.

Spanish Traditions

The Spanish conquest brought European customs and traditions to the region. The Spanish built their traditional square cities that surrounded plazas and included government buildings and churches. They honored their dead on All Saints' Day and All Souls' Day in November. They introduced foods such as oranges, wheat, beef, pork, sugar cane, coffee, and onions to the Mexican diet.

Food
Mexican sweet breads are made from wheat, which the Spaniards brought to Mexico.

Clothing
These dancers are dressed in traditional Spanish clothing from the colonial period.

Festivals
Mexican children participate in a procession celebrating Easter, a Roman Catholic holiday.

▲ *Spanish colonial church in Taxco, Mexico*

CRITICAL THINKING

1. **Evaluate** Why are Mexican traditions today a blend of Native American and Spanish traditions?

2. **Compare and Contrast** Based on the large photos, how do Native American and Spanish architecture compare?

Reading for Understanding

▶ Key Ideas

BEFORE, YOU LEARNED

The Mexican government has become more democratic with the elimination of the one-party system.

NOW YOU WILL LEARN

Mexico faces new challenges as the country takes steps to modernize its economy.

▶ Vocabulary

TERMS & NAMES

maquiladora factory in which materials are imported and assembled into products for export

global economy economy in which buying and selling occurs across national borders

North American Free Trade Agreement (NAFTA) agreement that reduced trade barriers among Mexico, Canada, and the United States

REVIEW

immigration process of coming to another country to live

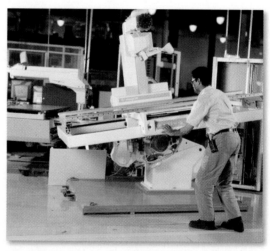

Visual Vocabulary X-ray table built in a *maquiladora*

▶ Reading Strategy

Re-create the web diagram shown at right. As you read and respond to the **KEY QUESTIONS**, find supporting details for each main idea in Section 3.

 See Skillbuilder Handbook, page R4

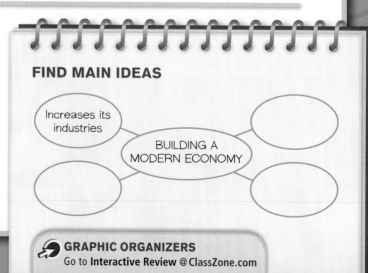

FIND MAIN IDEAS

Increases its industries

BUILDING A MODERN ECONOMY

GRAPHIC ORGANIZERS
Go to **Interactive Review** @ ClassZone.com

Creating a New Economy

3.02 Describe the environmental impact of regional activities such as deforestation, urbanization, and industrialization and evaluate their significance to the global community.
4.02 Identify the main commodities of trade over time in selected areas of South America and Europe, and evaluate their significance for the economic, political and social development of cultures and regions.

Connecting to Your World

Do you add tomatoes to a salad or to your favorite kind of sandwich? Chances are that the tomatoes you eat were grown in Mexico. Tomatoes make up the largest percentage of vegetables that Mexico exports to the United States. Agriculture is an important part of Mexico's economy. In this section, you will learn how Mexico has expanded its economy.

Building a Modern Economy

▼ **KEY QUESTION** How has Mexico created a strong modern economy?

Vicente Fox's election as president in 2000 changed Mexico from a one-party system to a multiparty democracy. With a stable government, Mexico is working to improve the quality of life for its people. It has been modernizing its industry and economy by cooperating with other North American countries.

Animated GEOGRAPHY

Mexican Industry
Workers perform their jobs on a floating oil-rig platform off the Mexican coast in the Gulf of Mexico.

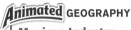 *Click here* for an interactive map of Mexican industry @ ClassZone.com

Vicente Fox promised as president to improve education, jobs, and opportunities in Mexico. For his official portrait, Fox posed with Mexican people from all walks of life to show, as the caption indicates, that "We are all Mexico." Read what Fox had to say in his inaugural speech.

> It is time we recognized that everything cannot be solved by the State [government]. . . . Quality education, employment and regional development are the levers to remove, once and for all, the signs of poverty.
>
> Source: Vicente Fox's inaugural speech

Vicente Fox

TODOS SOMOS MÉXICO

DOCUMENT–BASED QUESTION
What does Fox think is the best way to reduce poverty?

 ONLINE PRIMARY SOURCE To read more works of Vicente Fox, go to the **Research & Writing Center** @ ClassZone.com

Industrialization Traditionally, Mexico's economy depended upon agriculture and mining. But since the 1940s, Mexico has become more industrialized. Mexico continues to be one of the world's major producers of silver. Its most profitable industry is oil production. Today, Mexico is tied with China as the world's fifth largest producer of crude petroleum.

Other industries have also become important to Mexico's economy. In recent years, many factories have been located along Mexico's border with the United States. These factories are called *maquiladoras*. A **maquiladora** is a factory that assembles imported materials into finished goods that are exported. Jeans, appliances, car engines, and computers are some of the products manufactured in this way.

Global Economy In 1992, Mexico took a stronger role in the **global economy**, in which nations cooperate to trade goods and services. It signed the **North American Free Trade Agreement (NAFTA)** with the United States and Canada. NAFTA created rules about trade in North America. The agreement made it easier for the three countries to transport goods and services across their borders.

▲ **DRAW CONCLUSIONS** Discuss the steps Mexico has taken to build its economy.

Facing New Challenges

▼ **KEY QUESTION** What are some problems Mexico must solve in order to continue to develop a stronger economy?

Mexico faces two major challenges in continuing to develop a strong economy. It has to reduce pollution, and it has to create more jobs in order to improve conditions for its people and to slow migration to other countries.

Pollution Like other large international cities, Mexico City has had to deal with increased air pollution, brought on in large part by industrialization. Mexico City sits in a valley, almost completely surrounded by mountains. The mountains help produce a layer of warm air above the city. This layer keeps gases from car exhaust and thousands of industries from blowing away. These gases react with sunlight to form smog, a thick brown haze, over the city. The smog causes health problems for many people.

Recently, the Mexican government has taken steps to deal with the pollution problem. It has urged automobile manufacturers to produce cars that use cleaner fuels and helped companies develop smog controls. It has also encouraged public transportation.

CONNECT to Science

Like many modern cities, Mexico City became industrialized in the last 50 years. While developing a modern economy helps a country, the increase in industries often causes pollution problems. Many other cities have experienced situations similar to Mexico City's.

Mexico City Smog blankets the city.

Activity

Create a Pollution Hot Spot Map

Materials
- newspapers and magazines
- large blank world map
- markers

1. Find information about pollution problems in other parts of the world.

2. Locate and label the places on the world map. Include Mexico City on the map.

3. Choose one of the locations and find out what is being done to reduce pollution there.

4. Present your map and findings to the class.

Creation of Jobs The movement of people from rural to urban areas and across international borders presents a second challenge to Mexico's economy. Many Mexicans from rural areas move to cities for jobs. There, they often live in poor conditions, with no jobs or low-wage jobs.

Many Mexicans move to the United States for economic opportunities. Some risk the dangerous border crossing to the United States and enter the country illegally. Many earn money to help their families back home. Once in the United States, immigrants often work long hours at low-paying jobs, sometimes at more than one job.

As the Mexican economy creates more and better-paying jobs, the problem of illegal **immigration** may improve. In the meantime, Mexico and the United States continue to cooperate to strengthen security on their border and to find ways to resolve the immigration problems.

Providing Jobs These men are working on a large-scale construction project. **How might such projects help develop Mexico's economy?**

 IDENTIFY PROBLEMS AND SOLUTIONS Identify the challenges Mexico faces in developing its economy.

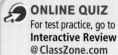 **ONLINE QUIZ** For test practice, go to **Interactive Review** @ ClassZone.com

Section ③ Assessment

TERMS & NAMES

1. Explain the importance of
- *maquiladora*
- NAFTA
- global economy
- immigration

USE YOUR READING NOTES

2. Find Main Ideas Use your completed chart to answer the following question:

What steps has Mexico taken to build a modern economy?

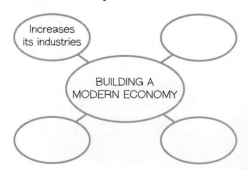

KEY IDEAS

3. What was Mexico's traditional economy based on until the 1940s?

4. What are Mexico's most important industries?

5. What are two challenges Mexico faces today?

CRITICAL THINKING

6. Evaluate What are the advantages and disadvantages of Mexico's membership in NAFTA?

7. Analyze Causes and Effects How did the growth of urban areas and industrialization contribute to Mexico's pollution problems?

8. CONNECT to Today Why is creating jobs important for Mexico today?

9. WRITING **Prepare a Report** Choose one of Mexico's major industries. Find out how many people are employed in the industry, its major locations, and how much money the industry brings to Mexico's economy. Prepare an illustrated report of your findings.

Interactive ← Review

Click here to complete these and other activities online @ ClassZone.com

CHAPTER SUMMARY

Key Idea 1
Mexico overcame many obstacles as the country moved toward establishing a democracy.

Key Idea 2
Three cultures blended to create the heritage and daily life of the Mexican people.

Key Idea 3
Mexico continues to face challenges as it tries to modernize its economy.

For **Review and Study Notes**, go to **Interactive Review** @ ClassZone.com

NAME GAME

Use the Terms & Names list to complete each sentence on paper or online.

1. I am the place that became independent from Mexico in 1837. __Republic of Texas__

2. I am the place where the cultural sources of modern Mexico can be seen. _____

3. I am a document that brought reforms to Mexico and is still in effect in Mexico today.

   _____

4. I am the president who broke Mexican one-party rule. _____

5. I am a neighborhood or suburb of a Mexican city. _____

6. I am an agreement made between North American countries._____

7. I am a person who lives on land that is not my own. _____

8. I am a tax on imported goods. _____

9. I am a Mexican writer who won the Nobel Prize for Literature. _____

10. I am a famous Mexican mural painter.

    _____

colonia
Constitution of 1917
Vicente Fox
Benito Juárez
maquiladora
NAFTA
Octavio Paz
Plaza of the Three Cultures
Republic of Texas
Diego Rivera
squatter
tariff

Activities

Flip Cards

Use the online flip cards to quiz yourself on the terms and names introduced in this chapter.

Benito Juárez

Mexican president and reformer who helped write the Constitution of 1857

Crossword Puzzle

Complete an online crossword puzzle to test your knowledge of the history and culture of Mexico.

ACROSS
1. a holiday celebrated with parades, games, and food

VOCABULARY

Explain the significance of each of the following.

1. Republic of Texas
2. annex
3. Plaza of the Three Cultures
4. *colonia*
5. squatter
6. mural
7. Diego Rivera
8. fiesta
9. Day of the Dead
10. immigration

Explain how the terms and names in each group are related.

11. Mexican Revolution and Constitution of 1917
12. Antonio López de Santa Anna, Benito Juárez, and Vicente Fox
13. *maquiladoras*, global economy, and NAFTA

KEY IDEAS

1 A Struggle Toward Democracy

14. Why was it difficult for Mexicans to rule themselves after independence?
15. What contributions did Benito Juárez make to Mexico?
16. How and why did the Mexican Revolution happen?
17. Why was the 2000 presidential election in Mexico significant?

2 A Blend of Traditions

18. What are three influences on Mexican culture today?
19. What conditions led Mexican people to move from rural to urban areas?
20. Why is Mexican mural painting a continuation of ancient Mexican tradition?
21. What do Mexicans celebrate on *Cinco de Mayo*?

3 Creating a New Economy

22. Why is oil important to Mexico's economy?
23. What steps did Mexico take to modernize its economy?
24. What factors contribute to air pollution in Mexico City?
25. Why do many Mexicans migrate to the United States?

CRITICAL THINKING

26. **Analyze Causes and Effects** Complete a cause and effect diagram to explain the effects of Mexico's conflicts with Texas and the United States in the 1800s.

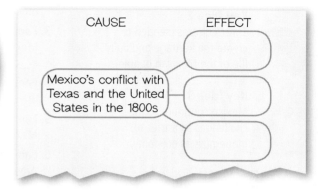

CAUSE   EFFECT

Mexico's conflict with Texas and the United States in the 1800s

27. **Make Inferences** How do Mexico's holidays and arts show the influence of Mexico's history?
28. **Draw Conclusions** How did Mexico's frequent changes in leaders before the Mexican Revolution affect the country?
29. **Connect History & Art** Why did so many Mexican artists and writers paint and write about Mexico's past?
30. **Five Themes: Location** How does Mexico City's location contribute to the problem of smog in the city?

Answer the ESSENTIAL QUESTION

How does Mexico reflect both ancient traditions and the demands of the modern world?

Written Response Write a two- or three-paragraph response to the Essential Question. Be sure to include a discussion of Mexican life, government, and economy. Use the rubric below to guide your thinking.

Response Rubric

A strong response will:

- describe how Mexican life reflects both ancient and modern traditions
- discuss the challenges Mexico faced in creating a democratic government and a modern economy

THEMATIC MAP

Use the map and your knowledge of Mexico to answer questions 1 and 2.

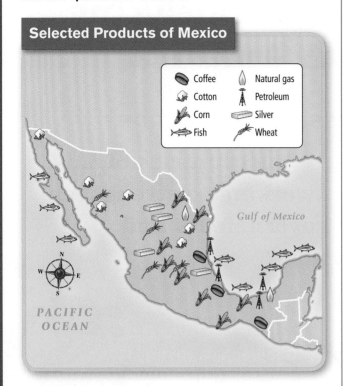

Selected Products of Mexico

- Coffee
- Cotton
- Corn
- Fish
- Natural gas
- Petroleum
- Silver
- Wheat

Gulf of Mexico

PACIFIC OCEAN

1. In what region of Mexico is petroleum produced?

A. along the Pacific coast
B. along the U.S. border
C. along the coast of the Gulf of Mexico
D. along the interior of the country

2. In what part of Mexico is cotton grown?

A. in the southern part
B. in the northern part
C. only on the western coast
D. only on the eastern coast

CIRCLE GRAPH

Examine the graph below. Use the information in the graph to answer questions 3 and 4.

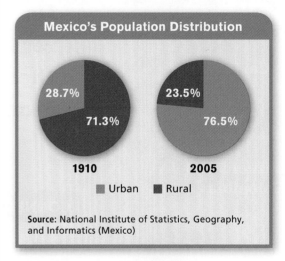

Mexico's Population Distribution

28.7% 71.3% — 1910

23.5% 76.5% — 2005

■ Urban ■ Rural

Source: National Institute of Statistics, Geography, and Informatics (Mexico)

3. What percentage of Mexico's population was urban in 1910? in 2005?

4. What does this tell you about changes that have taken place in Mexican society?

GeoActivity

1. INTERDISCIPLINARY ACTIVITY–SCIENCE

Find out about the habitat of the monarch butterfly in Mexico. Research the butterfly's migration pattern and life cycle. Find out what the Mexican government has done to protect these butterflies. Present your findings in an illustrated and captioned poster.

2. WRITING FOR SOCIAL STUDIES

Create a guide for visitors to Mexico City. Use the Internet to learn about places to visit, such as museums, and cultural institutions, such as the ballet. Write a description of each of these places, and include illustrations.

3. MENTAL MAPPING

Create an outline map of Mexico and label the following:

• Mexico City
• Rio Grande
• Sierra Madre Occidental
• Sierra Madre Oriental
• Gulf of Mexico
• Pacific Ocean

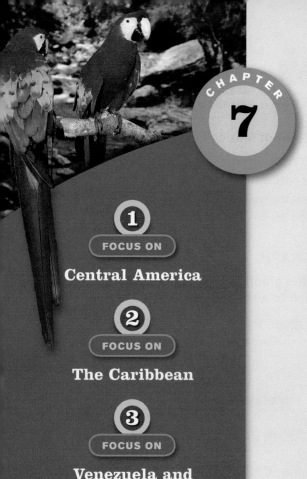

Middle America and Spanish-Speaking South America

 ESSENTIAL QUESTION

How are the countries of this region working to strengthen their governments and economies?

CONNECT → **Geography & History**

Use the map and the time line to answer the following questions.

1. What country connects Central and South America?
2. Who led the Cuban independence movement?

History
1804 Haiti is the first Caribbean Island to become independent. (Present-day Haitian flag) ▶

1800

History
1821 Central American countries gain independence from Spain.

History
◀ **1895** José Martí leads Cuban revolution against Spanish rule.

History
1902 Cuba gains independence.

Culture
1911 Archaeologist Hiram Bingham locates the site of Machu Picchu.
(Incan watchtower) ▼

Government
1959 Fidel Castro overthrows government of Fulgencio Batista.
(Fulgencio Batista) ▶

Culture
1992 Rigoberta Menchú wins the Nobel Peace Prize.

Today

History
1952 Puerto Rico becomes a U.S. commonwealth.

History
1990s Many Central American countries develop democracies.

Reading for Understanding

▶ Key Ideas

BEFORE, YOU LEARNED

Mexico faces many challenges as it modernizes its economy.

NOW YOU WILL LEARN

Central American countries also face challenges as they develop democratic governments and improve their economies.

▶ Vocabulary

TERMS & NAMES

ecotourism travel to a natural habitat in a way that does not damage the habitat

dictator a person with complete control over a country's government

subsistence farming a kind of farming in which farmers grow only enough to feed their families

Central America Free Trade Agreement (CAFTA) trade agreement to promote trade between the United States and countries of Central America

service industry an industry that provides services rather than objects

artisan a worker skilled in making products or art with his or her hands

REVIEW

maquiladora factory in which materials are imported and assembled into products for export

North American Free Trade Agreement (NAFTA) agreement that reduced trade barriers among Mexico, Canada, and the United States

mestizo person with mixed European and Indian ancestry

▶ Reading Strategy

Re-create the web diagram shown at right. As you read and respond to the **KEY QUESTIONS**, use the diagram to outline the major aspects of Central America's government, economy, and culture.

 See Skillbuilder Handbook, page R7

CATEGORIZE

Government — CENTRAL AMERICA — Economy — Culture

GRAPHIC ORGANIZERS
Go to **Interactive Review** @ClassZone.com

Central America

4.02 Identify the main commodities of trade over time in selected areas of South America and Europe, and evaluate their significance for the economic, political and social development of cultures and regions.

11.04 Identify examples of economic, political, and social changes, such as agrarian to industrial economies, monarchical to democratic governments, and the roles of women and minorities, and analyze their impact on culture.

Connecting to Your World

What is the most exotic animal you have ever seen? If you were to visit the rain forest in Costa Rica's Corcovado National Park, you would see many exotic animals, such as macaws, coatis, and anteaters. People's interest in visiting this and other natural habitats has led some countries in Central America to promote **ecotourism**, or travel to natural habitats in a way that does not damage the habitat. Ecotourism is just one way that Central American countries are expanding their economies.

Keel-billed Toucan
This bird makes its home in the treetops of the rain forests.

Government and Economy

▼ **KEY QUESTION** What steps have Central American countries taken to improve their economies?

Central America today faces major challenges. In most countries, a wide gap exists between the small number of wealthy people and the large number of poor people. A large percentage of the population is unemployed. In many areas, people lack basic services, such as running water and electricity. In recent years, Central American countries have been working to improve their economies and to develop democratic governments.

Ecotourism The people shown here are standing on a bridge, looking down over a rain forest in Costa Rica.

COSTA RICA

Path Toward Democracy Since gaining independence from Spain in 1821, most Central American countries have struggled to develop democratic governments. As in Mexico, the wealthy in Central America controlled most aspects of government. Most of the population remained poor, with no say in how they were governed.

Costa Rica is the only country in the region that has been a democracy since the early 1900s. Nearly all the other Central American countries have been under the rule of **dictators**, or leaders with complete control over their governments. Starting in the 1950s, civil wars fought for equal rights led to years of suffering in countries such as Guatemala, El Salvador, and Nicaragua (NIHK•uh•RAH•gwuh). Since the 1990s, however, many Central American nations have developed democracies in which more people participate in government.

Developing the Economy During the colonial period, Spain set up large plantations that focused on growing one kind of crop. Today, agriculture is the main economic activity in Central America. Large plantations still produce crops, mainly bananas, sugar cane, and coffee, for export. Cattle are raised on large ranches in the drier western parts of Central America. But most agriculture consists of **subsistence farming**, in which poor farmers grow a variety of crops, such as corn and vegetables, on small plots to feed their own families.

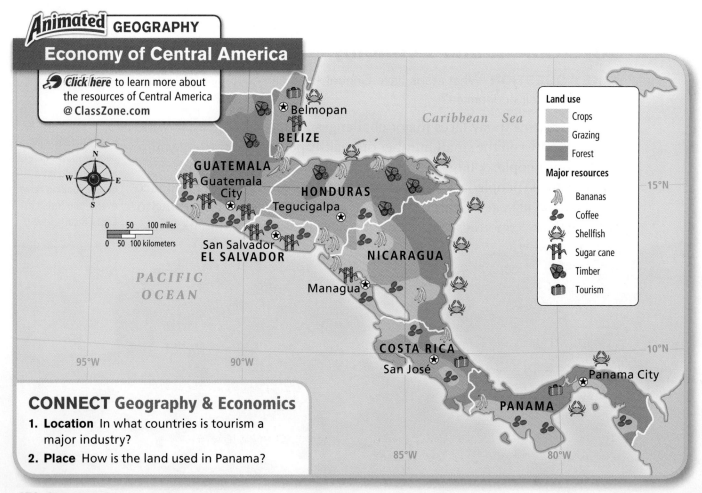

Animated GEOGRAPHY

Economy of Central America

Click here to learn more about the resources of Central America @ ClassZone.com

Land use
- Crops
- Grazing
- Forest

Major resources
- Bananas
- Coffee
- Shellfish
- Sugar cane
- Timber
- Tourism

CONNECT Geography & Economics

1. **Location** In what countries is tourism a major industry?
2. **Place** How is the land used in Panama?

COMPARING ⟩ Human-Made Waterways

	PANAMA CANAL	**ST. LAWRENCE SEAWAY**
Location	Central America	North America
Length	50 miles	2,340 miles
Tonnage	279 million tons	48 million tons
Average time to cross	8 hours	8 days
Average ships per year	14,000	4,000

◀ *Cargo ships passing through the locks of the Panama Canal*

CRITICAL THINKING

Compare and Contrast How do the two waterways compare in terms of the number of ships that pass through them every year?

As the map indicates, timber is an important economic activity in forested areas, such as in Costa Rica. Tourism, and in particular eco-tourism, has become a major industry in Costa Rica and Guatemala. *Maquiladoras* in Guatemala and Honduras produce goods such as clothing for export. In recent years, Central American countries have begun to develop technology and telecommunications industries to help expand their economies.

Promoting International Trade As you have learned, the Panama Canal is important to world trade. It is a crossroads for goods that travel between the western and eastern hemispheres. The economies of many Central American countries depend on the canal for shipping and receiving goods.

Today, Central American nations are trying to increase trade with other countries of the world. The United States, Costa Rica, Guatemala, El Salvador, Honduras, and Nicaragua have signed the **Central America Free Trade Agreement (CAFTA)**. Like **NAFTA**, this trade agreement will lower tariffs and make trade easier among member nations. The five Central American nations hope the flow of money into Central America from CAFTA will help to develop more jobs and strengthen their economies.

▲ **EVALUATE** Discuss the steps Central American countries have taken to strengthen their economies.

People and Culture

▼ **KEY QUESTION** How is the present-day culture of Central America a blend of several cultures?

The cultures of Central American countries are a blend of Spanish, Indian, and African cultures. Two-thirds of Central Americans are *mestizos*. Most Central Americans are Roman Catholics. Spanish is the official language of all the Central American countries except Belize, where English is the official language. Many people also speak Indian languages.

Rural and Urban Life Half of Central America's population is urban. Many people in rural areas live in small villages built on mountainsides. Because they plant small fields for food, they grow barely enough to feed their families.

Most Central American nations require children to attend school for nine years. However, rural schools are poorly equipped, and it is difficult to hire teachers to work in these areas. Children often do not attend school because they are needed to work on family farms.

Generally, Central American countries have one large capital city, where factories and service industries are located. **Service industries** provide services, such as banking, rather than objects. Open-air markets, where people buy and sell products, are found in large cities as well as in small villages throughout Central America. Market days are a time for people to shop and to socialize.

Daily Life The family is important in Central American life. A Central American family includes grandparents, parents, children, aunts, and uncles, who often live in houses built near one another. Family members frequently gather to celebrate family events and holidays.

Open-Air Market
Markets such as this one take place throughout Central America. **What kinds of activities are taking place in this market?**

Corn is the main ingredient in many Central American foods, such as tortillas. Meals include beans and vegetables such as chili peppers and avocados, and fruits such as guavas and mangoes.

The Arts Central American countries are known for the work of their **artisans**, people skilled in making things with their hands. The works include Panamanian molas, Nicaraguan painted gourds, and Honduran baskets.

Popular music includes calypso, salsa, and punta rock, a type of music created by Central Americans. It combines traditional rhythms with modern instruments. A popular instrument is the marimba, a kind of xylophone played throughout the region.

Famous Central American writers include Rigoberta Menchú, an Indian Guatemalan woman. She won the Nobel Peace Prize in 1992 for her work for the rights of Indians in Central America.

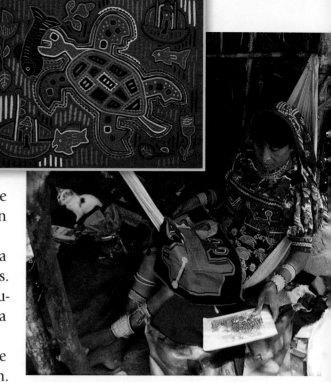

Making a Mola This Panamanian woman is making a mola, a cloth panel used for decorating such things as clothing.

 SUMMARIZE Explain how the culture of Central America is a blend of several cultures.

ONLINE QUIZ
For test practice, go to **Interactive Review** @ ClassZone.com

Section 1 Assessment

TERMS & NAMES

1. Explain the importance of
- ecotourism
- dictator
- CAFTA
- artisan

USE YOUR READING NOTES

2. Categorize Use your completed diagram to answer the following question:

What kinds of music are popular in Central American countries today?

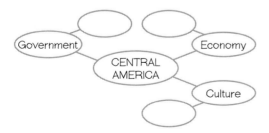

KEY IDEAS

3. What is the main economic activity in Central America?

4. What five Central American countries signed CAFTA?

5. What kinds of crafts do Central American artisans create?

CRITICAL THINKING

6. Draw Conclusions How did the civil wars in Central American countries affect attempts to establish strong governments?

7. Identify Problems and Solutions What problems do people in the rural areas of Central America face?

8. CONNECT to Today Many ecotourists visit the various natural habitats in Central America. Why do you think ecotourism has become so popular?

9. TECHNOLOGY Make a Multimedia Presentation Choose a Central American country and research its art, music, and other traditions. In a small group, prepare a multimedia presentation of your findings.

Reading for Understanding

▶ Key Ideas

BEFORE, YOU LEARNED

Mayan and Spanish influences are seen today in Central American cultures.

NOW YOU WILL LEARN

The influences of various European countries and Africa are reflected in the Caribbean island cultures.

▶ Vocabulary

TERMS & NAMES

Taino Indian group in the Caribbean islands

dependency a place governed by a country that it is not officially a part of

one-crop economy an economy that depends on a single crop for income

tourism industry that provides services for travelers

Caribbean Community and Common Market (CARICOM) a trade organization of several Caribbean nations

commonwealth a self-governing political unit that is associated with another country

REVIEW

Central America Free Trade Agreement (CAFTA) trade agreement to promote trade between the United States and countries of Central America

dictator person with complete control over a country's government

communism a type of government in which the Communist Party holds all political power and controls the economy

▶ Reading Strategy

Re-create the chart shown at right. As you read and respond to the **KEY QUESTIONS**, use the chart to summarize what you have learned about the economies, governments, and cultures of the Caribbean islands.

 See Skillbuilder Handbook, page R5

SUMMARIZE

ECONOMY	GOVERNMENT	CULTURE
1.	1.	1.
2.	2.	2.
3.	3.	3.

 GRAPHIC ORGANIZERS
Go to **Interactive Review** @ ClassZone.com

The Caribbean

8.01 Describe the role of key historical figures and evaluate their impact on past and present societies in South America and Europe.
11.04 Identify examples of economic, political, and social changes, such as agrarian to industrial economies, monarchical to democratic governments, and the roles of women and minorities, and analyze their impact on culture.

Connecting to Your World

What images come to mind when you hear the words Caribbean islands? Many people think of beautiful sandy beaches and clear blue water. Thousands of people from all over the world travel to the Caribbean islands each year to enjoy the warm climate and outdoor activities. But the Caribbean islands are home for many thousands more. These people are shaping the economy and culture of the islands today.

History and Economy

▼ **KEY QUESTION** How have Caribbean nations worked to develop their economies?

Although Spain ruled most of Central America, several other European nations claimed and settled the Caribbean islands. In addition, Africans were brought to the islands as enslaved persons. The influences of all these people contributed to the diverse cultures in the Caribbean islands today.

Beach in Varadero, Cuba

U.S.

CUBA

Caribbean Sea

SOUTH AMERICA

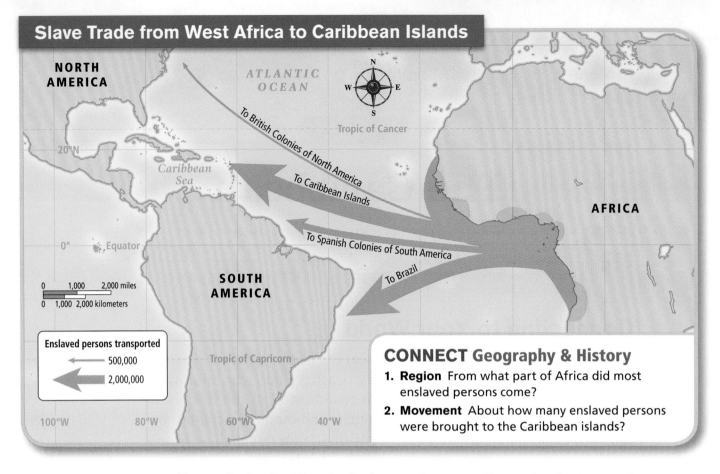

NORTH AMERICA

ATLANTIC OCEAN

Tropic of Cancer

To British Colonies of North America

To Caribbean Islands

Caribbean Sea

AFRICA

0° Equator

To Spanish Colonies of South America

To Brazil

0   1,000   2,000 miles
0   1,000 2,000 kilometers

SOUTH AMERICA

Tropic of Capricorn

Enslaved persons transported
500,000
2,000,000

100°W   80°W   60°W   40°W

CONNECT Geography & History

1. **Region** From what part of Africa did most enslaved persons come?
2. **Movement** About how many enslaved persons were brought to the Caribbean islands?

From Colonization to Independence After Columbus arrived in the Caribbean islands in 1492, the Spanish settled some of the islands and set up sugar cane plantations. They used the native **Taino** people as forced labor. By the 19th century, the French, British, and Dutch also claimed islands to profit from the sugar trade.

After nearly all the Taino people died due to disease and cruel treatment, Europeans looked to enslaved Africans to replace the Taino. Forty percent of all enslaved persons brought to the Americas were brought to the Caribbean islands.

In 1804, Haiti was the first island to achieve independence. The independence movement there started as a slave revolt against the French, who forced Africans to work on the sugar plantations. In 1898, Cuba gained independence from Spain, while Puerto Rico became a dependency of the United States. A **dependency** is a place governed by or closely connected with a country that it is not officially part of. Today, only a few islands are still under the direction of European nations or the United States.

Economic Activities During colonial times, the Caribbean islands focused mainly on developing the sugar cane industry. Sugar was so profitable that European plantation owners raised few other crops. A country that depends on a single crop for most of its income has a **one-crop economy**. This kind of economy can be unstable. If a crop fails or prices for the crop are low, the entire economy suffers.

In the late 1800s, the sugar industry in the Caribbean islands was in trouble. Places in other parts of the world that raised sugar cane charged lower prices for their sugar. As a result, the sugar trade in the Caribbean islands declined.

The Caribbean nations found they had to diversify their economies. They began to raise other crops, such as bananas, pineapples, and citrus fruits. They also developed industries such as fishing, mining, and chemical plants. **Tourism**, which provides services for travelers, has become a very important industry. Residents of the islands are able to find jobs in the hotels, restaurants, and resorts on the islands. They also work as guides on sailing trips, snorkeling, and other activities for tourists.

Several Caribbean nations today are members of the **Caribbean Community and Common Market (CARICOM)**, a trade organization similar to NAFTA and **CAFTA**. The purpose of the organization is to coordinate economic and trade relations among the member nations.

🔺 **DRAW CONCLUSIONS** Explain what Caribbean nations have done to develop their economies.

Two Different Governments

🔻 **KEY QUESTION** How are the Puerto Rican and Cuban governments different?

Most Caribbean nations have at some time been under the rule of **dictators**. Today, most nations have democratically elected governments. Two islands, however, Cuba and Puerto Rico, have developed two distinctly different forms of government.

Cuba Spain controlled Cuba until the United States defeated Spain in the Spanish-American War in 1898. The United States military occupied the island until Cuba became an independent country in 1902. However, U.S. influence continued until 1959, when rebel forces led by Fidel Castro overthrew an unpopular dictator. By 1961, Castro had established communism in Cuba, with close ties to the Soviet Union. **Communism** is a type of government in which the Communist Party holds all political power and controls the economy. Castro's government

HISTORY MAKERS

Fidel Castro born 1926

Castro was the son of a wealthy farmer. As a boy, he worked in his father's sugar cane fields. He attended private schools and received a law degree from the University of Havana in 1950. There he also developed an interest in politics. As a lawyer, Castro worked on behalf of poor people. In 1953, he unsuccessfully tried to overthrow Cuba's dictator, Batista. After succeeding in 1959, Castro himself has ruled as a dictator for more than 40 years.

🚀 **ONLINE BIOGRAPHY**
For more on the life of Fidel Castro, go to the
Research & Writing Center @ ClassZone.com

	PUERTO RICO	CUBA
Political Status	U.S. commonwealth	Independent country
Type of Government	Democracy	Communist state
Head of Government	Governor	President
Voting Age	18	16
Number of Political Parties	2	1
Political Divisions	Divided into 78 municipalities	Divided into 14 provinces
Relationship to U.S.	Non-voting commissioner in the U.S. House of Representatives	None

CRITICAL THINKING

Evaluate How does a two-party system help make a government more democratic?

improved health care and education for the Cuban people. However, Castro has ruled Cuba as a dictator and has denied Cubans many rights and freedoms.

Puerto Rico Like Cuba, Puerto Rico was a Spanish colony until 1898, when it became a U.S. territory. Puerto Rico, however, was never independent. In 1952, Puerto Rican voters approved a constitution that made Puerto Rico a commonwealth of the United States. As a **commonwealth**, Puerto Rico is self-governing but is still a part of the United States. Although Puerto Ricans are U.S. citizens, they cannot vote for the U.S. president.

▲ **COMPARE AND CONTRAST** Describe the similarities and differences between the governments of Cuba and Puerto Rico.

People and Culture

▼ **KEY QUESTION** Why has African culture been a major influence on Caribbean life?

The cultures of the Caribbean islands reflect Indian, African, and European influences. Because the region was the center of the slave trade, African influences have left a mark on many aspects of

Caribbean life. People in the islands speak a variety of languages. Spanish is the official language in Cuba, French in Haiti, and English in Jamaica.

Music in the Caribbean also reflects a blend of cultures. Calypso music began in Trinidad. It combines styles from Africa, Spain, and the Caribbean. Steel drums and guitars accompany calypso songs. Reggae developed in Jamaica in the 1960s. It blends African music, Caribbean music, and U.S. music to make its own unique style. Caribbean music includes many guitar-like instruments that have been created in the region, such as the Puerto Rican *cuatro* and the Cuban *tres*.

Most people in the Caribbean live in urban areas, where they hope to find jobs in the tourist industry. People celebrate festivals, such as Carnival. Artisans create folk art, such as oil drum art and papier-mâché sculptures. Popular sports are football, known as soccer in the United States, and baseball.

 EVALUATE Explain why African culture has been a major influence on life in the Caribbean.

STEEL DRUMS

The steel drum was first made in Trinidad from the end and part of the sides of a 55-gallon steel oil barrel. The surface was hammered in certain ways to produce various tones. The steel drum is one of the few acoustic musical instruments created in the 20th century.

Section ❷ Assessment

 **ONLINE QUIZ**
For test practice, go to
Interactive Review
@ ClassZone.com

TERMS & NAMES

1. Explain the importance of
- Taino
- dependency
- tourism
- commonwealth

USE YOUR READING NOTES

2. Summarize Use your completed chart to answer the following question:

Why did the Caribbean islands diversify their economies?

ECONOMY	GOVERNMENT	CULTURE
1.	1.	1.
2.	2.	2.
3.	3.	3.

KEY IDEAS

3. What was the main economic activity in the Caribbean islands during colonial times?

4. How did Fidel Castro come to power in Cuba?

5. Why do people in the Caribbean Islands speak a variety of languages?

CRITICAL THINKING

6. Compare and Contrast How is Cuba's government different from the U.S. government?

7. Draw Conclusions Why do most people in the Caribbean islands live in urban areas?

8. CONNECT to Today In recent years Puerto Ricans have debated the issue of becoming a state of the United States. Why might people support or oppose Puerto Rican statehood?

9. WRITING Write a Country Profile Choose one Caribbean island and prepare a country profile for its Web site. Include its location, the kind of government and economy it has, and tourist attractions.

Reading for Understanding

▶ Key Ideas

BEFORE, YOU LEARNED

Many Caribbean nations are working together to increase trade.

NOW YOU WILL LEARN

Venezuela's economy depends heavily on petroleum, while Colombia's economy depends more on agricultural products.

▶ Vocabulary

TERMS & NAMES

federal republic form of government in which power is divided between a national government and state governments

Caracas capital city of Venezuela

joropo (huh•ROH•poh) Venezuelan national folk dance

Bogotá capital city of Colombia

Gabriel García Márquez Colombian author and Nobel Prize winner

Fernando Botero Colombian artist known for portraits of people with exaggerated forms

REVIEW

Simón Bolívar (boh•LEE•vahr) leader for independence in northern South America

dictator person with complete control over a country's government

llanos (YAH•nohs) grasslands of South America's Central Plains

BACKGROUND VOCABULARY

mosaic a picture made by placing small, colored pieces of tile or glass on a surface

▶ Reading Strategy

Re-create the cluster diagram shown at right for Venezuela and Colombia. As you read and respond to the **KEY QUESTIONS**, use the diagram to record details about the two countries' government, economy, and people.

 Skillbuilder Handbook, page R4

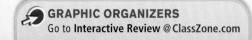

FIND MAIN IDEAS

VENEZUELA

Government
1. _____
2. _____

Economy
1. _____
2. _____

People
1. _____
2. _____

GRAPHIC ORGANIZERS
Go to **Interactive Review** @ ClassZone.com

Venezuela and Colombia

8.01 Describe the role of key historical figures and evaluate their impact on past and present societies in South America and Europe.
11.04 Identify examples of economic, political, and social changes, such as agrarian to industrial economies, monarchical to democratic governments, and the roles of women and minorities, and analyze their impact on culture.

Connecting to Your World

Many civilizations have created beautiful mosaic art. A **mosaic** involves placing small, colored pieces of stone, tile, or glass next to each other on a surface to make a picture or design. The countries of South America form a kind of mosaic of their own, a cultural mosaic. People from different cultural groups live near each other but keep their own cultural identities. *Mestizos*, Indians, and people of African ancestry form part of the cultural mosaic in Venezuela and Colombia.

Venezuela

Caracas
VENEZUELA

▼ **KEY QUESTION** What are the main economic activities of Venezuela?

Venezuela and Colombia are located in the northern and northwestern part of South America. Both countries border the Caribbean Sea, and Colombia also borders the Pacific Ocean. In both countries, most people live in urban areas. While Venezuela and Colombia share similar histories, their governments and economies have developed differently.

Cultural Mosaic
South Americans today reflect a blend of cultures.

Caracas, Venezuela

ANALYZING Primary Sources

Simón Bolívar (1783–1830) is known as the liberator of South America. But his dream of uniting South America into one nation failed. In a letter, he explained what kind of government he thought would be best for South America.

> Events . . . have proved that institutions which are wholly representative are not suited to our . . . customs, and present knowledge. . . . As long as our countrymen do not acquire the abilities and political virtues that distinguish our brothers of the north [the United States], . . . popular systems, far from working to our advantage, will, I greatly fear, bring about our downfall.
>
> Source: Jamaican Letter

DOCUMENT-BASED QUESTION

What "abilities" would be needed to set up a representative system?

Simón Bolívar

History and Government Venezuela became part of Spain's empire in the early 1500s. When Spanish explorers saw Indian villages built on stilts on Lake Maracaibo, they named the area "Venezuela" after Venice, an Italian city built on water. By the 1700s, Venezuela was a colony, and most residents had little control over their lives.

Led by the Venezuelan **Simón Bolívar**, Venezuela became the first colony to declare independence from Spain in 1811 and to win it in 1821. After independence, the country went through years of civil war and **dictators**. Although establishing a democracy was not easy, Venezuela's leaders have been democratically elected since 1958.

Today, Venezuela is a **federal republic**, a government in which power is divided between a national government and state governments. The national government consists of a president, a congress, and a supreme court. Venezuela has 22 states and a Federal District. Each state and the Federal District have a governor and a congress.

Economy Venezuela's economy today is dependent on oil production. Its oil fields are located in the Maracaibo Basin, the location of Lake Maracaibo (South America's largest lake), and on the eastern plains. Venezuela is one of the world's leading oil producers. About 75 percent of the nation's exports are oil exports, especially to the United States and Canada. But, like the Caribbean countries with one-crop economies, Venezuela's dependence on one product sometimes results in economic instability, as oil prices rise and fall.

About ten percent of Venezuela's workers are farmers. More than half of them cultivate small farms, where they raise enough food and animals to support their families. Larger farms and ranches supply most of Venezuela's commercial products. Large farms grow bananas, coffee, corn, oranges, and rice. Large cattle ranches are an important part of the economy of Venezuela's **llanos** (YAH•nohs).

People and Culture Like the majority of Central Americans, most Venezuelans are *mestizos*. Other Venezuelans are Indians or people of European or African ancestry. Because Venezuela is a former Spanish colony, the official language is Spanish, and most Venezuelans are Roman Catholics.

Most Venezuelans live in cities, such as the capital city, **Caracas**. Many city dwellers live comfortably in houses and apartment buildings and work as professionals such as doctors, government workers, and lawyers. However, as in many parts of Latin America, the gap between the rich and the poor continues to be large. Many poor people from rural areas travel to cities in search of jobs. They live as squatters in crowded settlements outside the cities. To encourage people to stay in rural areas, Venezuela's government has paved roads, created health and education services, and provided electrical service in many rural areas.

Venezuelans enjoy sports, music, and dancing. Football (soccer) and baseball are among the most popular sports. Rodeos are popular, especially in cattle-raising regions in the llanos. The plains also inspired the *joropo* (huh•ROH•poh), Venezuela's national folk dance. While Venezuelans love to dance to Caribbean salsa, meringue, and calypso, they change each dance to make it truly Venezuelan.

▲ **CATEGORIZE** Describe the economic activities of Venezuela.

Baseball Fans Venezuelans cheer on their baseball team as it plays Italy in the 2006 World Baseball Classic.

COLOMBIA

Colombia

▼ **KEY QUESTION** What are the characteristics of Colombia's population?

Colombia was named after Christopher Columbus. It is second in population and fourth in size among South American countries. The Andes Mountains stretch across western Colombia. Hot lowlands are located along the coasts of the Caribbean Sea and the Pacific Ocean, and plains are found in the eastern part of the country.

History and Government Like Venezuela, Colombia was a Spanish colony until 1819, when Simón Bolívar gained Colombia's independence. Periods of violence and civil war followed. Colombians could not agree on what kind of government to establish. Some people wanted a strong central government, and others supported strong regional governments. Political violence and civil war continue to threaten the nation today.

Today, Colombia is a republic. The national government is made up of a legislative, executive, and judicial branch. A president, elected to a four-year term, heads the executive branch. Colombia is divided into 32 departments and the district of **Bogotá**, the nation's capital. Each department has an elected legislature and governor.

CONNECT Geography & Economics

Coffee

Coffee was brought to Colombia in 1808. Colombia today is the world's second-leading coffee producer. Its land and climate are perfect for growing a certain type of coffee—Arabica. This coffee grows best in rainy regions near the equator, at elevations between 3,600 and 6,300 feet. One coffee tree produces only enough beans to make one pound of coffee a year!

Economy Unlike Venezuela, Colombia's economy relies on agricultural products. Coffee is Colombia's leading legal export. Large plantations produce bananas, corn, cotton, and sugar. Colombian ranches raise cattle for meat and for leather goods. Stopping the illegal cocaine trade has been a major economic challenge for Colombia. Over the past 30 years, Colombia has supported the cut-flower industry as an alternative to growing cocaine-producing coca plants. It has become the second-largest exporter of cut flowers in the world.

Manufacturing and service industries have become increasingly important to Colombia's economy. Manufactured goods include clothing, chemicals, and processed foods. Service industries employ about 45 percent of Colombian workers.

Colombia produces large amounts of coal and petroleum. Emeralds from Colombian mines account for more than 90 percent of the world's supply.

People and Culture Spanish is Colombia's official language, and most Colombians are Roman Catholics. Most people are *mestizos*. About 70 percent of Colombia's people live in the highland valley basins in western Colombia. Colombia's capital and largest city, Bogotá, is located in a basin in the Andes Mountains.

Most Colombians live in urban areas. People who work in the business, service, and government industries in the cities live quite comfortably. Since the mid-1900s, rural Colombians have moved to cities in search of a better life. However, their lack of education and skills make it difficult to find jobs. They sometimes end up living in poverty in squatter settlements that circle the cities.

Colombia has produced famous writers and artists. **Gabriel García Márquez**, a Nobel Prize winner, writes about Colombian life using a mixture of realism and fantasy. **Fernando Botero** is an artist known for portraits that show people in exaggerated forms.

Bogotá Colombia's capital city lies more than 8,000 feet above sea level and is home to nearly seven million people.

 SUMMARIZE Describe the characteristics of Colombia's population.

Section 3 Assessment

ONLINE QUIZ
For test practice, go to
Interactive Review
@ ClassZone.com

TERMS & NAMES

1. Explain the importance of
- federal republic
- Caracas
- *joropo*
- Bogotá

USE YOUR READING NOTES

2. Find Main Ideas Use your completed diagram to answer the following question:

What kind of government do Venezuela and Colombia have today?

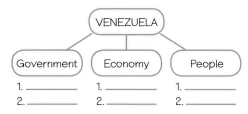

KEY IDEAS

3. What are Venezuela's main products and crops?

4. What three geographic regions are found in Colombia?

5. What industries are important to Colombia's economy?

CRITICAL THINKING

6. Identify Problems and Solutions How has the Venezuelan government attempted to curb the movement of people from rural to urban areas?

7. Compare and Contrast How are the histories of Venezuela and Colombia similar?

8. CONNECT to Today Much of Venezuela's income comes from oil production. How can that be both positive and negative for its economy?

9. WRITING Write a Marketing Campaign Ad Choose a product from Venezuela or Colombia, such as oil or cut flowers, and write an ad to convince other countries to buy this product.

Reading for Understanding

▶ Key Ideas

BEFORE, YOU LEARNED

The cultures of Venezuela and Colombia have been greatly influenced by their Spanish colonial heritage.

NOW YOU WILL LEARN

Indians and *mestizos* make up a large part of the population of Peru, Bolivia, and Ecuador.

▶ Vocabulary

TERMS & NAMES

llama a South American mammal related to the camel

alpaca a South American mammal related to the llama

selva Spanish name for the eastern Peruvian regions that contain rain forests

indigenous native to a region

landlocked surrounded by land with no access to a sea

quinoa a kind of weed from the Andean region that produces a small grain

REVIEW

altiplano the high plateau region of Bolivia

BACKGROUND VOCABULARY

edible fit for eating

Visual Vocabulary landlocked

▶ Reading Strategy

Re-create the chart shown at right. As you read and respond to the **KEY QUESTIONS**, use the chart to categorize details about Peru, Bolivia, and Ecuador.

 Skillbuilder Handbook, page R7

CATEGORIZE

	PERU	BOLIVIA	ECUADOR
Government			
Economy			
People			

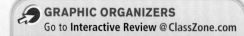
GRAPHIC ORGANIZERS
Go to **Interactive Review** @ ClassZone.com

Peru, Bolivia, and Ecuador

11.02 Examine the basic needs and wants of all human beings and assess the influence of factors such as environment, values, and beliefs in creating different cultural responses.
12.02 Describe the relationship between cultural values of selected societies of South America and Europe and their art, architecture, music, and literature, and assess their significance in contemporary culture.

Connecting to Your World

How would you adapt to living in a mountain region, where it was cold much of the time? For hundreds of years, Indians have lived in the Andes Mountains, where they developed innovative ways to deal with their harsh environment. They raised **llamas** and **alpacas**, small camel-like animals, on the mountainsides. The Inca used the freezing nighttime temperatures and the strong daytime sunlight to preserve and store potatoes and meat by freezing and drying them. Today, people in the Andes Mountains continue to adapt to their environment.

Peruvian Girl and Baby Alpaca

PERU

Peru

🔻 **KEY QUESTION** What products are made in Peru's coastal regions?

The Andes Mountains are located in Bolivia, Ecuador, and Peru. Peru is South America's third largest country. It has three land regions—the coast along the Pacific Ocean, the Andes Mountains, and the **selva**, an area of rain forests in eastern Peru.

Adapting to the Mountains Farmers in Bolivia plant crops on mountain terraces, such as these.

History and Government Between about 1200 and the early 1500s, Peru was home to the Inca civilization. The empire in the Andes Mountains extended from present-day Colombia to Argentina. In 1533, the Spanish conquered the Inca and ruled Peru for 300 years.

Since gaining independence in 1821, Peru has suffered military takeovers, dictatorships, and wars with neighboring countries and revolutionary groups. Today, Peru is a democratic republic. In 2001, Peruvians elected Alejandro Toledo, the first Indian president.

Economy Peru's rugged geography and scarce farmland have made it difficult for the country to create a strong economy. About one-third of the people are farmers. Coffee, potatoes, and grains are grown on high-land terraces. Sugar cane, cotton, and asparagus are grown in coastal valleys. Peru is one of the world's leading producers of asparagus.

Peru is a leading producer of copper, lead, silver, and zinc, which are mined in the Peruvian mountains. It also has a profitable fishing industry. Factories that process metals, fish, and sugar cane have been built along Peru's coast. Peru also exports petroleum.

Peruvian Weaver This woman weaves colorful yarns with a hand loom. **What do you think she will do with the products she creates?**

People and Culture *Mestizos* and **indigenous** people, or people native to a region, make up most of Peru's population. About ten percent are of European, African, or Asian ancestry. Spanish and Quechua (KEHCH•wuh) are Peru's official languages. About 75 percent of Peruvians speak Spanish, and about 25 percent speak Quechua or another Indian language.

Most Peruvians live in cities. While the middle and upper classes live in houses and apartment buildings, the poor live in slums or squatter settlements. Peru's government has tried to develop these settlements by providing running water and sewer systems.

Peruvians create beautiful sculpture, pottery, and textiles. Music and dancing are popular throughout Peru. As elsewhere in Latin America, football (soccer) is the most popular sport.

🔺 **CATEGORIZE** Identify the kinds of products that are produced in Peru's coastal regions.

The Lake Dwellers The Uros, descendants of an ancient people, live on floating islands on Lake Titicaca. Titicaca, the world's highest lake, is on the border of Peru and Bolivia. They use a kind of reed, or wetland grass, called *totora* (toh•TOH•rah) to make floating mats. They use the mats to create islands in the lake. The Uros also make reed boats and houses. They even have a floating soccer field!

CRITICAL THINKING
Make Inferences How might the Uros have contributed to making Lake Titicaca a popular tourist spot?

Bolivia and Ecuador

▼ **KEY QUESTION** How are Bolivia's and Ecuador's geographies, histories, and economies alike?

Bolivia is a **landlocked** country, surrounded entirely by land with no access to a sea. The country has two capital cities—Sucre, which is the official capital, and La Paz, which is the administrative capital. Ecuador is one of South America's smallest countries. Large plains are located in northern and eastern Bolivia and on Ecuador's Pacific coastal plain. The Andes Mountains circle a high plateau in western Bolivia and run through the center of Ecuador.

Evo Morales An Aymara, Morales was elected president of Bolivia by a large margin in December 2005. He took office in January 2006.

History and Government Both Bolivia and Ecuador were colonized by the Spanish and achieved independence in the 1800s. Bolivia was named for Simón Bolívar. *Ecuador* is the Spanish word for "equator," which crosses the country.

Both Bolivia and Ecuador struggled to develop democracies. Each country has had several constitutions that provided for free elections. But dictators and military leaders often took control.

Today, both Bolivia and Ecuador are democratic republics. Both governments include a national legislature, a supreme court, and an elected president. In 2005, Bolivians elected Evo Morales as president, the first indigenous person to be elected to that office in Bolivia.

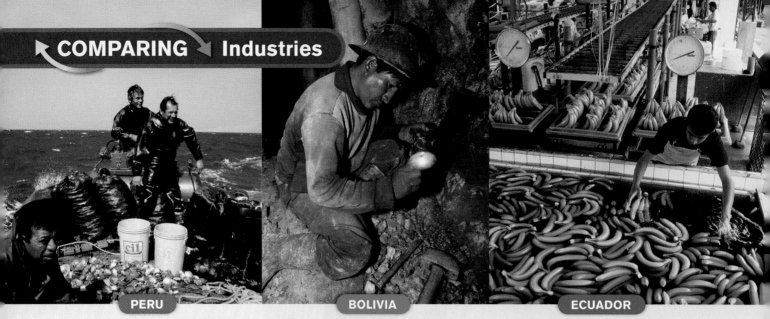

COMPARING Industries

PERU

- **Major industries:** mineral production, steel, petroleum refining, fishing (Above: fishing crew harvesting shellfish off the coast of Peru)
- **Major agricultural products:** coffee, cotton, sugar cane, asparagus
- **Major trading partner:** United States

BOLIVIA

- **Major industries:** mining, petroleum, food and beverages (Above: miner underground in Bolivian silver mine)
- **Major agricultural products:** soybeans, coffee, cotton, corn, potatoes
- **Major trading partner:** Brazil

ECUADOR

- **Major industries:** petroleum, food processing, textiles, wood products
- **Major agricultural products:** bananas, coffee, cacao, balsa wood, shrimp (Above: Ecuadorian workers in a banana-processing plant)
- **Major trading partner:** United States

CRITICAL THINKING

Compare and Contrast What agricultural products do Peru, Bolivia, and Ecuador have in common?

Economy Bolivia and Ecuador both have natural resources that have not been fully developed. Bolivia has many minerals and fertile soil. Ecuador's farm and timberland on the coast and in the eastern lowlands still need development. Both nations are working to develop their resources and help improve their economies.

One of Bolivia's leading exports is natural gas. Bolivia is also a leading producer of tin, but only a small percentage of the nation's workers are employed in this industry. About half of Bolivia's workers are farmers. Potatoes, wheat, and **quinoa**, a kind of weed that produces a small **edible** grain, are grown on the **altiplano**, the high plateau region of Bolivia, just east of the Andes Mountains. Bananas, beans, cacao, coffee, soybeans, and corn are also important agricultural products.

Ecuador's major export is petroleum. Gold is also an important mineral product. Most manufacturing in Ecuador takes place in Guayaquil (gwy•uh•KEEL), the nation's largest city, and in Quito, the capital. Ecuador's major manufacturing products include cement, processed foods, and textiles. Ecuador is the world's major supplier of balsa wood, used to make model airplanes. Like Bolivians, most Ecuadorians are farmers. They grow bananas, cacao, coffee, and sugar cane on the country's coastal plain.

People and Culture Spanish and the Indian languages Quechua and Aymara are Bolivia's three official languages. Most Bolivians practice subsistence farming. They have traditionally raised llamas to transport goods and alpacas to provide food, clothing, and fertilizer. In fact, Bolivia has more llamas than any other place in the world!

Most Ecuadorians are Indians or *mestizos*. Many Indians live in the Andes, speak Indian languages, and wear traditional clothes.

As they have for thousands of years, indigenous people in Bolivia today create jewelry, rugs, and shawls. Ecuadorian artists carve objects using the tagua plant. The tagua nut resembles ivory, which is a material that comes from elephant tusks. The tagua nut is used to make buttons and works of art. No animals are harmed to create tagua art.

Countries in the Andes Mountains are famous for pan-pipe music. Aymara and Quechua peoples play these flute-type instruments combined with drums and guitar-like instruments to create unique regional music.

Playing a Panpipe Peruvian musicians play panpipes, like the one this girl is playing.

 **COMPARE AND CONTRAST** Compare the geographies, histories, and economies of Bolivia and Ecuador.

 Section 4 Assessment

ONLINE QUIZ For test practice, go to **Interactive Review** @ ClassZone.com

TERMS & NAMES

1. Explain the importance of
- llama
- selva
- landlocked
- quinoa

USE YOUR READING NOTES

2. Categorize Use your chart to answer the following question:

How are Bolivia and Ecuador working to improve their economies?

	PERU	BOLIVIA	ECUADOR
Government			
Economy			
People			

KEY IDEAS

3. What kind of government do Peru, Ecuador, and Bolivia have?

4. How are most people in Peru, Ecuador, and Bolivia employed?

5. What groups of people make up a large percentage of the population of all three countries?

CRITICAL THINKING

6. Analyze Causes and Effects How do you think being a landlocked nation affects Bolivia's economy?

7. Make Inferences Why do you think that so many Indian communities have been able to keep their traditional customs and ways of life?

8. CONNECT to Today Why is it important for Bolivia and Ecuador to fully develop their natural resources?

9. WRITING Create a Picture Essay Choose an indigenous group in Peru, Bolivia, or Ecuador. Research their customs and ways of life. Create a captioned picture essay to present the information.

Tropical and mountain climates are both found in Middle America and Spanish-speaking South America. Each climate supports its own unique vegetation and animal life.

Tropical

The climate in tropical regions is hot year-round, with abundant rainfall. This climate produces the thick, green rain forests and the many exotic plants and animals that live in them. Farmers plant crops, such as sugar cane and bananas, that thrive in the tropical conditions.

Outdoor Activities

Scuba divers explore the coral reefs off the coast of Bonaire, one of the Caribbean islands.

Nevis Peak and Botanical Gardens on the Caribbean island of Nevis ▼

Agriculture

A farmer harvests sugar cane on the island nation of Barbados.

Wildlife

Sloths, such as this one hanging upside down from a branch, live in the tropical forests of Central America and South America and spend most of their lives in trees.

Mountain

Unlike the fairly constant climate of the tropical areas, the highland climate of the Andes Mountains varies with changes in elevation. Temperatures range from warm in the lower elevations to freezing in the highest elevations. Farming is difficult in this climate, but several crops, such as potatoes, barley, and wheat, grow well there. Various species of plants and animals have adapted to the mountain conditions.

Sacsayhuamán, an ancient Inca fortress, overlooks the city of Cuzco, Peru. ▼

Agriculture

These Ecuadorian farmers are harvesting barley.

Wildlife

The spectacled bear makes its home in the Andes Mountains. It gets its name from the markings around its eyes.

CRITICAL THINKING

1. **Compare and Contrast** What differences can be seen between tropical and mountain climate regions?

2. **Form an Opinion** Which climate region is more appealing to you? Why?

Reading for Understanding

▶ Key Ideas

BEFORE, YOU LEARNED

Geography has influenced the economies and people's ways of life in Peru, Bolivia, and Ecuador.

NOW YOU WILL LEARN

Geography has also influenced the economies of the nations in the Southern Cone.

▶ Vocabulary

TERMS & NAMES

gaucho Argentinian cowboy

Southern Cone South American nations located in the cone-shaped southernmost part of South America

estancia (eh•STAHN•syah) large farm or ranch in Argentina

Mercosur association of several South American countries to promote trade among the countries

REVIEW

José de San Martín leader for independence in southern South America

gross domestic product (GDP) the total value of all the goods and services produced in a country in a year

Pampas grassy plains in south-central South America

landlocked surrounded by land with no access to sea

Visual Vocabulary
Southern Cone

▶ Reading Strategy

Re-create the web diagram shown at right for each country in the section. As you read and respond to the **KEY QUESTIONS**, use the diagram to organize details about the nation's history and government, economy, and population.

 Skillbuilder Handbook, page R4

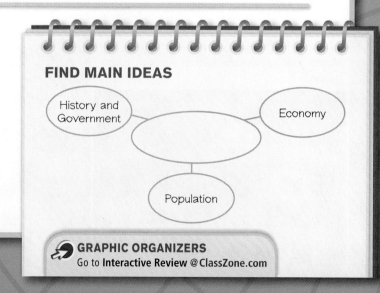

FIND MAIN IDEAS

History and Government

Economy

Population

⚡ GRAPHIC ORGANIZERS
Go to Interactive Review @ ClassZone.com

SECTION
5

FOCUS ON

The Southern Cone

8.01 Describe the role of key historical figures and evaluate their impact on past and present societies in South America and Europe.
11.04 Identify examples of economic, political, and social changes, such as agrarian to industrial economies, monarchical to democratic governments, and the roles of women and minorities, and analyze their impact on culture.

Connecting to Your World

Cowboys played an important role in cattle ranching in the American West in the 1800s. In Argentina, **gauchos**, or cowboys, also play an important role in cattle ranching. As in the United States, the life and culture of gauchos is the subject of many Argentinian stories and movies. But the gaucho is just one aspect of the culture of Argentina and its neighbors.

Argentina and Chile

🔻 **KEY QUESTION** How do Argentina's plains and Chile's mountains affect their economies?

Together with Paraguay and Uruguay, Argentina and Chile form part of South America's **Southern Cone**, the cone-shaped southernmost area of South America. The largest of the four countries is Argentina, a country of plains, plateaus, mountains, forests, and a long coastline. The Andes Mountains make up much of Chile, the world's longest and narrowest country. Argentina is bordered by Paraguay on the north and Uruguay on the east.

Argentinian gaucho

Patagonia Sheep farmers round up their sheep. **How would you describe the land on which this sheep ranch is located?**

Michelle Bachelet
Michelle Bachelet won more than 53 percent of the votes. She promised to bring more jobs to Chile and to work for social justice.

History and Government The Spanish who first arrived in Argentina expected to find gold and silver. In fact, *Argentina* comes from the Latin word *argentum*, which means "silver." *Chile* likely comes from the Native American word meaning "where the land ends." In the 1500s, the Spanish came looking for gold and silver in both regions. Later, **José de San Martín** of Argentina helped both countries gain independence from Spain by 1818.

Like other South American nations, Argentina was controlled by dictators into the 20th century. Chile's government, on the other hand, was more stable. Presidents were often elected because they promised social reforms. In 1973, however, General Augusto Pinochet took control of Chile's government and ruled as a military dictator until 1990. Today, Argentina and Chile are republics. In 2006, Chile elected its first female president, Michelle Bachelet.

Economy In both Argentina and Chile, service industries make up most of the nations' **gross domestic product (GDP)** and employ more than half of the nations' workers. Most of Argentina's manufacturing occurs in factories in and around Buenos Aires. The **Pampas** and Patagonia are important to Argentina's agriculture. Beef cattle and grain and fruits, such as wheat and grapes, are raised on large ranches and farms, called ***estancias*** (eh•STAHN-syahs), on the Pampas. Thousands of sheep graze in Patagonia. Petroleum from Patagonia is Argentina's main mineral. Fishing along Argentina's long coastline is also an important part of Argentina's economy.

CONNECT to Math

The GDP is an important indicator of the strength of a nation's economy. A strong GDP indicates a healthy economy and usually influences a nation's stock market in a positive way.

Stock market in Buenos Aires, Argentina

Activity

Make a GDP Bar Graph

Materials
• Gross domestic product figures for Argentina, Chile, Paraguay, and Uruguay
• Graph paper

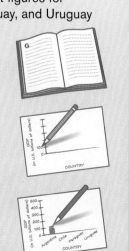

1. Research the latest GDP figures for Argentina, Chile, Paraguay, and Uruguay.

2. Make a graph. Label the horizontal axis "Country." Label the vertical axis "GDP in U.S. billions of dollars." Label the axis by 100s, starting from 0.

3. Draw a bar for each country to represent the GDP figure for that country.

Because only about three percent of Chile's land can be farmed, Chile developed copper mining in its mountains and fishing industries along its coast. Today, Chile is the world's leading copper producer. Both Argentina and Chile are part of **Mercosur**, an association of several South American countries, to promote trade among the countries.

People and Culture Argentina and Chile have large urban populations, particularly in the major cities of Buenos Aires and Santiago. Like other South American cities, these cities are surrounded by squatter settlements.

About 85 percent of Argentina's population is of European ancestry. Although gauchos still work on Argentina's ranches today, they are also celebrated, much like American cowboys, in Argentinian poetry, literature, painting, and music. The tango, a dance that combines European and African influences, is Argentina's national dance.

Chile's population, unlike Argentina's, is mostly *mestizo*. Many Chileans have left difficult conditions in rural areas for opportunities in the cities. Chile has produced many famous writers, such as poets Gabriela Mistral and Pablo Neruda. Chileans spend their leisure time going to the movies and playing and watching football (soccer), the most popular sport.

Dancing the Tango The tango involves alternating long, slow steps with quick, short steps.

▲ **DRAW CONCLUSIONS** Explain how geography affects parts of Argentina's and Chile's economies.

Paraguay and Uruguay

▼ **KEY QUESTION** How is the population of Paraguay different from Uruguay's?

Paraguay is a small **landlocked** country of rivers, hills, and forests. Hilly grasslands cover much of Uruguay, located southeast of Paraguay. Both countries won independence from the Spanish, experienced political turmoil, and today are constitutional republics.

Paraguay Most people in Paraguay work in service industries and in agriculture. Cattle raising and most farming take place in eastern Paraguay, where the richest soil is found. Forests cover much of eastern Paraguay, and wood products are important industries. Paraguay is a founding member of Mercosur.

Mestizos make up most of Paraguay's population, and the Guaraní (GWAH•ruh•NEE) are the nation's largest indigenous group. The Guaraní influence is reflected in Paraguay's arts, particularly in music and handicrafts. The Guaraní are especially known for nanduti lace, which incorporates a lace-making technique introduced by the Spanish.

Montevideo The Plaza Independencia is located in the center of Montevideo in Uruguay. **What other culture makes use of plazas in its cities?**

Uruguay More than 60 percent of Uruguay's people work in service industries. Uruguay's plains and grasslands are perfect for raising cattle and sheep. Meat, hides, and wools are the nation's biggest exports. Like other Southern Cone nations, Uruguay is a member of Mercosur.

Most of Uruguay's people are of Spanish and Italian ancestry. Most people live in cities, half in Montevideo, the capital city. Unlike many other South American nations, Uruguay's culture is influenced more by European traditions than by native ones. Gaucho folklore has inspired Uruguay's music and art and Montevideo's Gaucho Museum.

 COMPARE AND CONTRAST Compare the populations of Paraguay and Uruguay.

Section 5 Assessment

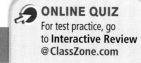 **ONLINE QUIZ** For test practice, go to **Interactive Review** @ ClassZone.com

TERMS & NAMES

1. Explain the importance of
- gaucho
- Southern Cone
- *estancia*
- Mercosur

USE YOUR READING NOTES

2. Find Main Ideas Use your completed diagram to answer the following question:

What products account for most of Uruguay's exports?

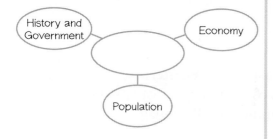

KEY IDEAS

3. How are the histories of the Southern Cone nations alike?

4. What industry employs a majority of the people in Argentina and Chile?

5. Why does most farming and cattle ranching occur in eastern Paraguay?

CRITICAL THINKING

6. Make Inferences Why have Southern Cone nations become members of Mercosur?

7. Draw Conclusions How might Argentina's geography and size contribute to its strong economy?

8. CONNECT to Today In 2006, Chileans elected their first female president. What do you think this says about women's role in Chilean politics?

9. MATH **Create a Pie Graph** Choose one of the Southern Cone nations and research its major exports. Make a pie graph to present the information.

Interactive ◄─ Review

Click here to complete these and other activities online @ ClassZone.com

CHAPTER SUMMARY

Key Idea 1
Central American countries face challenges as they improve their economies.

Key Idea 2
Europe and Africa have influenced Caribbean cultures.

Key Idea 3
Venezuela's economy depends heavily on petroleum, while Colombia's economy depends more on agricultural products.

Key Idea 4
Indians and *mestizos* make up a large part of Peru, Bolivia, and Ecuador.

Key Idea 5
Geography has influenced the economies of Southern Cone nations.

For **Review and Study Notes**, go to **Interactive Review** @ ClassZone.com

NAME GAME

Use the Terms & Names list to complete each sentence on paper or online.

1. I am a place that is ruled by or closely connected with another country.   **dependency**

2. I describe the countries in the southern part of South America. _____

3. I describe the countries of Bolivia and Paraguay. _____

4. I am the national folk dance of Venezuela. _____

5. I am a measure of a country's economy. _____

6. I am a trade agreement made between Central American countries._____

7. I am an important animal in the Andes Mountains. _____

8. I am a kind of grassy plain. _____

9. I draw tourists to a natural habitat without harming the environment. _____

10. I am a large farm in Argentina. _____

CAFTA
commonwealth
dependency
ecotourism
estancia
gaucho
gross domestic product, or GDP
joropo
landlocked
llama
llanos
Southern Cone

Activities

GeoGame

Use this online map to show what you know about the geography of Middle America and Spanish-Speaking South America. Drag and drop each place name to its location on the map.

Geo GAME

Bogotá

Caracas

Cuba

Panama

Andes Mountains

Present-Day Middle America and Spanish-Speaking South America

Caracas

To play the complete game, go to **Interactive Review** @ ClassZone.com

Crossword Puzzle

Complete an online crossword puzzle to test your knowledge of the region's history, culture, government, and economics.

ACROSS
1. a small camel-like animal, related to the llama

CHAPTER 7 Assessment

VOCABULARY

Explain the significance of each of the following.

1. ecotourism
2. one-crop economy
3. Taino
4. commonwealth
5. landlocked

Explain how the terms in each group are related.

6. CAFTA and Mercosur
7. dictator and communism
8. Pampas, gaucho, and *estancia*

KEY IDEAS

① Central America

9. What is Central America's main economic activity?
10. What group of people makes up most of Central America's population?

② The Caribbean

11. Why did the Spanish bring enslaved Africans to the Caribbean islands?
12. What kind of government does Puerto Rico have?

③ Venezuela and Colombia

13. What product is the most important to the economy of Venezuela?
14. What is Colombia's leading export?

④ Peru, Bolivia, and Ecuador

15. What are three economic activities in Peru?
16. What are the major mineral exports of Bolivia and Ecuador?

⑤ Argentina and Chile

17. What economic activity provides most of Argentina's and Chile's gross domestic product?
18. In what parts of Argentina does farming and ranching take place?
19. Where do most people in Uruguay live?

CRITICAL THINKING

20. **Compare and Contrast** Create a chart to compare the industries and major products of Venezuela, Peru, and Argentina.

COUNTRY	MAJOR INDUSTRIES/PRODUCTS
Venezuela	
Peru	
Argentina	

21. **Evaluate** What challenges do Central American countries face today?
22. **Identify Problems and Solutions** What have Central American and Caribbean nations done to help solve the problem of one-crop economies?
23. **Five Themes: Movement** How has the settlement of Caribbean nations affected the culture of those nations?
24. **Connect to History** What conditions created during the Spanish conquest of South America made it difficult for nations there to form stable governments?

Answer the ESSENTIAL QUESTION

How are the countries of this region working to strengthen their governments and economies?

Written response Write a two- or three- paragraph response to the Essential Question. Be sure to consider the key ideas of each section. Use the rubric below to guide your thinking.

Response Rubric
A strong response will:
- discuss ways in which the countries have strengthened their governments
- explain how the nations have strengthened their economies

✔ **Test Practice**
- Online Test Practice @ ClassZone.com
- Test-Taking Strategies and Practice at the front of this book

THEMATIC MAP

Use the map to answer questions 1 and 2.

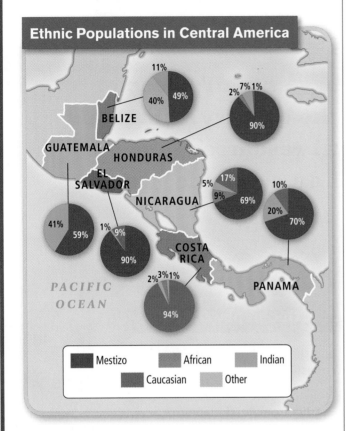

Ethnic Populations in Central America

Legend:
- Mestizo
- African
- Indian
- Caucasian
- Other

1. What percentage of Guatemalans are *mestizo*?

- **A.** about 59 percent
- **B.** about 33 percent
- **C.** about 3 percent
- **D.** about 1 percent

2. Which of the following countries has the largest percentage of *mestizos*?

- **A.** Belize
- **B.** Panama
- **C.** El Salvador
- **D.** Guatemala

TABLE

Use the table below to answer questions 3 and 4 on your paper.

Literacy and Life Expectancy in Selected Countries		
	Literacy Rate	**Life Expectancy**
Haiti	53 percent	53 years
Costa Rica	96 percent	77 years
Ecuador	93 percent	76 years
Argentina	97 percent	76 years

Source: *The World Factbook*, 2006

3. Which country has the lowest life expectancy?

4. What conclusion can you draw about the relationship between literacy rates and life expectancy?

GeoActivity

1. INTERDISCIPLINARY ACTIVITY–SCIENCE

Use the library or visit a zoo to find out about an animal that makes its home in the region, such as the Andean condor, spectacled bear, tapir, or toucan. Find out how the animal adapts to its environment. Present the information in an illustrated, captioned poster.

2. WRITING FOR SOCIAL STUDIES

Write an ad that encourages people to visit one of the countries discussed in the chapter. Your ad should focus on the landforms, people, and cultural features that visitors to the country would find interesting.

3. MENTAL MAPPING

Create an outline map of South America and label the following:

- Southern Cone nations
- llanos
- altiplano
- Pampas
- Andes Mountains
- coastal plains
- equator

1
HISTORY & GOVERNMENT

From Portuguese Colony to Modern Giant

2
CULTURE

A Multicultural Society

3
ECONOMICS

Developing an Abundant Land

ESSENTIAL QUESTION

How have Brazil's people used the country's abundant natural resources to make Brazil an economic giant?

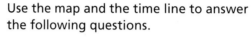
CONNECT → **Geography & History**

Use the map and the time line to answer the following questions.

1. When was Brazil claimed by Portugal?
2. How far is Brasília from Rio de Janeiro?

Geography
◄ **1494** Spain and Portugal sign the Treaty of Tordesillas.

1494

History
1500 Pedro Álvares Cabral claims Brazil for Portugal. ►

History
1822 Brazil declares independence from Portugal.

History
1888 Brazil abolishes slavery.

VENEZUELA

GUYANA

SURINAME

FRENCH
GUIANA

COLOMBIA

RORAIMA

AMAPÁ

Negro River

Amazon River

Manaus

AMAZONAS

Madeira River

Purús River

PARÁ

Tapajos River

Equator   0°

MARANHÃO

Fortaleza

CEARÁ

RIO GRANDE
DO NORTE

10°N

PIAUÍ

PARAÍBA

PERNAMBUCO

Recife

B R A Z I L

PERU

ACRE

RONDÔNIA

Xingu River

MATO
GROSSO

Tocantins River

TOCANTINS

ALAGOAS

SERGIPE

10°S

BAHIA

Salvador

BOLIVIA

Brasília

GOIÁS

ATLANTIC
OCEAN

DISTRITO
FEDERAL

MINAS
GERAIS

MATO
GROSSO
DO SUL

Belo
Horizonte

ESPÍRITO SANTO

PACIFIC
OCEAN

PARAGUAY

Paraná River

SÃO
PAULO

São Paulo

RIO DE JANEIRO

Rio de Janeiro

20°S

Tropic of Capricorn

PARANÁ

CHILE

ARGENTINA

SANTA
CATARINA

RIO GRANDE
DO SUL

Pôrto Alegre

URUGUAY

N   W   E   S

0   200   400 miles
0   200   400 kilometers

National border
State border
★ National capital
● Other cities

Government
1960 Brasília
becomes Brazil's
new capital.

Government
1985 Military rule
ends in Brazil.

Today

History
▲ 1889 Brazil
becomes a republic.

Culture
◄ 2002 Brazil wins its
fifth World Cup in soccer.

209

Reading for Understanding

▶ Key Ideas

BEFORE, YOU LEARNED

Geography plays an important role in the economic activities of the countries of the Southern Cone.

NOW YOU WILL LEARN

Brazil's government is dealing with the problems resulting from urbanization.

▶ Vocabulary

TERMS & NAMES

Treaty of Tordesillas (TAWR•day•SEEL•yahs) 1494 treaty that gave Portugal control over land that is now part of Brazil

Pedro Álvares Cabral Portuguese explorer who in 1500 claimed land that is now part of Brazil for Portugal

Dom Pedro I Brazil's first Portuguese emperor; declared Brazil's independence from Portugal in 1822

Dom Pedro II second emperor of Brazil, under whose rule slavery was abolished in Brazil in 1888

favelas Brazilian name for the poor neighborhoods that surround the cities

Rio de Janeiro (REE•oh day zhuh•NAYR•OH) Brazil's capital city from 1763 to 1960

Brasília Brazil's current capital city

REVIEW

urbanization growth in the number of people living in urban areas

Visual Vocabulary
Dom Pedro I

▶ Reading Strategy

Re-create the time line shown at right. As you read and respond to the **KEY QUESTIONS**, use the time line to show the major events in Brazil's history and the development of a democratic government.

 See Skillbuilder Handbook, page R6

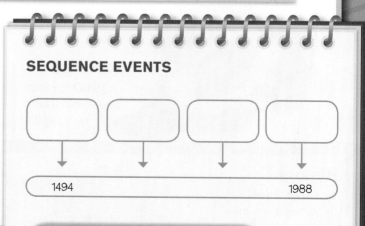

SEQUENCE EVENTS

1494   1988

GRAPHIC ORGANIZERS
Go to Interactive Review @ ClassZone.com

From Portuguese Colony to Modern Giant

8.01 Describe the role of key historical figures and evaluate their impact on past and present societies in South America and Europe.

9.04 Describe how different governments in South America and Europe select leaders and establish laws in comparison to the United States and analyze the strengths and weaknesses of each.

Connecting to Your World

What does the Statue of Liberty represent to you? For many people, it represents the United States, symbolizes freedom, and welcomes those who arrive at the nation's shores. In Brazil, a similar symbol is the statue of Christ the Redeemer, which welcomes people to Rio de Janeiro, Brazil's second largest city. Like the Statue of Liberty, it is one of the world's best-known and most-visited monuments.

Portuguese Build a Colony

▼ **KEY QUESTION** What helped to make Brazil a profitable colony for Portugal?

After Columbus' expeditions, Portugal feared that if Columbus had found a route to Asia, Spain might claim lands that Portugal had already claimed. So in 1494, both countries signed the **Treaty of Tordesillas** (TAWR•day•SEEL•yahs), which drew an imaginary line from north to south around the world. Spain could claim all lands west of the line, and Portugal those east of the line. This gave Portugal control of the land in what is now eastern Brazil. The treaty line is illustrated on the map on the next page.

Rio de Janeiro The statue of Christ the Redeemer overlooks Rio de Janeiro and Guanabara Bay. Sugarloaf Mountain is seen in the distance.

BRAZIL

Rio de Janeiro

211

Treaty of Tordesillas

Treaty of Tordesillas, 1494

EUROPE

PORTUGAL   SPAIN

AFRICA

SOUTH
AMERICA

N
W   E
S

Portuguese

Spanish

| 0 | 1,500 | 3,000 miles |
| 0 | 1,500 | 3,000 kilometers |

CONNECT Geography & History

Region In 1494, which country claimed most of the lands in North and South America?

The Colony Expands In 1500, **Pedro Álvares Cabral** landed on the coast of what is now eastern Brazil and claimed the land for Portugal. Like the Spanish in South America, the Portuguese came to find gold and silver. When they found neither, Portuguese colonists cleared out large areas of the land to establish sugar cane plantations. The huge demand for sugar made it an important export and a source of wealth for Portugal.

The Portuguese later developed tobacco and cotton plantations and cattle ranches for meat and hides. They forced the indigenous people to work on the plantations and ranches. Many died from disease and overwork, and others fled into the rain forest. African slaves were brought in to replace them.

The discovery of gold in the late 1600s and diamonds in the early 1700s west of present-day Rio de Janeiro attracted many people farther inland. Coffee plants were introduced in Brazil in 1727, and by the mid-1800s coffee had become Brazil's chief export.

Independence to Republic Portugal controlled Brazil from 1500 to 1822. In 1807, the French ruler, Napoleon, invaded Portugal. As a result, Prince John, the Portuguese ruler, fled to Brazil and established a monarchy there.

In 1821, Prince John returned to Portugal, leaving his son, Pedro, in charge of the colony. Pedro and other officials declared Brazil's independence from Portugal in 1822, and Pedro became **Dom Pedro I**, Brazil's first emperor. Unpopular with the people, he returned to Portugal in 1831, and his son became Emperor **Dom Pedro II**.

Under Dom Pedro II's rule, Brazil started to become industrialized. Railroads and telegraph lines improved transportation and communication. Pedro II worked to end slavery, which was abolished in 1888. This angered wealthy plantation owners, who forced Pedro II to give up the throne. Brazil became a constitutional republic in 1889.

🔺 **FIND MAIN IDEA** Explain what made Brazil a profitable Portuguese colony.

Dom Pedro II

	UNITED STATES	BRAZIL
Type of Government	federal republic	federal republic
Branches of Government	legislative, executive, judicial	legislative, executive, judicial
Election of President	elected directly by the people and the electoral college	elected directly by the people; must win 50 percent plus one votes
Voting	voters must be at least 18 years old; voting is a choice	voters must be at least 16 years old; voting is mandatory for citizens ages 18 to 70

CRITICAL THINKING

1. **Compare** How are the Brazilian and U.S. governments alike?

2. **Contrast** How are elections different in the two countries?

Challenges of a Modern Nation

▼ **KEY QUESTION** What challenges does the government of Brazil face today?

After adopting a constitution in 1891 that was based on the U.S. constitution, Brazil struggled to establish a democratic government. Dictators and military leaders ruled the nation until 1985. Today's government faces the problem of **urbanization** and the wide gap between the nation's rich and poor.

Establishing a Democratic Government After military rule ended, Brazilians voted for a president for the first time since 1960. Today, Brazil is ruled by the constitution established in 1988.

Brazil's federal government includes an executive branch led by a president, a two-house legislature, and a court system. The country is divided into 26 states and a federal district in Brasília. Since Brazil has many political parties with different viewpoints, elected officials have to work with all the parties in order to rule effectively.

Urbanization During the last half of the 20th century, millions of people from rural areas moved to Brazil's cities in search of jobs. Brazil's urban population more than doubled between 1950 and 2000. Several of Brazil's cities are among the largest cities in the world in population. All but two of Brazil's heavily populated cities are located near Brazil's eastern coast.

São Paulo

Tresópolis

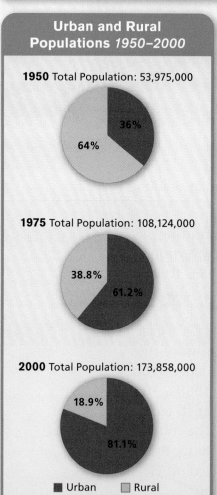

Urban and Rural Populations *1950–2000*

1950 Total Population: 53,975,000

36%
64%

1975 Total Population: 108,124,000

38.8%
61.2%

2000 Total Population: 173,858,000

18.9%
81.1%

■ Urban   ■ Rural

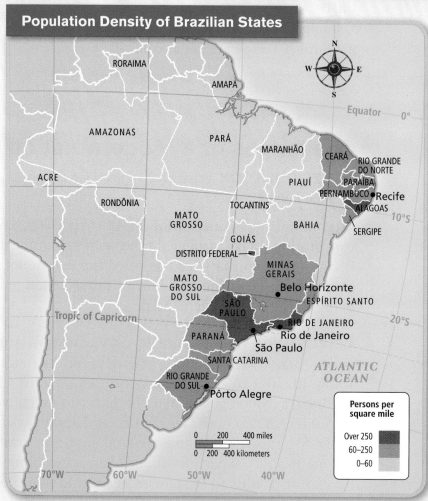

Population Density of Brazilian States

RORAIMA
AMAPÁ
Equator 0°
AMAZONAS
PARÁ
MARANHÃO
CEARÁ
RIO GRANDE DO NORTE
ACRE
PIAUÍ
PARAÍBA
PERNAMBUCO ● Recife
RONDÔNIA
TOCANTINS
ALAGOAS
MATO GROSSO
10°S
GOIÁS
BAHIA
SERGIPE
DISTRITO FEDERAL
MINAS GERAIS
MATO GROSSO DO SUL
Belo Horizonte
ESPÍRITO SANTO
SÃO PAULO
RIO DE JANEIRO
20°S
Tropic of Capricorn
Rio de Janeiro
PARANÁ
São Paulo
SANTA CATARINA
ATLANTIC OCEAN
RIO GRANDE DO SUL ● Pôrto Alegre

0   200   400 miles
0   200   400 kilometers

Persons per square mile
Over 250
60–250
0–60

70°W   60°W   50°W   40°W

Source: Population Division of the Department of Economic and Social Affairs of the United Nations Secretariat, *World Population Prospects: The 2004 Revision* and *World Urbanization Prospects: The 2003 Revision*

CRITICAL THINKING

1. Draw Conclusions What is the population density in most of Brazil?

2. Evaluate About how many people lived in urban areas in Brazil in 2000?

Many poor Brazilians who moved from rural areas work at low-income jobs or are unemployed. Most live in neighborhoods called *favelas*, located on the outskirts of cities. In 1960 the Brazilian government moved the capital city from **Rio de Janeiro** (REE•oh day zhuh•NAYR•oh) to **Brasília**, about 600 miles inland. The Brazilian government has encouraged people to move inland, even offering land to people who are willing to move to the nation's interior.

Favela This *favela* is located outside of Rio de Janeiro. **Why might it be located there?**

Bridging the Gap Between Rich and Poor Today, Brazil has one of the largest economies in the world. However, one of the major challenges facing Brazil is how to bridge the large gap between the rich and poor. A small number of Brazilians live comfortably or in luxury, but most Brazilians are poor. Brazil has one of the most uneven distributions of land in the world. Two percent of landowners own most of the land, while more than half of Brazil's farmers work on less than three percent of the land. To help narrow the income gap, Brazil will have to create more jobs for the nation's poor.

▲ **SUMMARIZE** Discuss some of the challenges facing Brazil today.

Section 1 Assessment

ONLINE QUIZ
For test practice, go to
Interactive Review
@ ClassZone.com

TERMS & NAMES

1. Explain the importance of
- Pedro Álvares Cabral
- *favela*
- Rio de Janeiro
- Brasília

USE YOUR READING NOTES

2. Sequence Events Use your time line to answer the following question:

How long after becoming a republic did military rule end in Brazil?

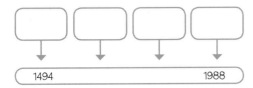

1494   1988

KEY IDEAS

3. What European nation developed Brazil as its colony?

4. Where do most people in Brazil live today?

5. Why did the Brazilian government offer land to people to move to the nation's interior?

CRITICAL THINKING

6. Make Inferences How has uneven land distribution contributed to poverty in Brazil?

7. Analyze Causes and Effects Why has urbanization resulted in the creation of *favelas* in Brazil's cities?

8. CONNECT to Today What is one action Brazil's government hopes to take to narrow the income gap between its rich and poor?

9. WRITING Write a Newspaper Article Research information about Brazil's government. Find out who is the current president, how the legislative branch is organized, and the term of office for both. Present your findings in the form of a newspaper article.

Reading for Understanding

▶ Key Ideas

BEFORE, YOU LEARNED
Brazil's government is dealing with problems resulting from urbanization.

NOW YOU WILL LEARN
Several cultures have influenced Brazil's unique culture.

▶ Vocabulary

TERMS & NAMES

Candomblé (kahn•duhm•BLEH) African religious practices that are mixed with Roman Catholic beliefs to produce a unique belief

quilombos (kih•LOHM•buhs) communities created by escaped African slaves

samba (SAM•buh) music and dance, with roots in African rhythms; the most famous form of Brazilian music worldwide

cuíca (kwee•kuh) a friction drum used in the samba

bossa nova (BAHS•uh NOH•vuh) a jazz version of the samba

capoeira (KAP•oh•AY•ruh) a Brazilian dance combined with martial arts

REVIEW

immigrant a person who leaves one area to settle in another

mural a wall painting

Visual Vocabulary *capoeira*

▶ Reading Strategy

Re-create the chart shown at right. As you read and respond to the **KEY QUESTIONS**, use the chart to organize important details about Brazil's people and culture.

 See Skillbuilder Handbook, page R7

CATEGORIZE

ART AND ARCHITECTURE	MUSIC	ENTERTAINMENT
1.	1.	1.
2.	2.	2.
3.	3.	3.

 GRAPHIC ORGANIZERS
Go to **Interactive Review** @ ClassZone.com

A Multicultural Society

12.02 Describe the relationship between cultural values of selected societies of South America and Europe and their art, architecture, music and literature, and assess their significance in contemporary culture.

12.03 Identify examples of cultural borrowing, such as language, traditions, and technology, and evaluate their importance in the development of selected societies in South America and Europe.

Connecting to Your World

Think about some of the foods you eat. Think about the music that you and your family enjoy. Chances are that many of the foods you enjoy and the music you listen to have their roots in a variety of cultures. If you visited Brazil, you would see how a variety of cultures has also influenced the foods, music, and other aspects of Brazilian culture today.

A Blend of Many Cultures

▼ **KEY QUESTION** What cultures have most influenced Brazil?

Brazilian culture includes European, African, Asian, and Indian influences. Portuguese is the official language. Most Brazilians are Roman Catholic. At the same time, Brazilians of African ancestry mix *Candomblé* (kahn•duhm•BLEH), West African religious practices, with Catholicism to create a unique Brazilian blend.

Brazilian Diversity
These Brazilian girls are getting ready to participate in Carnival in Rio de Janeiro.

Daniel Munduruku is a Munduruku Indian. He has written several books about his culture. Here he describes learning the ancient myths of his people.

Daniel Munduruku
Tales of the Amazon
How the Munduruku Indians Live

Illustrated by Laurabeatriz

> When I was a . . . boy, my grandfather would . . . tell the stories that explained the origins of our people and the vision of the universe. . . . Now . . . I realize that those ancient myths say what cannot be said. They are pure poetry, and through them I see how an identity can be created in the oral tradition.
>
> Source: *Tales of the Amazon, How the Munduruku Indians Live*

CRITICAL THINKING

Summarize How is storytelling important in the Munduruku culture?

Native Brazilians Up to 6 million Indians lived in Brazil before the Portuguese arrived. Tens of thousands died from diseases brought by the European colonists. Today, only about 700,000 Indians live in Brazil, mostly in the Amazon rain forest. They make up less than one percent of Brazil's population. The Tupi and Guarani make up the largest groups. Other tribes, such as the Yanomami and Bororo, still follow traditional ways of hunting and farming.

The Brazilian government has set up reservations to protect these cultures. But even isolated groups now have contact with outsiders, such as miners, loggers, and researchers, who move into the area to study native cultures. This increased contact threatens the groups' traditional ways of life, arts, crafts, and languages.

Yanomami Woman A Yanomami woman poses with her child. **How might being photographed threaten the Yanomami's traditional way of life?**

Africans Today, most Brazilians with African ancestry live in the nation's northern and coastal regions and make up about 6 percent of the population. The Portuguese brought Africans to Brazil between the 1500s and 1800s to work on the sugar plantations. In fact, of all the slaves brought to North and South America, more than a third were brought to Brazil.

Some of these slaves escaped to freedom in Brazil's inland northern region, where they established communities that were similar to their African homes. They called the settlements **quilombos** (kih•LOHM•buhs), an African word for "housing." By the end of the 1600s, as many as 25,000 Africans may have lived in these communities. *Quilombos* can still be found in parts of Brazil today, particularly in the northern part, where people continue their traditional way of life. Today most Brazilians of African ancestry live in the northeastern state of Bahia. Its capital, Salvador, was the center of the Portuguese empire, sugar industry, and slave trade.

African influences are evident in various parts of Brazilian culture. African slaves created Brazil's national food, *feijoada* (fayh•zhoo•AH•duh), a bean stew. African rhythms play an important role in Brazilian music. Brazil's art and literature also reflect an African influence.

Europeans and Asians In the 1700s, Europeans viewed Brazil as a place to acquire wealth. With the discovery of gold and diamonds, many immigrated to Brazil to make their fortunes. After Brazil declared its independence, many Europeans, including Italians, Spanish, Portuguese, and Germans, came to work in Brazil, mostly in the coffee industry. Today, people of European ancestry make up about half of Brazil's population. Most live in the southern part of the country.

Japanese **immigrants** first began arriving in Brazil in the early 1900s. Most came to work on coffee or tea farms. More Japanese arrived after World War II. Today Brazil has the largest Japanese population outside of Japan, with most making their homes in the state of São Paulo. In recent years, Asians from China and Korea have also immigrated to Brazil.

▲ **EVALUATE** Explain how Brazil's culture is a blend of several cultures.

CONNECT History & Culture

African Influence on Brazilian Food

Since most slaves brought to Brazil arrived from West Africa, West African cooking has had a strong influence on Brazilian food. Palm oil, called *dendê*, and chili peppers, called *malagueta*, are basic West African cooking ingredients. Today, Bahian cooks make *moqueca*, a popular stew. It is made with seafood, coconut, garlic, onion, parsley, *malagueta*, and *dendê*.

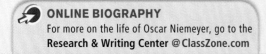
Arts and Entertainment

▼ **KEY QUESTION** What are some ways Brazilians enjoy holidays and leisure time?

Brazil's art, literature, music, and celebrations reflect the nation's blend of cultural traditions. Brazil's Carnival, in particular, highlights Brazil's cultural diversity.

Architecture and Art Brazil's earliest art included the crafts made by Brazil's Indian groups. Their work included such items as pottery, baskets, and jewelry. Native American groups today continue to make these handicrafts, many of which are sold to tourists in Brazilian markets.

António Francisco Lisboa, known as Aleijadinho, is a well known sculptor of the colonial period. He created religious sculptures for many churches in the mid- to late 1700s. Today, Mario Cravo Junior is an important sculptor who creates statues made with concrete.

Cândido Portinari is a famous Brazilian painter and muralist. His six largest **murals** are found in New York's United Nations building and in Washington's Library of Congress. Much of his art reflects rural life and social concerns.

Brazil is the home of Oscar Niemeyer, one of the world's most famous architects. He is best known for designing several buildings in Brasília, Brazil's capital. Niemeyer has also designed a variety of buildings in several countries throughout the world, including France, Ghana, Israel, and Lebanon. More recently, Niemeyer created a unique design for an art museum near the city of Rio de Janeiro.

Music and Dance Brazilian music is a blend of African, European, and Indian cultures. Brazilians enjoy dancing to the **samba** (SAM•buh), the most famous form of Brazilian music. The samba developed in the early 1900s and has its roots in African rhythms. The samba has many forms, but the most popular is the street samba danced during the celebrations of Carnival, a Brazilian holiday. The drum plays a major role in Brazilian music. Brazilian drums come in many shapes and sizes, each producing its own sound and rhythm. Drummers play the surdo, a bass drum, and the *cuíca* (kwee•kuh), a friction drum, to create samba rhythms.

Worldster
A Day in Pedro's Life

To learn more about Pedro and his world, go to the **Activity Center** @ ClassZone.com

Hi! My name is Pedro. I am 13 years old and live in São Paulo, the largest city in Brazil and the third largest city in the world in population. I attend a public school, a short walk from my apartment. Many of my friends live in the same apartment building, so there's always someone to do things with. Let me tell you about my day.

This is how to say "Hello, my name is Pedro" in Portuguese:

"Oi, meu nome é Pedro."

6 A.M. My family and I have breakfast before my parents go to work and my sister and I go to school. Today we're having cereal and papaya.

7 A.M.–noon My school day begins early. Because of overcrowded schools, many students go to school in two shifts. I like having the morning shift. My school year runs from March to December.

1 P.M. My family and I get together for the main meal of the day. Today I'm looking forward to *feijoada,* which is a dish made with black beans and beef.

6 P.M. After I finish my homework and have a small snack, I'm off to the local park to play soccer. Next to playing the game, my favorite thing to do is to watch our city's professional team play soccer.

CONNECT to Your Life

Journal Entry Think about your typical daily schedule. How are the meals you eat and the time you eat the same as and different from Pedro's? Record your ideas in your journal.

The *cuíca* and other percussion instruments create the energetic sounds of the samba during Carnival celebrations (shown below). The *cuíca* is an African friction drum made by attaching a stick to the center of a drum skin. The drummer holds the drum in one hand and puts the other arm inside the drum. The sound is made by rubbing the stick with a wet piece of cloth or leather. When the stick is rubbed, the drum skin vibrates, producing a distinctive sound.

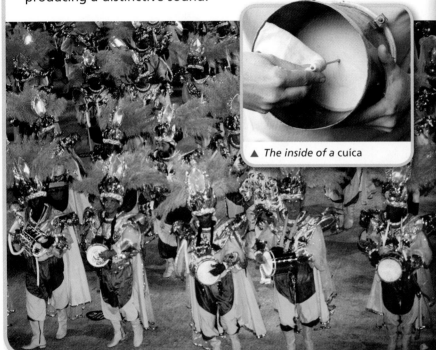

▲ *The inside of a cuíca*

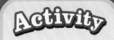

Make a *Cuíca*

Materials
- plastic cup or strong food container
- nail
- waxed dental floss

1. With a nail, make two holes, about an inch apart , in the bottom of the cup or container.

2. Push a three-foot piece of dental floss through both holes and make sure the two ends of the floss are the same length.

3. Tie the two ends into a knot as close to the hole inside the cup as possible so the string doesn't slip out.

4. Hold the cup in one hand and slide your fingers along the string with the other to make your own *cuíca* music.

Another popular form of Brazilian music and dance is the **bossa nova** (BAHS•uh NOH•vuh). It mixes the samba beat with the sounds of jazz. Brazilian jazz musicians popularized the bossa nova in the rest of the world. Brazilian samba-reggae is a popular form of music based on African drum traditions. **Capoeira** (kap•oh•AY•ruh) combines dance and the martial arts. It developed in Brazil from African origins. During Portuguese rule, the Portuguese forbade the African slaves to fight. So the Africans created fight dances, which developed into *capoeira*.

Festivals Brazilians are known for Carnival, celebrated every year for four days before the beginning of the Christian season of Lent. The holiday combines a Roman Catholic festival with African celebrations and includes parades and street parties. The world's most famous Carnival takes place in Rio de Janeiro. Thousands of spectators line the streets to watch costumed people ride elaborately decorated floats. In clubs and other places, thousands of dancers, who have been practicing for months, participate in samba dance competitions.

Recreation Brazil's thousands of miles of coastline provide extensive sandy beaches. On weekends, thousands of Brazilian families flock to the beaches to swim and enjoy picnics. Copacabana Beach in Rio de Janeiro attracts millions of tourists every year.

Brazil's most famous sport is football (soccer). It is played everywhere—in cities, beaches, and rural areas. People of all ages play it for fun. Professional football teams draw huge crowds of enthusiastic fans in football stadiums in many Brazilian cities. Maracana Stadium in Rio de Janeiro, one of the world's largest stadiums, holds more than 150,000 people. Brazil's teams have produced some of the world's top football players, such as Pelé and Ronaldo. Brazil's national football team has won 5 of the 17 World Cups ever awarded, the most for any football team. The World Cup is a trophy awarded to a nation's football team for winning the world championship.

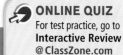
Beach in Recife, Brazil
Children enjoy playing in the waters of Boa Viagem beach, a popular beach in Recife.

▲ **SUMMARIZE** Describe the ways Brazilians enjoy holidays and their leisure time.

ONLINE QUIZ
For test practice, go to **Interactive Review** @ ClassZone.com

Section ② Assessment

TERMS & NAMES

1. Explain the importance of
- *Candomblé*
- *quilombos*
- *cuíca*
- *capoeira*

USE YOUR READING NOTES

2. Categorize Use your completed chart to answer the following question.

What contributions has Oscar Niemeyer made to Brazilian culture?

ART AND ARCHITECTURE	MUSIC	ENTERTAINMENT
1.	1.	1.
2.	2.	2.
3.	3.	3.

KEY IDEAS

3. What four cultures have contributed to modern Brazilian culture?

4. Where do most Brazilians of African ancestry live?

5. What type of music and dance is identified worldwide as Brazilian?

CRITICAL THINKING

6. Make Inferences Why are the traditional ways of life of some Indian groups in Brazil threatened?

7. Draw Conclusions How have Africans contributed to Brazilian culture?

8. CONNECT to Today Why do you think the Brazilian government has set up reservations to protect traditional Indian cultures?

9. ART Make a Collage Create a collage that illustrates ways people enjoy themselves in Brazil. Use the information in the section as well as in other sources. Then make a collage that features the various sources of entertainment in Brazil.

Reading for Understanding

Key Ideas

BEFORE, YOU LEARNED

The culture of Brazil today is a blend of many cultures.

NOW YOU WILL LEARN

An abundance of natural resources helps make Brazil a major industrial nation.

Vocabulary

TERMS & NAMES

hydroelectricity electric power generated by water

ethanol (EHTH•uh•NAWL) a liquid made by using a chemical process to convert sugar cane to a kind of alcohol that can be used for fuel

deforestation the cutting and clearing away of trees

boycott to stop buying and using products from certain sources as a way of protest

REVIEW

economy a system for producing and exchanging goods and services among a group of people

export a product or resource sold to another country

rain forest a broadleaf-tree region in a tropical climate

global warming an increase in the average temperature of the Earth's atmosphere

BACKGROUND VOCABULARY

mechanized equipped with machinery

self-sufficient able to provide for one's own needs without outside help

Reading Strategy

Re-create the web diagram shown at right. As you read and respond to the **KEY QUESTIONS**, use the diagram to organize main ideas and details about Brazil's economy.

 See Skillbuilder Handbook, page R4

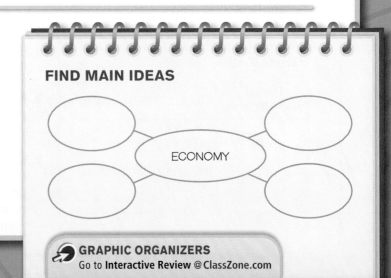

FIND MAIN IDEAS

ECONOMY

GRAPHIC ORGANIZERS
Go to **Interactive Review** @ ClassZone.com

Developing an Abundant Land

3.02 Describe the environmental impact of regional activities such as deforestation, urbanization, and industrialization and evaluate their significance to the global community.
11.04 Identify examples of economic, political, and social changes, such as agrarian to industrial economies, monarchical to democratic governments, and the roles of women and minorities, and analyze their impact on culture.

Connecting to Your World

In the early 1900s, Henry Ford invented a way to manufacture cars that would make them affordable for most people. His invention sparked the U.S. automobile industry and made the United States a major producer of automobiles. Today Brazil has become a leading maker of automobiles in the world and one of the most industrialized countries in South America.

Creating an Economic Giant

▼ **KEY QUESTION** What factors have helped Brazil become an important industrial nation?

Brazil's **economy** is the largest in South America and one of the largest in the world. Brazil's climate makes it possible for the nation to grow a wide range of crops. The abundance of natural resources, used to develop a variety of industries and manufactured goods, has helped to make Brazil a growing economic power. **Hydroelectricity**, or electric power generated by water, is provided by power plants along the Amazon River and many other rivers flowing through Brazil. Hydroelectricity supplies most of the energy needed to run these industries.

Itaipu Dam The dam, built on the Paraná River, provides about 25 percent of Brazil's power.

Agriculture About one-fifth of Brazil's workers are employed in agriculture. Most farming and livestock grazing takes place in the southern and southeastern parts of Brazil, which have the nation's best soil and climate for agriculture. Farms and ranches in this part of Brazil are generally large and **mechanized**. Farms in the northern part of Brazil, however, are smaller and generally depend on manual labor to produce crops.

Brazil is one of the world's leading exporters of agricultural products, second only to the United States. Brazil is the world's largest producer of sugar cane and coffee. It is a major producer of soybeans (the nation's primary farm **export**), oranges, wheat, corn, and beef, as well as a world leader in the raising of cattle, hogs, and poultry.

Industries Brazil is rich in minerals, and a major producer of the world's gold and diamonds. Brazil has large deposits of iron, manganese, and bauxite, which are important raw materials used in manufacturing. Most large manufacturing plants are located in Brazil's southeastern section. In recent years, Brazil has invested in high-tech equipment to run its manufacturing industries, which employ about 10 percent of its workers. Brazil has one of the largest steel plants in Latin America and is a world leader in automobile production.

CONNECT Geography & Economics

Deforestation More than half of the Amazon rain forest is located in Brazil. As Brazil's economy developed, many people moved to the Amazon region to develop its resources. Several economic activities have contributed to deforestation, including:

- logging by the timber industry to export woods such as mahogany
- clearing the forests for raising crops and livestock and for housing
- mining minerals for export and as raw materials

CRITICAL THINKING

Make Inferences How might the opportunity to make money contribute to deforestation?

Slash-and-Burn Agriculture Trees in the Amazon rain forest are burned to clear the land for farming and ranching.

Service industries employ about half of Brazil's workers. Many Brazilians work for government agencies, hotels and restaurants, and stores.

Brazil is leading the way in becoming energy **self-sufficient**. Hydroelectric power from Brazil's major rivers provide most of the nation's energy needs. In fact, Brazil expects to become energy-independent in the near future.

▲ **ANALYZE CAUSES AND EFFECTS** Explain why Brazil has become an important industrial nation.

Preserving the Rain Forest

▼ **KEY QUESTION** Why is preserving the rain forest important?

The Amazon **rain forest**, the world's largest rain forest, covers one-third of South America. In the past, rain forests covered about 14 percent of the Earth's surface. Today, because of **deforestation**, the cutting down and clearing away of trees, rain forests cover only 6 percent of the Earth's surface.

Sloth The sloth makes its home in the treetops of the rain forest. **How might deforestation affect this animal?**

Logging in the Rain Forest Although today logging in the Amazon rain forest is controlled by the Brazilian government, illegal logging continues.

Endangering Ways of Life Deforestation threatens the homes and ways of life of some of the people who live in the rain forests.

Why Save It? You read earlier in this book that the rain forest is an important resource. Rain forests help to regulate the world's climate by absorbing carbon dioxide and producing oxygen. As trees are cut down, less carbon dioxide is absorbed, which contributes to **global warming**. Rain forests are home to millions of species of plants and animals, more than half of the world's species. Many medicines are made from rain-forest plants. Destroying rain forests endangers the traditional ways of life of some of the people who live there.

Preserving the Brazilian Rain Forest These children are planting trees to reverse the effects of deforestation.

What Is Being Done? Many governments, groups, and individuals are working to preserve the rain forests. Recently, Brazil's government presented plans to declare about 193,000 square miles of the Amazon rain forest a protected area. Some groups raise money to buy land to create large rain forest reserves. Some organize protests against plans that might result in deforestation. Others organize boycotts of products that destroy the forests. To **boycott** is to stop buying or using certain products as a form of protest. Still others work to educate people about the importance of rain forests to the world.

 SUMMARIZE Explain why preserving rain forests is important.

ONLINE QUIZ For test practice, go to **Interactive Review** @ ClassZone.com

Section ③ Assessment

TERMS & NAMES

1. Explain the importance of
- hydroelectricity
- ethanol
- deforestation
- boycott

USE YOUR READING NOTES

2. Find Main Ideas Use your web diagram to answer the following question:

What industry employs half of Brazilian workers?

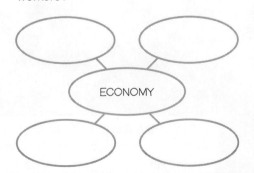

KEY IDEAS

3. What is Brazil's major export crop?

4. Where does most farming take place in Brazil?

5. How is Brazil becoming energy self-sufficient?

CRITICAL THINKING

6. Analyze Causes and Effects What effect has rain-forest deforestation had on the world's climate?

7. Identify Problems and Solutions What do you think is the best solution for curbing the deforestation of rain forests?

8. (CONNECT to Today) Brazil is becoming energy-independent. What effect might that have on Brazil's economy?

9. (LANGUAGE ARTS) **Write a Slogan** Imagine that you are working for an organization dedicated to preserving the rain forest. Write a slogan for the organization to use to educate people about the reasons that preserving rain forests is important.

Interactive ◄Review

Click here to complete these and other activities online @ ClassZone.com

CHAPTER SUMMARY

Key Idea 1
Brazil's government is dealing with the problems resulting from urbanization.

Key Idea 2
Several cultures have influenced Brazil's unique culture.

Key Idea 3
An abundance of natural resources helps make Brazil a major industrial nation.

For **Review and Study Notes**, go to **Interactive Review @ ClassZone.com**

NAME GAME

Use the Terms & Names list to complete each sentence on paper or online.

1. I am the capital of Brazil. __Brasília__
2. I am a community created by escaped African slaves. _____
3. I am the first emperor of Brazil. _____
4. I am a government official who helped abolish slavery in Brazil. _____
5. I am the city famous for Carnival. _____
6. I am the music of Brazil that is best known worldwide. _____
7. I am a neighborhood located in areas surrounding big cities. _____
8. I am a cleaner, renewable fuel for cars. _____
9. I am a religious practice brought from Africa to Brazil. _____
10. I destroy millions of acres of forest. _____

Brasília
Candomblé
capoeira
cuíca
deforestation
Dom Pedro I
Dom Pedro II
ethanol
favela
quilombo
Rio de Janeiro
samba

Activities

Flip Cards

Use the online flip cards to quiz yourself on the terms and names introduced in this chapter.

Pedro Álvares Cabral

? Portuguese explorer who claimed Brazil for Portugal

Crossword Puzzle

Complete an online puzzle to test your knowledge of Brazil's history, economy, and culture.

ACROSS
1. friction drum used in the samba

VOCABULARY

Explain the significance of each of the following.

1. Treaty of Tordesillas
2. Pedro Álvares Cabral
3. Dom Pedro I
4. Dom Pedro II
5. Brasília
6. Rio de Janeiro
7. hydroelectricity
8. ethanol
9. deforestation
10. boycott

Explain how the terms and names in each group are related.

11. *Candomblé, cuíca,* and *quilombos*
12. samba and *capoeira*

KEY IDEAS

1 **From Portuguese Colony to Modern Giant**

13. What explorer claimed Brazil for Portugal?
14. How did Brazil become independent?
15. What is Brazil's biggest economic challenge?
16. How has Brazil's urban population changed in the last half of the 20th century?

2 **A Multicultural Society**

17. What Portuguese influences are seen in Brazil today?
18. Where does the largest Japanese population live in Brazil today?
19. How have Africans influenced Brazilian culture?
20. Why is Carnival considered a blend of European and African traditions?

3 **Developing an Abundant Land**

21. How has having an abundance of natural resources benefited Brazil?
22. Why does most farming and ranching in Brazil take place in the southern and southeastern parts?
23. What provides most of Brazil's energy needs?
24. What actions are people taking today to help preserve the rain forest?

CRITICAL THINKING

25. **Analyze Causes and Effects** Create a diagram to explain the causes of deforestation of the Amazon rain forest.

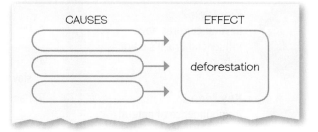

26. **Evaluate** How did the introduction of coffee plants in Brazil affect its economy?
27. **Summarize** What did Brazil's government do to try to relieve overcrowding in its cities?
28. **Five Themes: Human-Environment Interaction** How might deforestation affect the Indians of the Amazon rain forest?
29. **Connect to Economics** Why is narrowing the income gap important for Brazil's government to address?
30. **Connect Geography & History** What historical events have contributed to Brazil's cultural diversity?

Answer the ESSENTIAL QUESTION

How have Brazil's people used the country's abundant natural resources to make Brazil an economic giant?

Written response Write a two- or three-paragraph response to the Essential Question. Be sure to consider the key ideas of each section. Use the rubric below to guide your thinking.

Response Rubric
A strong response will:
- include how Brazil's natural resources have contributed to the growth of industries
- explain how Brazilian Indians, Africans, and European and Asian immigrants have helped make Brazil an economic power

PRIMARY SOURCE

Use the primary source below to answer questions 1 and 2.

> It is not just those who depend directly on the tropical forests who suffer from deforestation, but the entire population of tropical forest countries. The forests assist in the regulation of local climate patterns, protecting watersheds, preventing floods, guaranteeing and controlling huge flows of life-giving water. Strip away the forests and there is, first, too much water . . . and then too little.
>
> Source: Charles, Prince of Wales, from a speech given on February 6, 1990

1. What observation does the passage support?

A. Deforestation hurts no one.

B. Deforestation prevents flooding.

C. Rain forests help to prevent floods.

D. Rain forests affect only a few people.

2. What is the best title for this passage?

A. Prince Charles Helps the Rain Forests

B. Where Are the Rain Forests?

C. Deforestation–Is It Serious?

D. The Rain Forest and Water Supply

LINE GRAPH

Use the graph below to answer questions 3 and 4.

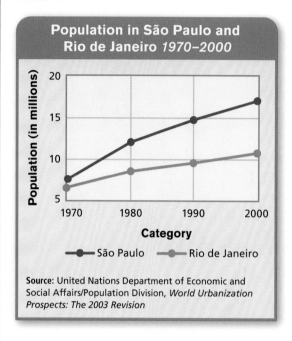

Population in São Paulo and Rio de Janeiro 1970–2000

Source: United Nations Department of Economic and Social Affairs/Population Division, *World Urbanization Prospects: The 2003 Revision*

3. What was the population of Rio de Janeiro in 2000?

4. Between what years did São Paulo's population increase the most?

GeoActivity

1. INTERDISCIPLINARY ACTIVITY–SCIENCE

Research the four layers of a tropical rain forest. Find out the differences in the four layers, the kinds of plants that grow there, and the kinds of animals that live in each layer. Include a diagram to illustrate the four layers.

2. WRITING FOR SOCIAL STUDIES

Unit Writing Project Decide on the place from your journal that you found most interesting, and find more information about it. Then write an article for a travel magazine describing the place and giving reasons for people to visit it.

3. MENTAL MAPPING

Create an outline map of Brazil and label the following:

- Bahia
- Salvador
- São Paulo
- Brasília
- Rio de Janeiro
- The Amazon River

UNIT 3

Europe

Why It Matters:

In the past, Europeans used the oceans and seas to make voyages for trade and to build empires. Their culture spread around the world. Today, Europeans still play a large part in world affairs.

The Alps

CHAPTER 9 Europe: Physical Geography and History

Notre Dame Cathedral

CHAPTER 10 Western Europe

London Street Scene

CHAPTER 11 United Kingdom

Prague, Czech Republic

CHAPTER 12 Eastern Europe

Europe

Europe occupies the western portion of the Eurasian landmass. Many people view the Ural Mountains as the eastern border of Europe, which means that Europe includes part of Russia. However, for historic and cultural reasons, Russia and the Eurasian republics are not considered in this unit.

As you study the graphs on this page, compare the landmass, population, rivers, and mountains of Europe with those of the United States and the world. Then jot down the answers to the following questions in your notebook.

Comparing Data

1. How does Europe compare in size to the United States?

2. Is Europe's population bigger or smaller than that of the United States? Given what you know about Europe's size, do you think that makes Europe more or less densely populated than the United States?

3. How does the Danube River compare to the Mississippi River in the United States?

4. What is the tallest peak in Europe? Is it taller or shorter than Mt. McKinley, the tallest mountain in the United States?

Comparing Data

Landmass

Europe
2,276,109 sq. mi.

Continental United States
3,165,630 sq. mi.

Population

Europe
584,413,424

United States
296,410,404

Population (in millions)
0   100   200   300   400   500   600

Rivers

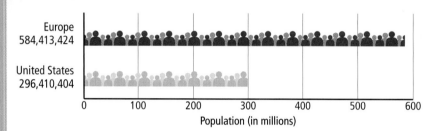

Rhine 820 mi.
Dnieper 1,367 mi.
Danube 1,776 mi.
Mississippi 2,357 mi.
Nile 4,160 mi.   World's Longest

Length (in miles)
0   1000   2000   3000   4000

Mountains

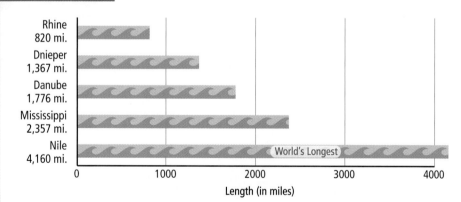

World's Tallest
Mt. Everest
Nepal-Tibet
29,035 ft.

U.S. Tallest
Mt. McKinley
United States
20,320 ft.

Mont Blanc
France-Italy
15,771 ft.

Monte Rosa
Switzerland-Italy
15,203 ft.

Dom
Switzerland
14,913 ft.

Population Density

Persons per square mile

- Over 520
- 260–519
- 130–259
- 25–129
- 1–24
- 0

Arctic Circle

Norwegian Sea

North Sea

ATLANTIC OCEAN

Bay of Biscay

Baltic Sea

Black Sea

Adriatic Sea

Mediterranean Sea

Oslo
Stockholm
Helsinki
Manchester
London
Amsterdam
Brussels
Paris
Berlin
Leipzig
Warsaw
Kiev
Budapest
Milan
Belgrade
Bucharest
Lisbon
Madrid
Rome
Naples
Athens

60°N
50°N
40°N
30°N
0°
10°E
20°E

0   125   250 miles
0   125   250 kilometers

THINK LIKE A GEOGRAPHER

1. **Place** Where on the continent is the population density highest?

2. **Region** Which is less densely populated, far northern or far southern Europe?

235

3
ATLAS

ICELAND

Dry
Semiarid

Mid-Latitude
Mediterranean
Marine west coast
Humid subtropical
Humid continental

High Latitude
Subarctic
Tundra
Icecap

Highland

Arctic Circle

Norwegian Sea

SWEDEN

FINLAND

NORWAY

North Sea

ESTONIA

Baltic Sea

LATVIA

IRELAND

UNITED KINGDOM

DENMARK

LITHUANIA

60°N

RUSSIA

NETHERLANDS

BELARUS

ATLANTIC OCEAN

BELGIUM

GERMANY

POLAND

50°N

CZECH REPUBLIC

UKRAINE

LUXEMBOURG

SLOVAKIA

Bay of Biscay

FRANCE

SWITZERLAND

AUSTRIA

HUNGARY

MOLDOVA

SLOVENIA

ROMANIA

PORTUGAL

CROATIA

Black Sea

SPAIN

BOSNIA and HERZEGOVINA

SERBIA

ITALY

Adriatic Sea

MONTENEGRO

BULGARIA

MACEDONIA

40°N

ALBANIA

TURKEY

GREECE

Mediterranean Sea

MALTA

THINK LIKE A GEOGRAPHER

1. **Region** What climate zone occurs most often in southern Europe?

2. **Human-Environment Interaction** Compare this map to the population density map on the previous page. What climate is most densely populated?

0	125	250 miles
0	125	250 kilometers

30°N

A F R I C A

10°E   20°E   30°E

Land use
- Commercial agriculture
- Dairying
- Livestock raising
- Nomadic herding
- Forestland
- Limited agriculture

Major resources
- Bauxite
- Coal
- Fish
- Iron ore
- Natural gas
- Oil
- Other minerals
- Timber
- Uranium
- Manufacturing center

ICELAND

Arctic Circle

Norwegian Sea

SWEDEN

FINLAND

NORWAY

Stockholm

ESTONIA

Baltic Sea

LATVIA

North Sea

LITHUANIA

IRELAND

UNITED KINGDOM

RUSSIA

DENMARK

BELARUS

Birmingham

NETHERLANDS

London

Amsterdam/ Rotterdam

BELGIUM

GERMANY

POLAND

ATLANTIC OCEAN

Essen

Katowice

50°N

Paris

CZECH REPUBLIC

UKRAINE

Donetsk

LUXEMBOURG

SLOVAKIA

Bay of Biscay

FRANCE

Munich

MOLDOVA

SWITZERLAND

AUSTRIA

HUNGARY

ROMANIA

Milan

SLOVENIA

PORTUGAL

Marseille

CROATIA

Black Sea

SPAIN

ITALY

BOSNIA and HERZEGOVINA

SERBIA

Barcelona

MONTENEGRO

BULGARIA

40°N

MACEDONIA

ALBANIA

TURKEY

GREECE

Mediterranean Sea

MALTA

| 0 | 125 | 250 miles |
| 0 | 125 | 250 kilometers |

THINK LIKE A GEOGRAPHER

1. **Human-Environment Interaction**
   What activity is the majority of the land in Europe used for?

2. **Region** Which sea is the source of many of Europe's energy resources? What countries are most likely to benefit from these resources?

AFRICA

30°N

0°   10°E   20°E   30°E

Regional Overview

Europe

Europe is the world's second smallest continent in area, but one of the largest in population. The population is diverse, with many different cultures developing on the small landmass. The chapters in this unit provide more information about the geography, history, culture, government, and economics of Europe.

GEOGRAPHY

Europe extends from the Arctic Ocean in the north to the Mediterranean Sea in the south. Geographically, the European continent stretches from the Atlantic Ocean all the way to the Ural Mountains in Russia, but in this unit, we will mark Europe's western border where Russia begins.

HISTORY

For centuries, different groups of people settled, lived in, and fought over the lands of Europe. Though some regions are still troubled by conflict, Europe is more unified than ever before.

CULTURE

Since the time of the ancient Greeks and Romans, Europe's culture has had a global influence. European ideas about politics, science, art, philosophy, and religion have spread around the world.

GOVERNMENT

The governments of Europe come in all shapes and sizes. Some are democracies. Other nations have monarchs who govern alongside a parliament chosen by the people.

ECONOMICS

Europe has many natural resources and abundant farmland that strengthen its economies. Many European countries are also highly industrialized. The European Union has worked to continue Europe's role as an economic power.

Leaning Tower of Pisa Construction started on this Italian monument in 1173. It began to tilt when only three of its eight stories were completed.

Country Almanac

🖰 *Click here* to compare the most recent data on countries @ ClassZone.com

Unit Writing Project

Imagine that your class is planning a trip to Europe. Choose a country from this unit that you would like to visit. Write a persuasive speech to convince your classmates to pick your country for their trip.

Think About:
- specific sites you would visit
- the people you would meet
- how it differs from your home

Europe

Europe is made up of 43 different countries.

Albania
GEOGRAPHY
Capital: Tiranë
Total Area: 11,100 sq. mi.
Population: 3,130,000
ECONOMY
Imports: food; machinery; minerals; clothing
Exports: clothing; metals
CULTURE
Language: Albanian
Religion: Muslim 39%; Catholic 17%

Andorra
GEOGRAPHY
Capital: Andorra la Vella
Total Area: 181 sq. mi.
Population: 70,549
ECONOMY
Imports: food; tobacco; machinery
Exports: motor vehicles; photo equipment
CULTURE
Language: Catalan
Religion: Catholic 89%; nonreligious 5%

Austria

GEOGRAPHY
Capital: Vienna
Total Area: 32,382 sq. mi.
Population: 8,189,000
ECONOMY
Imports: machinery; vehicles; chemicals
Exports: transportation equipment; steel
CULTURE
Language: German
Religion: Catholic 75%; nonreligious 9%; Protestant 5%

Belgium
GEOGRAPHY
Capital: Brussels
Total Area: 11,787 sq. mi.
Population: 10,419,000
ECONOMY
Imports: machinery; medicine; food
Exports: machinery; vehicles; medicine
CULTURE
Language: Dutch; French; German
Religion: Catholic 88%; Muslim 3%

Belarus
GEOGRAPHY
Capital: Minsk
Total Area: 80,155 sq. mi.
Population: 9,755,000
ECONOMY
Imports: petroleum; chemicals; food
Exports: food; petroleum; road vehicles
CULTURE
Language: Belarusian; Russian
Religion: Belarusian Orthodox 32%; Catholic 18%

Bosnia and Herzegovina
GEOGRAPHY
Capital: Sarajevo
Total Area: 19,741 sq. mi.
Population: 3,907,000
ECONOMY
Imports: machinery; chemicals; fuels
Exports: metals; clothing; wood products
CULTURE
Language: Bosnian
Religion: Sunni Muslim 43%; Serbian Orthodox 30%; Catholic 18%

Bulgaria
GEOGRAPHY
Capital: Sofia
Total Area: 42,823 sq. mi.
Population: 7,726,000
ECONOMY
Imports: textiles; crude petroleum; plastics
Exports: clothing; metals; mineral fuels
CULTURE
Language: Bulgarian
Religion: Bulgarian Orthodox 72%; Sunni Muslim 12%

Croatia
GEOGRAPHY
Capital: Zagreb
Total Area: 21,831 sq. mi.
Population: 4,551,000
ECONOMY
Imports: machinery; metals; petroleum
Exports: chemicals; clothing; petroleum
CULTURE
Language: Croatian
Religion: Catholic 89%; Eastern Orthodox 6%; Sunni Muslim 2%

 Czech Republic

GEOGRAPHY
Capital: Prague
Total Area: 30,450 sq. mi.
Population: 10,220,000

ECONOMY
Imports: machinery; chemicals; vehicles
Exports: computers; vehicles; metals

CULTURE
Language: Czech
Religion: Catholic 40%; nonreligious 32%; Protestant 3%

 Denmark

GEOGRAPHY
Capital: Copenhagen
Total Area: 16,639 sq. mi.
Population: 5,431,000

ECONOMY
Imports: machinery; food; tobacco
Exports: agricultural products; swine

CULTURE
Language: Danish
Religion: Evangelical Lutheran 86%; Muslim 2%

 Estonia

GEOGRAPHY
Capital: Tallinn
Total Area: 17,462 sq. mi.
Population: 1,330,000

ECONOMY
Imports: textiles; food
Exports: wood; textiles; paper

CULTURE
Language: Estonian
Religion: Orthodox 20%; Evangelical Lutheran 14%

 Finland

GEOGRAPHY
Capital: Helsinki
Total Area: 130,559 sq. mi.
Population: 5,249,000

ECONOMY
Imports: machinery; mineral fuels; vehicles
Exports: paper products; wood products

CULTURE
Language: Finnish; Swedish
Religion: Evangelical Lutheran 85%; nonreligious 13%

 France

GEOGRAPHY
Capital: Paris
Total Area: 211,209 sq. mi.
Population: 60,496,000

ECONOMY
Imports: machinery; chemicals; food
Exports: aircraft; perfumes; cosmetics

CULTURE
Language: French
Religion: Catholic 82%; Muslim 7%; Protestant 4%

 Germany

GEOGRAPHY
Capital: Berlin
Total Area: 137,847 sq. mi.
Population: 82,689,000

ECONOMY
Imports: televisions; computers; food
Exports: televisions; medical instruments

CULTURE
Language: German
Religion: Protestant 36%; Catholic 34%; nonreligious 17%

 Greece

GEOGRAPHY
Capital: Athens
Total Area: 50,942 sq. mi.
Population: 11,120,000

ECONOMY
Imports: chemicals; petroleum; ships
Exports: fruits and nuts; aluminum

CULTURE
Language: Greek
Religion: Eastern Orthodox 94%; Muslim 1%

 Hungary

GEOGRAPHY
Capital: Budapest
Total Area: 35,919 sq. mi.
Population: 10,098,000

ECONOMY
Imports: machinery; vehicles
Exports: telecommunications equipment

CULTURE
Language: Hungarian
Religion: Catholic 58%; Reformed 18%; nonreligious 19%

Tour de France Each year, about 200 riders compete in this famous bicycle race.

Iceland

GEOGRAPHY
Capital: Reykjavik
Total Area: 39,769 sq. mi.
Population: 295,000

ECONOMY
Imports: machinery; food; clothing
Exports: fish; aluminum; medicines

CULTURE
Language: Icelandic
Religion: Evangelical Lutheran 87%; Catholic 2%

Ireland

GEOGRAPHY
Capital: Dublin
Total Area: 27,135 sq. mi.
Population: 4,148,000

ECONOMY
Imports: computers; electronics; food
Exports: computers; recording devices

CULTURE
Language: Irish; English
Religion: Catholic 88%; Church of Ireland (Anglican) 3%

Italy

GEOGRAPHY
Capital: Rome
Total Area: 116,306 sq. mi.
Population: 58,093,000

ECONOMY
Imports: machinery; chemicals; iron; steel
Exports: chemicals; textile yarn and fabrics; food

CULTURE
Language: Italian
Religion: Catholic 80%; nonreligious 13%

Latvia

GEOGRAPHY
Capital: Riga
Total Area: 24,938 sq. mi.
Population: 2,307,000

ECONOMY
Imports: machinery; chemicals; vehicles
Exports: wood; metals; textiles

CULTURE
Language: Latvian
Religion: Catholic 15%; Lutheran 15%; Orthodox 8%

Liechtenstein

GEOGRAPHY
Capital: Vaduz
Total Area: 62 sq. mi.
Population: 33,717

ECONOMY
Imports: machinery; glass and ceramics
Exports: precision tools; food products

CULTURE
Language: German
Religion: Catholic 80%; Protestant 8%; Muslim 3%

Lithuania

GEOGRAPHY
Capital: Vilnius
Total Area: 25,174 sq. mi.
Population: 3,431,000

ECONOMY
Imports: chemicals; clothing
Exports: mineral fuels; clothing; food

CULTURE
Language: Lithuanian
Religion: Catholic 79%; nonreligious 10%; Orthodox 5%

Luxembourg

GEOGRAPHY
Capital: Luxembourg
Total Area: 998 sq. mi.
Population: 465,000

ECONOMY
Imports: machinery; metals; chemicals
Exports: metals; transport equipment; food

CULTURE
Language: Luxemburgian; French
Religion: Catholic 91%; Protestant 2%

Macedonia

GEOGRAPHY
Capital: Skopje
Total Area: 9,781 sq. mi.
Population: 2,034,000

ECONOMY
Imports: mineral fuels; food; live animals
Exports: clothing; iron; tobacco; beverages

CULTURE
Language: Macedonian; Albanian
Religion: Orthodox 59%; Sunni Muslim 28%

Malta

GEOGRAPHY
Capital: Valletta
Total Area: 122 sq. mi.
Population: 402,000

ECONOMY
Imports: electronics; petroleum; food
Exports: clothing; children's toys and games

CULTURE
Language: Maltese; English
Religion: Catholic 95%

Republic of Moldova

GEOGRAPHY
Capital: Chişinău
Total Area: 13,067 sq. mi.
Population: 4,206,000

ECONOMY
Imports: minerals; chemicals; textiles
Exports: food; textiles

CULTURE
Language: Romanian
Religion: Orthodox 46%; Muslim 6%; Catholic 2%; Protestant 2%

Monaco

GEOGRAPHY
Capital: Monaco
Total Area: 1 square mile
Population: 32,409

ECONOMY
Imports: perfumes; clothing; publishing
Exports: plastic products; glass; paper

CULTURE
Language: French
Religion: Catholic 89%; Jewish 2%

Montenegro

GEOGRAPHY
Capital: Podgorica
Total Area: 5,415 sq. mi.
Population: 630,548

ECONOMY
Imports: no information available
Exports: no information available

CULTURE
Language: Serbian
Religion: Orthodox, Muslim, Catholic

Netherlands

GEOGRAPHY
Capital: Amsterdam
Total Area: 16,033 sq. mi.
Population: 16,299,000

ECONOMY
Imports: computers; chemicals; food
Exports: chemicals; food; mineral fuels

CULTURE
Language: Dutch
Religion: nonreligious 43%; Catholic 31%; Reformed 14%

Norway

GEOGRAPHY
Capital: Oslo
Total Area: 125,182 sq. mi.
Population: 4,620,000

ECONOMY
Imports: road vehicles; ships; metals
Exports: crude petroleum; metals; fish

CULTURE
Language: Norwegian
Religion: Church of Norway 86%; Muslim 2%, Catholic 1%

Poland

GEOGRAPHY
Capital: Warsaw
Total Area: 120,728 sq. mi.
Population: 38,530,000

ECONOMY
Imports: machinery; textiles
Exports: food; furniture; ships

CULTURE
Language: Polish
Religion: Catholic 91%; Polish Orthodox 1%

Portugal

GEOGRAPHY
Capital: Lisbon
Total Area: 35,672 sq. mi.
Population: 10,495,000

ECONOMY
Imports: telecommunications equipment
Exports: road vehicles; clothing; fabrics

CULTURE
Language: Portuguese
Religion: Catholic 87%; nonreligious 7%

Romania

GEOGRAPHY
Capital: Bucharest
Total Area: 91,699 sq. mi.
Population: 21,711,000

ECONOMY
Imports: fabrics; chemicals; petroleum
Exports: clothing; iron and steel

CULTURE
Language: Romanian
Religion: Romanian Orthodox 87%; Protestant 6%; Catholic 5%

San Marino

GEOGRAPHY
Capital: San Marino
Total Area: 24 sq. mi.
Population: 28,880

ECONOMY
Imports: electricity; gold
Exports: postage stamps; leather goods; ceramics; wine

CULTURE
Language: Italian
Religion: Catholic 89%

Serbia

GEOGRAPHY
Capital: Belgrade
Total Area: 34,116 sq. mi.
Population: 9,396,400

ECONOMY
Imports: machinery; mineral fuels
Exports: food & live animals; machinery

CULTURE
Language: Serbian
Religion: Serbian Orthodox 63%; Muslim 19%; nonreligious 13%

Slovakia

GEOGRAPHY
Capital: Bratislava
Total Area: 18,859 sq. mi.
Population: 5,401,000

ECONOMY
Imports: machinery; fuels
Exports: road vehicles; machinery; metals

CULTURE
Language: Slovak
Religion: Catholic 69%; Slovak Evangelical 7%

Slovenia

GEOGRAPHY
Capital: Ljubljana
Total Area: 7,827 sq. mi.
Population: 1,967,000

ECONOMY
Imports: machinery; vehicles; fuels
Exports: medicines and pharmaceuticals; furniture

CULTURE
Language: Slovene
Religion: Catholic 84%; nonreligious 8%

Spain

GEOGRAPHY
Capital: Madrid
Total Area: 194,897 sq. mi.
Population: 43,064,000

ECONOMY
Imports: vehicles; chemicals; petroleum
Exports: fruits and vegetables; chemicals

CULTURE
Language: Castilian Spanish; Euskera (Basque); Catalan; Galician
Religion: Catholic 92%

Sweden

GEOGRAPHY
Capital: Stockholm
Total Area: 173,732 sq. mi.
Population: 9,041,000

ECONOMY
Imports: machinery; chemicals; vehicles
Exports: vehicles; electronics; medicines

CULTURE
Language: Swedish
Religion: Church of Sweden 87%; Muslim 2%; Catholic 2%

Switzerland

GEOGRAPHY
Capital: Bern
Total Area: 15,942 sq. mi.
Population: 7,252,000

ECONOMY
Imports: machinery; vehicles; food
Exports: precision instruments, watches

CULTURE
Language: French; German; Italian
Religion: Catholic 42%; Protestant 35%; Muslim 4%; Orthodox 2%

Ukraine

GEOGRAPHY
Capital: Kiev
Total Area: 233,090 sq. mi.
Population: 46,481,000

ECONOMY
Imports: natural gas; chemicals; food
Exports: metals; wood; food

CULTURE
Language: Ukrainian
Religion: Ukrainian Orthodox 29%; Catholic 7%; Protestant 4%

United Kingdom

GEOGRAPHY
Capital: London
Total Area: 94,526 sq. mi.
Population: 59,668,000

ECONOMY
Imports: radios; televisions; aircraft
Exports: computers; aircraft; petroleum

CULTURE
Language: English
Religion: Anglican 29%; nonreligious 16%; Catholic 11%

Vatican City

GEOGRAPHY
Capital: Vatican City
Total Area: 0.2 sq. mi.
Population: 921

ECONOMY
Imports: no information available
Exports: no information available

CULTURE
Language: Italian; Latin
Religion: Catholic

Majorca, Spain

Europe: Physical Geography and History

 ESSENTIAL QUESTION

What changes have taken place in Europe since ancient times?

CONNECT Geography & History

Use the map and the time line to answer the following questions.

1. What countries share borders with France?
2. The European Union's headquarters are in the capital of Belgium. What city is that?

History
◄ **27 B.C.** Augustus forms the Roman Empire, which lasts until A.D. **476.** (Coin showing Augustus)

2000 B.C.

Geography
A.D. 79 Eruption of Mount Vesuvius destroys Roman city of Pompeii.

History
400s Beginning of the Middle Ages ►

ARCTIC OCEAN

20°W

0°

20°E

N
W   E
S

ICELAND
Reykjavík

Arctic Circle

Norwegian Sea

Faroe Islands
(Den.)

Shetland Islands
(U.K.)

0   200   400 miles
0   200   400 kilometers

ATLANTIC OCEAN

SWEDEN

NORWAY

FINLAND

Helsinki

Oslo

Stockholm

Gulf of Bothnia

Gulf of Finland

Tallinn

ESTONIA

RUSSIA

60°N

North Sea

Baltic Sea

LATVIA
Riga

LITHUANIA
Vilnius

Minsk

50°N

Dublin

IRELAND

British Isles

UNITED KINGDOM

DENMARK
Copenhagen

NETHERLANDS

London

Amsterdam

Berlin

POLAND

Warsaw

BELARUS

Kiev

English Channel

Brussels

GERMANY

Channel Islands (U.K.)

BELGIUM

LUX.

Paris

Prague

CZECH REPUBLIC

SLOVAKIA

UKRAINE

FRANCE

Bern

SWITZ.

LIECH.

Vienna

AUSTRIA

Bratislava

Budapest

MOLDOVA
Chişinău

Bay of Biscay

SLOV.

Ljubljana

Zagreb

HUNGARY

ROMANIA

SAN MARINO

CROATIA

Bucharest

PORTUGAL

MONACO

B. & HER.

Belgrade

Black Sea

ANDORRA

Corsica (Fr.)

Sarajevo

SERBIA

Madrid

ITALY

MONT.

Sofia

BULGARIA

Lisbon

SPAIN

VATICAN CITY

Rome

Podgorica

Tiranë

Skopje

MAC.

ALB.

40°N

Balearic Islands (Sp.)

Sardinia (It.)

Adriatic Sea

ASIA

Strait of Gibraltar

GIBRALTAR (U.K.)

Tyrrhenian Sea

Ionian Sea

GREECE

Aegean Sea

Sicily (It.)

Mediterranean Sea

AFRICA

MALTA

Athens

Crete (Gr.)

Cyprus

★ National capital

ALB.	Albania
B.& HER.	Bosnia and Herzegovina
LEICH.	Leichtenstein
LUX.	Luxembourg
MAC.	Macedonia
MONT.	Montenegro
SLOV.	Slovenia
SWITZ.	Switzerland

Culture
c. 1300 The Renaissance begins in Italy.

Government
1799 Napoleon seizes power in France following the French Revolution. ▶

Economics
▲ **1992** Treaty forming the European Union is signed.

Today

Reading for Understanding

▶ Key Ideas

BEFORE, YOU LEARNED

The Earth's surface is covered with a variety of landforms, produced by internal and external forces.

NOW YOU WILL LEARN

Europe, too, has landforms ranging from mountains to plains. Its climate is influenced by its nearness to the ocean.

▶ Vocabulary

TERMS & NAMES

peninsula a body of land nearly surrounded by water

Alps Europe's tallest mountain range, stretching across southern Europe

Northern European Plain vast area of flat or gently rolling land from France to Russia

North Atlantic Drift warm ocean current that helps keep Europe's climate mild

fossil fuels sources of energy from ancient plant and animal remains

renewable energy sources sources of energy able to be replaced through ongoing natural processes

hydroelectric power electricity made by water-powered engines

BACKGROUND VOCABULARY

seafaring using the sea for transportation

Visual Vocabulary The Alps

▶ Reading Strategy

Re-create the chart shown at right. As you read and respond to the **KEY QUESTIONS**, use the chart to organize important details about the physical geography of Europe.

 See Skillbuilder Handbook, page R7

CATEGORIZE

PENINSULAS	MOUNTAINS	RIVERS
1.	1.	1.
2.	2.	2.
3.	3.	3.

 GRAPHIC ORGANIZERS
Go to **Interactive Review** @ ClassZone.com

Europe's Dramatic Landscape

 2.01 Identify key physical characteristics such as landforms, water forms, and climate, and evaluate their influence on the development of cultures in selected South American and European regions.
3.02 Describe the environmental impact of regional activities such as deforestation, urbanization, and industrialization and evaluate their significance to the global community.

Connecting to Your World

What comes to mind when you think of Europe? Snowcapped mountains on travel posters? Medieval castles next to winding rivers that you've seen in jigsaw puzzles? Or perhaps you've watched the Winter Olympics on television and seen skiers speeding down steep mountain slopes. Each of these images tells us something about Europe's physical geography. High mountain ranges, oceans, long broad rivers, and fertile plains are all a part of it. Let's see how they fit together.

Alcazar Castle Europe is famous for its castles, like this one in Segovia, Spain.

Peninsula of Peninsulas

🔻 **KEY QUESTION** Why is Europe called a peninsula of peninsulas?

A quick look at a map of Europe explains why it is called the "peninsula of peninsulas." A **peninsula** is a piece of land nearly surrounded by water. The entire continent of Europe is a peninsula with smaller peninsulas jutting out from it. Because of these peninsulas, most places in Europe are no more than 300 miles from an ocean or sea. Its nearness to these bodies of water has influenced Europe in many ways. The ocean modifies Europe's climate. Many Europeans use the ocean for both business and pleasure.

Opatija, Croatia This town is located on the Istria Peninsula in southern Europe.

Opatija

ISTRIA PENINSULA

Europe's Coastline Europe's peninsulas extend off the continent in all directions, as the map on the opposite page shows. Far to the north, the Scandinavian Peninsula Ⓐ juts out into the North Sea. Spain and Portugal occupy the Iberian Peninsula Ⓑ, which extends into the Mediterranean Sea in southern Europe. The Italian and Balkan Peninsulas also stretch into the Mediterranean Sea.

Europe's many bays and peninsulas give it a long, uneven coastline, dotted with islands and stretching almost 24,000 miles. Europe has more coastline than Africa, a much larger continent. Long ago, Europe's nearness to the sea and its many natural harbors encouraged **seafaring**, or the use of the sea for transportation. Europeans fished, traded, and in time set out to explore other parts of the world.

Mountains Mountains are another key landform in Europe. They affect climate, travel, and culture. The **Alps** Ⓒ, Europe's tallest mountain range, stretch across eight countries in southern Europe. The Pyrenees Ⓓ once formed a natural barrier between France and Spain. Europe also has smaller mountain ranges, such as the Apennines.

Europe's mountain ranges separated the groups of people who settled the land thousands of years ago. This is one reason different cultures developed in Europe. Mountain ranges also contain natural resources, such as timber, which influence where people settle.

Mountains surround the **Northern European Plain** Ⓔ, a vast area of flat or gently rolling land from France to Russia. Parts of the plain have fertile soil, making them Europe's major farming areas. Other parts are rich with coal. Industrial centers developed near the coal deposits. These variations have made settlement across the plain uneven.

▲ **SUMMARIZE** Explain why Europe is called a peninsula of peninsulas.

CONNECT ⟳ **Geography & Economics**

Seafaring Economies
Europe's vast coastline boosted its economy by encouraging exploration, fishing, and trade. Europe provides over half of the world's international shipping. Countries with large fleets, such as Great Britain, ship goods around the world. To do so, they use ports on rivers like the Thames in London, shown here.

Physical Geography of Europe

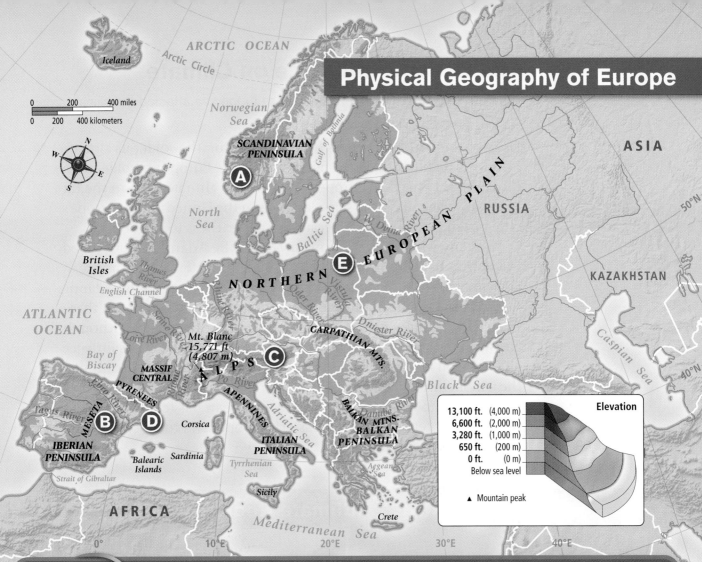

ARCTIC OCEAN
Arctic Circle
Iceland

Norwegian Sea

SCANDINAVIAN PENINSULA
(A)

North Sea

British Isles

English Channel

Thames River

ATLANTIC OCEAN

Bay of Biscay

Loire River

Seine River

Rhine River

Gulf of Bothnia

Baltic Sea

NORTHERN EUROPEAN PLAIN

Oder River

Vistula River

W. Dvina River

RUSSIA

ASIA

KAZAKHSTAN

50°N

Dniester River

CARPATHIAN MTS.

Mt. Blanc 15,771 ft (4,807 m)

MASSIF CENTRAL

PYRENEES

A L P S (C)

Po River

APENNINES

Rhone River

Black Sea

Caspian Sea

40°N

MESETA (B)

(D)

Corsica

Ebro River

IBERIAN PENINSULA

Tagus River

Balearic Islands

Sardinia

ITALIAN PENINSULA

Adriatic Sea

Tyrrhenian Sea

Danube River

BALKAN MTS. BALKAN PENINSULA

Aegean Sea

Strait of Gibraltar

AFRICA

Sicily

Mediterranean Sea

Crete

0°   10°E   20°E   30°E   40°E

Elevation	
13,100 ft.	(4,000 m)
6,600 ft.	(2,000 m)
3,280 ft.	(1,000 m)
650 ft.	(200 m)
0 ft.	(0 m)
Below sea level	

▲ Mountain peak

0   200   400 miles
0   200   400 kilometers

CONNECT — Geography & Economics

A Network of Rivers Europe's rivers are key trade and transportation networks. Goods are transported on rivers to and from coastal harbors. Cities sprang up along river-banks to take advantage of these benefits.

- The **Rhine River** travels north from the Swiss Alps into the North Sea.
- The **Danube River** flows southeast from Germany into the Black Sea.
- The **Thames River** in the United Kingdom runs east across southern England to the North Sea.

CRITICAL THINKING

1. **Find Main Ideas** What advantages result from Europe's network of rivers?

2. **Draw Conclusions** Why are rivers important to landlocked countries in Europe?

ARCTIC OCEAN
Arctic Circle

60°N

North Sea

Thames R.

London

Hamburg

Elbe R.

Oder R.

W. Dvina R.

Vistula R.

Dnieper R.

Kiev

ATLANTIC OCEAN

Paris

Seine R.

Rhine R.

Loire R.

Warsaw

Vienna

Budapest

Lisbon

Rhone R.

Po R.

Danube R.

Black Sea

Tagus R.

Ebro R.

Rome

Tiber R.

40°N

Mediterranean Sea

0   250   500 miles
0   250   500 kilometers

The Ocean's Influence on Climate

▼ **KEY QUESTION** How has nearness to the sea affected the climate and vegetation of Europe?

Usually, the farther a place is from the equator, the colder its climate is. Like the United States, the northern parts of Europe are colder than the southern parts. In Europe, however, the climate even in the far north is warmer than the same latitudes in the United States. Europe's climate tends to be milder because of its nearness to the ocean.

Westerly winds and a warm current in the Atlantic Ocean called the **North Atlantic Drift** influence Europe's climate. The warm ocean current heats the air above it. Winds blowing east across the Atlantic Ocean carry the heat and moisture to Europe. In the winter, these westerlies bring warm tropical air to parts of Europe. Although Norway is as far north as parts of Alaska and Canada, it gets little ice and snow on its coast during the winter months. During the summer, the winds shift and deliver cooler subarctic air, keeping temperatures from getting too hot. Farther inland, the ocean has less effect on climate. Winter temperatures in eastern Europe tend to be colder than those in western Europe.

▶ COMPARING ◀ Climate Regions of Europe

Mediterranean Palm trees grow in this Spanish garden. **1. What feature is this climate zone named for?**

Marine West Coast Grapevines thrive in France's scenic Loire Valley. **2. How might climate affect a country's exports?**

Humid Continental Forests cover about one-fourth of Romania. **3. How could humidity affect plant life?**

Tundra Finland's tundra often blooms in the summer. **4. How does it change in winter?**

Europe's plant and animal life varies with its climate. Parts of the Scandinavian Peninsula in the north are covered with tundra. Few plants can survive the cold winters. There are no trees on the tundra, but in the spring, mosses and a few wildflowers appear. Thick forests of fir trees cover large areas of northern Europe. Such trees remain green year-round. Central and eastern Europe once had forests of maple, oak, and elm trees. Today, most have been cut down for lumber or fuel. Far to the south, along the Mediterranean Sea, the climate is too warm and dry for the trees seen farther north. Instead, the wax-coated leaves of cork and olive trees retain water, helping these plants grow here.

In the Arctic region, elk and reindeer still roam, but most animals that once inhabited Europe's dense northern forests are gone. European brown bears, deer, foxes, and wolves live in parts of Europe. Two goatlike animals, the chamois (SHAM•ee) and ibex, inhabit high mountain areas in southern and southwestern Europe.

▲ **ANALYZE EFFECTS** Explain the effects of Europe's location on its climate and vegetation.

Fun Facts!

PALM TREES IN SCOTLAND?

Did you know that there are palm trees in Scotland? Even though Stranraer, Scotland is almost as far north as southern Alaska, palm trees thrive there. For this, Scots can thank the North Atlantic Drift. This ocean current brings mild weather to the region.

Tromsø, Norway
Latitude: 69° N

Valencia, Spain
Latitude: 39° N

Tromsø, Norway: Subarctic

Source: www.euroweather.net

Valencia, Spain: Mediterranean

Source: www.euroweather.net

Europe's Many Climates

Much of Europe's climate is mild as a result of the ocean, but differences in latitude still affect climate. Tromsø, Norway, far to the north, experiences the cool temperatures of a subarctic climate. Valencia, Spain, has a warm Mediterranean climate.

CRITICAL THINKING

1. **Evaluate** In both locations, more rain falls in October than in any other month. How does Valencia's October precipitation compare to Tromsø's?

2. **Compare and Contrast** How do the ranges of temperatures that each city experiences during the year compare to each other?

Europe: Physical Geography and History **251**

Europe's Resources

▼ **KEY QUESTION** Why are energy resources so important to Europe's growth?

Europe has a variety of natural resources, from fertile soils to mineral deposits. These resources have influenced where people settled on the continent. They have also contributed to Europe's industrialization.

Fertile Soil and Abundant Resources Soil is an important resource because it is used to grow food for people to eat. Europe's regions of rich soil allow farmers to produce plentiful crops. About one-third of Europe's land can be used for farming, three times more than the world average.

Europe's landscape also provides a wide variety of important mineral resources. Minerals like iron, copper, lead, zinc, and coal provide the raw materials and energy needed for manufacturing. For instance, both coal and iron ore are used to make steel. Large deposits of these minerals helped industry develop in the United Kingdom and the Ruhr Valley in Germany.

Fuel for Industry As Europe's industry developed, it required additional energy sources to power factories and move goods. Several countries in northern Europe tap into oil and natural gas deposits in the North Sea. Countries such as France and Ukraine have uranium, a rare, naturally occurring element used to fuel nuclear power plants.

However, coal, oil, and natural gas are **fossil fuels**, sources of energy from ancient plant and animal remains. All of these energy sources—even uranium—exist in limited quantities and will eventually run out. In addition, using these energy sources can harm the environment. Burning fossil fuels can pollute the air and is believed to contribute to global warming. Nuclear plants create toxic waste.

Geothermal Power Plant This power plant in Larderello, Italy, produces enough energy each year to power half a million homes. **Why might Italy want to develop more geothermal plants?**

Renewable Energy As an alternative to fossil fuels, many European nations are trying to find renewable sources of energy. **Renewable energy sources** can be replaced through ongoing natural processes, such as sunshine, wind, and flowing water. These types of energy sources are also sustainable, meaning that they can be utilized without being used up.

Hydroelectric power is a renewable energy source that uses water-powered engines to make electricity. Austria generates energy by damming Alpine rivers. Coastal countries such as Ireland and Portugal are developing technology to harness wave energy. Germany, Spain, and Denmark lead the pack in producing electricity from wind energy. Other nations, including the Netherlands, generate heat and electricity by collecting solar energy from the sun. Italy and Iceland tap geothermal energy by drilling into naturally hot groundwater. These alternative energy sources have many benefits. They are sustainable. They reduce pollution. They mean that European nations can rely less on importing energy from other countries.

▲ **DRAW CONCLUSIONS** Explain why energy resources are important to Europe's growth.

European Renewable Energy Sources

In 2001, 15 European countries used renewable energy sources to supply 15.2 percent of the energy they consumed. This pie graph shows how much energy came from each source.

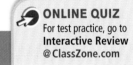

1.6% — 9.7%
8.8%
79.9%

- ■ Hydroelectric
- ■ Wind
- ■ Geothermal
- ■ Other

Source: European Commission, *Electricity from Renewable Energy Sources*, 2004

ONLINE QUIZ
For test practice, go to
Interactive Review
@ ClassZone.com

Section 1 Assessment

TERMS & NAMES

1. Explain the importance of
- Alps
- Northern European Plain
- North Atlantic Drift
- fossil fuels

USE YOUR READING NOTES

2. Categorize Use your completed chart to answer the following question:

What are the major mountain ranges of Europe?

PENINSULAS	MOUNTAINS	RIVERS
1.	1.	1.
2.	2.	2.
3.	3.	3.

KEY IDEAS

3. Why is the Northern European Plain important to Europe's economy?

4. How does the North Atlantic Drift affect the climate of Europe?

5. What are Europe's most important mineral resources?

CRITICAL THINKING

6. Draw Conclusions Why might mountains be both an asset and a disadvantage?

7. Make Inferences Why are coal and iron important to industrializing nations?

8. CONNECT to Today Why is Europe's network of rivers still important to its economy?

9. WRITING Write a Report Choose one of Europe's major rivers to write a report about. List the countries the river runs through. Include some major cities you might see if you sailed along the river. Finally, explain one way the river is important to Europe's economy.

Reading for Understanding

▶ Key Ideas

BEFORE, YOU LEARNED

Europe has diverse landforms. Its climate and vegetation vary by latitude and distance from the ocean.

NOW YOU WILL LEARN

Ancient Greek and Roman achievements in government, art and architecture, engineering, and law continue to influence Europe and the world today.

▶ Vocabulary

TERMS & NAMES

democracy a government in which the citizens make political decisions, either directly or through elected representatives

Peloponnesus (PEHL•uh•puh•NEE•suhs) the peninsula in southern Greece where Sparta was located

city-state a political unit made up of a city and its surrounding lands

tyrant someone who takes power illegally

oligarchy (AHL•ih•GAHR•kee) a government ruled by a few powerful individuals

republic a government in which citizens elect representatives to rule in their name

patrician (puh•TRIHSH•uhn) a wealthy land-owner who held a high government position in ancient Rome

plebeian (plih•BEE•uhn) a commoner who was allowed to vote but not to hold government office in ancient Rome

BACKGROUND VOCABULARY

isolate to cut off or set apart from a group

REVIEW

monarchy a type of government in which a ruling family headed by a king or queen holds political power

▶ Reading Strategy

Re-create the chart shown at right. As you read and respond to the **KEY QUESTIONS**, use the chart to help you compare and contrast the governments of ancient Greece, the Roman Republic, and the Roman Empire.

 See Skillbuilder Handbook, page R9

COMPARE AND CONTRAST

GOVERNMENT	WHO RULED	HOW CHOSEN	WHO PARTICIPATED
Greek Democracy			
Roman Republic			
Roman Empire			

 GRAPHIC ORGANIZERS
Go to **Interactive Review** @ ClassZone.com

Classical Greece and Rome

9.01 Trace the historical development of governments including traditional, colonial, and national in selected societies and assess the effects on the respective contemporary political systems.
11.03 Compare characteristics of political, economic, religious, and social institutions of selected cultures, and evaluate their similarities and differences.

Connecting to Your World

Have you ever been to the nation's capital, Washington, D.C.? It is the center of the U.S. government. The United States is a **democracy**, a government in which citizens make political decisions. You are about to learn about ancient Greece, the place where modern democracy began. Ideas about what democracy should be have changed over time. Democratic government in Greece stands as a remarkable first step.

Lincoln Memorial Some buildings in Washington, D.C., reflect ancient Greek architecture.

History of Ancient Greece

▼ **KEY QUESTION** How did ancient Greek culture spread?

Between 5000 and 3000 B.C., groups of people began settling on the **Peloponnesus** (PEHL•uh•puh•NEE•suhs), a mountainous peninsula in southern Europe. Almost 2,000 small islands surrounded the peninsula. Villages were **isolated**, or cut off, from each other. The rugged terrain and remote islands made it difficult to unite the villages under one government. In time, people had settled throughout what is now Greece.

The Acropolis This part of Athens held important buildings constructed in the second half of the fifth century B.C.

GREECE

Athens

Sparta

Rise of City-States: Athens and Sparta Eventually, Greek towns and cities became **city-states**, political units made up of a city and surrounding villages. Most people were farmers and herders, but where land was rocky and soil was poor, people made their living from the sea. They fished, sailed, and traded with other city-states.

Greek city-states shared a common culture and language, but each had unique features. They chose different forms of government. At first, many were monarchies, ruled by kings. Others were ruled by tyrants. In Greece, a **tyrant** was someone who took power illegally.

Athens and Sparta, the largest Greek city-states, had different governments. Sparta was an **oligarchy** (AHL•ih•GAHR•kee), a system ruled by a few powerful individuals. Two kings governed the state, making all major decisions with the help of a few officials. Sparta was a military state. Its large slave class farmed the land, freeing male citizens to serve in the army. Spartan boys began receiving military training at age seven. After decades of military service, they became citizens at 30. They faced losing their citizenship if they did not fight bravely.

At first, kings also governed Athens. Then, at the end of the sixth century B.C., Athens became a limited democracy. All citizens had the right to take part in the government and decide on laws. However, only free adult males were citizens. Women, slaves, and foreigners were not. Athens became a center of Greek culture. It attracted the finest scholars, artists, and philosophers from all over the Mediterranean.

ANALYZING Primary Sources

Pericles (495–429 B.C.) was an Athenian statesman and general. His "Funeral Oration" honors those who died in the Peloponnesian War and praises democracy. Pericles saw participation in government as a civic duty. Greek citizens often discussed politics in an agora, or marketplace, like the one shown at left.

> An Athenian citizen does not neglect public affairs when attending to his private business. . . . We consider a man who takes no interest in the state not as harmless, but as useless.
>
> Source: Thucydides, from *The Peloponnesian War*

DOCUMENT–BASED QUESTION

Why was an interest in politics considered a public duty?

Pericles ▲

Wars and Conquest In the early fifth century B.C., the rulers of Persia, the region in southwestern Asia that is now Iran, tried to conquer Greece. Led by Sparta and Athens, the Greeks resisted. Conflict between the Greeks and Persians lasted on and off for many years. The Greeks defeated the Persians, keeping Greek culture alive.

Decades later, Athens and Sparta fought each other in the Peloponnesian War. Sparta won the war, becoming the dominant power in Greece. Weakened by their internal conflict, the city-states paid little attention to neighboring Macedonia, a kingdom north of Greece that was preparing to attack.

In 338 B.C., King Philip II of Macedonia used his well-trained army to seize control of Greece. After Philip's death, his son Alexander took control. A brilliant military planner, Alexander conquered vast new territories and became known as Alexander the Great. His empire extended into North Africa, the Middle East, and Asia. As his empire expanded, Greek culture spread. When Alexander died, three of his generals divided his territory among themselves, ending one of the great empires of the ancient world.

▲ **EVALUATE** Explain the differences between Athens and Sparta.

History of Ancient Rome

▼ **KEY QUESTION** How were the governments of the Roman Republic and the Roman Empire different?

While Athens was creating a democracy, the people of Rome, located west of Greece on the Italian Peninsula, were also making changes to their government. They overthrew the foreign kings that ruled them and set up a **monarchy** of their own. Then, in 509 B.C., the Romans rejected rule by kings and created a new form of government.

From Republic to Empire The Romans set up a **republic**, a form of government in which citizens elect representatives to rule in their name. It was not a democracy. All male citizens could vote, but only **patricians** (puh•TRISH•uhnz), members of rich and powerful families, could hold the highest government offices. Farmers, merchants, and craftspeople made up the class known as **plebeians** (plih•BEE•uhnz). Over time, the plebeians gained more political power.

HISTORY MAKERS

Alexander 356–323 B.C.

One important effect of Alexander's conquest was the spread of Greek culture to other parts of the world. When Alexander was young, the great Greek thinker Aristotle was his teacher. Alexander came to know and admire Greek culture. His many conquests enabled him to spread Greek language, ideas, and beliefs far beyond the Greek peninsula. Greek culture influenced life throughout his vast empire.

ONLINE BIOGRAPHY
For more on the life of Alexander the Great, go to the **Research & Writing Center @ ClassZone.com**

Over centuries the Roman Republic grew, until it controlled the entire Italian Peninsula. As they conquered, the Romans offered citizenship to many groups, a policy that strengthened the republic. After almost 500 years, however, the republic began to fall apart. By 27 B.C., military leaders were fighting civil wars. Worn down by the conflict and seeking order at the cost of liberty, the Romans allowed Octavian—later known as Augustus—to take over the government. The republic became an empire, united under a supreme leader.

Augustus and later emperors greatly expanded the empire, as the map below shows. Palestine, a Jewish kingdom on the eastern edge of the Mediterranean, came under Roman control. It was here that Jesus was born and Christianity began. The new religion quickly spread across the empire, becoming its official religion in A.D. 380.

The Empire Falls Apart By the third century A.D., the Roman Empire faced serious problems, which you can see in the chart below. To make the empire easier to govern, it was divided it into two halves. Constantinople became the capital of the eastern empire. Rome remained the capital of the western part. Germanic tribes who lived outside of Rome's borders began pushing into Roman territory. In A.D. 476, the Western Roman Empire fell. The Eastern Roman Empire lasted about 1,000 years more.

▲ COMPARE AND CONTRAST Explain how the governments of the Roman Republic and the Roman Empire were different.

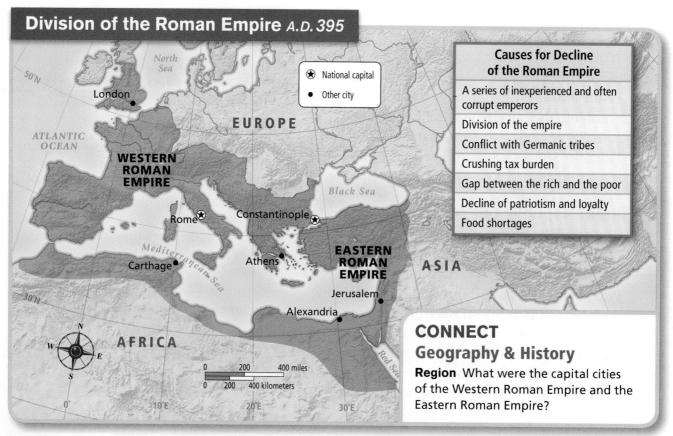

Division of the Roman Empire A.D. 395

★ National capital
● Other city

North Sea
London
EUROPE
ATLANTIC OCEAN
WESTERN ROMAN EMPIRE
Black Sea
Rome ★
Constantinople ★
Mediterranean Sea
Carthage ●
Athens ●
EASTERN ROMAN EMPIRE
ASIA
Jerusalem ●
Alexandria ●
AFRICA
Red Sea

0   200   400 miles
0   200   400 kilometers

Causes for Decline of the Roman Empire

A series of inexperienced and often corrupt emperors
Division of the empire
Conflict with Germanic tribes
Crushing tax burden
Gap between the rich and the poor
Decline of patriotism and loyalty
Food shortages

CONNECT
Geography & History
Region What were the capital cities of the Western Roman Empire and the Eastern Roman Empire?

Classical Culture

▼ **KEY QUESTION** What accomplishments of ancient Greece and Rome still influence modern life?

The ancient Greeks and Romans left a powerful legacy. The Greeks excelled as artists, writers, and philosophers. Their ideas led to developments in theater, science, and government that still influence life today. Perhaps the greatest legacy of the Greeks is democracy. Greek society was one of the first to give people a voice in government. Democracy is a goal for many countries.

The Romans adopted many aspects of Greek culture, but they also had many practical skills of their own. Roman engineers designed and built roads, aqueducts, and public buildings such as the Colosseum. Their system of roads helped expand trade networks and spread culture, including Christianity. The Romans invented the idea of the republic and created a written code of law, the Law of the Twelve Tables. These ideas later shaped legal systems throughout Europe and the Americas.

▲ **SUMMARIZE** Describe the achievements of ancient Greece and Rome that continue to influence modern life.

Animated GEOGRAPHY

Roman Aqueduct Their advances in engineering allowed the Romans to build aqueducts, like this one in France, which carried fresh water from distant sources into cities and towns.

Click here to see how aqueducts work @ ClassZone.com

Section 2 Assessment

ONLINE QUIZ For test practice, go to **Interactive Review** @ ClassZone.com

TERMS & NAMES

1. Explain the importance of
- democracy
- oligarchy
- patrician
- plebeian

USE YOUR READING NOTES

2. Compare and Contrast Use your completed chart to answer the following question:

Who participated in elections in the Roman Republic?

GOVERNMENT	WHO RULED	HOW CHOSEN	WHO PARTICIPATED
Greek Democracy			
Roman Republic			
Roman Empire			

KEY IDEAS

3. Why were the waters surrounding the Greek peninsulas an important resource for ancient Greece?

4. How did Alexander help spread Greek culture to foreign lands?

5. What role did patricians and plebeians play in the early Roman Republic?

CRITICAL THINKING

6. Compare and Contrast What are some differences between the achievements of the ancient Greek and Roman civilizations?

7. Analyze Causes Which of the causes of the fall of the Western Roman Empire do you think was most significant? Why?

8. CONNECT to Today How was the original Roman Republic similar to the U.S. government today?

9. WRITING Rewrite a Myth Pick a myth from Greek or Roman literature. Rewrite it as a poem or short story set in the present.

COMPARING Classical Cultures

The cultures of ancient Greece and Rome shaped the people who came after them. The influence of both cultures can still be seen today.

Greece

The Greeks developed new ideas about architecture and the gods. They created a new art form—the Greek drama. Other cultures, including ancient Rome, picked up many of these ideas. We can still see ancient Greece in ruins like the Acropolis, shown below, and reflected in our own culture.

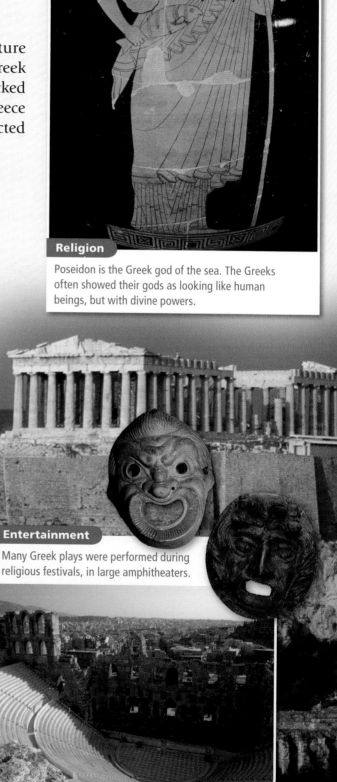

Religion

Poseidon is the Greek god of the sea. The Greeks often showed their gods as looking like human beings, but with divine powers.

Daily Life

Greek pottery provides a good record of daily life. This pot shows women collecting water from a public fountain.

Entertainment

Many Greek plays were performed during religious festivals, in large amphitheaters.

Rome

Roman culture was based on values of strength and loyalty. The Romans picked up some Greek ideas about the gods and architecture. They transformed these ideas into styles that were uniquely Roman, as seen in the Forum, shown below.

Religion

The Romans called the god of the sea Neptune. Roman depictions of their gods and goddesses frequently seem more realistic and three-dimensional than those of the Greeks.

Daily Life

Agriculture and trade formed the basis of the Roman economy. Shops occupied the ground story of many ancient buildings.

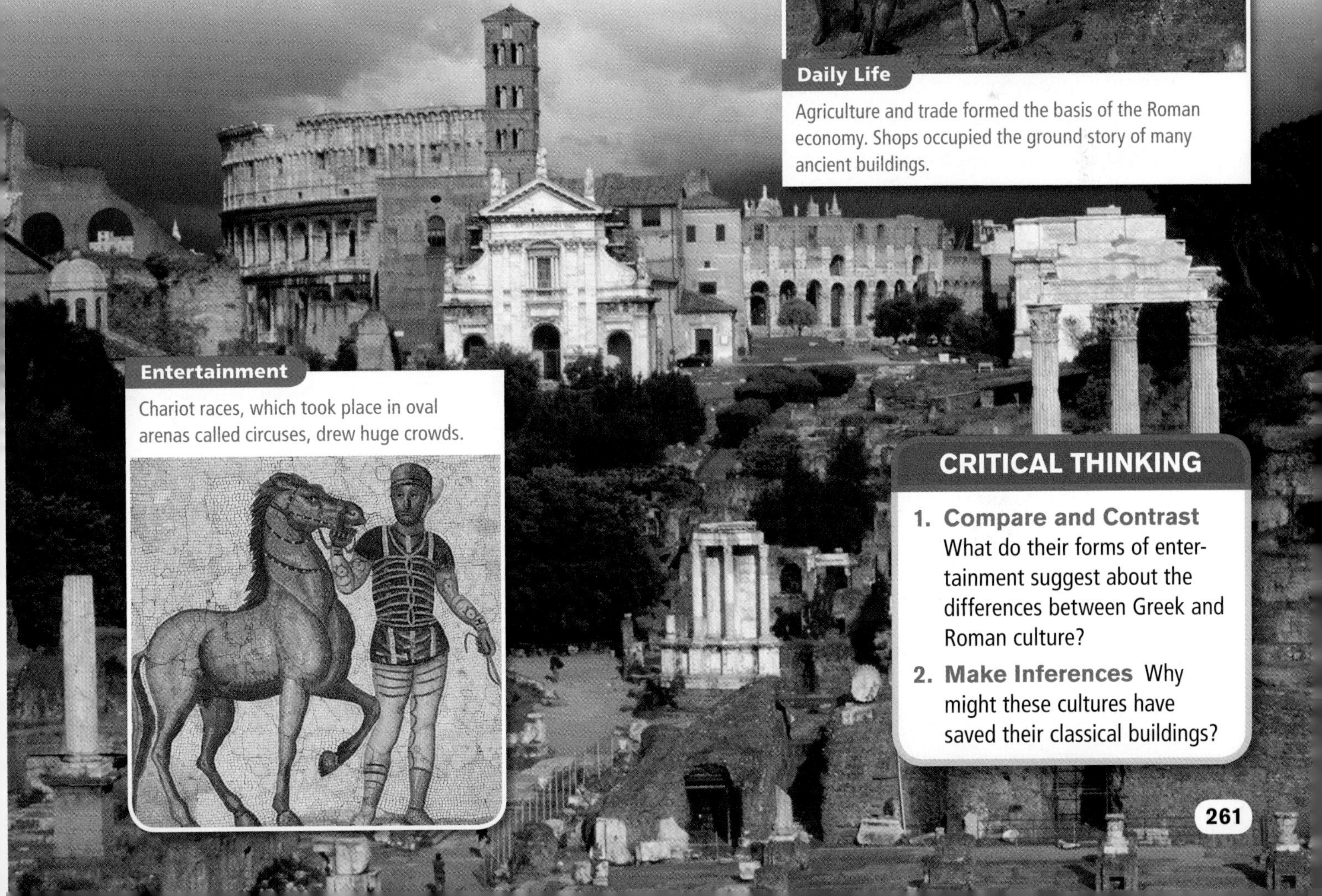

Entertainment

Chariot races, which took place in oval arenas called circuses, drew huge crowds.

CRITICAL THINKING

1. **Compare and Contrast** What do their forms of entertainment suggest about the differences between Greek and Roman culture?

2. **Make Inferences** Why might these cultures have saved their classical buildings?

Reading for Understanding

▶ Key Ideas

BEFORE, YOU LEARNED

Ancient Greek and Roman achievements continue to influence our world today.

NOW YOU WILL LEARN

Feudalism provided stability after the fall of the Roman Empire. The Renaissance marked a rebirth of creativity in Europe.

▶ Vocabulary

TERMS & NAMES

Middle Ages the period between the fall of the Roman Empire and the modern era, from about A.D. 476 to 1453

medieval from the Middle Ages

feudalism a political system in which lords gave land to vassals in exchange for services

lord a powerful landowner

vassal a less wealthy noble who paid taxes to and served a lord in exchange for land

knight a vassal trained in combat who fought on behalf of lords

serf a person who lived and worked on the manor of a lord or vassal

manor a noble's house and the villages on his land where the peasants lived

Renaissance (REHN•ih•SAHNS) a rebirth of creativity, literature, and learning in Europe from about 1300 to 1600

patron a wealthy or powerful person who provides money, support, and encouragement to an artist or a cause

secular worldly or not related to religion

perspective a technique used by artists to give the appearance of depth and distance

Reformation a movement in the 1500s to change practices in the Catholic Church

Protestant a member of a Christian Church founded on the principles of the Reformation

▶ Reading Strategy

Re-create the cause-and-effect diagram shown at right. As you read and respond to the **KEY QUESTIONS**, use the diagram to help you find the effect of the events listed in the first ovals in each pair.

 See Skillbuilder Handbook, page R8

ANALYZE CAUSE AND EFFECT

Fall of the Roman Empire → ◯

The Plague and the Crusades → ◯

Challenges to the Church → ◯

GRAPHIC ORGANIZERS
Go to **Interactive Review** @ ClassZone.com

The Middle Ages and Renaissance

7.02 Examine the causes of key historical events in selected areas of South America and Europe and analyze the short-and long-range effects on political, economic, and social institutions.
8.01 Describe the role of key historical figures and evaluate their impact on past and present societies in South America and Europe.

Connecting to Your World

Sometimes it can be difficult to imagine life without the ideas and technology that exist today. The pace of change seems to increase with every passing decade. Even 25 years ago, cell phones were just being invented. Now they are everywhere. At the beginning of the period in European history you are about to study, new ideas and inventions traveled much more slowly than they do today. Yet change did take place. In time, new ideas and discoveries challenged many Europeans' accepted beliefs about how the world worked and their place in it.

The Middle Ages

▼ **KEY QUESTION** Why did feudalism develop in Europe?

Historians call the period of history between the fall of the Roman Empire and the beginning of the modern era the **Middle Ages**. It is also called the **medieval** period, from the Latin words for "Middle Ages." The collapse of the Western Roman Empire made many people fearful and uncertain. Europeans no longer had a strong central government, an army to protect them, or a common culture and belief system to unite them. Many advances of the ancient world were lost.

Cell phones Many people today use cell phones.

Bayeux Tapestry This textile shows feudal knights during the Norman Conquest of England from 1064 to 1066.

NAN:CLAVES:POR REXIT: hIC:WILLELM: DEDIT:HAROLDO: ARMA   hIE   VVILLELM VENIT:BAGIAS   VBI hAROL

Medieval Society The Germanic tribes in western Europe were quite different from the Romans. They had no tradition of central government. At first, many small kingdoms replaced the Roman Empire. Roads and water systems were not kept up. Trade declined. As their economies slowed, western European towns shrank. Residents abandoned them, heading to the countryside to become farmers. Literacy—and with it the educated middle class—all but disappeared.

During the early Middle Ages, invaders such as the Huns, Moors, and Vikings threatened Europe. Constant conflict and warfare plagued the region. In the 700s, a ruler named Charlemagne (SHAHR•luh•MAYN) brought much of France and Germany under his control. Charlemagne was a strong military leader. He worked with the pope, the leader of the Roman Catholic Church, to strengthen the church and his own empire. Pope Leo III crowned him emperor in 800. However, Charlemagne died in 814. In 843, his three grandsons divided his empire among themselves. Europe again became a disorderly group of small kingdoms.

Faced with such disorder, Europeans turned to a political system called **feudalism**, which would remain in place from about the 9th to the 14th century. Feudalism created a new social structure in Europe. The king ruled at the top of society. Nobles, church officials, knights, and peasants had their places below the king.

Feudalism depended on an agreement between two groups of nobles—lords and vassals.

- **Lords**, or powerful landowners, gave some of their land to less-wealthy nobles called vassals.

- **Vassals** pledged to serve their lords. They paid taxes to the lords in exchange for their plots of land, called fiefs (feefs).

- Some vassals were warriors known as **knights**, who began combat training as young boys. Knights fought on behalf of their lords.

- The feudal structure also included peasants. Most were **serfs**, who lived and worked on a noble's land. Serfs received housing and protection in return.

This political system kept Europe divided into many small kingdoms and estates, with little trade between them. As a result, the nobles' lands became the center of most economic activity. The main part of a noble's land was called a **manor**. Often the manor was a fortified house, surrounded by farmland worked by serfs. Manors supplied much of what their residents needed. Towns grew less important, as townspeople left to work on manors.

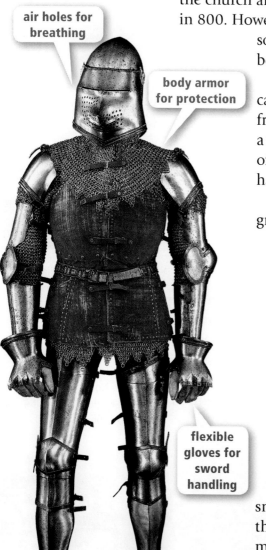

European Knight Knights often wore a suit of armor to protect themselves in battle. These suits made it difficult to move quickly—the average suit weighed 65 pounds! **What might the advantages and disadvantages of armor be?**

air holes for breathing

body armor for protection

flexible gloves for sword handling

The Role of the Church The Roman Catholic Church was one institution that survived the fall of Rome. After the division of the Roman Empire, Christianity split into several different churches. The Roman Catholic Church developed in the Western Roman Empire. Many of the Germanic tribes that invaded Rome converted to Christianity. The religion spread slowly across Europe. The church became the main source of education during the Middle Ages. Church officials built universities where nobles could go and study.

Eventually, the territory once controlled by Charlemagne became the Holy Roman Empire. It was a loose confederation of states associated with the Catholic Church, rather than a unified empire with a strong central government. Even so, the Holy Roman Empire helped to bring Europe back together after the divisions of the Middle Ages.

▲ **ANALYZE CAUSES** Explain how events in Europe contributed to the rise of feudalism.

Animated GEOGRAPHY

European Feudalism

Click here to hear from each level of feudal society @ ClassZone.com

King This man sat atop feudal society and ruled over large areas of land.

Church Officials and Lords These people owned land and therefore held much power.

Knights Many of these warriors were vassals who provided military service to lords in return for land.

Peasants Peasants known as serfs worked the land for nobles and performed other backbreaking tasks.

King

Church Officials and Lords

Knights

Peasants

Feudal castles were designed for defense against enemy attacks. Many included the following defensive features:

- Moats **A**, filled with water, prevented attackers from getting too close.
- Watchtowers **B** allowed guards to fire on approaching enemies from a protected position.
- Thick stone walls **C** kept enemies out of the castle's inner courtyard.

Design a Castle Floor Plan

Materials
- paper
- pencil
- ruler

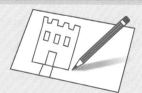

1. Be sure your castle has these features: walls, windows, and moat.

2. Research and add one other defensive feature to your castle.

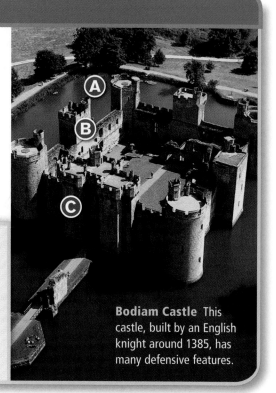

Bodiam Castle This castle, built by an English knight around 1385, has many defensive features.

The Renaissance

▼ **KEY QUESTION** How did the Renaissance change Europe?

Peace and stability were returning to Europe. Merchants again felt safe traveling on the roads. Trade began again. Towns grew. Travel spread new ideas, which set the stage for change.

Forces of Change At the end of the 11th century, thousands of western European Christians took part in the Crusades, a series of military expeditions to take back the Holy Land, Palestine, from the Muslims. The Crusades led to centuries of mistrust between Christians and Muslims and imposed economic burdens on many Europeans. However, they resulted in economic growth, increasing trade between towns on the Mediterranean Sea and in the Middle East.

The importance of towns increased during the Crusades, when towns were needed to supply armies. As towns grew into cities and serfs left manors to find better work, feudal lords lost power. In the 1300s, the deadly plague, known as the Black Death, swept through Europe. About one-third of Europe's population died. The high death rate led to a labor shortage, which further weakened feudal ties.

All these forces helped bring about the Renaissance. The **Renaissance** (REHN•ih•SAHNS) was a 300-year period of renewed interest in learning and art from about 1300 to 1600. The rediscovery of ancient Greek and Roman knowledge influenced the Renaissance. Europeans developed new ideas about art, science, and humanity.

The Rebirth of Europe The Renaissance began in the city-states of the Italian Peninsula. Increased trade between Italian towns and the Middle East after the Crusades had made many Italian merchants and bankers wealthy. They used their new wealth to build and furnish beautiful palaces. Some became **patrons** of the arts, supporting painters and writers. They showed their pride in their city by hiring architects to build churches, public fountains, and sculptures. City-states like Florence, Rome, and Venice competed to display the talents of Italy's finest artists, such as Michelangelo and Leonardo da Vinci.

Renaissance art reflected the beliefs of the period. Many scholars began to study humanity, prompting a new interest in the individual and in **secular**, or worldly, concerns. Many Renaissance paintings still had religious themes, but others depicted contemporary people instead of biblical figures. Painters also found new ways to create more lifelike portraits and realistic landscapes. The technique known as **perspective** gave objects in a painting the appearance of depth and distance. The Renaissance also produced notable writers. Many wrote in their national languages, rather than Latin, which was the practice before the Renaissance. For example, the poet Dante wrote his finest works in Italian.

Animated GEOGRAPHY

Mona Lisa Leonardo da Vinci's *Mona Lisa* is one of the most famous paintings of the Renaissance.

Click here to see more works by Renaissance artists @ ClassZone.com

COMPARING   Medieval and Renaissance Art

MEDIEVAL

Madonna Enthroned by Duccio di Buoninsegna

- Created art with religious themes, especially scenes from the Bible
- Created flat, two-dimensional art

RENAISSANCE

Peasant Wedding by Pieter Brueghel

- Created art about secular as well as religious themes, with more emphasis on the individual and daily life
- Created lifelike, realistic sculptures and paintings

CRITICAL THINKING

Form and Support Opinions Which artistic style seems more lifelike? Why?

The Printing Press The invention of the printing press had a huge impact on European society. Johann Gutenberg, a German, created a machine that pressed movable type against paper. Until then, Europeans copied books slowly by hand. The printing press allowed 500 times as many books to be printed in the same amount of time. The first book printed on Gutenberg's press was a Bible. Ideas spread as books became cheap enough for many to buy.

CRITICAL THINKING

Draw Conclusions How did the printing press help ideas spread during the Renaissance?

The Renaissance Spreads In the late 1400s, the Renaissance began to spread north from Italy to France, England, Germany, and Flanders, a region that today is part of Belgium. The Hundred Years' War, a series of battles between France and England, ended in 1453. With the conflict over, cities and trade routes expanded. A wealthy merchant class developed. Like the Italian merchants, they eagerly sponsored artists and writers. So did the monarchs of these countries, who viewed artistic achievements as a source of national pride.

Unlike the Italian artists, many northern European artists chose to paint scenes of everyday life. Pieter Brueghel the Elder, an artist from Flanders, painted peasants dancing and feasting. His paintings included many details of daily life. Authors such as William Shakespeare examined human nature. Many of Shakespeare's plays, including *Hamlet* and *Romeo and Juliet*, are still performed today. Scholars also made scientific advances, learning more about the human body and the minerals that make up the Earth's surface.

The scholars in northern Europe were also more interested in studying Christianity than ancient Greek and Roman art. Their studies led them to call for reforms to existing religious practices. They criticized the Catholic Church for caring more about wealth and power than about spiritual matters. Renaissance knowledge and ideas like these spread across Europe, aided by the printing press. People began to examine and question the institutions around them.

▲ **FIND MAIN IDEAS** Explain how the ideas of the Renaissance changed Europe.

The Reformation

▼ **KEY QUESTION** What concerns led Martin Luther and others to break with the Catholic Church?

During the 14th and 15th centuries, criticisms of the Catholic Church grew more intense. In the 1500s, these concerns set the stage for the **Reformation**, a movement to change church practices. Martin Luther, a German monk, led this movement. In 1517, Luther wrote his Ninety-Five Theses, a list of statements of belief. He attacked practices he saw as corrupt. Luther posted his theses on a church door in Wittenberg, Germany. His supporters sent copies throughout Europe.

Luther's ideas spread quickly. Many northern countries broke with the Catholic Church. Other reformers in Switzerland, Scotland, and England created their own **Protestant** sects, the name given to Christians who protested against the Catholic Church. The Catholic Church tried to slow the expansion of Protestantism. They began their own Catholic Reformation. Luther was excommunicated, or cast out of the Catholic Church. Church leaders sent missionaries overseas in an effort to spread Catholic ideas around the world.

Martin Luther Luther nails his Ninety-Five Theses to the church door in Wittenberg.

▲ **SUMMARIZE** Explain what concerns led Martin Luther and others to break with the Catholic Church.

Section ❸ Assessment

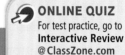

ONLINE QUIZ
For test practice, go to
Interactive Review
@ ClassZone.com

TERMS & NAMES

1. Explain the importance of
- Middle Ages
- feudalism
- Renaissance
- Reformation

USE YOUR READING NOTES

2. Analyze Cause and Effect Use your completed diagram to answer the following question:

How did the plague help bring about the Renaissance?

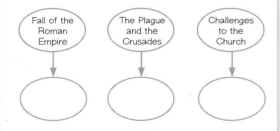

KEY IDEAS

3. In what ways did the Crusades contribute to the start of the Renaissance?

4. Where did the Renaissance begin?

5. What was Martin Luther's role in the Reformation?

CRITICAL THINKING

6. Compare and Contrast What were the main differences between the Italian Renaissance and the Renaissance in northern Europe?

7. Draw Conclusions What did the leaders of the Catholic Church hope to achieve with the Catholic Reformation?

8. CONNECT to Today How is the Internet similar to the printing press? How are they different?

9. WRITING Prepare an Art Lecture Choose a painting by a Renaissance artist. Visit an art museum or library to do research. Prepare a short talk for the class on the artist and the significance of the painting. Show the class a picture of the artwork.

Europe: Physical Geography and History **269**

Reading for Understanding

▶ Key Ideas

BEFORE, YOU LEARNED

Feudalism and religion provided stability during the Middle Ages. The Renaissance marked a rebirth of creativity in Europe.

NOW YOU WILL LEARN

Revolutions in science, politics, and industry transformed Western Europe. After two world wars, European nations found new ways to cooperate.

▶ Vocabulary

TERMS & NAMES

Scientific Revolution a major change in European thinking in the mid-1500s that led to the questioning of old theories

Enlightenment a philosophical movement in the 1600s and 1700s that was characterized by the use of reason and scientific methods

French Revolution a conflict in France between 1789 and 1799 that ended the monarchy and led to changes in the way France was governed

nationalism pride in and loyalty to one's nation

Industrial Revolution the shift that began in Britain in the 1760s from making goods by hand to making them by machine

imperialism the practice of one country controlling the government and economy of another country or terrritory

Holocaust the systematic murder of Jews and other minorities by the Nazis during World War II

European Union (EU) an organization of European nations whose members cooperate on economic, social, and political issues

▶ Reading Strategy

Re-create the time line shown at right. As you read and respond to the **KEY QUESTIONS**, use the time line to help you place the events of modern European history in order.

 See Skillbuilder Handbook, page R6

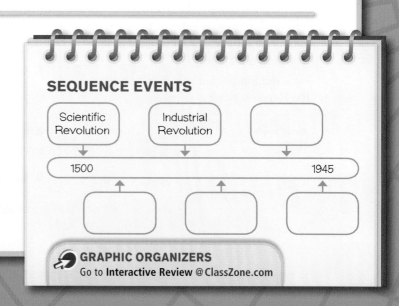

SEQUENCE EVENTS

Scientific Revolution → | Industrial Revolution → | →

1500   1945

GRAPHIC ORGANIZERS
Go to **Interactive Review** @ ClassZone.com

Modern European History

7.02 Examine the causes of key historical events in selected areas of South America and Europe and analyze the short-and long-range effects on political, economic, and social institutions.
11.04 Identify examples of economic, political, and social changes, such as agrarian to industrial economies, monarchical to democratic governments, and the roles of women and minorities, and analyze their impact on culture.

Connecting to Your World

How would you feel if you learned that what you knew about the world was wrong? Today, students aren't likely to disagree when a teacher describes how planets revolve around the sun. In the 1600s, when the Italian astronomer Galileo Galilei observed the sky through his telescope, he was looking for proof of this theory. Some things that seem obvious to us now weren't accepted as fact until a few hundred years ago. In this section, you will learn how new ideas changed Europeans' views of the world.

New Ideas Produce Change

▼ KEY QUESTION How did Enlightenment ideas affect the struggle for independence in many European countries?

In the 1500s and 1600s, scientists such as Galileo examined accepted scientific ideas using reason and careful observation. Knowledge grew rapidly in astronomy, anatomy, and other fields. These discoveries were part of the **Scientific Revolution**, which caused scientists to re-examine old theories.

In the 1600s, European philosophers began to question traditional beliefs and accepted ideas. They argued that reason could be used to study both human behavior and the natural world. Because of the influence of these ideas, this era is known as the **Enlightenment**, or the Age of Reason.

Telescope Galileo built his first telescope in 1609.

Accademia del Cimento This scientific academy was founded by students of Galileo in 1657.

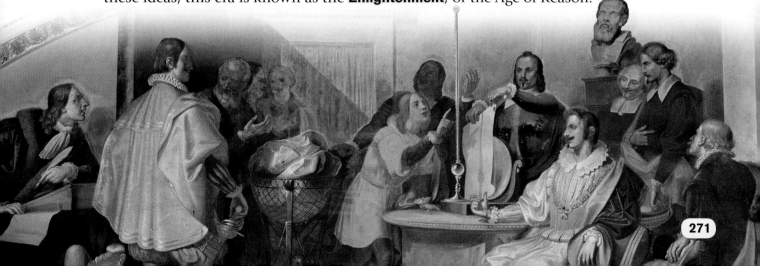

The Guillotine

Before the French Revolution, only nobles had the privilege of execution by beheading. Commoners faced hanging or more gruesome methods. In 1792, Dr. Joseph-Ignace Guillotin proposed a law requiring a machine to carry out executions. The guillotine, with its weighted blade that severed a victim's neck in one cut, was thought to be more humane and democratic than previous methods.

Enlightenment and Revolution The Enlightenment thinker John Locke argued that people had the rights to life, liberty, and property. The government's job was to protect these rights. When it failed to do so, people had the right to rebel. In 1789, Enlightenment ideas inspired French citizens to challenge the monarchy and the privileges of the wealthiest classes. Their protests led to the **French Revolution**. Radical revolutionary leaders took control of the government. They beheaded the king and abolished the monarchy.

Napoleon Seizes Power During the French Revolution, Napoleon Bonaparte distinguished himself as a brilliant leader of the French army. In 1799, Napoleon seized control of France. His goal was to create and rule a great empire. His army rapidly conquered most of Europe.

However, his hopes of a long-lasting empire ended after a poorly planned attack on Russia killed many of his soldiers. In 1815, Napoleon faced his final defeat against allied European troops at the Battle of Waterloo.

Nationalism Sweeps Europe

The French Revolution helped spread **nationalism**, pride and loyalty to one's nation. Many Europeans began to see themselves as citizens of a nation, not subjects of a king. Alarmed by the French Revolution, Europe's leaders sought to stop the spread of democracy. They put kings back on their thrones, but ideas of democracy and nationalism were too powerful to fade quickly. Many European countries revolted against their rulers. By the 1870s, the smaller states that made up Italy and Germany had become unified nations. Much of western Europe had achieved self-government, inspired by the spirit of nationalism.

🔺 **SUMMARIZE** Explain how Enlightenment ideals contributed to European revolutions.

Napoleon's Coronation Napoleon crowned himself emperor of France in an elaborate ceremony at Paris's Notre Dame Cathedral in 1804. **Why do you think Napoleon staged such an elaborate ceremony?**

Europe's Expanding Power

▼ **KEY QUESTION** How did the Industrial Revolution change Europe?

In the 1700s, new methods of making goods started a peaceful revolution. Industrialization led European nations to build empires.

Industrial Revolution Many of the inventions of the Scientific Revolution changed the way Europeans worked. New machines produced goods more quickly with fewer workers. The change became known as the **Industrial Revolution**. Factories were built near rivers, so that they could be powered by water. By the 1760s, steam powered the machines, and factories appeared in cities. People moved to cities from the countryside, in search of work. The Industrial Revolution began in Great Britain and spread to other European countries.

Imperialism The newly industrial nations of Europe needed raw materials and new markets for their products. Major European nations looked to Asia and Africa for valuable natural resources. Many nations made **imperialism** their foreign policy, seeking to control smaller, weaker countries politically and economically. European nations claimed overseas colonies without considering how their policies might affect the lives of the people living in these places.

▲ **UNDERSTAND EFFECTS** Explain how the Industrial Revolution changed Europe.

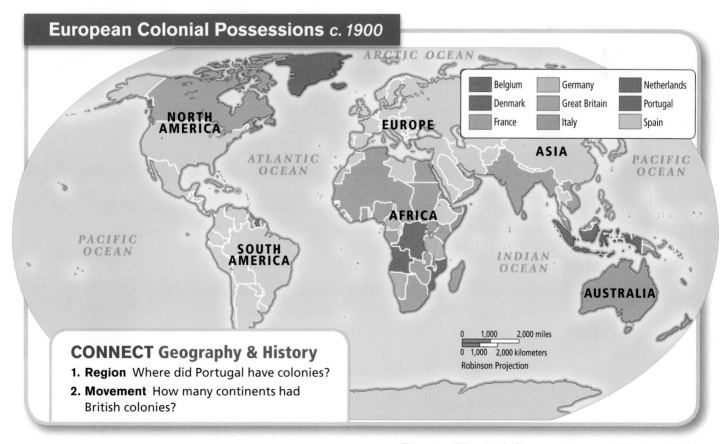

European Colonial Possessions c. 1900

Legend: Belgium, Denmark, France, Germany, Great Britain, Italy, Netherlands, Portugal, Spain

Robinson Projection

CONNECT Geography & History

1. **Region** Where did Portugal have colonies?
2. **Movement** How many continents had British colonies?

Europe: Physical Geography and History **273**

Europe in Conflict During the 20th century, tensions between European nations led to two devastating wars, World War I (1914–1918) and World War II (1939–1945). These wars left much of Europe in ruins.

WORLD WAR I		WORLD WAR II
1914–1918	Why	**1939–1945**

Why

WORLD WAR I (1914–1918)
- A rise in nationalism, imperialism, and military buildup increases tensions.
- European nations form mutual protection alliances.
- The assassination of Archduke Franz Ferdinand, shown at left, forces allied nations into war.

WORLD WAR II (1939–1945)
- A global economic depression worsens conditions in Europe.
- Adolf Hitler, leader of the Nazi Party, at right, gains control of Germany in 1933 and promises to expand German territory.
- Under Hitler's leadership, Germany invades Poland in 1939.

Who

Central Powers vs. Allies
- Central Powers: Germany, Austria-Hungary, and Turkey
- Allies: Russia, France, the United Kingdom, and the United States (in 1917)

Axis Powers vs. Allies
- Axis Powers: Germany, Italy, and Japan
- Allies: The United Kingdom, France, the Soviet Union, and the United States (in 1941)

THE UNITED NATIONS FIGHT FOR FREEDOM

How

World War I
- Machine guns make it difficult for forces to advance.
- Soldiers on both sides fight from defensive trenches.
- Trench warfare leads to development of new weapons, including poison gas and tanks, shown at left.

World War II
- The German strategy of *blitzkrieg* uses fast-moving tanks and airplanes followed by ground troops to overwhelm enemies.
- Airplanes like this one allow the war to be fought over great distances.
- Nazi labor and death camps carry out the **Holocaust**, the mass murder of Jews and others.

Outcomes

World War I
- About 8.5 million soldiers and 13 million civilians die.
- Fighting the war costs Europe over $330 billion and causes mass physical destruction, as seen in France at left.
- The peace treaty blames and punishes Germany for the war, causing German resentment.

World War II
- Historians estimate total deaths between 35 and 60 million. The Holocaust claims the lives of 6 million Jews. (right: concentration camp survivors)
- The war costs over $1 trillion.
- Two superpowers emerge after the war, the United States and the Soviet Union, leading to the Cold War.

CRITICAL THINKING

Sequence Events What led to the start of Europe's two world wars?

Uniting After War

▼ **KEY QUESTION** How did the two world wars encourage European nations to work together?

After World War II, Europe was devastated. European nations had been at war with each other for several years. Two goals emerged in the war's aftermath: to rebuild Europe's shattered nations and their economies and to work together to prevent future wars.

Creating a European Union In 1952, Belgium, France, Italy, Luxembourg, the Netherlands, and West Germany formed the European Coal and Steel Community (ECSC). Its six members agreed to combine their iron, steel, and coal industries. Their success with these commodities led them to drop trade barriers on others.

In 1967, they created the European Community (EC). Members worked to find ways to move goods, workers, and money more easily across their borders. Trade increased, and more countries wanted to join. In 1973, the EC began to admit other nations, paving the way for the European Union.

By 1992, 12 Western European nations belonged to the EC. That year, all of them signed the Maastricht (MAH-strikt) Treaty. The treaty formed the **European Union (EU)**, an organization of European nations whose members cooperate on economic, social, and political issues. By 2004, the EU had expanded to include Eastern European nations, bringing the total number of members to 25 countries. Candidate nations continue to apply.

How Does the EU Work? The goal of the European Union is to bring the people and countries of Europe closer together. Citizens of EU nations have European citizenship. They can travel freely throughout the EU. They can live and work anywhere in the union. They can vote in elections in the country they live in, even if they are citizens elsewhere.

The European Union member nations also work together on political and social matters such as immigration, law enforcement, and the environment. For instance, the EU sponsors many of Europe's efforts toward finding cleaner, sustainable sources of energy, which you read about earlier in the chapter. The EU also tries to protect the diverse cultures and traditions of its member nations. It funds cultural programs, including education in the languages of other EU nations.

Members of the European Union	
Date	**Country**
By 1952 (ECSC)	Belgium
	France
	Italy
	Luxembourg
	Netherlands
	West Germany
By 1973 (EC)	Denmark
	Ireland
	United Kingdom
By 1995	Greece
	Portugal
	Spain
	East Germany*
	Austria
	Finland
	Sweden
By 2004	Cyprus
	Czech Republic
	Estonia
	Hungary
	Latvia
	Lithuania
	Malta
	Poland
	Slovakia
	Slovenia
By 2007 or 2008	Bulgaria
	Romania

*East Germany joined through German reunification and not as a separate state.

Economic Unity One major area of EU cooperation is its economic policy. The EU is a single market, which means that its members can trade goods freely, without paying taxes on those goods. Many EU members also use the same currency, called the euro. In 1999, 11 EU nations adopted the euro. This decision made it easier for members to trade with each other.

As a single economic unit, the EU is powerful, more than any member nation on its own. However, the EU is weak in other ways. The countries that belong to the union remain independent. The EU does not yet have a constitution. Its leaders make decisions but have little authority to enforce them. So far, the member nations have cooperated on most issues, and the EU has been successful. However, keeping such a large organization unified could be challenging, especially as new countries join.

 SUMMARIZE Explain how two wars encouraged European nations to work together.

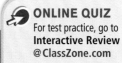 **ONLINE QUIZ** For test practice, go to **Interactive Review** @ ClassZone.com

Section 4 Assessment

TERMS & NAMES

1. Explain the importance of
- Enlightenment
- nationalism
- imperialism
- European Union

USE YOUR READING NOTES

2. Sequence Events Use your completed time line to answer the following question:

Which event occurred between the Scientific Revolution and the French Revolution?

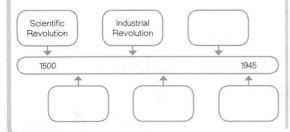

KEY IDEAS

3. How did Enlightenment ideas influence the French Revolution?

4. How did the Industrial Revolution affect imperialism?

5. What steps did the EU and its predecessors take to bring the nations of Europe closer together?

CRITICAL THINKING

6. Analyze Cause and Effect How did the Industrial Revolution change where people lived?

7. Compare and Contrast In what ways were World War I and World War II similar?

8. CONNECT to Today Why might Eastern European nations want to join the European Union?

9. WRITING Write a Speech Imagine that you have been asked to speak to EU members about why you think the nations of Europe should or should not form a "United States of Europe." Write a brief speech expressing your opinion.

Interactive ◀ Review

Click here to complete these and other activities online @ ClassZone.com

CHAPTER SUMMARY

Key Idea 1
Europe has diverse landforms ranging from mountains to plains. Its climate is influenced by its nearness to the ocean.

Key Idea 2
The achievements of the ancient Greeks and Romans continue to influence our modern world.

Key Idea 3
Feudalism provided stability after the fall of the Roman Empire. The Renaissance marked a rebirth of creativity.

Key Idea 4
Revolutions in science, politics, and industry transformed Europe. After two world wars, European nations found new ways to cooperate.

For **Review and Study Notes**, go to **Interactive Review @ ClassZone.com**

NAME GAME

Use the Terms & Names list to complete each sentence on paper or online.

1. I am Europe's tallest mountain range. ___Alps___
2. I am the vast area of flat or gently rolling land from France to Russia. _____
3. I make the climate in much of Europe warmer than it would be otherwise. _____
4. I am the form of government that originated in the Greek city-state of Athens. _____
5. I am the form of government that Rome had before it became an empire. _____
6. I am the medieval political system that gave nobles, peasants, and serfs protection in exchange for service. _____
7. I am a time of rebirth in creativity and the arts in Europe. _____
8. I am the religious protest and reform movement that split the Church in the 1500s. _____
9. I am a time of great interest in using reason to understand and improve society. _____
10. I am an organization made up of European nations that works together to solve common problems. _____

Alps
city-state
democracy
Enlightenment
European Union
feudalism
French Revolution
imperialism
Industrial Revolution
North Atlantic Drift
Northern European Plain
Peloponnesus
Reformation
Renaissance
republic

Activities

GeoGame

Use this online map to reinforce your understanding of Europe's physical geography. Drag and drop each place name in the list to its location on the map.

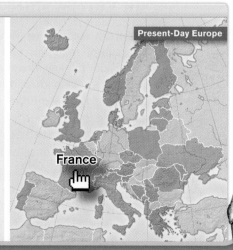

The Pyrenees
Danube River
Greece
Iberian Peninsula
France

To play the complete game, go to **Interactive Review @ ClassZone.com**

Crossword Puzzle

Complete an online crossword puzzle to test your knowledge of Europe's geography and history.

ACROSS
1. vassal trained in combat who fought on behalf of lords

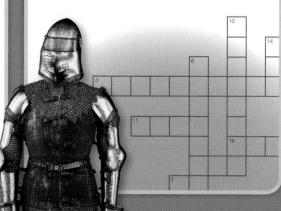

277

VOCABULARY

Explain the significance of each of the following.

1. fossil fuels
2. republic
3. manor
4. Renaissance
5. Holocaust
6. European Union

Choose the best answer from each pair.

7. This influences Europe's mild climate. (Northern European Plain/North Atlantic Drift)
8. This group of people could hold government office in ancient Rome. (patrician/plebeian)
9. This group of people pledged service to wealthy landowners in exchange for land under the feudal structure. (lords/vassals)
10. This is a feeling of pride for and loyalty to one's nation. (nationalism/imperialism)

KEY IDEAS

1 Europe's Dramatic Landscape

11. How does the North Atlantic Drift affect the climate of Europe?
12. How do Europe's waterways affect its economy?
13. Why is the Northern European Plain a valuable resource?

2 Classical Greece and Rome

14. Why is Athens considered the birthplace of modern democracy?
15. What did the Romans give conquered peoples?

3 The Middle Ages and Renaissance

16. How did feudalism benefit lords?
17. What contributed to the growth of towns before the Renaissance?
18. Why did the Renaissance begin in Italy?

4 Modern European History

19. How did the Industrial Revolution change the way goods were made?
20. Why were many European leaders upset by the French Revolution?

CRITICAL THINKING

21. **Form and Support Opinions** Create a graphic organizer like the one below. Include three factors that influence the mild climate of Europe.

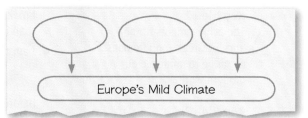

Europe's Mild Climate

22. **Connect Geography & History** What effect have Europe's peninsulas had on its development?
23. **Five Themes: Place** How did Athens and Sparta differ in their views of citizens?
24. **Connect Geography & Culture** How did feudalism affect trade and daily life in medieval Europe?
25. **Analyze Causes and Effects** How are the Renaissance and the Reformation related to each other?
26. **Make Inferences** How did the World War I peace agreement contribute to the start of World War II?

Answer the
ESSENTIAL QUESTION

What changes have taken place in Europe since ancient times?

Written Response Write a two- or three-paragraph response to the Essential Question. Consider the key ideas of each section as well as specific ideas about how Europe has changed. Use the rubric below to guide you.

Response Rubric

A strong response will:
- identify elements of ancient society and politics
- discuss three major historical events that occurred after the fall of the Roman Empire
- explain how each of those events changed European society and politics

STANDARDS-BASED ASSESSMENT

PHYSICAL MAP

Use the map to provide short answers to questions 1 and 2 on your paper.

European Peninsulas

1. **Which of the peninsulas is located farthest north?**

2. **Which of the peninsulas has a coastline on the Black Sea?**

PRIMARY SOURCE

The following excerpt is from Pericles's "Funeral Oration." Use context clues within the quotation to answer questions 3 and 4 on your paper.

> Our constitution is named a democracy, because it is in the hands not of the few but of the many. But our laws secure equal justice for all in their private disputes, and our public opinion welcomes and honors talent in every branch of achievement, not as a matter of privilege but on grounds of excellence alone.
>
> Source: Thucydides, from *The Peloponnesian War*

3. **According to Pericles, what made Athens a democracy?**

   A. It had laws that protect only the elite.
   B. It granted privileges to the rich.
   C. It was governed by a small group of leaders.
   D. It was governed by the many.

4. **Whom did the laws of Athens protect?**

   A. everyone
   B. government officials
   C. privileged citizens
   D. peasants

GeoActivity

1. INTERDISCIPLINARY ACTIVITY–HISTORY

With a small group, learn more about the events of the French Revolution. Create a political cartoon about one of these events such as the rioting by the poor, or Napoleon's takeover of government. Your cartoon should show a clear point of view.

2. WRITING FOR SOCIAL STUDIES

Reread the part of Section 4 on the growth of nationalism in Western Europe. Imagine that you live in a European monarchy in the mid-1800s. Write a letter to a friend telling why you believe in independence for your country.

3. MENTAL MAPPING

Create an outline map of France and label the following:

• Rhone River
• Pyrenees
• Massif Central
• Seine River
• English Channel
• Atlantic Ocean

CHAPTER 10

Western Europe

ESSENTIAL QUESTION

What geographic and cultural characteristics define the subregions of Western Europe?

CONNECT Geography & History

Use the map and the time line to answer the following questions.

1. How many Western European nations have territory that extends east of 20° E longitude?
2. What country is Berlin the capital of, and when did the city reunite?

476

History

▲ **476** Beginning of the Byzantine Empire (Empress Theodora)

Geography

1418 Prince Henry of Portugal begins sponsoring expeditions of exploration.

Culture

1880 Bastille Day is set aside as a French national holiday. ▶

Present-Day Western Europe

Click here to explore Western Europe @ ClassZone.com

National capital

ICELAND
Reykjavík

Arctic Circle

Norwegian Sea

Faroe Islands (Den.)

Shetland Islands (U.K.)

ATLANTIC OCEAN

North Sea

SCOTLAND

NOTHERN IRELAND

Dublin

IRELAND

UNITED KINGDOM

WALES   ENGLAND

British Isles

London

English Channel

Channel Islands (U.K.)

Bay of Biscay

PORTUGAL

Madrid

Lisbon   Tagus River

SPAIN

Strait of Gibraltar

GIBRALTAR (U.K.)

MOROCCO

Ebro River

Balearic Islands (Sp.)

ANDORRA

Corsica (Fr.)

Sardinia (It.)

SWEDEN

NORWAY

Oslo

Stockholm

Baltic Sea

Gulf of Bothnia

FINLAND

Helsinki

Gulf of Finland

ESTONIA

LATVIA

LITHUANIA

RUSSIA

BELARUS

RUSSIA

DENMARK

Copenhagen

NETHERLANDS

Amsterdam

Berlin

Brussels

BELGIUM

LUXEMBOURG

Elbe R.

Rhine

GERMANY

POLAND

CZECH REPUBLIC

SLOVAKIA

UKRAINE

MOLDOVA

Paris

Seine R.

Loire R.

FRANCE

Bern

SWITZERLAND

LIECHTENSTEIN

Danube R.

Vienna

AUSTRIA

HUNGARY

ROMANIA

Black Sea

Rhône R.

Po R.

SLOV.

CROATIA

BOSNIA & HERZ.

SERBIA

BULGARIA

SAN MARINO

MONACO

ITALY

Rome

VATICAN CITY

Adriatic Sea

MONT.

MAC.

ALB.

Tyrrhenian Sea

Ionian Sea

GREECE

Aegean Sea

Athens

Crete (Gr.)

TURKEY

Sicily (It.)

Mediterranean Sea

ALGERIA

TUNISIA

MALTA

0   200   400 miles
0   200   400 kilometers

Geography

1989 Berlin reunites after the opening of the Berlin Wall. ▶

Today

Government

1920 The Nazi Party forms in Germany.

Government

2006 Finland's first female president, Tarja Halonen, is elected to a second term. ▶

281

Reading for Understanding

▶ Key Ideas

BEFORE, YOU LEARNED

Ancient Greece began as many independent city-states with different ways of life. Ancient Rome began as a republic and expanded into a vast empire.

NOW YOU WILL LEARN

For many centuries, Greece and Italy were collections of small states. Fueled by nationalism, each struggled to gain independence and unite as a nation.

▶ Vocabulary

TERMS & NAMES

Byzantine Empire the eastern half of the Roman Empire that survived for a thousand years after the fall of Rome

fascism (FASH•IHZ•uhm) a political philosophy that promotes blind loyalty to the state and a strong central government controlled by a powerful dictator

Romance language any of the languages that developed from the Roman language, Latin, such as Spanish, Portuguese, French, Italian, and Romanian

Vatican the official residence of the pope in Vatican City, and the political and religious center of the Roman Catholic Church

coalition an alliance or partnership, often a temporary one

BACKGROUND VOCABULARY

compulsory required

REVIEW

nationalism pride in and loyalty to one's nation

European Union (EU) an organization of European nations whose members cooperate on economic, social, and political issues

▶ Reading Strategy

Re-create the chart shown at right. As you read and respond to the **KEY QUESTIONS**, use the chart to help you summarize what you learn about Greece and Italy.

 Skillbuilder Handbook, page R5

SUMMARIZE

	GREECE	ITALY
History		
Language		
Government		
Economy		

 GRAPHIC ORGANIZERS
Go to **Interactive Review** @ClassZone.com

Greece and Italy

1.02 Generate, interpret, and manipulate information from tools such as maps, globes, charts, graphs, databases, and models to pose and answer questions about space and place, environment and society, and spatial dynamics and connections.

11.01 Identify the concepts associated with culture such as language, religion, family, and ethnic identity, and analyze how they both link and separate societies.

Connecting to Your World

It's not surprising that Greece and Italy are popular tourist destinations. Stretching across southern peninsulas in the Mediterranean Sea, both countries have mild climates and warm, sunny weather much of the year. In both places, visitors can see the magnificent treasures of the distant past. While both countries were once part of the Roman Empire, after it divided, these nations developed different cultures. In the 1800s, both Greece and Italy fought for independence and tried to preserve their ancient heritage as they became modern nations.

Greece

▼ **KEY QUESTION** How has Greece's government changed since the Byzantine Empire?

As you learned in Chapter 11, ancient Greece began as a series of independent city-states. Eventually, it became part of the Roman Empire. When the Roman Empire divided, Greece was in the eastern half, called the **Byzantine Empire**. Most of the Byzantine Empire's inhabitants spoke Greek, not Latin, and followed the eastern traditions of Christianity. By 1453, the Byzantines had been conquered by the Islamic Ottoman Turks. Before declaring their independence in 1829, Greeks had lived under foreign rule for over 2,000 years.

Greek Pottery
Tourists come to Greece to see artifacts like this fifth century B.C. pot.

Byzantine Ruins in Greece

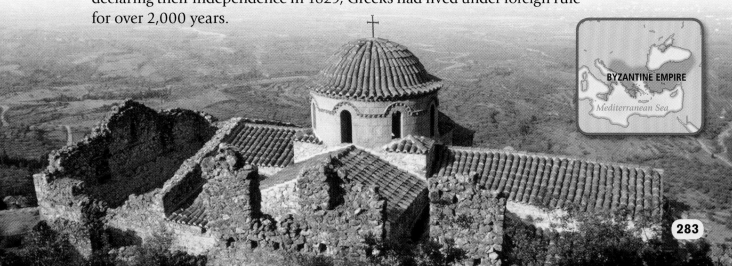

BYZANTINE EMPIRE

Mediterranean Sea

History When the Byzantine Empire fell, Greece became part of the Ottoman Empire for approximately 400 years. By the late 1700s, desire for independence was growing. **Nationalism** increased as more Greeks learned about their past. Interest and pride in Greece's history as a center of culture and democracy grew.

In 1829, after a long struggle, Greece broke free from Ottoman rule. Its leaders made the nation a monarchy. Then, in 1967, Greek military officers seized control of the government. When the military government collapsed, voters decided not to return to a monarchy. Since 1975, Greece has been a parliamentary democracy.

Culture Most Greeks share the same ethnic background, language, and religion. They speak Greek and belong to the Greek Orthodox Church, a form of Christianity. Every major town has a patron saint, and townspeople celebrate their saint with an annual festival. Easter is also an important religious holiday in Greece.

About two-thirds of Greeks live in cities. Many live in Athens, Greece's capital. Cities have both older sections with narrow streets and newer areas with high-rise apartments and shopping centers. Many cities have a coffee house, or *kafeneio*, where friends meet.

Government and Economics Greece is a parliamentary democracy. The president's job is mostly ceremonial. The country is governed by the prime minister, the cabinet, and the parliament. Voting in Greece is **compulsory**, or required. Failing to vote is against the law.

Greece has fewer high-tech industries and service jobs than many countries in Western Europe. Although it is a member of the **European Union (EU)**, its economy lags behind other nations. Agriculture makes up a greater percentage of its economy than wealthier nations. Because of Greece's position on the Mediterranean Sea, tourism, shipping, and fishing remain important.

🔺 **SEQUENCE EVENTS** Explain the changes to Greece's government since the Byzantine Empire.

Greek Orthodox Church This church, with its typical whitewashed walls and blue domes, is located in Oia on the island of Santorini.

The percentage of a nation's labor force employed in agriculture is a good indication of that country's economic development. Take a look at how Greece compares to these other Western European countries.

	GDP (Per Capita*)	Agriculture	Industry	Services
		(Percentage Employed in Selected Sectors)		
Denmark	$34,600	3	21	76
France	$29,900	4	24	72
Spain	$25,500	5	30	65
Greece	$22,200	12	20	68
Portugal	$19,300	10	30	60

*GDP: Gross Domestic Product
Source: *CIA World Factbook, 2006*

CRITICAL THINKING

Compare and Contrast How do Greece's GDP per capita and agricultural employment compare to the other countries listed in the chart?

ITALY

Italy

▼ **KEY QUESTION** What changes has Italian society experienced in recent years?

After the Western Roman Empire fell in the late 400s, the Italian peninsula split into many small kingdoms and city-states. Sometimes they were independent. At other times, France, Austria, and Spain ruled over them.

Benito Mussolini
Fascist dictator Mussolini took control of Italy in the early 1920s.

History In 1796, France conquered much of the Italian Peninsula. French rule led to new laws, better roads, and a common currency. Italians saw the benefits of unity and began to work toward independence. In 1861, Italian patriots such as Giuseppe Garibaldi and Camillo Cavour succeeded in unifying Italy.

In the early 1920s, Benito Mussolini took control of the Italian government. He promoted **fascism** (FASH•IHZ•uhm), a political system based on fierce nationalism and a strong central government led by a dictator. Mussolini gained support by promising a return to a powerful Roman Empire. During World War II, Italy fought with Germany against the Allies. After Italian forces suffered major defeats, Mussolini was forced out and killed as he tried to escape Italy. In 1946, Italians replaced the monarchy with democracy.

Culture Like Greece, modern Italy has been influenced by traditions. The official language is Italian, a Romance language. **Romance languages** come from Latin and are spoken in places that used to be part of the Roman Empire. Take a look at the map below to see where other Romance languages are spoken.

Most Italians are Roman Catholics. For many centuries, Catholic Church leaders and the Italian government were closely allied. The political and religious center of the Church, the **Vatican**, is located in Italy. Although it lies within the city of Rome, it is an independent country, the smallest such country in the world.

In recent years, Italy has become more diverse as immigrants have come from nearby Morocco and Tunisia in North Africa and Albania on the Balkan Peninsula. Much of Italy has changed from a rural, agricultural nation to a modern, urban society. However, life differs between northern and southern Italy. Northern Italy is richer, with more people employed in manufacturing than in the south, where more people work in agriculture.

Italian food changes depending on the region of the country, from pasta with tomato sauce in the south to a dish made of rice called *risotto* in the north. Sports are also important to Italian culture. Many Italians enjoy watching race car driving, cycling, and soccer.

Languages of Western Europe

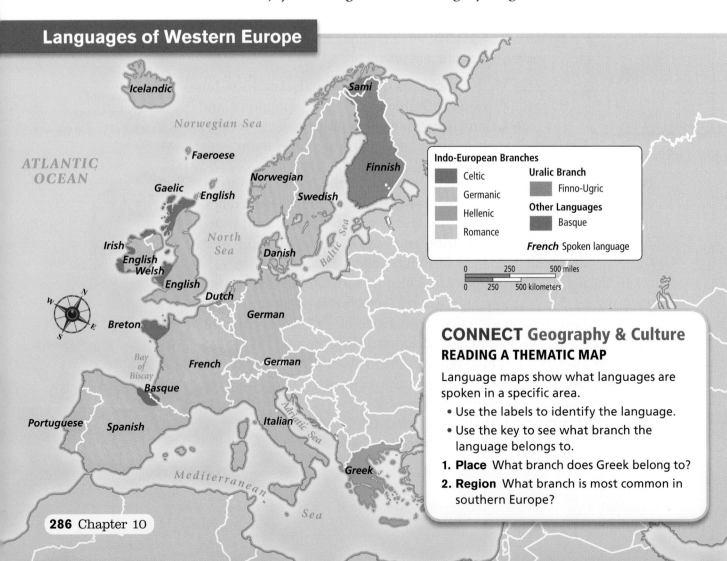

Indo-European Branches
- Celtic
- Germanic
- Hellenic
- Romance

Uralic Branch
- Finno-Ugric

Other Languages
- Basque

French Spoken language

0   250   500 miles
0   250   500 kilometers

CONNECT Geography & Culture
READING A THEMATIC MAP

Language maps show what languages are spoken in a specific area.

- Use the labels to identify the language.
- Use the key to see what branch the language belongs to.

1. **Place** What branch does Greek belong to?
2. **Region** What branch is most common in southern Europe?

Government and Economics Italy is a parliamentary democracy. Voters elect three-fourths of parliament members. The rest are assigned by a complex system designed to make sure each of Italy's many political parties is represented in the government. A prime minister heads the government. Usually this leader comes from the party that wins the most votes in the election. Because Italy has so many parties, leaders often have to form coalition governments. A **coalition** is an alliance or partnership, which is often temporary. Members of several parties agree to work together. If parties withdraw from a coalition, leaders have to form a new one. As a result, Italy has had many changes in government.

Once a mainly agricultural country, Italy is now a prosperous industrial nation. Only five percent of the population has a farm-related job. European Union membership has helped Italy grow, opening new markets for its products, which include fashionable clothing, shoes, and cars. Milan, in northern Italy, is world-famous for its fashion shows. However, economic growth for the country has been uneven. The north has many of Italy's factories, while the south remains largely farmland. Italy continues to look for ways to bring greater prosperity to the southern region.

Runway Model
A model walks the runway at a Milan fashion show.

 SUMMARIZE Describe the changes that Italian society has experienced in recent years.

ONLINE QUIZ
For test practice, go to
Interactive Review
@ ClassZone.com

Section ① Assessment

TERMS & NAMES

1. Explain the importance of
- Byzantine Empire
- fascism
- Vatican
- coalition

USE YOUR READING NOTES

2. Summarize Use your completed chart to answer the following question:

How is Greece's economy different from Italy's economy?

	GREECE	ITALY
History		
Language		
Government		
Economy		

KEY IDEAS

3. In what ways did Greek culture develop differently from Italian culture after the division of the Roman Empire?

4. Why are so many Italians members of the Catholic Church?

5. How has Italy's economy changed over time?

CRITICAL THINKING

6. Analyze Cause and Effect How did the Byzantine Empire influence Greek culture?

7. Make Inferences What are the disadvantages for Italy of having had so many coalition governments?

8. CONNECT to Today Why would it be an advantage for Italy to make sure that southern Italy is as prosperous as northern Italy?

9. MATH Create a Bar Graph Look at the chart on Western European economies in this section. Create a bar graph showing the percentage of workers employed in agriculture in each country.

Italy can be roughly divided into three regions: northern, central, and southern. While northern and southern Italy share aspects of Italian culture, they are also different.

Northern Italy

The craggy Alps of northern Italy are dotted with villages, such as St. Magdalena, shown below. Tourists often come to hike or ski in the mountains. The northern region is also highly industrialized, however, with major metropolitan areas such as Milan and Turin. Many of Italy's cities with populations of 100,000 or greater are in the north.

Recreation

Like these hikers, many people enjoy the rugged trails winding through the Italian Alps.

Work

Northern Italy has more factories than farms defining the region's major cities. Workers at this factory in Bologna manufacture Ducati motorcycles.

Southern Italy

Southern Italy also has mountains, but it benefits more from the coastline along the Mediterranean and Adriatic seas than does northern Italy. Many of the tourists visiting southern Italy come to relax on sandy beaches in towns such as Minori, shown below.

The south is also much less industrialized than the north. Southern Italy has fewer big cities and more people are employed in agriculture, such as growing and harvesting grapes and olives.

Recreation
Sunbathers lounge on the beach in Sorrento, enjoying its warm Mediterranean climate.

Work
These men are gathering olives to make olive oil in an orchard in Bisceglie. It is located in the southern region of Puglia, where the arid climate is particularly suited to growing olives.

CRITICAL THINKING

1. **Compare and Contrast** What geographic features are characteristic of each region?

2. **Make Inferences** Which region do you think is wealthier and why?

Reading for Understanding

▶ Key Ideas

BEFORE, YOU LEARNED

After the division and fall of the Roman Empire, Greece and Italy developed into different nations.

NOW YOU WILL LEARN

Like Greece and Italy, Spain and Portugal were ruled by foreigners. After gaining independence, both developed overseas empires to fuel their economies.

▶ Vocabulary

TERMS & NAMES

Moors the group of Muslims from North Africa who conquered Spain in the eighth century

Reconquista the successful effort by the Spanish to drive the Moors out of Spain

Christopher Columbus Italian navigator and explorer who sailed for Spain and explored the Caribbean and the coast of Central and South America

Basque (bask) an ethnic group living in the western Pyrenees and along the Bay of Biscay in Spain and France; also the name of their language

BACKGROUND VOCABULARY

separatist a person who wants a region to break away from the nation it is a part of

Visual Vocabulary Christopher Columbus reaches the New World.

▶ Reading Strategy

Re-create the Venn diagram shown at right. As you read and respond to the **KEY QUESTIONS**, use the diagram to help you compare and contrast Spain and Portugal.

 Skillbuilder Handbook, page R9

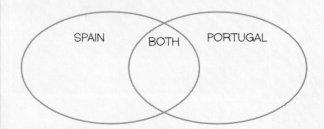

COMPARE AND CONTRAST

SPAIN   BOTH   PORTUGAL

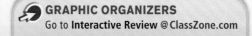

GRAPHIC ORGANIZERS
Go to **Interactive Review** @ ClassZone.com

Spain and Portugal

8.01 Describe the role of key historical figures and evaluate their impact on past and present societies in South America and Europe.
8.02 Describe the role of key groups and evaluate their impact on historical and contemporary societies of South America and Europe.

Connecting to Your World

Without ever visiting Spain, most Americans know more about Spanish culture than they think. For over 300 years, Spain had an empire in what is today Mexico and the southwestern United States. In places where Spain once ruled, the impact of Spanish culture is easy to see. Many southwestern cities have Spanish names and buildings influenced by Spanish architecture. Throughout the United States, many people speak Spanish and eat Spanish food. Spanish culture itself was the product of influences from many other cultures.

Spanish Food
Spanish food—including small appetizers called *tapas*, such as this squid dish—has become popular in the United States.

Spain

▼ **KEY QUESTION** What regional differences affect Spain's culture?

For centuries, Spain was part of the Roman Empire. When the empire fell, a Germanic tribe conquered the peninsula and established a Christian kingdom. It lasted until the early A.D. 700s, when the **Moors**, Muslim peoples from North Africa, took control of southern Spain. Spain's Moorish rulers brought a more advanced culture to medieval Europe. Muslim scholars made new discoveries in medicine, mathematics, and other fields. They remained there for almost eight centuries, when groups of Christians still living in northern Spain succeeded in driving them out of the region.

The Alhambra
Located in Granada, Spain, the Alhambra was a Moorish palace and fortress.

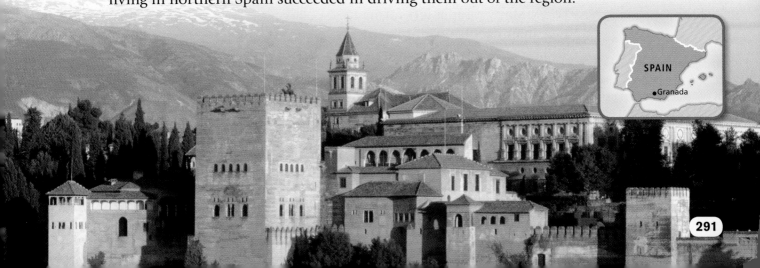

SPAIN
•Granada

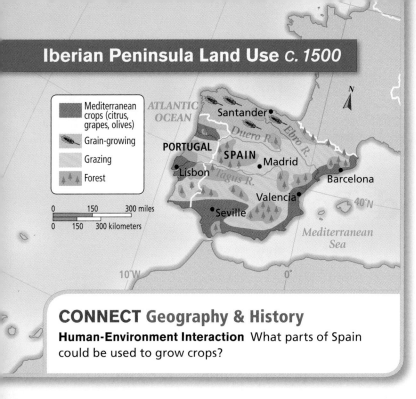

Iberian Peninsula Land Use c. 1500

Mediterranean crops (citrus, grapes, olives)

Grain-growing

Grazing

Forest

0   150   300 miles
0   150   300 kilometers

ATLANTIC OCEAN

Santander

Duero R.

Ebro R.

PORTUGAL   SPAIN

Madrid

Lisbon   Tagus R.

Barcelona

Valencia

Seville

Mediterranean Sea

N

40°N

10°W   0°

CONNECT Geography & History

Human-Environment Interaction What parts of Spain could be used to grow crops?

History In the 1000s, Christians in northern Spain began the **Reconquista**, the effort to drive the Moors out of Spain. It lasted until the 1400s, when King Ferdinand and Queen Isabella conquered the last Muslim kingdom. Once unified under its Catholic monarchs, Spain began to look beyond its territory, which was poor in resources and farmland. Spain turned to the sea, and sponsored **Christopher Columbus's** first voyage to the Americas in 1492. By the 1500s, Spain's conquests in the Americas had made it rich. Its colonies provided Spain with resources it lacked. For a time, Spain was the world's greatest power. By the 1800s, Spain's power had faded, and its colonies declared independence.

Spain remained neutral during World War I. In the 1930s, the Spanish fought a civil war over whether the country should be a monarchy or a republic. During the struggle, Francisco Franco of Spain's fascist party won control of the government. He ruled as a dictator for almost 40 years.

Culture The Spanish share many cultural traits. Until a few decades ago, however, most people identified more with the region they lived in than the country. Spain has many regional languages, such as Catalan and Valencian, which emphasize cultural differences. The Roman Catholic Church was the biggest common tie. Almost all Spaniards are Catholic.

In the 1950s and 1960s, Spain's economy developed quickly and changed the way many people lived. Many people left farms to take manufacturing jobs in cities. Today, most of Spain's people live in cities or towns. Their homes are apartments rather than houses. Even in rural areas, better farming methods and labor-saving machinery have made life easier.

Flamenco Flamenco, a traditional Spanish dance, consists of men and women in elaborate costumes performing intricate steps and gestures. **How do dances like the flamenco preserve Spanish culture?**

The Running of the Bulls Every July, tourists come to Pamplona in northern Spain for the Fiesta de San Fermín. The main attraction is the daily stampede of a half-dozen bulls through the city's narrow streets to the bullfighting ring. Runners sprint ahead, trying to avoid getting slashed by sharp horns. According to legend, the run may have started in the 1200s as a way to move the bulls through town to be sold at market.

CRITICAL THINKING

Make Inferences Why might some people object to the Running of the Bulls?

While the shift to an urban society threatened some Spanish traditions, many Spaniards still enjoy taking part in the old customs. *Paella* (pah•AY•yah), a flavorful dish of seafood, meat, and vegetables mixed with yellow rice, remains a popular choice. Spaniards like soccer, but bullfighting remains Spain's most famous traditional sport. Audiences also enjoy watching Spanish dances, such as the flamenco.

Government and Economics After Franco's death in 1975, Spain became a parliamentary monarchy. This change allowed the people to have a voice in their government. King Juan Carlos I has ruled the country alongside elected officials since the monarchy was formed.

Today, Spain's leaders face demands by some in the **Basque** (bask) ethnic group to create a separate Basque nation. The Basque people live in the Pyrenees Mountains. They have lived in Spain longer than any other group and have kept a distinct language and customs. Some Basque **separatist** groups have tried violence to further their cause.

For centuries, Spain's economy depended heavily on fishing and farming. It lagged behind most of Western Europe in industrial growth. After World War II, Spain's economy grew more rapidly. Factories began turning out cars and steel, and tourism increased. In the 1980s, Spain joined the EU. Membership boosted the economy by promoting trade and by making financial aid from the EU available.

▲ **EVALUATE** Explain some of the regional differences that exist within Spanish culture.

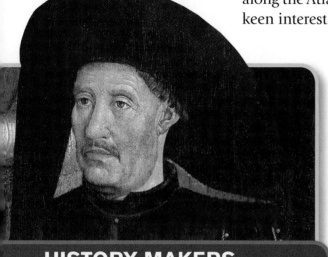
PORTUGAL
SPAIN

Portugal

▼ **KEY QUESTION** How did Portugal's location contribute to its role as a leader in the Age of Exploration?

Portugal shares the Iberian Peninsula with Spain, but occupies a much smaller area. It is located on Europe's western coastline along the Atlantic Ocean. Despite its small size, its location and keen interest in exploration helped it build an empire.

History For many centuries, the region that is now Portugal was, like Spain, under Muslim rule. In 1143, Portugal became an independent kingdom. Because of its coastal location, the Portuguese became skilled sailors, navigators, and shipbuilders. In the 1400s and 1500s, Portugal played a key role in Europe's Age of Exploration. Prince Henry of Portugal sponsored many expeditions. Portuguese explorers helped their country build an empire.

For a time, overseas colonies brought prosperity. Portugal profited from the spice trade with Asia and the gold, diamonds, and other resources taken from its African and South American colonies. By the 1800s, however, Portugal had lost its position as a world power to larger European nations. In 1822, Brazil, Portugal's richest colony, declared independence.

In 1908, revolutionaries overthrew Portugal's king and made the country a republic, but political unrest continued. In 1926, military leaders seized control. Dictators ruled until 1976, when Portugal became a parliamentary democracy in a peaceful revolution.

Culture The official language of Portugal is Portuguese. Like Spanish, Portuguese is a Romance language. Most Portuguese are Roman Catholics. Especially in rural areas, Catholic priests play a key role in political and social life. Traditional Catholic celebrations are important. Unlike much of Western Europe, Portugal today is still a largely rural country with many small farming and fishing villages. Just under half of its citizens live in rural areas. Although Portugal remains a rural country, its cities are growing. Each year, many people move from the countryside in search of jobs in the cities.

HISTORY MAKERS

Prince Henry 1349–1460

Historians call Prince Henry "the Navigator" because he made major contributions to maritime exploration. He wasn't a sailor, and he rarely traveled far from his homeland of Portugal. During his lifetime, he sponsored more than 50 voyages of exploration. His dedication to exploration eventually led Portugal to discover valuable trade routes to Asia. These voyages greatly advanced European knowledge of the world. Prince Henry's efforts helped make Portugal a major sea power and put the nation on the path to empire.

ONLINE BIOGRAPHY
For more on the life of Prince Henry, go to the
Research & Writing Center @ ClassZone.com

One-third of the population lives in or near its two largest cities, Lisbon and Porto. Lisbon, in southern Portugal, is the nation's capital and largest city. It is a center of tourism and commerce. Porto is a major seaport and industrial center.

Government and Economics Since 1976, Portugal has been a parliamentary democracy. Citizens elect members of parliament and the president. Candidates from many political parties compete for seats in its parliament.

Portugal's colonies once made it the richest nation in Europe. Today, it is one of the poorest, with the lowest per capita GDP in Western Europe. For decades, leaders failed to strengthen its economy and neglected its roads, ports, and factories. Lack of energy resources and a poor educational system also slowed its growth. Since joining the EU in 1986, however, Portugal has worked hard to improve its economy. It has diversified and expanded the role of service industries. Membership in the EU has helped increase trade. Today, Portugal continues its efforts to develop its economy.

Albufeira, Portugal Two fishermen tend to their nets in this fishing village. Fishing remains an important part of the Portuguese economy. **What geographic trait makes Portugal a major fishing nation?**

🔺 **ANALYZE EFFECTS** Explain how Portugal's location contributed to its role as a leader in the Age of Exploration.

ONLINE QUIZ
For test practice, go to **Interactive Review** @ ClassZone.com

Section 2 Assessment

TERMS & NAMES

1. Explain the importance of
- Moors
- Reconquista
- Christopher Columbus
- Basque

USE YOUR READING NOTES

2. Compare and Contrast Use your completed diagram to answer the following question:

How is Spain's government different from Portugal's government?

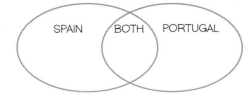

KEY IDEAS

3. What major event in Spain's history occurred in 1492?

4. What role did Portugal play in the Age of Exploration?

5. In what ways are the cultures and histories of Spain and Portugal similar?

CRITICAL THINKING

6. Analyze Causes What are some reasons for Portugal's slow economic growth?

7. Summarize How has EU membership changed Spain's economy?

8. CONNECT to Today How has increased urbanization affected the societies of Spain and Portugal?

9. WRITING Plan an Itinerary Plan a cultural and historical tour of a city in Spain. Choose two places that show its diverse religious and ethnic heritage. Tell why you have chosen each place and explain its importance to the history of the city.

Reading for Understanding

SECTION 3

▶ Key Ideas

BEFORE, YOU LEARNED

Spain and Portugal both created empires to supplement the natural resources of the Iberian Peninsula. Spain's economy is stronger than Portugal's economy.

NOW YOU WILL LEARN

Over the centuries, France's natural resources have helped it prosper. Through economic union, Belgium, Luxembourg, and the Netherlands have also prospered.

▶ Vocabulary

TERMS & NAMES

Benelux (BEHN•uh•LUHKS) name for the economic union formed by Belgium, the Netherlands, and Luxembourg to ensure the fast and efficient movement of people, goods, and services within these nations

polders (POHL•durz) land reclaimed by draining it of water with the use of a dam and pump

duchy the territory ruled by a duke or duchess

multilingual able to speak many languages

BACKGROUND VOCABULARY

autonomy self-governance or independence

REVIEW

Northern European Plain vast area of flat or gently rolling land from France to Russia

Visual Vocabulary polders in the Netherlands

▶ Reading Strategy

Re-create the web diagram shown at right. As you read and respond to the **KEY QUESTIONS**, use the diagram to help you find the main ideas about France and the Benelux countries.

 Skillbuilder Handbook, page R4

FIND MAIN IDEAS

FRANCE AND THE BENELUX COUNTRIES

France

Benelux Countries

GRAPHIC ORGANIZERS
Go to **Interactive Review** @ ClassZone.com

France and the Benelux Countries

9.01 Trace the historical development of governments including traditional, colonial, and national in selected societies and assess the effects on the respective contemporary political systems.
13.02 Describe the diverse cultural connections that have influenced the development of language, art, music, and belief systems in North Carolina and the United States and assess their role in creating a changing cultural mosaic.

Connecting to Your World

Can you imagine spending three weeks riding your bike from Chicago to Los Angeles? Every July, about 200 riders in the Tour de France bicycle race cover that distance and more in one of the world's most watched sporting events. The course of the race runs through much of France and some of the surrounding countries. Riders cover terrain from the mountainous roads of the Alps to the cobbled streets of Paris. The race is a great source of national pride for the French people.

Tour de France
Cyclists race down a curvy mountain road in western France.

France

🔻 **KEY QUESTION** How has its colonial empire changed the population of France?

France is the largest country in Western Europe. Its landscape ranges from the peaks of the Alps and the beaches on the Mediterranean Sea to cities such as Paris and fishing villages along the Atlantic Ocean. For much of its history, kings ruled this territory. Then, in 1789, the French were inspired to fight for their independence. Since then, France has gone back and forth many times between monarchy and democracy.

Arc de Triomphe
This monument in Paris celebrates military victories.

Paris

FRANCE

History In 1792, French revolutionaries decided to make France a democracy. Soon after, Napoleon Bonaparte seized power and ruled as emperor until his defeat in 1815. France then returned briefly to a monarchy. In 1848, a second, less violent revolt occurred that led to another democracy. Voters chose Louis Napoleon Bonaparte, a nephew of Napoleon, as president of the new government, but like his famous uncle, he declared himself emperor. After his armies suffered major defeats, he was forced to step down, and France once again became a republic. Political instability and frequent changes in government continued. Then, in 1958, French voters agreed to a new constitution that gave their president greater power.

Despite its many changes in government, France became a powerful nation. Like other major powers, it developed a colonial empire in Africa and Asia that boosted its economy. In the 1900s, however, many battles of World War I and World War II were fought on French soil. These conflicts devastated France. Millions died, and the destruction of factories, farms, and cities shattered the French economy. In the 1960s and 1970s, the French colonies overseas gained their independence, another blow to the French economy. It has since recovered, as a result of hard work and access to natural resources.

CONNECT to History

Bastille Day is celebrated each year on July 14. It marks the beginning of the French Revolution. On July 14, 1789, an angry mob took control of the Bastille, a French prison. On August 4, 1789, frightened French nobles allowed the common people a greater role in government. In June 1791, fearing for his life, King Louis XVI tried to escape from France. He was imprisoned in August 1792. In January 1793, revolutionaries beheaded the king. Three constitutions were adopted during the revolution, one in 1791, one in 1793, and the last in 1795. In October 1799, Napoleon Bonaparte seized power, ending the revolution.

Bastille Day parade in Paris

Activity

Make an Illustrated Time Line

Materials
• markers
• butcher paper

1. To create a French Revolution time line, pick beginning and end dates.

2. Draw a line and divide it into segments. Leave room to illustrate each event.

3. Choose three or four events to show on the time line.

4. Use markers to create drawings and write short captions describing each event.

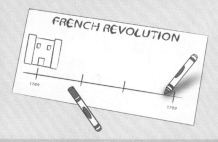

Culture Most French citizens have a very strong cultural identity, and take pride in French culture, history, and language. In recent decades, France has become more diverse. People have emigrated from its former colonies in North Africa and Asia. Many Muslims now live in this primarily Roman Catholic nation.

France, like much of Western Europe, is highly urbanized and densely settled. Three out of four people live in cities. Because space is scarce, apartments are more common than houses. People often walk or ride public transportation. In fact, many cities limit car use and parking on city streets.

French culture has had a global influence. French painters such as Claude Monet and Pierre-Auguste Renoir influenced the popular Impressionist style of painting in the late 1800s. French chefs are well-known for creating culinary masterpieces. Chefs in restaurants around the world try to master French techniques. Each year on July 14, the French celebrate their nation and its culture on Bastille Day. Fireworks displays and parades commemorate French independence.

Government and Economics Today, France is a parliamentary democracy with power concentrated at the national level. Its government spreads power across executive, legislative, and judicial branches, like the United States. In France, however, the executive branch includes a president and a prime minister. France's president serves a five-year term and oversees foreign affairs. He or she appoints a prime minister to take care of the daily operation of the government.

After the devastation of World War II, France worked hard to modernize its economy. Now, its economy is one of the world's strongest. Although a small percentage of French workers are farmers, France is Europe's largest exporter of farm produce. This is because of the fertile soil of the **Northern European Plain** that covers much of France, as well as modern farming methods. France, an EU member, is a major producer of cars, high-speed trains, and airplanes.

Tourism is a key industry. France has been the world's top tourist destination for several years running. Many people travel to France to visit its museums, castles, and cathedrals. Visitors also wait in long lines to go to the top of the most famous landmark in Paris, the Eiffel Tower.

▲ **ANALYZE EFFECTS** Explain how France's colonial empire has changed its population.

THE EIFFEL TOWER

Height: 1,063 feet

Weight: 10,100 tons

Date Completed: March 31, 1889

Elevators: Seven elevators travel over 64,000 miles each year, equal to more than two and a half times around the Earth.

Materials: The tower is made of iron, and is painted about every 5 years with 50 to 60 tons of paint to keep it from rusting.

Composition: It consists of 18,038 pieces, joined together by 2.5 million rivets.

NETHERLANDS

BELGIUM

LUXEMBOURG

The Benelux Countries

▼ **KEY QUESTION** How has belonging to an economic union helped the Benelux countries?

The Netherlands, Belgium, and Luxembourg belong to an economic union known as the **Benelux** (BEHN•uh•LUHKS) countries. The name was created by combining the first few letters of each country's name. The Benelux nations are alike in many ways. All are constitutional monarchies. All are highly urbanized with well-developed economies. All belong to the EU and depend on trade with larger neighbors.

The Netherlands Following centuries of foreign rule, the Dutch declared their independence from Spain in 1581. Spain finally recognized the Netherlands as an independent nation in 1648. The 1600s were an era of prosperity and achievement for the Dutch. They became a great sea power with colonies in Southeast Asia and the Americas. Dutch is the official language of the Netherlands. Many people also speak English, German, or French. Most Dutch are Christians, though many Muslim immigrants have come from former Dutch colonies in Indonesia and Suriname.

The Netherlands is very densely populated. Because nearly half of its land is below sea level, living space is scarce. The Dutch have used dikes, dams, canals, and pumping systems to reclaim land that is below sea level. The drained lands, called **polders** (POHL•durz), have rich soil and are often used for farming. The Dutch also build factories and towns on them. Forty percent of the land in the Netherlands is from polders.

The Netherlands is also highly urbanized. Because of the shortage of land, Dutch rural areas are close to cities. Bicycles are very common, both for recreation and as a means of transportation in crowded cities.

Belgium and Luxembourg For many years, Belgium was part of the Netherlands. It gained its independence in 1830. Belgium's central location has been both an advantage and a disadvantage. It has enabled Belgium to prosper through trade with its neighbors. But it also made Belgium a battleground during the two world wars, which caused great destruction and loss of life.

CONNECT ⟳ **Geography & Economics**

Tulip Mania

In the early 1600s in the Netherlands, people went crazy over tulips imported from Turkey. Dutch families bought rare varieties of bulbs, not for their gardens but as an investment. Tulip prices soared. One man traded his mansion for just three bulbs. When prices dropped, many people lost everything. The craze ended, but tulips were in the Netherlands to stay. Today, the country is one of the world's biggest exporters of tulip bulbs.

At one time, cultural differences between Dutch-speaking Flemings in the north and French-speaking Walloons in the south caused serious tensions. In recent years, the government has eased tensions by giving both ethnic groups greater **autonomy**. Now, the Belgian constitution recognizes separate cultural communities based on language, as well as separate economic regions for the two groups.

Luxembourg is one of the smallest countries in Europe. In 1890, it broke away from the Netherlands to become a **duchy**, a state ruled by a duke or duchess. The country has three official languages: French, used in government; German, used in newspapers; and Luxembourgish, used for everyday matters. Many of its people are **multilingual**, or able to speak several languages. This has made Luxembourg attractive to foreign companies looking for new locations. At one time, steel was Luxembourg's most important product. Today, its economy is more diversified, with banking and other financial services making up a key segment of its economy.

Antwerp, Belgium
The cafés in this square in the heart of Antwerp's historic district are typical of Europe's outdoor cafés.

 MAKE INFERENCES Explain how belonging to an economic union has helped the Benelux countries.

 ONLINE QUIZ
For test practice, go to
Interactive Review
@ ClassZone.com

Section 3 Assessment

TERMS & NAMES

1. Explain the importance of
- Benelux
- polders
- duchy
- multilingual

USE YOUR READING NOTES

2. Find Main Ideas Use your completed web diagram to answer the following question:

How are France and the Benelux countries similar?

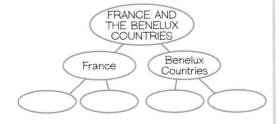

KEY IDEAS

3. What are France's leading industrial products and services?

4. How have the people of the Netherlands used technology to reshape their environment?

5. What cultural differences have caused problems within Belgium?

CRITICAL THINKING

6. Make Inferences How has France's location been beneficial for its economy?

7. Analyze Effects How do the Benelux countries benefit from their nearness to Germany and France?

8. CONNECT to Today Why might France object to trade barriers on farm produce?

9. WRITING Create an Advertisement You have been asked by a French travel agency to make a list of the top five reasons to visit France. Create an advertisement explaining why France is an interesting and fun place to visit.

SECTION 4

Reading for Understanding

▶ Key Ideas

BEFORE, YOU LEARNED

France prospered as a result of natural resources. The Benelux countries have benefited from their economic union.

NOW YOU WILL LEARN

Germany's central location helped it to dominate neighboring lands. Germany and the Alpine countries are linked in many ways.

▶ Vocabulary

TERMS & NAMES

Prussia the most powerful German state in the Holy Roman Empire

Adolf Hitler German head of state from 1933 to 1945

Berlin Wall a wall built by East Germany's Communist government to close off East Berlin from West Berlin

Alpine having to do with the Alps mountain range

neutrality a policy of not taking part in war

BACKGROUND VOCABULARY

reunify to bring something that has been separated back together

REVIEW

Holocaust the systematic murder of Jews and other minorities by the Nazis during World War II

market economy an economic system in which the production of goods and services is decided by supply and the demand of consumers

▶ Reading Strategy

Re-create the time line shown at right. As you read and respond to the **KEY QUESTIONS**, use the time line to help you sequence the events that have shaped Germany and the Alpine countries.

 See Skillbuilder Handbook, page R6

SEQUENCE EVENTS

1648   2005

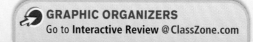

GRAPHIC ORGANIZERS
Go to **Interactive Review** @ ClassZone.com

Germany and the Alpine Countries

2.01 Identify key physical characteristics such as landforms, water forms, and climate, and evaluate their influence on the development of cultures in selected South American and European regions.
8.01 Describe the role of key historical figures and evaluate their impact on past and present societies in South America and Europe.

Connecting to Your World

Germany has had a big influence on the United States, and for good reason. In 1990, more Americans reported that their ancestors came from Germany than from any other country. It's no wonder that Americans enjoy eating hot dogs, or frankfurters—a sausage named after Frankfurt, Germany. American children go to kindergarten, a type of school borrowed from Germany. And in December, many Americans decorate trees for the holidays, a German tradition.

Germany

🔻 **KEY QUESTION** How was Germany reshaped after World War II?

German traditions are part of Germany's strong national identity. For a long time, military strength was another aspect of Germany's identity. Germany is a large country centrally located on the European continent. It is well-positioned to dominate other nations and has conquered surrounding lands several times.

Neuschwanstein Castle King Ludwig II began building this fairy-tale castle in 1869.

GERMANY
○ Neuschwanstein Castle

History Like Italy, Germany was once a collection of small states instead of a united nation. **Prussia** was the most powerful German state. In 1871, Prussia unified the German states into one nation. Germany was a military power until its defeat in World War I, which weakened its economy and reduced its territory.

Many Germans, frustrated by the poor economy, began to support the fascist Nazi Party. The Nazis promised to make Germany the world power it had once been. In 1933, **Adolf Hitler**, the party's leader, became Germany's head of state. Hitler began a movement to gain more territory for Germany that eventually led to World War II. The war devastated Germany and much of Europe. The Nazis also carried out the **Holocaust**, the systematic murder of millions of Jews and other ethnic minorities.

The Allies defeated the Germans and divided Germany into four zones. The United States, France, and Britain merged their zones into the democratic West Germany. The Soviet Union's zone became East Germany, a Communist country. Berlin, located in East Germany, was divided into east and west sides. In 1961, the East German government built the **Berlin Wall** to formally divide the city in two. East Germany's government fell in 1989, and the Berlin Wall came down. In 1990, Germany decided to **reunify**, ending the east-west division.

ONLINE PRIMARY SOURCE To read more eyewitness accounts, go to the **Research & Writing Center** @ClassZone.com

ANALYZING Primary Sources

Andreas Ramos traveled from Denmark to Germany in 1989. He was one of the five million people in Berlin to witness the fall of the Berlin Wall. Afterwards, he wrote the following.

Everything was out of control. . . . There were fireworks, kites, flags and flags and flags, dogs, children. The wall was finally breaking. . . .
I saw an indescribable joy in people's faces. It was the end of the government telling people what not to do, it was the end of the Wall, the war, the East, the West.

Source: Andreas Ramos, *A Personal Account of The Fall of the Berlin Wall*

DOCUMENT-BASED QUESTION

What do you think Ramos meant by "it was the end . . . of the East, the West"?

Culture Germany has the largest population in Western Europe. German is the official language, though different forms of the language are spoken. Catholics and Protestants each account for about one-third of Germany's population. About four percent are Muslims.

Today, approximately 90 percent of Germany's population lives in cities and their surrounding suburbs. Cities offer greater employment opportunities and more varied entertainment. German culture has a strong musical tradition. Some great classical composers, including Bach, Beethoven, and Brahms, were German. Richard Wagner wrote spectacular operas based on German myths. With teenagers, American music is popular. Many German pop stars sing in English.

Government and Economics Germany is a federal republic—a union of states similar to that of the United States. Germany's president acts as the country's formal chief of state, mainly performing ceremonial duties. The chancellor heads the government. The German people elect the president, but the chancellor is selected by parliament. In 2005, Angela Merkel became Germany's first female chancellor.

Germany has had to overcome some serious economic problems. At the time of reunification, East German industries were outdated. Almost half of East Germany's workers were unemployed. In 1990, East Germany adopted West Germany's currency and **market economy**. The German economy continues to adjust and is getting stronger.

▲ **EVALUATE** Explain how World War II reshaped Germany.

Angela Merkel Germany's first female chancellor

CONNECT ⟳ Government & Culture

The Reichstag When East and West Germany reunited in 1990, they chose Berlin as their capital. In 1999, the German legislature began meeting in Berlin's renovated Reichstag building (shown at right). The building's prominent glass dome contains a ramp leading to an observation platform. It is a symbol of the people being able to raise themselves above their leaders, who meet in the chamber below.

CRITICAL THINKING

Make Inferences What else could the Reichstag building symbolize about Germany and its government?

LIECHTENSTEIN
AUSTRIA
SWITZERLAND

The Alpine Countries

▼ **KEY QUESTION** How has Austrian history been tied to war?

Austria, Switzerland, and Liechtenstein are **Alpine** countries, named for the Alps Mountains common to all three. The Alpine countries have historic and cultural ties to Germany. All three, like Germany, once were part of the Holy Roman Empire. All three share a common border with Germany. They also share the German language.

Austria Austria was once a powerful nation. In 1804, Austria became an empire. For a time, it was the leader of the German states. But in 1866, Austria lost a war with Prussia. The next year, it joined a dual monarchy with Hungary. The two countries cooperated in foreign affairs but had separate governments. Then, Austria fought on the losing side in World War I. Following its defeat, Austria separated from Hungary. After World War II, the nation adopted a policy of **neutrality**, meaning that it does not participate in military conflicts.

Almost all Austrians speak German, and the majority are Roman Catholics. Although most Austrians live in cities or towns, they still manage to enjoy the outdoors. Austria, about three-fourths of which is covered by mountains, is a nation of skiers. The Austrian Alps offer nearly perfect conditions for this winter sport. In the summer, the scenic beauty of the Alps attracts many hikers and backpackers.

After World War II, Austria became a federal republic with both a president and a chancellor. Austria belongs to the European Union. One of its major industries is iron and steel production. Tourism also plays a major role in Austria's economy. Many people visit the mountainous country to ski, hike, and admire the scenery.

Skiing Like the other Alpine countries, many tourists visit Austria to ski its many slopes. Tourism is a billion-euro industry for Austria. **What are the economic disadvantages of a seasonal industry?**

Switzerland and Liechtenstein Switzerland and Liechtenstein are small countries that share a border. They were once part of the Holy Roman Empire. Switzerland became independent in 1648, and Liechtenstein in 1866. Both are officially neutral.

German, French, and Italian are Switzerland's official languages. Liechtenstein's official language is German. Switzerland has a mix of Catholics and Protestants, while most Liechtensteiners are Catholic. Switzerland is famous for the high-quality chocolate and watches it produces. Liechtenstein is known for its postage stamps, which are prized by collectors all over the world. Both countries are popular tourist destinations because of their beautiful Alpine landscapes. Both have reputations as centers of international finance. Tiny Liechtenstein uses Swiss money.

Switzerland is a federal republic, like Austria and Germany. The Swiss government is very democratic. The Swiss can vote to change laws passed by their legislature. Liechtenstein is a constitutional monarchy ruled by a prince. It also has a prime minister and parliament.

Swiss Watches The intricate works of many Swiss watches are still made and repaired by hand.

🔺 **SUMMARIZE** Explain how Austrian history has been tied to war.

Section ④ Assessment

ONLINE QUIZ
For test practice, go to
Interactive Review
@ ClassZone.com

TERMS & NAMES

1. Explain the importance of
- Adolf Hitler
- Berlin Wall
- Alpine
- neutrality

USE YOUR READING NOTES

2. Sequence Events Use your completed time line to answer the following question:

What significant event occurred in Germany in 1961?

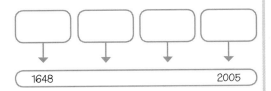

1648   2005

KEY IDEAS

3. What role has geographic location played in Germany's rise to power?

4. How did Prussia's actions strengthen the German states?

5. What do the Alpine countries have in common?

CRITICAL THINKING

6. Make Inferences What did the fall of the Berlin Wall symbolize for Germany?

7. Draw Conclusions How have the Alps helped shape the cultures and economies of the Alpine countries?

8. CONNECT to Today Why would it be important for the Alpine countries to maintain good relations with Germany?

9. TECHNOLOGY Prepare an Oral Presentation Choose one of Germany's many famous musicians—Bach, Beethoven, or Brahms—and do research to create a short biography of his life. Choose one of his songs to play during your presentation.

Reading for Understanding

▶ Key Ideas

BEFORE, YOU LEARNED

Germany and the Alpine countries share common borders and a common language. They are linked in many ways.

NOW YOU WILL LEARN

The Nordic countries have histories and cultures that are closely intertwined.

▶ Vocabulary

TERMS & NAMES

Vikings a seafaring Scandinavian people who raided northern and western Europe from the 9th to the 11th century

Sami people of northern Scandinavia who traditionally herd reindeer; also the name of their language

ombudsman an official who investigates citizens' complaints against the government

welfare state a social system in which the government provides for many of its citizens' needs

BACKGROUND VOCABULARY

Nordic relating to Scandinavia

REVIEW

hydroelectric power electricity made by water-powered engines

Visual Vocabulary Sami with a reindeer

▶ Reading Strategy

Re-create the chart shown at right. As you read and respond to the **KEY QUESTIONS**, use the chart to help you organize important details about the Nordic countries.

 See Skillbuilder Handbook, page R7

CATEGORIZE

	Language	Government	Economy
Sweden			
Norway			
Finland			
Denmark			
Iceland			

 GRAPHIC ORGANIZERS
Go to **Interactive Review** @ ClassZone.com

The Nordic Countries

5.01 Describe the relationship between the location of natural resources and economic development, and assess the impact on selected cultures, countries, and regions in South America and Europe.
9.02 Describe how different types of governments such as democracies, dictatorships, monarchies, and oligarchies in selected areas of South America and Europe carry out legislative, executive, and judicial functions, and evaluate the effectiveness of each.

Connecting to Your World

Who were the first Europeans to reach North America? Many think that Columbus and his crew were the first to do so. In fact, Leif Ericson, a Viking, was probably the first. According to an ancient account from Greenland, Ericson hoped to find a forested land glimpsed by an Icelandic trader and sailor. Ericson and his men sailed west from Greenland. They landed and spent the winter on the North American continent, at a place Ericson called Vinland.

Leif Ericson

Sweden and Norway

▼ **KEY QUESTION** Why do Sweden and Norway have so much in common?

Five nations in northernmost Europe make up the **Nordic**, or Scandinavian, countries: Sweden, Norway, Finland, Denmark, and Iceland. These lands were first settled thousands of years ago. Sweden and Norway share the same landmass, the Scandinavian Peninsula. Their histories are intertwined. Sweden and Norway were both influenced by the **Vikings**, seafaring Scandinavians who raided Europe from the 9th to the 11th century.

Viking Ship
This Viking longship was recovered from a farm in Slagen, Norway, in 1904.

History The Vikings were some of the world's best sailors and ship-builders. They also were pirates and fierce warriors. During the three centuries that the Vikings lived in Scandinavia, they invaded much of Europe, as you can see from the map here.

The Viking Invasions of Western Europe 820–941

CONNECT Geography & History

1. **Region** Where was the Viking homeland?
2. **Movement** What was the southernmost city reached by the Vikings?

In the late 1000s, the Vikings converted to Christianity and settled down. Sweden and Norway became monarchies. Finland became part of Sweden in 1323. In 1397, Denmark's Queen Margaret formed a union with Sweden and Norway, which lasted until Sweden withdrew in 1523. Sweden had become a great power, often battling Denmark, Russia, and Poland for territory. In 1700, those three countries attacked Sweden. Sweden's king, Charles XII, fell in battle in 1718, bringing Sweden's domination to an end. In 1809, Sweden lost control of Finland to Russia.

Norway came under Sweden's control in 1814. In 1905, Sweden recognized Norway's independence. During the two world wars, Sweden and Norway remained neutral. However, during World War II, Norway was invaded and occupied by the Germans.

Culture Although Swedes and Norwegians speak different languages, Swedish and Norwegian are similar. As a result, speakers of the two languages often are able to communicate with each other. In both countries, Lutheranism is the official state religion. However, Swedes and Norwegians have the freedom to practice different religions.

In Sweden, Finns make up the largest immigrant population, while immigrants in Norway come from many nations. In the northern regions of Sweden and Norway, there is a large minority population of **Sami**, whose traditional way of life involves caring for herds of reindeer. Their native language is also called Sami.

Because of their climates, Sweden and Norway are less densely populated than other European countries. Most people live in the countries' southern and central regions. About 80 percent of Swedes and 75 percent of Norwegians live in urban areas. Many people in both countries own vacation homes. Swedes and Norwegians enjoy outdoor sports year round. Skiing and ice skating are both popular.

Worldster
A Day in Ulrika's Life

 To learn more about Ulrika and her world, go to the **Activity Center @ ClassZone.com**

To introduce herself, Ulrika says:

"Hello, mitt namn är Ulrika."

Hi! My name is Ulrika. I am 14 years old and live in Uppsala, a city of 180,000 people. Uppsala is about 50 miles north of Stockholm, Sweden's capital. I like to read and play computer games. On the weekends, I leave the city with some of my friends to take horseback-riding lessons. Riding is really popular here. Of course, like you, I go to school. Here's what my day is usually like.

School At my school, all of our books and school supplies are free—even paper! We also get a free lunch every day. This year, one of my favorite classes is metal working. I'm making a modern sculpture for our yard.

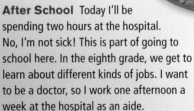

Break Time We have a lot of breaks during the day. Usually, we go outside and play soccer, field hockey, or another game or sport. It's great to be able to go outdoors.

After School Today I'll be spending two hours at the hospital. No, I'm not sick! This is part of going to school here. In the eighth grade, we get to learn about different kinds of jobs. I want to be a doctor, so I work one afternoon a week at the hospital as an aide.

Dinner Time I'm meeting my family for dinner at my aunt and uncle's house. It's Thursday so I know what we're having—pea soup, with pancakes and lingonberries for dessert. That's a traditional Thursday meal in Sweden!

CONNECT to Your Life

Journal Entry Do you know what kind of job you want when you're older? Would volunteering like Ulrika does help you decide? Record your thoughts in your journal.

Government and Economics Sweden and Norway are constitutional monarchies. Although both have monarchs, their prime ministers and cabinets hold most of the executive power. Both Sweden and Norway appoint ombudsmen to protect their citizens. An **ombudsman** investigates complaints against the government and makes sure that governmental power is not abused.

Sweden and Norway are welfare states. **Welfare states** use taxes to provide a wide range of services to their citizens. Families with children under age 16 are given money to care for them. Workers receive good retirement and unemployment plans.

Sweden has a highly industrialized economy. It also has a reputation for modern design, which has spread to other countries through two major Swedish companies, household goods store IKEA and clothing store H&M. Norway took longer to develop manufacturing because it did not have enough energy resources to power factories. By 1900, Norway was able to use hydroelectric power from its rivers. Today, Norway also has access to North Sea oil. Sweden joined the European Union in 1995, but Norway's citizens voted not to join.

Scandinavian Design
Scandinavian design, known for its use of simple forms, has become popular in the United States.

▼ **DRAW CONCLUSIONS** Explain why Sweden and Norway share so many similarities.

Finland

▼ **KEY QUESTION** How did Finland's neighbors affect its history?

Finland's location between Sweden and Russia has played a major role in Finland's history. Both countries have influenced its culture.

History and Culture In 1155, Finland became part of Sweden. It remained under Swedish control until 1809, when Russia conquered Finland. In 1917, Finland gained its independence from Russia. During World War II, Finland had to fight off two invasions by the Soviet Union.

Because of its history, Finland's culture is strongly influenced by Sweden. Finland's two official languages are Finnish and Swedish. Most people in Finland are Finnish. Swedes make up the largest minority group. Small groups of Sami also live in Finland.

About three out of five Finns live in urban areas. Still, many of them find opportunities to enjoy outdoor recreation. With snow on the ground for almost half the year, sports like cross-country skiing and ice hockey are especially popular. Northern Finland even has reindeer races!

Government and Economics Finland is a democratic republic. A president and prime minister share executive power. Voters elect the president, who appoints the prime minister. In 2000, Finland elected its first female president, Tarja Halonen. Finland is a welfare state.

Finland's forests are its most plentiful natural resource. Forests cover almost two-thirds of the land, more than in any other European country. Paper and other forest products make up 30 percent of Finland's exports. Finland also produces mobile phones and other high-tech items. In 1995, Finland joined the European Union.

▼ **SUMMARIZE** Explain how Finland's neighbors affected its history.

Denmark and Iceland

▼ **KEY QUESTION** How are Denmark and Iceland similar?

Denmark occupies the Jutland Peninsula and over 400 small islands surrounding the peninsula. The nation also includes Greenland and the Faroe Islands. Denmark is a small country, but it has played a large role in Scandinavian history. Iceland is an island nation just south of the Arctic Circle. It was ruled by Denmark for over 500 years.

History Viking raids on other countries shaped Denmark's early history. Denmark's power expanded during the late 1100s and early 1200s. For a time, Denmark controlled Sweden, Norway, and Iceland. Sweden withdrew from the union in 1523. Denmark continued to rule Norway until 1814. Iceland gained its independence in 1944.

Culture Most Danes have Danish ancestry, though some are descended from Germans. Icelanders are mainly of Norwegian or Celtic descent. Over 90 percent of Iceland's population lives in urban areas, as do most Danes. The Evangelical Lutheran Church is the official religion of both countries. Danish is spoken in Denmark, and Icelandic in Iceland.

Nyhavn Harbor These colorful old sailors' quarters in Copenhagen, Denmark, have been converted to cafés and dance clubs.

Government and Economics Denmark is a constitutional monarchy. The Danish monarch has mainly ceremonial duties. The prime minister serves as the head of government. Like other Scandinavian nations, Denmark and Iceland have welfare systems that provide for many of their citizens' needs. Iceland is a republic. Its people elect a president, who serves a four-year term and has limited powers. The prime minister and cabinet perform most executive functions.

Despite lacking natural resources, Denmark has a strong, modern economy. The cost of living in Iceland is high because so many goods have to be imported to the small island nation. Denmark belongs to the EU but has not adopted the euro. Iceland is not an EU member.

▼ **COMPARE AND CONTRAST** Explain how Denmark and Iceland are similar to each other.

Section 5 Assessment

ONLINE QUIZ
For test practice, go to
Interactive Review
@ ClassZone.com

TERMS & NAMES

1. Explain the importance of
- Vikings
- Sami
- ombudsman
- welfare state

USE YOUR READING NOTES

2. Categorize Use your completed chart to answer the following question:

Which of the Nordic countries are welfare states?

	Language	Government	Economy
Sweden			
Norway			
Finland			
Denmark			
Iceland			

KEY IDEAS

3. What cultural characteristics do Sweden and Norway share?

4. How has Finland's location affected its history?

5. Why is Iceland's cost of living so high?

CRITICAL THINKING

6. Make Inferences How has the climate of the Scandinavian countries helped define their cultures?

7. Summarize What benefits do welfare states offer their citizens?

8. **CONNECT to Today** How do you think having ombudsmen would change the U.S. government?

9. **WRITING** **Write a Speech** Use appropriate sources to research and prepare a speech explaining three advantages and disadvantages of welfare states like those in Scandinavia. Then explain why you would or would not like to live in a country with that kind of economy.

Interactive ◄ Review

Click here to complete these and other activities online @ ClassZone.com

CHAPTER SUMMARY

Key Idea 1
Greece and Italy began as collections of small states that gained independence.

Key Idea 2
Both Spain and Portugal were ruled by foreigners and developed colonial empires.

Key Idea 3
France and the Benelux nations have prospered.

Key Idea 4
Germany and the Alpine countries are linked in many ways.

Key Idea 5
The Nordic countries have histories and cultures that are closely intertwined.

For **Review and Study Notes**, go to **Interactive Review** @ ClassZone.com

NAME GAME

Use the Terms & Names list to complete each sentence on paper or online.

1. I was a barrier that divided a city in half.
   _____ Berlin Wall _____

2. I investigate complaints against the government.
   _____

3. I was the eastern half of the Roman Empire after the fall of Rome. _____

4. I am a political system based on a strong central government led by a dictator. _____

5. I am one of a group of people living in Sweden's far north. _____

6. I am an ethnic group living in the northern Pyrenees. _____

7. I am the official home of the Pope.
   _____

8. I was Germany's leader during World War II.
   _____

9. I am an economic union formed by three western European nations. _____

10. I was a powerful German state in the Holy Roman Empire. _____

Adolf Hitler
Basque
Benelux
Berlin Wall
Byzantine Empire
Christopher Columbus
coalition
fascism
Moors
ombudsman
Prussia
Reconquista
Sami
Vatican
Vikings

Activities

GeoGame

Use this online map to reinforce your understanding of the countries and cities of Western Europe. Drag and drop each place name in the list to its location on the map.

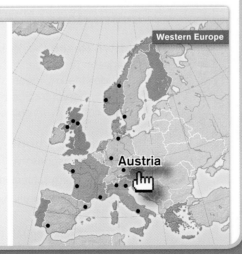

Geo GAME

Greece

Spain

Paris

Berlin

Austria

To play the complete game, go to **Interactive Review** @ ClassZone.com

Western Europe

Austria

Crossword Puzzle

Complete an online crossword puzzle to test your knowledge of Western Europe.

ACROSS
1. seafaring Scandinavians who raided Europe from the 9th to 11th century

VOCABULARY

Explain the significance of each of the following.

1. Byzantine Empire
2. Romance language
3. coalition
4. Christopher Columbus
5. Benelux
6. Berlin Wall
7. neutrality

Explain how the terms and names in each group are related.

8. Moors, Reconquista
9. Basque, Sami
10. Adolf Hitler, Holocaust
11. ombudsman, welfare state

KEY IDEAS

1 Greece and Italy

12. How has Greece's geography defined some of its major economic activities?
13. Why has the Catholic Church had such a strong impact on Italian culture?

2 Spain and Portugal

14. What was the Reconquista?
15. How has Portugal improved its economy?

3 France and the Benelux Countries

16. How is the French government similar to and different from the U.S. government?
17. How are the three Benelux countries alike?

4 Germany and the Alpine Countries

18. How did World War II affect Germany's economy?
19. What geographical characteristic most clearly defines the Alpine countries?

5 The Nordic Countries

20. Why did Norway's manufacturing sector lag behind other Scandinavian countries?
21. Who were the Vikings?

CRITICAL THINKING

22. **Compare and Contrast** Create a table to compare and contrast the geography, work, and recreation of northern and southern Italy.

NORTHERN ITALY	SOUTHERN ITALY

23. **Analyze Causes and Effects** Why did Spain begin exploring the world by sea?
24. **Connect Geography & History** What geographical factor helped Portugal to establish an empire despite its small size?
25. **Compare** How do France's experiences with its eastern neighbor Germany compare to Finland's experiences with Russia?
26. **Connect Geography & Economics** How has the presence of offshore oil contributed to Norway's economy?
27. **Five Themes: Location** How has Scandinavia's northern location helped shape its culture?

Answer the
ESSENTIAL QUESTION

What geographic and cultural characteristics define the subregions of Western Europe?

Written Response Write a two- or three-paragraph response to the Essential Question. Consider the key ideas of each section and the specific characteristics of each subregion. Use the rubric below to guide your thinking.

Response Rubric
A strong response will:
- identify each subregion
- explain how geographic characteristics define each subregion
- compare and contrast cultural characteristics within each subregion

THEMATIC MAP

Use the map and your knowledge of Europe to answer questions 1 and 2 on your paper.

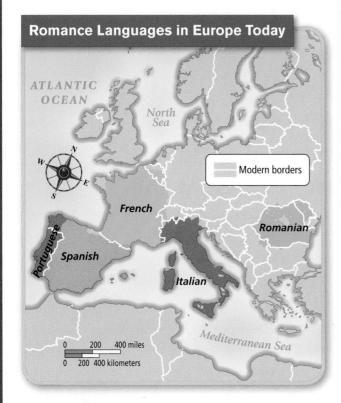

Romance Languages in Europe Today

ATLANTIC OCEAN

North Sea

Modern borders

French

Romanian

Portuguese

Spanish

Italian

Mediterranean Sea

0   200   400 miles
0   200 400 kilometers

1. The Romance languages are concentrated in which part of Europe?

A. north
B. east
C. southwest
D. southeast

2. Which statement best describes the pattern of Romance languages?

A. They are not spoken along the Mediterranean Sea.
B. They are found in the former Roman Empire.
C. They are dying out.
D. They are spoken only in northern Europe.

BAR GRAPH

Use the information in the graph below to answer questions 3 and 4 on your paper.

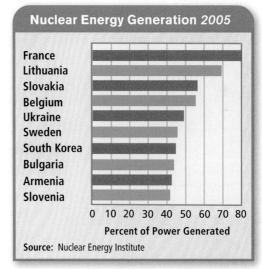

Nuclear Energy Generation *2005*

France
Lithuania
Slovakia
Belgium
Ukraine
Sweden
South Korea
Bulgaria
Armenia
Slovenia

0 10 20 30 40 50 60 70 80
Percent of Power Generated

Source: Nuclear Energy Institute

3. How many countries get more of their energy from nuclear power than France?

4. How many of the top ten nuclear energy producers are in Western Europe?

GeoActivity

1. INTERDISCIPLINARY ACTIVITY–HISTORY

With a small group, research Viking ships and create a poster about them. Be sure your poster shows how the ship was built, what materials were used, and when and where the Vikings traveled.

2. WRITING FOR SOCIAL STUDIES

Reread the part of Section 5 that describes Ulrika's day. Then write a letter to Ulrika about how you spend a typical day. Use interesting details to describe your activities and point out how your day differs from Ulrika's day.

3. MENTAL MAPPING

Create an outline map of Scandinavia and label the following:

• Denmark   • Sweden
• Finland   • Greenland
• Norway   • Faroe Islands
• Iceland

Western Europe **317**

United Kingdom

 ESSENTIAL QUESTION

How did being an island nation influence the development of the United Kingdom?

CONNECT Geography & History

Use the map and the time line to answer the following questions.

1. What is the capital of the United Kingdom?
2. Under what body of water would a railroad tunnel between England and France run?

8000 B.C.

Geography
 ◄ **8000 B.C.** People begin settling the British Isles.
(rock formation in Cornwall)

Government
 **1689** Parliament passes the English Bill of Rights.

Government
 ◄ **1215** King John signs the Magna Carta.

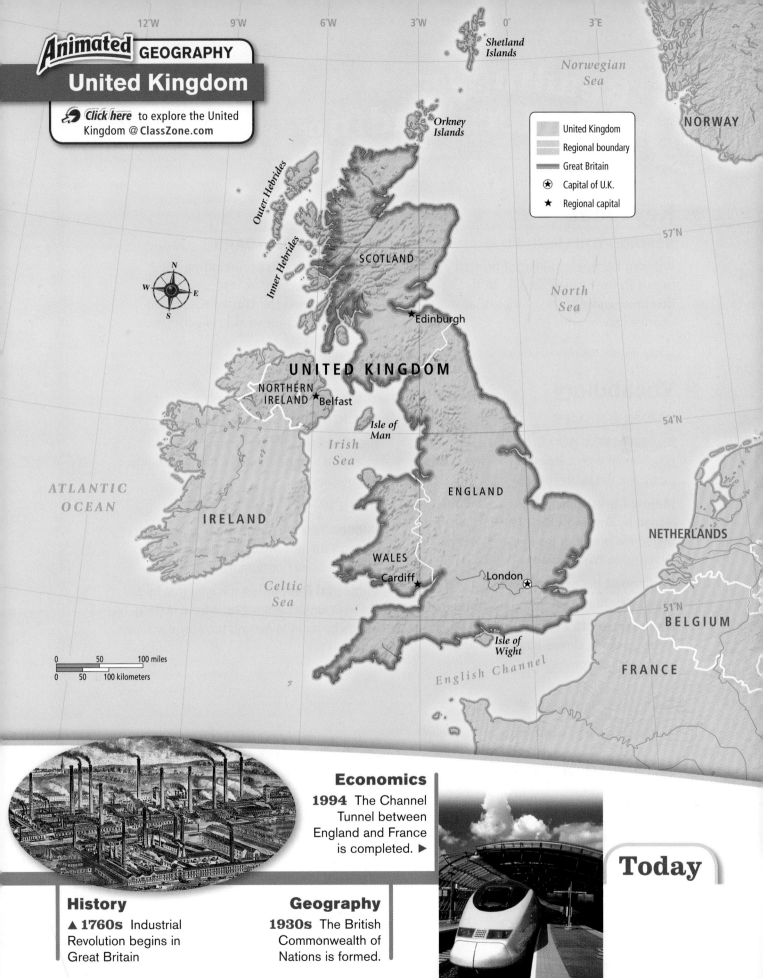

Legend:
- United Kingdom
- Regional boundary
- Great Britain
- ⊛ Capital of U.K.
- ★ Regional capital

NORWAY

Shetland Islands

Norwegian Sea

Orkney Islands

Outer Hebrides

Inner Hebrides

SCOTLAND

★ Edinburgh

North Sea

UNITED KINGDOM

NORTHERN IRELAND ★ Belfast

Isle of Man

Irish Sea

IRELAND

ATLANTIC OCEAN

ENGLAND

WALES

Cardiff ★

London ⊛

Celtic Sea

Isle of Wight

English Channel

NETHERLANDS

BELGIUM

FRANCE

0   50   100 miles
0   50   100 kilometers

Economics
1994 The Channel Tunnel between England and France is completed. ▶

Today

History
▲ **1760s** Industrial Revolution begins in Great Britain

Geography
1930s The British Commonwealth of Nations is formed.

319

Reading for Understanding

▶ Key Ideas

BEFORE, YOU LEARNED

Western Europe's industrial growth began in the United Kingdom. Its inventors caused a revolution that changed the world.

NOW YOU WILL LEARN

Many developments, including the Industrial Revolution and a colonial empire, helped the United Kingdom grow into a major world power.

▶ Vocabulary

TERMS & NAMES

representative government a system of government with a legislature that is at least partly elected by the people

Magna Carta a charter, or document, signed by England's King John in 1215 that limited the power of the monarch and guaranteed nobles basic rights

Parliament the national legislature of the United Kingdom

Commonwealth of Nations an association made up of the United Kingdom and many former British colonies

BACKGROUND VOCABULARY

mainland the primary landmass of a continent or territory rather than its islands or peninsulas

REVIEW

imperialism the policy where one country controls the government and economy of another country or territory

Industrial Revolution the shift that began in Great Britain in the 1760s from making goods by hand to making them by machine

▶ Reading Strategy

Re-create the chart shown at right. As you read and respond to the **KEY QUESTIONS**, use the chart to help you identify the solutions to problems faced by the United Kingdom.

 Skillbuilder Handbook, page R10

IDENTIFY PROBLEMS AND SOLUTIONS

PROBLEMS	SOLUTIONS
Divided Territory	
Monarchy Too Powerful	
Need for Resources	

 GRAPHIC ORGANIZERS
Go to **Interactive Review** @ ClassZone.com

Building a British Empire

9.01 Trace the historical development of governments, including traditional, colonial, and national in selected societies, and assess the effects on the respective contemporary political systems.
10.01 Trace the development of relationships between individuals and their governments in selected cultures of South America and Europe, and evaluate the changes that have evolved over time.

Connecting to Your World

When someone asks you what country you live in, do you say America, the United States, or the U.S.? Our country has many names. So does the United Kingdom. Few use its official name, the United Kingdom of Great Britain and Northern Ireland. Some say the United Kingdom. Some call it Great Britain, the name of the island shared by England, Scotland, and Wales. Others just use Britain. Its different names reflect its history.

Patriotic Teen An American teenager displays one of her country's names.

Creating a United Kingdom

▼ **KEY QUESTION** What aspects of culture did Britain's settlers influence?

Different groups settled the British Isles over time. The Celts, the Romans, Germanic tribes called the Angles and the Saxons, and the Normans from France all inhabited the region. Each contributed to British culture. They shaped its language, government, and customs. By the late 1200s, English kings wanted to bring the British Isles under their control. They conquered Wales and much of Ireland. In 1707, England, Wales, and Scotland united as the Kingdom of Great Britain. Ireland became part of the union in 1801, creating the United Kingdom of Great Britain and Ireland. Ireland split into two parts in 1949, and Northern Ireland stayed in the union.

Stonehenge Early settlers of the British Isles built Stonehenge between about 3100 and 1500 B.C.

[Map showing WALES, ENGLAND, and Stonehenge location]

Although the United Kingdom is a small island group, it has had an influence on world affairs far greater than its size would suggest. At the height of its power, its colonies spanned the globe. As it became a world leader, the United Kingdom's location set it apart from nations on the European **mainland**, allowing it to create a unique identity.

▲ **SUMMARIZE** Explain the aspects of culture that Britain's early settlers influenced.

Influencing the Modern Age

▼ **KEY QUESTION** How did British governmental and economic ideas influence the rest of the world?

British ideas and customs have had a lasting influence on the way people around the world live. The British policy of **imperialism** helped spread new developments, such as representative government and the Industrial Revolution, which still affect political and economic life.

Representative Government In 1215, the kingdom took steps toward **representative government**, a system in which the legislature is at least partly elected by the people. British nobles forced King John to sign the **Magna Carta**. This document outlined nobles' rights and limited the king's powers. British kings gradually acknowledged that they needed the people's support to govern. A group of representatives called **Parliament** was established. Some call King Edward's 1295 Parliament a "model parliament" because it was more representative of British society than earlier versions. Today, several other European governments, such as Greece and Hungary, also have parliaments.

In 1689, the English Bill of Rights strengthened the rights of citizens. This document outlined the relationship between the monarchy and Parliament. In doing so, it limited the power of the monarch and guaranteed basic freedoms to English citizens. It became a model for other nations, including the United States. Many countries have been influenced by British advances in representative government.

Houses of Parliament
This building in London, finished in 1860, contains the chambers where the United Kindom's Parliament meets. **How might the building's exterior show that an important group meets inside?**

English Bill of Rights In 1689, Parliament passed the English Bill of Rights. They presented the document to King William III and Queen Mary, who agreed to uphold it.

> That the . . . suspending of laws, or the execution of laws, by regal authority, without consent of parliament, is illegal . . .
>
> That election of members of parliament ought to be free . . .
>
> And that for redress [remedy] of all grievances, and for the amending, strengthening, and preserving of the laws, parliaments ought to be held frequently.
>
> Source: English Bill of Rights

XXVIII. WILLIAM *the* THIRD *and* MARY *the* SECOND, *from* 1688 *to* 1702.

WILLIAM the hero, with MARIA mild,
(He James's nephew, she his eldest child)
Fix'd freedom and the church, reform'd the coin;
Oppos'd the French, and settled Brunswick's line.

▲ *King William III and Queen Mary with the English Bill of Rights*

DOCUMENT–BASED QUESTION
How did the English Bill of Rights protect English citizens?

The British Empire In the 1500s, Britain joined other European nations in the race to claim overseas colonies in order to gain resources and expand trade networks. By the 1800s, Great Britain used its strong navy to control a prosperous empire. At its height, the empire covered one-fourth of the globe. British colonies included Canada, Australia, New Zealand, Singapore, India, and Pakistan, as well as parts of Africa and the Caribbean. They provided raw materials needed for industrialization and markets for British goods. As British control spread, so did its language and culture.

Commonwealth of Nations This World War II poster shows soldiers from several Commonwealth nations, including India, South Africa, New Zealand, Canada, and Australia.

In the 1920s, several British colonies controlled their internal affairs, but also wanted to manage their foreign policy and defense. In response, the United Kingdom created the **Commonwealth of Nations**, an association of countries that had been part of the British empire. Original members included Australia, Canada, and South Africa. Members of the Commonwealth were independent, but agreed to cooperate in trade and political matters. The British empire still controlled many other territories.

THE BRITISH COMMONWEALTH OF NATIONS

TOGETHER

The Industrial Revolution The **Industrial Revolution** that you read about earlier began in Great Britain in the 1760s. The country's geographic advantages helped make it the world's first industrial nation. Early on, rivers provided power to fuel machines. Rivers and harbors on the Atlantic Ocean offered ways to transport raw materials from British colonies to factories and finished goods to overseas markets. The nation also had ample supplies of coal and iron ore.

By the 1800s, the United Kingdom had become the world's leading industrial power. Although Britain tried to keep its new technology to itself, other nations sought to industrialize. British knowledge spread first to nearby Belgium and France, then to much of the world.

▲ ANALYZE EFFECTS Explain how British governmental and economic ideas influenced the world.

Britain in Today's World

▼ KEY QUESTION How has Great Britain's position in world politics changed?

At the beginning of the 1900s, Great Britain was a major world power. Its leaders governed a prosperous nation and a vast empire. Today, the United Kingdom is no longer the world's richest or most powerful nation. However, it remains a respected world leader.

Fighting Two World Wars The United Kingdom played a major role in two world wars. As you learned earlier, it served as a leader of the Allies in both struggles. The British people showed great courage. During World War II, civilians faced massive German air raids on their cities. British and Commonwealth soldiers fought bravely in Europe, North Africa, and Asia. In stirring radio addresses, Prime Minister Winston Churchill inspired confidence as the British people faced the threat of a German invasion.

The two wars had a devastating effect on the United Kingdom's economy. Bombs had destroyed large parts of London and other cities. When the war ended, Britain had huge debts. All the industry that had been devoted to the war effort had to be converted back to manufacturing consumer goods. It took the British economy years to recover fully.

HISTORY MAKERS

Winston Churchill 1874–1965

A brilliant speaker and enemy of Nazi Germany, Prime Minister Winston Churchill led the United Kingdom during World War II. His stirring speeches on the radio and in the British Parliament rallied the British people. As the British prepared for an expected invasion by Germany, Churchill urged them to show courage and make this "their finest hour." His confidence that democratic government would in the end win out over dictatorships inspired the United Kingdom and its allies to work hard for victory.

 ONLINE BIOGRAPHY
For more on the life of Winston Churchill, go to the
Research & Writing Center @ ClassZone.com

The End of the Empire In the postwar period, many British colonies in Africa and Asia began demanding independence. Great Britain was struggling to recover from the war. Its leaders lacked the time or resources to maintain its colonies. Between 1947 and 1980, about 40 British colonies became independent. Almost all of them joined the Commonwealth of Nations.

Today, the United Kingdom works closely with its former colonies and with other European nations. Its ties to Commonwealth nations have strengthened its role in world affairs. The United Kingdom is also a member of the European Union. However, some British citizens think that their country should be less involved with the rest of Europe, which is a source of tension for the government.

The Struggle for Independence

Colonial Independence This time line shows when some of Great Britain's many colonies achieved their independence from the empire.

India   Ghana   Kenya   The Bahamas

1947   1957   **1962**   1963   **1965**   1973   **1981**

Pakistan   Jamaica   Singapore   Belize

▲ **EVALUATE** Explain how Britain's role in world politics has changed.

Section ① Assessment

ONLINE QUIZ
For test practice, go to
Interactive Review
@ ClassZone.com

TERMS & NAMES

1. Explain the importance of
- Magna Carta
- Parliament
- Commonwealth of Nations

USE YOUR READING NOTES

2. Identify Problems and Solutions
Use your completed chart to answer the following question:

How did the United Kingdom meet its needs for more natural resources?

PROBLEMS	SOLUTIONS
Divided Territory	
Monarchy Too Powerful	
Need for Resources	

KEY IDEAS

3. How did the creation of Parliament change the British monarchy?

4. What were the effects of Industrial Revolution on the way the British lived?

5. What benefits did the Commonwealth of Nations have for British colonies?

CRITICAL THINKING

6. Analyze Causes and Effects Why did the United Kingdom have to give up its colonial empire?

7. Make Inferences How did the British overcome the disadvantages of being an island nation?

8. CONNECT to Today Why might the United Kingdom want to maintain ties with former colonies?

9. ART Design a Memorial Research the experiences of British soldiers or civilians during World War II. Create a design for a war memorial honoring their part in the war.

Click here to enter Victorian London
@ ClassZone.com

LONDON AROUND 1890

London grew rapidly during the 19th century. By 1901, over 6.5 million people lived there. All these people required services, such as transportation and law enforcement. Rapid growth also affected London society as different social classes interacted.

Click here to experience what daily life in Victorian London would have been like. Learn more about the different social classes that shared the city, such as the upper-class residents shown above. See some of the public services needed to keep the city running, including electricity and the London Underground.

Click here to learn more about the economic activities that might have taken place in this important commercial center. Connected to the world by the Thames River, the city attracted all types of businesses, from street stalls to major factories.

COFFEE & TEA

GEORGE JONES

Growth of London

0   2.5   5 miles
0 2.5 5 kilometers

Thames River

- London, 1700
- Growth to 1800
- Growth to 1900
- Greater London, 2007

N

GOODMAN'S DENTISTS

Men's Wear

JAMES BEASLEY & SONS

CITY MANSION HOUSE

NATIONAL & STATION HOTEL

SEAL JACKETS MILLINERY

METROPOLITAN RAILWAY

MOORGATE STREET STATION

McGUINNESS FLINT

JOSEPH KIMICH

ALBERT'S BOOKSHOP

GeoActivity

A Victorian Talk Show
Break into groups of four. One
person will pretend to be someone
from this London street who is
appearing on a talk show. The rest
of the group will interview him
or her. Choose the best question
and answer from your group and
share it with the class.

Reading for Understanding

▶ Key Ideas

BEFORE, YOU LEARNED

Great Britain became an industrial leader with a worldwide empire. Today, it no longer has a great empire, but it remains a respected European power.

NOW YOU WILL LEARN

Britain's history as an industrial and colonial power has shaped its culture. Britain's increasingly diverse population continues to enrich its cultural life.

▶ Vocabulary

TERMS & NAMES

Briton a British person

Gaelic any of the Celtic family of languages spoken in Ireland or Scotland

multicultural relating to or including many different cultures

Church of England the official church of England headed by the Archbishop of Canterbury

William Shakespeare an English playwright and poet during the late 16th and early 17th centuries

REVIEW

immigrant a person who leaves one area to settle in another

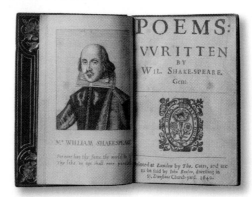

Visual Vocabulary William Shakespeare

▶ Reading Strategy

Re-create the web diagram shown at right. As you read and respond to the **KEY QUESTIONS**, use the diagram to help you find main ideas about British culture.

 Skillbuilder Handbook, page R4

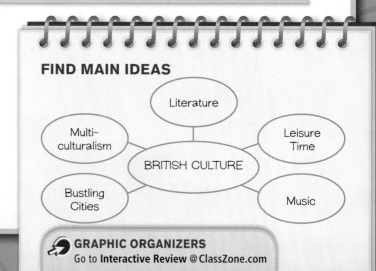

FIND MAIN IDEAS

Literature · Multi-culturalism · BRITISH CULTURE · Leisure Time · Bustling Cities · Music

GRAPHIC ORGANIZERS
Go to **Interactive Review** @ ClassZone.com

From Shakespeare to J.K. Rowling

11.01 Identify the concepts associated with culture such as language, religion, family, and ethnic identity, and analyze how they both link and separate societies.
13.02 Describe the diverse cultural connections that have influenced the development of language, art, music, and belief systems in North Carolina and the United States and assess their role in creating a changing cultural mosaic.

Connecting to Your World

Have you ever read a Harry Potter book? One day in 1990, an idea for a book popped into the head of J. K. Rowling, a British author. She wanted to write about a young boy named Harry who could do magic. Today, millions of people around the world know about this boy. Rowling's Harry Potter books have made publishing history, selling out at bookstores hours after they are put on the shelves. Rowling is just one part of Great Britain's rich cultural heritage.

Harry Potter Fans Like these boys, many fans dress up as their favorite Harry Potter characters.

Life in the United Kingdom

🔻 **KEY QUESTION** What influences have made British culture more diverse in recent years?

Before World War II, most British people shared the same ethnicity and religious beliefs. Today, people of many different faiths and customs make their home in the United Kingdom. Many of them have immigrated from the former colonies of the British empire. The influence of these newcomers can be seen throughout Britain. Although some changes have caused tensions, the mix of old and new traditions is making many British cities lively places to live.

Tower Bridge The Tower Bridge, built in 1894, spans the Thames River near London's modern City Hall, the round building at right.

Bustling Cities For many centuries, Great Britain was a largely rural country. The Industrial Revolution sparked urban growth. Today, nine out of ten **Britons**, or British people, live in cities. London, the capital of the United Kingdom, is by far the largest city, with over 7 million residents. While London is the biggest, the nation has several other major cities. The map below shows the location of Britain's largest cities by population, most of which fall within industrial areas.

By the 1800s, London was already a busy city. Today, it is a multi-level city with a subway system below ground and skyscrapers above. It is a global center of culture and commerce. It also has many tourist attractions that draw millions of visitors each year.

Edinburgh People stroll down a street in Edinburgh, Scotland, during a festival.

10 Biggest Cities in Great Britain

Industrial area

ATLANTIC OCEAN

UNITED KINGDOM

IRELAND

North Sea

Edinburgh
Glasgow
Bradford • Leeds
Liverpool • Manchester
Sheffield
Birmingham
London
Bristol

0   100   200 miles
0   100   200 kilometers

City	Population
London	7,172,036
Birmingham	977,091
Leeds	715,404
Glasgow	629,501
Sheffield	513,234
Bradford	467,668
Liverpool	439,476
Edinburgh	430,082
Manchester	392,819
Bristol	380,615

Sources: National Statistics UK Census 2001 and Scotland Census 2001

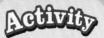

Would you know what to do if someone told you to go find a bobby? If you were British, you would know to look for a police officer, like those shown below. Although British English and American English are similar, some of the words used by Britons are very different—and some can be difficult to translate.

Activity

Translate British to American English

Materials

- flipcards
- pencil
- dictionary

1. Write each of the words listed below on one side of a flipcard: *biscuit, bloke, boot, chemist, jumper, lift, lorry, mate, petrol,* and *zebra crossing*.

2. Think about what each word might mean. Write your guess next to each one.

3. Look up each word in the dictionary. Look for the definition identified as British. Write the definition on the other side of each flipcard.

Multiculturalism Each region in the United Kingdom—England, Scotland, Wales, and Northern Ireland—has its own customs. English is Great Britain's official language. In Scotland and Ireland, however, some speak **Gaelic**, the language brought to the British Isles by the Celtic people. In Wales, about one-fifth of the population speaks Welsh, another Celtic language.

Over the years, the United Kingdom has welcomed **immigrants** from around the world. After World War II, the nation saw an increase in immigration from former colonies in South Asia, Africa, and the Caribbean. Today, about one in ten people in Britain is an immigrant. These newcomers have added variety to British culture and influenced tastes in food and music. They have made the United Kingdom one of the most **multicultural** countries in the world, meaning that it includes many cultures. This has also caused tensions, however, as diverse customs and viewpoints occasionally clash.

Immigration has also had an impact on religion in the United Kingdom. Many Britons belong to the **Church of England**. As the nation's official church, it combines both Catholic and Protestant traditions. In Northern Ireland, about two-fifths of the population are Roman Catholics. However, Great Britain also has many religious minorities, such as Hindus, Muslims, and Sikhs. Their faiths are reflected in the temples and mosques found in many British cities.

▲ **EVALUATE** Explain why British culture has become more diverse.

Fun Facts!

CHICKEN TIKKA MASALA

At one time fish and chips was England's favorite dish, but no more. Now Britons prefer an Indian-influenced dish called chicken tikka masala. The dish is an Indian meal called chicken tikka, to which the Britons have added a masala sauce to satisfy their love of gravy. The new creation is a true combination of British and Indian culture.

A Rich Cultural Heritage

▼ **KEY QUESTION** What cultural achievements is Britain known for?

Many of the United Kingdom's most treasured exports don't come from factories. Literature, music, and popular culture make up a rich cultural heritage. With its history as an imperial power, the nation has been exporting its culture around the world for centuries.

Literature Many consider English playwright and poet **William Shakespeare** the finest writer of all time. His plays have entertained audiences for over 400 years. In 1997, a replica of the Globe Theatre—where Shakespeare's plays were originally performed—opened in London, introducing a new generation of Britons to his work.

Many talented authors followed Shakespeare. Jane Austen wrote about British life in the late 1700s and early 1800s in such books as *Pride and Prejudice*. In books such as *Oliver Twist* and *A Christmas Carol*, Charles Dickens explored Britain's social problems. Modern British authors have written many stories for young people. C. S. Lewis crafted fantastic tales in the *Chronicles of Narnia*. J. R. R. Tolkien created the magical world of the *Lord of the Rings* series. Most recently, J. K. Rowling's young wizard Harry Potter has charmed readers of all ages.

Leisure Time Many Britons are sports fans. Soccer, known as football in Europe, is the nation's favorite sport. The modern form of the game played worldwide is thought to have originated in England.

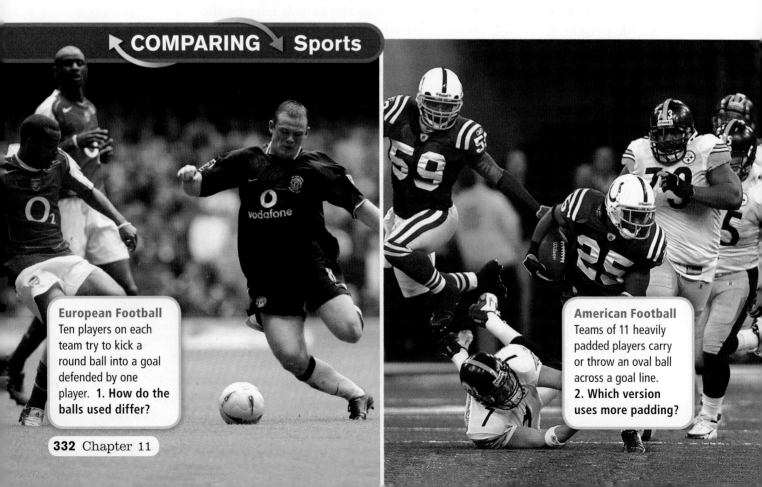

COMPARING Sports

European Football
Ten players on each team try to kick a round ball into a goal defended by one player. **1. How do the balls used differ?**

American Football
Teams of 11 heavily padded players carry or throw an oval ball across a goal line. **2. Which version uses more padding?**

Two other games invented in Britain have become popular in its former colonies. Cricket is played with a bat and a ball. Teams from the United Kingdom and other Commonwealth nations such as India and Pakistan often compete in international games. Rugby, a sport like football, is popular in Australia and South Africa.

The United Kingdom has also produced some well-known films and television shows that have been exported around the world. One British reality television program, *Pop Idol*, allowed viewers to vote for their favorite singers each week. The show was an instant success. Versions of it spread to over 30 countries, including the United States.

Music In the 1960s, the United States faced an unusual kind of invasion, not by soldiers but by music. American teenagers went crazy for British rock 'n' roll. Mobs of screaming fans greeted "British Invasion" bands like the Beatles and the Rolling Stones wherever they performed. Since then, many other British bands, such as Coldplay, have gained popularity with Americans.

Playing Cricket Some Pakistani Muslim boys use a traffic cone to play cricket on a London street.

 SUMMARIZE Describe British cultural achievements that have had a global impact.

ONLINE QUIZ
For test practice, go to **Interactive Review** @ ClassZone.com

Section 2 Assessment

TERMS & NAMES

1. Explain the importance of
- Briton
- Gaelic
- multicultural
- Church of England

USE YOUR READING NOTES

2. Find Main Ideas Use your completed web diagram to answer the following question:

What British authors have written books for young people?

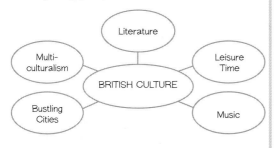

KEY IDEAS

3. In addition to English, what other languages are spoken in the United Kingdom?

4. How have immigrants changed British culture?

5. What early writer helped make the United Kingdom well known for its literary achievements?

CRITICAL THINKING

6. Draw Conclusions How did British sports become popular in countries like India and Australia?

7. Form and Support Opinions What are the advantages of having a diverse British population?

8. CONNECT to Today What challenges might the United Kingdom face if the diversity of its population continues to grow?

9. WRITING Create a Brochure In 2012, London will host the Summer Olympic Games. Use a word processor to create a brochure telling Americans why they should come to London for the 2012 Olympics. Find a picture to illustrate your brochure.

United Kingdom **333**

Reading for Understanding

▶ Key Ideas

BEFORE, YOU LEARNED

British culture is changing as the population becomes more diverse.

NOW YOU WILL LEARN

The United Kingdom's government is a constitutional monarchy. Its economy is strong and adapts to global changes.

▶ Vocabulary

TERMS & NAMES

constitutional monarchy a government in which the powers of the king or queen are limited by a constitution

unwritten constitution a framework for government that is not a single written document but includes many different laws, court decisions, and political customs

devolution the process of shifting some power from national to regional government

Good Friday Agreement an agreement between Northern Ireland's unionists and nationalists that set up a new government

wind farm a power plant that uses windmills to generate electricity

Channel Tunnel the underwater railroad tunnel between France and England under the English Channel

Visual Vocabulary wind farm

▶ Reading Strategy

Re-create the web diagram shown at right. As you read and respond to the **KEY QUESTIONS**, use the web diagram to help you summarize information about the government and economy of the United Kingdom.

 Skillbuilder Handbook, page R5

SUMMARIZE

```
┌──────────────┐        ┌──────────────┐
│  GOVERNMENT  │        │   ECONOMY    │
└──────────────┘        └──────────────┘
   ┌────┐ ┌────┐          ┌────┐ ┌────┐
   │    │ │    │          │    │ │    │
   └────┘ └────┘          └────┘ └────┘
```

GRAPHIC ORGANIZERS
Go to **Interactive Review** @ ClassZone.com

Parliament and Free Enterprise

9.02 Describe how different types of governments such as democracies, dictatorships, monarchies, and oligarchies in selected areas of South America and Europe carry out legislative, executive, and judicial functions, and evaluate the effectiveness of each.

11.04 Identify examples of economic, political, and social changes, such as agrarian to industrial economies, monarchical to democratic governments, and the roles of women and minorities, and analyze their impact on culture.

Connecting to Your World

Most Americans know that the United Kingdom has a monarch, Queen Elizabeth II. You may have seen pictures of her, her son Prince Charles, or her grandsons Prince William and Prince Harry. While most Americans have heard of Queen Elizabeth II, many aren't sure exactly what role she plays in British political life. Does she help govern Britain? Does she control the nation's foreign policy or manage its economy? Keep reading to learn more about how the British government works and how monarchs and elected leaders fit into it.

Queen and Parliament

🔻 **KEY QUESTION** How are the regions of the United Kingdom governed?

The British sovereign, or monarch, serves as an important symbol of the British nation, but not as the leader of the government. Elected leaders govern the country. The sovereign is not above the law, and he or she rules and acts with Parliament's approval. The king or queen performs mostly ceremonial duties, which can include attending formal dinners or appointing ambassadors to other countries.

The Royal Family Queen Elizabeth II (above) with her grandsons, William and Harry. The queen uses this gold coach (below) for special occasions, such as a parade celebrating her reign.

Constitutional Monarchy The United Kingdom is a **constitutional monarchy**, in which the monarch's power is limited by a constitution. Unlike most countries, it has an **unwritten constitution** made up of laws, court decisions, and political customs. Parliament, the United Kingdom's legislature, can change it as needed.

Parliament is made up of two houses and the sovereign. Members of the House of Lords are mostly appointed. This house has little real power. The House of Commons, the key lawmaking body, consists of elected officials. Usually, the leader of the party with the most seats in the House of Commons becomes prime minister. The prime minister heads the executive branch of the government. He or she governs with the support of the Cabinet. Tony Blair served as prime minister until 2007, when he was replaced by Gordon Brown.

Regional Governments All four regions of the United Kingdom—England, Wales, Scotland, and Northern Ireland—are represented in Parliament. In the late 1990s, Parliament shifted some power from the national level to regional governments, a process called **devolution**. Scotland and Wales set up parliaments. They took over their domestic affairs, while Parliament kept charge of foreign policy and defense.

◀ COMPARING ▶ U.S. and British Governments

U.S. GOVERNMENT
U.S. citizens elect representatives and the President for the national government.

BRITISH GOVERNMENT
British citizens elect members of the House of Commons. The Prime Minister is the leader of the majority party.

CITIZENS

elect

CONGRESS

PRESIDENT

CITIZENS

elect

leader of majority party becomes

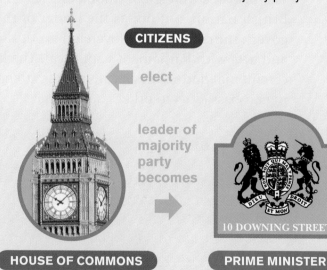

10 DOWNING STREET

HOUSE OF COMMONS

PRIME MINISTER

CRITICAL THINKING
Compare and Contrast Where do citizens more directly choose their leader?

Establishing a government in Northern Ireland has been more difficult. The English first expanded into Ireland in the 1100s. The Irish, who had their own culture, bitterly resented the English. In 1949, the southern part of Ireland became the Republic of Ireland. Since the 1920s, Northern Ireland has been divided by conflict between two groups. The nationalists, who are mostly Catholic, believe Northern Ireland should unite with the Republic of Ireland. The unionists, mainly Protestants, want to stay part of the United Kingdom. In 1998, both sides signed the **Good Friday Agreement**, which set up a new government. In 2002, however, renewed violence led to the government's shutdown. Recent efforts toward self-government have failed, but violence between the two sides has decreased and talks continue.

▲ **SUMMARIZE** Explain how the United Kingdom governs its regions.

The British Economy

▼ **KEY QUESTION** How has the United Kingdom's economy changed?

Today, the United Kingdom is a densely populated urban nation. Cities cover most areas that were once farmland. The country also lost its empire, which had boosted its economy. These changes have forced it to adapt.

A Powerful Economy For decades, manufacturing formed the basis of Great Britain's economy. It was fueled by natural resources such as iron ore, coal, and oil deposits in the North Sea. As these resources are depleted, British scientists have begun looking for sustainable energy sources, including wind energy. The map at right shows Britain's development of **wind farms**, power plants that use windmills to generate electricity.

At one time, Great Britain was known for its textile and steel industries. While it remains a leader in the production of textiles, chemicals, and motor vehicles, it has fewer manufacturing jobs than before. Over three-fourths of Britain's labor force now works in service industries. The nation is a world leader in insurance and financial services. London's banks and stock exchange have made it one of Europe's leading business centers.

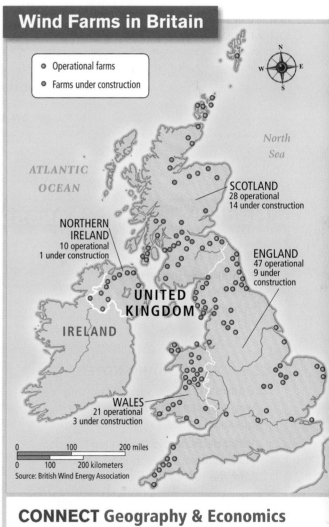

Wind Farms in Britain

- Operational farms
- Farms under construction

ATLANTIC OCEAN

North Sea

SCOTLAND
28 operational
14 under construction

NORTHERN IRELAND
10 operational
1 under construction

ENGLAND
47 operational
9 under construction

UNITED KINGDOM

IRELAND

WALES
21 operational
3 under construction

0   100   200 miles
0   100   200 kilometers
Source: British Wind Energy Association

CONNECT Geography & Economics

1. **Human-Environment Interaction** Are more wind farms located inland or near the coast?
2. **Region** Which of the four regions has the most wind farms under construction?

The Channel Tunnel Trains like this one, operated by a company called Eurotunnel, shuttle passengers and freight through the Channel Tunnel. In June 2006, the 100 millionth passenger traveled on the train.

Participating in the Global Economy Winston Churchill once said of Great Britain, "We are with Europe but not of it." In some ways the nation still stands apart. In 2002, most European Union members agreed to replace their own currency with the euro. Britain chose to continue using its national currency, the pound.

In most other ways, however, the United Kingdom is now closely tied to Europe through participation in the European Union and trade with industrial and developing nations. The nation has a trillion-dollar economy. Because of its prosperity, it can trade with other countries. It has goods and services that other nations want. Most of the United Kingdom's trade is with other EU members.

Technology has also drawn the United Kingdom closer to its neighbors in Europe. In 1994, British and French workers completed construction of the 31-mile undersea **Channel Tunnel**. The tunnel links Britain to France by train. Every day, an average of 45,000 people make the 35-minute journey to the European mainland.

 ANALYZE EFFECTS Explain how the United Kingdom's economy has changed.

 **ONLINE QUIZ**
For test practice, go to
Interactive Review
@ ClassZone.com

Section 3 Assessment

TERMS & NAMES

1. Explain the importance of
- constitutional monarchy
- unwritten constitution
- Good Friday Agreement
- Channel Tunnel

USE YOUR READING NOTES

2. Summarize Use your completed web diagram to answer the following question:

What decision did the United Kingdom make that kept its economy separate from the rest of the European Union?

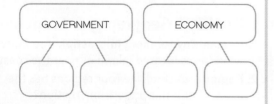

KEY IDEAS

3. Why is the United Kingdom said to have an unwritten constitution?

4. What are the roles of the monarch, prime minister, and Parliament within the British government?

5. What are the United Kingdom's most important service industries?

CRITICAL THINKING

6. Compare and Contrast How are the British Parliament and the U.S. Congress alike and different?

7. Analyze Causes and Effects Why might a long history of conflict make it hard for Northern Ireland to set up a workable government?

8. CONNECT to Today How might London's growing cultural diversity help it expand its global financial and business services?

9. WRITING Write a Report Choose a major British industry to research. Write a paragraph explaining why it is important to the United Kingdom's economy.

Interactive ← Review

Click here to complete these and other activities online @ ClassZone.com

CHAPTER SUMMARY

Key Idea 1
Many developments, including the Industrial Revolution and a colonial empire, helped the United Kingdom grow into a major world power.

Key Idea 2
Britain's long history as an industrial and colonial power has shaped its culture. Britain's increasingly diverse population continues to enrich its cultural life.

Key Idea 3
The United Kingdom's government is a constitutional monarchy. Its economy is strong and adapts to global changes.

 For **Review and Study Notes**, go to **Interactive Review** @ ClassZone.com

NAME GAME

Use the Terms & Names list to complete each sentence on paper or online.

1. I am a famous English playwright.
   __William Shakespeare__

2. I connect Britain with France by rail.
   _____

3. I am the United Kingdom's official church.
   _____

4. I am a British person. _____

5. I am a government in which the powers of the king and queen are limited by a constitution.
   _____

6. I am a document written in 1215 that limited the power of the English monarch. _____

7. I am the language spoken by some people in Scotland and Ireland along with English.
   _____

8. I am the process of shifting power from national to regional government. _____

9. I am the legislative branch of the British government. _____

10. I am the organization made up of former British colonies. _____

Briton
Channel Tunnel
Church of England
Commonwealth of Nations
constitutional monarchy
devolution
Gaelic
Good Friday Agreement
imperialism
Magna Carta
multicultural
Parliament
unwritten constitution
William Shakespeare

Activities

GeoGame

Use this online map to reinforce your understanding of the United Kingdom. Drag and drop each place name in the list to its location on the map.

To play the complete game, go to **Interactive Review** @ ClassZone.com

Crossword Puzzle

Complete an online crossword puzzle to test your knowledge of the United Kingdom.

ACROSS
1. a power plant that uses windmills to generate electricity

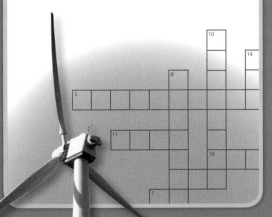

VOCABULARY

Explain the significance of each of the following.

1. Parliament
2. multicultural
3. Church of England
4. William Shakespeare
5. unwritten constitution
6. Good Friday Agreement

Match the item on the left with its description on the right.

7. Magna Carta	A. spoken in Scotland and Ireland
8. Gaelic	B. limited the power of the monarchy
9. Briton	C. connects Britain to France underwater
10. devolution	D. a British person
11. Channel Tunnel	E. shifting power from national to regional government

KEY IDEAS

1 Building a British Empire

12. What four regions make up the United Kingdom?
13. How did Great Britain benefit from its empire?
14. What geographic factors led to the start of the Industrial Revolution in Great Britain?
15. Why did Great Britain's standing as a world power change after World War II?

2 From Shakespeare to Harry Potter

16. What is Great Britain's largest city?
17. What languages are spoken in Wales, Ireland, and Scotland besides English?
18. How did Shakespeare contribute to British culture?
19. In what areas has British culture influenced popular culture in the United States in recent decades?

3 Parliament and Free Enterprise

20. What has the United Kingdom done to give more self-government to the regions of Scotland, Wales, and Northern Ireland?
21. Which part of the United Kingdom's economy is expanding, and which has become smaller?
22. How does the United Kingdom participate in the global economy?

CRITICAL THINKING

23. **Draw Conclusions** Create a diagram and include two factors that led to British industrial growth.

British Industrial Growth

24. **Five Themes: Movement** How did the Industrial Revolution contribute to the urbanization of the United Kingdom?
25. **Connect Geography & Culture** How do sports keep Great Britain tied to its former colonies?
26. **Compare and Contrast** How does the selection of the British prime minister differ from that of the U.S. president?
27. **Connect to Economics** What effect might a decline in North Sea oil have on the United Kingdom's economy?
28. **Draw Conclusions** How is Britain's role in the global economy different today from its role during the height of the British Empire?

Answer the ESSENTIAL QUESTION

How did being an island nation influence the development of the United Kingdom?

Written Response Write a two- or three-paragraph response to the Essential Question. Be sure to consider the key ideas of each section as well as specific ideas about the United Kingdom. Use the rubric below to guide your thinking.

Response Rubric

A strong response will:

• discuss how Britain's location, waterways, and natural resources influenced its development
• explain why Britain needed to look beyond its island home for resources and how it met this need through empire building and trade

✔ **Test Practice**

• Online Test Practice @ ClassZone.com
• Test-Taking Strategies and Practice at the front of this book

THEMATIC MAP

Use the map below to answer questions 1 and 2 on your paper.

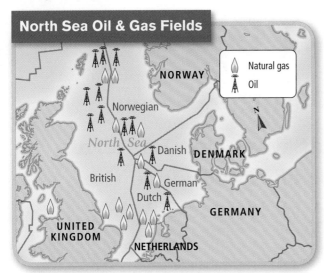

North Sea Oil & Gas Fields

△ Natural gas
⚱ Oil

NORWAY

Norwegian

North Sea

Danish DENMARK

British

German

Dutch

GERMANY

UNITED KINGDOM

NETHERLANDS

1. The map above shows sectors of natural gas and oil fields in the North Sea. Which sector has the fewest oil fields?

A. Norwegian Sector

B. German Sector

C. British Sector

D. Dutch Sector

2. How many oil fields are shown in the British Sector of the North Sea?

A. four   **C.** nine

B. seven   **D.** ten

LINE GRAPH

Examine the graph below. Use the graph to answer questions 3 and 4 on your paper.

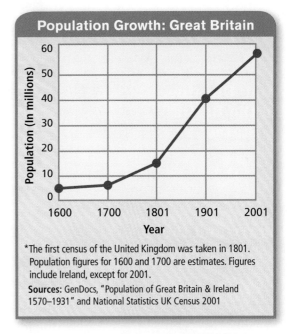

Population Growth: Great Britain

Population (In millions)

60
50
40
30
20
10
0

1600   1700   1801   1901   2001

Year

*The first census of the United Kingdom was taken in 1801. Population figures for 1600 and 1700 are estimates. Figures include Ireland, except for 2001.

Sources: GenDocs, "Population of Great Britain & Ireland 1570–1931" and National Statistics UK Census 2001

3. When did Great Britain experience the greatest population growth?

A. 1600s   **C.** 1800s

B. 1700s   **D.** 1900s

4. What was the British population in 1901?

A. 416,000   **C.** 16.3 million

B. 4.8 million   **D.** 41.6 million

GeoActivity

1. INTERDISCIPLINARY ACTIVITY–LANGUAGE ARTS

Review the section on British literature. Pick one writer in this section. Find a short excerpt from one of his or her works to read aloud to the class. Introduce your choice and provide some information about the writer.

2. WRITING FOR SOCIAL STUDIES

Reread the part of Section 2 on British culture. Pick three things described in this section and write a paragraph on each explaining how they are similar to and different from your own culture.

3. MENTAL MAPPING

Create an outline map of the United Kingdom and label the following:

• England
• Scotland
• Wales
• Northern Ireland
• London
• English Channel
• Atlantic Ocean

12

Eastern Europe

ESSENTIAL QUESTION

In what ways has Eastern Europe changed since the end of World War II?

① **FOCUS ON**

Poland, Ukraine, and the Baltic States

② **FOCUS ON**

Hungary and the Czech Republic

③ **FOCUS ON**

The Balkans

CONNECT ➤ Geography & History

Use the map and the time line to answer the following questions.

1. What four Eastern European countries border the Baltic Sea?

2. What city in the Ukraine still carries the name of an early Slavic state?

800

Geography
800s Kievan Rus, the first eastern Slavic state, is established.

Government
◄ **970** Magyar leaders establish a stable kingdom in Hungary. (Magyar artifact)

History
1918 Yugoslavia is formed at the end of World War I. (King Peter I) ►

NORWAY
SWEDEN
FINLAND
20°E
30°E
DENMARK
Baltic Sea
RUSSIA
ESTONIA ★ Tallinn
★ Riga LATVIA
LITHUANIA
Vilnius ★
RUSSIA
Minsk ●
BELARUS
NETHERLANDS
BELGIUM
GERMANY
LUXEMBOURG
POLAND
Warsaw ★
Łódź ●
Oder River
Vistula River
Chernobyl ●
Kiev ★
Kharkiv ●
50°N
Prague ★
CZECH REPUBLIC
Kraków ●
SLOVAKIA
Bratislava ★
UKRAINE
Dnieper River
Dnipropetrovsk ●
Donetsk ●
Dniester River
SWITZERLAND
AUSTRIA
Budapest ★
HUNGARY
MOLDOVA
Chişinău ★
SLOVENIA
Ljubljana ★
Zagreb ★
CROATIA
Odessa ●
BOSNIA AND HERZEGOVINA
Belgrade ★
ROMANIA
Bucharest ★
Danube River
Black Sea
Sarajevo ●
SERBIA
ITALY
Adriatic Sea
MONTENEGRO
Podgorica ●
BULGARIA
Sofia ●
★ National capital
● Other city
Skopje ★
Tiranë ●
MACEDONIA
ALBANIA
GREECE
Aegean Sea
TURKEY
40°N

0   200   400 miles
0   200   400 kilometers

History
1940s Communists gain power in Eastern Europe. (Josip Broz Tito) ▼

Economics
2004 The first Eastern European nations—the Czech Republic, Hungary, Poland, Slovenia, and the Baltic states—join the EU.

Geography
1986 Chernobyl nuclear disaster in Ukraine ▶

Today

DANGER
НЕБЕЗПЕКА

Reading for Understanding

▶ Key Ideas

BEFORE, YOU LEARNED

European nations experienced many changes after World War II.

NOW YOU WILL LEARN

Poland, Ukraine, and the Baltic States faced many challenges after shaking off Communist rule.

▶ Vocabulary

TERMS & NAMES

Baltic States Latvia, Lithuania, and Estonia, three countries that border the Baltic Sea

Lech Walesa (lehk wah•LEHN•suh) Polish leader who cofounded Solidarity and served as president of Poland from 1990 to 1995

Solidarity Poland's first independent labor union, cofounded by Lech Walesa

Russification the effort to make countries occupied by the Soviet Union more Russian by replacing local languages and customs

bread basket an abundant grain-producing region

deport to expel from a country

BACKGROUND VOCABULARY

brain drain the loss of skilled workers who move in search of better opportunities

REVIEW

communism a type of government in which the Communist Party holds all political power and controls the economy

command economy an economic system in which the production of goods and services is decided by a central government

market economy an economic system in which the production of goods and services is decided by the supply of goods and the demand of consumers

▶ Reading Strategy

Re-create the chart shown at right. As you read and respond to the **KEY QUESTIONS**, use the chart to help you categorize information about the Eastern European nations in this chapter.

 Skillbuilder Handbook, page R7

CATEGORIZE

	LANGUAGE	GOVERNMENT	ECONOMY
Poland			
Ukraine			
Latvia			
Lithuania			
Estonia			

 GRAPHIC ORGANIZERS
Go to **Interactive Review** @ ClassZone.com

Poland, Ukraine, and the Baltic States

1.03 Use tools such as maps, globes, graphs, charts, databases, models, and artifacts to compare data on different countries of South America and Europe and to identify patterns as well as similarities and differences among them.

7.02 Examine the causes of key historical events in selected areas of South America and Europe and analyze the short- and long-range effects on political, economic, and social institutions.

Connecting to Your World

After the American Revolution, Americans quickly learned that building a strong independent nation was not easy. It took time to create a stable government and prosperous economy. In this section, you will read about Poland, Ukraine, and the three **Baltic States**, Latvia, Lithuania, and Estonia. Along with the rest of Eastern Europe, they gained independence from **communism** in the 1990s. Like the United States, they faced difficult choices. Many countries found the new freedom challenging.

Poland

▼ **KEY QUESTION** What actions did government leaders take to prepare Poland for a market economy?

Poland's name comes from the Slavic word *Polanie*, which means plain or field. The Northern European Plain covers much of Poland. Its flat, fertile land began attracting Slavic settlers as early as 2000 B.C. During the Middle Ages, Poland ruled an empire that covered much of central and eastern Europe. By the late 18th century, however, Poland was conquered by its neighbors. It did not regain its independence until after World War I.

Polish Countryside
Freshly plowed fields cover these gently rolling hills in the Roztocze region of southeast Poland.

POLAND
Roztocze

History During World War II, both Germany and the Soviet Union, a union of Communist republics led by Russia, invaded Poland. At the end of the war, Soviet troops drove the Germans out of Poland and supported Communists in gaining control of the government. By the 1950s, Communist rule was firmly established in Poland and throughout Eastern Europe. Communist leaders took over the economy and limited the rights of citizens.

During the 1970s, Poland faced food shortages and rising prices. As economic conditions worsened, people questioned Communist rule. In 1980, thousands of Polish workers went on strike, led by **Lech Walesa** (lehk wah•LEHN•suh). They demanded better pay, greater political freedom, and recognition of **Solidarity**, the nation's first independent labor union. Communist leaders saw public support for Solidarity growing. In 1989, they reached an agreement with Solidarity that led to government reform. Poland held its first free elections. The new government lifted many restrictions on Polish citizens.

Culture Before World War II, Poland was a diverse nation, with Germans, Jews, Ukrainians, and other ethnic groups. However, the war caused many groups to migrate and shifted Poland's borders. Almost all of the 3 million Jews living in Poland were killed during the Holocaust. Today, most people in Poland are Poles. Their ancestors belonged to the Slavic tribes that settled in Poland long ago. Polish, a Slavic language, is spoken throughout the country.

Catholic Mourners
People gather in Pilsudski Square in Warsaw, Poland, to mourn the death of Pope John Paul II.

Most Poles are Roman Catholics, which unites the Polish people. During Communist rule, when religious practice was restricted, many continued to practice the Catholic faith. In 1978, Cardinal Karol Wojtyla (voy•TIH•wah) became the world's first Polish pope, Pope John Paul II. He made Catholic Poles very proud. In visits to Poland, he encouraged efforts to gain greater freedom.

Poland has a rich cultural tradition, with a strong emphasis on education. Many outstanding scientists, such as Nicolaus Copernicus and Marie Curie, were Polish. Like other nations, Poland has to work hard to preserve its folk culture in the face of mass media and urbanization.

Government and Economics In 1990, Lech Walesa became Poland's first president. He helped Poland shift to democracy. In 1997, Poland adopted a new constitution to reflect its democratic government. Today, Poland is a republic. Voters elect the nation's president and legislature. The prime minister runs the government.

In the 1990s, Poland's leaders enacted a series of economic reforms to pave the way from a **command economy** to a **market economy**. Polish leaders sold government-owned industries to private companies. They shut down many old and inefficient factories and invited foreign companies to invest in Poland. Today, the country's major industries include production of coal, iron, steel, and machinery. Poland also has a large shipbuilding industry. Poland joined the European Union in 2004. Membership gave it new markets for such farm products as potatoes and rye and for manufactured goods.

Although Poland's transition to a market economy was more successful than that of many Eastern European nations, it still faces many economic challenges. High unemployment remains a serious problem. Factory closings have left many workers without jobs. Lack of good jobs for skilled workers has caused a serious **brain drain**, as many of Poland's bright young people leave the country in search of better job opportunities in Western Europe or the United States.

🔺 **SUMMARIZE** Explain how Poland became a market economy.

➔ **ONLINE PRIMARY SOURCE** To read the rest of Walesa's speech, go to the **Research & Writing Center** @ClassZone.com

ANALYZING Primary Sources

Lech Walesa (born 1943) led the struggle to form Solidarity. His peaceful resistance helped end Communist rule in Poland.

> We respect the dignity and the rights of every man and every nation. The path to a brighter future of the world leads through honest reconciliation [resolution] of the conflicting interests and not through hatred and bloodshed.
>
> Source: Lech Walesa, Nobel Peace Prize acceptance speech, 1983

DOCUMENT-BASED QUESTION
How does Walesa suggest conflicts among nations should be settled?

347

UKRAINE

Ukraine

▼ **KEY QUESTION** How did Soviet control affect the economy and culture of Ukraine?

For Ukraine, once a part of the Soviet Union, independence has not been easy. Nearby Russia still plays a part in its political and economic life. Ukraine faces many challenges as it seeks ties with the West while maintaining good relations with Russia.

History In the 800s, the town of Kiev in Ukraine was the center of the first eastern Slavic state, Kievan Rus. After 400 years as a powerful state, invading nomads conquered the territory. Ukraine came under foreign rule for centuries. By the late 1700s, it was part of the Russian Empire. In 1922, Ukraine became one of the first Soviet republics.

Soviet policies caused great hardships for the nation. In the 1930s, the Soviets took land from Ukrainian farmers to form huge, government-run farms called collectives. They required almost all crops to be sent to cities to feed the workers there. Millions of farm families starved. On April 26, 1986, the world's worst nuclear power accident occurred in Ukraine at the Chernobyl power plant. Radiation from Chernobyl has affected an estimated 7 million people in and around Ukraine.

Ukrainians had been protesting Soviet rule since the 1960s. When the Soviet Union collapsed in 1991, Ukraine finally gained its independence and began to rebuild.

CONNECT to Science

The Chernobyl explosion put large amounts of radiation into the atmosphere. The chart below shows the radiation released by a form of radioactive iodine during the week after the accident. The petabecquerel, or PBq, is a measure of radioactivity. For reference, a household smoke detector, which is very safe, emits 0.00000000003 PBq of radiation.

Date of Release	Amount (in PBq)
April 26	704
April 27	204
April 28	150
April 29	102
April 30	69
May 1	62
May 2	102

Source: Nuclear Energy Agency, "Chernobyl: Assessment of Radiological and Health Impacts"

◀ *radiation inspectors*

Activity

Make a Line Graph

Materials
• Graph paper
• Markers

1. Draw two lines for your graph. Label the vertical axis "Level of Radiation" and the horizontal axis "Date of Radiation Release."

2. Divide the horizontal axis into ten segments and label each. Divide the vertical axis into units of 100. Put a dot on the graph that represents the radiation measured for each date. Connect the dots. Title your line graph.

Culture About three-fourths of Ukraine's population is ethnic Ukrainian. Russians are the largest ethnic minority, at about one-fifth of the population. Under Soviet rule, the government imposed a **Russification** policy on the country. The Russian language replaced Ukrainian in schools, newspapers, and the government. After decades of speaking Russian, many Ukrainians knew it better than their native language. In 1991, Ukrainian became the official language, but Russian is still widely spoken.

About two-thirds of Ukrainians live in Kiev and other cities. Western Ukraine is heavily rural. Most people in rural areas live in large villages. They are employed in farming or in making small handicrafts, such as the traditional decorated eggs known as *pysanky*.

Government and Economics In 1990, Ukraine held its first free, multiparty election. Today, Ukraine is a democracy with a president, prime minister, and legislature. Ukrainians are committed to free elections. In 2004, tens of thousands of them took part in the Orange Revolution, a peaceful protest against fraud in the presidential election.

Ukrainians remain divided on plans for reform. Some favor closer ties to Russia. Others hope for EU membership and trade with Western Europe. Ukraine maintains good relations with Russia, whom it depends on for oil and natural gas. Ukraine belongs to the Commonwealth of Independent States (CIS), a group of former Soviet republics that cooperate on political and economic matters.

Ukraine is rich in natural resources and fertile soil. Most heavy industries are in eastern Ukraine near the nation's coal deposits. Ukraine's rich soil has made it the **bread basket**, or major grain-producing region, of Europe. However, Ukraine has lagged behind many former Communist countries in converting to private ownership. Many farms and factories also lack modern equipment.

▲ **ANALYZE EFFECTS**
Identify how Soviet control affected Ukraine's economy and culture.

CONNECT ⟶ **History & Culture**

Pysanky

Beautifully decorated Easter eggs known as *pysanky* are among the most famous Ukrainian crafts. The word *pysanky* means "written egg." Artists create intricate and colorful designs by drawing patterns on the eggs with wax and then dipping them in different-colored dyes. The wax prevents parts of the egg from picking up color. Many of the images and colors on the egg have special meaning. Designs are often passed down within a family for generations. The eggs are given as gifts during the Easter holiday.

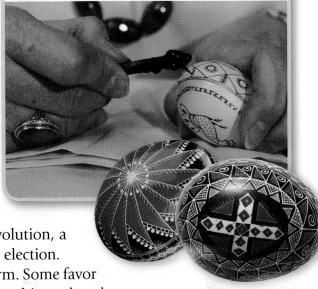

Ukrainian Farm
Farmers harvest wheat on a collective farm near Lvov, Ukraine. **How does equipment affect farm production?**

The Baltic States

▼ **KEY QUESTION** How are the Baltic States alike and different from each other?

The Baltic States—Estonia, Latvia, and Lithuania—share a coastline on the Baltic Sea. They also share the challenge of becoming part of prosperous, modern Europe.

Striving for Independence The Baltic States have a long history of foreign rule. At different times, Danes, Swedes, Poles, and Germans have controlled them. By the late 1700s, they belonged to the vast Russian Empire. They remained a part of it until it ended in 1918. In 1940, the Soviet Union occupied the Baltic States and forced them to join it. In all three countries, the Soviets decided to **deport**, or expel, the thousands of people who resisted their rule. The Soviets brought in Russian workers to replace them. In 1990, the Baltic States became the first Soviet republics to declare independence. The Soviet Union formally recognized their claims in September 1991.

Culture Although they share a common history, each Baltic state has its own language and customs. In Lithuania, most people speak Lithuanian and are Roman Catholics. The people of Latvia speak Latvian, while Estonians speak Estonian, a language related to Finnish. Most Estonians and Latvians are Lutheran Protestants.

Throughout the Baltic States, the Soviet policy of Russification brought population changes. For instance, before Soviet rule, Latvians made up three-fourths of that country's population. Now they make up just over half. In each country, Russians are the largest minority. During the Soviet era, many people left farms and villages to work in urban factories. Today, two-thirds of the people in the Baltic States live in cities. The people of Latvia, Lithuania, and Estonia have had to work to preserve their own languages, customs, and traditions.

Song Festival These girls are dressed up to participate in the All-Estonian Song Festival, held every five years in the capital city of Tallinn.

Government and Economics The Baltic States are republics with an elected president and legislature. A prime minister heads the government and carries out government operations.

The Baltic States are now successful market economies. Most industries and farms are privately owned. In 2004 all became EU members. Germany has become a key trade partner, while trade with Russia is decreasing. Estonia's major industries are electronics, wood products, and textiles. Latvia's factories make vehicles, farm machinery, and fertilizers. Lithuania produces machine tools, appliances, and electric motors.

During decades of Communist rule, government leaders ignored many serious environmental problems. Old and faulty wastewater-treatment plants, leaking sewers, and fertilizer, oil, and chemical run-off from factories and farms have polluted the Baltic Sea. All Baltic countries are now involved in the cleanup.

Independence Rally Many Eastern European nations held rallies to protest Communist rule, such as this one in Kaunas in southern Lithuania in 1989.

 COMPARE AND CONTRAST Explain how the Baltic States are similar to and different from each other.

Section 1 Assessment

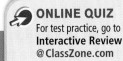 **ONLINE QUIZ** For test practice, go to **Interactive Review** @ ClassZone.com

TERMS & NAMES

1. Explain the importance of
- Baltic States
- Solidarity
- Russification
- deport

USE YOUR READING NOTES

2. Categorize Use your completed chart to answer the following question:

What kind of government does Poland have?

	LANGUAGE	GOVERNMENT	ECONOMY
Poland			
Ukraine			
Latvia			
Lithuania			
Estonia			

KEY IDEAS

3. What were the goals of Solidarity in Poland?

4. How did the Soviet Union carry out its Russification policy in the Ukraine?

5. What environmental issue do the Baltic States face today?

CRITICAL THINKING

6. Form and Support Opinions Why do many Eastern European countries want to join the European Union?

7. Analyze Causes and Effects Why are many people in the Baltic States concerned about each country's national identity?

8. CONNECT to Today Why might Polish leaders want to encourage young people to stay in Poland?

9. ART Give a Presentation Do research to learn more about one of the folk arts of the countries in this section. Give a short presentation on where and how this craft is made, how it is used, and any customs associated with it. Show pictures of the craft.

Reading for Understanding

▶ Key Ideas

BEFORE, YOU LEARNED

Independence brought political and economic changes and new challenges for Poland, Ukraine, and the Baltic States.

NOW YOU WILL LEARN

After decades of Communist rule, Hungary and the Czech Republic made economic and political reforms.

▶ Vocabulary

TERMS & NAMES

Magyar an ethnic Hungarian person or the Hungarian language

Czechoslovakia (CHEHK•uh•sluh•VAH•kee•uh) former country in Eastern Europe that existed from 1918 until 1993, when it split into the Czech Republic and Slovakia

Velvet Revolution the peaceful protest by the Czech people that led to the smooth end of communism in Czechoslovakia

BACKGROUND VOCABULARY

strategic relating to a plan of action designed to achieve a specific goal

standard of living an economic measure relating to the quality and amount of goods available to a group of people and how those goods are distributed across the group

eclectic made up of parts from a variety of sources

Visual Vocabulary Velvet Revolution

▶ Reading Strategy

Re-create the Venn diagram shown at right. As you read and respond to the **KEY QUESTIONS**, use the diagram to help you compare and contrast Hungary and the Czech Republic.

 Skillbuilder Handbook, page R9

COMPARE AND CONTRAST

HUNGARY   BOTH   CZECH REPUBLIC

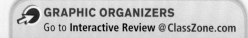

GRAPHIC ORGANIZERS
Go to **Interactive Review** @ ClassZone.com

Hungary and the Czech Republic

1.02 Generate, interpret, and manipulate information from tools such as maps, globes, charts, graphs, databases, and models to pose and answer questions about space and place, environment and society, and spatial dynamics and connections.
8.01 Describe the role of key historical figures and evaluate their impact on past and present societies in South America and Europe.

Connecting to Your World

Have you ever played chess or checkers? In these games, the player who controls the middle of the board can have a **strategic** advantage. That player can move in many different directions. Hungary sits right between the eastern and western regions of Europe and shares borders with seven other countries. It can choose which neighbors to befriend. Unlike good chess players, however, Hungary did not always have a choice about which way it moved.

Hungary

▼ **KEY QUESTION** How is Hungary's location an advantage in rebuilding its economy?

Hungary's central location attracted many groups. Hungary's earliest settlers were the **Magyar**, or ethnic Hungarian, people. In the late tenth century, Magyar leaders created a stable and prosperous kingdom. Then, in 1526, the Ottoman Turks and Austria conquered and divided Hungary's territory. Eventually, Austria drove out the Ottomans and took over. Hungary fought for independence from Austria's harsh rule.

Playing Chess A boy learns to play chess from his father.

Budapest The Széchenyi Chain Bridge was the first to cross the Danube River in Budapest.

History By 1867, Austria had been weakened by many costly wars, and it was forced to share power with Hungary. Together they ruled an empire known as Austria-Hungary. During World War I, Austria-Hungary fought on the losing side. After its defeat, its territory was divided up. Hungary was independent but lost much of its land.

During World War II, Soviet troops invaded Hungary. They were followed by Communist Party agents, who wanted to make sure the Communists gained control of the government. Many Hungarians opposed Communist rule. They resented the loss of their freedom. In 1956, thousands of protesters flooded the streets of Budapest, the nation's capital, demanding that Soviet troops leave. The Soviet Union responded by sending more troops and tanks to crush the uprising. Thousands of protesters died in the fighting.

In later decades, Communist Party officials gave Hungarians greater economic freedom, allowing some private ownership of business. In 1989, as the Soviet government began to fall apart, the Hungarian government agreed to allow other political parties. A year later, Hungarian reformers removed the Communists from power in the country's first free elections.

Culture Most Hungarians are Magyars, descendants of Hungary's early settlers. Hungarians speak Hungarian, also called Magyar, a language related to Finnish and Estonian. As you can see from the map at right, Hungarian is different from the languages spoken in surrounding countries. About two-thirds of Hungarians are Roman Catholics. One-fourth are Protestants. Other ethnic groups include Croats, Roma (also called Gypsies), Romanians, and Slovaks.

During the Communist era, many Hungarians moved from farms to cities. Everyday life changed as a result. In cities today, modern influences like blue jeans and pop music clash with traditional dress and folk songs. Budapest is a good example of Hungary's mix of old and new. It is actually two cities divided by the Danube River. Medieval Buda sits on the western bank and Pest, which underwent a surge of development in the 18th century, sits on the eastern bank.

Fun Facts!

PAPRIKA AND VITAMIN C

Paprika is a very popular spice in Hungarian food. It comes from a pepper that flavors food and also fights the common cold. When a cold starts, many people drink orange juice for extra vitamin C. In 1932, Hungarian scientist Albert Szent-Gyorgyi found that a paprika pepper contains five to six times more vitamin C than an orange.

Traditional and Modern (left) Teenagers perform at a Hungarian folk dance. (right) The crowd enjoys the show at the Sziget Music Festival in Budapest.

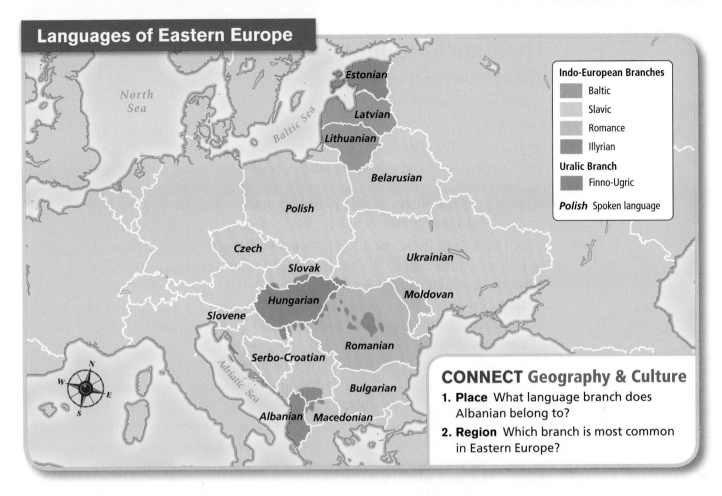

Languages of Eastern Europe

North Sea

Baltic Sea

Estonian

Latvian

Lithuanian

Belarusian

Polish

Czech

Slovak

Ukrainian

Hungarian

Moldovan

Slovene

Serbo-Croatian

Romanian

Adriatic Sea

Bulgarian

Albanian   Macedonian

Indo-European Branches
- Baltic
- Slavic
- Romance
- Illyrian

Uralic Branch
- Finno-Ugric

Polish Spoken language

CONNECT Geography & Culture
1. **Place** What language branch does Albanian belong to?
2. **Region** Which branch is most common in Eastern Europe?

Government and Economics Hungary is a parliamentary democracy. Voters elect the members of parliament, called the National Assembly, to serve four-year terms. The National Assembly elects the president and the prime minister. The president—who serves a five-year term—is the commander in chief of the armed forces, but has little power. The prime minister is the head of government.

Before World War II, most Hungarians were farmers living in rural villages. Under Communist rule, officials worked hard to expand industry. As industry increased, many Hungarians moved to cities to work in government-run factories. By the 1990s, employment in agriculture decreased from over half to one-eighth of the population.

In the decades after the failed Hungarian revolt in 1956, the government began to allow some private businesses to operate. After the Communists lost the 1990 elections, Hungary's new leaders lifted many government controls on business and sold most remaining state-owned businesses and farms. The country moved rapidly toward a market economy. Today, it has one of the highest **standards of living** in Eastern Europe. Hungary joined the EU in 2004. The nation's central location and the Danube River help boost trade. EU members Germany, Austria, France, and Italy are its main trade partners.

▲ **FIND MAIN IDEAS** Explain how Hungary's location is helpful in rebuilding its economy.

Eastern Europe **355**

CZECH
REPUBLIC SLOVAKIA

The Czech Republic

▼ **KEY QUESTION** How did freedom from Communist rule change the Czech Republic?

Like Hungary, the Czech Republic was once part of Austria-Hungary. It also spent many decades controlled by a Communist government. Today, it is one of the most prosperous countries in Eastern Europe.

History In the 900s, Slavic peoples established the kingdom of Bohemia alongside two other regions, Moravia and Slovakia. The Czech regions of Bohemia and Moravia maintained close ties throughout their histories. Both became part of the Austrian empire in 1526. Slovakia, a region of Slovaks, became part of Hungary. In 1918, after Austria-Hungary's defeat in World War I, Europe's leaders made the lands that had been Bohemia, Moravia, and Slovakia into the nation of **Czechoslovakia** (CHEHK•uh•sluh•VAH•kee•uh). Czechs and Slovaks were thrown together within the new borders.

Czechoslovakia lasted only a few decades as an independent nation. In 1948, Communists took over the country. In 1968, the Soviet Union crushed efforts by Czech Communist leaders to give citizens greater freedom. Fearing their own people might demand more freedom, the Soviets sent troops and tanks to end protests.

In 1989, thousands of protesters filled the streets of Prague calling for an end to Communist rule. Massive protests convinced Communist leaders to resign. The end of Communist rule took place so smoothly, that this protest became known as the **Velvet Revolution**. In 1990, voters elected protest leader Václav Havel president. Three years later, Czech and Slovak leaders agreed to divide the country into the Czech Republic and Slovakia. Some call this friendly split the "Velvet Divorce."

Culture Most people in the Czech Republic are Czechs. They speak Czech, a Slavic language. The country has many smaller ethnic groups including Slovaks, Germans, Roma (Gypsies), Hungarians, and Poles. Before World War II, Czechoslovakia had a large Jewish population. Almost all the nation's Jews were killed during the Holocaust. Roman Catholics are the largest religious group in the Czech Republic.

HISTORY MAKERS

Václav Havel (born 1936)

Václav Havel's (VAHT-slahv HAH-vuhl) admirers call him a hero for his role in leading the Velvet Revolution. During Czechoslovakia's years of Communist rule, the country's leaders called him a danger to society. A well-known playwright, he spent several years in prison for openly opposing Communist rule. After the end of communism, grateful citizens chose Havel as Czechoslovakia's first president. He later served as the first president of the new Czech Republic.

 ONLINE BIOGRAPHY
For more on the life of Václav Havel, go to the
Research & Writing Center @ ClassZone.com

The Czech Republic has a tradition of fine art. Composer Antonin Dvorák (DVAWR•zhahk) wrote music inspired by the Czech landscape and folk music. Famous Czech writers include Franz Kafka and Milan Kundera, whose books explore the human condition. For centuries, Czech artists have crafted beautiful glassware. Glittering Czech crystal chandeliers hang in opera houses, palaces, and mansions around the world today.

Prague Residents and tourists alike use the Charles Bridge to cross the Vltava River and get around Prague.

The culture of the Czech Republic is a vibrant mix of old and new. Prague is the nation's capital and largest city. In the 1300s, it became a center of art and learning in Europe. The city has many beautiful Renaissance buildings. It is known as the "City of a Hundred Spires" because of the churches that dot its streets. Contemporary influences are making their marks on Prague. Young people dance to modern pop music in clubs that have opened in basements in the historic sections of town. Each year, millions of tourists add to the **eclectic** atmosphere of the Czech Republic.

CONNECT ➤ Geography & Culture

The Dancing House Prague is known for its architecture. A popular stop on any tour of Prague is the Rasin Building, nicknamed the Dancing House. Although it is made of concrete, steel, and glass, it seems to swirl and twist, like a couple dancing.

Not everyone is a fan of the building, built by American architect Frank Gehry and Czech architect Vlado Milunic in 1996. Some feel it clashes with the older historic buildings that surround it. However, supporters find it lively and exciting, a symbol of the new Czech Republic.

CRITICAL THINKING

Make Inferences Why might some Prague residents want the city to build more new buildings like the Dancing House?

Worldster
A Day in Radek's Life

To learn more about Radek and his world, go to the **Activity Center @ ClassZone.com**

Hello! My name is Radek. I am 14 years old and live in Brno in the southeastern part of the Czech Republic. With almost 400,000 people, it is the second largest city after Prague. We live in a small apartment. On weekends, I like to read, listen to music, or watch television. Sometimes my family takes the train to Prague. Here's my day.

To introduce himself, Radek says:

"Dobrý den. Jmenuju se Radek."

7 A.M. My sister and I eat breakfast with our parents. They both have to go to work and we go to school. I have rye bread or a roll with butter and jam and a glass of milk. Sometimes we have slices of cheese or salami, too.

8 A.M.–4 P.M. I have to work hard at school, especially in my English class. Everyone has to take courses in at least one foreign language. My school has many after-school activities. I joined the gymnastics club. I'm looking forward to our first competition!

6 P.M. In the evening, my family eats dinner. Sometimes, my grandmother comes over and helps my mother make roast duck with *knedlíky*, or potato dumplings, and cabbage. It's one of my favorite meals.

7 P.M. Today is my name day. In the Czech Republic, each day of the year has a different name assigned to it. It's traditional to celebrate your birthday and your name day. Some of my friends and I are going out for ice cream sundaes to celebrate.

CONNECT to Your Life

Journal Entry Think about your own birthday. How do you celebrate it? Do you have other special occasions, like Radek, that you celebrate with your family? Record your ideas in your journal.

Government and Economics The Czech Republic is a parliamentary democracy. Voters elect members of parliament. The parliament elects the president, who serves as the head of state. The president appoints a prime minister to oversee the daily operations of government.

Before Communist rule, the Czech economy was diverse and balanced. Under communism, however, the government shifted the economy toward heavy industry. After Communist control ended, the country's new leaders had to regain the balance that it once had. This has led to some unemployment as factory jobs decline.

On the whole, however, the Czech Republic's transition from a command to a market economy has been a smooth one. Most farms and factories have been sold to private owners. The Czech Republic joined the EU in 2004. Foreign investment and exports of Czech products, especially to Germany, have helped the economy continue growing. It has been among the most successful economies of the former Communist nations in Eastern Europe.

Škoda Auto This Czech company has been manufacturing cars for over 100 years. When Communist rule ended, the industry privatized and Volkswagen took over the company.

▲ **SUMMARIZE** Explain how the Czech Republic changed after gaining freedom from Communist rule.

Section ② Assessment

ONLINE QUIZ
For test practice, go to
Interactive Review
@ ClassZone.com

TERMS & NAMES

1. Explain the importance of
- Magyar
- Czechoslovakia
- Velvet Revolution

USE YOUR READING NOTES

2. Compare and Contrast Use your completed chart to answer the following question:

How did Hungary's fight for independence differ from the Czech Republic's and how were they similar?

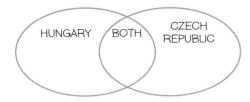

HUNGARY   BOTH   CZECH REPUBLIC

KEY IDEAS

3. What ethnic group do many Hungarians belong to?

4. How was Czechoslovakia formed?

5. How did the Velvet Revolution change Czechoslovakia?

CRITICAL THINKING

6. Analyze Causes and Effects How do you think the failure of the 1956 Hungarian revolt affected other Eastern European nations?

7. Find Main Ideas How did Václav Havel influence Czechoslovakia?

8. CONNECT to Today Why do you think the Czech Republic recently built new expressways and rail links to Germany?

9. WRITING Express an Opinion The young people who led the Hungarian revolt in 1956 were called freedom fighters by some and lawbreakers and traitors by others. Write a paragraph telling how you think they should be remembered.

Reading for Understanding

▶ Key Ideas

BEFORE, YOU LEARNED

The Czech Republic and Slovakia became independent countries without conflict or bloodshed.

NOW YOU WILL LEARN

In the 1990s the breakup of Yugoslavia was violent. Ethnic divisions and economic and political issues led to war.

▶ Vocabulary

TERMS & NAMES

Yugoslavia a country on the Balkan Peninsula from 1918 to 1991

Josip Broz Tito the Communist leader of Yugoslavia from 1953 to 1980

ethnic cleansing removing an ethnic or religious group from an area by force or the mass killing of members of such a group

Kosovo a self-governing province within Serbia

Slobodan Milosevic president of Serbia from 1989 to 1997 and of Yugoslavia from 1997 to 2000; a key figure in the ethnic conflicts in the Balkans in the 1990s

BACKGROUND VOCABULARY

Bosniac an ethnic Muslim from Bosnia and Herzegovina

refugee a person who flees a place to find safety

Visual Vocabulary Josip Broz Tito

▶ Reading Strategy

Re-create the web diagram shown at right. As you read and respond to the **KEY QUESTIONS**, use the diagram to help you find main ideas about the Balkans.

 Skillbuilder Handbook, page R4

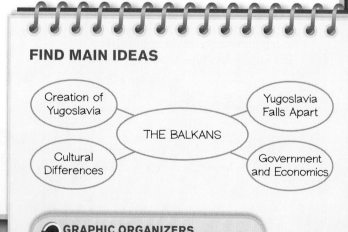

FIND MAIN IDEAS

Creation of Yugoslavia

Yugoslavia Falls Apart

THE BALKANS

Cultural Differences

Government and Economics

GRAPHIC ORGANIZERS
Go to **Interactive Review** @ ClassZone.com

The Balkans

1.02 Generate, interpret, and manipulate information from tools such as maps, globes, charts, graphs, databases, and models to pose and answer questions about space and place, environment and society, and spatial dynamics and connections.
8.01 Describe the role of key historical figures and evaluate their impact on past and present societies in South America and Europe.

Connecting to Your World

At the opening ceremonies of the Olympic Games, athletes from around the globe proudly display their national flags as they march around a packed stadium. The games demonstrate that people of different religions, languages, and beliefs can come together without conflict. In 1984, the Winter Olympic Games took place in Sarajevo, a city in what was then Yugoslavia on the Balkan Peninsula. In the 1990s, wars caused by ethnic conflict destroyed much of the city, including the Olympic facilities. Sarajevo has been rebuilt, but memories of the violence that destroyed it remain.

Sarajevo The flame is lit (above) at the 1984 Winter Olympics opening ceremonies. This Muslim cemetery (below) is in Sarajevo.

History and Culture

▼ **KEY QUESTION** What caused the breakup of Yugoslavia?

In the 500s, various groups of Slavic peoples settled the Balkan Peninsula. Centuries of foreign rule created differences in the religion, language, and customs of these Slavic groups. When these groups joined together in one nation in the 20th century, their ethnic differences became a time bomb waiting to explode.

BOSNIA AND HERZEGOVINA • Sarajevo

POJATA AZIZ 1956–1996

NIŠANE PODIŽU OTAC MAJKA BRAĆA I SESTRE

ČIBER MUHAMED 1921–1996

PORODICA I PRIJATELJI

361

Creation of Yugoslavia After World War I, Slavic groups formed a country on the Balkan Peninsula called the Kingdom of Croats, Serbs, and Slovenes. It was renamed **Yugoslavia** in 1929. When World War II ended, **Josip Broz Tito** took over Yugoslavia. It became a Communist state consisting of six republics: Bosnia-Herzegovina, Croatia, Macedonia, Montenegro, Serbia, and Slovenia. Within each republic, the majority of people belonged to the same ethnic group. Tito's tight control brought political stability and helped unite Yugoslavia.

Yugoslavia Falls Apart After Tito died in 1980, Yugoslavia faced many economic and political problems. The other republics felt Serbia was trying to take control. In 1991, Slovenia, Macedonia, Croatia, and Bosnia-Herzegovina each declared independence. War broke out in Bosnia, as Serbs clashed with **Bosniacs** and Croats. Serbian troops occupied parts of Bosnia, using force to drive all non-Serbs out. This tactic, known as **ethnic cleansing**, left thousands dead or homeless. A 1995 peace plan gave most of Bosnia to the Bosniacs and Croats and the rest to the Bosnian Serbs. In 1998, rebels in the Serbian province of **Kosovo** began fighting for independence. Violence between Serb forces and the Albanian majority in Kosovo lasted until late 1999. In 2002, Serbian leader **Slobodan Milosevic** was tried for war crimes related to ethnic cleansing in Bosnia and Kosovo. He died in prison before his trial ended. By 2003, Yugoslavia no longer existed.

Cultural Differences Five new nations resulted from the breakup of Yugoslavia: Bosnia and Herzegovina, Croatia, Macedonia, Serbia and Montenegro, and Slovenia. As the map on the next page suggests, most of the former Yugoslav republics are dominated by one ethnic group. Most Balkan peoples speak Slavic languages. The biggest difference among ethnic groups is in religion. These countries have had to find ways to accept their differences. They have also had to work to return their cities to the cultural centers they once were.

▲ **ANALYZE CAUSES** Explain why Yugoslavia collapsed.

Dubrovnik, Croatia
Dubrovnik is known for its terra cotta roofs, some of which were damaged in the ethnic conflict in the 1990s and needed to be repaired.

COMPARING ► Ethnic Distribution in the Balkans

Similarities and Differences Yugoslavia brought many ethnic groups together in one nation. In the 1990s, differences in language, religion, and culture overwhelmed similarities, until the region erupted in conflict. Today, these groups must find ways to live together.

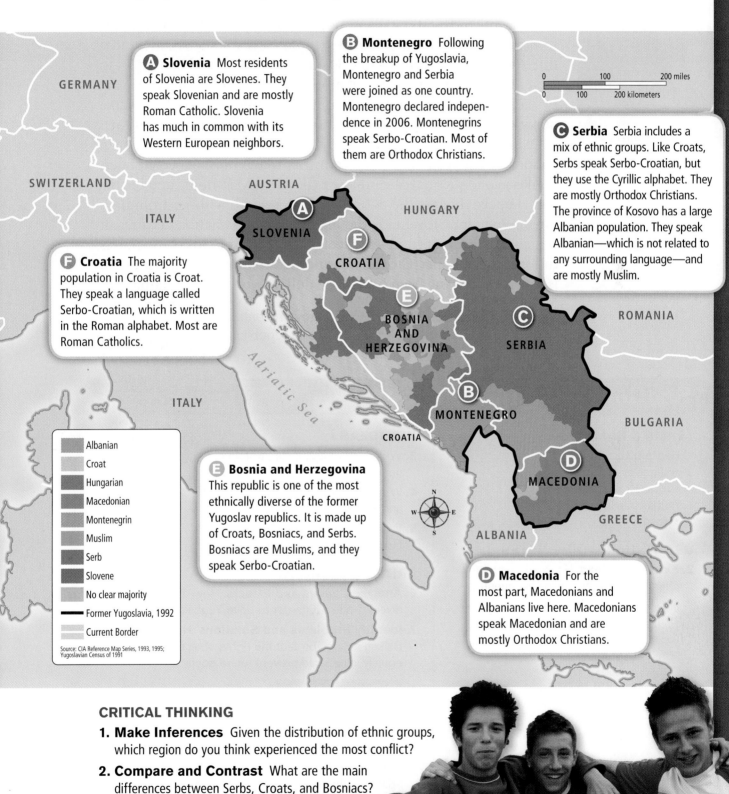

A Slovenia Most residents of Slovenia are Slovenes. They speak Slovenian and are mostly Roman Catholic. Slovenia has much in common with its Western European neighbors.

B Montenegro Following the breakup of Yugoslavia, Montenegro and Serbia were joined as one country. Montenegro declared independence in 2006. Montenegrins speak Serbo-Croatian. Most of them are Orthodox Christians.

C Serbia Serbia includes a mix of ethnic groups. Like Croats, Serbs speak Serbo-Croatian, but they use the Cyrillic alphabet. They are mostly Orthodox Christians. The province of Kosovo has a large Albanian population. They speak Albanian—which is not related to any surrounding language—and are mostly Muslim.

F Croatia The majority population in Croatia is Croat. They speak a language called Serbo-Croatian, which is written in the Roman alphabet. Most are Roman Catholics.

E Bosnia and Herzegovina This republic is one of the most ethnically diverse of the former Yugoslav republics. It is made up of Croats, Bosniacs, and Serbs. Bosniacs are Muslims, and they speak Serbo-Croatian.

D Macedonia For the most part, Macedonians and Albanians live here. Macedonians speak Macedonian and are mostly Orthodox Christians.

Legend:
- Albanian
- Croat
- Hungarian
- Macedonian
- Montenegrin
- Muslim
- Serb
- Slovene
- No clear majority
- Former Yugoslavia, 1992
- Current Border

Source: CIA Reference Map Series, 1993, 1995; Yugoslavian Census of 1991

CRITICAL THINKING

1. **Make Inferences** Given the distribution of ethnic groups, which region do you think experienced the most conflict?

2. **Compare and Contrast** What are the main differences between Serbs, Croats, and Bosniacs?

363

Government and Economics

 KEY QUESTION What governmental and economic problems do many former Yugoslav republics face?

Today, the remaining ethnic tensions have made it difficult for the former Yugoslav republics to form stable governments. One concern is protecting the rights of all ethnic groups to prevent future conflicts. In Bosnia and Herzegovina, the people elect the legislature and a three-member presidency—one Bosniac, one Croat, and one Serb—to represent the country's ethnic majorities. Serbia and Montenegro are two republics that formed one country in 2003. In 2006, however, a majority of Montenegrins voted to become an independent nation.

Wartime destruction and the movement of **refugees** between nations have forced the Balkan countries to rebuild their economies. Market economies have been slow to develop. Macedonia and Bosnia and Herzegovina are the poorest. Like Serbia, they suffer from high unemployment. Slovenia is the most prosperous nation, as a result of stable government and less involvement in the 1990s conflict. It is the only EU member. Croatia was another wealthy republic. Today, it is slowly recovering from billions of dollars worth of war damage.

Ljubljana, Slovenia
Visitors enjoy the sights on this street in Slovenia's capital. **Why is tourism important to the former Yugoslav republics' economies?**

△ **ANALYZE EFFECTS** Explain the governmental and economic problems faced by the former Yugoslav republics.

Section 3 Assessment

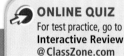 **ONLINE QUIZ** For test practice, go to **Interactive Review** @ ClassZone.com

TERMS & NAMES

1. Explain the importance of
- Yugoslavia
- Josip Broz Tito
- ethnic cleansing
- Kosovo

USE YOUR READING NOTES

2. Find Main Ideas Use your completed chart to answer the following question:

How did Tito's death affect Yugoslavia?

KEY IDEAS

3. What kind of economic system did Yugoslavia have under Tito?

4. Why did much of the ethnic fighting occur in Bosnia and Kosovo?

5. What economic problem is shared by many of the former Yugoslav republics?

CRITICAL THINKING

6. Analyze Causes and Effects How did ethnic diversity make it harder to unite Yugoslavia?

7. Identify Problems and Solutions How might Balkan nations protect the rights of all ethnic groups equally in order to prevent future conflicts?

8. CONNECT to Today What might be the benefits of EU membership for Slovenia?

9. GOVERNMENT Draft a Bill of Rights Draft a Bill of Rights for the ethnic groups living in the Balkans. List ten rights these groups should have. Consider the rights of ethnic minorities in these countries.

Interactive ◀Review

CHAPTER SUMMARY

Key Idea 1
Poland, Ukraine, and the Baltic states faced challenges after shaking off Communist rule.

Key Idea 2
After decades of Communist rule, Hungary and the Czech Republic made economic and political reforms.

Key Idea 3
In the 1990s the breakup of Yugoslavia was violent. Ethnic divisions and economic and political issues led to war.

For **Review and Study Notes**, go to **Interactive Review** @ ClassZone.com

NAME GAME

Use the Terms & Names list to complete each sentence on paper or online.

1. I am a self-governing province within Serbia and Montenegro. ___Kosovo___

2. I am the Communist leader who kept Yugoslavia from splitting apart for over 40 years. _____

3. I am a region where grain production thrives. _____

4. I am the policy practiced by the Soviet Union in an effort to make occupied countries more Russian. _____

5. I am another name for the countries of Latvia, Lithuania, and Estonia. _____

6. I am another term for ethnic Hungarians. _____

7. I mean to expel someone from a country. _____

8. I am the leader who helped start Poland's first independent trade union. _____

9. I am the Serbian leader who was charged with war crimes. _____

10. I am the Balkan country that split into six nations. _____

Baltic States
bread basket
crossroads
Czechoslovakia
deport
ethnic cleansing
Josip Broz Tito
Kosovo
Lech Walesa
Magyar
Russification
Slobodan Milosevic
Solidarity
Václav Havel
Yugoslavia

Activities

GeoGame

Use this online map to reinforce your understanding of Eastern Europe. Drag and drop each place name in the list to its location on the map.

Geo GAME

Poland
Kiev
Budapest
Czech Republic
Ukraine

To play the complete game, go to **Interactive Review** @ClassZone.com

Present-Day Eastern Europe

Ukraine

⊙ National capital

Crossword Puzzle

Complete an online crossword puzzle to test your knowledge of Eastern Europe.

ACROSS
1. Communist leader of Yugoslavia from 1953 to 1980

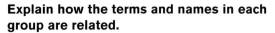

VOCABULARY

Explain the significance of each of the following.

1. Lech Walesa
2. bread basket
3. Magyar
4. Velvet Revolution
5. ethnic cleansing
6. Kosovo

Explain how the terms and names in each group are related.

7. Baltic States and Russification
8. Yugoslavia and Czechoslovakia
9. Josip Broz Tito and Slobodan Milosevic

KEY IDEAS

1 Poland, Ukraine, and the Baltic States

10. Which Eastern European countries were part of the Soviet Union before it collapsed?
11. What effect did Solidarity have on Polish resistance to Communist rule in the 1980s?
12. How did the ownership of farms and factories in Poland, Ukraine, and the Baltic States change after the collapse of communism?
13. How did the Soviet policy of Russification affect Ukraine and the Baltic States?

2 Hungary and the Czech Republic

14. Why did the 1956 Hungarian revolt fail?
15. How has industrial growth affected where people in Hungary and the Czech Republic live?
16. What is the Czech Republic's capital and largest city?
17. How was the Czech Republic able to move peacefully from Communist rule to democratic government?

3 The Balkans

18. How did Yugoslavia change during Tito's rule?
19. What led to the violence in Kosovo?
20. In what way are many of the languages spoken in the Balkans similar?
21. What helped Slovenia make a smooth transition to a market economy?

CRITICAL THINKING

22. **Compare and Contrast** How have Poland, Hungary, and the Czech Republic changed from command to market economies?

COMMAND ECONOMY	MARKET ECONOMY

23. **Form and Support Opinions** Why have many former Communist countries wanted closer ties with Western Europe?
24. **Compare and Contrast** How were the roles of Lech Walesa and Václav Havel in their nations' history similar?
25. **Connect Geography & Government** What effect did the collapse of Communist governments have on Eastern Europe?
26. **Connect Geography & History** How do the new governments of the former Yugoslav republics reflect their recent history?
27. **Five Themes: Place** How were the breakups of Czechoslovakia and Yugoslavia different?

Answer the ESSENTIAL QUESTION

In what ways has Eastern Europe changed since the end of World War II?

Written Response Write a two- or three-paragraph response to the Essential Question. Consider the key ideas of each section as well as specific ideas about Eastern Europe. Use the rubric below to guide your thinking.

Response Rubric
A strong response will:
- discuss changes in government and civil rights
- discuss changes in economies
- discuss the impact of Communist rule on language and national identity

Test Practice

• Online Test Practice @ClassZone.com

• Test-Taking Strategies and Practice at the front of this book

HISTORICAL MAP

Use the map to answer questions 1 and 2 on your paper.

Division of Poland *1795*

SWEDEN

Baltic Sea

Gdansk

R U S S I A

P R U S S I A
Warsaw•

•Kiev

A U S T R I A

HUNGARY

OTTOMAN EMPIRE

OTTOMAN EMPIRE

0   100   200 miles
0   100   200 kilometers

| | To Russia | | To Austria |
| | To Prussia | —— | Poland before partition, 1772 |

1. What three countries divided Poland among them?

A. Russia, Prussia, and Austria

B. Sweden, Prussia, and Hungary

C. Sweden, Russia, and Prussia

D. Russia, Hungary, and the Ottoman Empire

2. Which country gained the majority of Polish territory?

A. Austria

B. Russia

C. Prussia

D. Sweden

BAR GRAPH

Examine the graph below. Use the graph to answer questions 3 and 4 on your paper.

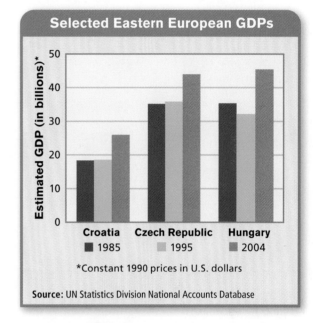

Selected Eastern European GDPs

Estimated GDP (in billions)*

Croatia   Czech Republic   Hungary

■ 1985   ■ 1995   ■ 2004

*Constant 1990 prices in U.S. dollars

Source: UN Statistics Division National Accounts Database

3. Which country's GDP dropped between 1985 and 1995?

4. During which time period did all three nations see the biggest increase in GDP?

GeoActivity

1. INTERDISCIPLINARY ACTIVITY–MATHEMATICS

With a small group, pick a country in this section. Find information on the religious makeup of the country, the percentage of people who live in urban and rural areas, and the percentage of people who can read. Use the information to create three pie graphs.

2. WRITING FOR SOCIAL STUDIES

Unit Writing Project Review your presentation about the European country you want to visit. Write a journal entry that describes how you spent your favorite day there, after your class decided to make the trip.

3. MENTAL MAPPING

Create an outline map of Eastern Europe and label the following:

• Hungary
• Poland
• Czech Republic
• Ukraine
• Latvia
• Lithuania
• Estonia
• Prague
• Chernobyl

UNIT 4

Russia and the Eurasian Republics

Why It Matters:

Since gaining their independence, Russia and the Eurasian republics have worked to stabilize their governments and economies. Achieving these goals will help ensure peace in the region and strengthen Russia's position as a world leader.

Moscow's Red Square

CHAPTER 13 Russia

Registan Square in Uzbekistan

CHAPTER 14 The Eurasian Republics

◄ Meet Zuhura

In this unit, you will meet Zuhura, a middle-school girl from Uzbekistan. Learn more about her on **Worldster** @ ClassZone.com

Russia and the Eurasian Republics

Russia and the Eurasian republics span two continents. The part of the region that lies to the west of the Ural Mountains is part of Europe. The part of the region that lies to the east of the Urals is part of Asia. As you study the maps, notice geographic patterns and specific details about the region. Answer the questions on each map in your notebook.

As you study the graphs on this page, compare the landmass, population, and lakes of Russia and the Eurasian republics with those of the United States. Then jot down the answers to the following questions in your notebook.

Comparing Data

1. Compare the landmass and population of Russia and the Eurasian republics with those of the United States. Based on these data, which region do you think has a higher population density? Why?

2. How much deeper is Lake Baikal than the deepest lake in the United States?

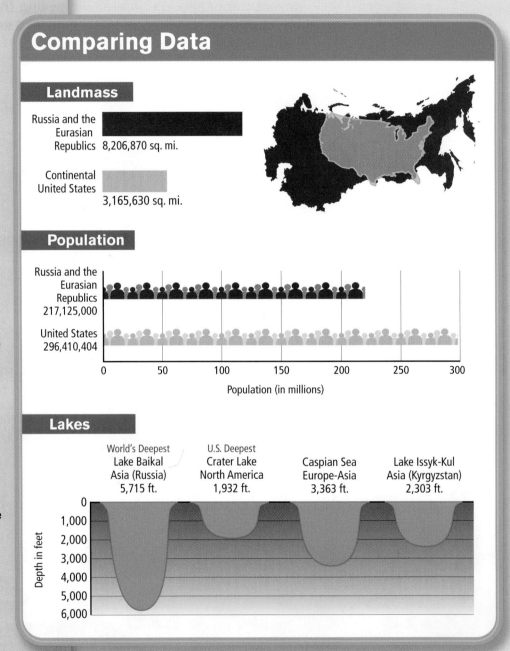

Comparing Data

Landmass

Russia and the Eurasian Republics 8,206,870 sq. mi.

Continental United States 3,165,630 sq. mi.

Population

Russia and the Eurasian Republics 217,125,000

United States 296,410,404

Population (in millions)
0   50   100   150   200   250   300

Lakes

World's Deepest
Lake Baikal
Asia (Russia)
5,715 ft.

U.S. Deepest
Crater Lake
North America
1,932 ft.

Caspian Sea
Europe-Asia
3,363 ft.

Lake Issyk-Kul
Asia (Kyrgyzstan)
2,303 ft.

Depth in feet
0
1,000
2,000
3,000
4,000
5,000
6,000

ICELAND
GREENLAND

ARCTIC OCEAN

Bering
Sea

180°

Arctic Circle

NORWAY

SWEDEN

FINLAND

Baltic Sea

RUSSIA
ESTONIA
LATVIA
LITHUANIA

BELARUS

St. Petersburg

Novgorod

NORTHERN

⊛ Moscow

EUROPEAN

UKRAINE

PLAIN

Black
Sea

Volga R.

CAUCASUS MTS.

Mt. Elbrus
18,510 ft.
(5,642 m)

GEORGIA

⊛ Tbilisi
Yerevan

AZERBAIJAN

ARMENIA

⊛ Baku

Caspian Sea

TURKMENISTAN

Ashgabat

IRAN

URAL MOUNTAINS

WEST

RUSSIA

SIBERIAN

PLAIN

Omsk

Astana

KAZAKHSTAN

Aral
Sea

Lake
Balkhash

UZBEKISTAN

Tashkent

Bishkek

KYRGYZSTAN

TIAN SHAN

Dushanbe ⊛ TAJIKISTAN

PAMIRS

AFGHANISTAN

Ob R.

Novosibirsk

Yenisey R.

S I B E R I A

CENTRAL

SIBERIAN

PLATEAU

Lena R.

Lena R.

Irkutsk

Lake
Baikal

MONGOLIA

CHINA

Yakutsk

Amur R.

Vladivostok

KAMCHATKA
PENINSULA

160°E

Sea of
Okhotsk

140°E

NORTH
KOREA

SOUTH
KOREA

Sea of
Japan
(East
Sea)

JAPAN

40°N

PACIFIC
OCEAN

PAKISTAN

INDIA

NEPAL

BHUTAN

BANGLADESH

MYANMAR

LAOS

THAILAND

OMAN

Tropic of Cancer

TAIWAN

20°N

80°N

60°N

Elevation

13,100 ft. (4,000 m)
6,600 ft. (2,000 m)
3,280 ft. (1,000 m)
650 ft. (200 m)
0 ft. (0 m)
Below sea level

▲ Mountain peak

0   500   1,000 miles
0   500   1,000 kilometers

THINK LIKE A GEOGRAPHER

1. **Location** On which landform is Russia's
   capital located?

2. **Place** How would you describe much of
   the elevation in Tajikistan?

60°E   80°E   100°E

371

Population Density

ARCTIC OCEAN

Bering Sea

Arctic Circle

80°N

60°N

180°

160°E

Sea of Okhotsk

Baltic Sea

St. Petersburg

Moscow

Nizhniy Novgorod

Yekaterinburg

Omsk

Novosibirsk

Lake Baikal

140°E

40°N

Sea of Japan (East Sea)

Black Sea

Tbilisi

Caspian Sea

Aral Sea

Lake Balkhash

Tashkent

Almaty

Persons per square mile

Over 520
260–519
130–259
25–129
1–24
0

Tropic of Cancer

20°N

THINK LIKE A GEOGRAPHER

1. **Region** In what part of Russia is the population most dense?

2. **Place** How would you describe the population between the Caspian and Aral seas?

0   500   1,000 miles
0   500   1,000 kilometers

80°E

100°E

120°E

ICELAND
GREENLAND

ARCTIC OCEAN

Arctic Circle

Bering Sea

80°N

180°

60°N

NORWAY

SWEDEN

FINLAND

Baltic Sea

RUSSIA   ESTONIA
LATVIA
LITHUANIA

BELARUS

UKRAINE

R U S S I A

Sea of Okhotsk

160°E

Black Sea

GEORGIA

ARMENIA

AZERBAIJAN

Caspian Sea

Aral Sea

KAZAKHSTAN

Lake Balkhash

Lake Baikal

140°E

40°N

Sea of Japan (East Sea)

JAPAN

UZBEKISTAN

TURKMENISTAN

KYRGYZSTAN

TAJIKISTAN

MONGOLIA

NORTH KOREA

SOUTH KOREA

IRAN

AFGHANISTAN

PAKISTAN

C H I N A

BHUTAN

NEPAL

TAIWAN

Tropic of Cancer

20°N

BANGLADESH

I N D I A

MYANMAR

LAOS

THAILAND

PHILIPPINES

SRI LANKA

Dry
Desert
Semiarid

Mid-Latitude
Mediterranean
Humid subtropical
Humid continental

High Latitude
Subarctic
Tundra

Highland

0   500   1,000 miles

0   500   1,000 kilometers

THINK LIKE A GEOGRAPHER

1. **Place** What is the climate of the area that is closest to the Arctic Ocean?

2. **Region** What area has a desert climate?

60°E   80°E   100°E

373

GREENLAND

ARCTIC OCEAN

Arctic Circle

Bering Sea

180°

80°N

60°N

160°E

NORWAY
SWEDEN
FINLAND

Baltic Sea

RUSSIA
ESTONIA
LATVIA
LITHUANIA

● St. Petersburg

BELARUS

● Moscow

UKRAINE

Black Sea

Perm ●

RUSSIA

Sea of Okhotsk

● Yekaterinburg

140°E

GEORGIA

Aral Sea

KAZAKHSTAN

Novosibirsk ●

Krasnoyarsk

Lake Baikal

40°N

Sea of Japan (East Sea)

JAPAN

ARMENIA
AZERBAIJAN

Caspian Sea

UZBEKISTAN

Lake Balkhash

NORTH KOREA

SOUTH KOREA

TURKMENISTAN

KYRGYZSTAN

MONGOLIA

TAJIKISTAN

IRAN

AFGHANISTAN

CHINA

PAKISTAN

Tropic of Cancer

20°N

TAIWAN

NEPAL

BHUTAN

BANGLADESH

INDIA

MYANMAR
LAOS

PHILIPPINES

THAILAND
VIETNAM

SRI LANKA

Land use

- Commercial agriculture
- Livestock raising
- Nomadic herding
- Forestland
- Limited agriculture

Major resources

- Bauxite
- Coal
- Diamonds
- Gold
- Iron ore
- Natural gas
- Oil
- Other minerals
- ● Manufacturing center

0   500   1,000 miles
0   500   1,000 kilometers

THINK LIKE A GEOGRAPHER

1. **Human-Environment Interaction**
   Where in Russia is most of the land used for commercial agriculture?

2. **Region** Around what body of water is oil a major resource?

80°E   100°E   120°E

Regional Overview

Russia and the Eurasian Republics

Russia and the Eurasian republics span two continents: Europe and Asia. Both continents have had a significant influence on the regions' histories and cultures.

GEOGRAPHY

Both Russia and the Eurasian republics contain rugged areas, with towering mountains, wide deserts, and vast plains. The climates in these regions range from the frigid weather in Siberia to more mild temperatures in Georgia.

Frozen Water A group of boys plays hockey on Lake Baikal.

HISTORY

Many groups have influenced Russia and the Eurasian republics. Throughout their histories, the regions have often been divided between holding onto Eastern, or Asian, traditions and adopting more modern ideas from the West, or Europe.

CULTURE

The blend of East and West is reflected in the culture of both regions. More than 100 ethnic groups from both Asia and Europe live in Russia and the Eurasian republics.

GOVERNMENT

When the Soviet Union dissolved in 1991, Russia and 14 other republics formed. Since then, Russia and the Eurasian republics have struggled to establish democratic governments.

ECONOMICS

Russia's economy has boomed as a result of its abundant energy resources. The countries of the Eurasian republics also have vast supplies of oil and coal. However, these countries are only beginning to benefit economically from their natural resources.

Country Almanac

Click here to compare the most recent data on countries @ ClassZone.com

Unit Writing Project

Travel Itinerary

As you read this unit, pick a country or region that interests you. Then imagine that you are planning a trip to this place. Write an itinerary for a week-long stay.

Think About:

- the clothes you should bring
- what specific sites you would like to visit
- what foods you would like to eat
- the questions you would like to ask the people who live there

Russia and the Eurasian Republics

The country cards on these pages contain information about Russia and the Eurasian republics. As you study the land area of Russia, consider that the country is bigger than the continents of Europe and Antarctica combined.

Russian Federation

GEOGRAPHY
Capital: Moscow
Total Area: 6,592,772 sq. mi.
Population: 143,202,000

ECONOMY
Imports: food; chemicals; cars
Exports: fuels; metals; chemicals

CULTURE
Language: Russian
Religion: Christian 57%; Muslim 8%; nonreligious 27%; atheist 5%

Russian Bear The brown bear of Eurasia is sometimes considered the symbol of Russia.

Russia and the Eurasian Republics

   Armenia

GEOGRAPHY
Capital: Yerevan
Total Area: 11,506 sq. mi.
Population: 3,016,000

ECONOMY
Imports: mineral fuels; rough diamonds
Exports: alcohol; cut diamonds

CULTURE
Language: Armenian
Religion: Armenian Apostolic 65%

 Azerbaijan

GEOGRAPHY
Capital: Baku
Total Area: 33,436 sq. mi.
Population: 8,411,000

ECONOMY
Imports: natural gas; iron and steel
Exports: petroleum; food

CULTURE
Language: Azerbaijani
Religion: Muslim 93%; Russian Orthodox 1%; Armenian Apostolic 1%

 Georgia

GEOGRAPHY
Capital: Tbilisi
Total Area: 26,911 sq. mi.
Population: 4,474,000

ECONOMY
Imports: food; mineral fuels
Exports: aircraft; food; mineral fuels

CULTURE
Language: Georgian
Religion: Christian 46%; Sunni Muslim 11%

 Kazakhstan

GEOGRAPHY
Capital: Astana
Total Area: 1,049,155 sq. mi.
Population: 14,825,000

ECONOMY
Imports: mineral fuels; chemicals
Exports: petroleum; metals; food

CULTURE
Language: Kazakh
Religion: Muslim 47%; Russian Orthodox 8%; Protestant 2%

 Kyrgyzstan

GEOGRAPHY
Capital: Bishkek
Total Area: 76,641 sq. mi.
Population: 5,264,000

ECONOMY
Imports: petroleum; food; chemicals
Exports: metals; electricity; tobacco

CULTURE
Language: Kyrgyz; Russian
Religion: Muslim 75%; Christian 7%

 Tajikistan

GEOGRAPHY
Capital: Dushanbe
Total Area: 55,251 sq. mi.
Population: 6,507,000

ECONOMY
Imports: natural gas; grain and flour
Exports: aluminum; electricity

CULTURE
Language: Tajik
Religion: Sunni Muslim 80%; Shi'a Muslim 5%; Russian Orthodox 2%

 Turkmenistan

GEOGRAPHY
Capital: Ashgabat
Total Area: 188,456 sq. mi.
Population: 4,833,000

ECONOMY
Imports: chemicals; food
Exports: natural gas; fabrics; raw cotton

CULTURE
Language: Turkmen
Religion: Muslim 87%; Russian Orthodox 2%

 Uzbekistan

GEOGRAPHY
Capital: Tashkent
Total Area: 172,742 sq. mi.
Population: 26,593,000

ECONOMY
Imports: food; metalworking products
Exports: cotton fiber; food; gold; metals

CULTURE
Language: Uzbek
Religion: Muslim 76%; nonreligious 18%

Ural Mountains The Urals extend from the Arctic Ocean to the Caspian Sea and contain a wealth of mineral resources.

CHAPTER 13 Russia

ESSENTIAL QUESTION

How is Russia preserving its Eastern culture while adapting to Western influences?

1
GEOGRAPHY
Sweeping Across Eurasia

2
HISTORY
Governing a Vast Land

3
CULTURE
Blending Europe and Asia

4
GOVERNMENT & ECONOMICS
The Struggle for Reform

CONNECT Geography & History

Use the map and the time line to answer the following questions.

1. What is the capital of Russia today?

2. What was the capital in 1703?

Culture
◄ **988** Orthodox Christianity becomes the official religion of Russia.

950

History
1237 Mongols conquer Russian lands.

Geography
1703 St. Petersburg is founded and becomes Russia's capital.
(Palace of Catherine the Great) ▼

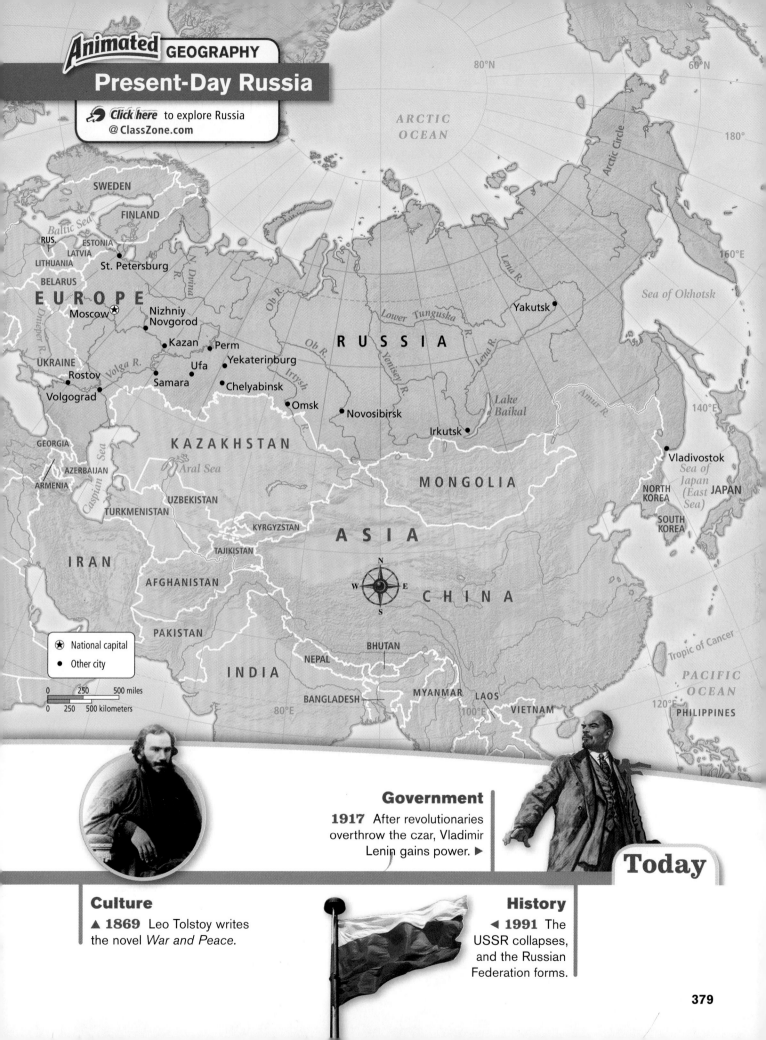

ARCTIC OCEAN

80°N   60°N

180°

Arctic Circle

160°E

SWEDEN

FINLAND

Baltic Sea

RUS.

ESTONIA

LATVIA

LITHUANIA

St. Petersburg

BELARUS

EUROPE

Moscow ✪

Nizhniy Novgorod

Kazan   Perm

UKRAINE   Ufa   Yekaterinburg

Rostov   Samara   Chelyabinsk

Volgograd   Omsk   Novosibirsk

Sea of Okhotsk

Yakutsk

RUSSIA

Lena R.

N. Dvina R.

Ob R.

Lower Tunguska R.

Ob R.

Yenisey R.

Irtysh R.

Volga R.

Dnieper R.

GEORGIA

AZERBAIJAN

ARMENIA

Caspian Sea

Aral Sea

KAZAKHSTAN

UZBEKISTAN

TURKMENISTAN

KYRGYZSTAN

TAJIKISTAN

Irkutsk

Lake Baikal

MONGOLIA

Amur R.

140°E

Vladivostok

Sea of Japan (East Sea)

NORTH KOREA   JAPAN

SOUTH KOREA

IRAN

AFGHANISTAN

ASIA

CHINA

N W E S

PAKISTAN

BHUTAN

NEPAL

INDIA

BANGLADESH

MYANMAR   LAOS

VIETNAM

Tropic of Cancer

PACIFIC OCEAN

120°E   PHILIPPINES

100°E

80°E

★ National capital

• Other city

0   250   500 miles

0   250   500 kilometers

Government

1917 After revolutionaries overthrow the czar, Vladimir Lenin gains power. ▶

Today

Culture

▲ **1869** Leo Tolstoy writes the novel *War and Peace*.

History

◀ **1991** The USSR collapses, and the Russian Federation forms.

379

Reading for Understanding

▶ Key Ideas

BEFORE, YOU LEARNED

The smaller nations of Eastern Europe have been greatly influenced by their overpowering neighbor, Russia.

NOW YOU WILL LEARN

Russia is a vast country that contains a variety of landforms, climates, vegetation regions, and natural resources.

▶ Vocabulary

TERMS & NAMES

Eurasia a term used to refer to a single continent made up of Europe and Asia

Ural Mountains a north–south mountain range that forms the border between European and Asian Russia

Caspian Sea a large body of water bordering Russia to the south

Volga River the longest river in Europe, flowing through European Russia

Siberia a huge region in Asian Russia

tundra a treeless plain around the Arctic Ocean; in Russia, located in the far north

taiga (TY•guh) a vast forest in Russia that lies south of the tundra

steppe a grassy plain; in Russia, this area lies south of the taiga

BACKGROUND VOCABULARY

permafrost ground that is frozen throughout the year

Visual Vocabulary Eurasia

▶ Reading Strategy

Re-create the chart shown at right. As you read and respond to the **KEY QUESTIONS**, use the chart to organize important details about the physical geography of Russia.

 Skillbuilder Handbook, page R7

CATEGORIZE

GEOGRAPHIC FEATURES	EUROPEAN RUSSIA	ASIAN RUSSIA
Climate		
Plants and Animals		
Agriculture		
Resources		

 GRAPHIC ORGANIZERS
Go to **Interactive Review** @ClassZone.com

Sweeping Across Eurasia

2.01 Identify key physical characteristics such as landforms, water forms, and climate and evaluate their influence on the development of cultures in selected African, Asian and Australian regions.
3.02 Describe the environmental impact of regional activities such as deforestation, urbanization, and industrialization and evaluate their significance to the global community.

Connecting to Your World

Russia is huge. It is the largest country in the world and spans 11 time zones. However, many parts of the country have few people. In fact, even though Russia is nearly twice the size of the United States, it has less than half as many people. Like the United States, Russia contains a variety of landforms, including vast forests, snow-capped mountains, and wind-swept plains. But, because of its location, the climate is much colder. The size, geography, and climate of Russia have a major impact on its people.

Crossing Two Continents

🔻 **KEY QUESTION** How are western and eastern Russia similar and different?

Does Russia lie on one continent or on two? Some geographers recognize the Ural Mountains as a dividing line between Europe and Asia. Since Russia crosses the Urals, these geographers claim that the country lies in both Europe and Asia. Others view Europe and Asia as a single continent called **Eurasia**. These geographers divide Russia into western and eastern regions. This book shares that view. In this chapter, the two regions are referred to as European (or western) Russia and Asian (or eastern) Russia.

Lake Baikal This very deep lake in eastern Russia holds over 20 percent of Earth's fresh water. **What can you tell about the physical geography of the area from this picture?**

RUSSIA

Lake Baikal

CHINA

European, or Western, Russia Study the map on the opposite page. Note that the borders of European Russia are formed by the Arctic Ocean and Baltic Sea to the north, the **Ural Mountains Ⓐ** to the east, and the Caucasus Mountains, the Black Sea, and the **Caspian Sea Ⓑ** to the south. To the west lie the European countries of Finland, Estonia, Latvia, Belarus, and Ukraine. Most of European Russia consists of a very flat expanse of land called the Northern European Plain Ⓒ. This plain contains rich farmland but does not provide any natural barriers to the west. As a result, the landform offers no protection from invaders.

Many rivers flow through European Russia, including the **Volga Ⓓ**, Europe's longest. Several canals and overland routes connect these rivers and form a transport system that carries two-thirds of Russia's waterway traffic. Another important body of water in western Russia is the Black Sea. It contains the country's busiest port.

Asian, or Eastern, Russia By far the largest part of Russia lies to the east of the Urals in Asian Russia. This region is bordered by the Urals to the west, the Arctic Ocean to the north, the Pacific Ocean to the east, and a series of mountain ranges to the south.

Most of Asian Russia is made up of a huge expanse of land called **Siberia Ⓔ**. Siberia contains the largest flat region in the world. Other parts of Siberia are not at all flat. Southeastern Siberia has mountain ranges with some of the world's highest peaks. Kamchatka Peninsula Ⓕ, in the far eastern part of Russia, has about 20 active volcanoes.

Asian Russia has several major rivers, including the Lena and the Yenisey rivers. Some of these rivers are frozen for much of the year and so limit transportation. Thousands of lakes are also found in Asian Russia. One of these, Lake Baikal Ⓖ, is the deepest in the world at 5,715 feet.

▲ **COMPARE AND CONTRAST** Explain how western and eastern Russia are similar and different.

Fun Facts!

FRESHWATER SEALS

Lake Baikal is home to the world's only freshwater seal—the nerpa. Nerpas are very graceful and can remain underwater for nearly 70 minutes. Scientists don't know how the seals ended up in a lake in the middle of Asia. But in Lake Baikal, the seals have found an ideal habitat with plenty of food.

Physical Geography of Russia

ARCTIC OCEAN

FINLAND

C

RUSSIA

NORTHERN

EUROPEAN

PLAIN

UKRAINE

Baltic Sea

N. Dvina R.

Volga R.

URAL MTS.

D

A

STEPPE

Black Sea

CAUCASUS MTS.

Mt. Elbrus
18,510 ft
(5,642 m)

TURKEY

B

Caspian Sea

60°E

KAZAKHSTAN

80°E

Ob R.

Irtysh R.

WEST

R U S S I A

SIBERIAN

PLAIN

ALTAI SHAN

MONGOLIA

100°E

S I B E R I A

CENTRAL

SIBERIAN

PLATEAU

Lower Tunguska

Yenisey R.

Lena R.

CHINA

E

G

Lake
Baikal

Amur R.

120°E

Arctic Circle

60°N

180°

F

**KAMCHATKA
PENINSULA**

PACIFIC
OCEAN

160°E

Kuril Islands

40°N

Sea of
Japan
(East Sea)

JAPAN

D Volga River, Western Russia

F Kamchatka, Eastern Russia

0   250   500 miles
0   250   500 kilometers

Elevation

13,100 ft.	(4,000 m)
6,600 ft.	(2,000 m)
3,280 ft.	(1,000 m)
650 ft.	(200 m)
0 ft.	(0 m)
Below sea level	

▲ Mountain peak

CONNECT Geography & Culture
READING A PHYSICAL MAP

Locate the Ural Mountains on the
map above. This mountain range
separates European Russia to the
west from Asian Russia to the east.
As you study these two regions,

- contrast their respective sizes
- compare their landforms and elevation
- consider how these features affect population

1. **Region** How do the landforms in Asian Russia
   differ from those in European Russia?

2. **Human-Environment Interaction** Which
   region do you think is more heavily
   populated? Why?

Climate, Vegetation, and Resources

▼ KEY QUESTION What types of natural resources are found in Russia?

Although Russia has many climates, it is mainly a cold-weather country. One Siberian town has recorded temperatures as low as –96°F. Such cold can burst tires and crack steel.

Extreme Climate All of Siberia has frigid weather during the winter. Temperatures remain so low in some areas that they are covered by a layer of permanently frozen ground called **permafrost**. However, the region can also have temperatures of nearly 100°F during the summer. These extreme temperature ranges are caused by two factors: Russia's northern latitude and its distance from any ocean. Much of the country lies many miles away from the oceans, which help moderate temperatures.

The climate is milder in European Russia. As a result, this region is more densely populated. However, even here the climate can be challenging. For example, the area around Moscow has snow on the ground for about five months of the year.

CONNECT ➤ to Math

Siberian winters are very cold. As you can see in the photo below, boiling water tossed into the region's wintry air can explode into a shower of ice crystals. Find out just how cold the winter is in Siberia. Follow the steps shown here to calculate the average temperature for each season in the Siberian town of Yakutsk.

Activity

Calculate Averages

1. Study the graph below.

2. Add the temperatures for the months in each season. For winter, you would add together: 18 + 40 + 45 + 33 + 8. Place a negative sign before the sum of these numbers.

3. Divide by the number of months in each season. For winter, you would divide by 5. Place the negative sign before the result. This is the average winter temperature in Yakutsk.

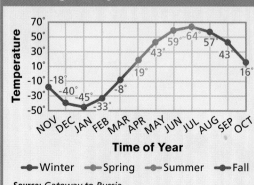

Average Temperatures in Yakutsk

Winter — Spring — Summer — Fall

Source: *Gateway to Russia*

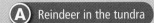
Ⓐ Reindeer in the tundra

Ⓑ Autumn in the taiga

Ⓐ **Tundra** The **tundra** in far northern Russia is a flat, treeless plain with long, harsh winters and short summers.

Ⓒ **Steppe** The **steppe** is the grassland plain that stretches south of the taiga. Rich, fertile soil covers much of the steppe.

Ⓑ **Taiga** The **taiga** (TY•guh) is a vast forest that lies south of the tundra. It is the largest forestland in the world.

Ⓓ **Semidesert & Mountain** This area in the far southwest of Russia has dry lowlands around the Caspian Sea and rich vegetation near the Caucasus Mountains.

CRITICAL THINKING
Evaluate Which region probably provides the best farmland?

Ⓒ Steppe in south-central Siberia

Ⓓ Wildflowers in the central Caucasus Mountains

Varied Wildlife A wide variety of wildlife survives in Russia's four vegetation regions.

- Although few people live in the tundra, it is home to many animals, including reindeer, Arctic foxes, and snowy owls.
- The taiga also has a small human population. Bears, deer, and wolves thrive in the region because there are so few people.
- The animals in the steppe region are largely grazing animals. These include cattle, antelope, and wild horses.
- Only animals that can survive very dry conditions live in Russia's semidesert region. Lizards, snakes, rodents, and camels adapt well to this environment.

Abundant Natural Resources Russia has some of the largest reserves of natural gas, oil, and coal in the world. Despite this, the vast majority of these riches remains untouched. Many of Russia's resources are located in remote areas of northern Siberia. The geography and climate in these areas make it difficult to remove and transport the resources. However, Russia is able to take better advantage of other resources. These include iron ore in the south and west, as well as gold, diamonds, copper, and lumber in both the east and the west.

▲ **SUMMARIZE** Describe Russia's natural resources.

Snowy Owl The snowy owl lives in the tundra for about half of the year. Although the birds are excellent fliers, they nest on the ground.

Animated GEOGRAPHY

Russia's Natural Resources

Click here to see an interactive map of Russia's natural resources and vegetation @ ClassZone.com

Timber Industry Russia's taiga region holds one-fifth of the world's timber resources.

Copper Foundry A Russian worker in western Siberia pours melted copper into molds.

Oil Field This pump is extracting oil from an area in western Siberia that produces about six percent of the world's oil.

Human-Environment Interaction

▼ **KEY QUESTION** What has caused some of the environmental problems in Russia?

As you have learned, Russia has some of the world's most abundant natural resources. Unfortunately, the process of extracting and developing some of these resources has created many environmental problems. Mining operations, in particular, have caused great damage. The mining sites have polluted the air in surrounding areas and contaminated nearby rivers. Industries that extract oil and gas have also added to the air and water pollution. In addition, overcutting trees in the taiga has caused problems. The loss of much of this forestland has endangered many plant and animal species.

Russia has taken steps to clean up its environment and prevent further damage. For example, the country has begun to enforce stricter rules on oil industries. The government has also discussed spending more money on solving environmental problems. Like other modern nations, Russia will have to balance its need for economic growth with its responsibility to protect the environment.

▲ **ANALYZE CAUSES** Detail what has caused some of Russia's environmental problems.

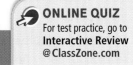

ONLINE QUIZ
For test practice, go to
Interactive Review
@ ClassZone.com

Section 1 Assessment

TERMS & NAMES

1. Explain the importance of
- Ural Mountains
- Siberia
- tundra
- steppe

USE YOUR READING NOTES

2. Categorize Use your completed chart to answer the following question:

Why do more people live in European Russia than in Asian Russia?

GEOGRAPHIC FEATURES	EUROPEAN RUSSIA	ASIAN RUSSIA
Climate		
Plants and Animals		
Agriculture		
Resources		

KEY IDEAS

3. How do the rivers of European Russia provide the region with a transportation network?

4. Why does Siberia have extremely cold weather?

5. Why have many of Russia's natural resources remained untouched?

CRITICAL THINKING

6. Draw Conclusions Do you think many people live on the Kamchatka Peninsula? Why or why not?

7. Analyze Causes and Effects Why do you think that only plants with short roots grow in the tundra?

8. CONNECT to Today In 2006, Russia held a contest to develop a technology to turn coal-processing waste into usable energy. What impact might such a technology have on Russia's pollution problems?

9. WRITING Make a Poster Design and write a poster on the animal and plant life found in one of the four vegetation regions of Russia. Include pictures and captions.

Reading for Understanding

▶ Key Ideas

BEFORE, YOU LEARNED

Russia sprawls across Eurasia, a landmass that includes both Europe and Asia.

NOW YOU WILL LEARN

The sometimes conflicting influences of the East and West have helped shape Russian history.

▶ Vocabulary

TERMS & NAMES

czar (zahr) title for the rulers of Russia from the mid-1500s to the early 1900s

serf a peasant who is bound to the land

Peter the Great a czar who ruled Russia from 1682 to 1725 and tried to make Russia more European

Bolsheviks (BOHL•shuh•VIHKS) a group of revolutionaries who took control of the Russian government in 1917

communism a government and economic system in which nearly all political power and means of production are held by the government in the name of the people

Union of Soviet Socialist Republics (USSR), or **Soviet Union** a new nation with a Communist government created by the Bolsheviks in 1922; dissolved in 1991

Joseph Stalin a cruel 20th-century dictator who had millions of his political enemies executed

totalitarian (toh•TAL•ih•TAIR•ee•uhn) a government that controls public and private life

Cold War a conflict between the United States and the Soviet Union after World War II that never developed into open warfare

Mikhail Gorbachev (GAWR•buh•CHAWF) Soviet leader from 1985 to 1991 who increased freedoms for the Russian people

▶ Reading Strategy

Re-create the chart shown at right. As you read and respond to the **KEY QUESTIONS**, use the chart to help you analyze causes and effects in Russia's history.

 See Skillbuilder Handbook, page R8

ANALYZE CAUSES AND EFFECTS

CAUSES	EFFECTS
Rise of the czars	
Russian expansion	
Communist revolution	
Collapse of Soviet Union	

 GRAPHIC ORGANIZERS
Go to **Interactive Review** @ ClassZone.com

Governing a Vast Land

8.01 Describe the role of key historical figures and evaluate their impact on past and present societies in Africa, Asia, and Australia.

9.01 Trace the historical development of governments, including traditional, colonial, and national in selected societies, and assess their effects on the respective contemporary political systems.

Connecting to Your World

Think about a country that started out being settled by a few groups of people. Gradually the country expanded until it covered a vast area. As this happened, more and more ethnic groups influenced this country's culture. Sound familiar? If you guessed that the country is the United States, you're right. However, Russia has followed a similar pattern. Russia was settled mainly by the Slavs, people of eastern Europe. But as Russia expanded, it was strongly influenced by groups from both the East and the West.

The Rise of an Empire

▼ **KEY QUESTION** How did the Russian Empire develop?

By the 800s, Slavic groups established many settlements in what is now called European Russia. In the 900s, the region came under the control of the Varangians. These people, also called Rus, were most likely Vikings from Scandinavia. The name "Russia" is taken from this group. Eventually, civil war weakened the Rus. In the 1200s, they fell to invaders from Mongolia, a region to the southeast.

Kremlin During the 1100s, the Rus began to develop a fortified town, or Kremlin. The walled fortress complex stands today in Moscow.

MOSCOW
Kremlin

Moscow's Princes Gain Power The Mongols allowed the grand prince of Moscow to collect taxes and keep a portion of them. This money, along with wealth gained through trade, helped Moscow to grow in power. At the same time, Mongol control weakened. Led by Ivan III, the Moscow state broke away from the Mongols in 1480.

Ivan IV became the grand prince of Moscow and, in 1547, the first ruler to be officially called **czar** (zahr). The word *czar* comes from "caesar," the title used for Roman emperors. Ivan IV came to be known as Ivan the Terrible because he was a harsh and suspicious ruler. He murdered hundreds of aristocrats and even killed his eldest son.

Ivan IV and the other czars who came after him passed several laws that bound peasants to the land. These peasants were called **serfs**. Serfdom formed the basis of the Russian economy until the late 1800s. Because of their poverty, harsh working conditions, and the strict controls on their lives, the serfs resented the czars' authority.

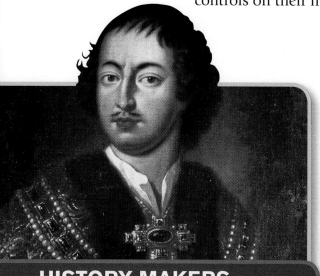

HISTORY MAKERS

Peter the Great 1672–1725

As a child, Peter had a lot of energy and curiosity. He would often organize his friends into an army and then play at war. As an adult, Peter still showed many of his childhood qualities. A dynamic ruler, he built up the navy and army. His enthusiasm for Western ways was extreme. He insisted that nobles shave off their beards, wear European fashions, and study the sciences. Those who opposed these changes were often punished.

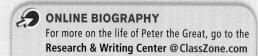

ONLINE BIOGRAPHY
For more on the life of Peter the Great, go to the
Research & Writing Center @ClassZone.com

Peter the Great After Ivan IV's death, Russia suffered under a series of weak rulers. Then in 1682, two half-brothers, Peter I (later known as **Peter the Great**) and Ivan, ruled together. Peter assumed full power when Ivan died in 1696.

The new czar was strongly influenced by the West and worked hard to modernize Russia. Peter believed that a more modern Russia would be better able to compete with Europe militarily and economically. As a result, he introduced European-style customs, factories, and schools in Russia. Peter even moved Russia's capital west from Moscow to an area on the Gulf of Finland. Architects modeled the new capital, called St. Petersburg, after European cities. Its construction cost huge amounts of money and the lives of about 30,000 workers.

Peter also reorganized Russia's government. He replaced inefficient administrative departments with a system of well-organized units. Each one had authority in a certain area, such as finances or justice.

In spite of Peter's efforts, many Russians remained suspicious of western Europeans. They considered western Europeans outsiders. Religious differences widened the gap. The Russians had adopted the Eastern Orthodox branch of Christianity, while western Europeans were mostly Catholics or Protestants.

Russia Expands After Peter's death in 1725, several rivals struggled to gain the throne. Eventually, in 1762, Empress Catherine II (known as Catherine the Great) came to power.

Catherine acquired the northern shore of the Black Sea and the Crimea through a series of wars with the Ottoman Empire. By gaining access to the Black Sea, Russia secured a warm-water port, one in which the water does not freeze in winter. As a result, the port could be used all year for trade. Also, through political deals, Russia obtained much of Poland and its territory.

Like Peter, Catherine admired European culture. She supported the arts, such as ballet and Italian opera. She also tried to pass legal reforms but did little to improve the life of the Russian serfs. In fact, when discontented serfs rebelled in 1773 and 1774, Catherine brutally crushed the revolt. She then tightened control over the serfs.

Catherine the Great died in 1796. Succeeding czars continued to expand Russia's territory. The empire also survived an invasion by the French emperor Napoleon I in 1812. By the late 1800s, Russia controlled land across Central Asia to the Pacific. To connect this vast expanse, Russia started to build the Trans-Siberian Railroad. Completed in 1916, it extended nearly 6,000 miles and greatly helped develop Siberia. You will learn more about this railroad in Animated Geography at the end of this section.

▲ **SUMMARIZE** Explain how the Russian Empire developed.

CONNECT ➜ History & Geography

Napoleon's 1812 March to Russia

In June 1812, Emperor Napoleon I of France and his army of about 600,000 men invaded Russia. Napoleon and his forces advanced on Moscow and occupied it for a time, but Napoleon knew the harsh Russian winter was quickly approaching. Soon he ordered his army to retreat. His soldiers fought against snowstorms, freezing temperatures, and attacking Russian soldiers. By the time Napoleon got out of Russia, only about 10,000 of his men had survived.

CRITICAL THINKING

Analyze Causes In what ways did Russia's geography bring about Napoleon's defeat?

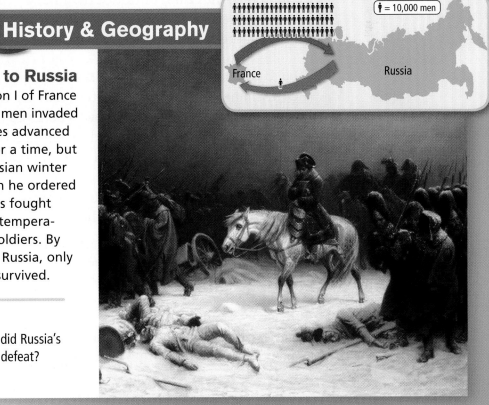

👤 = 10,000 men

France   Russia

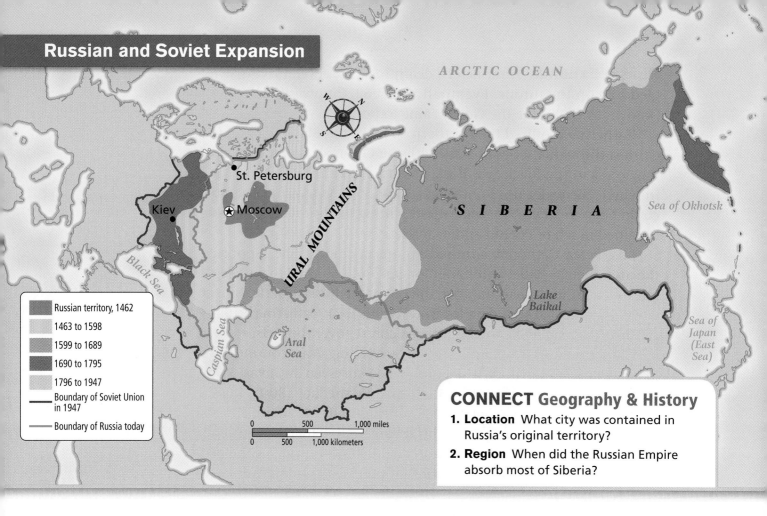

ARCTIC OCEAN

St. Petersburg

Kiev • Moscow

SIBERIA

Sea of Okhotsk

URAL MOUNTAINS

Black Sea

Caspian Sea

Aral Sea

Lake Baikal

Sea of Japan (East Sea)

Russian territory, 1462
1463 to 1598
1599 to 1689
1690 to 1795
1796 to 1947
Boundary of Soviet Union in 1947
Boundary of Russia today

0   500   1,000 miles
0   500   1,000 kilometers

CONNECT Geography & History

1. **Location** What city was contained in Russia's original territory?

2. **Region** When did the Russian Empire absorb most of Siberia?

Revolution Brings Communism

▼ **KEY QUESTION** Why did the Soviet Union rise and fall?

In the 1800s, the czars continued their harsh rule. A few reforms, such as freeing the serfs, were carried out. Many people, though, did not think that these reforms went far enough.

The Bolshevik Revolution Then, in 1917, the Bolshevik (BOHL•shuh•VIHK) Party overthrew czar Nicholas II, and Vladimir Lenin came to power. The **Bolsheviks** believed that all political power and means of production should be held by the government in the name of the people. This type of system is called **communism**.

In 1922, the Bolsheviks created a new Communist nation called the **Union of the Soviet Socialist Republics (USSR)**, or **Soviet Union**. By 1929, **Joseph Stalin** had become dictator. Stalin was a cruel ruler who had millions of his political enemies executed. As dictator, Stalin also set up a **totalitarian** (toh•TAL•ih•TAIR•ee•uhn) government. This form of government controls every aspect of public and private life. Stalin controlled all newspapers, film, radio, and other sources of information. He also censored writers, composers, and other artists who did not glorify his achievements. Stalin's control even extended to education and religion. He built a police state to enforce his power.

Superpower and Collapse The Soviet Union joined the Allies during World War II and gained control of many countries in Eastern Europe during and after the war. Before long, deep distrust developed between the Soviet Union and the West. The United States and the Soviet Union each began to produce more and more powerful nuclear weapons. However, open warfare between the two never broke out. This conflict is called the **Cold War**. The buildup of military weapons during the Cold War drained money from the Soviet Union. As a result, food and other basic items were in short supply. Soviet citizens had to wait in line for hours to buy ordinary items.

In 1985, Soviet leader **Mikhail Gorbachev** (GAWR•buh•CHAWF) tried to revive the nation's economy by reducing government control. He also began allowing more freedom of expression and a free flow of information. However, Gorbachev's policy of openness had an unexpected result. It allowed Soviet citizens the right to complain about economic problems. They also began to call for more freedom.

The efforts to reform the Soviet Union led to its breakup. In 1991, the Soviet Union collapsed, and the Cold War ended. Russia continues to be a world leader. But, as you will learn in Section 4, Russia is still struggling to overcome many problems.

Mikhail Gorbachev
Gorbachev brought about great change, but he did not want to end communism.

▲ **ANALYZE CAUSES AND EFFECTS** Tell why the Soviet Union rose and fell.

ONLINE QUIZ
For test practice, go to
Interactive Review
@ ClassZone.com

Section 2 Assessment

TERMS & NAMES

1. Explain the importance of
- czar
- Bolsheviks
- totalitarian
- Cold War

USE YOUR READING NOTES

2. Analyze Causes and Effects Use your completed chart to answer the following question:

What effect do you think the Cold War had on Western people and on the people of the Soviet Union?

CAUSES	EFFECTS
Rise of the czars	
Russian expansion	
Communist revolution	
Collapse of Soviet Union	

KEY IDEAS

3. Why was the Moscow state able to break away from Mongol rule?

4. What were the major accomplishments of Catherine the Great?

5. What caused the Cold War?

CRITICAL THINKING

6. Make Inferences Why do you think Peter the Great wanted to westernize Russia?

7. Compare and Contrast How were the collapses of czarist Russia and of the Soviet Union similar and different?

8. **CONNECT to Today** The Trans-Siberian Railroad continues to be a popular means of transportation today. Why do you think the railroad is still important?

9. **HISTORY** **Prepare an Oral Report** In your report, contrast western Europe and Eastern-influenced Russia during the time of Peter the Great. Include information on government, economy, and culture.

Animated GEOGRAPHY
The Trans-Siberian Railroad

Click here to to explore the
Trans-Siberian Railroad @ ClassZone.com

CONNECTING EAST AND WEST

In the 1800s, Siberia was Russia's frontier. The region had plentiful natural resources, but these remained largely untapped—until 1891. That's when construction on the Trans-Siberian Railroad began, and the process of linking East and West got under way.

Click here to see how the railroad helped small villages develop into large cities.

Click here to learn how the workers lived, laid tracks, and blasted through the ice.

The Trans-Siberian Railroad Is Built

The first line of the Trans-Siberian Railroad was built between 1891 and 1916.

- Work began at both ends of the line: in Moscow and in Vladivostok.
- One of the greatest obstacles to completion was Lake Baikal, where for a time, a ferry carried the train across the water.
- When the line was completed, it became—and still is—the longest single track in the world.

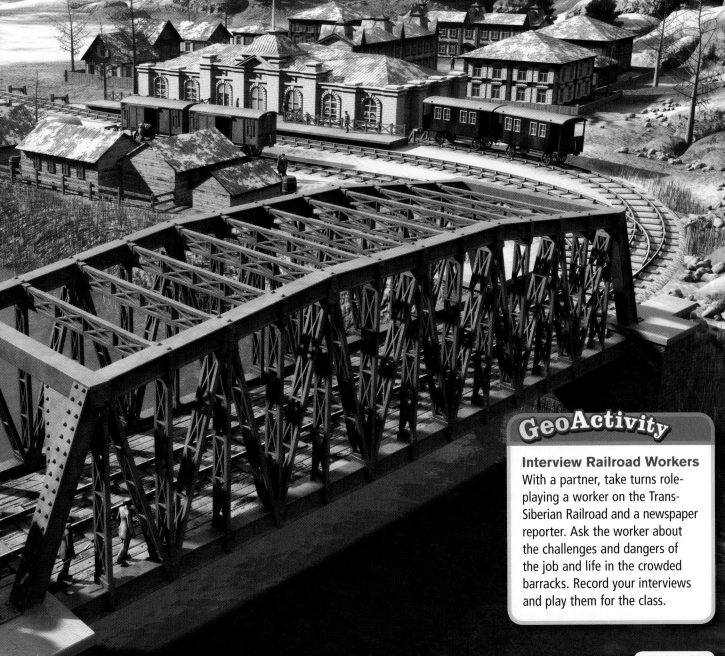

GeoActivity

Interview Railroad Workers
With a partner, take turns role-playing a worker on the Trans-Siberian Railroad and a newspaper reporter. Ask the worker about the challenges and dangers of the job and life in the crowded barracks. Record your interviews and play them for the class.

Reading for Understanding

▶ Key Ideas

BEFORE, YOU LEARNED

Russia has struggled to unite European and Asian influences throughout its history.

NOW YOU WILL LEARN

The influences of Europe and Asia are reflected in the people and culture of Russia.

▶ Vocabulary

TERMS & NAMES

Cyrillic (suh•RIHL•ihk) **alphabet** the official writing system of Russia

icon religious image used by Orthodox Christians in their worship

Leo Tolstoy (TOHL•stoy) a 19th-century writer who is one of Russia's greatest novelists

propaganda information that deliberately tries to influence opinion

BACKGROUND VOCABULARY

Orthodox Christianity the Eastern branch of Christianity that spread to Russia in the 900s and became the state religion

Islam a religion based on the teachings of the prophet Muhammad

Buddhism a religion that began in India and that is based on the teachings of Siddhartha Gautama

Judaism a religion based on the Hebrew Scriptures, whose followers are called Jews

REVIEW

ethnic group a group of people who share language, customs, and a common heritage

Visual Vocabulary dual-language sign depicting the Cyrillic alphabet

▶ Reading Strategy

Re-create the diagram shown at right. As you read and respond to the **KEY QUESTIONS**, use the diagram to record main ideas about Russian culture. Use a new diagram for each aspect of Russian culture you learn about.

 Skillbuilder Handbook, page R4

FIND MAIN IDEAS

RUSSIAN CULTURE

🔎 **GRAPHIC ORGANIZERS**
Go to **Interactive Review** @ ClassZone.com

Blending Europe and Asia

12.02 Describe the relationship between and cultural values of selected societies of Africa, Asia, and Australia and their art, architecture, music, and literature, and assess their significance in contemporary culture.

13.02 Describe the diverse cultural connections that have influenced the development of language, art, music, and belief systems in North Carolina and the United States and analyze their role in creating a changing cultural mosaic.

Connecting to Your World

The United States is made up of **ethnic groups** from all over the world. Their influence has shaped our country. You can see this in many big cities. There, you will find signs and advertisements in many different languages, including Spanish, Korean, and Arabic. Another country that has been strongly influenced by ethnic groups is Russia. In fact, the immense territory of Russia contains more than a hundred different ethnic groups. Most of these groups come from Europe and Asia and have made many cultural contributions.

The Russian People

▼ **KEY QUESTION** What elements shape the daily lives of the Russian people?

Most Russians live in western, or European, Russia. The rugged terrain and harsh climate in eastern Russia have kept populations low in that part of the country. Eighty percent of Russia's people are ethnic Russians, who are descended from the Slavs. Other ethnic groups include the Tatars, Ukrainians, Belarusians, and Chechens (CHECH•uhnz).

Ethnic Russians Russian women relax in front of Kazan Cathedral in St. Petersburg. Ethnic Russians form one of the largest ethnic groups in the world, with over 160 million people worldwide.

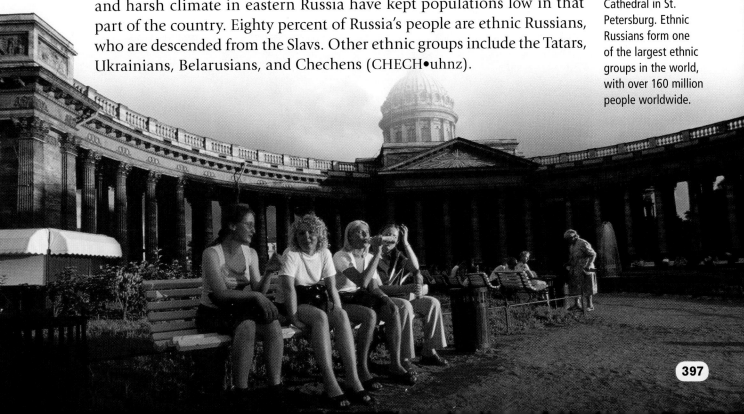

City and Country Life About three-fourths of Russia's people live in cities. The two largest cities are Moscow and St. Petersburg. Red Square in Moscow is the most famous city square in Russia. It was built in the late 1400s and served as a meeting place for the Russian people. The name of the square comes from an old Russian word for "beautiful," which today also means "red." You can see some of Red Square's most famous buildings on the opposite page.

During World War II, many of the buildings in Russia's urban areas were destroyed. After the war, Russia had housing shortages. The Soviet government tried to solve this shortage by building huge high-rises. Many people still live in these dwellings.

In the country, more people live in single-family homes. However, in remote areas, some homes lack plumbing, running water, gas, and electric power. The quality of health care and education is lower in rural areas than in cities. As a result, many people from rural areas have moved to the cities in search of jobs.

Religion By far the most common religion in Russia is **Orthodox Christianity**. During the 900s, missionaries brought this religion to Russia, and with it, the **Cyrillic** (suh•RIHL•ihk) **alphabet**. This alphabet was soon adopted and used to write the Russian language. Around 988, Vladimir I made Orthodox Christianity the state religion.

Before long, Russian Orthodox churches were constructed in the Byzantine style. These churches have distinctive onion-shaped domes. St. Basil's Cathedral in Moscow's Red Square, shown on the opposite page, is a famous example of Russia's Byzantine church style. The churches also usually contain religious paintings called **icons**. Icons are often painted according to strict rules set up by the church authorities and frequently depict God, Jesus, angels, or saints.

Orthodox Christmas
Russian girls light candles inside a church near Moscow during a midnight Christmas service. Orthodox Christians celebrate Christmas on January 7.

Moscow's Red Square

Red Square lies just outside the Kremlin's eastern wall. For over 500 years, the huge square (over 500,000 square feet) has served as a meeting place for the Russian people. Over the centuries, they have gathered there to celebrate festivals, hear announcements from the czar, and witness parades of Soviet military might. Today, Red Square is a popular spot for both Russians and tourists. The images here show some of the square's most legendary sites.

GUM Department Store Moscow's "State Department Store" is actually a huge mall that contains over 150 stores.

St. Basil's Cathedral St. Basil's was built in the 1550s to celebrate military victories over the Mongols.

Lenin's Mausoleum Lenin's body—or at least a wax copy—lies in state in this red and black pyramid.

Islam, **Buddhism**, **Judaism**, and other forms of Christianity are also practiced. In fact, over 15 percent of the population practices Islam. However, many Jews left Russia for the United States and Israel because they were persecuted for practicing their religion.

Food Russians generally eat a hearty diet that uses a lot of root vegetables, such as beets, carrots, onions, and potatoes. These vegetables grow well in the cool Russian climate. They are also warm and filling foods for the cold Russian winters.

Traditional Russian dishes are eaten throughout the world. They include thin pancakes, served with smoked salmon and sour cream, called *blinis* (BLEE•neez), and beet soup called *borscht* (bawrsht). Tea is a traditional beverage, which Russians enjoy piping hot and strong.

Sports Not surprisingly, winter sports, such as hockey, ice skating, and skiing, are popular in Russia. However, the most popular sport is soccer. Tennis has also soared in popularity. In fact, in 2006, five of the top 15 women tennis players in the world were Russian, including tennis star Maria Sharapova. Russian athletes also compete seriously in the Olympics.

🔺 **FIND MAIN IDEAS** Identify some of the elements that shape the daily lives of the Russian people.

CONNECT 🔄 History & Culture

Russia and the Olympics During the Soviet era, Russian Olympic athletes were supported by the government. The athletes excelled in ice skating, ice hockey, and gymnastics. Today, the old Soviet system of supporting athletes no longer exists. Nonetheless, between the time of the Soviet breakup and 2006, Russia has won four Olympic gold medals in men's figure skating and four in pairs skating. The Russians who won the 2006 Olympic gold medal in pairs figure skating are shown here.

Gold medalists Tatiana Totmianina and Maxim Marinin ▼

CRITICAL THINKING

Make Inferences What can you infer about the dedication of the Russian athletes who compete in the Olympics?

Cultural Heritage

▼ **KEY QUESTION** Who are some of the great Russian writers, artists, and composers of the 1800s and 1900s?

As you have learned, rulers such as Peter the Great and Catherine the Great encouraged the Russian people to adopt European customs. As a result, European culture gradually influenced Russian culture. Eventually, Russian literature and music that blended European and traditional styles began to emerge during the early 1800s. Soon Russia began to produce important works of literature, music, and art that are still highly regarded today.

Literature **Leo Tolstoy** (TOHL•stoy) is one of Russia's greatest novelists. In novels such as *War and Peace* (1869), Tolstoy showed deep concern for moral issues and for the welfare of the Russian people. In fact, the writer influenced Indian leader Mohandas Gandhi and his nonviolent independence movement. In turn, Gandhi inspired the nonviolent activism of civil rights leader Martin Luther King Jr.

Russia also boasted one of the best playwrights of the early 1900s. Anton Chekhov (CHEHK•awf) wrote insightful plays, including *The Three Sisters* (1901) and *The Cherry Orchard* (1904). Later in the century, Alexander Solzhenitsyn (SOHL•zhuh•NEET•sihn) described life in a Soviet labor camp under Stalin's rule in his short novel, *One Day in the Life of Ivan Denisovich* (1962). This novel led the Soviet Union to increase censorship.

ANALYZING Primary Sources

Alexander Solzhenitsyn (born 1918) is a Russian novelist who was arrested in 1945 for criticizing Stalin and spent eight years in prisons and labor camps like the one shown here. In this essay, Solzhenitsyn writes about what freedom means to him.

> This, I believe, is the single most precious freedom that prison takes away from us: the freedom to breathe freely, as I now can. No food on earth . . . is sweeter to me than this air steeped in the fragrance of flowers, of moisture and freshness.
>
> Source: "Freedom to Breathe," essay by Alexander Solzhenitsyn

DOCUMENT–BASED QUESTION
What do you think Solzhenitsyn means by "the freedom to breathe freely"?

Marc Chagall In this 1925 painting called *Peasant Life*, Chagall uses vivid colors to celebrate rural Jewish life.

Art Russian painting was slower to adopt European influences than was Russian literature. However, around 1911, Wassily Kandinsky (kan•DIHN•skee) became one of the first artists to paint in the abstract style. Abstract painting does not represent objects using realistic forms. Instead, Kandinsky used bold colors and shapes. Around the same time, Jewish artist Marc Chagall (shuh•GAHL) created imaginative paintings in which the figures often seem to float in the air.

Music and Dance Russian music flowered during the 1800s. Using traditional Russian melodies, Peter Ilich Tchaikovsky (chy•KAWF•skee) wrote many great works, including the ballet *Swan Lake* (1877). Igor Stravinsky introduced modern forms of musical expression with his bold compositions, including the ballet *Rite of Spring* (1913).

You may have noticed that both Tchaikovsky and Stravinsky wrote ballets. That is because dance, especially ballet, had become very popular in Russia. In fact, by the mid-1800s, Russia boasted two world-class ballet companies: the Bolshoi (BOHL•shoy) Ballet and a company that came to be known as the Kirov (KEE•RAWF).

▲ **SUMMARIZE** Explain what Russian writers, artists, and composers of the 1800s and 1900s contributed to Russian culture.

Bolshoi Ballet *Bolshoi* is Russian for "grand." The company first performed *Swan Lake* in 1877. **Why do you think the Bolshoi is popular outside of Russia?**

Soviet Arts

▼ **KEY QUESTION** What purpose did Soviet propaganda serve?

The establishment of the Soviet government in the early 1920s led to the censorship of literature in Russia. The Soviet era, though, did produce some strong works of art in other media. For instance, the films of Sergei Eisenstein, such as *Battleship Potemkim* (1925), influenced the art of filmmaking.

The Soviets also used the arts for propaganda. **Propaganda** is information that deliberately tries to influence opinion. Much of Soviet propaganda was conveyed through posters. Artists were required to create posters that supported and glorified the Communist Party and its programs. These posters were mass-produced and placed in very visible areas. They were constant reminders of Communist policy and guides for proper thought. Under Stalin's rule, the Communist Party outlawed artists who did not promote Communist ideals.

Soviet Poster This 1930s poster shows Soviet citizens waving a flag with Stalin's image and looking toward a bright future. **What feelings do you think posters like this one were meant to inspire in Soviet citizens?**

▲ **RECOGNIZE BIAS AND PROPAGANDA** Discuss the purpose of propaganda and how the Soviets used it.

Section ③ Assessment

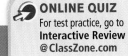
ONLINE QUIZ
For test practice, go to
Interactive Review
@ ClassZone.com

TERMS & NAMES

1. Explain the importance of
- Cyrillic alphabet
- Leo Tolstoy
- icon
- ethnic group

USE YOUR READING NOTES

2. Find Main Ideas Use your completed diagram to answer the following question:

How do Russian people blend Western and Eastern cultures?

RUSSIAN CULTURE

KEY IDEAS

3. What are some of the distinctive features of Russian Orthodox churches?

4. Why are winter sports so popular in Russia?

5. What impact did the Soviet era have on the arts?

CRITICAL THINKING

6. Make Inferences Why do you think Russia has developed so many great tennis players?

7. Compare and Contrast How does life in the country compare with city life in Russia?

8. CONNECT to Today Fast food and soft drinks are popular in Russia today. What does this fact suggest about Western influence in Russia?

9. TECHNOLOGY Present a Slide Show Use pictures to present a slide show about Russian culture. Listen to music by Tchaikovsky and Stravinsky and select your favorite piece. Play the piece as you present your slide show.

Throughout its history, Russia has adopted cultural influences from the West. That cultural exchange continues today. But even as Russia changes, it maintains its character. As these pictures show, the country mixes Western styles with a definite Russian flavor.

Traditional Russia

For hundreds of years, Russians have retreated to their country houses, or dachas, to work in their vegetable gardens. They might also boil water for their tea in a samovar or listen to music played on a balalaika (BAL•uh•LY•kuh). Who knows? The house might even be decorated with nesting Matryoshka (MA•tree•OHSH•kuh) dolls.

Matryoshka Dolls
Traditional dolls nestle one inside the other and depict a round-faced peasant girl.

Beverages
Since the mid-1700s, beautifully decorated samovars have been used in Russia to prepare tea.

◀ *A traditional dacha in western Russia*

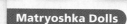

Music
This triangular folk guitar comes in many sizes, including the bass balalaika shown here.

Modern Russia

Many people in Russian cities live in high-rise apartment buildings built during the Soviet era. Further Western influence can be seen in the vending machines and music clubs that dot the cities. Even some traditional Matryoshka dolls now have a Western twist.

Matryoshka Dolls

Today, Matryoshka dolls can depict anyone, including George W. Bush and Vladimir Putin.

Soviet-style apartment blocks in a suburb of Moscow ▼

Beverages

Russians enjoy American-style soft drinks, but the machines dispense the soda into real glasses.

Music

Russian rock musicians often play unusual instruments, such as the cello seen here, in addition to electric guitars and drums.

CRITICAL THINKING

1. **Compare and Contrast** What different lifestyles do the dacha and apartment building suggest?

2. **Draw Conclusions** Which pictures best represent a blend of traditional and modern Russia?

Reading for Understanding

▶ Key Ideas

BEFORE, YOU LEARNED

The Communist government in Russia controlled the country's economy for most of the 20th century.

NOW YOU WILL LEARN

Russia is on its way to establishing a market economy but has struggled to change its government.

▶ Vocabulary

TERMS & NAMES

Vladimir Putin (POOT•ihn) president of Russia who increased executive power in the 2000s

Chechnya (CHEHCH•nee•uh) a largely Islamic republic in southwestern Russia that continues to fight for its independence

command economy an economic system in which the production of goods and services is controlled by a central government

market economy an economic system in which the production of goods and services is decided by the supply and demand of consumers

privatization (pry•vuh•tih•ZAY•shuhn) the process of selling government-owned businesses to private individuals

Boris Yeltsin (YEHLT•sihn) president who abruptly transformed the Russian economy after the Soviet Union collapsed

shock therapy term applied to Yeltsin's economic plan, which called for an abrupt shift from a command economy to a market economy

▶ Reading Strategy

Re-create the chart shown at right. As you read and respond to the **KEY QUESTIONS**, use the chart to identify the problems the Russian government faced after the collapse of the Soviet Union and the solutions they came up with.

 Skillbuilder Handbook, page R10

IDENTIFY PROBLEMS AND SOLUTIONS

PROBLEMS	SOLUTIONS
Establishing a new government	
Responding to internal troubles	
Changing the economy	

 GRAPHIC ORGANIZERS
Go to **Interactive Review** @ ClassZone.com

The Struggle for Reform

 5.02 Examine the different economic systems, (traditional, command, and market), developed in selected societies in Africa, Asia, and Australia, and assess their effectiveness in meeting basic needs.
9.02 Describe how different types of governments such as democracies, dictatorships, monarchies, and oligarchies in selected areas of South America and Europe carry out legislative, executive, and judicial functions and evaluate the effectiveness of each.

Connecting to Your World

Freedom of speech. Freedom of the press. Freedom of religion. These are some of the freedoms we enjoy under a democracy. You probably take them for granted. But the Russian people are still trying to gain many of these freedoms. Since the breakup of the Soviet Union, Russia has worked to establish a new form of government. But internal conflicts and violence have threatened to tear the country apart. In addition, Russia has abruptly changed its economic system. In the midst of these problems and changes, democratic reform has proved difficult to achieve.

A New Government

▼ **KEY QUESTION** Why did Russian democratic reform slow at the beginning of the 21st century?

After the breakup of the Soviet Union in 1991, Russians introduced many democratic reforms to their government. They set up several political parties, elected a president, and reorganized the structure of the government. However, while Russia has taken some steps forward, the country has also taken some steps back. In the early part of the 21st century, the government reversed some earlier reforms and seized more control.

Vladimir Putin Putin worked for 15 years in the KGB, the Soviet Union's intelligence agency, before he entered politics.

Pro-Putin Rally Young people demonstrate their support for Putin in a rally in 2002. The word on the banner means "Russia."

COMPARING ▸ U.S. and Russian Governments

U.S. GOVERNMENT

U.S. citizens elect the president, but the Constitution imposes a series of checks and balances on the president.

appoints federal judges

can declare executive acts unconstitutional

PRESIDENT

can veto acts of Congress

can override veto

can refuse to confirm judicial appointments

SUPREME COURT

CONGRESS

can declare acts of Congress unconstitutional

RUSSIAN GOVERNMENT

Russian citizens directly elect the president, but the Russian Constitution gives the president a great deal of power.

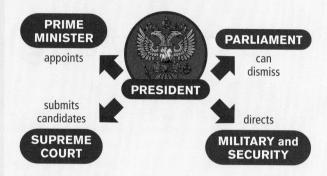

PRIME MINISTER

appoints

submits candidates

SUPREME COURT

PRESIDENT

PARLIAMENT

can dismiss

directs

MILITARY and SECURITY

CRITICAL THINKING

Compare and Contrast What are some similarities and differences between the powers of the president of Russia and those of the president of the United States?

Presidential Power The structure of the Russian government has much in common with that of the U.S. government. For example, the legislative branch of each government consists of two sections. Also, both governments' legislatures propose laws that they then submit to the president. However, the powers of the presidents differ. As you can see from the graphic above, the Russian president has more power than the U.S. president. By the early 2000s, President **Vladimir Putin** (POOT•ihn) of Russia had steadily begun to increase those powers.

When he became president, Putin made many changes to Russia's political system. He decreased the power of rival political parties and greatly increased the power of his own. He also took powers away from elected representatives and restricted the freedom of Russia's newspapers and other media. Today, some fear that Russia may return to the one-party system that ruled the Soviet Union.

Internal Troubles The Russian government restricted freedom, in part, in response to the rise in lawlessness and organized crime that occurred after 1991. The sudden social, political, and economic changes that followed independence encouraged this lawlessness. To combat crime in their country, many Russians have been willing to sacrifice their own liberty for order and the rule of law.

The Russian government also reversed some of its earlier reforms in reaction to terrorism and war with Chechnya. **Chechnya** (CHEHCH•nee•uh) is a largely Islamic region in southwestern Russia. When the people of Chechnya demanded their independence in 1991, Russia refused. Russia invaded the region in 1994 and again in 1999. Militants from Chechnya have also committed many acts of violence. The struggle between Russia and Chechnya continues today.

▲ **ANALYZE EFFECTS** Explain why Russia's democratic reforms have slowed.

Building a Market Economy

▼ **KEY QUESTION** What led to Russia's economic boom?

Although Russia has struggled to establish a democratic government, the country has had greater success reforming its economy. Russia is changing from a **command economy**, which is controlled by the government, to a **market economy**. This is an economic system in which private individuals own most of the businesses and operate them with little government control. The process of selling government-owned businesses to private individuals is called **privatization**.

Making the Transition Privatization has not been easy, however. When the Soviet Union broke apart, the economy was in a state of confusion. Encouraged by Western economists, Russian president **Boris Yeltsin** (YEHLT•sihn) adopted a plan to establish a market economy that involved **shock therapy**. This plan called for abrupt, widespread privatization. Many workers, though, were unwilling to privatize industries and farms. Soon industrial production fell, prices rose, businesses closed, and thousands of people lost work. Some critics of Yeltsin's plan complained that Russia got a lot of "shock" but no "therapy." In time, however, the economy began to prosper.

Moscow Mall Russia's new prosperity can be seen in this Western-style shopping mall. **How does this mall compare with those in your town?**

From Bust to Boom

The graph shown here measures Russia's economic growth. As you can see, the economy has experienced many ups and downs since the breakup of the Soviet Union. But, overall, Yeltsin's shock therapy plan and the country's move toward a market economy have been a success.

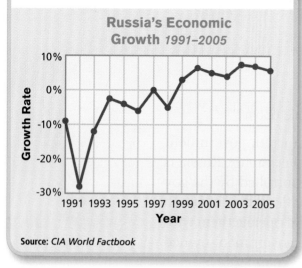

Russia's Economic Growth *1991–2005*

Source: *CIA World Factbook*

An Economic Boom Economic prosperity was not easy to achieve, though. In 1998, the country's money lost value, and the Russian stock market crashed. Economic hardships caused a steep rise in homelessness and a decline in life expectancy. But by 2001, Russia's economy showed steady growth and began to boom. The boom was largely due to Russian exports of oil.

As a result of the surging economy, salaries rose, unemployment decreased, and the Russian people could afford to buy goods. A growing middle class began to emerge. Unfortunately, not everyone has been able to take part in Russia's economic success. Many Russians are still unemployed or underpaid. But Russia has come a long way in a short amount of time.

 SEQUENCE EVENTS Identify the series of events that led to Russia's economic boom.

Section 4 Assessment

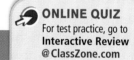
ONLINE QUIZ
For test practice, go to
Interactive Review
@ ClassZone.com

TERMS & NAMES

1. Explain the importance of
- shock therapy
- market economy
- command economy
- privatization

USE YOUR READING NOTES

2. Identify Problems and Solutions
Use your completed problem-solution chart to answer the following question:

How successful was Boris Yeltsin's shock therapy plan?

PROBLEMS	SOLUTIONS
Establishing a new government	
Responding to internal troubles	
Changing the economy	

KEY IDEAS

3. How did President Putin increase the powers of the Russian president?

4. How did Russia begin the shift from a command economy to a market economy?

5. How have the Russian people benefited from their country's economic boom?

CRITICAL THINKING

6. Make Inferences Why might Russians be willing to accept a very powerful president?

7. Evaluate What connection can you draw between Russia's physical geography and its economic boom?

8. CONNECT to Today What appears to be the most positive development in today's Russia?

9. MATH **Create Graphs** Use the Internet and your library to look up data on the unemployment rates for several years in the Soviet Union and in Russia. Then create a graph for each. Write a summary that compares and contrasts the graphs.

Interactive ← Review

Click here to complete these and other activities online @ ClassZone.com

CHAPTER SUMMARY

Key Idea 1
Russia is a vast country that contains a variety of land-forms, climates, vegetation regions, and natural resources.

Key Idea 2
The sometimes conflicting influences of the East and West have helped shape Russian history.

Key Idea 3
The influences of Europe and Asia are reflected in the people and culture of Russia.

Key Idea 4
Russia is on its way to establishing a market economy but has struggled to change its government.

For **Review and Study Notes**, go to **Interactive Review @ ClassZone.com**

NAME GAME

Use the Terms & Names list to complete each sentence on paper or online.

1. I separate European Russia from Asian Russia. _____ **Ural Mountains** 🖑

2. I am a large body of water bordering Russia to the south. _____

3. I am the longest river in Europe. _____

4. I am a vast forest that lies south of the tundra in Russia. _____

5. I am a peasant who is bound to the land. _____

6. I am the title for the ruler of Russia from the mid-1500s to the early 1900s. _____

7. I am a type of government that controls every aspect of public and private life. _____

8. I am the official writing system of Russia.

   _____

9. I am an economic system in which the production of goods and services is controlled by a central government. _____

10. I am the process in which government-owned businesses are sold to private individuals.

   _____

Caspian Sea
command economy
Cyrillic alphabet
czar
Eurasia
icon
market economy
privatization
serf
Slav
steppe
taiga
totalitarian
Ural Mountains
Volga River

Activities

GeoGame

Use this online map to show what you know about Russia's location, geographic features, and important places. Drag and drop each place name to its location on the map.

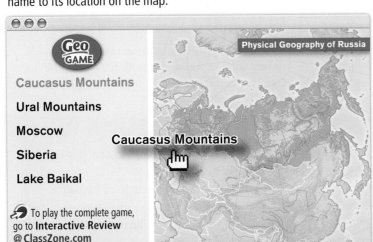

Geo GAME

Caucasus Mountains

Ural Mountains

Moscow

Siberia

Lake Baikal

To play the complete game, go to **Interactive Review @ ClassZone.com**

Physical Geography of Russia

Caucasus Mountains 🖑

Crossword Puzzle

Complete an online crossword puzzle to test your knowledge of Russia.

ACROSS
1. czar who tried to make Russia more European

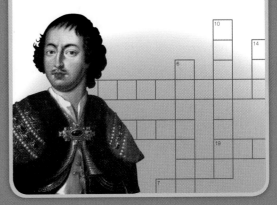

VOCABULARY

Explain the significance of each of the following.

1. Eurasia
2. Ural Mountains
3. czar
4. serf
5. Bolsheviks
6. Joseph Stalin
7. totalitarian
8. Cyrillic alphabet
9. icon
10. command economy

Explain how the terms and names in each group are related.

11. tundra, taiga, and steppe
12. market economy and privatization

KEY IDEAS

1 **Sweeping Across Eurasia**

13. Why has the Northern European Plain in Russia been both a blessing and a curse?
14. Why are many of the main rivers in Siberia hardly ever used for transportation?
15. Why do few people live on the tundra?

2 **Governing a Vast Land**

16. How did the serf system arise in Russia?
17. How did Peter the Great attempt to make Russia's government run efficiently?
18. What was the Cold War?

3 **Blending Europe and Asia**

19. What are icons and how are they used?
20. What winter sports are popular in Russia?
21. Who did Leo Tolstoy inspire?

4 **The Struggle for Reform**

22. What are some of the Russian president's powers?
23. What was the purpose of President Boris Yeltsin's shock therapy plan?
24. What helped bring about Russia's economic boom?

CRITICAL THINKING

25. **Compare and Contrast** Create a chart to compare and contrast the landforms, climate, and natural resources of European Russia and Asian Russia.

EUROPEAN RUSSIA	ASIAN RUSSIA

26. **Analyze Causes** What led to the overthrow of the czar in 1917?
27. **Draw Conclusions** How did the censorship of Solzhenitsyn reflect totalitarianism?
28. **Connect to Economics** How did privatization change Russia?
29. **Connect History & Culture** How do Peter the Great's efforts to westernize Russia affect the country's culture today?
30. **Five Themes: Movement** How did the Trans-Siberian Railroad help unite western and eastern Russia?

Answer the ESSENTIAL QUESTION

How is Russia preserving its Eastern culture while adapting to Western influences?

Written Response Write a two- or three-paragraph response to the Essential Question. Use the rubric below to guide your thinking.

Response Rubric
A strong response will:

• discuss the history of Eastern and Western influence in Russia
• identify Western characteristics Russia has adopted
• explain ways in which Russia maintains its Eastern flavor today

Test Practice
- Online Test Practice @ ClassZone.com
- Test-Taking Strategies and Practice at the front of this book

THEMATIC MAP

Use the map to answer questions 1 and 2 on your paper.

Vegetation Regions of Russia

ARCTIC OCEAN

Black Sea

- Tundra
- Taiga
- Steppe
- Semidesert

0   500   1,000 miles
0   500 1,000 kilometers

1. Which vegetation region covers most of Russia?

A. tundra

B. taiga

C. steppe

D. semidesert

2. Which region is closest to the Arctic Ocean?

A. tundra

B. taiga

C. steppe

D. semidesert

LINE GRAPH

Examine the graph below. Use the information in the graph to answer questions 3 and 4.

Russian Male Life Expectancy

Age

Year

Source: U.N. World Population Division

3. What was the life expectancy in 1990?

A. about 60

B. about 65

C. about 63

D. about 67

4. When did the life expectancy of Russian men decline the most?

A. between 1985 and 1990

B. between 1990 and 1995

C. between 1995 and 2000

D. between 2000 and 2005

GeoActivity

1. INTERDISCIPLINARY ACTIVITY–ECONOMICS

With a small group, prepare a short speech that President Boris Yeltsin might have given to the Russian people about his shock therapy plan. In the speech, explain the long-term benefits of the plan, but also warn the people about the short-term harm it may cause.

2. WRITING FOR SOCIAL STUDIES

Recall what you have learned about censorship under a totalitarian government. Do you think government should ever have the power to control what citizens say or create? Examine the conflicting viewpoints and then explain your position.

3. MENTAL MAPPING

Create a physical map of Russia and label the following:

- Volga River
- Ural Mountains
- Black Sea
- Caspian Sea
- Siberia
- Arctic Ocean
- Lake Baikal
- Kamchatka Peninsula

The Eurasian Republics

ESSENTIAL QUESTION

How can the Eurasian republics meet the challenges of independence?

1
GEOGRAPHY

Center of a Landmass

2
HISTORY & CULTURE

Historic Crossroads

3
GOVERNMENT & ECONOMICS

The Challenge of Independence

CONNECT ⟳ Geography & History

Use the map and the time line to answer the following questions.

1. When did the Mongols conquer Central Asia?

2. What body of water lies between Azerbaijan and Turkmenistan?

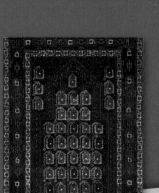

Culture

◄ **600s** Arabs spread Islam to Transcaucasia and Central Asia.
(Muslim prayer rug)

600

Culture

700s Turkish peoples migrate to Central Asia.

History

1200s Mongols conquer Central Asia and stabilize trade along Silk Roads.
(Mongol conqueror Timur the Lame) ►

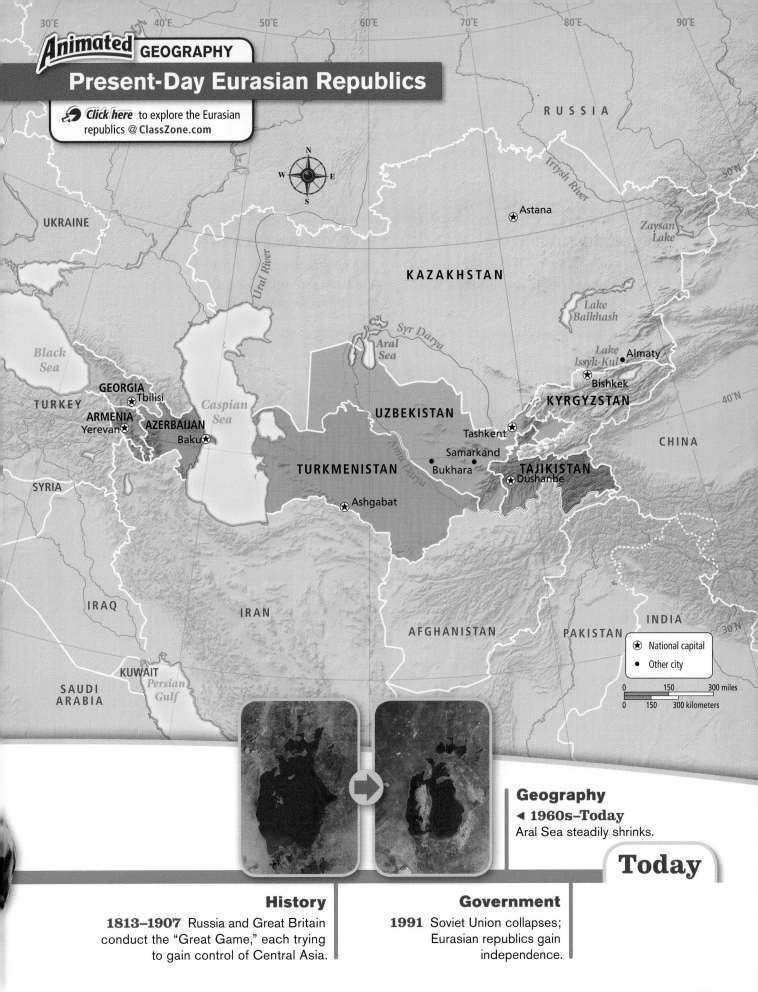

Animated GEOGRAPHY
Present-Day Eurasian Republics

Click here to explore the Eurasian republics @ ClassZone.com

RUSSIA

UKRAINE

Irtysh River

N
W   E
S

• Astana

KAZAKHSTAN

Zaysan Lake

50°N

Ural River

Black Sea

Aral Sea

Syr Darya

Lake Balkhash

GEORGIA • Tbilisi

TURKEY

Caspian Sea

Lake Issyk-Kul • Almaty

• Bishkek

ARMENIA   AZERBAIJAN
Yerevan •   Baku •

UZBEKISTAN

KYRGYZSTAN

40°N

SYRIA

TURKMENISTAN

Tashkent •
Samarkand •
Bukhara •

CHINA

TAJIKISTAN
• Dushanbe

Amu Darya

• Ashgabat

IRAQ

IRAN

AFGHANISTAN

PAKISTAN

INDIA

30°N

KUWAIT

Persian Gulf

SAUDI ARABIA

★ National capital
• Other city

0   150   300 miles
0   150   300 kilometers

Geography
◄ 1960s–Today
Aral Sea steadily shrinks.

Today

History
1813–1907 Russia and Great Britain conduct the "Great Game," each trying to gain control of Central Asia.

Government
1991 Soviet Union collapses; Eurasian republics gain independence.

415

Reading for Understanding

SECTION 1

▶ Key Ideas

BEFORE, YOU LEARNED

Russia's vast geography and variety of climates form a land of great diversity.

NOW YOU WILL LEARN

The geography and climate of the Eurasian republics pose challenges, but the countries are rich in natural resources.

▶ Vocabulary

TERMS & NAMES

Transcaucasia (TRANS•kaw•KAY•zhuh) a region between the Black and Caspian seas that contains the republics of Armenia, Azerbaijan (AZ•uhr•by•JAHN), and Georgia

Central Asia a region that contains the republics of Kazakhstan (KAH•zahk•STAN), Kyrgyzstan (KEER•gee•STAN), Tajikistan (tah•JIHK•ih•STAN), Turkmenistan (TURK•mehn•ih•STAN), and Uzbekistan (uz•BEHK•ih•STAN)

Caucasus (KAW•kuh•suhs) **Mountains** a mountain range that runs between the Black Sea and the Caspian Sea

landlocked completely surrounded by land

Tian Shan (TYAHN SHAHN) a mountain range that runs across Kyrgyzstan and Tajikistan

Kara Kum a huge desert that covers most of Turkmenistan

Aral Sea an inland body of water in Central Asia that has been steadily shrinking

Lake Balkhash a lake in eastern Kazakhstan

REVIEW

Eurasia a term used to refer to a single continent that is made up of Europe and Asia

Caspian Sea a sea situated between Transcaucasia and Central Asia; the largest inland body of water in the world

▶ Reading Strategy

Re-create the Venn diagram shown at right. As you read and respond to the **KEY QUESTIONS**, use the diagram to compare and contrast the landforms, climates, and resources of Transcaucasia and Central Asia.

 See Skillbuilder Handbook, page R9

COMPARE AND CONTRAST

TRANSCAUCASIA   BOTH   CENTRAL ASIA

GRAPHIC ORGANIZERS
Go to **Interactive Review @ ClassZone.com**

Center of a Landmass

3.01 Identify ways in which people of selected areas in Africa, Asia, and Australia have used, altered, and adapted to their environments in order to meet their needs and evaluate the impact of their actions on the development of cultures and regions.
5.01 Describe the relationship between the location of natural resources, and economic development, and analyze the impact on selected cultures, countries, and regions in Africa, Asia, and Australia.

Connecting to Your World

You have already learned that the Soviet Union was a Communist country that consisted of Russia and the surrounding republics. Remember that some geographers place this enormous nation in a region they call **Eurasia**, a landmass made up of both Europe and Asia. When the Soviet Union broke apart in 1991, 15 independent republics were formed. Three of these republics are located between the Black and Caspian seas in a region called Transcaucasia. Five more independent republics lie in Central Asia, a region east of the Caspian Sea.

Landforms and Bodies of Water

▼ **KEY QUESTION** What are the major landforms and bodies of water in Transcaucasia and Central Asia?

Transcaucasia consists of the republics of Armenia, Azerbaijan, and Georgia. **Central Asia** contains the republics of Kazakhstan, Kyrgyzstan, Tajikistan, Turkmenistan, and Uzbekistan. Both regions are very mountainous and boast some of the largest lakes in the world.

Tian Shan The Tian Shan, which is Chinese for "Heavenly Mountains," stretch for nearly 1,500 miles.

TIAN SHAN

417

Transcaucasia As you can see on the map on the opposite page, Transcaucasia is bounded by Turkey and Iran to the south. The **Caucasus Mountains** Ⓐ rise in the north and form the border between Russia and Transcaucasia. These mountains lie between two bodies of water. The Black Sea borders Georgia on the west. The **Caspian Sea** Ⓑ, which is actually a saltwater lake, borders Azerbaijan on the east. It is the largest inland body of water in the world.

Armenia lies between Georgia and Azerbaijan. In fact, Armenia is **landlocked**, or completely surrounded by land. The country contains fertile volcanic soil on a southern plateau. Fertile coastal plains lie in Georgia on the Black Sea and along the Caspian Sea in Azerbaijan.

Central Asia This region is bordered by Russia to the north, the Caspian Sea to the west, a series of mountain ranges to the south, and China to the east. Mountains dominate Kyrgyzstan and Tajikistan. Most of this rugged terrain is part of the Alay and **Tian Shan** Ⓒ mountain ranges. The towering Tian Shan range contains some of the largest alpine glaciers in the world. An even higher mountain range, called the Pamirs, is located in southeastern Tajikistan.

Kazakhstan has a variety of landforms. The mountainous terrain in the east lowers to a large steppe in the north and a desert in the south. Then the land lowers even more toward the Caspian Sea, where it sinks to about 433 feet below sea level. The huge desert of **Kara Kum** Ⓓ covers most of Turkmenistan. Another vast desert, the Kyzyl Kum, occupies much of Uzbekistan.

The two most important rivers of Central Asia, the Syr Darya and the Amu Darya, flow into the **Aral Sea** Ⓔ. *Darya* means "river." Much of the water from these rivers is used for irrigation. You will learn about the impact of this irrigation on the Aral Sea later in this section. **Lake Balkhash** Ⓕ is situated in eastern Kazakhstan. It is unusual because the lake is composed of fresh water in its western half and salt water in its eastern half.

Kara Kum The few people who live in this desert are mainly sheep and camel herders. **Why do you think the Kara Kum is sparsely populated?**

▲ **CATEGORIZE** Describe the major landforms and bodies of water in Transcaucasia and Central Asia.

Physical Geography of the Eurasian Republics

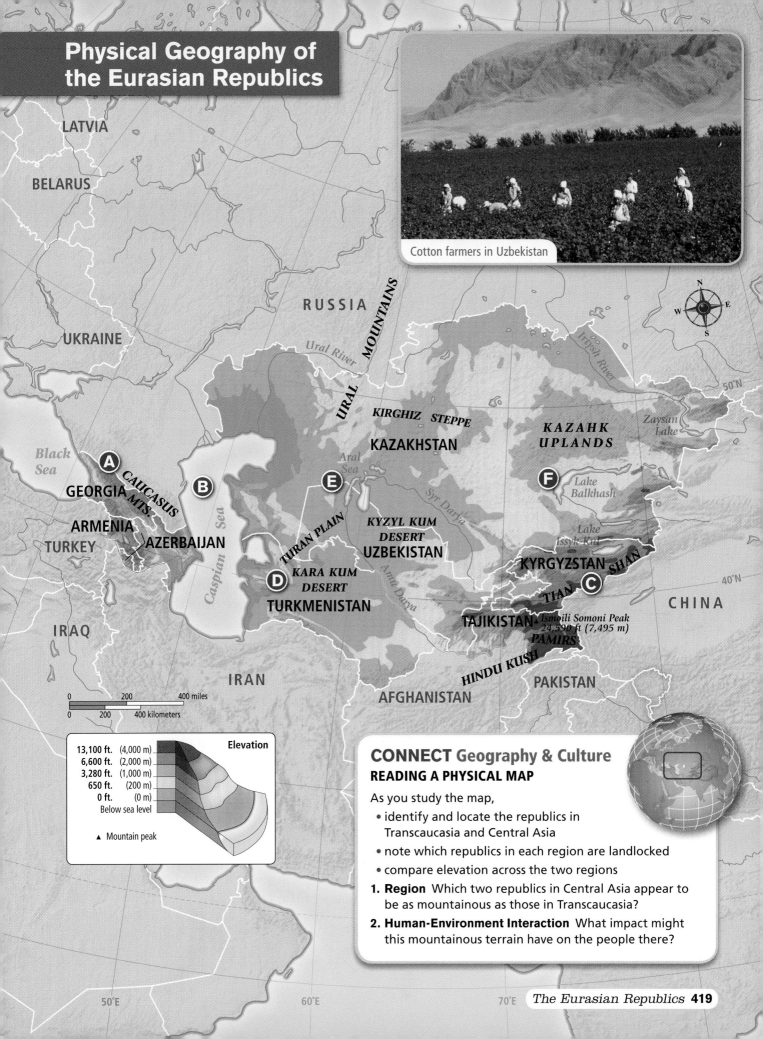

Cotton farmers in Uzbekistan

LATVIA

BELARUS

UKRAINE

RUSSIA

URAL MOUNTAINS

Ural River

Irtysh River

KIRGHIZ   STEPPE

KAZAKHSTAN

Aral Sea

Zaysan Lake

KAZAHK UPLANDS

Black Sea

Ⓐ

Ⓑ

Ⓔ

Ⓕ

Lake Balkhash

GEORGIA   *CAUCASUS MTS.*

Syr Darya

Lake Issyk-Kul

ARMENIA

TURKEY   AZERBAIJAN

Caspian Sea

TURAN PLAIN

KYZYL KUM DESERT
UZBEKISTAN

KYRGYZSTAN   *TIAN   SHAN*

Ⓒ

CHINA

Ⓓ   *KARA KUM DESERT*

TURKMENISTAN

Amu Darya

TAJIKISTAN   *Ismoili Somoni Peak 24,590 ft (7,495 m)*

PAMIRS

IRAQ

IRAN

HINDU KUSH

PAKISTAN

AFGHANISTAN

50°N

40°N

| 0 | 200 | 400 miles |
| 0 | 200 | 400 kilometers |

Elevation

13,100 ft.	(4,000 m)
6,600 ft.	(2,000 m)
3,280 ft.	(1,000 m)
650 ft.	(200 m)
0 ft.	(0 m)
Below sea level	

▲ Mountain peak

CONNECT Geography & Culture
READING A PHYSICAL MAP

As you study the map,
- identify and locate the republics in Transcaucasia and Central Asia
- note which republics in each region are landlocked
- compare elevation across the two regions

1. **Region** Which two republics in Central Asia appear to be as mountainous as those in Transcaucasia?

2. **Human-Environment Interaction** What impact might this mountainous terrain have on the people there?

50°E   60°E   70°E

Transcaucasia
Visitors enjoy a day on Georgia's Black Sea coast. **1. How does this image reflect the area's climate?**

Central Asia
Kyrgyzstan averages less than 20 inches of rain a year. **2. How might this climate affect vegetation?**

Climate

🔺 **KEY QUESTION** How do the climates in Transcaucasia and Central Asia differ?

Climate in the two regions ranges from the subtropical areas of Transcaucasia to the semiarid and desert climates of Central Asia. The high elevations of the mountains and distance from the sea have a big impact on climate in both regions.

Transcaucasia In the lowlands of Azerbaijan, winters are mild and summers are hot. In the mountainous areas of Armenia, on the other hand, temperatures are colder, and snow in the winter can be heavy. Georgia has a milder climate than either Armenia or Azerbaijan. The Caucasus Mountains protect the coastal areas from too much rain. In addition, moist air from the Black Sea moderates Georgia's climate.

Central Asia Like Armenia, the nations of Central Asia are land-locked. They are many miles from the moderating influence of the world's oceans. As a result, Central Asia has a much harsher climate than Transcaucasia, with extreme high and low temperatures. Southern and southeastern mountain ranges block any moist air and contribute to the semiarid and desert climates of the region.

🔻 **COMPARE AND CONTRAST** Compare the climates of Transcaucasia and Central Asia.

Resources

▼ **KEY QUESTION** What resources are abundant in Transcaucasia and Central Asia?

Both Transcaucasia and Central Asia are rich in natural resources. The regions have huge reserves of coal and metals, but oil and natural gas are especially plentiful. In fact, the petroleum deposits around and under the Caspian Sea are among the world's largest. The development of the oil resources in both regions should help the young nations thrive.

Transcaucasia Most of the oil in Transcaucasia lies in Azerbaijan. In fact, the country's name means "land of flames." The name refers to fires that erupted from the rocks and the rivers leading to the Caspian Sea. The fires were the result of underground oil and gas deposits.

The Transcaucasian republics also have fertile farmland. In the rich soil along the coastal plain of Georgia, farmers grow grapes, citrus fruit, and tea. In the highlands of Armenia, farm products include peaches, apricots, walnuts, and wheat. Because of the lack of precipitation, many of the farms in Azerbaijan require irrigation.

Central Asia Much of the oil in Central Asia can be found in Kazakhstan and Turkmenistan. Nations all over the world are interested in buying this oil, which may eventually bring great wealth to the region. In addition, rich deposits of highly valued energy resources, such as coal and natural gas, are plentiful. Mines also provide valuable minerals, including gold, copper, and lead.

Unlike Transcaucasia, Central Asia has little fertile soil, and many areas do not receive much rain. For that reason, water often has to be brought in to irrigate crops. Cotton is an important crop for all of the Central Asian republics. Other crops include grain, fruits, and vegetables.

CONNECT ➘ Geography & Economics

Oil and the Caspian Sea

For years, the five countries that border the Caspian Sea have argued over rights to the oil-rich area. In 2003, Azerbaijan, Kazakhstan, and Russia agreed to a division of the sea and its resources. However, Iran and Turkmenistan did not agree to the plan. Nonetheless, progress has been made in extracting the oil. In 2005, a pipeline was built to pump oil from Azerbaijan to Turkey. In this photograph, a mosque in the Azerbaijan capital of Baku overlooks oil derricks in the Caspian.

▲ **SUMMARIZE** Identify the resources that are abundant in Transcaucasia and Central Asia.

Human-Environment Interaction

▼ **KEY QUESTION** What has led to some of the environmental problems in Central Asia?

For decades the Soviet Union attempted to overcome its geographic limits by trying to increase its farmable land. The government also took advantage of some of its vast, uninhabited areas by carrying out experimental projects in them. Unfortunately, these projects sometimes had unintended negative results, particularly in Central Asia.

Aral Sea In the 1960s, the Soviet Union began using river water from the Syr Darya and Amu Darya for an irrigation project. This project was part of a plan to convert areas of Central Asian desert into thriving cotton farms. Indeed, the production of cotton soon soared. However, since the Aral Sea received most of its water from the two rivers, the irrigation caused the sea to drastically shrink. The sea even split into two, the small Aral and the large Aral. Recent efforts have helped raise the level of the small Aral. As a result, fish, jobs, and people have begun to return to the area. But the Soviet plan caused one of Earth's greatest environmental disasters.

CONNECT to Science

By the end of the 20th century, irrigation and evaporation had caused the Aral Sea to shrink about 75 percent. The retreating waters left behind dry beds filled with salt, fertilizers, and pesticides. These chemicals had washed into the sea from the cotton farms. Windstorms then blew the chemicals into the surrounding area. As a result, the rates of cancer and other diseases greatly increased in the nearby population.

Disappearing Sea A camel stands before an abandoned ship on what was once the floor of the Aral Sea.

Activity

Conduct an Evaporation Experiment

Materials
- 2 tablespoons of salt
- measuring cup of water
- spoon
- shallow bowl

1. Place salt into the measuring cup.

2. Fill the cup with warm water and stir to dissolve the salt.

3. Pour the mixture into the bowl and place near a window.

4. Check the bowl every day for a week. Note what evaporates and what remains behind.

Nuclear Testing Other Soviet programs have caused problems in Central Asia. As you may recall, the Soviet Union and the United States engaged in a weapons race during the Cold War. Between 1949 and 1990, the Soviet government used part of the vast steppes in northern Kazakhstan to test their nuclear weapons. Unfortunately, radiation from this testing poisoned the soil, food, and water over about a 7,000-square-mile area. The radiation caused dramatic increases in the rates of leukemia, birth defects, and mental illness in the area.

Recently, the nations of Central Asia have taken steps to avoid more environmental problems. For example, Kazakhstan has started to develop more light industry to prevent an overdependence on heavy industries. This measure should help decrease the region's air and water pollution problems.

 ANALYZE CAUSES Explain what led to some of the environmental problems in Central Asia.

Nuclear Blast The Soviets conducted about 715 nuclear tests. In this picture, a test site is destroyed in Kazakhstan in 2000.

 **ONLINE QUIZ**
For test practice, go to
Interactive Review
@ ClassZone.com

Section 1 Assessment

TERMS & NAMES

1. Explain the importance of
- Transcaucasia
- Central Asia
- Kara Kum
- Aral Sea

USE YOUR READING NOTES

2. Compare and Contrast Use your completed Venn diagram to answer the following question:

What element of their physical geography offers great promise for the futures of both Transcaucasia and Central Asia?

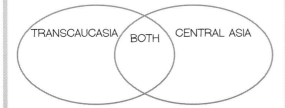

KEY IDEAS

3. What types of landforms are found in Kazakhstan?

4. Why does Central Asia have a harsh climate?

5. What areas of Transcaucasia have rich soil?

CRITICAL THINKING

6. Make Inferences Which region do you think is more densely populated, Transcaucasia or Central Asia? Explain your answer.

7. Compare and Contrast How are the landforms and bodies of water of Georgia and Armenia similar and different?

8. CONNECT to Today What lessons can be learned today from the Aral Sea environmental disaster?

9. WRITING Prepare an Environmental Report Do further research about the causes and effects of pollution in Central Asia. Also find out about possible solutions for these problems. Then write an environmental report that summarizes your research.

Reading for Understanding

▶ Key Ideas

BEFORE, YOU LEARNED

The Eurasian republics are largely mountainous and desert regions with harsh climates.

NOW YOU WILL LEARN

The geographic location of the Eurasian republics has attracted many different cultures, ideas, and conquerors.

▶ Vocabulary

TERMS & NAMES

nomad member of a group who makes a living by herding animals and moving from place to place as the seasons change

Islam a religion that is based on the teachings of the prophet Muhammad

Muslim a follower of Islam

Silk Roads major trade routes that ran from China to the rest of East Asia, through Central Asia, and into Europe

Russification the process of making a culture more Russian

yurt a portable, tentlike structure used by the nomads of Central Asia

REVIEW

ethnic group a group of people who share language, customs, and a common heritage

Visual Vocabulary Russification

▶ Reading Strategy

Re-create the web diagram shown at right. As you read and respond to the **KEY QUESTIONS**, use the diagram to record main ideas about the history and culture of the Eurasian republics. Add ovals as needed.

 See Skillbuilder Handbook, page R4

FIND MAIN IDEAS

Influenced by many ethnic groups

HISTORY AND CULTURE IN EURASIAN REPUBLICS

GRAPHIC ORGANIZERS
Go to **Interactive Review** @ ClassZone.com

Historic Crossroads

8.02 Describe the role of key groups such as Mongols, Arabs, and Bantu and evaluate their impact on historical and contemporary societies of Africa, Asia, and Australia.

11.01 Identify the concepts associated with culture such as language, religion, family, and ethnic identity, and analyze how they can link and separate societies.

Connecting to Your World

Imagine that you had to move every few months. In the summer, you might live in New England. Then in the fall, you would move to the Midwest. Finally, in the winter, you would go to the Southwest. In the spring, you would start the cycle all over again. This way of life probably sounds very different from your own, but it is similar to the way thousands of nomads live. **Nomads** are people who make a living by herding animals and moving from place to place as the seasons change. The people who first lived in Transcaucasia and Central Asia led a nomadic way of life.

Nomadic Man This man's weather-beaten face reflects a life lived largely out of doors.

Nomadic Home Nomads live in yurts, portable tents that usually consist of several layers of felt stretched around a wooden frame.

Regions of Exchange

🔻 **KEY QUESTION** How have various groups of people and trade influenced Transcaucasia and Central Asia?

For centuries, many groups of people moved through Transcaucasia and Central Asia. Some of them settled in these regions and had a major influence on culture. Three main reasons for this movement were military conquest, migration, and trade.

Migrations, Invasions, and Trade Three groups that had a major impact on the cultures of Transcaucasia and Central Asia were the Arabs, the Turks, and the Mongols.

In the 600s, Arabs moved into Transcaucasia in great numbers and introduced Islam. **Islam** is a religion based on the teachings of the prophet Muhammad. The followers of Islam are called **Muslims**. During the 1000s, tribes from Turkey moved into the region. Eventually, Transcaucasia became part of the Ottoman Empire, which ruled the area until World War I. In addition, Mongols raided Georgian lands from the 1200s to the early 1400s.

Central Asia followed a similar pattern of migration and invasion. Arabs spread Islam to parts of Central Asia. Turkish peoples began to migrate into Central Asia during the 700s. In the 1200s, the Mongols conquered the region.

The Mongol Empire brought stability to Central Asia. This stability encouraged trade in the region. A network of major trade routes, called the **Silk Roads**, flourished. They ran from China to the rest of East Asia, through Central Asia, and into Europe. Cities, such as Samarkand in present-day Uzbekistan and Merv in present-day Turkmenistan, sprang up along the Silk Roads. Central Asian nomads helped stimulate trade by traveling along the routes and exchanging livestock for food and manufactured products. Goods traded included jade, gold, horses, wool, and, of course, silk. Religions, including Islam, and inventions, such as the compass and gunpowder, also spread along these routes.

The Silk Roads

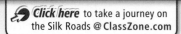

Click here to take a journey on the Silk Roads @ ClassZone.com

Travel along the demanding terrain of the Silk Roads was difficult and often dangerous. Traders avoided the harsh Taklimakan Desert as much as possible. Temperatures in the desert often reach 120°F in the summer. Even caravans that traveled along the edge of the desert often dealt with fierce sandstorms.

After the Taklimakan, caravans had to cross the steep Pamir Mountains. Caravans that traveled on southern routes had to cross over the Himalayas on narrow passes that dropped off into deep ravines.

CONNECT Geography & History

Human-Environment Interaction What do the difficulties along the Silk Roads suggest about the traders who traveled them?

Geographic Challenges A camel train winds through the Taklimakan Desert under the hot sun.

Ethnic Groups The movement of the Arabs, Turks, and Mongols into Transcaucasia and Central Asia had a major impact on the ethnic makeup of these regions. For example, in Central Asia, many people are descended from Turkish and Mongol tribes. The Silk Roads also brought many different ethnic groups to the regions. Remember that an **ethnic group** is made up of people who share a common heritage.

As a result of this migration and trade, people belonging to many different ethnic groups live in the Eurasian republics today. The pie graphs at right show the ethnic distributions in Transcaucasia and Central Asia. Most of the people practice Islam or Orthodox Christianity.

In Transcaucasia, Armenian, Azerbaijani, and Georgian are the most common languages. Russian and various languages related to Turkish are commonly spoken in Central Asia.

Like people in other parts of the world, those in Transcaucasia and Central Asia do not always get along. Allegiance to their ethnic group is often of greater importance than loyalty to their country. For instance, in Georgia, the Ossetians continue to fight for their independence from the republic. In Central Asia, the Kyrgyz and the Uzbeks have had conflicts over territorial claims.

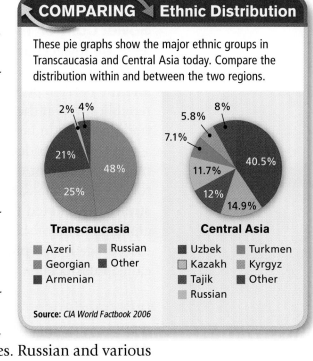

COMPARING **Ethnic Distribution**

These pie graphs show the major ethnic groups in Transcaucasia and Central Asia today. Compare the distribution within and between the two regions.

Transcaucasia
2% 4%
21%
25%
48%

- Azeri
- Georgian
- Armenian
- Russian
- Other

Central Asia
8%
5.8%
7.1%
40.5%
11.7%
12%
14.9%

- Uzbek
- Kazakh
- Tajik
- Russian
- Turkmen
- Kyrgyz
- Other

Source: *CIA World Factbook 2006*

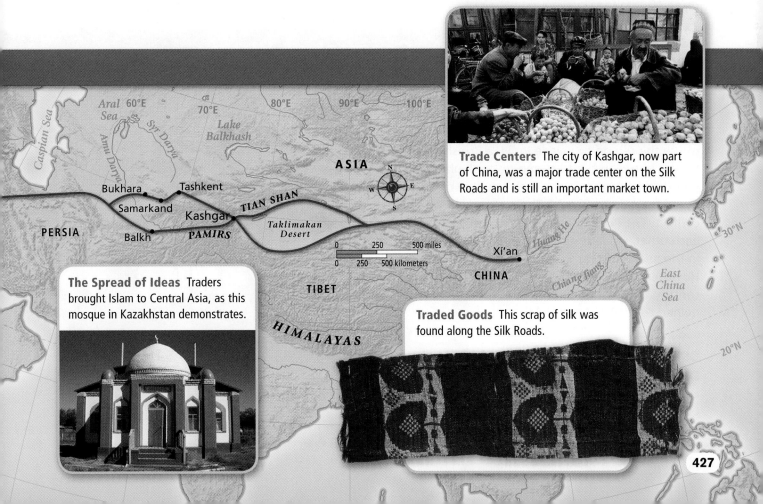

Trade Centers The city of Kashgar, now part of China, was a major trade center on the Silk Roads and is still an important market town.

The Spread of Ideas Traders brought Islam to Central Asia, as this mosque in Kazakhstan demonstrates.

Traded Goods This scrap of silk was found along the Silk Roads.

Soviet Control In 1922, Russia joined with three other territories to form the Soviet Union. These territories came to include Transcaucasia, Central Asia, and the western republics—Belarus, Moldova, Ukraine, and the Baltic republics. The Soviets then divided their land into 15 republics. When they divided the land, however, they often ignored traditional boundaries. This policy created deep resentment.

As the Soviets developed their republics, they tried to make them more Russian. For example, they forced a large number of Russians to move to Kazakhstan to work on farms and in cities. They also strongly promoted the Russian language and the use of the Cyrillic alphabet in all of their republics. Traditional ethnic ways of life were discouraged. This process of making other cultures more Russian is called **Russification**.

Independence When the Soviet Union collapsed in 1991, the republics in Transcaucasia and Central Asia gained their independence. Since then, they have begun to move toward market economies. However, widespread poverty and ethnic disputes are still common. As a result, many people have migrated from the former Soviet republics into Russia, seeking better conditions.

▲ **EVALUATE** Explain how trade and various groups of people have influenced Transcaucasia and Central Asia.

CONNECT ⟳ Geography & History

The Great Game From about 1813 to 1907, the Russian Empire and Great Britain competed for control of Central Asia. The Russian Empire wanted to use the region to invade India, a British colony. Battles between the two empires took place in the Kingdom of Afghanistan. Their struggle came to be called the "Great Game." The cartoon illustrates the conflict. The Russian bear and the British lion stare at each other, while the ruler of Afghanistan is caught in the middle. Great Britain managed to protect India. However, by the end of the 19th century, the Russian Empire had gained control of Central Asia.

CRITICAL THINKING
Draw Conclusions What lasting impact did the Great Game have on Central Asia in the 20th century?

PUNCH, OR THE LONDON CHARIVARI.—November 30, 1878.

"SAVE ME FROM MY FRIENDS!"

◀ *The empires in 1900*

RUSSIAN EMPIRE

KINGDOM OF AFGHANISTAN

BRITISH INDIA

People and Traditions

▼ **KEY QUESTION** What are some of the characteristics of life in Transcaucasia and Central Asia?

Many of the people of the Eurasian republics follow the same traditions as their ancestors. Most people in Central Asia live in rural areas, where they farm or herd livestock. In Transcaucasia, on the other hand, more than half the people live in urban areas. These people often work in offices or factories.

Family Life In both Transcaucasia and Central Asia, family life is very important. In many countries, extended families live together. These families include parents, grandparents, aunts, and uncles.

In the cities of Armenia and Azerbaijan, many families live in large apartment buildings. One- or two-story houses and apartment buildings are common in the cities of Georgia. Apartment buildings are also common in the cities of Central Asia.

In rural areas of Central Asia, however, nomads often live in a dwelling called a yurt. A **yurt** is a portable, tentlike structure covered with hides or textiles. Inside, yurts are lined with decorative rugs. When nomads search for good pasture for their livestock, they carry their yurts with them on horseback or in wagons.

In the Eurasian republics, families observe many ethnic and religious holidays. In Central Asia, the Muslim spring holiday of Noruz is widely celebrated. Orthodox Easter is a popular Christian holiday in Armenia and Georgia. Since gaining independence, the people of the Eurasian republics value the freedom to celebrate their ethnic and religious holidays. Under Soviet rule, these holidays were often banned.

Kazakh Picnic Many generations gather to enjoy a feast that includes meat dumplings, rice with roasted garlic, and bread. **What does the picture suggest about family life in Kazakhstan?**

Worldster
A Day in Zuhura's Life

 To learn more about Zuhura and her world, go to the **Activity Center** @ ClassZone.com

Hi! My name is Zuhura. I am 14 years old and live in a rural town in Uzbekistan. School and doing chores are an important part of my life. But I also have fun with my friends. I enjoy watching Bollywood movies, which are films made in India. In fact, I have covered my school notebook with stickers of Bollywood movie stars. This is what my day is like.

This is how to say "My name is Zuhura" in Uzbek:

"Mening ismim Zuhura."

6:30–7:30 A.M. I wake up and eat a breakfast of tea and bread with jam. Then I feed the chickens and milk the family cow. When I'm done, I head off to school with my brothers and sisters.

8 A.M.–2:30 P.M. School has seven 45-minute periods. Our school doesn't have heat. In the winter, it gets really cold. So we keep our coats on while we sit at our desks.

3 P.M. When I get home, I eat a snack of bread and tea and then help clean house and wash clothes by hand. Later, we all help my mother prepare dinner. Only then do I have time to spend with my friends.

8 P.M. We're having my favorite meal tonight: soup made of broth, carrots, potatoes, and meat. In the winter, we eat a lot of cabbage soup, which I don't like as well. After dinner, I do homework and watch TV.

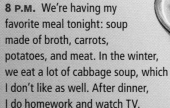
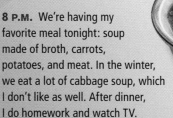

CONNECT to Your Life

Journal Entry In your journal, write a schedule detailing your typical school day. Then compare your schedule with Zuhura's. How are the two schedules similar and how are they different?

Traditions People in the Eurasian republics eat a variety of foods. Many of the dishes in Central Asia and Transcaucasia use meat and milk products. This diet is part of the heritage of the nomadic life. Traditional foods of Kyrgyzstan include lamb, noodles with broth and mutton, and vegetable soup. In Kazakhstan, the people drink *kumiss*, which is made from horse's milk. In Transcaucasia, Georgians and Armenians enjoy shish kabob. In Azerbaijan, pilaf (a rice dish) and grilled goat and lamb are popular. Pilaf is also a popular dish in Central Asia.

Traditional arts thrive in Transcaucasia and Central Asia. For hundreds of years, Armenian artisans have constructed beautiful stone churches with many domes. The craftspeople of Turkmenistan, Uzbekistan, and Azerbaijan are known for weaving decorative rugs and tapestries.

HORSEBACK SPORTS

Many of Central Asia's sports involve horses. These include *kokpar*, a type of polo, and horseback wrestling. In Kazakhstan, riders still practice the ancient art of eagle hunting, as shown above. These traditional sports reflect the importance of horses and riding in the region's culture.

 FIND MAIN IDEAS Identify some of the characteristics of life in Transcaucasia and Central Asia.

Section 2 Assessment

 ONLINE QUIZ
For test practice, go to **Interactive Review** @ ClassZone.com

TERMS & NAMES

1. Explain the importance of
- nomad
- Silk Roads
- Russification
- yurt

USE YOUR READING NOTES

2. Find Main Ideas Use your completed diagram to answer the following question:

Why does traditional ethnic culture play such a large role in the lives of the people of the Eurasian republics?

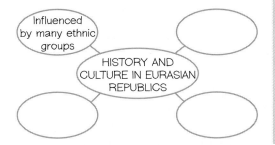

KEY IDEAS

3. What three groups had major impacts on the cultures of Transcaucasia and Central Asia?

4. How did the Soviet Union attempt to make its republics more Russian?

5. How do the dishes of the Eurasian republics reflect the region's nomadic heritage?

CRITICAL THINKING

6. Make Inferences Why did the Soviet Union ignore traditional boundaries when setting up its republics?

7. Compare and Contrast How do the dwellings of urban people and nomads in Central Asia compare?

8. CONNECT to Today After living under Soviet rule, why do you think the people in the Eurasian republics today value the freedom to celebrate their holidays?

9. ART Design a Rug Research rug making in Turkmenistan, Uzbekistan, and Azerbaijan. Draw a picture illustrating one of the rug designs. Then write a brief summary explaining what the design represents.

The Eurasian Republics **431**

Reading for Understanding

▶ Key Ideas

BEFORE, YOU LEARNED

The Eurasian republics gained their independence after many years under the control of the Soviet Union.

NOW YOU WILL LEARN

The republics are working to overcome internal problems and establish democratic governments and market economies.

▶ Vocabulary

TERMS & NAMES

Rose Revolution a peaceful uprising in Georgia that helped force a corrupt president to resign

Nagorno-Karabakh (nuh•GAWR•noh KAHR•uh•BAHK) a province in Azerbaijan that Armenians believe should be a part of their country

foreign investment money put into a business by people from another country

one-crop economy an economy that relies on one crop for much of its earnings

REVIEW

Joseph Stalin Soviet Union dictator who was born in Georgia

command economy an economic system in which the production of goods and services is controlled by a central government

market economy an economic system in which the production of goods and services is decided by the supply and demand of consumers

privatize to sell government-owned businesses to private individuals

▶ Reading Strategy

Re-create the problem-solution chart shown at right. As you read and respond to the **KEY QUESTIONS**, use the chart to identify some of the solutions the Eurasian republics have come up with to settle their problems.

 See Skillbuilder Handbook, page R10

IDENTIFY PROBLEMS AND SOLUTIONS

PROBLEMS	SOLUTIONS
Establishing democracies	
Changing their economies	
Developing their resources	

 GRAPHIC ORGANIZERS
Go to **Interactive Review** @ ClassZone.com

The Challenge of Independence

5.01 Describe the relationship between the location of natural resources, and economic development, and analyze the impact on selected cultures, countries, and regions in Africa, Asia, and Australia.
11.04 Identify examples of economic, political, and social changes, such as agrarian to industrial economies, monarchical to democratic governments, and the roles of women and minorities, and analyze their impact on culture.

Connecting to Your World

Imagine that you are one of the founders of a new country. What challenges will you face? Well, to begin with, you will have to form a new government and economic system. Suppose you want to establish a democracy. What will you do if your people have no previous experience with democratic rule? How will you make democracy work? This is one of the challenges faced by the people of the Eurasian republics today.

Mixed Success with Democracy

🔻 **KEY QUESTION** What obstacles have the Eurasian republics faced in their efforts to establish democracies?

For centuries, the peoples of Transcaucasia and Central Asia have sought independence. In the 800s, for example, Armenia established an independent kingdom that lasted for more than one hundred years. In the early 1900s, many Eurasian groups fought for independence—first from czarist Russia and then from the Soviet Union. The republics did not gain their independence until 1991, when the Soviet Union collapsed.

Elected Presidents Many of the presidents of former Soviet republics pose before their countries' flags in 2004.

Overcoming the Soviet Past The Eurasian republics had little experience with democracy. Under Soviet dictators such as **Joseph Stalin**, the Communist Party had controlled all aspects of the government. As a result, most of the politicians in the Eurasian republics were Communists. After independence, these officials often remained in office and ran the governments. In addition, Russia has continued to try to exert its influence over the Eurasian republics.

Many times, the Eurasian republics have taken on the appearance of democracies. Kyrgyzstan, for instance, adopted a parliament and allowed a free press. But in reality, the people had little voice in the government. Throughout the Eurasian republics, in fact, most people have very little political power.

Recently, however, some progress has been made. For example, in 2003, Mikhail Saakashvili (SAH•kahsh•VEE•lee) led a campaign against government corruption under Georgia's president and forced him to resign. Saakashvili himself became president. This peaceful uprising is known as the **Rose Revolution**.

Dealing with Conflicts As you know, the Soviet Union paid little attention to traditional boundaries when setting up the republics. For example, the Soviet government created a province named **Nagorno-Karabakh**, in which 76 percent of the people were Armenians, but placed it within the borders of Azerbaijan. After Armenia and Azerbaijan gained their independence, Nagorno-Karabakh remained in Azerbaijan. Fighting between Armenia and Azerbaijan over this territory soon began. A cease-fire was declared in 1994, but the dispute remains unresolved.

In Georgia, two ethnic groups—the Ossetians and the Abkhazians (ab•KAY•zhuhnz)—believe they should each have independent states. Both of these groups have fought with the Georgians over this issue, which also remains unresolved.

During the 1990s in Tajikistan, former Communist officials fought anti-Communists and Islamic groups for control of the country. This civil war killed thousands of people. Eventually, a peace agreement was reached.

▲ **IDENTIFY PROBLEMS** Identify the obstacles the Eurasian republics have faced in their efforts to establish democracies.

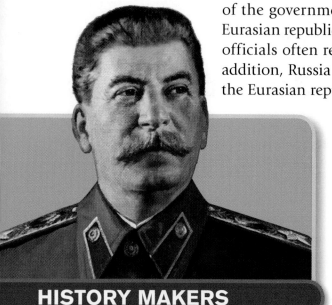

HISTORY MAKERS

Joseph Stalin 1879–1953

Joseph Stalin was born in a small town near Tbilisi, Georgia. He spent most of his childhood in this region. However, after he became dictator of the Soviet Union in 1929, he did not show a preference for Georgia. Indeed, he believed that it would be better off under Soviet rule. Stalin even enforced the same economic policy with Georgia that he put into effect in other Soviet republics. This policy required Georgia to change from a farm-based to an industry-based society.

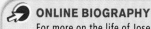

ONLINE BIOGRAPHY
For more on the life of Joseph Stalin, go to the
Research & Writing Center @ ClassZone.com

Heydar Aliyev (1923?–2003) served as president of Azerbaijan for the last ten years of his life. His son became president when he died. The image here shows an Azeri man casting his ballot in a parliamentary election under a portrait of Heydar Aliyev. In the following speech, Aliyev talks about the difficulties of establishing a democracy.

> Some people think we should be able to establish democracy in a short time, but that's impossible. Azerbaijan is a young nation and democracy is a new concept. . . . Democracy is not an apple you buy at the market and bring back home.
>
> Source: Heydar Aliyev, Speech at Georgetown University, July 30, 1997

DOCUMENT–BASED QUESTION

What does Aliyev suggest about the process of establishing a democracy?

Changing to a Market Economy

▼ **KEY QUESTION** What steps have the Eurasian republics taken toward developing their economies?

The Eurasian republics have many highly desired resources, including oil, natural gas, and coal. To take greater advantage of these resources, the Eurasian republics are attempting to develop market economies.

Controlling the Economy How does a country change from a command economy to a market economy? As you may recall, a **command economy** is one in which the government controls all businesses. In a **market economy**, private individuals own most of the businesses. To develop this type of economy, many Eurasian republics have started to **privatize** their businesses, or sell government-owned businesses to private individuals.

In addition, most of them have aggressively tried to obtain **foreign investments**. That means that they have encouraged people from other countries to put money into their businesses. Unfortunately, some republics are held back by being one-crop economies. A country with a **one-crop economy** relies on one crop for much of its earnings. The economy of Uzbekistan, for example, relies heavily on the country's production of cotton.

Energy Resources Drive the Future The people of the Eurasian republics believe that developing their resources will greatly benefit their economies. As a result, Azerbaijan has worked for several years with many countries to build a $4 billion pipeline from Baku to Turkey's Mediterranean coast. In 2006, one million barrels of oil a day began to pump through it. Georgia also benefits from the pipeline because it extends through that republic. The pipeline has brought Georgia many job opportunities and much foreign investment. In addition, Kazakhstan reached an agreement with China in 2005 that involves building an oil pipeline from the Caspian Sea eastward into China.

Tajikistan is also attempting to develop its natural resources. The republic has a great potential for water power. As a result, it is planning to build several huge dams to increase its production of electricity. If completed, these dams would be the largest in the world.

Azerbaijan Pipeline The president of Turkey has called the 1,100-mile oil pipeline "the Silk Road of the 21st century." **How will the pipeline encourage trade in the region?**

 EVALUATE Describe the steps that the Eurasian republics have taken toward developing their economies.

Section ③ Assessment

ONLINE QUIZ
For test practice, go to
Interactive Review
@ ClassZone.com

TERMS & NAMES

1. **Explain the importance of**
   • Rose Revolution
   • Nagorno-Karabakh
   • foreign investment
   • one-crop economy

USE YOUR READING NOTES

2. **Identify Problems and Solutions**
   Use your completed chart to answer the following question:

   Why was the Rose Revolution a good step toward establishing a democracy in Georgia?

PROBLEMS	SOLUTIONS
Establishing democracies	
Changing their economies	
Developing their resources	

KEY IDEAS

3. How did the Nagorno-Karabakh conflict develop?

4. Why have many of the Eurasian republics pursued foreign investment?

5. How has the Azerbaijan pipeline benefited Georgia?

CRITICAL THINKING

6. **Make Inferences** Why might Uzbekistan's reliance on cotton production hold back its economy?

7. **Form and Support Opinions** Do you think there are any drawbacks to obtaining foreign investments? Explain your answer.

8. **CONNECT to Today** In 2006, Azerbaijan began to pump one million barrels of oil a day through its pipeline. What effect do you think this pipeline will have on Azerbaijan's economy?

9. **TECHNOLOGY** **Create a Multimedia Presentation** Show how an oil pipeline works. Include a diagram showing where it starts and where it ends, and illustrations of the machinery used.

Interactive ← Review

Click here to complete these and other activities online @ ClassZone.com

CHAPTER SUMMARY

Key Idea 1
The geography and climate of the Eurasian republics pose challenges, but the countries are rich in natural resources.

Key Idea 2
The geographic location of the Eurasian republics has attracted many different cultures, ideas, and conquerors.

Key Idea 3
The republics are working to overcome internal problems and establish democratic governments and market economies.

For **Review and Study Notes**, go to **Interactive Review** @ ClassZone.com

NAME GAME

Use the Terms & Names list to complete each sentence on paper or online.

1. I describe a country that is completely surrounded by land. **landlocked** _____

2. I contain some of the largest alpine glaciers in the world. _____

3. I have been steadily shrinking as a result of irrigation. _____

4. I make my living by moving from place to place. _____

5. I am a huge desert that covers much of Turkmenistan. _____

6. I am a peaceful uprising that took place in Georgia. _____

7. I am the process of making a culture more Russian. _____

8. I am a portable, tentlike dwelling. _____

9. I am an area that Azerbaijan and Armenia have fought over. _____

10. I am money put into businesses in other countries. _____

Aral Sea
Caucasus Mountains
foreign investment
Islam
Kara Kum
Lake Balkhash
landlocked
Muslim
Nagorno-Karabakh
nomad
Rose Revolution
Russification
Silk Roads
Tian Shan
yurt

Activities

Flip Cards

Use the online flip cards to quiz yourself on the terms and names introduced in this chapter.

Tian Shan

? mountain range that runs across Kyrgyzstan and Tajikistan

Crossword Puzzle

Complete an online crossword puzzle to test your knowledge of the Eurasian republics.

ACROSS
1. major trading routes in Central Asia

VOCABULARY

Explain the significance of each of the following.

1. Transcaucasia
2. Central Asia
3. Caucasus Mountains
4. Aral Sea
5. nomad
6. Islam
7. Silk Roads
8. Russification
9. Rose Revolution
10. foreign investment

Explain how the terms and names in each group are related.

11. Transcaucasia, Central Asia, and Russification
12. Rose Revolution and Nagorno-Karabakh

KEY IDEAS

❶ Center of a Landmass

13. What bodies of water border Transcaucasia?
14. How do mountains affect Georgia's precipitation?
15. What deserts lie in Turkmenistan and Uzbekistan?
16. What effect did Soviet policies have on Central Asia?

❷ Historic Crossroads

17. How did the Mongol Empire affect trade in Central Asia?
18. What was exchanged on the Silk Roads?
19. How did the Soviets create resentment among ethnic groups in the Eurasian republics?
20. What are the craftspeople of Turkmenistan, Uzbekistan, and Azerbaijan known for?

❸ The Challenge of Independence

21. Why did many Communists continue to run the governments in the Eurasian republics after 1991?
22. What conflicts have arisen in Georgia?
23. How have the Eurasian republics attempted to change from command economies to market economies?
24. Which countries are working to market their natural resources?

CRITICAL THINKING

25. **Analyze Causes and Effects** Create a cause-and-effect chart to identify some of the policies of the Soviet Union and their impact on the Eurasian republics.

CAUSES	EFFECTS

26. **Identify Problems** What do you think are the biggest problems facing the Eurasian republics today?
27. **Make Inferences** Why do you think the Soviet Union promoted Russification?
28. **Evaluate** What aspects of Central Asian culture reflect its nomadic heritage?
29. **Connect Geography & Economics** How have geographic factors helped and hindered the republics' economies?
30. **Five Themes: Location** How did the location of Central Asia promote trade in the region?

Answer the
ESSENTIAL QUESTION

How can the Eurasian republics meet the challenges of independence?

Written Response Write a two- or three-paragraph response to the Essential Question. Be sure to consider specific ideas about the challenges the Eurasian republics face. Use the rubric below to guide your thinking.

Response Rubric
A strong response will:
- identify the resources of the Eurasian republics
- discuss the problems confronting the republics
- explain the steps the republics have taken to modernize their governments and economies

STANDARDS-BASED ASSESSMENT

THEMATIC MAP

Use the map to answer questions 1 and 2 on your paper.

Industries in the Eurasian Republics

KAZAKHSTAN

Aral Sea

Caspian Sea

GEORGIA

ARMENIA AZERBAIJAN

UZBEKISTAN KYRGYZSTAN

TURKMENISTAN TAJIKISTAN

Chemicals — Machinery
Coal — Oil and gas
Food processing — Textiles

1. Which republic contains the only coal industry in the two regions?

A. Kazakhstan
B. Azerbaijan
C. Turkmenistan
D. Uzbekistan

2. Where is most of the oil and gas produced?

A. in Kazakhstan
B. in Turkmenistan
C. around the Caspian Sea
D. around the Aral Sea

PHOTOGRAPH

Examine the photograph below showing the inside of a yurt. Use the photograph to write brief answers for questions 3 and 4 on your paper.

3. What might the carpets in this yurt be used for?

4. Why is it important that the yurt and all of its furnishings be lightweight?

GeoActivity

1. INTERDISCIPLINARY ACTIVITY–SCIENCE

With a small group, review the information you read on the Aral Sea in Section 1. Then research further to learn about the evaporation of the sea. Present your findings on a poster. Include pictures and information on the effects of the evaporation.

2. WRITING FOR SOCIAL STUDIES

Unit Writing Project Review the itinerary you created for a week-long stay in a country in this unit. Add a hike along the old Silk Roads to your travel plans. Write a journal entry about your experiences and the people you meet there.

3. MENTAL MAPPING

Create an outline map of Transcaucasia and Central Asia and label the following:

• Tian Shan
• Kara Kum
• Kyzyl Kum
• Caspian Sea
• Aral Sea
• Lake Balkhash
• Syr Darya
• Amu Darya

Reference Section

World Cultures *and* GEOGRAPHY

Skillbuilder Handbook

Contents

1.1 Taking Notes

Defining the Skill

When you **take notes,** you write down the important ideas and details of a passage. A chart or an outline can help you organize your notes to use in the future.

Applying the Skill

The following passage describes several different types of bodies of water. Use the strategies listed below to help you take notes on the passage.

How to Take and Organize Notes

Strategy ① Look at the title to find the main topic of the passage.

Strategy ② Identify the main ideas and details of the passage. Then summarize the main ideas and details in your notes.

Strategy ③ Identify key terms and define them. The term *hydrosphere* is shown in boldface type and highlighted; both techniques signal that it is a key term.

Strategy ④ In your notes, use abbreviations to save time and space. You can abbreviate words such as *gulf (G.), river (R.),* and *lake (L.),* as long as you write the proper name of the body of water with the abbreviation.

① **BODIES OF WATER**

② All the bodies of water on Earth form what is called ③ the **hydrosphere.** The world's ② oceans make up the largest part of the hydrosphere. Oceans have smaller regions. ② Gulfs, such as the Gulf of Tonkin, and seas, such as the Sea of Japan, are extensions of oceans. Land partially encloses these waters.

② Oceans and seas contain salt water, but most lakes and rivers contain fresh water. The water in rivers, such as the ② Nile River in Africa, flows down a channel in one direction. This movement is the current. Lake water, such as that found in ② Lake Victoria in Africa, can have currents too, even though the water is surrounded by land. Some lakes feed into rivers, and some rivers supply water to lakes.

Make a Chart

Making a chart can help you take notes on a passage. The chart below contains notes from the passage you just read.

② Item	Notes
1. ③ hydrosphere	all water on Earth
a. oceans	salt water; largest part of hydrosphere
b. gulfs and seas	④G. of Tonkin; ④S. of Japan; part of ocean
c. lakes and rivers	usually fresh water; ④Nile R. flows; ④L. Victoria surrounded by land

Practicing the Skill

Turn to the chapter "Understanding the Earth and Its Peoples," Section 2. Read "The Science of Mapmaking," and use a chart to take notes on the passage.

1.2 Finding Main Ideas

Defining the Skill

A **main idea** is a statement that summarizes the subject of a speech, an article, a section of a book, or a paragraph. Main ideas can be stated or unstated. The main idea of a paragraph is often stated in the first or last sentence. If it is the first sentence, it is followed by sentences that support that main idea. If it is the last sentence, the details build up to the main idea. To find an unstated idea, use the details of the paragraph as clues.

Applying the Skill

The passage below describes the economic system of Spain's colonies in Latin America. Use the strategies listed below to help you identify the main idea.

How to Find the Main Idea

Strategy ❶ Identify what you think may be the stated main idea. Check the first and last sentences of the paragraph to see if either could be the stated main idea.

Strategy ❷ Identify details that support the main idea. Some details explain that idea. Others give examples of what is stated in the main idea.

COLONIAL ECONOMY

❶ One of Spain's main purposes in developing colonies in Latin America was to make Spain wealthy. ❷ To do so, Spain set up the *encomienda* system. Under this system, ❷ the Spanish established huge ranches, plantations, and mines in various parts of Latin America. Indians ranched, farmed, and mined for Spanish landlords. ❷ The Indians lived in poverty and hardship, essentially enslaved. Spain, however, grew wealthy. ❷ The Spanish made huge profits on cattle and sheep from the ranches; sugar cane, coffee, and cacao from the plantations; and gold and silver from Mexican mines.

Make a Chart

Making a chart can help you identify the main idea and details in a passage or paragraph. The chart below identifies the main idea and details in the paragraph you just read.

> **Main Idea:** One of the main reasons to establish colonies in Latin America was to increase Spain's wealth.
> **Detail:** Spain set up the *encomienda* system to do so.
> **Detail:** Spain established ranches, plantations, and mines worked by the Indians.
> **Detail:** The Indians were poor and essentially enslaved.
> **Detail:** The Spanish made huge profits on products from the ranches, plantations, and mines.

Practicing the Skill

Turn to the chapter "Latin America: Physical Geography and History," Section 2. Read "Mountain Climates." Make a chart identifying the main idea and the supporting details.

1.3 Summarizing

Defining the Skill

When you **summarize,** you restate a paragraph, passage, or chapter in fewer words. You include only the main ideas and most important details. It is important to use your own words when summarizing.

Applying the Skill

The passage below describes the composition of Earth's interior. Use the strategies listed below to help you summarize the passage.

How to Summarize

Strategy ❶ Look for topic sentences stating the main idea or ideas. These are often at the beginning of a section or paragraph. Briefly restate each main idea in your own words.

Strategy ❷ Include key facts and any names, dates, numbers, amounts, or percentages from the text.

Strategy ❸ After writing your summary, review it to see that you have included only the most important details.

EARTH'S INTERIOR

❶ Earth is made up of several layers. ❷ The center of Earth's interior is a solid, hot metal layer called the inner core. ❷ Above it is the outer core, which is liquid because the metal has melted. Lying just above the core is the mantle. ❷ The mantle is a soft layer of hot rock, some of which is molten, or melted. It is the largest of Earth's layers.

❶ The crust, Earth's thin outer layer, forms the planet's shell. ❷ It is the solid, rocky surface of Earth that forms the ocean floors and the landmasses called continents. The crust is the part of Earth on which people live. It floats on top of the mantle.

Write a Summary

You should be able to write your summary in a short paragraph. The paragraph at right summarizes the passage you just read.

❸ Earth is made up of several layers. The inner core, outer core, and mantle are covered by Earth's crust, where we live.

Practicing the Skill

Turn to the chapter "Latin America: Physical Geography and History," Section 4. Read "Colonial Rule," and write a short paragraph summarizing the passage.

1.4 Sequencing Events

Defining the Skill

Sequence is the order in which events occur. Learning to follow the sequence of events through history will help you to better understand how events relate to one another.

Applying the Skill

The passage below describes Mexico's efforts to establish a stable government. Use the strategies listed below to help you follow the sequence of events.

How to Find the Sequence of Events

Strategy ① Look for specific dates provided in the text. The dates may not always read from earliest to latest, so be sure to match an event with the date.

Strategy ② Look for clues about time that allow you to order events according to sequence. Words and phrases, such as *later*, *before*, *today*, *then*, *until*, and *year*, and different tenses, such as *are*, *were*, or *would*, may help to sequence the events.

A STABLE MEXICAN GOVERNMENT

① After gaining independence from Spain in 1821, Mexico had trouble establishing a stable government. ① In 1846, a dispute over territory led to a war between Mexico and the United States that ② *lasted two years*. The Mexican War left the government in disorder. ① In 1876, General Porfirio Díaz took over as a dictator. ① By 1910, Mexicans were protesting Díaz's rule. ② *That same year*, the Mexican Revolution began. The revolution turned into a civil war, which finally ended ① in 1920.

① *During* the revolution, the Constitution of 1917 was adopted to meet the demands of Mexico's various groups. The Constitution of 1917 is still in effect ② *today*.

Make a Time Line

Making a time line can help you sequence events. The time line below shows the sequence of events in the passage you just read.

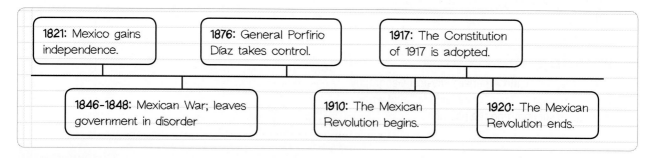

1821: Mexico gains independence.

1846-1848: Mexican War; leaves government in disorder

1876: General Porfirio Díaz takes control.

1910: The Mexican Revolution begins.

1917: The Constitution of 1917 is adopted.

1920: The Mexican Revolution ends.

Practicing the Skill

Turn to the chapter "Latin America: Physical Geography and History," Section 4. Read "Mexico's Path to Independence," and make a time line showing the sequence of events in the passage.

1.5 Categorizing

Defining the Skill

To **categorize** is to sort people, objects, ideas, or other information into groups, called categories. Geographers categorize information to help them identify and understand patterns in geographical data.

Applying the Skill

The passage below describes the natural resources available on Earth. Use the strategies listed below to help you categorize information.

How to Categorize

Strategy ① First, decide what kind of information needs to be categorized. Decide what the passage is about and how that information can be sorted into categories. For example, this passage discusses the different kinds of natural resources.

Strategy ② Then find out what the categories will be. If it is unclear, look for general words that could be category headings.

Strategy ③ Once you have chosen the categories, sort information into them. What are the characteristics of each category of natural resources? What are some examples of each?

NATURAL RESOURCES

① Geographers divide natural resources into three main categories. ② Renewable resources are those that nature can replace, such as trees or plants. These can be lost if they are used faster than they can be replaced. ② Non-renewable resources can't be easily replaced, so when they are used up, there aren't additional resources. Minerals and fuels such as coal and oil fall into this category. ② Unlimited resources are things such as sunlight and wind. They are always available no matter what amount is used. Unlimited resources often are used to produce energy.

Make a Chart

Making a chart can help you categorize information. The chart below shows how the information from the passage you just read can be categorized.

③

Resource Type	Renewable	Non-Renewable	Unlimited
Characteristics	can be replaced through natural processes; can be lost if used faster than replaced	can't be replaced once removed from the ground; gone forever once used	always available no matter what amount used; used to produce energy
Examples	trees, plants	coal, oil	sun, wind

Practicing the Skill

Turn to the chapter "Earth's Interlocking Systems," Section 1. Read "External Forces Shaping the Earth." Make a chart categorizing the external forces shaping Earth.

1.6 Analyzing Causes and Effects

Defining the Skill

A **cause** is an action that makes something happen. An **effect** is the event that is the result of the cause. A single event may have several causes. It is also possible for one cause to result in several effects. Geographers identify cause-and-effect relationships to help them understand patterns in human movement and interaction.

Applying the Skill

The following paragraph describes events that caused changes in the way of life of the ancient Maya people of Central America. Use the strategies below to help you identify the cause-and-effect relationships.

How to Analyze Causes and Effects

Strategy 1 Ask why an action took place. Ask yourself a question about the title and topic sentence, such as, "What caused Mayan civilization to decline?"

Strategy 2 Look for effects. Ask yourself, "What happened?" (the effect). Then ask, "Why did it happen?" (the cause). For example, "What caused the Maya to abandon their cities?"

Strategy 3 Look for clue words that signal causes, such as *caused*, *contributed to*, and *led to*.

---

1 DECLINE OF MAYAN CIVILIZATION

1 The civilization of the Maya went into a mysterious decline around A.D. 900. **2** Mayan cities in the southern lowlands were abandoned, trade ceased, and the huge stone pyramids of the Maya fell into ruin. No one really understands what happened to the Maya, but there are many theories.

3 Some believe that a change in climate *caused* the decline of Mayan civilization. Three long droughts between 810 and 910 meant that there was not enough water for Mayan crops. **2** As a result, the Maya abandoned their cities. **3** Other researchers believe that additional problems *contributed to* the crisis. They include overpopulation and warfare among the Mayan nobility.

Make a Diagram

Making a diagram can help you analyze causes and effects. The diagram below shows two causes and an effect for the passage you just read.

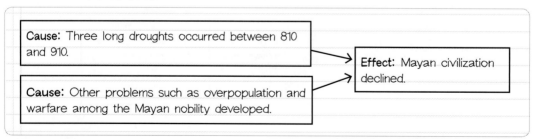

Cause: Three long droughts occurred between 810 and 910.

Cause: Other problems such as overpopulation and warfare among the Mayan nobility developed.

Effect: Mayan civilization declined.

Practicing the Skill

Turn to the chapter "Human Geography," Section 1. Read "Population Growth" and "Growth Challenges." Make a diagram about causes and effects of population growth.

1.7 Comparing and Contrasting

Defining the Skill

Comparing means looking at the similarities and differences between two or more things.
Contrasting means examining only the differences between them. Geographers compare and
contrast physical features, regions, cultures, beliefs, and situations in order to understand them.

Applying the Skill

The following passage describes the similarities and differences between the governments of
Cuba and Puerto Rico. Use the strategies listed below to help you compare and contrast the
two nations.

How to Compare and Contrast

Strategy ❶ Look for two
aspects of the subject that can be
compared and contrasted. This passage compares Cuba and Puerto
Rico, two Caribbean islands with
distinct governments.

Strategy ❷ To find similarities,
look for clue words indicating that
two things are alike. Clue words
include *both*, *together*, and *similarly*.

Strategy ❸ To contrast, look
for clue words that show how two
things differ. Clue words include
however, *but*, *on the other hand*,
and *yet*.

TWO DIFFERENT GOVERNMENTS

❶ Cuba and Puerto Rico, both Caribbean islands, have similar
histories but developed different forms of government. Spain
controlled Cuba until 1898, when the United States won the
Spanish-American War. The U.S. military occupied the island
until it gained independence in 1902. Then, in 1959, rebels led
by Fidel Castro overthrew Cuba's dictator. By 1961, Castro had
established a Communist government.

❷ *Like* Cuba, Puerto Rico was a Spanish colony until 1898,
when it became a U.S. territory. ❸ *However*, Puerto Rico was
never independent. In 1952, Puerto Rican voters approved a
constitution making it a commonwealth of the United States.

Make a Venn Diagram

Making a Venn diagram can help you identify similarities and differences between
two things. In the overlapping area, list
characteristics shared by both subjects.
Then, in the separate ovals, list the characteristics of each subject not shared by
the other. This Venn diagram compares
and contrasts Cuba and Puerto Rico.

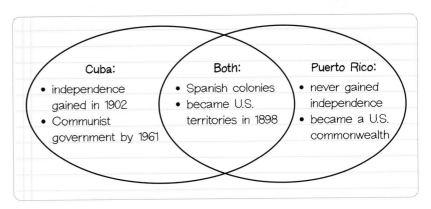

Cuba:
• independence gained in 1902
• Communist government by 1961

Both:
• Spanish colonies
• became U.S. territories in 1898

Puerto Rico:
• never gained independence
• became a U.S. commonwealth

Practicing the Skill

Turn to the chapter "Human Geography," Section 3. Read "Measuring Economic Development,"
and make a Venn diagram showing similarities and differences between developed and
developing nations.

1.8 Identifying Problems and Solutions

Defining the Skill

Identifying problems means finding and understanding the difficulties faced by a particular group of people during a certain time. **Identifying solutions** means understanding how people tried to remedy those problems. By studying how people solved problems in the past, you can learn ways to solve problems today.

Applying the Skill

The passage below describes the problem of pollution in Mexico. Use the strategies listed below to find and understand this problem.

How to Identify Problems and Solutions

Strategy ➊ Look for the difficulties or problems faced by a group of people.

Strategy ➋ Consider how situations that existed at that time and place contributed to these problems.

Strategy ➌ Look for the solutions that people or groups employed to deal with the problems. Think about whether the solutions were good ones.

POLLUTION IN MEXICO CITY

➊ Like other large industrial cities, Mexico City has had to deal with increased air pollution caused by industrialization. Mexico City is almost surrounded by mountains. ➋ The mountains produce a layer of warm air above the city, which keeps pollutants such as car and factory exhaust from blowing away. ➋ These gases then react with sunlight to form smog, which causes health problems.

The Mexican government has taken steps to deal with pollution. ➌ It has urged automobile manufacturers to produce cars that use cleaner fuels and helped companies develop smog controls. ➌ It has also encouraged public transportation.

Make a Chart

Making a chart can help you identify information about problems and solutions. The chart below shows the problem, contributing factors, and solutions in the passage you just read.

➊ Problem	➋ Contributing Factors	➌ Solutions
Mexico City faces problems with pollution and smog.	Warm air from the surrounding mountains traps pollutants. Polluted gases react with sunlight to form smog.	Leaders have urged use of cleaner fuels and helped develop smog controls. Leaders have encouraged public transportation.

Practicing the Skill

Turn to the chapter "Earth's Interlocking Systems," Section 4. Read "Desertification." Then make a chart that summarizes the problems faced by many arid and semiarid areas and the solutions that people who live in these areas are applying.

1.9 Making Inferences

Defining the Skill

Inferences are ideas that the author has not directly stated. **Making inferences** involves reading between the lines to interpret the information you read. You can make inferences by studying what is stated and using your common sense and previous knowledge.

Applying the Skill

This passage examines the cities of the Maya. Use the strategies below to help you make inferences from the passage.

How to Make Inferences

Strategy ❶ Read to find statements of fact. Knowing the facts will help you make inferences.

Strategy ❷ Use your knowledge, logic, and common sense to make inferences that are based on facts. Ask yourself, "What does the author want me to understand?" For example, from the presence of temples in Mayan cities, you can make the inference that religion was important to the Maya.

MAYAN CITIES

The Maya built more than 40 cities. ❶ Each Mayan city contained pyramids with temples on top of them. Many of the cities also had steles, or large stone monuments. ❶ On these monuments, the Maya carved glyphs that represented important dates and great events. ❶ Mayan cities also contained palaces, plazas, and ball courts. Larger Mayan cities included Copán, Tikal, Palenque, Bonampak, and Chichén Itzá. ❶ A different king governed each Mayan city and the surrounding areas. In about A.D. 900, the Maya started abandoning their cities. The reasons remain unclear. However, descendants of the Maya still live in the region.

Make a Chart

Making a chart can help you organize information and make logical inferences. The chart below organizes information from the passage you just read.

❶ Stated Facts and Ideas	❷ Inferences
Each Mayan city contained pyramids with temples on top of them.	Religion was important to the Maya.
On these monuments, the Maya carved glyphs that represented important dates and great events.	The Maya believed that history was important.
Mayan cities also contained palaces, plazas, and ball courts.	The Maya were skilled engineers and architects.

Practicing the Skill

Turn to the chapter "Latin America: Physical Geography and History," Section 3. Read "Inca, Mountain Empire." Use a chart like the one above to make inferences about the Incan civilization.

1.10 Making Generalizations

Defining the Skill

To **make generalizations** means to make broad judgments based on information. When you make generalizations, you should gather information from several sources.

Applying the Skill

The following three passages describe culture. Use the strategies below to make a generalization about these ideas.

How to Make Generalizations

**Strategy ① Look for information that the sources have in common. These three sources all look at the components of culture.

**Strategy ② Form a generalization that describes this relationship in a way that all three sources would agree with. State your generalization in a sentence.

COMPONENTS OF CULTURE

Culture is the way of life of a group of people. ① Culture includes common practices of a society, its shared understandings, and its social organization.

—*World History: Patterns of Interaction*

① . . . Culture should be regarded as the set of distinctive spiritual, material, intellectual, and emotional features of society or a social group.

—UNESCO, "Universal Declaration on Cultural Diversity"

① Human cultures are made up of many different parts, such as language, technology, religious beliefs. . . . These elements interact with one another to form . . . systems.

—*The Encyclopedia of World History*

Make a Diagram

Using a diagram can help you make generalizations. The diagram below shows how information you just read can be used to generalize about culture.

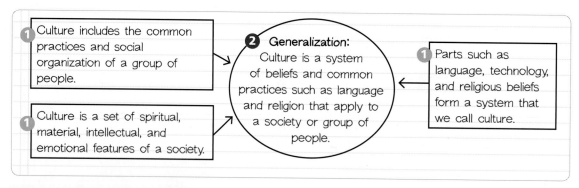

① Culture includes the common practices and social organization of a group of people.

① Culture is a set of spiritual, material, intellectual, and emotional features of a society.

② Generalization: Culture is a system of beliefs and common practices such as language and religion that apply to a society or group of people.

① Parts such as language, technology, and religious beliefs form a system that we call culture.

Practicing the Skill

Turn to the chapter "Brazil," Section 1. Read "Urbanization," and look at "Comparing Urban and Rural Populations." Use a diagram to make a generalization about where people live in Brazil.

1.11 Drawing Conclusions

Defining the Skill

Drawing conclusions means analyzing what you have read and forming an opinion about its meaning. To draw conclusions, look at the facts and then use your own common sense and experience to decide what the facts mean.

Applying the Skill

The following passage presents information about the spread of culture. Use the strategies listed below to help you draw conclusions about how culture spreads.

How to Draw Conclusions

Strategy 1 Read carefully to identify and understand all the facts.

Strategy 2 List the facts in a diagram and review them. Use your own experiences and common sense to understand how the facts relate to each other.

Strategy 3 After reviewing the facts, write down the conclusions you have drawn about them.

THE SPREAD OF CULTURE

Cultural exchange occurs when elements of culture are transferred between two groups. **1** In the past, the spread of culture was usually slow because of geographic barriers. Large bodies of water, mountains, or deserts often made it difficult for people to interact with others. **1** Sometimes political boundaries limited contact between peoples. Today, it is almost impossible to avoid some kind of interaction with other groups of people. **1** Satellite television, the Internet, and other forms of mass communication speed new ideas, practices, and inventions around the globe.

Make a Diagram

Making a diagram can help you draw conclusions. The diagram below shows how to organize facts to draw a conclusion about the passage you just read.

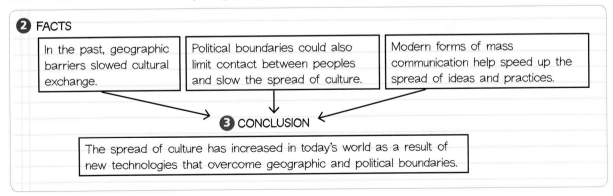

2 FACTS

| In the past, geographic barriers slowed cultural exchange. | Political boundaries could also limit contact between peoples and slow the spread of culture. | Modern forms of mass communication help speed up the spread of ideas and practices. |

3 CONCLUSION

The spread of culture has increased in today's world as a result of new technologies that overcome geographic and political boundaries.

Practicing the Skill

Turn to the chapter "Brazil," Section 2. Read "Africans." Then make a diagram to help you draw conclusions about African influences on Brazilian culture.

1.12 Making Decisions

Defining the Skill

Making decisions involves choosing between two or more options, or courses of action. In most cases, decisions have consequences, or results. Sometimes decisions may lead to new problems. By understanding how historical figures made decisions, you can learn how to improve your own decision-making skills.

Applying the Skill

The passage below explains the decision Father Hidalgo made to rebel against Spanish rule in Mexico. Use the strategies below to analyze his decision.

How to Make Decisions

Strategy ❶ Identify a decision that needs to be made. Think about what factors make the decision difficult.

Strategy ❷ Identify possible consequences of the decision. Remember that there can be more than one consequence to a decision.

Strategy ❸ Identify the decision that was made.

Strategy ❹ Identify actual consequences that resulted from the decision.

> **FATHER OF MEXICAN INDEPENDENCE**
>
> Many people in Mexico wanted independence from Spain. Father Hidalgo, a priest in the village of Dolores, belonged to a secret society that was plotting to rebel. ❶ When the Spanish discovered the plot, Father Hidalgo had to choose. ❷ He could flee to safety, but Mexico would stay under Spanish rule. ❷ If he went ahead with the rebellion, it could end Spanish rule. ❸ Father Hidalgo urged his parishioners to rebel. ❹ Thousands joined his army, but they were no match for Spanish soldiers. Father Hidalgo was captured and executed, but he inspired many and is known as the father of Mexican independence.

Make a Flow Chart

Making a flow chart can help you identify the process of making a decision. The flow chart below shows the decision-making process in the passage you just read.

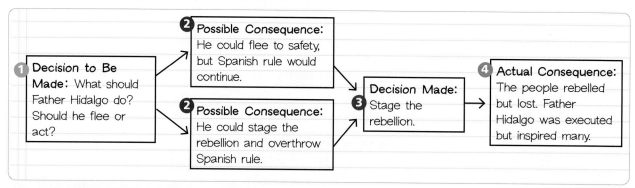

❶ **Decision to Be Made:** What should Father Hidalgo do? Should he flee or act?

❷ **Possible Consequence:** He could flee to safety, but Spanish rule would continue.

❷ **Possible Consequence:** He could stage the rebellion and overthrow Spanish rule.

❸ **Decision Made:** Stage the rebellion.

❹ **Actual Consequence:** The people rebelled but lost. Father Hidalgo was executed but inspired many.

Practicing the Skill

Turn to the chapter "Middle America and Spanish-Speaking South America," Section 2. Read "Economic Activities." Make a flow chart to identify the Caribbean nations' decision about one-crop economies and its consequences.

1.13 Evaluating

Defining the Skill

To **evaluate** is to make a judgment about something. Geographers evaluate the actions of people in history. One way to do this is to examine both the positives and the negatives of an action, and then decide which is stronger—the positive or the negative.

Applying the Skill

The following passage examines the decision to move Brazil's capital in the 1950s. Use the strategies listed below to help you evaluate the decision's success.

How to Evaluate

Strategy ❶ Before you evaluate a decision or action, first determine what it was meant to do. In this case, think about what Brazil's leaders wanted to accomplish.

Strategy ❷ Look for statements that show the positive, or successful, results of the action. For example, did the leaders achieve their goals?

Strategy ❸ Also look for statements that show the negative, or unsuccessful, results of the action. Did the decision fail to achieve something or create additional problems?

Strategy ❹ Write an overall evaluation of the decision made or the action taken.

BRAZIL MOVES ITS CAPITAL

During the last half of the 20th century, millions moved from rural areas to cities along Brazil's eastern coast in search of jobs. ❶ The coastal cities could not provide jobs for everyone, and overcrowding became a problem. In 1956, the Brazilian government began construction of a new capital city, Brasília, located 600 miles from the coast. ❶ Brasília was intended to encourage development of Brazil's untapped interior. ❷ Major highways constructed to connect Brasília with the rest of the country brought more settlement to the region. ❸ However, overcrowding and unemployment are still problems for Brazil's coastal cities.

Make a Diagram

Making a diagram can help you evaluate. List the positives and negatives of an action or decision. Then make an overall judgment. The diagram below shows how the information from the passage you just read can be evaluated.

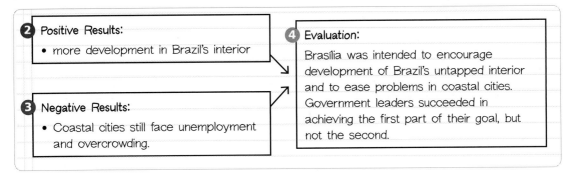

❷ Positive Results:
• more development in Brazil's interior

❸ Negative Results:
• Coastal cities still face unemployment and overcrowding.

❹ Evaluation:
Brasília was intended to encourage development of Brazil's untapped interior and to ease problems in coastal cities. Government leaders succeeded in achieving the first part of their goal, but not the second.

Practicing the Skill

Turn to the chapter "Middle America and Spanish-Speaking South America," Section 2. Read "Cuba," and make a diagram to evaluate Castro's government in Cuba.

1.14 Distinguishing Fact from Opinion

Defining the Skill

Facts are events, dates, statistics, or statements that can be proved to be true. **Opinions** are judgments, beliefs, and feelings. By identifying facts and opinions, you will be able to think critically when a person is trying to influence your own opinion.

Applying the Skill

The passage below describes the Aztec city of Tenochtitlán. Use the strategies listed below to help you distinguish fact from opinion.

How to Distinguish Fact from Opinion

Strategy ① Look for specific information that can be proved or checked for accuracy.

Strategy ② Look for assertions, claims, and judgments that express opinions. In this case, one speaker's opinion is addressed in a direct quote.

Strategy ③ Think about whether statements can be checked for accuracy. Then, identify the facts and opinions in a chart.

A BUSTLING CITY

By the early 1500s, Tenochtitlán was an urban center. ① With a population between 200,000 and 400,000 people, it was larger than any European capital of the time. Located on an island, it was connected to the mainland by three causeways, or raised roads, built by Aztec engineers. ① At the center of Tenochtitlán was a massive walled complex, filled with palaces, temples, government buildings, and a huge market. Bernal Díaz, one of the Spanish soldiers conquering Mexico, was amazed to see this bustling urban center. ② He observed, "These great towns and cues [pyramids] and buildings rising from the water, all made of stone, seemed like an enchanted vision."

Make a Chart

Making a chart can help you distinguish fact from opinion. The chart below analyzes the facts and opinions in the passage above.

Statement	③ Can It Be Proved?	③ Fact or Opinion
Tenochtitlán was larger than any European capital of the time.	Yes. Check population records.	fact
The city center contained a massive walled complex.	Yes. Check historical documents.	fact
The city seemed like an enchanted vision.	No. It is one person's belief.	opinion

Practicing the Skill

Turn to the chapter "Middle America and Spanish-Speaking South America," Section 4. Read "People and Culture" under "Peru." Then make a chart analyzing key statements about Peruvian culture to determine whether they are facts or opinions.

1.15 Analyzing Points of View

Defining the Skill

Analyzing points of view means looking closely at a person's arguments to understand the reasons behind that person's beliefs. The goal of analyzing a point of view is to understand different thoughts, opinions, and beliefs about a topic.

Applying the Skill

The following passage presents two views about slavery in Brazil in the 19th century. Use the strategies listed below to help you analyze the points of view.

How to Analyze Points of View

Strategy ❶ Look for statements that show you a particular point of view on an issue. For example, Dom Pedro II believed that slavery should be abolished. Plantation owners disagreed.

Strategy ❷ Think about why different peoples or groups held a particular point of view. Ask yourself what they valued. What were they trying to gain or protect? What were they willing to sacrifice?

Strategy ❸ Write a summary that explains why different people might take different positions on this issue.

> **DOM PEDRO II ABOLISHES SLAVERY**
>
> As emperor of Brazil, Dom Pedro II brought stability and progress to the country. One of his goals was to abolish slavery in Brazil. ❶ Pedro II opposed slavery. He freed his own slaves in 1840. He did not want to upset the wealthy plantation owners, an important part of Brazil's agriculturally based economy, so he worked to gradually end slavery. In 1888, the practice was outlawed. By then, 700,000 enslaved persons had been freed. ❶ However, the plantation owners were upset at the loss of labor to work their land. They were also angry because they were not paid for the freed slaves. In 1889, they forced Dom Pedro II to give up his throne.

Make a Diagram

Making a diagram can help you analyze points of view. The diagram below shows the points of view of Dom Pedro II and the plantation owners in the passage you just read.

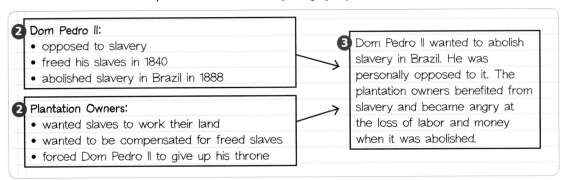

❷ Dom Pedro II:
- opposed to slavery
- freed his slaves in 1840
- abolished slavery in Brazil in 1888

❷ Plantation Owners:
- wanted slaves to work their land
- wanted to be compensated for freed slaves
- forced Dom Pedro II to give up his throne

❸ Dom Pedro II wanted to abolish slavery in Brazil. He was personally opposed to it. The plantation owners benefited from slavery and became angry at the loss of labor and money when it was abolished.

Practicing the Skill

Turn to the chapter "Mexico," Section 1. Read "Fight for Reforms." Make a diagram to analyze the points of view of the liberals and the conservatives.

1.16 Recognizing Bias

Defining the Skill

Bias is a prejudiced point of view. Accounts that are biased tend to present only one side of an issue and reflect the opinions of the writer. Recognizing bias will help you understand how much to trust the primary and secondary sources that you find.

Applying the Skill

The following passage is from explorer Amerigo Vespucci's observations of the Brazilian people. Use the strategies listed below to help you recognize bias in the passage.

How to Recognize Bias

Strategy ❶ Identify the author and examine any information about him or her. Does the author belong to a group, social class, or political party that might lead to a one-sided view of the subject?

Strategy ❷ Think about the opinions the author is presenting. Look for words, phrases, statements, or images that might convey a positive or negative slant.

Strategy ❸ Examine the evidence provided to support the author's opinions. Is the opinion correct? Would the same information appear in another account of the same event?

> ❶ **VESPUCCI ENCOUNTERS THE PEOPLE OF BRAZIL**
>
> Having no laws and no religious faith, they live according to nature. ❷ They understand nothing of the immortality of the soul. . . .
>
> They are also ❷ a warlike people and very cruel to their own kind. . . . That which made me . . . astonished at their wars and cruelty was that I could not understand why they made war upon each other, considering that they held no private property or sovereignty of empire and kingdoms and ❸ did not know any such thing as a lust for possession . . . or a desire to rule.
>
> ❶ —Amerigo Vespucci, 1502

Make a Chart

Making a chart can help you recognize bias in primary and secondary sources. The chart below analyzes the bias in the passage you just read.

Author	Amerigo Vespucci
Occasion and Purpose	exploration of coast of Brazil on second voyage to Americas, describing the native peoples
Tone	judging, negative, superior
Slanted Language	"Having no laws and no religious faith;" "understand nothing of the immortality of the soul;" "a warlike people and very cruel to their own kind"
Description of Bias	Vespucci's comments about religion show a bias toward his own religious beliefs. He also reveals a prejudice that European customs are superior to all others.

Practicing the Skill

Look through newspapers and news magazines to find an article related to geography. Then use a chart like the one above to analyze the article for bias.

1.17 Synthesizing

Defining the Skill

Synthesizing involves putting together clues, information, and ideas to form an overall picture. Geographers synthesize information in order to develop interpretations of important facts.

Applying the Skill

The following passage describes the agricultural revolution. The highlighting indicates the different kinds of information that will help you synthesize.

How to Synthesize

Strategy ❶ Look carefully for facts that will help you base your interpretations on evidence.

Strategy ❷ Look for explanations that link the facts together. This statement is based on the evidence of ancient tools mentioned in the next sentence.

Strategy ❸ Consider what you already know that could apply. Your knowledge will probably lead you to accept this statement.

Strategy ❹ Bring together the information you have about the subject. This interpretation brings together different kinds of information to arrive at a new understanding.

THE AGRICULTURAL REVOLUTION

❶ Flaked arrowheads found with mammoth bones at ancient sites suggest that some early people lived as big game hunters. ❷ After the big game became extinct, people shifted to hunting smaller game. They made tools, such as bows and arrows for hunting small game as well as baskets for collecting nuts.

About 10,000 years ago, people began to farm. ❸ The rise of agriculture brought tremendous change. More people lived in settled villages, and the storage of surplus food became more important. As their surplus increased, people had time to develop specialized skills and think about the world. ❹ From this agricultural base rose larger, more stable, and more complex societies.

Make a Diagram

Making a diagram can help you organize the facts, examples, and interpretations that you need to synthesize. The diagram below synthesizes the passage you just read.

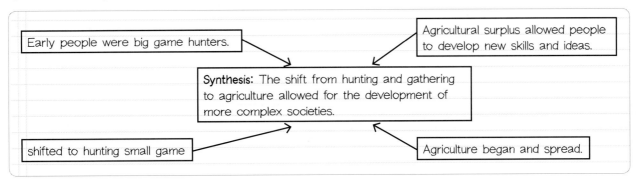

Practicing the Skill

Turn to the chapter "Human Geography," Section 2. Read "Causes of Migration." Then use a diagram like the one above to form a synthesis about why people migrate.

2.1 Reading Maps: Physical

Defining the Skill

Physical maps represent the landforms, or physical features, on Earth's surface, such as mountains or bodies of water. By learning about the different elements of maps, it will be easier for you to read them.

Applying the Skill

A physical map of Peru is shown below. Use the strategies to help you read the map.

How to Read a Physical Map

Strategy ① Read the title. This will tell you what place or region is represented by the map.

Strategy ② Look for the gridlines that form a pattern of squares over the map. These numbered lines represent latitude (horizontal) and longitude (vertical). They indicate the location of the area on Earth.

Strategy ③ Read the map legend. On a physical map, the legend often includes a scale to help you determine elevation as well as information about physical features.

Strategy ④ Use the scale and the pointer or compass rose to determine distance and direction.

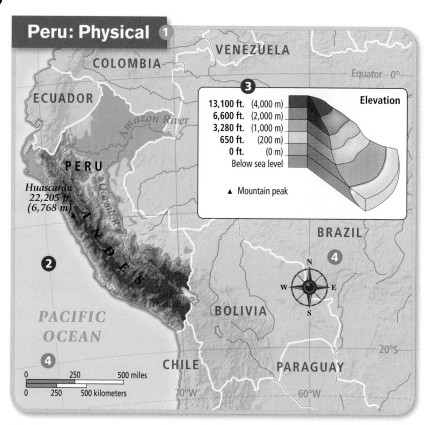

Make a Chart

Making a chart can help you organize the information given on a map. The chart below summarizes information about the physical map you just studied.

Title	Peru: Physical
Location	the Pacific coast of South America, near the equator and latitude 70° W
Legend Information	colors = elevation
Scale	1 in. = 500 miles, 5/8 in. = 500 km
Summary	Peru is located on the Pacific Ocean. The Andes run along the west coast, and the Amazon River and Ucayalí River flow through the country.

Practicing the Skill

Turn to the chapter "Latin America: Physical Geography and History," Section 1. Study the physical map of Mexico, Central America, and the Caribbean. Make a chart to identify the information on the map.

2.2 Reading Maps: Political

Defining the Skill

Political maps represent political features of various places, such as national borders and capital cities. The countries on political maps are often shaded in different colors to make them easier to distinguish from each other.

Applying the Skill

A political map of Peru is shown below. Use the strategies to help you read the map.

How to Read a Political Map

Strategy ① Read the title. This identifies the main idea of the map and will tell you what place or region the map represents.

Strategy ② Look for the gridlines that form a pattern of squares over the map. These numbered lines represent latitude (horizontal) and longitude (vertical). They indicate the location of the area on Earth.

Strategy ③ Read the map legend. The legend will help you to interpret the symbols on the map. On a political map, these symbols often include icons for major and capital cities.

Strategy ④ Use the scale and the pointer or compass rose to determine distance and direction.

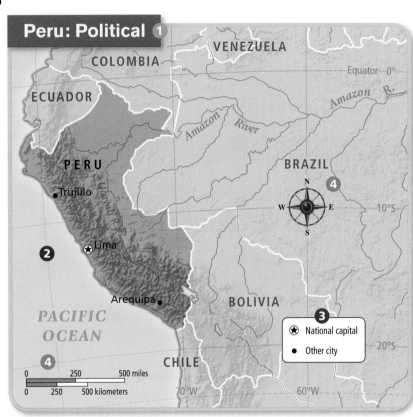

Make a Chart

Making a chart can help you organize the information given on a map. The chart below summarizes information about the political map you just studied.

Title	Peru: Political
Location	the Pacific coast of South America, near the equator and latitude 70° W
Legend Information	star icon = national capital; dot = other city
Scale	1 in. = 500 miles, 5/8 in. = 500 km
Summary	Peru, located on the Pacific Ocean, borders Ecuador, Colombia, Brazil, Bolivia, and Chile. Its capital is Lima.

Practicing the Skill

Turn to the chapter "Mexico," and study the political map of Mexico at the front of the chapter. Make a chart to identify the information on the map.

2.3 Reading Maps: Thematic

Defining the Skill

Thematic maps represent specific themes, or ideas. Climate, language, migration, population density, and economic activity maps are all different kinds of thematic maps.

Applying the Skill

The following map shows selected products of Mexico. Use the strategies listed below to help you read the map.

How to Read a Thematic Map

Strategy ● Read the title. This identifies the theme of the map and will tell you what place or region is represented by the map.

Strategy ❷ Some thematic maps have latitude (horizontal) and longitude (vertical) lines. They can help indicate the location of the area on Earth.

Strategy ❸ Read the map legend. On a thematic map, the legend is very important because the colors and symbols on the map are specific to the theme. The legend will help you interpret them.

Strategy ❹ Use the pointer or compass rose to determine direction. If the map has a scale, it can help you determine distance.

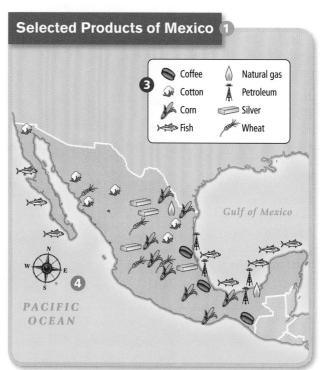

Selected Products of Mexico ❶

Coffee — Natural gas
Cotton — Petroleum
Corn — Silver
Fish — Wheat

Gulf of Mexico

PACIFIC OCEAN

Make a Chart

Making a chart can help you organize the information given on a map. The chart below summarizes information about the thematic map you just studied.

Title	Selected Products of Mexico
Location	Mexico, which borders the Pacific Ocean and the Gulf of Mexico
Legend Information	Icons represent specific products.
Summary	Mexico's different regions produce a variety of goods and crops, including coffee, corn, fish, petroleum, and silver.

Practicing the Skill

Turn to the chapter "Human Geography," Section 2. Study the thematic map "Bantu Migrations," and make a chart to identify the information on the map.

2.4 Reading Maps: Cartograms

Defining the Skill

A **cartogram** takes statistical data and represents it visually in the form of a map. Rather than representing land area, a cartogram shows a different set of data about a country, such as population or gross domestic product. The size of the nations on the cartogram are adjusted to reflect the selected data for each one.

Applying the Skill

The following cartogram shows world population. Use the strategies listed below to help you read the cartogram.

How to Read a Cartogram

Strategy ❶ Read the title. This identifies the data and region represented by the cartogram.

Strategy ❷ Look at the sizes of the countries shown to see how they compare to each other. Cartograms adjust the sizes of countries to convey relative data. Because of this, the countries' shapes are altered.

Strategy ❸ Compare the cartogram to a conventional map such as the world political map on pp. A16–A17. This will help you determine how much more or less of the selected data a particular country has by comparing its relative size on the cartogram to its size on the map.

Make a Chart

Making a chart can help you organize the information given on a cartogram. The chart below summarizes information about the cartogram you just studied.

Title	World Population
Location	the world
Summary	Countries are shown either smaller or larger than their actual area depending on their population. For instance, India and Japan are shown larger than normal because they have high populations. Canada and Russia, which are more sparsely populated, are smaller than normal.

2.5 Reading Graphs and Charts

Defining the Skill

Graphs and charts translate information into a visual form. Graphs take numerical information and present it using pictures and symbols instead of words. Different kinds of graphs include bar graphs, line graphs, and pie graphs. Charts are created by simplifying, summarizing, and organizing information. This information is then presented in a format that is easy to understand. Tables and diagrams are examples of commonly used charts.

Applying the Skill

Use the strategies listed to read the graphs and chart on these pages.

How to Read Graphs

Strategy ① Read the title to identify the main idea of the graph. Ask yourself what kind of information the graph shows. Check the graph's source line to make sure the data is reliable.

Strategy ② Read the labels on the graph. Bar and line graphs have labels on their vertical axis and horizontal axis. Pie graphs have labels for each wedge of the pie. These labels tell you what data the graph represents.

Strategy ③ Look at the graph. Try to find patterns, such as similarities and differences or increases and decreases.

Strategy ④ Summarize the information shown on the graph. Use the title to help you focus on what information the graph is presenting.

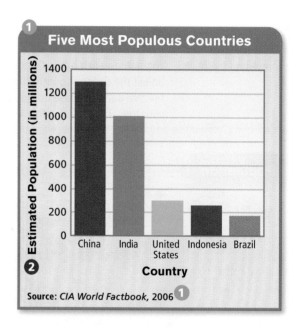

Five Most Populous Countries

Source: *CIA World Factbook*, 2006

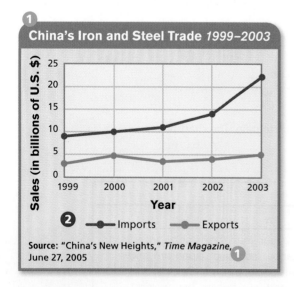

China's Iron and Steel Trade *1999–2003*

Imports — Exports

Source: "China's New Heights," *Time Magazine*, June 27, 2005

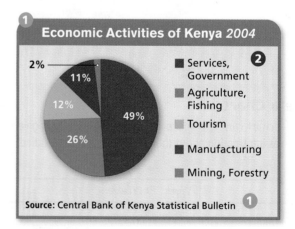

Economic Activities of Kenya *2004*

- Services, Government
- Agriculture, Fishing
- Tourism
- Manufacturing
- Mining, Forestry

Source: Central Bank of Kenya Statistical Bulletin

How to Read Charts

Strategy ❶ Read the title to find out what the chart is about. Ask yourself what kind of information the chart shows.

Strategy ❷ Read the headings to see how the chart is organized.

Strategy ❸ Study the data in the chart to understand the facts that it was designed to show.

Strategy ❹ Summarize the information shown in each part of the chart. Use the title to help you focus on what information the chart is presenting.

❶	World Economic Development						
❷ **Country**	**Status**	**GDP** in US Dollars*	**GDP/ Person** in US Dollars*	**Infant Mortality** per 1,000 Live Births	**Life Expectancy** at Birth	**Literacy Rate** (Percent)
❸ **Burkina Faso**	developing	5.4 billion	1,300	91.35	48.9	26.6
India	developing	719.8 billion	3,400	54.63	64.7	59.5
Uruguay	developing	13.2 billion	9,600	11.61	76.3	98.0
Germany	developed	2.8 trillion	30,400	4.12	78.8	99.0
Japan	developed	4.9 trillion	31,500	3.24	81.3	99.0
United States	developed	12.5 trillion	42,000	6.43	77.9	99.0

Source: *CIA World Factbook*, 2006   * official exchange rate

Write a Summary

Writing a summary can help you understand the information contained in graphs and charts. The paragraph below summarizes information from the chart above.

 The chart compares several indicators of economic development for three developing and three developed nations: Burkina Faso, India, Uruguay, Germany, Japan, and the United States. The developed nations have higher GDPs and literacy rates, longer life expectancies, and lower infant mortality than the developing nations. Of the countries shown, the United States has the highest GDP per person, Burkina Faso the lowest.

Practicing the Skill

Turn to the chapter "Brazil," Section 1. Look at "Comparing Urban and Rural Populations," and study the population pie graphs. Then write a paragraph summarizing what you learned from the graphs.

2.6 Interpreting Political Cartoons

Defining the Skill

Political cartoons express an opinion about a serious subject. A political cartoonist uses symbols, familiar objects, and people to make his or her point quickly and visually. Sometimes words used in the cartoon will help to clarify its meaning.

Applying the Skill

The cartoon below is about military dictatorships in Latin America. Use the strategies listed below to help you interpret this and other political cartoons.

How to Interpret Political Cartoons

Strategy ❶ Identify the subject of the cartoon. Look at the cartoon as a whole. If the cartoon has them, read the title and caption.

Strategy ❷ Look for symbols that the cartoonist used to communicate ideas. In this cartoon, the man's uniform is meant to convey that he is a military dictator.

Strategy ❸ Analyze the other visual details of the cartoon. A huge crowd of people has gathered at the balcony to express their desire for democracy. They appear surprised by his words, perhaps because dictators are not known for following the will of the people and voluntarily stepping down.

"My goodness, if I'd known how badly you wanted democracy I'd have given it to you ages ago."

Make a Chart

Making a chart can help you interpret a political cartoon. The chart below summarizes the information from the cartoon above.

Subject	military dictatorships in Latin America
Symbols and Details	The uniform conveys that the man is a military dictator. The crowd appears surprised that he supports their desire for democracy.
Message	In most Latin American military dictatorships, the will of the people was ignored by those in power.

Practicing the Skill

Look through newspapers to find a political cartoon about current events. Then use a chart like the one above to summarize information from the cartoon to help you interpret its meaning.

2.7 Creating a Map

Defining the Skill

When you **create a map,** you can choose what geographical information to include. You can show political information, such as the area covered by empires or countries. Your map can also be a thematic map, showing data on climates, population, or resources.

Applying the Skill

Below is a map that a student created that shows South American gross domestic product. Use the strategies listed below to learn how to create your own map.

How to Create a Map

Strategy ❶ Select a title that identifies the map's geographical area and purpose.

Strategy ❷ Use dashes to draw latitude and longitude lines. Using these as a guide, draw the area you are representing.

Strategy ❸ Create a legend that identifies the map's colors or icons.

Strategy ❹ Draw the colors or icons on the map to show information.

Strategy ❺ Draw a compass rose and scale.

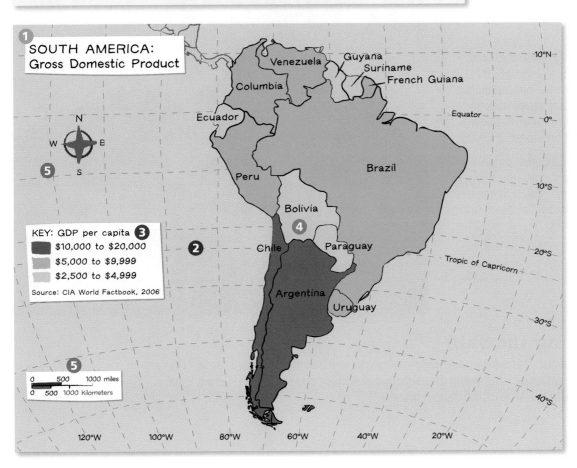

❶ SOUTH AMERICA: Gross Domestic Product

KEY: GDP per capita ❸
$10,000 to $20,000
$5,000 to $9,999
$2,500 to $4,999
Source: CIA World Factbook, 2006

Practicing the Skill

Turn to the chapter "Middle America and Spanish-Speaking South America," Section 1. Read "Promoting International Trade." Then, using the map at the front of the chapter as a guide, create a map showing the nations that signed CAFTA.

2.8 Creating a Model

Defining the Skill

When you **create a model,** you use information and ideas to show an event, situation, or place in a visual way. A model might be a poster or diagram that explains something. Or, it might be a three-dimensional model, such as a diorama, that depicts an important scene or situation.

Applying the Skill

The following sketch shows a model of a volcano. Use the strategies listed below to help you create your own model.

How to Create a Model

Strategy ❶ Gather the information you need to understand the situation or event. In this case, you need to be able to show the interior of a volcano and its parts.

Strategy ❷ Visualize an idea for your model. Once you have created a picture in your mind, make an actual sketch to plan how it might look.

Strategy ❸ Think of symbols you may want to use. Since the model should give information in a visual way, think about ways you can use color, pictures, or other visuals to tell the story.

Strategy ❹ Gather supplies you will need. Then create the model. To make this model, you would need a description of how volcanoes work and art supplies.

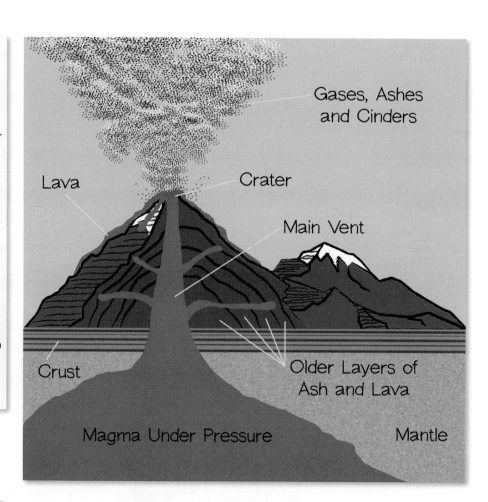

Gases, Ashes and Cinders

Lava

Crater

Main Vent

Crust

Older Layers of Ash and Lava

Magma Under Pressure

Mantle

Practicing the Skill

Turn to the chapter "Latin America: Physical Geography and History," Section 3. Read "The Aztec, a Military Culture," and look at the *chinampas* illustration that follows the section. Then create a model of the Atzec capital, Tenochtitlán.

3.1 Outlining

Defining the Skill

Outlining is a method of organizing information. Once you have settled on a topic for a report or paper, you must do research. When you have all the information you need, then you have to organize it. An outline lists your report's main ideas in the order in which they will appear. It also organizes main ideas and supporting details according to their importance.

Applying the Skill

The outline at right is for a research report about the causes and effects of earthquakes. Use the strategies listed below to help you make an outline.

How to Outline

Strategy ❶ Read the main ideas of this report. They are listed on the left and labeled with capital Roman numerals. Each main idea will need at least one paragraph in your report.

Strategy ❷ Read the supporting ideas for each main idea. These are indented and labeled with capital letters. Notice that some main ideas require more supporting ideas than others.

Strategy ❸ Read the supporting details in the outline. They are indented farther and labeled with numerals. Some supporting ideas will not have supporting details. It is not necessary to include every piece of information that you have. An outline is merely a guide to follow as you write your report.

Strategy ❹ Reports can be organized in different ways. This report is arranged to show the causes and effects of earthquakes. The outline should clearly reflect the way the report is organized.

❶ I. Causes of Earthquakes
    A. Shifting tectonic plates
❷   B. Volcanoes
    C. Human activities
❸   1. Large underground nuclear explosions, deep mine excavations, and filling large reservoirs can all cause earthquakes.

II. Effects of Earthquakes
    A. Earthquakes usually do not kill people directly.
    B. Damage to natural features
      1. shifting of large blocks of Earth's crust
        a. can cause landslides
        b. can break down the banks of rivers and lakes and cause flooding
    C. Damage to man-made structures
      1. Ground shaking causes structures to sway, bounce, and possibly collapse.
    D. Cause other catastrophic events
      1. Fires
        a. San Francisco, 1906
      2. Tsunamis
        a. Indian Ocean, 2004

Practicing the Skill

Turn to the chapter "Human Geography," Section 2. Read "The Effects of Migration," and gather information from it about the effects of human migration. Write an outline for a report about the topic using correct outline form.

3.2 Writing for Social Studies

Defining the Skill

Writing is an important skill to learn. It allows you to communicate your thoughts and ideas. There are many different kinds of writing used in social studies.

Narrative Writing

Narrative writing tells a story. Some narratives are fictional, but historians and geographers write narratives about events that really happened. A narrative has three basic parts. The beginning sets the scene. The body presents a conflict. The resolution settles the conflict and ends the narrative. The sample below describes the volcano Krakatoa.

> One of the most destructive volcanic eruptions in recorded history happened in 1883, when two-thirds of the Indonesian island of Krakatoa was blown apart. The explosion sent volcanic ash 50 miles into the air. The surrounding area was plunged into darkness for two days. Krakatoa was uninhabited by humans, but the eruption buried all life on the island under a layer of ash. It took five years for plants and animals to thrive again on Krakatoa.

Persuasive Writing

Persuasive writing is writing whose purpose is to convince another person to adopt your opinion or position. People use persuasive writing for many reasons, such as convincing a government to adopt a proposal. Geographers and historians use persuasive writing to propose interpretations of facts. The sample below presents arguments for establishing a tsunami warning system in the Indian Ocean. The system began operations in 2006.

> In December 2004, a catastrophic tsunami struck Southeast Asia. Massive losses underline the need for a tsunami early warning system in the Indian Ocean. Such a system would predict and detect tsunamis and communicate warnings to the region's inhabitants. It will cost millions of dollars and require the cooperation of nations already monitoring seismic activity. However, many feel it is worth the effort to reduce destruction from tsunamis.

Expository Writing

Expository writing is meant to explain. It might examine a process or event, compare and contrast two different regions or civilizations, explain causes and effects, or explore problems and solutions. Expository writing has three main parts. The introduction states the main idea. The body supports the main idea with facts and examples. The conclusion summarizes the information and restates the main idea. In the sample below, the author explains some of the major causes of earthquakes.

> Earthquakes, the sudden movement of Earth's crust followed by a series of vibrations, have several causes. Most are caused by shifts in tectonic plates. Stress builds up along fault lines until it is finally released, making the ground shake. Earthquakes can also be triggered by the explosive action of a volcano. Human activities, such as deep mining, can prompt earthquakes as well. No matter the cause, earthquakes can have dramatic effects.

Applying the Skill

No matter what kind of writing you are doing—whether it is narrative, persuasive, or expository writing or something more complicated such as a research report—it needs to be clear, concise, and factually accurate. The strategies listed below will help you achieve your goal. The following passage is part of a larger research report about earthquakes. Notice how using these strategies helped the author convey information about the effects of earthquakes.

How to Write for Social Studies

Strategy ❶ Focus on your topic. Be sure that you clearly state the main idea of your piece so that your readers know what you intend to say.

Strategy ❷ Collect and organize facts and supporting details. Gather accurate information about your topic to support the narrative you are crafting or the point you are trying to make. Creating an outline can help you organize your thoughts and information.

Strategy ❸ Write a first draft, using standard grammar, spelling, sentence structure, and punctuation. Proofread your writing. Make sure it is well organized and grammatically correct. Make any necessary revisions in your final draft.

EFFECTS OF EARTHQUAKES

❶ Earthquakes usually do not kill people directly. Instead, most deaths and injuries occur as a result of damage to natural features and man-made structures. Earthquakes can also cause other catastrophes that harm people.

❷ During an earthquake, large blocks of Earth's crust shift. These shifts can cause landslides or break down the banks of rivers and lakes and cause flooding. ❷ The ground shaking that occurs during an earthquake can make buildings sway and bounce. The stress causes some buildings to collapse. All of these situations are dangerous for people.

Sometimes, earthquakes can cause other disasters, such as tsunamis or fires. ❷ A 1906 quake in San Francisco started a fire that burned for three days. About 3,000 people died in this event. ❷ An undersea earthquake caused the Indian Ocean tsunami in 2004, which claimed at least 280,000 lives.

Practicing the Skill

Turn to the chapter "Earth's Interlocking Systems," Section 4. Read "Global Warming." Then write a persuasive paragraph convincing government leaders to try to reduce greenhouse gases. Use the strategies listed above to help you make your paragraph clear and informative.

3.3 Forming and Supporting Opinions

Defining the Skill

When you **form opinions,** you interpret and judge the importance of events and people in history. You should always **support your opinions** with facts, examples, and quotations.

Applying the Skill

The passage below describes deforestation of the Amazon rain forest. Use the strategies listed below to form and support an opinion about the practice.

How to Form and Support Opinions

Strategy ❶ Look for important information about the subject. Information can include facts, quotations, and examples.

Strategy ❷ Form an opinion about the subject by asking yourself questions about the information. For example, how important was the subject? How does it relate to similar subjects in your own experience?

Strategy ❸ Support your opinions with facts, quotations, and examples. If the facts do not support the opinion, then rewrite your opinion so that it is supported by the facts.

DEFORESTATION IN THE AMAZON

The Amazon rain forest—the world's largest—covers one-third of South America. ❶ The practice of deforestation has reduced the area of Earth's surface covered by rain forests from 14 to 6 percent. ❶ Rain forests are important because they help regulate the world's climate by absorbing carbon dioxide and producing oxygen. As trees are cut down, less carbon dioxide is absorbed, which can contribute to global warming. ❶ Destroying rain forests also endangers the millions of species of plants and animals that live there, at least half of the world's species. Today, many people are working to preserve the rain forests.

Make a Chart

Making a chart can help you organize your opinions and supporting facts. The chart below summarizes one possible opinion about the deforestation of the Amazon rain forest.

❷	Opinion	Efforts should be made to slow deforestation and protect the Amazon rain forest.
❸	Facts	Deforestation has reduced the area of Earth covered by rain forests from 14 to 6 percent.
		Rain forests absorb carbon dioxide and produce oxygen.
		Rain forests are home to at least half the world's species of plants and animals.

Practicing the Skill

Turn to the chapter "Mexico," Section 3. Read "Creation of Jobs," and form your own opinion about the importance of creating new jobs in Mexico. Make a chart like the one above to summarize your opinion and the supporting facts and examples.

3.4 Using Primary and Secondary Sources

Defining the Skill

Primary sources are materials written or created by people who lived during historical events. The writers might have been participants or witnesses. Primary sources include letters, journals, articles, and artwork. **Secondary sources** are materials that teach about an event, such as textbooks. When you research, you will use both kinds of sources.

Applying the Skill

The following passage uses primary and secondary sources to describe European diseases in the Americas. Use the strategies below to help you learn how to use these sources.

How to Use Primary and Secondary Sources

Strategy 1 Distinguish secondary sources from primary sources. Most of the paragraph is a secondary source. The observation by de Sahagun is a primary source. The primary source supports the point the secondary source is making.

Strategy 2 Determine the thesis, or main idea, of the secondary source. Look for details that support the main idea.

Strategy 3 Identify the author of the primary source and consider why the author produced it. What was the document supposed to achieve? Is it credible? Is it promoting a particular viewpoint? In this case, de Sahagun seems to be an objective observer.

DISEASES IN THE NEW WORLD

1 After Christopher Columbus landed in the New World and the Spanish came to the Americas, plants and animals were traded between Europe and the Americas. Both cultures introduced new goods and ideas to the other. **2** Unfortunately, the Europeans also brought diseases with them. These diseases, which included smallpox, influenza, and measles, led to the deaths of millions of Native Americans. **3** Spanish missionary Bernardino de Sahagun saw the diseases' effects firsthand, observing, "There was a great havoc. Very many died of it. . . . Great was its destruction."

Make a Chart

Making a chart can help you assess information from primary and secondary sources. The chart below summarizes information from the passage above.

Questions	Answers
What is the main idea?	Europeans brought diseases to the Americas.
What are the supporting details?	The diseases included smallpox, influenza, and measles. Millions of Native Americans died from them.
Who wrote the primary source?	Bernardino de Sahagun
What can you tell about the primary source?	De Sahagun appears to be an objective observer. The source seems credible.

Practicing the Skill

Turn to the chapter "Mexico," Section 3. Read "Building a Modern Economy" and the primary source by Vicente Fox. Make a chart to summarize the information found in the sources and to help you read them.

3.5 Using a Database

Defining the Skill

A **database** is a collection of data, or information, that is organized so that you can find and retrieve information on a specific topic quickly and easily. Once a computerized database is set up, you can search it to find specific information without going through the entire database. The database will provide a list of all information in the database related to your topic. Learning how to use a database will help you learn how to create one.

Applying the Skill

The chart below is a database for famous mountains in the Western Hemisphere. Use the strategies below to help you understand and use the database.

How to Use a Database

Strategy ❶ Identify the topic of the database. The most important words in this title are *Mountains* and *Western Hemisphere*. These words were used to begin the research for this database.

Strategy ❷ Identify the kinds of data you need to enter in your database. These will be the column headings of your database. The keywords *Mountain*, *Location*, *Height*, and *Interesting Facts* were chosen to focus the research.

Strategy ❸ Identify the entries included under each heading.

Strategy ❹ Use the database to help you find information quickly. For example, in this database, you could search for "volcanoes" to find a list of famous mountains that are also volcanoes.

❶ FAMOUS MOUNTAINS OF THE WESTERN HEMISPHERE			
❷ MOUNTAIN	LOCATION	HEIGHT ABOVE SEA LEVEL (FEET)	INTERESTING FACTS
❸ Aconcagua	Argentina	22,834	tallest mountain in Western Hemisphere
Cotopaxi	Ecuador	❹ 19,347	one of tallest active volcanoes
Logan	Canada	19,524	tallest mountain in Canada
Mauna Kea	Hawaii	13,796	tallest mountain in world from ocean floor to peak
Mauna Loa	Hawaii	❹ 13,677	largest volcano in the world
McKinley	Alaska	20,320	tallest mountain in North America
Orizaba	Mexico	18,700	tallest mountain in Mexico
Shasta	California	14,162	symmetrically shaped peak

Practicing the Skill

Create a database of countries in Latin America that shows the name of each country, its capital, its land area, and its population. Use the information in the "Country Almanac" of the "Latin America" unit atlas to provide the data. Use a format like the one above for your database.

3.6 Creating a Multimedia Presentation

Defining the Skill

Audio and video recordings, photographs, CD-ROMs, television, and computer software are all different kinds of media. To **create a multimedia presentation,** you need to collect information in different media and organize them into one presentation so that your audience watches, listens, and learns.

Applying the Skill

The photographs below show students using computers to create multimedia presentations. A multimedia presentation can incorporate computers, but it does not have to. Use the strategies listed below to help you create your own multimedia presentation.

How to Create a Multimedia Presentation

Strategy 1 Identify the topic of your presentation and decide which media are best for an effective presentation. For example, you may want to use video or photographic images to show the dry character of a desert. Or, you may want to use CDs or audio tapes to provide music or to make sounds that go with your presentation, such as the sounds of a camel.

Strategy 2 Research the topic in a variety of sources. Images, text, props, and background music should reflect the region and the historical period of your topic.

Strategy 3 Write the script for the presentation. You could use a narrator and characters' voices to tell the story. Primary sources are an excellent source for script material.

Strategy 4 Put together your presentation. Supplement your script with the images, props, music, and other media that you selected from your research. If you create your presentation on your computer, you can save the file for future viewing.

Practicing the Skill

Create a multimedia presentation about one of the ancient civilizations of Latin America. Turn to the chapter "Latin America: Physical Geography and History," Section 3, and choose one of the four civilizations discussed there. Use the text and images provided in the section for ideas about what your presentation might include.

4.1 Using a Search Engine

Defining the Skill

Using a **search engine** can be a useful way to do research on the Internet. A search engine is a tool designed to find information on the Internet. There are billions of Web sites and documents available on the Internet. Using a search engine properly can help you sort through the vast amount of information.

Applying the Skill

The screen below shows a popular search engine. Use the strategies listed below to help you search the Internet.

How to Use a Search Engine

Strategy ❶ Brainstorm keywords to enter into the search engine. Make a list of possible search terms. It often helps to try to be specific. If your research topic is what careers geographers can have, try entering *careers in geography* instead of just *geography*. This will narrow the results to relevant information.

Strategy ❷ Many search engines will provide an excerpt of a Web site below the link to the site. Read these to help you determine if the Web site is relevant to your topic and worth visiting.

Strategy ❸ Click on the link to go to the Web site you are interested in exploring in depth. If you can, open the new Web site in a separate window, so that it is easier to come back to your original search.

Practicing the Skill

Choose a topic from Unit 1 that you would like to learn more about. Develop a list of keywords to help you search the Internet for information about that topic. Visit a search engine, and enter your keywords. Take a look at your search results, and consider which keywords were the most useful and why.

4.2 Evaluating Internet Sources

Defining the Skill

By **evaluating Internet sources** for credibility, you can make sure that you are only using the most accurate, reliable information as a resource.

Applying the Skill

The screen below shows a Web site about geography. Use the strategies listed below to learn how to assess its credibility.

How to Evaluate Internet Sources

Strategy ❶ Look at the Web site's Internet address. The three-letter code in it will help you determine who created the site. Almost anyone can set up a Web site with a ".com," or commercial, address. School Web sites use ".edu," or education, addresses. Addresses that end with ".org" are used by nonprofit organizations. Official government Web sites end in ".gov." These last three will often be more reliable than commercial Web sites.

Strategy ❷ Try to identify the author of the Web site and when it was last updated. This information does not always appear. Some sites are anonymous, or created by an unidentified author. You should not use these as sources because the information could be outdated, or the author might not know much about the Web site's topic.

Strategy ❸ Use another source to verify the information you find on the Internet. Online encyclopedias contain accurate information. Sources with .gov and .edu addresses are usually reliable. So is information from newspaper, magazine, and television news channel Web sites. Search several sites, and try to find two or three sources with the same information.

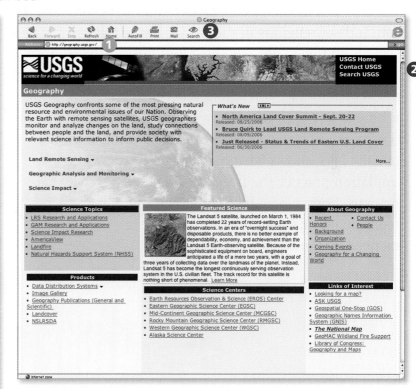

Practicing the Skill

Choose one of the Web sites that you found in your search from "Practicing the Skill" for "Using a Search Engine" on page R36 of this handbook. Evaluate the Web site to assess its credibility and its usefulness as a resource. Use the strategies listed above to help you.

World Religions and Ethical Systems

A Global View

A religion is an organized system of beliefs and practices, often centered on one or more gods. In this book, you have learned about many different religions and their impact on the world. Religions have guided people's beliefs and actions for thousands of years. They have brought people together. But they have also torn them apart.

Religions are powerful forces today as well. They affect everything from what people wear to how they behave. There are thousands of religions in the world. In the following pages, you will learn about five major religions: Buddhism, Christianity, Hinduism, Islam, and Judaism. You will also learn about Confucianism, an ethical system. Like a religion, an ethical system provides guidance on how to live your life. However, unlike religions, ethical systems do not center on the worship of gods. The chart on the opposite page shows what percentages of the world population practice the five major religions. The map shows where these religions are predominant or where they are practiced by significant numbers.

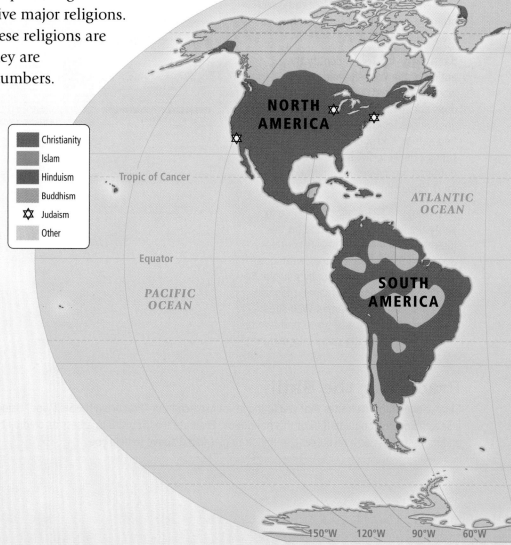

Christianity
Islam
Hinduism
Buddhism
✡ Judaism
Other

NORTH AMERICA

Tropic of Cancer

ATLANTIC OCEAN

Equator

PACIFIC OCEAN

SOUTH AMERICA

150°W   120°W   90°W   60°W

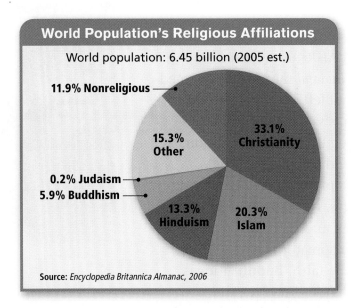

World Population's Religious Affiliations

World population: 6.45 billion (2005 est.)

- 11.9% Nonreligious
- 15.3% Other
- 0.2% Judaism
- 5.9% Buddhism
- 13.3% Hinduism
- 33.1% Christianity
- 20.3% Islam

Source: *Encyclopedia Britannica Almanac, 2006*

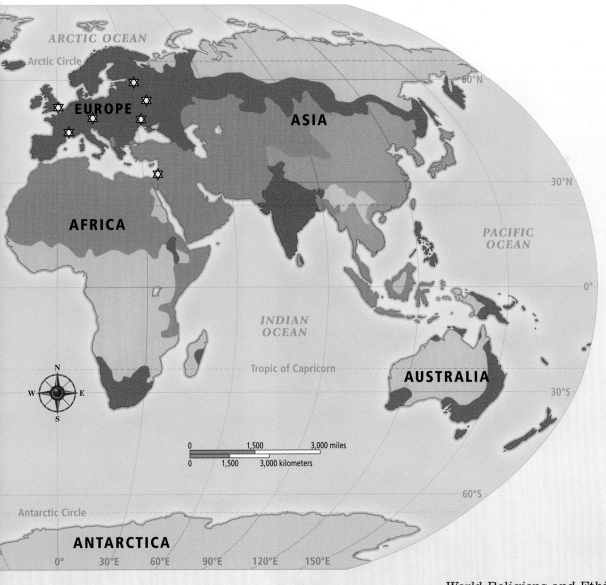

Buddhism

Buddhism began in India in the sixth century B.C. The religion was founded by Siddhartha Gautama (sihd•DAHR•tuh GOW•tuh•muh), who came to be known as the Buddha. *Buddha* means "enlightened one." He was born into a noble family but left home to search for enlightenment, or wisdom. The Buddha is said to have achieved enlightenment after long study. According to Buddhist tradition, he taught his followers that the way to end suffering was by practicing the Noble Eightfold Path. This path involved observing the following: right opinions, right desires, right speech, right action, right job, right effort, right concentration, and right meditation.

After the Buddha's death, Buddhism spread in India, Ceylon, and Central Asia. Missionaries spread the faith. Buddhist ideas also traveled along trade routes. The religion, however, did not survive on Indian soil. Today, most Buddhists live in Sri Lanka (formerly Ceylon), East Asia, Southeast Asia, and Japan.

▼ **Monks**
Buddhist monks dedicate their entire lives to the teachings of the Buddha. They live together in religious communities called monasteries. There, the monks lead lives of poverty, meditation, and study. In this photograph, Buddhist monks in Myanmar hold their begging bowls.

▼ **Buddha**
Statues of the Buddha, such as this one in Japan, appear in shrines throughout Asia. Buddhists try to follow the Buddha's teachings by meditating, a way of emptying the mind of thought. They also make offerings at shrines, temples, and monasteries.

▲ **Pilgrimage**
For centuries, Buddhists have come to visit places in India and Nepal associated with the Buddha's life. These sites include the Buddha's birthplace and the fig tree where he achieved his enlightenment. Worshipers also visit the Dhamekha Stupa in Sarnath, India, the site of the Buddha's first sermon, shown here.

Symbol The Buddha's teaching, known as the dharma, is often symbolized by a wheel because his teaching was intended to end the cycle of births and deaths. The Buddha is said to have "set in motion the wheel of the dharma" during his first sermon.

Primary Source

The Buddha called his insight into the nature of suffering the Four Noble Truths. In the following selection, the Buddha tells his followers how they can end suffering and find enlightenment. The path involves understanding that life on Earth is brief and full of sadness. It also involves giving up selfish desire.

All created things are transitory [short-lived]; those who realize this are freed from suffering. This is the path that leads to pure wisdom.

All created beings are involved in sorrow; those who realize this are freed from suffering. This is the path that leads to pure wisdom.

All states are without self; those who realize this are freed from suffering. This is the path that leads to pure wisdom.

from the *Dhammapada*
Translated by Eknath Easwaran

Christianity

Christianity is the largest religion in the world, with about 2 billion followers. It is based on the life and teachings of Jesus, as described in the Bible's New Testament. Jesus, a Jew, taught many ideas from the Jewish tradition. Some biblical prophets had spoken of a day when a promised figure would come to save all of humankind. By the end of the first century A.D., many Jews and non-Jews had come to believe that Jesus was the one who would make this happen. Now called "Christians," they spread their faith throughout the Roman Empire.

Christians regard Jesus as the Son of God. They believe that Jesus entered the world and died to save humanity.

▼ **Easter and Palm Sunday**
On Easter, Christians celebrate their belief in Jesus' resurrection, or his being raised to heavenly life after he was put to death. The Sunday before Easter, Christians observe Palm Sunday. This day celebrates Jesus' triumphal entry into Jerusalem. Palm branches, like those carried in this procession in El Salvador, were spread before him.

▲ **Jesus and the Disciples**
Jesus' followers included 12 disciples, or pupils. Jesus passed on his teachings to his disciples. This painting from the 1400s shows Jesus with his disciples.

▼ **St. Paul's Cathedral**
Paul was a missionary who spread Christian beliefs throughout the Roman Empire. He started churches almost everywhere he went. Many churches today, such as this great cathedral in London, are named for Paul.

Symbol According to the New Testament, Jesus was crucified, or put to death on a cross. As a result, the cross became an important symbol of Christianity. It represents the belief that Jesus died to save humanity.

Primary Source

One of Jesus' most famous sermons is the Sermon on the Mount. In this talk, Jesus provided guidance to his followers. His words were written down in the New Testament, the part of the Bible that describes the teachings of Jesus. In the following verses, Jesus explains that people can be saved by opening their hearts to God and by treating others as they would like to be treated.

Ask, and it will be given you; seek, and you will find; knock, and it will be opened to you. For every one who asks receives, and he who seeks finds, and to him who knocks it will be opened. Or what man of you, if his son asks him for a loaf, will give him a stone? Or if he asks for a fish, will give him a serpent? If you then, who are evil, know how to give good gifts to your children, how much more will your Father who is in heaven give good things to those who ask him? So whatever you wish that men would do to you, do so to them; for this is the law and the prophets.

Matthew 7:7–12

Hinduism

Hinduism is a way of life guided by religious beliefs and practices that developed over thousands of years. Hindus believe that a supreme being called Brahman is the soul of the universe. The same presence, they believe, can also be found within each person. People can be freed from suffering and desires once they understand the nature of Brahman. The religious practices of Hindus include prayer, meditation, selfless acts, and worship of the various Hindu deities.

Today, Hinduism is the major religion of India and Nepal. It also has followers in Indonesia, Africa, Europe, and the Western Hemisphere.

▼ **Festival of Diwali**
Diwali, the Festival of Lights, is the most important festival in India. Diwali may have begun as a harvest festival in ancient India. Today, it marks the beginning of the year for many Hindus. They celebrate the festival by lighting candles and lamps, as shown in this photograph.

▲ Deities
Brahman often takes the form of three deities in Hinduism. Brahma is the creator of the universe. Vishnu is its protector. Shiva is its destroyer. All three deities are represented in this sculpture.

▼ Brahmin Priest
Brahmin priests, like the one shown here, are among Hinduism's religious leaders. These priests take care of the holy images in temples and read from the religion's sacred books.

Learn More About Hinduism

Symbol The syllable *Om* (or *Aum*) is often recited at the beginning of Hindu prayers. *Om* is the most sacred sound in Hinduism because it is believed to contain all other sounds. The syllable is represented by the symbol shown below.

Primary Source

Hinduism has many sacred texts. The Vedas, four collections of prayers, rituals, and other sacred texts, are the oldest Hindu scriptures. They are believed to contain all knowledge, past and future.

The *Bhagavad-Gita* is another sacred Hindu text. In this work, Vishnu takes on the personality of a chariot driver named Krishna. Krishna and the warrior Arjuna discuss the meaning of life and religious faith. In this selection, Krishna explains that Brahman cannot be destroyed.

> Weapons do not cut it,
> fire does not burn it,
> waters do not wet it,
> wind does not wither it.
>
> It cannot be cut or burned;
> it cannot be wet or withered;
> it is enduring, all-pervasive,
> fixed, immovable, and timeless.
>
> *Bhagavad-Gita* 2:23–24

Islam

Islam is a religion based on the teachings of the Qur'an, the religion's holy book. Followers of Islam, known as Muslims, believe that God revealed these teachings to the prophet Muhammad through the angel Gabriel around A.D. 610. Islam teaches that there is only one God—the same God that is worshiped in Christianity and Judaism. In Arabic, God is called Allah. Muslims also believe in the prophets of Judaism and Christianity. In fact, Muslims traditionally refer to Christians and Jews as "people of the book." That is because Christians and Jews have received divine revelations from scriptures in the Bible.

Today, most Muslims live in southwestern and central Asia and parts of Africa. Islam also has many followers in Southeast Asia. Muslims show their devotion by performing acts of worship known as the Five Pillars of Islam. These include faith, prayer, charity, fasting, and a pilgrimage to Mecca.

▲ **Muslim Prayer**
Five times a day—dawn, noon, mid-afternoon, sunset, and evening—Muslims face toward Mecca to pray. Like the people in this photograph, Muslims stop what they are doing when they hear the call to prayer. Everything comes to a halt—even traffic.

▼ **The Dome of the Rock**
The Dome of the Rock in Jerusalem is one of Islam's holiest sites. The rock on the site is the spot from which Muslims say Muhammad rose to heaven to learn Allah's will. With Allah's blessing, Muhammad returned to Earth to bring God's message to all people.

▼ Ramadan

During the holy month of Ramadan, Muslims fast, or do not eat or drink, from dawn to sunset. The family shown here is ending their fast. The most important night of Ramadan is called the Night of Power. This is believed to be the night the angel Gabriel first spoke to Muhammad.

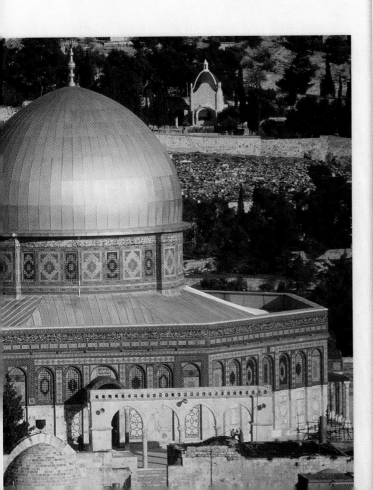

Learn More About Islam

Symbol The crescent moon has become a symbol of Islam. The symbol may be related to the new moon that begins each month in the Islamic lunar calendar.

Primary Source

The Qur'an is the spiritual guide for Muslims. It also contains teachings for Muslim daily life. The following chapter is called the Exordium (introduction). It is also called Al-Fatihah. Muslims recite this short chapter, as well as other passages from the Qur'an, when they pray.

In the Name of God, the Compassionate, the Merciful

Praise be to God, Lord of the Universe,
The Compassionate, the Merciful,
Sovereign of the Day of Judgment!
You alone we worship, and to You alone
  we turn for help.
Guide us to the straight path,
The path of those whom You have favored,
Not of those who have incurred Your wrath,
Nor of those who have gone astray.

Qur'an 1:1–6

World Religions and Ethical Systems **R47**

Judaism

Judaism was the first major monotheistic religion—that is, based on the concept of one God. The basic teachings of Judaism come from the Torah, the first five books of the Hebrew Bible. Judaism teaches that a person serves God by studying the Torah and living by its teachings. The Torah became the basis for the civil and religious laws of Judaism. The followers of Judaism, or Jews, also believe that God set down many moral laws for all of humanity with the Ten Commandments.

Today, there are more than 15 million Jews throughout the world. Many live in Israel, where a Jewish state was created in 1948.

▼ Abraham

According to the Torah, God chose a Hebrew shepherd named Abraham to be the "father" of the Hebrew people. In the 19th century B.C., Abraham led his family to a land that he believed God had promised them. This painting illustrates their journey.

▲ Rabbi
Rabbis are the Jewish people's spiritual leaders and teachers. A rabbi often conducts the services in a synagogue, or Jewish house of worship. Like the rabbi shown here, he or she may also conduct the ceremony that marks Jewish children's entrance into the religious community.

▼ Western Wall
Many Jews make the pilgrimage to the Western Wall, shown here. The sacred wall formed the western wall of the courtyard of the Second Temple of Jerusalem. The temple was built in the second century B.C. The Romans destroyed it in A.D. 70.

Learn More About Judaism

Symbol The Star of David, also called the Shield of David, is a very important symbol of Judaism. The symbol honors King David, who ruled the kingdom of Israel about 1000–962 B.C.

Primary Source

The Book of Genesis is the first book of the Hebrew Bible and of the Torah. Genesis tells the history of the Hebrew people. It focuses on the individuals with whom God had a special relationship. In the following verses, God speaks to Abraham. His words express a promise of land and a special pledge to the Hebrew people.

Now the Lord said to Abram [Abraham], "Go from your country and your kindred and your father's house to the land that I will show you. And I will make of you a great nation, and I will bless you, and make your name great, so that you will be a blessing. I will bless those who bless you, and him who curses you I will curse; and by you all the families of the earth will bless themselves."

Genesis 12:1–3

Confucianism

Confucianism is an ethical system based on the teachings of the Chinese scholar Confucius. It stresses social and civic responsibility. Confucius was born in 551 B.C., during a time of crisis in China. He hoped his ideas and teachings would restore the order of earlier times to his society. But although Confucius was active in politics, he never had enough political power to put his ideas into practice. After his death, Confucius' students spread his teachings. As a result, his ideas became the foundation of Chinese thought for more than 2,000 years.

Today, Confucianism guides the actions of millions of Chinese people and other peoples of the East. It has also greatly influenced people's spiritual beliefs. While East Asians declare themselves to follow a number of religions, many also claim to be Confucians.

▼ **Temple**
Although Confucianism has no clergy or gods to worship, temples, like this one in Taiwan, have been built to honor Confucius. In ancient times, the temples provided schools of higher education. Today, many have been turned into museums.

◀ Confucius

Confucius believed that society should be organized around five basic relationships. These are the relationships between (1) ruler and subject, (2) father and son, (3) husband and wife, (4) elder brother and junior brother, and (5) friend and friend.

▲ Confucius' Birthday

Historians do not know for certain the day when Confucius was born, but people in East Asia celebrate his birthday on September 28. In Taiwan and China, it is an official holiday known as Teachers' Day. The holiday pays tribute to teachers because Confucius himself was a teacher. Here, students in Beijing take part in a ceremony honoring their teachers.

Learn More About Confucianism

Symbol The yin-and-yang symbol represents opposite forces in the world working together. Yin represents all that is cold, dark, soft, and mysterious. Yang represents everything that is warm, bright, hard, and clear. The yin-and-yang symbol represents the harmony that Confucius hoped to restore to society.

Primary Source

Confucius' teachings were collected by his students in a book called the *Analects*. In the following selections from the *Analects*, Confucius (called the Master) instructs his students about living a moral and thoughtful life.

The Master said: "Even in the midst of eating coarse rice and drinking water and using a bent arm for a pillow happiness is surely to be found; riches and honors acquired by unrighteous means are to me like the floating clouds." (7.16)

The Master said: "When I walk with two others, I always receive instruction from them. I select their good qualities and copy them, and improve on their bad qualities." (7.22)

The Master said: "The people may be made to follow something, but may not be made to understand it." (8.9)

from the *Analects*
Translated by Raymond Dawson

Other Important Religions

You have learned about the five major world religions. Now find out about some other important religions: Bahaism, Shinto, Sikhism, and Zoroastrianism. These religions are important both historically and because they have many followers today.

▼ Shinto

Shinto, meaning "way of the gods," is Japan's oldest and only native religion. Shintoists worship many gods, called *kami*. They believe that kami are spirits found in mountains, rivers, rocks, trees, and other parts of nature. Shintoists often worship the kami at shrines in their homes. They also celebrate the gods during special festivals, such as the one shown here. Today, there are about 3 million Shintoists, mostly in Japan.

▲ Bahaism

Bahaism (buh•HAH•IHZ•uhm) is a young religion, with more than 7 million followers throughout the world. It was founded in 1863 in Persia (modern-day Iran) by a man known as Bahaullah, which means "splendor of God" in Arabic. Followers believe that, in time, God will break down barriers of race, class, and nation. When this happens, people will form a single, united society. All of the Baha'i houses of worship have nine sides and a central dome, symbolizing this unity. The Baha'i house of worship shown here is located in Illinois.

◄ Sikhism

Sikhism was founded in India over 500 years ago by Guru Nanak. The religion's 24 million followers, called Sikhs, believe in one God. Like Buddhists and Hindus, Sikhs believe that the soul goes through repeated cycles of life and death. However, Sikhs do not believe that they have to live outside the world to end the cycle. Rather, they can achieve salvation by living a good and simple life. Uncut hair symbolizes this simple life. Many Sikh men cover their long hair with a turban, like the one worn by this man.

▲ Zoroastrianism

Zoroastrianism (ZAWR•oh•AS•tree•uh•NIHZ•uhm) was founded in ancient Persia around 600 B.C. by a prophet named Zoroaster. This prophet taught that Earth is a battleground where a great struggle is fought between the forces of good and the forces of evil. Each person is expected to take part in this struggle. At death, the Zoroastrian god, called Ahura Mazda (ah•HUR•uh MAZ•duh), will judge the person on how well he or she fought. This stone relief shows Ahura Mazda (*right*) giving the crown to a Persian king. Today, there are about 2.5 million Zoroastrians throughout the world.

Comparing World Religions and Ethical Systems

	Buddhism	Christianity	Hinduism	Islam	Judaism	Confucianism
Followers worldwide (estimated 2005 figures)	379 million	2.1 billion	860 million	1.3 billion	15.1 million	6.5 million
Name of god	no god	God	Brahman	Allah	God	no god
Founder	the Buddha	Jesus	no founder	no founder but spread by Muhammad	Abraham	Confucius
Holy book	many sacred books, including the Dhammapada	Bible, including Old Testament and New Testament	many sacred texts, including the Upanishads	Qur'an	Hebrew Bible, including the Torah	*Analects*
Clergy	Buddhist monks	priests, ministers, monks, and nuns	Brahmin priests, monks, and gurus	no clergy but a scholar class, called the ulama, and imams, who may lead prayers	rabbis	no clergy
Basic beliefs	• Followers can achieve enlightenment by understanding the Four Noble Truths and by following the Noble Eightfold Path of right opinions, right desires, right speech, right action, right jobs, right effort, right concentration, and right meditation.	• There is only one God, who watches over and cares for his people. • Jesus is the Son of God. He died to save humanity. His death and resurrection made eternal life possible for others.	• The soul never dies but is continually reborn until it becomes divinely enlightened. • Persons achieve happiness and divine enlightenment after they free themselves from their earthly desires. • Freedom from earthly desires comes from many lifetimes of worship, knowledge, and virtuous acts.	• There is only one God, who watches over and cares for his people. • Persons achieve salvation by following the Five Pillars of Islam and living a just life. The pillars are faith, prayer, charity, fasting, and pilgrimage to Mecca.	• There is only one God, who watches over and cares for his people. • God loves and protects his people but also holds people accountable for their sins and shortcomings. • Persons serve God by studying the Torah and living by its teachings.	• Social order, harmony, and good government should be based on strong family relationships. • Respect for parents and elders is important to a well-ordered society. • Education is important for the welfare of both the individual and society.

Source: *Encyclopedia Britannica Almanac, 2006*

Review

KEY IDEAS

Buddhism (pages R40–R41)

1. How did the Buddha believe that his followers could end their suffering?

2. How did Buddhism spread?

Christianity (pages R42–R43)

3. Why is Jesus important to the Christian religion?

4. What are some Christian beliefs?

Hinduism (pages R44–R45)

5. What is the importance of Brahman in Hinduism?

6. What three deities does Brahman often take the form of?

Islam (pages R46–R47)

7. How do Muslims believe the teachings of the Qur'an were revealed?

8. Why do Muslims traditionally refer to Christians and Jews as "people of the book"?

Judaism (pages R48–R49)

9. What does it mean to say that Judaism is a monotheistic religion?

10. What are the Ten Commandments?

Confucianism (pages R50–R51)

11. What did Confucius hope to restore?

12. What five relationships are important in Confucianism?

Other Important Religions (pages R52–R53)

13. How does Shinto differ from Bahaism, Sikhism, and Zoroastrianism?

14. How is Sikhism similar to Buddhism and Hinduism?

CRITICAL THINKING

15. **Compare and Contrast** What goal do Buddhists and Hindus share?

16. **Draw Conclusions** How does Islam affect the everyday lives of its followers?

INTERPRETING A PIE CHART

The pie chart below shows what percentages of the population of India practice the major religions. Use the pie chart to answer the following questions.

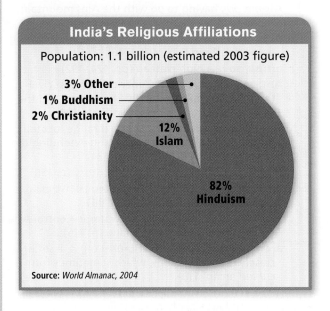

India's Religious Affiliations

Population: 1.1 billion (estimated 2003 figure)

3% Other
1% Buddhism
2% Christianity
12% Islam
82% Hinduism

Source: *World Almanac, 2004*

1. **What percentage of the people in India practice Hinduism?**

   A. 1 percent
   B. 2 percent
   C. 12 percent
   D. 82 percent

2. **Which religion is practiced by 12 percent of the population?**

   A. Buddhism
   B. Christianity
   C. Hinduism
   D. Islam

Glossary

A

agricultural revolution *n.* the shift from gathering food to raising food (p. 96)

alpaca *n.* a South American mammal related to the llama (p. 192)

Alpine *adj.* having to do with the Alps mountain range (p. 302)

Alps *n.* Europe's tallest mountain range, stretching across southern Europe (p. 246)

altiplano *n.* a high plateau (pp. 124, 192)

Amazon River *n.* South America's longest river (about 4,000 miles, or 6,400 kilometers) and the second-longest river in the world (p. 124)

Andes Mountains *n.* a mountain range located on South America's west coast and extending the full length of the continent (p. 124)

annex *v.* to add to an existing territory (p. 150)

anthropologist (AN•thruh•PAHL•uh•jihst) *n.* a scientist who studies culture (p. 88)

Aral Sea *n.* an inland body of water in Central Asia that has been steadily shrinking (p. 416)

archipelago (AHR•kuh•PEHL•uh•GOH) *n.* a set of closely grouped islands, which sometimes form a curved arc (p. 118)

artisan *n.* a worker skilled in making products or art with his or her hands (p. 174)

atmosphere *n.* the layer of gases that surround the Earth (p. 34)

autonomy *n.* self-governance or independence (p. 296)

Aztec *n.* an early civilization in the Valley of Mexico (p. 132)

B

Baltic States *n.* Latvia, Lithuania, and Estonia, three countries that border the Baltic Sea (p. 344)

Basque (bask) *n.* an ethnic group living in the western Pyrenees and along the Bay of Biscay in Spain and France; also the name of their language (p. 290)

Benelux (BEHN•uh•LUHKS) *n.* name for the economic union formed by Belgium, the Netherlands, and Luxembourg to ensure the fast and efficient movement of people, goods, and services within these nations (p. 296)

Berlin Wall *n.* a wall built by East Germany's Communist government to close off East Berlin from West Berlin; torn down in 1991 (p. 302)

birth rate *n.* the number of births per 1,000 people per year (p. 58)

Bogotá *n.* capital city of Colombia (p. 186)

Bolívar, Simón (boh•LEE•vahr, see•MOHN) *n.* leader for independence in northern South America (pp. 140, 186)

Bolsheviks (BOHL•shuh•VIHKS) *n.* a group of revolutionaries who took control of the Russian government in 1917 (p. 388)

Bosniac *n.* an ethnic Muslim from Bosnia and Herzegovnia (p. 360)

bossa nova (BAHS•uh NOH•vuh) *n.* a jazz version of the samba, a Brazilian dance (p. 216)

Botero, Fernando *n.* Colombian artist known for portraits of people with exaggerated forms (p. 186)

boycott *v.* to stop buying and using products from certain sources as a way of protest (p. 224)

brain drain *n.* the loss of skilled workers who move in search of better opportunities (p. 344)

Brasília *n.* Brazil's current capital city (p. 210)

bread basket *n.* an abundant grain-producing region (p. 344)

Briton *n.* a British person (p. 328)

Buddhism *n.* a major world religion that began in India and is based on the teachings of Siddhartha Gautama (p. 396)

Byzantine Empire *n.* the eastern half of the Roman Empire that survived for a thousand years after the fall of Rome (p. 282)

C

Cabral, Pedro Álvares *n.* Portuguese explorer who in 1500 claimed land that is now part of Brazil for Portugal (p. 210)

Candomblé (kahn•duhm•BLEH) *n.* African religious practices that are mixed with Roman Catholic beliefs to produce a unique belief system (p. 216)

capoeira (KAP•oh•AY•ruh) *n.* a Brazilian dance combined with martial arts (p. 216)

Caracas *n.* capital city of Venezuela (p. 186)

carbon dioxide *n.* a gas composed of carbon and oxygen (p. 48)

Caribbean Community and Common Market (CARICOM) *n.* a trade organization of several Caribbean nations (p. 180)

cartographer (kahr•TAHG•ruh•fur) *n.* a geographer who creates maps (p. 10)

Caspian Sea *n.* a large body of water bordering Russia to the south and situated between Transcaucasia and Central Asia (pp. 380, 416)

Caucasus (KAW•kuh•suhs) **Mountains** *n.* a mountain range that runs between the Black Sea and the Caspian Sea (p. 416)

Central America Free Trade Agreement (CAFTA) *n.* an agreement to promote trade between the United States and countries of Central America (pp. 174, 180)

Central Asia *n.* a region that contains the republics of Kazakhstan (KAH•zahk•STAN), Kyrgyzstan (KEER•gee•STAN), Tajikistan (tah•JIHK•ih•STAN), Turkmenistan (TURK•mehn•ih•STAN), and Uzbekistan (uz•BEHK•ih•STAN) (p. 416)

cession *n.* surrendered territory (p. 150)

Channel Tunnel *n.* the underwater railroad tunnel between France and England under the English Channel (p. 334)

Chechnya (CHEHCH•nee•uh) *n.* a largely Islamic republic in southwestern Russia that continues to fight for its independence (p. 406)

chinampas *n.* in Mexico, artificial islands used for farming (p. 132)

Church of England *n.* the official church of England headed by the Archbishop of Canterbury (p. 328)

citizen *n.* a person who owes loyalty to a country and receives its protection (p. 78)

city-state *n.* a political unit made up of a city and its surrounding lands (p. 254)

climate *n.* the typical weather conditions of a region over a long period of time (p. 40)

climatologist *n.* a geographer who studies climates (p. 16)

coalition *n.* an alliance or partnership, often a temporary one (p. 282)

Cold War *n.* a conflict between the United States and the Soviet Union after World War II that never developed into open warfare (p. 388)

colonia *n.* a neighborhood in Mexico (p. 156)

colony *n.* overseas territory ruled by a nation, such as Mexico from the 1500s to 1821 (p. 140)

Columbian Exchange *n.* the movement of plants and animals between Latin America and Europe after Columbus' voyage to the Americas in A.D. 1492 (p. 140)

Columbus, Christopher *n.* Italian navigator and explorer who sailed for Spain and explored the Caribbean and the coast of Central and South America (p. 290)

command economy *n.* an economic system in which the production of goods and services is decided by a central government (pp. 72, 344, 406, 432)

commonwealth *n.* a self-governing political unit that is associated with another country (p. 180)

Commonwealth of Nations *n.* an association made up of the United Kingdom and many former British colonies (p. 320)

communism *n.* a type of government in which the Communist Party holds all political power and controls the economy (pp. 78, 180, 344, 388)

compulsory *adj.* required (p. 282)

conquistador (kahn•KWIHS•tuh•DAWR) *n.* Spanish word for "conqueror" (p. 140)

constitution *n.* the set of laws and principles that defines the nature of a government (p. 150)

Constitution of 1917 *n.* Mexican constitution written during the revolution that is still in effect today (p. 150)

constitutional monarchy *n.* a government in which the powers of the king or queen are limited by the constitution (p. 334)

continent *n.* one of seven large landmasses on the Earth's surface (p. 26)

continental shelf *n.* the submerged land at the edge of a continent (p. 34)

cuíca (KWEE•kuh) *n.* a friction drum used in the samba, a Brazilian dance (p. 216)

cultural hearth *n.* the heartland of a major culture; an area where a culture originated and spread to other areas (pp. 96, 132)

culture *n.* the shared attitudes, knowledge, and behaviors of a group (pp. 66, 88, 132)

Cyrillic (suh•RIHL•ihk) **alphabet** *n.* the official writing system of Russia (p. 396)

czar (zahr) *n.* title for the rulers of Russia from the mid-1500s to the early 1900s (p. 388)

Czechoslovakia (CHEHK•uh•sluh•VAH•kee•uh) *n.* former country in Eastern Europe that existed from 1918 until 1993, when it split into the Czech Republic and Slovakia (p. 352)

D

database *n.* a collection of information that can be analyzed (p. 10)

Day of the Dead *n.* holiday to remember loved ones who have died (p. 156)

death rate *n.* the number of deaths per 1,000 people per year (p. 58)

debris (duh•BREE) *n.* the scattered remains of something broken or destroyed (p. 10)

deforestation *n.* the cutting and clearing away of trees (p. 224)

degraded *adj.* of a lower quality than previously existed (p. 48)

democracy *n.* a government in which the citizens make political decisions, either directly or through elected representatives (p. 254)

demographer *n.* a geographer who studies the characteristics of human populations (p. 58)

dependency *n.* a place governed by a country that it is not officially a part of (p. 180)

deport *v.* to expel from a country (p. 344)

desert *n.* a region with plants specially adapted to dry conditions (p. 40)

desertification *n.* the process in which farmland becomes less productive because the land is degraded (p. 48)

devolution *n.* the process of shifting some power from national to regional government (p. 334)

dictator *n.* a person with complete control over a country's government (pp. 174, 180, 186)

dictatorship *n.* a state or government ruled by a leader with absolute power (p. 78)

diffusion *n.* the spread of ideas, inventions, and patterns of behavior from one group to another (p. 96)

discrimination *n.* actions that might be hurtful to an individual or a group (p. 66)

diversity *n.* having many different ways to think or to do something, or a variety of people (p. 66)

Dom Pedro I *n.* Brazil's first Portuguese emperor; declared Brazil's independence from Portugal in 1822 (p. 210)

Dom Pedro II *n.* second emperor of Brazil, under whose rule slavery was abolished in Brazil in 1888 (p. 210)

domestication *n.* the raising and tending of a plant or an animal to be of use to humans (p. 96)

drainage basin *n.* the area drained by a major river (p. 34)

duchy (DUHCH•ee) *n.* the territory ruled by a duke or duchess (p. 296)

E

earthquake *n.* a sudden movement of the Earth's crust followed by a series of shocks (p. 26)

eclectic *adj.* made up of parts from a variety of sources (p. 352)

economic system *n.* a way people use resources to make and exchange goods (p. 72)

economy *n.* a system for producing and exchanging goods and services among a group of people (pp. 72, 224)

ecotourism *n.* travel to unique environments by people who take care to preserve them in their natural state (p. 174)

edible *adj.* fit for eating (p. 192)

emissions *n.* substances discharged into the air (p. 48)

empire *n.* a political system in which people or lands are controlled by one ruler (pp. 132, 140)

Enlightenment *n.* a philosophical movement in the 1600s and 1700s that was characterized by the use of reason and scientific methods (p. 270)

environment *n.* the physical surroundings of a location (p. 4)

equinox *n.* one of the two times a year when the sun's rays are over the equator and days and nights around the world are equal in length (p. 40)

erosion *n.* the wearing away and movement of weathered materials by water, wind, or ice (p. 26)

estancia (eh•STAHN•see•ah) *n.* large farm or ranch in Argentina (p. 200)

ethanol (EHTH•uh•NAWL) *n.* a liquid made by using a chemical process to convert sugar cane to a kind of alcohol that can be used for fuel (p. 224)

ethnic cleansing *n.* removing an ethnic or religious group from an area by force or the mass killing of members of such a group (p. 360)

ethnic group *n.* a group of people who share language, customs, and a common heritage (pp. 88, 396, 424)

Eurasia *n.* a term used to refer to a single continent made up of Europe and Asia (pp. 380, 416)

European Union (EU) *n.* an organization of European nations whose members cooperate on economic, social, and political issues (pp. 270, 282)

export *n.* a product or resource sold to another country (pp. 72, 224)

F

fascism (FASH•IHZ•uhm) *n.* a political philosophy that promotes blind loyalty to the state and a strong central government controlled by a powerful dictator (p. 282)

favelas (fuh•VEH•lahs) *n.* Brazilian name for the poor neighborhoods that surround the cities (p. 210)

federal republic *n.* form of government in which power is divided between a national government and state governments (p. 186)

feudalism *n.* a political system in which lords gave land to vassals in exchange for services (p. 262)

fiesta *n.* a holiday celebrated with parades, games, and food (p. 156)

foreign investment *n.* money put into a business by people from another country (p. 432)

fossil fuels *n.* sources of energy from ancient plant and animal remains; includes fuels such as coal, oil, and natural gas (pp. 48, 246)

Fox, Vicente *n.* Mexican president from the National Action Party who was elected in 2000 (p. 150)

French Revolution *n.* a conflict in France between 1789 and 1799 that ended the monarchy and led to changes in the way France was governed (p. 270)

G

Gaelic *n.* any of the Celtic family of languages spoken in Ireland or Scotland (p. 328)

García Márquez, Gabriel *n.* Colombian author and Nobel Prize winner (p. 186)

gaucho (GAOW•choh) *n.* Argentinian cowboy (p. 200)

Geographic Information Systems (GIS) *n.* a computer- or Internet-based mapping technology (pp. 10, 16)

geography *n.* the study of people, places, and environments (p. 4)

geomorphology (JEE•oh•mawr•FAHL•uh•jee) *n.* the study of how the shape of the Earth changes (p. 16)

glacier *n.* a large, slow-moving mass of ice (p. 26)

global economy *n.* economy in which buying and selling occurs across national borders (p. 164)

Global Positioning System (GPS) *n.* a system that uses a network of Earth-orbiting satellites to pinpoint location (p. 10)

global warming *n.* an increase in the average temperature of the Earth's atmosphere (pp. 48, 224)

globe *n.* a model of the Earth in the shape of a sphere (p. 10)

glyph *n.* a carved or engraved symbol that stands for a syllable or a word (p. 132)

Good Friday Agreement *n.* an agreement between Northern Ireland's unionists and nationalists that set up a new government (p. 334)

Gorbachev (GAWR•buh•CHAWF), **Mikhail** *n.* Soviet leader from 1985 to 1991 who increased freedoms for the Russian people (p. 388)

government *n.* an organization set up to make and enforce rules for a society (p. 78)

Greater Antilles *n.* the northern largest Caribbean islands that include Cuba, Jamaica, Hispaniola (which includes Haiti and the Dominican Republic), and Puerto Rico (p. 118)

greenhouse effect *n.* the trapping of the sun's heat by gases in the Earth's atmosphere (p. 48)

greenhouse gas *n.* any gas in the atmosphere that contributes to the greenhouse effect (p. 48)

Gross Domestic Product (GDP) *n.* the total value of all the goods and services produced in a country in a year (pp. 72, 200)

ground water *n.* water found beneath the Earth's surface (p. 34)

H

habitable lands *n.* lands suitable for human living (p. 58)

Hidalgo, Miguel ("Father Hidalgo") *n.* father of Mexican independence (p. 140)

highlands *n.* mountainous or hilly sections of a country (pp. 118, 124)

Hitler, Adolf *n.* German head of state from 1933 to 1945 (p. 302)

Holocaust *n.* the systematic murder of Jews and other minorities by the Nazis during World War II (pp. 270, 302)

hydroelectricity *n.* electric power generated by water (p. 224)

hydroelectric power *n.* electricity made by water-powered engines (p. 246)

hydrologic cycle *n.* the circulation of water between the Earth, the oceans, and the atmosphere (p. 34)

I

icon *n.* religious image used by Orthodox Christians in their worship (p. 396)

immigrant *n.* a person who leaves one area to settle in another (pp. 66, 216, 328)

immigration *n.* process of coming to another country to live (p. 164)

imperialism *n.* the practice of one country controlling the government and economy of another country or territory (pp. 270, 320)

import *n.* a product or resource that comes into a country (p. 72)

Inca *n.* an early civilization in the Andes Mountains of Peru (p. 132)

indigenous *n.* native to a region (p. 192)

Industrial Revolution *n.* the shift that began in Great Britain in the 1760s from making goods by hand to making them by machine (pp. 270, 320)

innovation *n.* something new that is introduced for the first time (p. 96)

Islam *n.* a monotheistic religion based on the teachings of Muhammad and the writings of the Qur'an, the Muslim holy book (pp. 396, 424)

isolate *v.* to cut off or set apart from a group (p. 254)

isthmus *n.* strip of land that connects two landmasses (p. 118)

J

jaguar *n.* a large cat mainly found in Central and South America (p. 132)

joropo (huh•ROH•poh) *n.* Venezuelan national folk dance (p. 186)

Juárez, Benito (1806–1872) *n.* Indian who became president and a Mexican national hero (p. 150)

Judaism (JOO•day•IHZ•uhm) *n.* the monotheistic religion of the Jews, based on the writings of the Hebrew Bible (p. 396)

K

Kara Kum *n.* a huge desert that covers most of Turkmenistan (p. 416)

knight *n.* a vassal trained in combat who fought on behalf of lords (p. 262)

Kosovo *n.* a self-governing province within Serbia (p. 360)

L

Lake Balkhash *n.* a lake in eastern Kazakhstan (p. 416)

landform *n.* a feature on the Earth's surface formed by physical force (p. 34)

landlocked *adj.* surrounded by land with no access to an ocean or sea (pp. 192, 200, 416)

Landsat *n.* a series of information-gathering satellites that orbit above Earth (p. 10)

language *n.* human communication, either written, spoken, or signed (p. 88)

language family *n.* a group of languages that have a common origin (p. 88)

Latin America *n.* the region that includes Mexico, Central America, the Caribbean Islands, and South America (p. 118)

Lesser Antilles *n.* the smaller Caribbean islands southeast of the Greater Antilles (p. 118)

llama *n.* a South American mammal related to the camel (p. 192)

llanos (YAH•nohs) *n.* grasslands of South America's Central Plains (pp. 124, 186)

location analyst *n.* a person who studies an area to find the best location for a client (p. 16)

location *n.* an exact position using latitude and longitude, or a description of a place in relation to places around it (p. 4)

lord *n.* a powerful landowner (p. 262)

M

magma *n.* molten rock (p. 26)

Magna Carta *n.* a charter, or document, signed by England's King John in 1215 that limited the power of the monarch and guaranteed nobles basic rights (p. 320)

Magyar *n.* an ethnic Hungarian person or the Hungarian language (p. 352)

mainland *n.* the primary landmass of a continent or territory rather than its islands or peninsulas (p. 320)

manor *n.* a noble's house and the villages on his land where the peasants lived (p. 262)

map *n.* a representation of a part of the Earth (p. 10)

maquiladora (mah•kee•la•DOHR•uh) *n.* factory in which materials are imported and assembled into products for export (pp. 164, 174)

market economy *n.* an economic system in which the production of goods and services is decided by supply and the demand of consumers (pp. 72, 302, 344, 406, 432)

Maya *n.* an early civilization located in what is now the Yucatán Peninsula, Guatemala, and northern Belize (p. 132)

mechanized *adj.* equipped with machinery (p. 224)

medieval *adj.* from the Middle Ages (p. 262)

Mercosur *n.* association of several South American countries to promote trade among the countries (p. 200)

mestizo (mehs•TEE•zoh) *n.* person with mixed European and Native American ancestry (pp. 140, 174)

Mexican Revolution *n.* a fight for reforms in Mexico from 1910 to 1920 (p. 150)

Middle Ages *n.* the period between the fall of the Roman Empire and the modern era, from about A.D. 476 to 1453 (p. 262)

migration *n.* the process of relocating to a new region (p. 66)

Milosevic, Slobodan (muh•LOH•suh•VICH, SLAW•baw•dahn) *n.* president of Serbia from 1989 to 1997 and of Yugoslavia from 1997 to 2000; a key figure in the ethnic conflicts in the Balkans in the 1990s (p. 360)

missionary *n.* a person sent to do religious work in another place (p. 88)

monarchy *n.* a type of government in which a ruling family headed by a king or queen holds political power (pp. 78, 254)

Moors *n.* the group of Muslims from North Africa who conquered Spain in the eighth century (p. 290)

mosaic *n.* a picture made by placing small, colored pieces of stone, tile, or glass on a surface (p. 186)

multicultural *adj.* relating to or including many different cultures (p. 328)

multilingual *n.* able to speak many languages (p. 296)

mural *n.* a wall painting (pp. 156, 216)

Muslim *n.* a follower of Islam (p. 424)

N

Nagorno-Karabakh (nuh•GAWR•noh-KARH•uh•BAHK) *n.* a province in Azerbaijan that Armenians believe should be a part of their country (p. 432)

nationalism *n.* pride in and loyalty to one's nation (pp. 270, 282)

natural resource *n.* something that is found in nature that is necessary or useful to humans (p. 72)

neutrality *n.* a policy of not taking part in war (p. 302)

nomad *n.* member of a group who makes a living by herding animals and moving from place to place as the seasons change (pp. 96, 424)

Nordic *adj.* relating to Scandinavia (p. 308)

North American Free Trade Agreement (NAFTA) *n.* agreement that reduced trade barriers among Mexico, Canada, and the United States (pp. 164, 174)

North Atlantic Drift *n.* warm ocean current that helps keep Europe's climate mild (p. 246)

Northern European Plain *n.* vast area of flat or gently rolling land from France to Russia (pp. 246, 296)

O

oligarchy (AHL•ih•GAHR•kee) *n.* a government ruled by a few powerful individuals (pp. 78, 254)

Olmec *n.* an early civilization along the Gulf Coast of what is now southern Mexico (p. 132)

ombudsman *n.* an official who investigates citizens' complaints against the government (p. 308)

one-crop economy *n.* an economy that depends on a single crop for income (pp. 180, 432)

Orthodox Christianity *n.* the Eastern branch of Christianity that spread to Russia in the 900s and became the state religion (p. 396)

P

Pampas *n.* grassy plains in south-central South America (pp. 124, 200)

Parliament *n.* the national legislature of the United Kingdom (p. 320)

patrician (puh•TRIHSH•uhn) *n.* a wealthy landowner who held a high government position in ancient Rome (p. 254)

patron *n.* a wealthy or powerful person who provides money, support, and encouragement to an artist or a cause (p. 262)

Peloponnesus (PEHL•uh•puh•NEE•suhs) *n.* the peninsula in southern Greece where Sparta was located (p. 254)

peninsula *n.* a body of land nearly surrounded by water (p. 246)

permafrost *n.* ground that is frozen throughout the year (p. 380)

persecution *n.* cruel treatment on the basis of religion, race, ethnic group, nationality, political views, gender, or class (p. 66)

perspective *n.* a technique used by artists to give the appearance of depth and distance (p. 262)

Peter the Great *n.* a czar who ruled Russia from 1682 to 1725 and tried to make Russia more European (p. 388)

place *n.* a geographical term that describes the physical and human characteristics of a location (p. 4)

plateau *n.* a high area of flat land (pp. 34, 118)

Plaza of the Three Cultures *n.* plaza in Mexico City that shows parts of Aztec, Spanish, and modern influences in Mexico (p. 156)

plebeian (plih•BEE•uhn) *n.* a commoner who was allowed to vote but not to hold government office in ancient Rome (p. 254)

polders (POHL•durz) *n.* land reclaimed by draining it of water with the use of a dam and pump (p. 296)

population *n.* the number of people who live in a specified area (p. 58)

population density *n.* the average number of people who live in a certain area (p. 58)

precipitation *n.* falling water droplets in the form of rain, snow, sleet, or hail (p. 40)

privatization (PRY•vuh•tih•ZAY•shuhn) *n.* the process of selling government-owned businesses to private individuals (p. 406)

privatize *v.* to sell government-owned businesses to private individuals (p. 432)

propaganda *n.* distorted or inaccurate information that is deliberately used to influence opinion (p. 396)

Protestant *n.* a member of a Christian Church founded on the principles of the Reformation (p. 262)

Prussia *n.* the most powerful German state in the Holy Roman Empire (p. 302)

pull factor *n.* a reason that attracts people to another area (p. 66)

push factor *n.* a reason that causes people to leave an area (pp. 66, 156)

Putin (POOT•ihn), **Vladimir** *n.* president of Russia who increased executive power in the 2000s (p. 406)

Q

quilombos (kih•LOHM•buhs) *n.* communities created by escaped African slaves (p. 216)

quinoa (kih•NOH•uh) *n.* a kind of weed from the Andean region that produces a small grain (p. 192)

R

rain forest *n.* a broadleaf tree region in a tropical climate (pp. 124, 224)

rate of natural increase *n.* the death rate subtracted from the birth rate (p. 58)

raw material *n.* an unprocessed natural resource that will be converted to a finished product (p. 72)

Reconquista *n.* the successful effort by the Spanish to drive the Moors out of Spain (p. 290)

Reformation *n.* a movement in the 1500s to change practices in the Catholic Church (p. 262)

refugee *n.* a person who flees a place to find safety (pp. 66, 360)

region *n.* an area that has one or more common characteristics that unite or connect it with other areas (p. 4)

relief *n.* the difference in the elevation of a landform from its lowest point to its highest point (p. 34)

religion *n.* an organized system of beliefs and practices, often centered on one or more gods (p. 88)

remote sensing *n.* obtaining information about a site by using an instrument that is not physically in contact with the site (p. 10)

Renaissance (REHN•ih•SAHNS) *n.* a rebirth of creativity, literature, and learning in Europe from about 1300 to 1600 (p. 262)

renewable energy sources *n.* sources of energy able to be replaced through ongoing natural processes (p. 246)

representative democracy *n.* a type of government in which citizens hold political power through elected representatives (p. 78)

representative government *n.* a system of government with a legislature that is at least partly elected by the people (p. 320)

republic *n.* a government in which citizens elect representatives to rule in their name; another term for representative democracy (p. 254)

Republic of Texas *n.* constitutional government of Texas after independence from Mexico (p. 150)

reunify *v.* to bring something that has been separated back together (p. 302)

revolution *n.* the overthrow of a ruler or government; a major change in ideas (p. 150)

Ring of Fire *n.* a geographic zone that extends along the rim of the Pacific Ocean and has numerous volcanoes and earthquakes (p. 26)

Rio de Janeiro (REE•oh day zhuh•NAYR•OH) *n.* Brazil's capital city from 1763 to 1960 (p. 210)

Rivera, Diego *n.* famous muralist who painted the history of Mexico on the walls of the National Palace (p. 156)

Romance language *n.* any of the languages that developed from the Roman language, Latin, such as Spanish, Portuguese, French, Italian, and Romanian (p. 282)

Rose Revolution *n.* a peaceful uprising in Soviet Georgia that helped force a corrupt president to resign (p. 432)

rural *adj.* having to do with the countryside (pp. 58, 156)

Russification *n.* the effort to make countries occupied by the Soviet Union more Russian by replacing local languages and customs (pp. 344, 424)

S

samba (SAM•buh) *n.* music and dance, with roots in African rhythms; the most famous form of Brazilian music worldwide (p. 216)

Sami *n.* people of northern Scandinavia who traditionally herd reindeer; also the name of their language (p. 308)

San Martín, José de *n.* leader for independence in southern South America (pp. 140, 200)

Santa Anna, Antonio López de (1794–1876) *n.* Mexican general, president, and leader of Mexican independence from Spain (p. 150)

savanna *n.* a vegetation region in the tropics or subtropics with a mix of grassland and scattered trees (p. 40)

Scientific Revolution *n.* a major change in European thinking in the mid-1500s that led to the questioning of old theories (p. 270)

seafaring *adj.* using the sea for transportation (p. 246)

secular *adj.* worldly or not related to religion (p. 262)

sediment *n.* pieces of rock in the form of sand, stone, or silt deposited by wind, water, or ice (p. 26)

self-sufficient *adj.* able to provide for one's own needs without outside help (p. 224)

selva *n.* Spanish name for the eastern Peruvian regions that contain rain forests (p. 192)

separatist *n.* a person who wants a region to break away from the nation it is a part of (p. 290)

serf *n.* in Europe, a person who lived and worked on the manor of a lord or vassal; in Russia, a peasant who is bound to the land (pp. 262, 388)

service industry *n.* an industry that provides services rather than objects (p. 174)

Shakespeare, William *n.* English playwright and poet during the late 16th and early 17th centuries (p. 328)

shock therapy *n.* in Russia, term applied to Yeltsin's economic plan, which called for an abrupt shift from a command economy to a market economy (p. 406)

Siberia *n.* a huge region in Asian Russia (p. 380)

Sierra Madre Occidental *n.* mountain range that runs from north to south down the western part of Mexico (p. 118)

Sierra Madre Oriental *n.* mountain range that runs from north to south down the eastern part of Mexico (p. 118)

Silk Roads *n.* major trade routes that ran from China to the rest of East Asia, through Central Asia, and into Europe (p. 424)

Solidarity *n.* Poland's first independent labor union, cofounded by Lech Walesa (p. 344)

solstice *n.* the time during the year when the sun reaches the farthest northern or southern point in the sky (p. 40)

Southern Cone *n.* South American nations located in the cone-shaped southernmost part of South America (p. 200)

spatial *adj.* referring to where a place is located and its physical relationship to other places, people, or environments (p. 4)

specialization *n.* a focus on producing a limited number of a specific product (p. 72)

squatter *n.* person who settles on unoccupied land without having legal claim to it (p. 156)

Stalin, Joseph *n.* a cruel 20th-century dictator who had millions of his political enemies executed (pp. 388, 432)

standard of living *n.* an economic measure relating to the quality and amount of goods available to a group of people and how those goods are distributed across the group (p. 352)

steppe *n.* a grassy plain; in Russia, this area lies south of the taiga (p. 380)

strategic *adj.* relating to a plan of action designed to achieve a specific goal (p. 352)

subsistence farming *n.* farming that produces just enough to feed the farmer's family, with little or nothing left over to sell (p. 174)

surveyor *n.* a person who maps and measures the land (pp. 10, 16)

sustainable *adj.* refers to using natural resources in such a way that they exist for future generations (p. 48)

T

taiga *n.* (TY•guh) a vast forest in Russia that lies south of the tundra (p. 380)

Taino (TY•noh) *n.* Indian group in the Caribbean islands (p. 180)

technology *n.* people's application of knowledge, tools, and inventions to meet their needs (p. 96)

tectonic plate *n.* a large rigid section of the Earth's crust that is in constant motion (pp. 26, 118)

three-dimensional *adj.* describing an image in which there is a sense of depth and perspective (p. 4)

Tian Shan (TYAHN SHAHN) *n.* a mountain range that runs across Kyrgyzstan and Tajikistan (p. 416)

Tito, Josip Broz *n.* the Communist leader of Yugoslavia from 1953 to 1980 (p. 360)

Tolstoy (TOHL•stoy), **Leo** *n.* a 19th-century writer who is one of Russia's greatest novelists (p. 396)

totalitarian (toh•tal•ih•TAIR•ee•uhn) *adj.* referring to a type of government that controls every aspect of public and private life (p. 388)

tourism *n.* industry that provides services for travelers (p. 180)

Transcaucasia (TRANS•kaw•KAY•zhuh) *n.* a region between the Black and Caspian seas that contains the republics of Armenia, Azerbaijan (AZ•uhr•by•ZHYAHN), and Georgia (p. 416)

Treaty of Tordesillas (TAWR•day•SEEL•yahs) *n.* 1494 treaty between Spain and Portugal that gave Portugal control over land that is now Brazil (p. 210)

tundra *n.* a cold, dry climate and vegetation adapted to the climate in the Arctic Circle; in Russia, located in the far north (p. 380)

tyrant *n.* someone who takes power illegally (p. 254)

U

Union of Soviet Socialist Republics (USSR), or **Soviet Union** *n.* a nation with a Communist government created by the Bolsheviks in 1922; dissolved in 1991 (p. 388)

unwritten constitution *n.* a framework for government that is not a single written document but includes many different laws, court decisions, and political customs (p. 334)

Ural Mountains *n.* a north-south mountain range that forms the border between European and Asian Russia (p. 380)

urban *adj.* having to do with a city (pp. 16, 58, 156)

urban planner *n.* a person who creates plans for developing and improving parts of a city (p. 16)

urbanization *n.* growth in the number of people living in urban areas; the process of city development (pp. 58, 210)

V

vassal *n.* a less wealthy noble who paid taxes to and served a lord in exchange for land (p. 262)

Vatican *n.* the official residence of the pope in Vatican City, and the political and religious center of the Roman Catholic Church (p. 282)

vegetation region *n.* an area that has similar plants (p. 40)

Velvet Revolution *n.* the peaceful protest by the Czech people that led to the smooth end of communism in Czechoslovakia (p. 352)

Vikings *n.* a seafaring Scandinavian people who raided northern and western Europe from the 9th to the 11th century (p. 308)

volcano *n.* an opening in the Earth's crust from which molten rock, ash, and hot gases flow or are thrown out (p. 26)

Volga River *n.* the longest river in Europe, flowing through European Russia (p. 380)

W

Walesa, Lech (wah•LEHN•suh, lehk) *n.* Polish leader who cofounded Solidarity and served as president of Poland from 1990 to 1995 (p. 344)

weather *n.* the condition of the Earth's atmosphere at a given time and place (p. 40)

weathering *n.* the gradual physical and chemical breakdown of rocks on the surface of the Earth (p. 26)

welfare state *n.* a social system in which the government provides for many of its citizens' needs (p. 308)

wind farm *n.* a power plant that uses windmills to generate electricity (p. 334)

Y

Yeltsin (YEHLT•sihn), **Boris** *n.* president who abruptly transformed the Russian economy after the Soviet Union collapsed (p. 406)

Yugoslavia *n.* a country on the Balkan Peninsula from 1918 to 1991 (p. 360)

yurt *n.* a portable, tentlike structure used by the nomads of Central Asia (p. 424)

Spanish Glossary

A

agricultural revolution [revolución agrícola] *s.* el cambio de recolectar alimentos a cultivarlos (pág. 96)

alpaca *s.* mamífero suramericano de la misma familia que la llama (pág. 192)

Alpine [alpino] *adj.* relativo a la cadena montañosa de los Alpes (pág. 302)

Alps [Alpes, los] *s.* la cadena montañosa más alta de Europa, que se extiende por el sur de Europa (pág. 246)

altiplano *s.* meseta situada a gran altitud (págs. 124, 192)

Amazon River [río Amazonas] *s.* el río más extenso de Suramérica (aproximadamente 4,000 millas o 6,400 kilómetros) y el segundo más extenso del mundo (pág. 124)

Andes Mountains [Cordillera de los Andes] *s.* cadena montañosa ubicada en la costa oeste de Suramérica, que se extiende a lo largo de todo el continente (pág. 124)

annex [anexar] *v.* añadir a un territorio existente (pág. 150)

anthropologist [antropólogo] *s.* científico que estudia la cultura (pág. 88)

Aral Sea [Mar de Aral] *s.* cuerpo de agua interior ubicado en Asia central que se está reduciendo de manera continua (pág. 416)

archipelago [archipiélago] *s.* conjunto de islas agrupadas, que a veces toma la forma de un arco curvo (pág. 118)

artisan [artesano] *s.* trabajador hábil en fabricar con sus manos productos o arte (pág. 174)

atmosphere [atmósfera] *s.* capa de gases que rodea la Tierra (pág. 34)

autonomy [autonomía] *s.* gobernabilidad propia o independencia (pág. 296)

Aztec [azteca] *s.* antigua civilización del valle de México (pág. 132)

B

Baltic States [Países Bálticos] *s.* Letonia, Lituania y Estonia, tres países cuyas costas dan al mar Báltico (pág. 344)

Basque [vasco] *s.* grupo étnico que vive en los Pirineos occidentales y a lo largo del golfo de Vizcaya, en España y Francia; también el nombre de su idioma (pág. 290)

Benelux *s.* nombre de la unión económica formada por Bélgica, los Países Bajos y Luxemburgo para asegurar la rapidez y la eficiencia en el movimiento de personas, bienes y servicios entre los tres países (pág. 296)

Berlin Wall [Muro de Berlín] *s.* muro construido por el gobierno comunista de Alemania Oriental para separar Berlín Oriental de Berlín Occidental; derribado en 1991 (pág. 302)

birth rate [tasa de natalidad] *s.* cantidad de nacimientos por año, por cada 1,000 personas (pág. 58)

Bogotá *s.* capital de Colombia (pág. 186)

Bolívar, Simón *s.* líder independentista del norte de Suramérica (págs. 140, 186)

Bolsheviks [bolcheviques] *s.* grupo de revolucionarios que tomó el control del gobierno de Rusia en 1917 (pág. 388)

Bosniac [bosnio] *s.* grupo étnico musulmán de Bosnia-Herzegovina (pág. 360)

bossa nova *s.* versión estilo *jazz* de la samba, un baile brasileño (pág. 216)

Botero, Fernando *s.* artista colombiano famoso por sus retratos de personas con figuras exageradas (pág. 186)

boycott [boicotear] *v.* dejar de comprar y de usar productos de ciertos orígenes, a modo de protesta (pág. 224)

brain drain [fuga de cerebros] *s.* pérdida de trabajadores calificados que emigran en búsqueda de mejores oportunidades laborales (pág. 344)

Brasília [Brasilia] *s.* capital actual de Brasil (pág. 210)

bread basket [granero] *s.* región de producción abundante de granos (pág. 344)

Briton [británico] *s.* natural de Gran Bretaña (pág. 328)

Buddhism [budismo] *s.* una de las principales religiones del mundo, que se inició en la India y se basa en las enseñanzas de Siddhartha Gautama (pág. 396)

Byzantine Empire [Imperio Bizantino] *s.* la mitad oriental del Imperio Romano, que sobrevivió más de mil años después de la caída de Roma (pág. 282)

C

Cabral, Pedro Álvares *s.* explorador portugués que en el año 1500 reclamó como posesión portuguesa parte del territorio actual de Brasil (pág. 210)

candomblé *s.* prácticas religiosas africanas que se mezclan con creencias católicas para crear un sistema único de creencias (pág. 216)

capoeira *s.* danza brasileña combinada con artes marciales (pág. 216)

Caracas *s.* capital de Venezuela (pág. 186)

carbon dioxide [dióxido de carbono] *s.* gas compuesto de carbono y oxígeno (pág. 48)

Caribbean Community and Common Market (CARICOM) [Comunidad del Caribe] *s.* organización comercial de varias naciones del Caribe (pág. 180)

cartographer [cartógrafo] *s.* geógrafo que traza mapas (pág. 10)

Caspian Sea [Mar Caspio] *s.* gran cuerpo de agua en el límite sur de Rusia, ubicado entre Transcaucasia y Asia Central (págs. 380, 416)

Caucasus Mountains [cordillera del Cáucaso] *s.* cadena montañosa que se extiende entre el mar Negro y el mar Caspio (pág. 416)

Central America Free Trade Agreement (CAFTA) [Tratado de Libre Comercio entre Estados Unidos y América Central] *s.* acuerdo para fomentar el comercio entre los Estados Unidos y los países de América Central (págs. 174, 180)

Central Asia [Asia Central] *s.* región que comprende las repúblicas de Kazajistán, Kirguistán, Tayikistán, Turkmenistán y Uzbekistán (pág. 416)

cession [cesión] *s.* territorio entregado (pág. 150)

Channel Tunnel [*Eurotúnel*] *s.* túnel ferroviario entre Francia e Inglaterra que corre bajo el Canal de la Mancha (pág. 334)

Chechnya [Chechenia] *s.* república mayormente islámica del sudoeste de Rusia que continúa su lucha por la independencia (pág. 406)

chinampas s. en México, islas artificiales utilizadas para la agricultura (pág. 132)

Church of England [Iglesia de Inglaterra o Anglicana] *s.* iglesia oficial de Inglaterra, cuya cabeza es el Arzobispo de Canterbury (pág. 328)

citizen [ciudadano] *s.* persona que debe lealtad a un país y recibe su protección (pág. 78)

city-state [ciudad estado] *s.* unidad política compuesta de una ciudad y las tierras a su alrededor (pág. 254)

climate [clima] *s.* condiciones habituales del tiempo de una región durante un largo período de tiempo (pág. 40)

climatologist [climatólogo] *s.* geógrafo que estudia los climas (pág. 16)

coalition [coalición] *s.* alianza o asociación, habitualmente transitoria (pág. 282)

Cold War [Guerra Fría] *s.* conflicto entre los Estados Unidos y la Unión Soviética tras la Segunda Guerra Mundial, que nunca se desarrolló en forma de combate armado explícito (pág. 388)

colonia s. un vecindario de México (pág. 156)

colony [colonia] *s.* territorio de ultramar gobernado por una nación, como México desde el siglo XVI hasta 1821 (pág. 140)

Columbian Exchange [intercambio colombino] *s.* traslado de plantas y animales entre América Latina y Europa, después del viaje de Colón a América en 1492 d.C. (pág. 140)

Columbus, Christopher [Cristobal Colón] *s.* navegante y explorador italiano que navegaba al servicio de España y exploró el Caribe y las costas de América Central y de Suramérica (pág. 290)

command economy [economía planificada] *s.* sistema económico en donde la producción de bienes y servicios es decidida por un gobierno central (págs. 72, 344, 406, 432)

commonwealth [mancomunidad] *s.* unidad política de gobierno autónomo que está asociada a otro país (pág. 180)

Commonwealth of Nations [Mancomunidad Británica de Naciones] *s.* asociación compuesta por el Reino Unido y muchas antiguas colonias británicas (pág. 320)

communism [comunismo] *s.* tipo de gobierno en donde el Partido Comunista posee la totalidad del poder político y controla la economía (págs. 78, 180, 344, 388)

compulsory [obligatorio] *adj.* exigido (pág. 282)

conquistador s. explorador y guerrero español que llegó al continente americano en el siglo XVI (pág. 140)

constitution [constitución] *s.* conjunto de leyes y principios que definen la naturaleza de un gobierno (pág. 150)

Constitution of 1917 [Constitución de 1917] *s.* constitución mexicana redactada durante la revolución que aún está en vigencia (pág. 150)

constitutional monarchy [monarquía constitucional] *s.* gobierno donde los poderes del rey o la reina están limitados por la constitución (pág. 334)

continent [continente] *s.* una de las siete enormes extensiones de tierra de la superficie de la Tierra (pág. 26)

continental shelf [plataforma continental] *s.* tierra sumergida al borde de un continente (pág. 34)

cuíca s. zambomba utilizada en la samba, una danza brasileña (pág. 216)

cultural hearth [núcleo cultural] *s.* la zona central de una cultura importante; el área en la cual una cultura se originó y se expandió a otras áreas (págs. 96, 132)

culture [cultura] *s.* actitudes, conocimientos y comportamientos compartidos por un grupo de personas (págs. 66, 88, 132)

Cyrillic alphabet [alfabeto cirílico] *s.* el sistema oficial de escritura de Rusia (pág. 396)

czar [zar] *s.* título de los soberanos de Rusia desde mediados del siglo XVI hasta comienzos del siglo XX (pág. 388)

Czechoslovakia [Checoslovaquia] *s.* antiguo país de Europa del Este que existió desde 1918 hasta 1993, cuando se dividió en la República Checa y Eslovaquia (pág. 352)

D

database [base de datos] *s.* recopilación de información que puede analizarse (pág. 10)

Day of the Dead [Día de Muertos] *s.* día feriado para recordar a los seres queridos que han fallecido (pág. 156)

death rate [tasa de mortalidad] *s.* cantidad de muertes por año, por cada 1,000 personas (pág. 58)

debris [escombros] *s.* restos dispersos de algo roto o destruido (pág. 10)

deforestation [deforestación] *s.* tala y eliminación de árboles (pág. 224)

degraded [degradado] *adj.* de calidad menor a la que existía previamente (pág. 48)

democracy [democracia] *s.* gobierno en el cual los ciudadanos toman decisiones políticas, ya sea de manera directa o a través de los representantes que han elegido (pág. 254)

demographer [demógrafo] *s.* geógrafo que estudia las características de las poblaciones humanas (pág. 58)

dependency [dependencia] *s.* lugar gobernado por un país del cual oficialmente no forma parte (pág. 180)

deport [deportar] *v.* expulsar de un país (pág. 344)

desert [desierto] *s.* región con plantas especialmente adaptadas a condiciones secas (pág. 40)

desertification [desertificación] *s.* proceso por el cual la tierra de cultivo pierde su productividad debido a que la tierra se degrada (pág. 48)

devolution [traspaso] *s.* proceso por el cual se transfiere algo del poder del gobierno nacional al gobierno regional (pág. 334)

dictator [dictador] *s.* persona que tiene el control absoluto sobre el gobierno de un país (págs. 174, 180, 186)

dictatorship [dictadura] *s.* estado o gobierno regido por un líder con poder absoluto (pág. 78)

diffusion [difusión] *s.* propagación de ideas, inventos y pautas de conducta de un grupo a otro (pág. 96)

discrimination [discriminación] *s.* acciones que pueden herir a un individuo o a un grupo (pág. 66)

diversity [diversidad] *s.* tener muchas maneras diferentes de pensar o de hacer algo, o una variedad de personas (pág. 66)

Dom Pedro I [Pedro I] *s.* primer emperador portugués de Brasil; proclamó Brasil independiente de Portugal en 1822 (pág. 210)

Dom Pedro II [Pedro II] *s.* segundo emperador de Brasil; durante su reinado, en 1888, se abolió la esclavitud en Brasil (pág. 210)

domestication [domesticación] *s.* cría y cuidado de una planta o un animal para ser de utilidad a los seres humanos (pág. 96)

drainage basin [cuenca de drenaje] *s.* área drenada por un río principal (pág. 34)

duchy [ducado] *s.* territorio regido por un duque o una duquesa (pág. 296)

E

earthquake [terremoto] *s.* movimiento repentino de la corteza terrestre seguido de una serie de sacudidas (pág. 26)

eclectic [ecléctico] *adj.* compuesto a partir de partes de diversos orígenes (pág. 352)

economic system [sistema económico] *s.* manera en que las personas usan los recursos para fabricar e intercambiar bienes (pág. 72)

economy [economía] *s.* sistema de producción e intercambio de bienes y servicios entre un grupo de personas (págs. 72, 224)

ecotourism [ecoturismo] *s.* viajes que algunas personas realizan a medio ambientes únicos, en los que se preocupan por preservarlos en su estado natural (pág. 174)

edible [comestible] *adj.* apto para ser comido (pág. 192)

emissions [emisiones] *s.* sustancias liberadas en el aire (pág. 48)

empire [imperio] *s.* sistema político en donde las personas o las tierras son controladas por un soberano único (págs. 132, 140)

Enlightenment [Ilustración] *s.* movimiento filosófico de los siglos XVII y XVIII que se caracterizó por el uso de la razón y los métodos científicos (pág. 270)

environment [medio ambiente] *s.* el entorno físico de una ubicación (pág. 4)

equinox [equinoccio] *s.* una de las dos ocasiones en el año en que los rayos del sol caen directamente sobre el ecuador y los días y las noches tienen la misma duración en todo el mundo (pág. 40)

erosion [erosión] *s.* desgaste y movimiento de materiales desgastados por el agua, el viento o el hielo (pág. 26)

estancia *s.* hacienda o finca agrícola de gran tamaño de la Argentina (pág. 200)

ethanol [etanol] *s.* líquido que se obtiene mediante un proceso químico que convierte la caña de azúcar en un tipo de alcohol que se puede usar como combustible (pág. 224)

ethnic cleansing [limpieza étnica] *s.* eliminar un grupo étnico o religioso de un área a través de la fuerza o del asesinato en masa de los miembros del grupo (pág. 360)

ethnic group [grupo étnico] *s.* grupo de personas que comparten un idioma, costumbres y un patrimonio cultural común (págs. 88, 396, 424)

Eurasia *s.* término usado para designar a un único continente compuesto por Europa y Asia (págs. 380, 416)

European Union (EU) [Unión Europea (UE)] *s.* organización de naciones europeas cuyos miembros cooperan en asuntos económicos, sociales y políticos (págs. 270, 282)

export [exportación] *s.* producto o recurso vendido a otro país (págs. 72, 224)

F

fascism [fascismo] *s.* filosofía política que fomenta la lealtad ciega hacia el estado y un fuerte gobierno central controlado por un dictador poderoso (pág. 282)

favelas [*favelas*] *s.* término brasileño para designar a los vecindarios pobres que rodean las ciudades (pág. 210)

federal republic [república federal] *s.* forma de gobierno donde el poder está dividido entre un gobierno nacional y los gobiernos estatales (pág. 186)

feudalism [feudalismo] *s.* sistema político en el cual los señores feudales daban tierras a sus vasallos a cambio de servicios (pág. 262)

fiesta *s.* día feriado que se celebra con desfiles, juegos y comida (pág. 156)

foreign investment [inversión extranjera] *s.* dinero aportado a una empresa por personas de otro país (pág. 432)

fossil fuels [combustibles fósiles] *s.* fuentes de energía a partir de restos antiguos de animales y plantas; se incluyen los combustibles como el carbón, el petróleo y el gas natural (págs. 48, 246)

Fox, Vicente *s.* presidente mexicano perteneciente al Partido de Acción Nacional, elegido en 2000 (pág. 150)

French Revolution [Revolución Francesa] *s.* conflicto ocurrido en Francia, entre 1789 y 1799, que puso fin a la monarquía y produjo cambios en la manera de gobernar Francia (pág. 270)

G

Gaelic [gaélico] *s.* cualquiera de los dialectos de la familia de lenguas celtas habladas en Irlanda o Escocia (pág. 328)

García Márquez, Gabriel *s.* autor colombiano ganador del Premio Nobel (pág. 186)

gaucho *s.* vaquero argentino (pág. 200)

Geographic Information Systems (GIS) [Sistemas de Información Geográfica] *s.* tecnología de mapeo basada en las computadoras o Internet (págs. 10, 16)

geography [geografía] *s.* estudio de las personas, los lugares y los medios ambientes (pág. 4)

geomorphology [geomorfología] *s.* estudio de cómo cambia la forma de la Tierra (pág. 16)

glacier [glaciar] *s.* gran masa de hielo de movimiento lento (pág. 26)

global economy [economía global] *s.* economía en la cual se compra y vende atravesando las fronteras nacionales (pág. 164)

Global Positioning System (GPS) [Sistema de Posicionamiento Global] *s.* sistema que usa una red de satélites que orbitan la Tierra para dar una ubicación exacta (pág. 10)

global warming [calentamiento global] *s.* aumento de la temperatura promedio de la atmósfera terrestre (págs. 48, 224)

globe [globo] *s.* modelo de la Tierra con forma esférica (pág. 10)

glyph [glifo] *s.* símbolo tallado o grabado que representa una sílaba o una palabra (pág. 132)

Good Friday Agreement [Acuerdo de Viernes Santo] *s.* acuerdo entre los unionistas y nacionalistas de Irlanda del Norte que estableció un nuevo gobierno (pág. 334)

Gorbachev, Mikhail *s.* líder soviético de 1985 a 1991 que incrementó las libertades del pueblo ruso (pág. 388)

government [gobierno] *s.* organización establecida para crear y hacer cumplir las reglas de una sociedad (pág. 78)

Greater Antilles [Antillas Mayores] *s.* las islas más grandes del norte del Caribe, entre las que se incluyen Cuba, Jamaica, La Española (la cual incluye Haití y la República Dominicana) y Puerto Rico (pág. 118)

greenhouse effect [efecto invernadero] *s.* retención del calor del sol producido por los gases de la atmósfera terrestre (pág. 48)

greenhouse gas [gas invernadero] *s.* cualquier gas de la atmósfera que contribuye al efecto invernadero (pág. 48)

Gross Domestic Product (GDP) [Producto Bruto Interno (PBI)] *s.* valor total de todos los bienes y servicios producidos por un país en un año (págs. 72, 200)

ground water [agua subterránea] *s.* agua que se encuentra debajo de la superficie terrestre (pág. 34)

H

habitable lands [tierras habitables] *s.* tierras apropiadas para ser habitadas por los seres humanos (pág. 58)

Hidalgo, Miguel ("Padre Hidalgo") *s.* padre de la independencia mexicana (pág. 140)

highlands [tierras altas] *s.* regiones montañosas o accidentadas de un país (págs. 118, 124)

Hitler, Adolf *s.* jefe de estado alemán desde 1933 a 1945 (pág. 302)

Holocaust [Holocausto] *s.* asesinato sistemático de judíos y otras minorías por parte de los nazis durante la Segunda Guerra Mundial (págs. 270, 302)

hydroelectricity [hidroelectricidad] *s.* energía eléctrica generada por el agua (pág. 224)

hydroelectric power [energía hidroeléctrica] *s.* electricidad generada por motores que funcionan gracias a la fuerza del agua (pág. 246)

hydrologic cycle [ciclo hidrológico] *s.* circulación del agua entre la Tierra, los océanos y la atmósfera (pág. 34)

I

icon [ícono] *s.* imagen religiosa usada por los cristianos ortodoxos en su culto (pág. 396)

immigrant [inmigrante] *s.* persona que deja un área para habitar en otra (págs. 66, 216, 328)

immigration [inmigración] *s.* proceso de ir a vivir a otro país (pág. 164)

imperialism [imperialismo] *s.* la práctica de un país de controlar el gobierno y la economía de otro país o territorio (págs. 270, 320)

import [importación] *s.* producto o recurso que llega a un país (pág. 72)

Inca [inca] *s.* civilización antigua que se desarrolló en la Cordillera de los Andes, en Perú (pág. 132)

indigenous [indígena] *s.* nativo de una región (pág. 192)

Industrial Revolution [Revolución Industrial] *s.* cambio que comenzó en Gran Bretaña en la década de 1760 de producir bienes a mano a hacerlo mediante máquinas (págs. 270, 320)

innovation [innovación] *s.* algo nuevo que es presentado por primera vez (pág. 96)

Islam [islam] *s.* religión monoteísta basada en las enseñanzas de Mahoma y los escritos del Corán, el libro sagrado de los musulmanes (págs. 396, 424)

isolate [aislar] *v.* separar o apartar de un grupo (pág. 254)

isthmus [istmo] *s.* franja de tierra que conecta dos territorios (pág. 118)

J

jaguar *s.* felino de gran tamaño que habita principalmente en América Central y del Sur (pág. 132)

joropo *s.* baile folklórico nacional de Venezuela (pág. 186)

Juárez, Benito (1806–1872) *s.* indio que se convirtió en presidente y héroe nacional mexicano (pág. 150)

Judaism [judaísmo] *s.* religión monoteísta de los judíos, basada principalmente en los escritos de la Biblia hebrea (pág. 396)

K

Kara Kum *s.* desierto inmenso que cubre la mayor parte de Turkmenistán (pág. 416)

knight [caballero] *s.* vasallo entrenado en el combate que peleaba en nombre de un señor feudal (pág. 262)

Kosovo *s.* provincia autónoma dentro de Serbia (pág. 360)

L

Lake Balkhash [lago Balkhash] *s.* lago del este de Kazakstán (pág. 416)

landform [accidente geográfico] *s.* rasgo de la superficie terrestre formado por la fuerza física (pág. 34)

landlocked [mediterráneo] *adj.* rodeado por tierra sin acceso a un océano o mar (págs. 192, 200, 416)

Landsat [*Landsat*] *s.* serie de satélites que reúnen información y orbitan sobre la Tierra (pág. 10)

language [lenguaje] *s.* comunicación humana ya sea escrita, hablada o por señas (pág. 88)

language family [familia de lenguas] *s.* conjuntos de lenguas que derivan de una misma lengua originaria (pág. 88)

Latin America [Latinoamérica] *s.* región que incluye México, América Central, las islas del Caribe y Suramérica (pág. 118)

Lesser Antilles [Antillas Menores] *s.* las islas del Caribe más pequeñas ubicadas al sureste de las Antillas Mayores (pág. 118)

llama *s.* mamífero suramericano emparentado con el camello (pág. 192)

llanos *s.* prados de las planicies centrales de Suramérica (págs. 124, 186)

location analyst [analista de ubicación] *s.* persona que estudia un área para encontrar la mejor ubicación para un cliente (pág. 16)

location [ubicación] *s.* posición exacta según la latitud y longitud, o la descripción de un lugar en relación a los lugares que lo rodean (pág. 4)

lord [señor] *s.* terrateniente poderoso (pág. 262)

M

magma *s.* roca fundida (pág. 26)

Magna Carta [Carta Magna] *s.* carta, o documento, firmado por el rey Juan de Inglaterra en 1215 que limitaba el poder del monarca y le garantizaba derechos básicos a los nobles (pág. 320)

Magyar [magiar] *s.* persona de la etnia húngara o el idioma húngaro (pág. 352)

mainland [continente] *s.* masa terrestre principal de un continente o territorio, excluyendo a sus islas o penínsulas (pág. 320)

manor [finca solariega] *s.* casa del noble y las aldeas ubicadas en sus tierras donde vivían los campesinos (pág. 262)

map [mapa] *s.* representación de una parte de la Tierra (pág. 10)

maquiladora *s.* fábrica en la que los materiales son importados y ensamblados para producir bienes de exportación (págs. 164, 174)

market economy [economía de mercado] *s.* sistema económico en el que la producción de bienes y servicios se determina según la oferta y la demanda de los consumidores (págs. 72, 302, 344, 406, 432)

Maya [maya] *s.* civilización antigua ubicada en lo que hoy es la Península de Yucatán, Guatemala y el norte de Belice (pág. 132)

mechanized [mecanizado] *adj.* equipado con maquinaria (pág. 224)

medieval *adj.* relativo a la Edad Media (pág. 262)

Mercosur *s.* asociación de varios países de Suramérica con el fin de promover el comercio entre los países (pág. 200)

mestizo *s.* persona con mezcla de ancestros europeos y americanos nativos (págs. 140, 174)

Mexican Revolution [Revolución Mexicana] *s.* lucha por lograr reformas en México entre 1910 y 1920 (pág. 150)

Middle Ages [Edad Media] *s.* período entre la caída del Imperio Romano y la Edad Moderna, desde aproximadamente el 476 d.C. hasta 1453 (pág. 262)

migration [migración] *s.* proceso de trasladarse a una nueva región (pág. 66)

Milosevic, Slobodan *s.* presidente de Serbia desde 1989 a 1997, y de Yugoslavia desde 1997 a 2000; una figura clave en los conflictos étnicos de los países balcánicos en la década de 1990 (pág. 360)

missionary [misionero] *s.* persona enviada para realizar trabajo religioso en otro lugar (pág. 88)

monarchy [monarquía] *s.* tipo de gobierno en el cual una familia gobernante encabezada por un rey o una reina ejerce el poder político (págs. 78, 254)

Moors [moros] *s.* grupo de musulmanes de África del Norte que conquistó España en el siglo VIII (pág. 290)

mosaic [mosaico] *s.* imagen creada al colocar pequeñas piezas coloreadas de piedra, azulejo o vidrio sobre una superficie (pág. 186)

multicultural [multicultural] *adj.* relativo a muchas culturas diferentes o que las incluye (pág. 328)

multilingual [multilingüe] *s.* capaz de hablar muchos idiomas (pág. 296)

mural *s.* pintura hecha sobre una pared (págs. 156, 216)

Muslim [musulmán] *s.* seguidor del islam (pág. 424)

N

Nagorno-Karabakh [Nagorno Karabaj] *s.* provincia de Azerbaiyán sobre la que los armenios tienen reclamos territoriales, pues creen que debe ser parte de su país (pág. 432)

nationalism [nacionalismo] *s.* orgullo por la propia nación y lealtad a ella (págs. 270, 282)

natural resource [recurso natural] *s.* algo que se halla en la naturaleza que es necesario o útil para los seres humanos (pág. 72)

neutrality [neutralidad] *s.* política de no tomar parte en la guerra (pág. 302)

nomad [nómada] *s.* miembro de un grupo que vive del pastoreo de animales y que se desplaza de un lugar a otro con el cambio de estación (págs. 96, 424)

Nordic [nórdico] *adj.* relativo a Escandinavia (pág. 308)

North American Free Trade Agreement (NAFTA) [Tratado de Libre Comercio de América del Norte] *s.* acuerdo que redujo las barreras comerciales aduaneras entre México, Canadá y los Estados Unidos (págs. 164, 174)

North Atlantic Drift [Corriente del Atlántico Norte] *s.* corriente oceánica cálida que ayuda a mantener moderado el clima de Europa (pág. 246)

Northern European Plain [Planicie del Norte de Europa] *s.* área vasta de tierras llanas o de relieve leve que se extiende desde Francia hasta Rusia (págs. 246, 296)

O

oligarchy [oligarquía] *s.* gobierno regido por unos pocos individuos poderosos (págs. 78, 254)

Olmec [olmeca] *s.* civilización antigua a lo largo de la Costa del Golfo en lo que hoy es el sur de México (pág. 132)

ombudsman [defensor del pueblo] *s.* funcionario que investiga las quejas de los ciudadanos contra el gobierno (pág. 308)

one-crop economy [economía de monocultivo] *s.* economía que depende de un único cultivo para obtener ingresos (págs. 180, 432)

Orthodox Christianity [cristianismo ortodoxo] *s.* rama oriental del cristianismo que se difundió en Rusia en el siglo X y se convirtió en su religión oficial (pág. 396)

P

Pampas *s.* llanuras cubiertas de pasto en la zona central del sur de Suramérica (págs. 124, 200)

Parliament [Parlamento] *s.* legislatura nacional del Reino Unido (pág. 320)

patrician [patricio] *s.* terrateniente acaudalado que ocupaba un alto puesto gubernamental en la antigua Roma (pág. 254)

patron [mecenas] *s.* persona acaudalada o poderosa que provee dinero, apoyo y ánimo a un artista o a una causa (pág. 262)

Peloponnesus [Peloponeso] *s.* la península del sur de Grecia donde se encontraba Esparta (pág. 254)

peninsula [península] *s.* una masa de tierra rodeada casi completamente por agua (pág. 246)

permafrost [permahielo] *s.* suelo que se mantiene congelado a lo largo del año (pág. 380)

persecution [persecución] *s.* trato cruel por motivo de religión, raza, grupo étnico, nacionalidad, opiniones políticas, género o clase (pág. 66)

perspective [perspectiva] *s.* técnica usada por los artistas para dar la impresión de profundidad y distancia (pág. 262)

Peter the Great [Pedro el Grande] *s.* zar que gobernó Rusia desde 1682 a 1725 y trató de hacerla más europea (pág. 388)

place [lugar] *s.* término geográfico que describe las características físicas y humanas de una ubicación (pág. 4)

plateau [meseta] *s.* área plana situada a considerable altura (págs. 34, 118)

Plaza of the Three Cultures [Plaza de las Tres Culturas] *s.* plaza de la Ciudad de México que muestra partes de las influencias azteca, española y moderna en México (pág. 156)

plebeian [plebeyo] *s.* persona humilde a la que se le permitía votar pero no podía ocupar un cargo gubernamental en la antigua Roma (pág. 254)

polders [pólder] *s.* terreno pantanoso ganado al mar drenándole el agua con el uso de una presa y una bomba y que una vez desecado se dedica al cultivo (pág. 296)

population [población] *s.* número promedio de personas que viven en una área determinada (pág. 58)

population density [densidad de población] *s.* número promedio de personas que vive en una determinada área (pág. 58)

precipitation [precipitación] *s.* agua que cae en forma de lluvia, nieve, aguanieve o granizo (pág. 40)

privatization [privatización] *s.* el proceso de vender empresas que son propiedad del gobierno a individuos (pág. 406)

privatize [privatizar] *v.* vender empresas que son propiedad del gobierno a individuos (pág. 432)

propaganda *s.* información tergiversada o imprecisa que se usa deliberadamente para influenciar la opinión pública (pág. 396)

Protestant [protestante] *s.* miembro de una iglesia cristiana basada en los principios de la Reforma (pág. 262)

Prussia [Prusia] *s.* el estado alemán más poderoso del Sacro Imperio Romano (pág. 302)

pull factor [factor de atracción] *s.* motivo que atrae a la gente a otra área (pág. 66)

push factor [factor de exclusión] *s.* motivo que hace que la gente abandone un área (págs. 66, 156)

Putin, Vladimir *s.* presidente de Rusia que incrementó el poder ejecutivo en la década de 2000 (pág. 406)

Q

quilombos *s.* comunidades creadas por esclavos africanos fugitivos (pág. 216)

quinoa [quinua] *s.* tipo de planta de la región andina que produce semillas pequeñas comestibles (pág. 192)

R

rain forest [bosque tropical] *s.* región poblada de árboles en un clima tropical (págs. 124, 224)

rate of natural increase [tasa de crecimiento natural] *s.* tasa de muertes restada de la tasa de nacimientos (pág. 58)

raw material [materia prima] *s.* recurso natural no procesado que será convertido en un producto acabado (pág. 72)

Reconquista *s.* esfuerzo exitoso realizado por los españoles para expulsar de España a los moros (pág. 290)

Reformation [Reforma] *s.* movimiento del siglo XVI que buscó cambiar las prácticas de la Iglesia Católica (pág. 262)

refugee [refugiado] *s.* persona que huye de un lugar para encontrar seguridad (págs. 66, 360)

region [región] *s.* área que tiene una o más características en común que la unen o conectan con otras áreas (pág. 4)

relief [relieve] *s.* diferencia en la elevación de un accidente geográfico desde su punto más bajo a su punto más alto (pág. 34)

religion [religión] *s.* sistema organizado de creencias y prácticas, a menudo centrado en uno o más dioses (pág. 88)

remote sensing [detección remota] *s.* obtención de información sobre un sitio mediante el uso de un instrumento que no está en contacto físico con el mismo (pág. 10)

Renaissance [Renacimiento] *s.* renacimiento de la creatividad, la literatura y el aprendizaje en Europa desde aproximadamente el siglo XIV hasta el siglo XVII (pág. 262)

renewable energy sources [fuentes de energía renovables] *s.* fuentes de energía que pueden ser reemplazadas a través de procesos naturales en curso (pág. 246)

representative democracy [democracia representativa] *s.* sistema de gobierno en el cual los ciudadanos ejercen el poder político a través de representantes elegidos (pág. 78)

representative government [gobierno representativo] *s.* sistema de gobierno con una legislatura que es al menos en parte elegida por el pueblo (pág. 320)

republic [república] *s.* gobierno en el que los ciudadanos eligen representantes para que gobiernen en su nombre; otro término para la democracia representativa (pág. 254)

Republic of Texas [República de Texas] *s.* gobierno constitucional de Texas luego de la independencia de México (pág. 150)

reunify [reunificar] *v.* volver a unir algo que había sido separado (pág. 302)

revolution [revolución] *s.* el derrocamiento de un gobernante o gobierno; un cambio importante en las ideas (pág. 150)

Ring of Fire [Anillo de Fuego] *s.* zona geográfica que se extiende a lo largo del borde del Océano Pacífico y tiene numerosos volcanes y terremotos (pág. 26)

Rio de Janeiro [Río de Janeiro] *s.* capital de Brasil desde 1763 a 1960 (pág. 210)

Rivera, Diego *s.* muralista famoso que pintó la historia de México sobre las paredes del Palacio Nacional (pág. 156)

Romance language [lengua romance] *s.* cualquiera de las lenguas que se desarrollaron a partir de la lengua romana, el latín, tales como el español, el portugués, el francés, el italiano y el rumano (pág. 282)

Rose Revolution [Revolución de las Rosas] *s.* levantamiento pacífico en la Georgia soviética que contribuyó a forzar la renuncia de un presidente corrupto (pág. 432)

rural *adj.* relativo al campo (págs. 58, 156)

Russification [rusificación] *s.* esfuerzo en hacer que los países ocupados por la Unión Soviética se volvieran similares a Rusia mediante la sustitución de los idiomas y costumbres locales (págs. 344, 424)

S

samba *s.* música y baile, con raíces en los ritmos africanos; el estilo de música brasileña más famosa en el mundo (pág. 216)

Sami [sami] *s.* pueblo del norte de Escandinavia que tradicionalmente arrea renos; también es el nombre de su idioma (pág. 308)

San Martín, José de *s.* líder de la independencia en el sur de Suramérica (págs. 140, 200)

Santa Anna, Antonio López de (1794–1876) *s.* general mexicano, presidente y líder de la independencia mexicana de España (pág. 150)

savanna [sabana] *s.* región de vegetación en los trópicos o subtrópicos con una mezcla de pastizales y árboles dispersos (pág. 40)

Scientific Revolution [Revolución Científica] *s.* cambio rotundo en el pensamiento europeo a mediados del siglo XVI que llevó al cuestionamiento de viejas teorías (pág. 270)

seafaring [marinero] *adj.* que usa el mar para transportarse (pág. 246)

secular *adj.* mundano, no relacionado con la religión (pág. 262)

sediment [sedimento] *s.* pedazos de roca en forma de arena, piedra o cieno depositados por el viento, el agua o el hielo (pág. 26)

self-sufficient [autosuficiente] *adj.* capaz de satisfacer las propias necesidades sin ayuda externa (pág. 224)

selva *s.* nombre que se le da en español a la región al este de Perú que contiene bosques tropicales (pág. 192)

separatist [separatista] *s.* persona que quiere que una región se separe de la nación de la que forma parte (pág. 290)

serf [siervo] *s.* en Europa, persona que vivía y trabajaba en la finca de un señor feudal o de un vasallo; en Rusia, campesino atado a la tierra (págs. 262, 388)

service industry [industria de servicios] *s.* industria que provee servicios en lugar de objetos (pág. 174)

Shakespeare, William *s.* dramaturgo y poeta inglés de finales del siglo XVI y principios del siglo XVII (pág. 328)

shock therapy [terapia de choque] *s.* en Rusia, término dado al plan económico de Yeltsin, el cual exigía un cambio abrupto desde una economía dirigida a una economía de mercado (pág. 406)

Siberia [Siberia] *s.* inmensa región de Rusia asiática (pág. 380)

Sierra Madre Occidental *s.* cordillera que se extiende de norte a sur por la parte oeste de México (pág. 118)

Sierra Madre Oriental *s.* cordillera que se extiende de norte a sur por la parte este de México (pág. 118)

Silk Roads [Rutas de la seda] *s.* principales rutas de comercio que iban desde China hasta el resto del este de Asia, a través de Asia Central y hasta Europa (pág. 424)

Solidarity [Solidaridad] *s.* primer sindicato independiente de Polonia, cuyo cofundador fue Lech Walesa (pág. 344)

solstice [solsticio] *s.* época del año en la que el Sol alcanza en el cielo su punto extremo al norte o al sur (pág. 40)

Southern Cone [Cono Sur] *s.* naciones de Suramérica ubicadas en la parte con forma de cono del extremo sur de Suramérica (pág. 200)

spatial [espacial] *adj.* relativo a la ubicación de un lugar y a su relación física con otros lugares, personas o ambientes (pág. 4)

specialization [especialización] *s.* énfasis en producir una cantidad limitada de un producto específico (pág. 72)

squatter [ocupante ilegal] *s.* persona que se asienta en tierras sin ocupar sin tener un derecho legal sobre ellas (pág. 156)

Stalin, Joseph *s.* cruel dictador del siglo XX que hizo ejecutar a millones de sus enemigos políticos (págs. 388, 432)

standard of living [estándar de vida] *s.* medida económica relativa a la calidad y cantidad de bienes disponibles para un grupo de personas y cómo se distribuyen esos bienes en el grupo (pág. 352)

steppe [estepa] *s.* planicie cubierta de hierba; en Rusia, esta área se ubica al sur de la taiga (pág. 380)

strategic [estratégico] *adj.* relativo a un plan de acción diseñado para alcanzar una meta específica (pág. 352)

subsistence farming [agricultura de subsistencia] *s.* agricultura que produce tan sólo lo suficiente para alimentar a la familia del agricultor, quedando poco excedente o nada para vender (pág. 174)

surveyor [agrimensor] *s.* persona que traza un mapa del terreno y lo mide (págs. 10, 16)

sustainable [sostenible] *adj.* relativo al uso de recursos naturales de tal manera que existan para las generaciones futuras (pág. 48)

T

taiga *s.* extenso bosque de Rusia que se ubica al sur de la tundra (pág. 380)

Taino [taíno] *s.* pueblo indígena de las islas del Caribe (pág. 180)

technology [tecnología] *s.* aplicación del conocimiento, herramientas e inventos de las personas para satisfacer sus necesidades (pág. 96)

tectonic plate [placa tectónica] *s.* sección rígida de gran tamaño en la corteza terrestre que se encuentra en movimiento constante (págs. 26, 118)

three-dimensional [tridimensional] *adj.* que describe una imagen en la que hay un sentido de profundidad y perspectiva (pág. 4)

Tian Shan *s.* cordillera que se extiende a través de Kirguistán y Tayikistán (pág. 416)

Tito, Josip Broz *s.* líder comunista de Yugoslavia desde 1953 a 1980 (pág. 360)

Tolstoy, Leo *s.* escritor del siglo XIX que es uno de los más grandes novelistas rusos (pág. 396)

totalitarian [totalitario] *adj.* relativo a un tipo de gobierno que controla todos los aspectos de la vida pública y privada (pág. 388)

tourism [turismo] *s.* industria que provee servicios para los viajeros (pág. 180)

Transcaucasia *s.* región entre los mares Negro y Caspio que comprende las repúblicas de Armenia, Azerbaiyán y Georgia (pág. 416)

Treaty of Tordesillas [Tratado de Tordesillas] *s.* tratado de 1494 entre España y Portugal que le dio a Portugal el control sobre la tierra que hoy es Brasil (pág. 210)

tundra *s.* clima seco y frío y vegetación adaptada a tal clima que se halla en el Círculo Polar Ártico; en Rusia, ubicada en el extremo norte (pág. 380)

tyrant [tirano] *s.* alguien que toma el poder ilegalmente (pág. 254)

U

Union of Soviet Socialist Republics (USSR), o Soviet Union [Unión de Repúblicas Socialistas Soviéticas (URSS), o Unión Soviética] *s.* nación con un gobierno comunista creada por los bolcheviques en 1922; disuelta en 1991 (pág. 388)

unwritten constitution [constitución no escrita] *s.* marco de gobierno que no es un único documento escrito sino que incluye muchas leyes diferentes, decisiones judiciales y costumbres políticas (pág. 334)

Ural Mountains [montes Urales] *s.* cordillera que se extiende de norte a sur y forma la frontera entre la Rusia europea y la asiática (pág. 380)

urban [urbano] *adj.* relativo a la ciudad (págs. 16, 58, 156)

urban planner [urbanista] *s.* persona que crea planes para desarrollar y mejorar partes de una ciudad (pág. 16)

urbanization [urbanización] *s.* crecimiento en el número de personas que viven en áreas urbanas; el proceso de desarrollo de las ciudades (págs. 58, 210)

V

vassal [vasallo] *s.* noble menos acaudalado que pagaba impuestos y servía a un señor feudal a cambio de tierras (pág. 262)

Vatican [Vaticano] *s.* la residencia oficial del Papa en la Ciudad de Vaticano y el centro político y religioso de la Iglesia Católica Romana (pág. 282)

vegetation region [región de vegetación] *s.* un área que tiene plantas similares (pág. 40)

Velvet Revolution [Revolución de Terciopelo] *s.* protesta pacífica del pueblo checo que condujo al fin paulatino del comunismo en Checoslovaquia (pág. 352)

Vikings [vikingos] *s.* pueblo marinero escandinavo que realizó incursiones en Europa occidental y del norte desde el siglo IX al siglo XI (pág. 308)

volcano [volcán] *s.* abertura en la corteza terrestre de la que fluyen o salen expelidos roca fundida, ceniza y gases calientes (pág. 26)

Volga River [río Volga] *s.* río más largo de Europa, que fluye a través de la Rusia europea (pág. 380)

W

Walesa, Lech *s.* líder polaco, cofundador de Solidaridad, que fue presidente de Polonia desde 1990 a 1995 (pág. 344)

weather [tiempo] *s.* la condición de la atmósfera terrestre en un momento y lugar dados (pág. 40)

weathering [desgaste] *s.* erosión física y química gradual de las rocas en la superficie de la Tierra (pág. 26)

welfare state [estado de bienestar] *s.* sistema social en el que el gobierno satisface muchas de las necesidades de sus ciudadanos (pág. 308)

wind farm [parque eólico] *s.* central de energía que usa molinos de viento para generar electricidad (pág. 334)

Y

Yeltsin, Boris *s.* presidente que transformó abruptamente la economía rusa después del colapso de la Unión Soviética (pág. 406)

Yugoslavia *s.* país en la Península de los Balcanes desde 1918 a 1991 (pág. 360)

yurt [yurta] *s.* estructura portátil semejante a una tienda usada por los nómadas de Asia Central (pág. 424)

Index

Page references in **boldface** indicate Key Terms & Names and Background Vocabulary that are highlighted in the main text.

Page references in *italics* indicate illustrations, charts, and maps.

Index

L

M

T

taiga, **380**, *385, 385*, 386
Taino, **180, 182**
Tajikistan, 377, 418, 434, 436
taking notes, R3
Taklimakan Desert, *426*
tango, 203, *203*
Taxco, *163*
Tchaikovsky, Peter Ilich, 402
teapickers, *7*
technology, **96, 98**
tectonic plate, *25, 26, 29, 29*–30, 38–39, **118, 120**
telescope, *271*
temperature
  global warming and, 49–50
  in Siberia, 384, *384*
Tenochtitlán, 136, *136*
test-taking strategies
  charts, S16–S17
  constructed response, S28–S29
  document-based questions, S32–S35
  extended response, S30–S31
  line and bar graphs, S18–S19
  multiple choice, S10–S11
  pie graphs, S20–S21
  political cartoons, S14–S15
  political maps, S22–S23
  primary and secondary sources, S12–S13
  thematic maps, S24–S25
  time lines, S26–S27
Texas, Republic of, **150**, *152*, **152**
Texas Annexation, 152, *152*
textiles, 337
Thames River, *249*
thematic maps, reading, S24–S25, R22
three-dimensional image, **4**, *5*
Tian Shan, **416**, *417*, **418**
Tikal Pyramid, *133*
timber, *386*
time line, S26–S27
Tito, Josip Broz, **360, 362**
Toledo, Alejandro, 194
Tolkien, J.R.R., 332
Tolstoy, Leo, **396, 401**
Torah, R48
totalitarian government, **388, 392**
Totmianina, Tatiana, *400*
toucan, *175*
Tour de France, 297
tourism, **180, 183**
  ecotourism, **174, 175**
Tower Bridge, *329*
trade, 77
  economic systems and, **75**–77
  Silk Roads, **424, 426**, *426*–*427*
  slave, 212, 219

traditional economy, 75
Transcaucasia, **416, 417**–421, *420*, 426–428. *See also* Eurasian republics.
transportation
  Amish, *100*
  Australia, *64*
  Indonesia, *65*
Trans-Siberian Railroad, 391, *394*–*395*
Treaty of Tordesillas, **210, 211**, *212*
tree frog, *123*
Tresópolis, *214*
tributary, 36
Trinidad and Tobago, 115
Tromsø, *251*
tropical latitude, 43–45, *44*
tropic of Cancer, 43
tropic of Capricorn, 43
tsunami, 31
Tsunami Warning System (TWS), 82
tulips, *300*
tundra, *250*, 380, *385*, **385**, 386
Tupi, 218
Turkmenistan, 377, 418
Turks, 426
Twelve Tables, Law of the, 259
tyrant, **254, 256**

U

Ukraine, 243, 348–349
Union of the Soviet Socialist Republics (USSR), **388, 392**
United Kingdom, 243, 318–338
  cities of, 330, *330*
  colonies and, 323, 325, *325*
  culture of, 332–333
  early settlers of, 321
  government and economy, 322, *323*, 335–338, *336*
  immigration, 331
  Industrial Revolution in, 324
  Northern Ireland, 336–337
  political map of, *319*
  religion in, 331
  Russia and, *428*
  wind, 337, *337*
  World Wars and, 324
United Nations (UN), 82, *82*
United States
  Brazil and, 77
  government, *336, 408*
  immigration, 168
  landforms, 38
  Mexico and, 152, *152*, 168
  political map of, *S22*
  population density, 63
  religion in, 93
  Soviet Union and, 393
unwritten constitution, **334, 336**

Uppsala, *311*
Ural Mountains, **380, 382**
uranium, 252
urban area, 58, *61, 63*, 69, **156**
  in Brazil, 213–215, *214*
  Mexico, *158*, **158**
urbanization, **58, 63, 210, 213**
urban planner, *16*, **16**, *17, 19*, **19**
Uros, *195*
Uruguay, 115, 203–204
U.S. Capitol, 79
Uzbekistan, 377, 418, *430*, 435

V

Valencia, *251*
Varangians, 389
vassal, **262, 264**
Vatican City, 243, **282, 286**
vegetation
  in Latin America, 122–123
  in Russia, *385*, 386
  in South America, 128–131
vegetation region, **40**, 43–45, *44*, **45**
Velvet Revolution, **352, 356**
Venezuela, 115, 187–189
Venice, 267
Vikings, **308**, *309*, **309**–310, *310*
Villa, Pancho, 154, *154*
Vladim, 398
volcanoes, 8–9, **26**, *31*, **31**
  in Latin America, 120
  in Russia, 382
  specialist in, *7*
Volga River, **380, 382**, *383*
voting, compulsory, 284

W

Wagner, Richard, 305
Wales, 321, 331, 336
Walesa, Lech, **344, 346**, 347, *347*
Walloons, 301
Warsaw, *346*
Washington, D.C., 7, *13*
water, 35–36, *37*
water vapor, 43
weather, **40**, 42–43. *See also* climate.
weathering, **26, 32**
Wegener, Alfred, 30
welfare state, **308, 312**, 314
West Africa
  Brazil and, 219, *219*
Western Europe, 280–314
  Alpine countries, **302, 306**–307
  Benelux countries, **296, 300**–301
  economies of, *285*
  France, 297–299
  Germany, 303–305

Acknowledgments

Text Acknowledgments

Front Matter
Houghton Mifflin: Adaption of line graph from "Exports of English Manufactured Goods, 1700-1774," from *A History of World Societies*, Fifth Edition by John P. McKay, Bennett D. Hill, John Buckler, and Patricia Buckley Ebrey. Copyright © 2000 by Houghton Mifflin Company. All rights reserved. Used by permission.

Unit 1
Christian Science Monitor: Excerpt from "As English Spreads, Speakers Morph It Into World Tongue," by David Rohde from *Christian Science Monitor*, May 17, 1995. Copyright © 1995 by the *Christian Science Monitor*. Reprinted by permission of the *Christian Science Monitor* (www.csmonitor.com). All rights reserved.

Unit 2
John Bierhorst: Excerpt from "The Eagle On the Prickly Pear," from by John Bierhorst. Copyright © 1984 by John Bierhorst. Reprinted by permission of the author.

Rhett A. Butler: Excerpt from Interview with William F. Laurance by Rhett A. Butler. Copyright © 2006 by Rhett A. Butler. Reprinted by permission of Rhett A. Butler, mongabay.com.

Unit 3
Andreas Ramos: Excerpt from "A Personal Account of The Fall of the Berlin Wall," by Andreas Ramos from www.andreas.com/berlin.html. Copyright © by Andreas Ramos. Reprinted by permission of the author.

Photography

Front Matter
cover *front to back* © Wolfgang Kaehler/Alamy; © BananaStock/Alamy; © Robert Fried/Alamy; © Ian Thraves/Alamy; © David Sanger Photography/Alamy; *background* © David Madison/Getty Images; **NC3** *top left* © Keren Su/Getty Images; *top right background* © Corbis; *top right foreground* © Beth Dixson/Getty Images; *center* © Rick Gomez/Masterfile; *bottom* © Panoramic Images/Getty Images; **NC4** *top* Photograph by Robert S. Bednarz; *center* Photograph by Marci Smith Deal; *bottom* Photograph by Inés M. Miyares; **NC5** *top* Photograph by Rob Caron; *center* Photograph by Erica Houskeeper; *bottom* Photograph by Joe Wieszczyk; **NC7** Photograph by Bac To Trong; **NC10** *top left* © Joeseph Sohm-Visions of America/Getty Images; *top right* © Tibor Bognar/Alamy; **NC11** *top left* © Getty Images; *top right background* © Royalty-Free/Corbis; *top right, small dolphin* © David Tipling/Alamy; *top right foreground* © Stuart Westmorland/Corbis; **NC12** *top left* © Simon Reddy/Alamy; *top right* © Bill Bachmann/Index Stock Imagery/Jupiter Images; **NC13** *top left foreground* © Pavel Filatov/Alamy; *top left background* © Pavel Filatov/Alamy; *top right background* © Pavel Filatov/Alamy; *top right foreground* © Royalty-Free/Corbis; **NC14** *bottom right* Photograph by Ed-Imaging; **NC15** *top* © Rob Melnychuk/Getty Images; *center* © Getty Images; **NC22** *top* © Comstock Images/Alamy; **NC26** *top right* © Photodisc/Punchstock; *bottom right* © Richard Sheppard/Alamy; *background* © Brand X Pictures/Alamy; *center right* © Photograph by Ed-Imaging; **S36** NASA Goddard Space Flight Center; **A11** *bottom left* © Getty Images, Inc.; *top right* © Bruce Roberts/Photo Researchers, Inc.; *center right* © Frans Lanting/Corbis; *bottom right* © David R. Frazier/Photo Researchers, Inc.; **A12–13** Image created by Reto Stockli with the help of Alan Nelson, under the leadership of Fritz Hasler/NASA.

Unit 1 Opener
1 *top right* © Getty Images; *top left* © Digital Vision/Getty Images; *bottom right* © Peter Horree/Alamy; *bottom left* © Philip and Karen Smith/Getty Images.

Chapter 1
2-3 NASA Goddard Space Flight Center; **2** *bottom left* Strabo (1584). Engraving. The Granger Collection, New York; *bottom right* © Science Museum/Science and Society Picture Library; *top left* © Peter Horree/Alamy; **3** *bottom left* © Science Museum/Science and Society Picture Library; *bottom right* © Photolibrary/Alamy; *center right* © Peter Horree/Alamy; *center left* © Photo Researchers, Inc.; **5** *bottom* NASA; *top left* © Keren Su/Getty Images; *top center* © Corbis; *top right* © Beth Dixson/Getty Images; **6** *top* © Silvestre Machado/Getty Images; *second from top* © Gavin Hellier/Getty Images; *center* © Danita Delimont/Alamy; *second from bottom* © Lester Lefkowitz/Corbis; *bottom* © Phil Schermeister/Peter Arnold, Inc.; **7** *second from top* © David R. Frazier/Photo Researchers, Inc.; *center left* © Craig Lovell/Eagle Visions Photography/Alamy; *second from bottom* © Frans Lanting/Corbis; *bottom* © Bruce Roberts/Photo Researchers, Inc.; **8** © Mark Segal/Panoramic Images/NGSImages.

com; **11** *center right* © The Image Works, Inc.; *bottom* © Rob Matheson/Corbis; *top left* © Keren Su/Getty Images; *top center* © Corbis; *top right* © Beth Dixson/Getty Images; **12** *bottom left* Strabo (1584). Engraving. The Granger Collection, New York; *bottom right* Horace L. Jones. trans., *The Geography of Strabo*, 8 vols. (New York: G.P. Putnam's Sons, (1917), vol. 1, pp. 451-455, 501-503, 277-385, passim; **13** *bottom center* © NASA/Angela King/Geology.com; *bottom right* © Max Dannenbaum/Getty Images; **14** *center* © David R. Frazier Photolibrary, Inc./Alamy; **15** © Craig Lovell/Eagle Visions Photography/Alamy; **16** © David Vaughan/Photo Researchers, Inc.; **17** *center* © Mark Gibson/Alamy; *bottom* © Mark Edwards/Peter Arnold, Inc.; *top left* © Keren Su/Getty Images; *top center* © Corbis; *top right* © Beth Dixson/Getty Images; **18** © Johnathan Smith; Cordaiy Photo Library Ltd./Corbis; **19** *top* © age fotostock/SuperStock; *bottom* © Jeff Greenberg/Alamy; **20** © Erin Cigliano; **21** *bottom left* © NASA/Angela King/Geology.com; *bottom right* © Scott Rothstein/ShutterStock; **22** © Scott Rothstein/ShutterStock.

Chapter 2
24 *bottom* The Granger Collection, New York; *top left* © Peter Horree/Alamy; **25** © Gary Braasch/Corbis; **26** © Gregory G. Dimijian, M.D./Photo Researchers, Inc.; **27** *bottom* © Roger Ressmeyer/Corbis; *top left* © Robert Glusic/Getty Images; *top center* © Getty Images; *top right* © Royalty-Free/Corbis; *top right inset* © Peter Arnold, Inc./Alamy; **31** *background* © George Steinmetz/Corbis; *bottom* © Roger Ressmeyer/Corbis; **32-33** © James Randklev/Getty Images; **33** © Corbis; **34** D. Brown/PanStock/Panoramic Images/National Geographic Image Collection; **35** *center right* NASA; *bottom* © David Lyons/Alamy; *top left* © Robert Glusic/Getty Images; *top center* © Getty Images; *top right* © Royalty-Free/Corbis; *top right inset* © Peter Arnold, Inc./Alamy; **36** © Scott T. Smith/Corbis; **38** Sitki Tarlan/Panoramic Images/National Geographic Image Collection; **39** © James D. Watt/Image Quest Marine; **40** © Jeff Lepore/Photo Researchers, Inc.; **41** *center right* © Jeff Schultz/AlaskaStock.com; *bottom* © Arend/Soucek/AlaskaStock.com; *top left* © Robert Glusic/Getty Images; *top center* © Getty Images; *top right* © Royalty-Free/Corbis; *top right inset* © Peter Arnold, Inc./Alamy; **43** *all* © Getty Images; © Getty Images; © Getty Images; **46** *center left* © Ed George/NGSImages.com; *bottom left* © Mark Moffett/Minden Pictures; **48** © Frank Kroenke/Peter Arnold, Inc.; **49** *bottom* © Knut Mueller/Peter Arnold, Inc.; *top left* © Robert Glusic/Getty Images; *top center* © Getty Images; *top right* © Royalty-Free/Corbis; *top right inset* © Peter Arnold, Inc./Alamy; **51** Fritz Reiss/AP/Wide World Photos; **52** © William Campbell/Corbis; **53** *bottom left* © Douglas Peebles/Corbis; *bottom right* Sitki Tarlan/Panoramic Images/National Geographic Image Collection; **54** NASA.

Chapter 3
56 *top left* © Peter Adams Photography/Alamy; *bottom left* Kuba mask. Kuba related peoples, Zaire. Wood, pigment. Private collection. Photo © Aldo Tutino/Art Resource, New York; *bottom right* © The British Museum/HIP/The Image Works, Inc.; **57** *center* NASA; *bottom left* © Gary Randall/Getty Images; *bottom center* © First/zefa/Corbis; **58** © Royalty-Free/Corbis; **59** *bottom* © David Lawrence; *top left* © Joseph Sohm-Visions of America/Getty Images; *top right* © Tibor Bognar/Alamy; **60** © Art Kowalsky/Alamy; **61** © Peter Adams Photography/Alamy; **62** © PCL/Alamy; **64** *center left* © Dave G. Houser/Post-Houserstock/Corbis; *center right* © Australian Scenics; *bottom* © John Hay/Lonely Planet Images; **65** *center left* © Robin Moyer/OnAsia; *center right* © Dan Bigelow/Getty Images; *bottom* © Robert Harding Picture Library Ltd/Alamy; **66** © Yellow Dog Productions/Getty Images; **67** *center right* © Alexander Walter/Getty Images; *bottom* The Granger Collection, New York; *top left* © Joeseph Sohm-Visions of America/Getty Images; *top right* © Tibor Bognar/Alamy; **68** The Granger Collection, New York; **69** Kuba mask. Kuba related peoples, Zaire. Wood, pigment. Private collection. Photo © Aldo Tutino/Art Resource, New York; **70** Brennan Linsley/AP/Wide World Photos; **71** © Beatrice Mategwa/Reuters/Corbis; **73** *bottom* © Photo Researchers, Inc.; **74** *top left* © Joeseph Sohm-Visions of America/Getty Images; *top right* © Tibor Bognar/Alamy; **75** Steve Raymer/National Geographic Image Collection; **76** © Sue Cunningham Photographic/Alamy; **77** © Authors Image/Alamy; **78** © Le Segretain Pascal/Corbis; **79** *top left* © Joeseph Sohm-Visions of America/Getty Images; *top right* © Tibor Bognar/Alamy; *center right* © Denise Kappa/ShutterStock; *bottom* © Marc Muench/Getty Images; **81** © Majid/Getty Images; **82** Gregory Bull/AP/Wide World Photos; **83** *bottom left* © Le Segretain Pascal/Corbis; *bottom right* © Dan Lamont/Corbis; **84** © Bettmann/Corbis.

Chapter 4
86 *bottom center* © The British Museum/Topham-HIP/The Image Works, Inc.; *bottom right* © Jane Sweeney/Lonely Planet Images; *top left* © Philip and Karen Smith/Getty Images; *bottom left* © Louis Fox/Getty Images; **87** *bottom left* Limestone tablet with Sumerian pictographic script. Symbol of the hand indicates the proprietor.

End of 4th millenium. Mesopotamia. 5 x 4.2 cm. A) 19936. Louvre, Paris. Photo © Erich Lessing/Art Resource, New York; *bottom right* © Peter Horree/Alamy; *top left* © Nathan Benn/Corbis; *center* Benin aquamanile in the shape of a leopard (1700s). British Museum, London. Photo © Art Resource, New York; *top right* © Lowell Georgia/Corbis; **88** © Pascal Goetgheluck/Photo Researchers, Inc.; **89** *bottom* © David L. Brown/PanStock/Jupiter Images; *top left* © Joe Sohm/Pan America/Jupiter Images; *top center* © David Jones/Alamy; *top right* © Kevin Schafer/Alamy; **90** © Sergio Gaudenti/Kipa/Corbis; **91** *bottom left* © Rob Melnychuk/Getty Images; *top left* © Yellow Dog Productions/Getty Images; *top center* © Jeff Greenberg/PhotoEdit; *second from right* © Michael Newman/PhotoEdit; *bottom right* © Getty Images; **92** Boddhisatva Kuan-Yin (Avalokitesvara) (1271-1368 B.C.). Porcelain Ch'ing Pai ware with blue glaze. National Museum, Beijing. Photo © Erich Lessing/Art Resource, New York; **96** © Images&Stories/Alamy; **97** *center right* © Bill Bachman/Danita Delimont; *bottom* © Robert Azzi/Woodfin Camp and Associates, Inc.; *top left* © Joe Sohm/Pan America/Jupiter Images; *top center* © David Jones/Alamy; *top right* © Kevin Schafer/Alamy; **98** *left* Pot with handles, ribbon-ornaments and animal scenes. Baked clay with white incrustations. The Louvre, Paris. Photo © Erich Lessing/Art Resource, New York; *center* Basket woven with a killer whale crest. Spruce root. Museum of Anthropology, University of British Columbia, Vancouver, British Columbia, Canada. Photo © Werner Forman/Art Resource, New York; *right* Pouch (1800s). Mixed media. 30cm. Peabody Essex Museum, Salem, Massachusetts. Photo © Bridgeman Art Library; **100** © David Noble Photography/Alamy; **101** *bottom right* Limestone tablet with Sumerian pictographic script. Symbol of the hand indicates the proprietor. End of 4th millenium. Mesopotamia. 5 x 4.2 cm. A) 19936. Louvre, Paris. Photo © Erich Lessing/Art Resource, New York; *bottom left* © Pascal Goetgheluck/Photo Researchers, Inc.; *center left* © Dynamic Graphics Group/IT Stock Free/Alamy; **102** © J. Marshall - Tribaleye Images/Alamy.

Unit 2 Opener

105 *top right* © Peter M. Wilson/Alamy; *top left* © Ian Cumming/Axiom; *bottom left* © Mauritius/SuperStock; *bottom right* © Rachael Bowes/Alamy; **110-111** © Wide Group/Iconica/Getty Images; **111** © eStock Photo/Alamy; **113** © Larry Fisher/Masterfile; **114** © Andoni Canela/ASA/IPNstock; **115** © Carol Barrington/IPNstock.

Chapter 5

116 *bottom left* © Werner Forman/Corbis; *bottom right* Chalchihuitlicue. Sculpture. British Museum, London. Photo © Werner Forman/Art Resource, New York; *top left* © Dynamic Graphics Group/IT Stock Free/Alamy; **117** *bottom left* The Granger Collection, New York; *bottom right* The Granger Collection, New York; **119** *top left* © Royalty-Free/Corbis; *top center* © Getty Images; *bottom* © Toby Maudsley/Getty Images; *top waterfall* © imagebroker/Alamy; *top macaw* © Getty Images; *top leaves* © Getty Images; **120** © Jeff Hunter/Getty Images; **121** © Danny Lehman/Corbis; **122** *left* © Getty Images; *center* © eStock Photo/Alamy; *right* © Robert Everts/Getty Images; **123** © Gail Shumway/Getty Images; **124** © Gary Cook/Alamy; **125** *top left* © Royalty-Free/Corbis; *top center* © Getty Images; *bottom* © Peter Adams Photography/Alamy; *top waterfall* © imagebroker/Alamy; *top macaw* © Getty Images; *top leaves* © Getty Images; **126** © Jay Dickman/Corbis; **128** © Keith Dannemiller/Alamy; **129** *top left* © Simon Littlejohn/Alamy; *top right* © Derrick Francis Furlong/Alamy; *bottom left* © Pixonnet.com/Alamy; *bottom right* © Jeremy Horner/Corbis; **130** © Hemis/Alamy; **131** © H. Sitton/zefa/Corbis; **133** *top left* © Royalty-Free/Corbis; *top center* © Getty Images; *center right* © SEF/Art Resource, New York; *bottom* © Vanni/Art Resource, New York; *top waterfall* © imagebroker/Alamy; *top macaw* © Getty Images; *top leaves* © Getty Images; **134** *center left* Photo by Fernando Rochaix, University of Texas/Courtesy of the Naachtun Archaeological Project; *bottom left* Drawing by Peter L. Mathews, La Trobe University, Australia/Courtesy of the Naachtun Archaeological Project; *bottom center* Photo by Fernando Rochaix, University of Texas/Courtesy of the Naachtun Archaeological Project; **135** *center right* © Loren McIntyre-Woodfin Camp/IPNstock; © Getty Images; *center left* © Werner Forman/Art Resource, New York; The Granger Collection, New York; *left* Detail of a page from the Codex Becker depicting two war-chiefs. Museum fuer Voelkerkunde, Vienna, Austria. Photo © Werner Forman/Art Resource, New York; **136** © Dagli Orti/Museo Ciudad Mexico/The Art Archive; **137** © Wolfgang Kaehler/Corbis; **138** *bottom left* © Danny Lehman/Corbis; **140** The Granger Collection, New York; **141** *top left* © Royalty-Free/Corbis; *top center* © Getty Images; *top waterfall* © imagebroker/Alamy; *top macaw* © Getty Images; *top leaves* © Getty Images; **142** © James Quine/Alamy; **143** Father Hidalgo at the Battle of Monte de las Cruces, 1810 (1865), Joaquin Ramirez. National Palace, Mexico City. Photo © Art Resource, New York; **144** © J. Marshall - Tribaleye Images/Alamy.

Chapter 6

148 *bottom left* Portrait of Emperor Maximilian of Mexico (1865), Albert Graefle. Museo Nacional de Historia, Castillo de Chapultepec, Mexico City. Photo © Schalkwijk/Art Resource, New York; *bottom right* The Granger Collection, New York; *top left* © Tom Bean/Getty Images; **149** *bottom right* © Reuters/Corbis; **151** *center right* Santa Anna (1849). Lithograph. Photo The Granger Collection, New York; *bottom* Encounter of the Armies (1964), David Alfaro Siqueiros. Mural. Museo Nacional de Historia, Castillo de Chapultepec, Mexico City. Photo © Schalkwijk/Art Resource, New York; *top left* © Macduff Everton/Getty Images; *top center* © blickwinkel/Alamy; *pine* © Getty Images; *top right, large butterfly* © Getty Images; *top right, group of butterflies* © Elvele Images/Alamy; **153** Benito Juarez (1870). Steel engraving. Photo The Granger Collection, New York; **154** Francisco "Pancho" Villa (1914). Oil over a photograph. Photo The Granger Collection, New York; **155** © Janet Schwartz/Getty Images; **156** © Tony Anderson/Getty Images; **157** *bottom* © Royalty-Free/Corbis; *top left* © Macduff Everton/Getty Images; *top center* © blickwinkel/Alamy; *pine* © Getty Images; *top right, large butterfly* © Getty Images; *top right, group of butterflies* © Elvele Images/Alamy; **158** *left* © John Mitchell Stock Photography, photographersdirect.com; *right* © Viviane Moos/Corbis; **159** Self Portrait with Changuito (1945), Frida Kahlo. Fundacion Dolores Olmedo, Mexico City. © Banco de Mexico Trust. Photo © Schalkwijk/Art Resource, New York; **160** *top left* © JupiterMedia/Alamy; *center right* © Danita Delimont/Alamy; *bottom left* © Danita Delimont/Alamy; *bottom right* © Spike Mafford/Getty Images; **161** © Henry Romero/Reuters/Corbis; **162** *top right* © Kathleen Finlay/Masterfile; *center left* © David Hiser/Getty Images; *bottom right* © Kayte Deioma Photography, photographersdirect.com; *background* © Irfan Parvez, http://pg.photos.yahoo.com/ph/iparvezfareast/my_photos; **163** *top left* © Steve Hamblin/Alamy; *bottom* © Russell Monk/Masterfile; *center right* © Rommel/Masterfile; *background* © Chris Barton Travel Photography/photographersdirect.com; **164** © Keith Dannemiller/Corbis; **165** *bottom* © Lynsey Addario/Corbis; *top left* © Macduff Everton/Getty Images; *top center* © blickwinkel/Alamy; *pine* © Getty Images; *top right, large butterfly* © Getty Images; *top right, group of butterflies* © Elvele Images/Alamy; **166** © Reuters/Corbis; **167** © Oxford Scientific/Jupiter Images; **168** © Tom Tracy Photography/Alamy; **169** *bottom left* Benito Juarez (1870). Steel engraving. Photo The Granger Collection, New York; *bottom right* © Tony Anderson/Getty Images; *center left* © Blend Images/Veer; **170** © Danita Delimont/Alamy.

Chapter 7

172 *top left* © Stuart Westmorland/Getty Images; *bottom left* © Royalty-Free/Corbis; *bottom right* © Bettmann/Corbis; **173** *bottom left* © Brian A. Vikander/Corbis; *bottom right* © Bettmann/Corbis; **175** *center right* © Stuart Westmorland/Getty Images; *bottom* © Hemis/Alamy; *top left* © Getty Images; *top, reef* © Royalty-Free/Corbis; *top, small dolphin* © David Tipling/Alamy; *top, big dolphin* © Stuart Westmorland/Corbis; **177** © Matthew Johnston/Alamy; **178** © Mauritius/SuperStock; **179** *top right* © Justine Evans, photographersdirect.com; *top* © Kevin Schafer/Getty Images; **181** *bottom* © Look GMBH/eStock Photo; *top left* © Getty Images; *top, reef* © Royalty-Free/Corbis; *top, small dolphin* © David Tipling/Alamy; *top, big dolphin* © Stuart Westmorland/Corbis; **183** © Alejandro Ernesto/epa/Corbis; **185** © Bob Krist/Corbis; **187** *bottom* © Hisham Ibrahim/Getty Images; *center left two* © Pablo Corral V/Corbis; *center right* © age fotostock/SuperStock; *top left* © Getty Images; *top, reef* © Royalty-Free/Corbis; *top, small dolphin* © David Tipling/Alamy; *top, big dolphin* © Stuart Westmorland/Corbis; **188** Simon Bolivar. Painting. The Granger Collection, New York; **189** © Charles W Luzier/Corbis; **190** © Reuters/Corbis; **191** © Carl & Ann Purcell/Corbis; **193** *center right* © Michael J. P. Scott/Getty Images; *bottom* © Eye Ubiquitous/Corbis; *top left* © Getty Images; *top, reef* © Royalty-Free/Corbis; *top, small dolphin* © David Tipling/Alamy; *top, big dolphin* © Stuart Westmorland/Corbis; **194** © David Noton Photography/Alamy; **195** *top left* © Steve Vidler/eStock Photo; *bottom right* Victor R. Caivano/AP/Wide World Photos; **196** *top left* © Ed Kashi/Corbis; *top center* © Alistair Berg/Alamy; *top right* © Owen Franken/Corbis; **197** © Steve Vidler/eStock Photo; **198** © Nik Wheeler/Corbis; *top right* © Stephen Frink/Corbis; *center left* © Ted Spiegel/Corbis; *bottom right* © Danita Delimont/Alamy; **199** *top left* © Robert Harding World Imagery/Corbis; *center right* © Pablo Corral V/Corbis; *bottom left* © Juniors Bildarchiv/Alamy; *background* © Fridmar Damm/zefa/Corbis; **201** *center right* © Hemis/Alamy; *bottom* © Jon Crwys-Williams/Alamy; *top left* © Getty Images; *top, reef* © Royalty-Free/Corbis; *top, small dolphin* © David Tipling/Alamy; *top, big dolphin* © Stuart Westmorland/Corbis; **202** *bottom left* © Chad Ehlers/Alamy; *top left* Jesus Inostroza/AP/Wide World Photos; **203** *right* © Danita Delimont/Alamy; *top left* © Claudia Raschke-Robinson/Just One Productions/The Kobal Collection; **204** © Richard Wareham Fotografie/Alamy; **205** *bottom right* © Michael J. P. Scott/Getty Images; **206** © Hemis/Alamy.

Chapter 8

208 *top left* © Theo Allofs/Getty Images; *bottom left* © Newberry Library/SuperStock; *bottom center* © Roger Day/Alamy; **209** *bottom left* © Luis Pacheco/Getty Images; *bottom right* © Christian Liewig/Tempsport/Corbis; **210** Dom Pedro I of Brazil (1800s). Lithograph. The Granger Collection, New York; **211** *top left* © Panoramic Images/Getty Images; *top right* © Luiz C. Marigo/Peter Arnold, Inc./Alamy; *top, ants* © Digital Archive Japan/Alamy; *top center* © Getty Images; *bottom* © Ary Diesendruck/Getty Images; **212** © The Granger Collection, New York; **214** *top left* © ImageState/Jupiter Images; *top right* © Eduardo Garcia/SuperStock; **215** © Adrian Lascom/Alamy; **216** © Terry Winn Photography, photographersdirect.com; **217** *top left* © Panoramic Images/Getty Images; *top right* © Luiz C. Marigo/Peter Arnold, Inc./Alamy; *top, ants* © Digital Archive Japan/Alamy; *top center* © Getty Images; *bottom* © Edward Parker/EASI-Images/CFWiages.com/photographersdirect.com; **218** *top right* Cover Illustration from *Tales of the Amazon: How the Munduruku Indians Live.* Text © 1996 by Daniel Munduruku. Illustrations © 1996 by Laurabeatriz. First published in Canada by Groundwood Books Ltd. Reprinted by permission of the publisher.; *bottom* © Images&Stories, photographersdirect.com; **219** © James Davis Photography/Alamy; **220** *top inset* © Paulo Fridman/Corbis; *top* © Cassio Vasconcellos/Getty Images; **221** *bottom left* © Rick Gomez/Masterfile; *second from top left* © Julia Waterlow/Eye Ubiquitous/Hutchison; *second from right* © Martina Urban/Getty Images; *bottom right* © Rainer Raffalski Photography, photographersdirect.com; *top left* © David R. Frazier Photolibrary, Inc./Alamy; **222** *left* © Sue Cunningham Photographic/Alamy; *inset* Photograph by Ed-Imaging; **223** © Tom Cockrem Photography, photographersdirect.com; **225** *top left* © Panoramic Images/Getty Images; *top right* © Luiz C. Marigo/Peter Arnold, Inc./Alamy; *top, ants* © Digital Archive Japan/Alamy; *top center* © Getty Images; *bottom* © mediacolor's/Alamy; **226-227** *bottom* © Will and Deni McIntyre/Getty Images; **226** *bottom inset* © Stephen Ferry/Getty Images; *top left* © Reuters News Picture Archive; **227** *top right* © Paulo Backes Fotografia e Paisagismo, photographersdirect.com; *bottom left* © Ricardo Beliel/BrazilPhotos/Alamy; *bottom right* © James Davis Photography/Alamy; **228** © Paulo Backes Fotografia e Paisagismo, photographersdirect.com; **229** *bottom left* © Roger Day/Alamy; *bottom right* © Lebrecht Music and Arts Photo Library/Alamy; *center left* © Creatas; **230** © The Granger Collection, New York.

Unit 3 Opener

233 *top left* © BL Images Ltd/Alamy; *top right* © David Sailors/Corbis; *bottom left* © Kieran Doherty/Reuters/Corbis; *bottom right* © William Manning/Corbis; **238** © Getty Images; **240** Peter Dejong/AP/Wide World Photos; **243** © Peter Adams Photography/Alamy.

Chapter 9

244 *top left* © nagelestock.com/Alamy; *bottom left* The Granger Collection, New York; *bottom right* © Metropolitan Museum of Art; **245** *bottom left* Napoleon Crossing the Alps (1801), Jacques Louis David. Oil on canvas. 259 cm x 221 cm. Chateaux de Malmaison et Bois-Preau, Rueil-Malmaison, France. Photo © Réunion des Musées Nationaux/Art Resource, New York; *bottom right* © First/zefa/Corbis; **246** © K. Yamashita/PanStock/Panoramic Images/NGSImages.com; **247** *center right* © Jon Arnold Images/Alamy; *bottom* © Nik Wheeler/Corbis; *top left* © Josef Beck/Getty Images; *top right* © Su Davies/Life File/Getty Images; *top swan* © David Martyn Hughes/Alamy; **248** © Paul Hardy/Corbis; **250** *left* © Hortus/Alamy; *second from left* © images-of-france/Alamy; *second from right* © Stan Kujawa/Alamy; *right* © Jorma Jaemsen/zefa/Corbis; **251** © Doug Houghton/Alamy; **252** © nagelestock.com/Alamy; **255** *center right* © Ted Russell/Getty Images; *bottom* © Frank Chmura/Panoramic Images/National Geographic Image Collection; *top left* © Josef Beck/Getty Images; *top right* © Su Davies/Life File/Getty Images; *top, swan* © David Martyn Hughes/Alamy; **256** *bottom* © Peter Grumann/Alamy; *bottom right* The Granger Collection, New York; **257** Detail from the Alexander battle. Mosaic. Museo Archeologico Nazionale, Naples, Italy. Photo © Erich Lessing/Art Resource, New York; **259** © Hideo Kurihara/Alamy; **260** *top right* Kleophrades Painter (500-490 B.C.). Attic red figure amphora. 37 cm. Antikensammlung, Staatliche Museen zu Berlin, Berlin, Germany. Photo © Bildarchiv Preussischer Kulturbesitz/Art Resource, New York; *center left* Greek hydria from Vulci (530 B.C.). Museo Nazionale di Villa Giulia, Rome. Photo © Scala/Art Resource, New York; *left mask* © Ancient Art and Architecture; *right mask* © The Lowe Art Museum, The University of Miami/Superstock; *bottom right* © Buddy Mays/Corbis; *background* © John Elk III/Lonely Planet Images; **261** *top left* Neptune Calming the Waves (1757), Lambert-Sigisbert Adam. Marble sculpture. Louvre, Paris. Photo © Giraudon/Bridgeman Art Library; *top right* Breadseller in Public Square, from *House of the Baker.* Fresco. Museo Archeologico Nazionale, Naples, Italy. Photo © Scala/Art Resource, New York; *bottom left* © Gianni Dagli Orti/Corbis; *background* © Art Kowalsky/Alamy; **263** *center*

right © Royalty-Free/Corbis; *bottom* Detail from the Bayeux Tapestry (1000s). Wool embroidery on linen. Musee de la Tapisserie, Bayeux, France. Photo © Bridgeman Art Library; *top left* © Josef Beck/Getty Images; *top right* © Su Davies/Life File/Getty Images; *top, swan* © David Martyn Hughes/Alamy; **264** © Metropolitan Museum of Art; **266** © Jason Hawkes/Corbis; **267** *top right* Mona Lisa (1503-1506), Leonardo da Vinci. Oil on wood. 77 x 53 cm. Inv. 779. Louvre, Paris. Photo © Erich Lessing/Art Resource, New York; *bottom left* Maesta (Madonna Enthroned), Duccio di Buoninsegna. Museo dell'Opera Metropolitana, Siena, Italy. Photo © Scala/Art Resource, New York; *bottom right* The Peasants' Wedding (1568), Pieter Brueghel, the Elder. Oil on oakwood. 114 cm x 164 cm. Kunsthistorisches Museum, Vienna, Austria. Photo © Erich Lessing/Art Resource, New York; **269** © akg-images; **271** *center right* © akg-images; *bottom* An Experiment at the Accademia del Cimento, Gaspero Martellini. Tribuna di Galileo, Museo della Scenza, Florence, Italy. Photo © Scala/Art Resource, New York; *top left* © Josef Beck/Getty Images; *top right* © Su Davies/Life File/Getty Images; *top, swan* © David Martyn Hughes/Alamy; **272** *top left* Execution of King Louis XVI of France (1793). Colored etching. Photo The Granger Collection, New York; *bottom right* Napoleon in Coronation Robe (1810), François Gerard. Oil on canvas 205 cm x 150.5 cm. Chateaux de Malmaison et Bois-Preau, Rueil-Malmaison, France. Photo © Réunion des Musées Nationaux/Art Resource, New York; **274** *left column, top* © Bettmann/Corbis; *left column, second from top* © Swim Ink 2, LLC/Corbis; *left column, second from bottom* © Corbis; *left column, bottom* © Bettmann/Corbis; *second column, top* © Hulton-Deutsch Collection/Corbis; *second column, second from top* © Swim Ink 2, LLC/Corbis; *second column, second from bottom* © Bettmann/Corbis; *second column, bottom* © Corbis; **276** © Photograph by Sharon Hoogstraten; **277** © Metropolitan Museum of Art; **278** © Photograph by Sharon Hoogstraten.

Chapter 10

280 *top left* © Rohan/Getty Images; *bottom left* Detail from Theodora's Court, bust of Theodora. S. Vitale, Ravenna, Italy. Photo © Scala/Art Resource, New York; *bottom right* The Taking of the Bastille, July 14, 1789 Anonymous French painter. Musée National du Chateau, Versailles, France. Photo © Erich Lessing/Art Resource, New York; **281** *bottom left* © Tom Stoddart Archive/Getty Images; *bottom right* © Suomen Kuvapalveluoy/Corbis; **283** *top left* © Adrian Neal/Getty Images; *top right* © Westend61/Alamy; *center right* Polynices and Eriphyle (about 450-440 B.C.). Red figure oinochoe. Louvre, Paris. Photo © Réunion des Musées Nationaux/Art Resource, New York; *bottom* © Roger Wood/Corbis; **284** © Sergio Pitamitz/Corbis; **285** © New York Times Co./Getty Images; **287** Luca Bruno/AP/Wide World Photos; **288** *center left* © Franco Origlia/Getty Images; *top right* © Gareth McCormack/Lonely Planet Images; *bottom* © Jose Fuste Raga/Corbis; **289** *top left* © MedioImages/Getty Images; *bottom left* © Robert Harding Picture Library Ltd/Alamy; *bottom* © Atlantide Phototravel/Corbis; **290** The Granger Collection, New York; **291** *top left* © Adrian Neal/Getty Images; *top right* © Westend61/Alamy; *center right* © Iraida Icaza/Getty Images; *bottom* © John Heseltine/Corbis; **292** © Pete Saloutos/Corbis; **293** Jon Dimis/AP/Wide World Photos; **294** Henry the Navigator (1400s), Nuno Goncalves. Museu Nacional de Arte Antiga, Lisbon, Portugal. Photo © Bridgeman-Giraudon/Art Resource, New York; **295** © Buddy Mays/Corbis; **296** © K. M. Westermann/Corbis; **297** *top left* © Adrian Neal/Getty Images; *top right* © Westend61/Alamy; *center right* © Wolfgang Rattay/Reuters/Corbis; *bottom* © Stock Connection/Jupiter Images; **298** Jacques Brinon/AP/Wide World Photos; **299** *right* © Angelo Cavalli/zefa/Corbis; *inset* © char abumansoor/Alamy; **300** *bottom center* © Brand X Pictures/Alamy; *bottom left* © Greg Stott/Masterfile; **301** © David Noble Photography/Alamy; **303** *top left* © Adrian Neal/Getty Images; *top right* © Westend61/Alamy; *bottom* © Josef Beck/Getty Images; **304** © Robert Maass/Corbis; **305** *bottom* © ImageState/Alamy; *center right* © David Bathgate/Corbis; **306-307** © Stefan Matzke/NewSport/Corbis; **307** © Denis Balibouse/Reuters/Corbis; **308** © Corbis; **309** *top left* © Adrian Neal/Getty Images; *top right* © Westend61/Alamy; *center right* © Nik Wheeler/Corbis; *bottom* © Chris Lisle/Corbis; **311** *bottom left* © Royalty-Free/Corbis; *top left* © Maskot; *second from top left* © P. Manner/zefa/Corbis; *second from right* © Jonathan Blair/Corbis; *bottom right* © FoodPix/Jupiter Images; **312** © Royalty-Free/Corbis; **313** © Nik Wheeler/Corbis; **314** © Rohan/Getty Images; **315** *bottom right* © Nik Wheeler/Corbis; **316** Detail from Theodora's Court, bust of Theodora. S. Vitale, Ravenna, Italy. Photo © Scala/Art Resource, New York.

Chapter 11

318 *bottom right* Signing the Magna Carta (1800s). Engraving. The Granger Collection, New York; *top left* © Kim Sayer/Corbis; *bottom left* © David Noble Photography/Alamy; **319** *bottom left* Factories: England (about 1850). Engraving. The Granger Collection, New York; *bottom right* © Tim Hawkins/Eye Ubiquitous/Corbis; **321** *bottom* © Panoramic Images/Getty Images; *top left* © Hideo Kurihara/Alamy;

R88 Acknowledgments

top center © images-of-france/Alamy; *top right* © Getty Images; *center right* © Peter Casolino/Alamy; **322** © PanStock/Jupiter Images; **323** *top* King William III and Queen Mary II. The Granger Collection; *bottom* © Swim Ink 2, LLC/Corbis; **324** © Hulton-Deutsch Collection/Corbis; **328** © Nathan Benn/Corbis; **329** *center right* © Daemmrich Bob/Corbis; *top left* © Hideo Kurihara/Alamy; *top center* © images-of-france/Alamy; *top right* © Getty Images; *bottom* © Panoramic Images/Getty Images; **330** © Grant Pritchard/britainonview; **331** *top* © Scott Barbour/Getty Images; *bottom* © Simon Reddy/Alamy; **332** *left* © Christian Liewig/Corbis; *right* © Steve C. Michell/epa/Corbis; **333** © Ashley Cooper/Corbis; **334** © Photo Researchers, Inc.; **335** *center right* © Tim Graham/Corbis; *bottom* © Julian Calder/Corbis; *top left* © Hideo Kurihara/Alamy; *top center* © images-of-france/Alamy; *top right* © Getty Images; **336** *second from right* © Sergio Pitamitz/zefa/Corbis; *left* © Free Agents Limited/Corbis; *second from left* © Photo 24/Brand X Pictures/Getty Images; *right* © Tim Graham/Corbis; **338** © qaphotos.com/Alamy; **339** © Robert Brook/Photo Researchers, Inc.; **340** © Visual Arts Library (London)/Alamy.

Chapter 12

342 *bottom left* Boar (400-300 B.C.). Bronze statuette. Hungarian National Museum, Budapest, Hungary. Photo © Erich Lessing/Art Resource, New York; *bottom right* © Bettmann/Corbis; *top left* © ML Sinibaldi/Corbis; **343** *bottom right* © James Reeve/Corbis; **345** *bottom* © Momatiuk-Eastcott/Corbis; *top left* © Simon Reddy/Alamy; *top right* © Bill Bachmann/Index Stock Imagery/Jupiter Images; **346** © Konrad Zelazowski/Alamy; **347** *bottom right* John Maniaci/Wisconsin State Journal/AP/Wide World Photos; *bottom* © Bernard Bisson/Corbis; **348** © Reuters/Corbis; **349** *hand with egg* © Jim Sugar/Corbis; *right egg* © Ingram Publishing/Alamy; *bottom* © Peter Turnley/Corbis; *left egg* © Hemera Technologies/Alamy; **350** © Tiit Veermae/Alamy; **351** © Peter Turnley/Corbis; **352** © Peter Turnley/Corbis; **353** *center right* © Stock Connection Distribution/Alamy; *bottom* © Panoramic Images/Getty Images; *top left* © Simon Reddy/Alamy; *top right* © Bill Bachmann/Index Stock Imagery/Jupiter Images; **354** *pepper* © imagebroker/Alamy; *can* © Danita Delimont/Alamy; *bottom left* © Catherine Karnow/Corbis; *bottom right* © Ivan Zupic/Alamy; **356** © Reuters/Corbis; **357** *top* © ML Sinibaldi/Corbis; *bottom* © Robert Harding World Imagery/Corbis; **358** *bottom left* © Jose Luis Pelaez Inc/Getty Images; *top left* © Janine Wiedel Photolibrary/Alamy; *top center* © David Young-Wolff/PhotoEdit; *top right* © Simon Reddy/Alamy; *bottom right* © Mario Ponta/Alamy; **359** *top* © Justin Leighton/Alamy; *top inset* © Motoring Picture Library/Alamy; **360** © Bettmann/Corbis; **361** *center right* AP/Wide World Photos; *bottom* © FAN travelstock/Alamy; *top left* © Simon Reddy/Alamy; *top right* © Bill Bachmann/Index Stock Imagery/Jupiter Images; **362** © Jon Hicks/Corbis; **363** © WoodyStock/Alamy; **364** © CapitalCity Images/Alamy; **365** © Bettmann/Corbis; **366** John Maniaci/Wisconsin State Journal/AP/Wide World Photos.

Unit 4 Opener

369 *bottom left* © 2004 Adrienne McGrath; *top right* © John Lamb/Getty Images; *bottom right* © Eitan Simanor/Alamy; **375** © Dean Conger/Corbis; **376** © Klaus Nigge/National Geographic/Getty Images; **377** © Sovfoto/Eastfoto, photographersdirect.com.

Chapter 13

378 *top left* © Ellen Rooney/Getty Images; *bottom left* © Diego Lezama Orezzoli/Corbis; *bottom right* © SIME s.a.s./eStock Photo; **379** *bottom right* The Granger Collection, New York; *bottom center* © Steve Allen Travel Photography/Alamy; *bottom left* © Corbis; **381** *bottom* © Ralph White/Corbis; *top left* © Pavel Filatov/Alamy; *top center* © Pavel Filatov/Alamy; *top right* © Pavel Filatov/Alamy; *top right inset* © Royalty-Free/Corbis; **382** © Boyd Norton; **383** *center left* © Michel Setboun/Corbis; *bottom left* © Carsten Peter/Getty Images; **384** © Bryan & Cherry Alexander Photography; **385** *top left* © Bryan & Cherry Alexander Photography/Alamy; *top right* © Pavel Filatov/Alamy; *bottom left* © Boyd Norton/Evergreen Photo Alliance; *bottom right* © Pat O'Hara/Corbis; **386** *bottom left* © Bryan & Cherry Alexander Photography/Alamy; *bottom center* © Peter Arnold, Inc./Alamy; *bottom right* © Bryan & Cherry Alexander Photography/Alamy; *top left* © Royalty-Free/Corbis; **389** *top left* © Pavel Filatov/Alamy; *top center* © Pavel Filatov/Alamy; *top right* © Pavel Filatov/Alamy; *top right inset* © Royalty-Free/Corbis; *bottom* © Gavin Hellier/Jon Arnold Images/Alamy; **390** © SuperStock; **391** © By courtesy of Sotheby's Picture Library, London; **393** © Bernard Bisson & Thierry Orban/Sygma/Corbis; **394** *top left* © JTB Photo/Alamy; **396** © Mark Sykes/Alamy; **397** *bottom* © Picture Contact/Alamy; *top left* © Pavel Filatov/Alamy; *top center* © Pavel Filatov/Alamy; *top right* © Pavel Filatov/Alamy; *top right inset* © Royalty-Free/Corbis; **398** © Reuters/Corbis; **399** *top right* © Mark Sykes/Alamy; *center inset* © Reuters/Corbis; *center left* © Douglas Armand/Getty Images; *background* © José Fuste Raga/zefa/Corbis; *bottom right* © AFP/Getty Images; **400** *bottom inset* © Franck Fife/AFP/Getty Images; **401** *bottom inset*

© Lesegretain/Corbis; *bottom* © Pierre Perrin/Corbis; **402** *top* © 2006 Artists Rights Society (ARS), New York/ADAGP, Paris. Photo © Albright-Knox Art Gallery/Corbis; *bottom* © Kurov Alexander/Itar-Tass/Corbis; **403** © Thomas Johnson/Corbis; **404** *top left* © Bryan & Cherry Alexander; *background* © Marc Garanger/Corbis; *bottom right* © Nick Haslam/Alamy; *top right* © Jack Sullivan/Alamy; **405** *top left* © Iain Masterton/Alamy; *top right* © Peter Turnley/Corbis; *background* © Bryan & Cherry Alexander Photography/Alamy; *bottom left* © Steve Raymer/Corbis; *second from top left* © Iain Masterton/Alamy; **407** *center right* © Panov Alexei/ITAR-TASS/Corbis; *bottom* © Jeremy Nicholl/Alamy; *top left* © Pavel Filatov/Alamy; *top center* © Pavel Filatov/Alamy; *top right* © Pavel Filatov/Alamy; *top right inset* © Royalty-Free/Corbis; **408** *right* © Reuters/Corbis; **409** © Jeremy Nicholl/Alamy; **411** © SuperStock; **412** © Mark Sykes/Alamy.

Chapter 14

414 *top left* © Keren Su/China Span/Alamy; *bottom left* © Paul H. Kuiper/Corbis; *bottom right* Portrait of Timur (1780), Pierre Duflos. © Stapleton Collection/Corbis; **415** *left* © WorldSat International, Inc.; *right* © WorldSat International, Inc.; **417** *bottom* © Marc Garanger/Corbis; *top left* © Upperhall/Robert Harding World Imagery/Getty Images; *top right* © Imageshop/Alamy; *top right inset* © Creatas/Dynamic Graphics Group/Alamy; **418** © Jerry Kobalenko/Getty Images; **419** © Charles and Josette Lenars/Corbis; **420** *left* © Zurab Kurtsikidze/epa/Corbis; *right* © Tony Allen Photography, photographersdirect.com; **421** © Reuters/Corbis; **422** © AFP/Getty Images; **423** © Reuters/Corbis; **424** © Charles and Josette Lenars/Corbis; **425** *bottom* Temp. Credit: © Ludovic Maisant/Corbis; *top left* © Upperhall/Robert Harding World Imagery/Getty Images; *top right* © Imageshop/Alamy; *top right inset* © Creatas/Dynamic Graphics Group/Alamy; *center right* © Nevada Wier/Corbis; **426** © Robert Harding Picture Library Ltd./Alamy; **427** *bottom left* © Titus Moser/Eye Ubiquitous/Hutchison; *center right* © Marco Brivio/Alamy; *bottom right* Robert Harding Picture Library; **428** © HIP-Archive/Topham/The Image Works, Inc.; **429** *bottom* © Simon Richmond/Lonely Planet Images; *top right* © Vladimir Sidoropolev Photography, photographersdirect.com; *center right* © Vladimir Sidoropolev Photography, photographersdirect.com; *bottom right* © James Strachan/Getty Images; **430** *bottom left* © Photo © 2004 Adrienne McGrath; *top left* © Eliane Farray-Sulle/Alamy; *second from top left* © Antoine Gyori/Corbis; *second from view* © Antoine Gyori/Corbis; *right* © Index Stock Imagery/Jupiter Images; **431** © Reuters/Corbis; **433** *bottom* © Alexey Panov/AFP/Getty Images; *top left* © Upperhall/Robert Harding World Imagery/Getty Images; *top right* © Imageshop/Alamy; *top right inset* © Creatas/Dynamic Graphics Group/Alamy; **434** Joseph Stalin (1935), Nikolaj Vasilevic Tomskij. Oil on canvas. © SuperStock; **435** © Sergei Karpukhin/Reuters/Corbis; **436** © Staton R. Winter/Getty Images; **437** *bottom left* © Marc Garanger/Corbis; *bottom right* Robert Harding Picture Library; **438** © Nevada Wier/Corbis; **439** © David Samuel Robbins/Corbis.

End Matter

R1 Photograph by Ed-Imaging; **R23** © Mark Newman/University of Michigan; **R26** © J. B. Handelsman/The Cartoon Bank; **R35** *top* © Michael Newman/PhotoEdit; *bottom* © Bob Daemmrich/PhotoEdit; **R36** Screenshot © Google Inc. and is used with permission; **R37** Courtesy of USGS; **R40-R41** *top* © Lindsay Hebberd/Corbis; *bottom* © Dave Bartruff/Corbis; **R40** *bottom* © Comstock; **R41** *top right* © David Samuel Robbins/Corbis; **R42-R43** *top* The Tribute Money, Masaccio (Maso di San Giovanni). S. Maria del Carmine, Florence, Italy. Photo © Scala/Art Resource, New York; **R42** *bottom left* Luis Romero/AP/Wide World Photos; **R43** *bottom left* © Angelo Hornak/Corbis; *top right* © Comstock Images/Jupiter Images; **R44** © Reuters/Corbis; **R45** *top left* Heads of Brahma, Vichnu and Shiva (late 800's). Phnom Bok (Siemreap). Musée des Arts Asiatiques-Guimet, Paris. Photo © Erich Lessing/Art Resource, New York; *bottom left* © Bennett Dean; Eye Ubiquitous/Corbis; *top right* © ArkReligion.com/Alamy; **R46-R47** © Richard T. Nowitz/Corbis; **R46** *bottom left* Muslim men praying in the street. Photo © Arthur Thévenart/Corbis; **R47** *top left* Jassim Mohammed/AP/Wide World Photos; *top right* © Michael S. Yamashita/Corbis; **R48-R49** *top* Photograph by Bill Aron; **R48** *bottom left* © The Art Archive/Corbis; **R49** *bottom left* © Christie's Images/Corbis; *top right* © Nathan Benn/Corbis; **R50** *bottom* © Yoshio Tomii/SuperStock Inc.; © SuperStock Inc.; **R51** *left* © ImagineChina; *top right* Chinese ying and yang (200's). Roman. Mosaic. Archaeological Museum, Sousse, Tunisia. Photo © Dagli Orti/Art Archive; **R52-R53** © Bob Krist/Corbis; **R52** © Royalty-Free/Corbis; **R53** *top* © Chris Lisle/Corbis; *center right* © Paul Almasy/Corbis.

Illustrations

Maps by Rand McNally **A14-A37**

All other maps, locators and globe locators by GeoNova LLC

Illustration by Peter Bull **138-139, 138** *both,* **394-395, 394**

Illustration by Peter Dennis **268**

Illustration by Ken Goldammer **A8-A9**

Illustration by Martin Hargraves **265**

Illustration by Bob Kayganich **46-47, 46** *top left*

Illustration by Precision Graphics **28, 29, 37, 42, 50**

Illustration by Robert Sikora **326-327, 326** *both*

All other illustrations by McDougal Littell/Houghton Mifflin Co.

The editors have made every effort to trace the ownership of
all copyrighted material found in this book and to make full
acknowledgment for its use. Omissions brought to our attention will
be corrected in a subsequent edition.

Complete North Carolina Competency Goals and Objectives for South America and Europe

▶ North Carolina's Standard Course of Study for 6th Grade Social Studies is divided into thirteen competency goals.

▶ Each competency goal is divided into objectives.

Competency Goals and Objectives

COMPETENCY GOAL 1:
The learner will use the five themes of geography and geographic tools to answer geographic questions and analyze geographic concepts.

Objective

1.01 Create maps, charts, graphs, databases, and models as tools to illustrate information about different people, places and regions in South America and Europe.

Competency Goals are the broad categories of information you need to learn.

Objectives narrow the focus of what you need to learn.

SIXTH GRADE SOUTH AMERICA AND EUROPE

SOCIAL STUDIES SKILL COMPETENCY GOALS AND OBJECTIVES: K–12

In all social studies courses, knowledge and skills depend upon and enrich each other while emphasizing potential connections and applications. In addition to the skills specific to social studies, there are skills that generally enhance students' abilities to learn, to make decisions, and to develop as competent, self-directed citizens that can be all the more meaningful when used and developed within the context of social studies.

It is important that students be exposed to a continuum of skill development from kindergarten through grade twelve. As they encounter and reencounter these core skills in a variety of environments and contexts that are intellectually and developmentally appropriate, their competency in using them increases.

SKILL COMPETENCY GOAL 1: The learner will acquire strategies for reading social studies materials and for increasing social studies vocabulary.

Objectives

1.01   Read for literal meaning.
1.02   Summarize to select main ideas.
1.03   Draw inferences.
1.04   Detect cause and effect.
1.05   Recognize bias and propaganda.
1.06   Recognize and use social studies terms in written and oral reports.
1.07   Distinguish fact and fiction.
1.08   Use context clues and appropriate sources such as glossaries, texts, and dictionaries to gain meaning.

SKILL COMPETENCY GOAL 2: The learner will acquire strategies to access a variety of sources, and use appropriate research skills to gather, synthesize, and report information using diverse modalities to demonstrate the knowledge acquired.

Objectives

2.01   Use appropriate sources of information.
2.02   Explore print and non-print materials.
2.03   Utilize different types of technology.
2.04   Utilize community-related resources such as field trips, guest speakers, and interviews.
2.05   Transfer information from one medium to another such as written to visual and statistical to written.
2.06   Create written, oral, musical, visual, and theatrical presentations of social studies information.

SKILL COMPETENCY GOAL 3: The learner will acquire strategies to analyze, interpret, create, and use resources and materials.

Objectives

3.01   Use map and globe reading skills.
3.02   Interpret graphs and charts.
3.03   Detect bias.
3.04   Interpret social and political messages of cartoons.
3.05   Interpret history through artifacts, arts, and media.

SKILL COMPETENCY GOAL 4: The learner will acquire strategies needed for applying decision-making and problem-solving techniques both orally and in writing to historic, contemporary, and controversial world issues.

Objectives

4.01 Use hypothetical reasoning processes.
4.02 Examine, understand, and evaluate conflicting viewpoints.
4.03 Recognize and analyze values upon which judgments are made.
4.04 Apply conflict resolutions.
4.05 Predict possible outcomes.
4.06 Draw conclusions.
4.07 Offer solutions.
4.09 Develop hypotheses.

SKILL COMPETENCY GOAL 5: The learner will acquire strategies needed for effective incorporation of computer technology in the learning process.

Objectives

5.01 Use word processing to create, format, and produce classroom assignments/projects.
5.02 Create and modify a database for class assignments.
5.03 Create, modify, and use spreadsheets to examine real-world problems.
5.04 Create nonlinear projects related to the social studies content area via multimedia presentations.

SIXTH GRADE SOUTH AMERICA AND EUROPE
COMPETENCY GOALS AND OBJECTIVES

The focus for sixth grade is on the continued development of knowledge and skills acquired in the fourth and fifth grade studies of North Carolina and the United States by considering, comparing, and connecting those studies to the study of South America and Europe, including Russia. As students examine social, economic, and political institutions they analyze similarities and differences among societies. While concepts are drawn from history and the social sciences, the primary discipline is geography, especially cultural geography. This focus provides students with a framework for studying local, regional, national, and global issues that concern them, for understanding the interdependence of the world in which they live, and for making informed judgments as active citizens.

Strands: Geographic Relationships, Historic Perspectives, Economics and Development, Government and Active Citizenship, Global Connections, Technological Influences and Society, Individual Identity and Development, Cultures and Diversity

COMPETENCY GOAL 1: The learner will use the five themes of geography and geographic tools to answer geographic questions and analyze geographic concepts.

Objectives

1.01 Create maps, charts, graphs, databases, and models as tools to illustrate information about different people, places and regions in South America and Europe.
1.02 Generate, interpret, and manipulate information from tools such as maps, globes, charts, graphs, databases, and models to pose and answer questions about space and place, environment and society, and spatial dynamics and connections.
1.03 Use tools such as maps, globes, graphs, charts, databases, models, and artifacts to compare data on different countries of South America and Europe and to identify patterns as well as similarities and differences among them.

COMPETENCY GOAL 2: The learner will assess the relationship between physical environment and cultural characteristics of selected societies and regions of South America and Europe.

Objectives

2.01 Identify key physical characteristics such as landforms, water forms, and climate, and evaluate their influence on the development of cultures in selected South American and European regions.
2.02 Describe factors that influence changes in distribution patterns of population, resources, and climate in selected regions of South America and Europe and evaluate their impact on the environment.
2.03 Examine factors such as climate change, location of resources, and environmental challenges that influence human migration and assess their significance in the development of selected cultures in South America and Europe.

COMPETENCY GOAL 3: The learner will analyze the impact of interactions between humans and their physical environments in South America and Europe.

Objectives

3.01 Identify ways in which people of selected areas in South America and Europe have used, altered, and adapted to their environments in order to meet their needs, and evaluate the impact of their actions on the development of cultures and regions.

3.02   Describe the environmental impact of regional activities such as deforestation, urbanization, and industrialization and evaluate their significance to the global community.

3.03   Examine the development and use of tools and technologies and assess their influence on the human ability to use, modify, or adapt to their environment.

3.04   Describe how physical processes such as erosion, earthquakes, and volcanoes have resulted in physical patterns on the earth's surface and analyze their effects on human activities.

COMPETENCY GOAL 4: The learner will identify significant patterns in the movement of people, goods and ideas over time and place in South America and Europe.

Objectives

4.01   Describe the patterns of and motives for the migrations of people, and evaluate their impact on the political, economic, and social development of selected societies and regions.

4.02   Identify the main commodities of trade over time in selected areas of South America and Europe, and evaluate their significance for the economic, political and social development of cultures and regions.

4.03   Examine key ethical ideas and values deriving from religious, artistic, political, economic, and educational traditions, as well as their diffusion over time, and assess their influence on the development of selected societies and regions in South America and Europe.

COMPETENCY GOAL 5: The learner will evaluate the ways people of South America and Europe make decisions about the allocation and use of economic resources.

Objectives

5.01   Describe the relationship between the location of natural resources and economic development, and assess the impact on selected cultures, countries, and regions in South America and Europe.

5.02   Examine the different economic systems, (traditional, command, and market), developed in selected societies in South America and Europe, and analyze their effectiveness in meeting basic needs.

5.03   Explain how the allocation of scarce resources requires economic systems to make basic decisions regarding the production and distribution of goods and services, and evaluate the impact on the standard of living in selected societies and regions of South America and Europe.

5.04   Describe the relationship between specialization and interdependence, and analyze its influence on the development of regional and global trade patterns.

COMPETENCY GOAL 6: The learner will recognize the relationship between economic activity and the quality of life in South America and Europe.

Objectives

6.01   Describe different levels of economic development and assess their connections to standard of living indicators such as purchasing power, literacy rate, and life expectancy.

6.02   Examine the influence of education and technology on productivity and economic development in selected nations and regions of South America and Europe.

6.03   Describe the effects of over-specialization and assess their impact on the standard of living.

COMPETENCY GOAL 7: The learner will assess connections between historical events and contemporary issues.

Objectives

7.01   Identify historical events such as invasions, conquests, and migrations and evaluate their relationship to current issues.

7.02   Examine the causes of key historical events in selected areas of South America and Europe and analyze the short- and long-range effects on political, economic, and social institutions.

COMPETENCY GOAL 8: The learner will assess the influence and contributions of individuals and cultural groups in South America and Europe.

Objectives

8.01 Describe the role of key historical figures and evaluate their impact on past and present societies in South America and Europe.

8.02 Describe the role of key groups and evaluate their impact on historical and contemporary societies of South America and Europe.

8.03 Identify major discoveries, innovations, and inventions, and assess their influence on societies past and present.

COMPETENCY GOAL 9: The learner will analyze the different forms of government developed in South America and Europe.

Objectives

9.01 Trace the historical development of governments including traditional, colonial, and national in selected societies and assess the effects on the respective contemporary political systems.

9.02 Describe how different types of governments such as democracies, dictatorships, monarchies, and oligarchies in selected areas of South America and Europe carry out legislative, executive, and judicial functions, and evaluate the effectiveness of each.

9.03 Identify the ways in which governments in selected areas of South America and Europe deal with issues of justice and injustice, and assess the influence of cultural values on their practices and expectations.

9.04 Describe how different governments in South America and Europe select leaders and establish laws in comparison to the United States and analyze the strengths and weaknesses of each.

COMPETENCY GOAL 10: The learner will compare the rights and civic responsibilities of individuals in political structures in South America and Europe.

Objectives

10.01 Trace the development of relationships between individuals and their governments in selected cultures of South America and Europe, and evaluate the changes that have evolved over time.

10.02 Identify various sources of citizens' rights and responsibilities, such as constitutions, traditions, and religious law, and analyze how they are incorporated into different government structures.

10.03 Describe rights and responsibilities of citizens in selected contemporary societies in South America and Europe, comparing them to each other and to the United States.

10.04 Examine the rights, roles, and status of individuals in selected cultures of South America and Europe, and assess their importance in relation to the general welfare.

COMPETENCY GOAL 11: The learner will recognize the common characteristics of different cultures in South America and Europe.

Objectives

11.01 Identify the concepts associated with culture such as language, religion, family, and ethnic identity, and analyze how they both link and separate societies.

11.02 Examine the basic needs and wants of all human beings and assess the influence of factors such as environment, values and beliefs in creating different cultural responses.

11.03 Compare characteristics of political, economic, religious, and social institutions of selected cultures, and evaluate their similarities and differences.

11.04 Identify examples of economic, political, and social changes, such as agrarian to industrial economies, monarchical to democratic governments, and the roles of women and minorities, and analyze their impact on culture.

COMPETENCY GOAL 12: The learner will assess the influence of major religions, ethical beliefs, and values on cultures in South America and Europe.

Objectives

12.01 Examine the major belief systems in selected regions of South America and Europe, and analyze their impact on cultural values, practices, and institutions.

12.02 Describe the relationship between cultural values of selected societies of South America and Europe and their art, architecture, music and literature, and assess their significance in contemporary culture.

12.03 Identify examples of cultural borrowing, such as language, traditions, and technology, and evaluate their importance in the development of selected societies in South America and Europe.

COMPETENCY GOAL 13: The learner will describe the historic, economic, and cultural connections among North Carolina, the United States, South America, and Europe.

Objectives

13.01 Identify historical movements such as colonization, revolution, emerging democracies, migration, and immigration that link North Carolina and the United States to selected societies of South America and Europe and evaluate their influence on local, state, regional, national, and international communities.

13.02 Describe the diverse cultural connections that have influenced the development of language, art, music, and belief systems in North Carolina and the United States and assess their role in creating a changing cultural mosaic.

13.03 Examine the role and importance of foreign-owned businesses and trade between North Carolina and the nations of South America and Europe, and evaluate the effects on local, state, regional, and national economies and cultures.

COMPETENCY GOALS AND OBJECTIVES